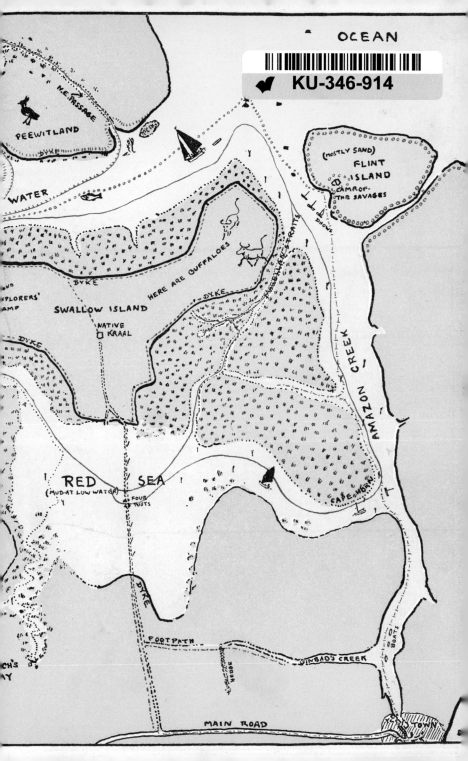

Betty J. Roscoe
1939.

SECRET WATER

Also by Arthur Ransome

WHAT SUSAN FOUND IN THE CAMP

SECRET WATER

by

ARTHUR RANSOME

JONATHAN CAPE
THIRTY BEDFORD SQUARE, LONDON
AND AT TORONTO

FIRST PUBLISHED 1939

JONATHAN CAPE LTD.   30 BEDFORD SQUARE, LONDON
AND 91 WELLINGTON STREET WEST, TORONTO

PRINTED IN GREAT BRITAIN IN THE CITY OF OXFORD
AT THE ALDEN PRESS
PAPER MADE BY JOHN DICKINSON & CO. LTD.
BOUND BY A. W. BAIN & CO. LTD.

CONTENTS

ILLUSTRATIONS

ILLUSTRATIONS

TO

THE BUSK FAMILY

SECRET WATER

FAREWELL TO ADVENTURE

T HE First Lord of the Admiralty was unpopular at Pin Mill.

"I hate him," said Roger, sitting on the foredeck of the *Goblin*, with his legs dangling over the side.

"Who?" said Titty.

"The first of those lords," said Roger.

"We all hate him," said Titty.

John and Susan, perhaps, did not hate the First Lord in particular, but their thoughts about the Admiralty were as bitter as Roger's.

"I don't see the good of Daddy's coming home," said Bridget.

That was it. Daddy had come home and had been looking forward to a week or so of freedom before settling down to work at Shotley. The last thing Jim Brading had done before being whisked off home by an aunt (who had said that a young man with concussion would be better there than in a yacht, even if it had been turned into a hospital ship), had been to lend Daddy the *Goblin*. More: he had given Daddy a chart of a place, quite near by, where there were inland seas and dozens of islands. Everything had been fixed. The whole family of the Walkers were to sail round in the *Goblin*, to land at the place where Jim had marked a cross on the chart. Daddy and Mummy were to sleep afloat in the *Goblin*. The five Swallows and Sinbad the kitten were to camp ashore. They were going to do real exploring and make their own maps of those secret waters and unknown islands. Daddy, who had been looking forward to exploring as much as if he had not spent half his life at sea, had made a blank map on which their discoveries were to be put down. He had sent to the north for their camping things. He had got them bamboos for surveying poles. He and Mother had laid in stores as if they were planning an expedition into the desert. The little inner room at Alma Cottage was crammed with tents and sleeping bags and packages of all sorts. Everything was ready, and then, that morning, the postman had handed over the letters, and Daddy, who had been ragging John about taking a compass bearing of the coffeepot from the cruet, saw the O.H.M.S. on one of them, tore it open, and said one "Damn" as if he really meant it.

"What is it?" Mummy had asked.

"We can't go. It's all off. The First Lord's chucked a spanner in the works."

"Not really?"

He had passed the letter to her.

"There it is. They want this and they want that. It means going up to London the day after to-morrow. And they want me to start in at Shotley as soon as I get back. You'll have to come to London with me, Mary, if you're to get all you want in time. I'm awfully sorry, you people. It just can't be helped. Orders is orders. The expedition's off. No exploring for us till next year."

It was as if the curtain had been rung down at the very beginning of the first act of the pantomime.

*

Breakfast was hardly over before a young man in naval uniform had stopped his little car at the foot of the lane, run up the steps to the cottage, saluted, given a message, and taken Daddy and Mummy away. John, Susan, Titty, Roger, Bridget and Sinbad, the kitten, had rowed off to the *Goblin*,

to keep their promise to her owner and, even if they were not
going to sail in her, keep his little ship clean for him.

*

Titty was sitting on the cabin top.

"The Admiralty just likes spoiling everything," she said.
"That lieutenant who came and took them off to Shotley
was fairly gloating. I saw his horrid grin."

"And everything planned," said Susan. "And Daddy and
Mother were just as keen on it as us."

"By the time they let him go, we'll be getting ready to
go back to school," said John. "Well, it's no good sitting about.
Let's get to work and tidy her up."

"If it wasn't for that beastly Admiralty we'd be stowing
cargo instead," said Roger.

"Keep Sinbad out of the way," said John. "We don't want
to sweep him o.b."

Work made everybody feel a little better, though not
much. John dipped the big mop over the side and sent the
water shooting along the decks and pouring out of the
scuppers in the low rail. Susan found that the *Goblin's* sauce-
pans, though clean enough inside, had smoky patches outside
that took a lot of rubbing off. Roger and Titty with a tin of
metal polish between them settled down to smarten up portholes and cleats. Sinbad walked about on the cabin roof and
on the decks, lifting first one paw and then another and giving
it a shake after treading in the damper places left by John's
sluicing. Bridget told Sinbad he ought to be wearing sea-
boots. There was not much talking among the others. They
all knew that this tidying up of the *Goblin* instead of being
a beginning was like the words "THE END" on the last page of a
book.

Work went steadily on all morning. Decks grew spotless.
Coils of ropes were re-coiled so beautifully that they looked

like carved ornaments. John and Susan joined the polishers and porthole after porthole that had been dull with salt and verdigris glittered in the sun. Even Bridget did her bit and rubbed at a porthole till she could see her face in it.

Now and then barges with their tall sails towered past, going up to Ipswich with the tide. Yachts came in from the sea, and the workers on the *Goblin* watched each in turn round up into the wind, with someone on the foredeck dropping the staysail and reaching with a boathook for a mooring buoy.

"Gosh," said Roger at last, "isn't it awful not to be going anywhere after all."

"Hullo," said Titty. "Look at that little boat, just like *Swallow* only with a white sail."

"Two of them," said John.

"Three," said Roger. "There's another just leaving the hard. Getting her sail up."

The two small white sailed dinghies met the third, and then all three ran together through the fleet of moored yachts. Work stopped aboard the *Goblin*. There was a girl in one of the boats and a boy in each of the other two. They sailed close by.

"Pudding faces," said Roger, not because of any special likeness to puddings in the faces of the helmsmen, but simply because he envied them.

"They'd call you a pudding face if they knew you'd been to Holland," said John. "Gosh! They did that pretty neatly."

The three little sailing dinghies had run up alongside one of the anchored yachts, a big yellow cutter, two on one side of her and one on the other. There was not the slightest bump. Eggshells would not have been cracked if they had been hanging over the side instead of fenders. Sails were coming down, and presently the three skippers climbed aboard the

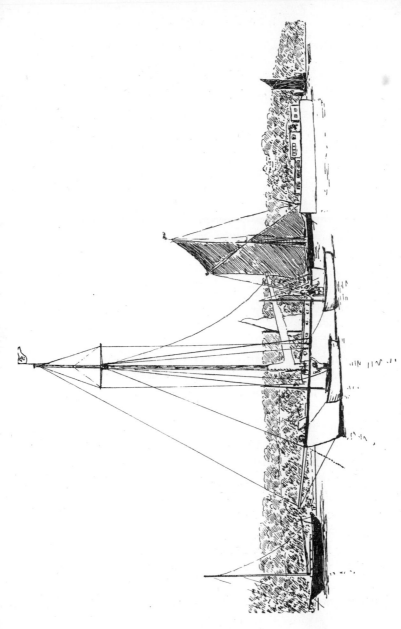

"PUDDING FACES," SAID ROGER. "PROBABLY GOING SOMEWHERE, AND WE'RE NOT"

big yellow cutter, and disappeared one after another down into the cabin.

"Pudding faces," said Roger again. "They're probably going somewhere, and we're not."

The sight of those little boats reminded them of other little boats on the lake in the far away north.

"I wonder what the Amazons and D's are doing," said Titty.

"Houseboat battle anyway," said Roger. "And they've got Timothy to walk the plank as well as Captain Flint."

"Bother everything," said John. "It wouldn't have mattered so much if we weren't all ready to start."

"Hang that first lord," said Roger. "I say, I wish we had him here, with a good springy plank and the water thick with sharks."

"Brrrrrrrrrrrrrrrrrrr."

Susan's alarm clock that had been brought aboard the *Goblin* went off down in the cabin.

"Come on," said Susan. "I set it for ten minutes to one. Daddy and Mother'll be back and you know how Miss Powell hates people to let her cooking get cold."

In two minutes they were all in the dinghy and John was pulling for the hard.

Daddy met them at the top of the hard.

"Well, what have you been up to?" he said.

"Cleaning up the *Goblin*," said Roger.

"Polishing," said Bridget.

"I wish I could take her for a sail," said Daddy. "But I can't. I've got to go back to Shotley this afternoon. That lad's coming for me after lunch."

"That beast?" said Titty. "That gloating beast?"

"Oh come, Titty," said Daddy. "He can't help it. Even sub-lieutenants are God's creatures, though it's hard to believe it sometimes."

They were just following Daddy up the steps to Alma Cottage, when Titty saw a woman coming down the lane and waving to them. She stopped.

"Isn't this for your mother?" said the woman, holding out a letter. "Postman left it at mine by mistake."

Titty looked at the envelope. "Yes," she said, and then, seeing the postmark, she ran up to the cottage calling, "Mother, Mother, here's a letter from Beckfoot."

Mother was already at the round table in the parlour, cutting slices of roast mutton. She took the letter and looked at Daddy. "Oh dear," she said, "I do hope it's to say 'No'."

"No to what?" asked Roger.

"Just something I asked her," said Mother. She opened the envelope, took out the letter, read it through, and passed it across to Daddy. "What on earth am I to say?" she asked.

"Is one of them ill?" said Susan, seeing Mother's face.

"Oh no, it's not that," said Mother. "They're all quite well and Mrs. Blackett sends her love to you."

"What about the D's," said Titty.

"They've gone home."

"Oh well," said Titty. "There's still Timothy and Captain Flint."

Daddy finished reading the letter. "Can't be helped," he said. "Impossible. I can't get out of going to London, and it'll take us all our time anyhow, and I shall be up to the ears after I get back. . . .'

"In water?" said Roger.

"In work," said Daddy, and then, seriously, looking at Mother. "You'll just have to tell her the sort of fix we're in."

He folded up the letter and passed it across the table. Mother folded it up and put it in its envelope.

As she did so, she found that it would not slip in comfortably. There was something in the way at the bottom of the envelope. She turned the envelope upside down, and shook out a narrow card with a picture on it. There was no writing, not even an address, only a skull and crossbones in one corner and a picture of dancing savages.

"I expect this is for you people," said Mother, and gave the card to Susan.

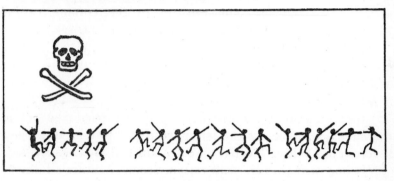

NANCY'S MESSAGE[1]

Susan looked at it. "What's that first one, John?" she said.

"Left arm over his head. Right arm pointing at half-past ten. ... That's T. ... The next one's H. ... Both arms straight out. ... That's R. ... Half a minute. ..."

"Let me see too," said Titty.

John pulled a pencil out of his pocket and scribbled a letter of the alphabet under each of the dancing figures. T.H.R.E.E ... M.I.L.L.I.O.N ... C.H.E.E.R.S ... Three million cheers."

Commander Walker burst out laughing. "Right under your very nose," he said. "We ought to have that young woman to teach signalling to naval cadets."

"Three million cheers," said Titty. "What for? She must have done something and thinks we know all about it."

"Captured the houseboat I should think," said Roger.

[1] See page 263 for Semaphore Alphabet.

"Or drowned the Great Aunt. She wouldn't send three million cheers about nothing at all."

Nobody at Pin Mill felt like three million cheers. They felt about Nancy's message almost as Roger had felt about the "pudding faces". It was not fair. Three million cheers, indeed. Who could be expected to cheer about anything on a day when the best plan ever made had been wiped out by stony-hearted Lords of the Admiralty.

From the round table in the parlour they could see through into that inner room, with the bamboo poles for surveying leaning up in a corner, the bundles of blankets, the cases of provisions, the tent-rolls and all the other things they had got ready for the expedition.

Titty got up from her chair and quietly closed the door.

Dinner was hardly finished before Daddy was taken off to Shotley again. And then Mother said she could not come out with them, because of letters to write. Bridget and Sinbad played in the garden. The others had no heart for boats, and went for a walk along the woods above the river. But even there, they could not forget what had happened. Yachts were coming up the river. Yachts were going down. Each one of them was going somewhere, or coming back, and Roger, until the others told him to shut up, kept telling them he was sure this yacht or that was carrying an expedition like the one Daddy had planned, on its way to the very islands they had meant to explore.

And then, when they had come back for high tea at Miss Powell's they learnt that something had happened that had made Daddy at least feel quite different. Tea was over before he came in smiling to himself.

"Get out," he said jovially as if nothing was wrong with the world. "Committee meeting with your Mother."

They went, and as they went, heard just two sentences.

"Been sending a few telegrams," said Daddy. "Must

have sent half a dozen I should think. One thing after another."

"Have a look at my letter and see if it'll do," said Mother.

"It won't," said Daddy. "Not after my telegrams."

"Oh Ted," said Mother. "What have you gone and done?"

And then they heard their father's cheerful laughter. Cheerful and rather mischievous.

"Daddy's up to something," said Titty.

"I say," said Roger. "You don't think he's thought of a way of dishing the first of those lords?"

They went back aboard the *Goblin*, watched Roger's pudding faces racing their three dinghies, gave another rub round to the portholes and finally, though there was really no need, lit the *Goblin's* riding light before coming ashore. She lay there, with her light twinkling below her forestay, just as it had twinkled in the evening when they had been at anchor with Jim Brading in command.

"Awful to think we shan't sail until next year," said Titty.

"But if Daddy's squashed that lord . . ." said Roger.

"He can't have done that," said John.

Daddy was putting away a map as they came in. He and Mother went upstairs together to see Bridget into bed.

"They've got a secret," said Titty.

"They've got lots probably," said Susan.

"Something to do with us," said Titty. "Didn't you hear what he was saying?"

"What did he say?"

"He said, 'Better keep mum about it till the morning'."

CHAPTER II

ADVENTURE AHEAD

"ALL hands!" said Daddy, as they sat down to breakfast.

"Wait till they've had their porridge," said Mother.

Daddy laughed.

"Oh do tell us now," said Titty.

"You heard what your Mother said."

"Oh Mother!"

"You get your porridge down," said Mother. "But don't go and eat it too quickly."

"Or too slowly," said Roger, swallowing fast. "Slop it in, Bridget. Bridget doesn't know how to eat porridge. When you've got a mouthful in, don't just wave the spoon about. Get it filled while you're swallowing."

"Don't you hurry, Bridgie," said Daddy. "News'll keep."

"Anybody want any more porridge?" said Mother presently.

"Nobody does," said Titty.

"What about Roger?"

For a minute or two everybody had been watching Bridget, whose eyes wandered from face to face as she worked steadily on, spoonful by spoonful. Roger looked at the porridge still left in her plate. He could have a little more and yet be done as soon as she was.

"Yes, please," said Roger, and passed his plate.

Bridget eyed him balefully and put on speed. It was a very close thing. Roger was still swallowing his last mouthful while Susan was wiping a stray bit off Bridget's chin.

Daddy looked at Mummy. She nodded.

There was a breathless pause.

"Now, look here," said Daddy. "Mummy and I have been talking it over. We can't come. I've got to be in London. Mummy's got to come with me for part of the time anyhow. It all depends on John and Susan. If John and Susan will guarantee to keep the rest of you out of trouble, how would you like to take on that bit of exploration for yourselves?"

"Gosh!" said Roger.

"We won't need to be kept out of trouble," said Titty.

"Well, John?" said Daddy.

"But would Jim Brading let us have the *Goblin* without you?"

"No, he jolly well wouldn't. Not if he could help it. Once was quite enough for him. What I propose to do is to take you round in her, dump the lot of you at the place he told us about, and come back and take you off as soon as my Lords of the Admiralty give me a chance. What about it, Susan?"

"We'll be awfully careful," said Susan.

"You'll have to be," said Daddy. "Tidal water. This won't be like camping in the lakes. Where's that chart? And the blank map?"

Daddy showed them the chart Jim had lent him, with a cross marking the best place for landing. "That's where we'll land," he said putting his finger on the spot. "And there's a farm here, where you see that little square."

"Native kraal," said Titty.

"Are we going to have the chart?" asked John.

Daddy showed them the blank map he had made for the expedition when he had thought that he and not John would be in charge of it. "No," he said. "You'll have this instead. I've copied it roughly from the chart, but that's all. It's the sort of map people might have of a place that had never been explored. Those round lumps may be islands or they may not. Tide'll make a lot of difference. A lot of it's marsh covered at high water. I've marked just three things on it. Two of them

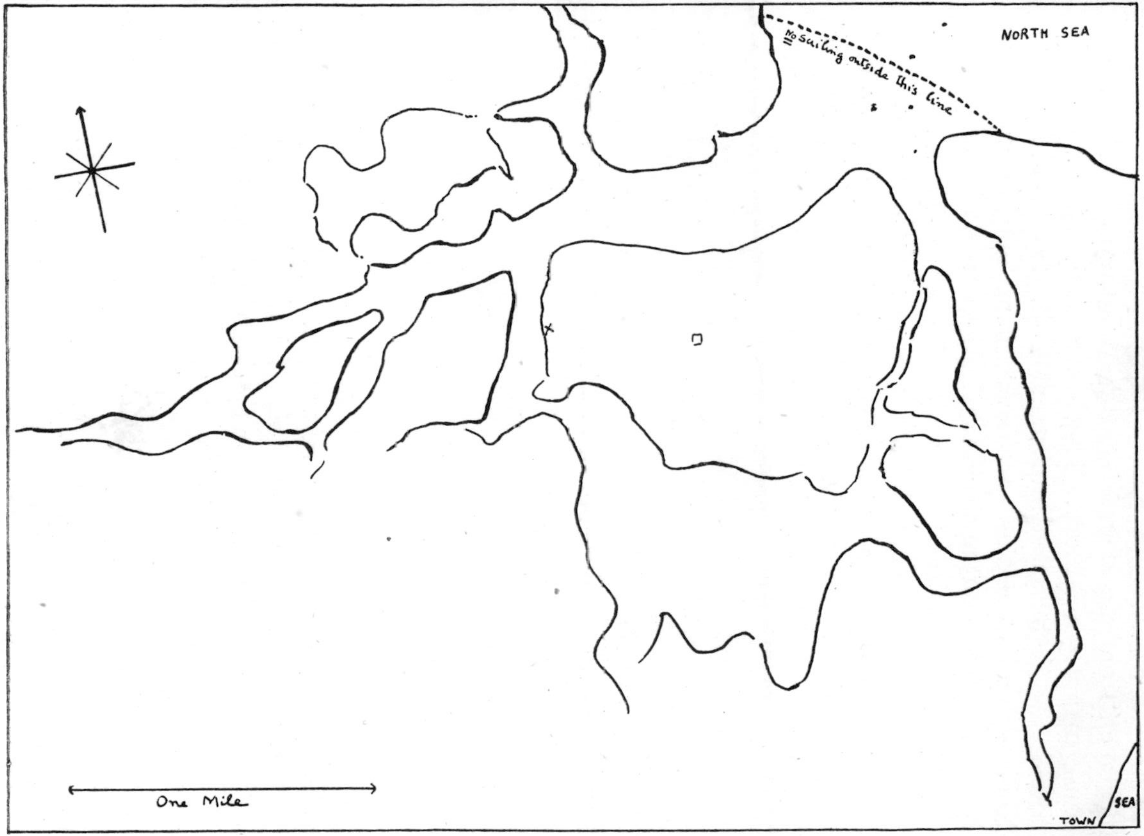

NORTH SEA

No sailing outside this line

TOWN

SEA

One Mile

THE BLANK MAP

are taken from the chart. That cross is the place where I'm going to put you ashore. That square is the farm, but this dotted line is the most important of all. See it, everybody? Nobody, on any excuse whatever, goes outside that line. No more drifting out to sea in fogs. Agreed? "

"Agreed."

"How can we drift at all without a boat?" said Roger.

"You couldn't explore islands without one, could you?" said Daddy. "I've borrowed a boat for you, and we'll tow her round."

"Brown sail?" asked Roger. "Like *Swallow's*."

"What's her name?' asked Titty.

"Where is she?" asked John and began to get up from the table.

"Plenty of time after breakfast," said Mother. John sat down again and looked out of the window. Close to the boat-builders' shed two men were cleaning a dinghy, and a brown sail, wrapped round its spars, was propped against the wall beside them.

"Is that her?" asked John.

"Maybe."

"But no sailing outside the dotted line," said Mother. "No going out to sea, even without meaning to."

"It won't happen again," said Susan.

"Anyway not in a dinghy," said John.

"Going to let me finish what I was saying?" asked Daddy.

"Do go on," said Titty.

"You'll start with a blank map, that doesn't do more than show roughly what's water and what isn't. You'll have your tents, stores, everything we'd got ready when we thought we were all going together. You'll be just a wee bit better off than Columbus. And with all the practice you've had at exploring, I think you'll do pretty well. But you'll be marooned fair and square. You'll have to depend on yourselves alone. There'll be nobody coming along everyday to see that you're all right."

"Marooned?" said Roger.

"What happened to Ben Gunn," said Titty. "They gave him a gun and put him on an island and sailed away and never came back."

"Oh," said Roger.

"We'll come back for you all right some day," said Daddy.

"When?" said Susan.

"Don't say," said Titty. "Much better if we don't know. We'll grow old and grey watching for a distant sail. . . .'

"Not very old," said Daddy. "And you won't have time to get very grey before you have to stop being explorers and go back to school."

"Don't spoil it," said Titty.

"Do you really think you'll be all right there by yourselves?" said Mother.

"We will," said almost everybody at once.

"Hullo, Bridget," said Daddy, "what's the matter?"

"What's going to happen to me?" said Bridget, who had been growing more and more solemn. "You said you were going to take me when we were all going. Don't let them leave me behind again. I'm quite old enough to go."

"Ask Susan if she'll have you," said Daddy. "I'll be glad if she will. May as well maroon the lot while we're about it."

"You'll be a strong expedition," said Mother, half smiling, and half comforting herself. "A captain and a mate and two able seamen and a ship's baby."

"What about Sinbad?" asked Titty.

"We can't ask Miss Powell to look after him," said Mother. "There'll have to be a ship's kitten as well."

"Then I won't be the youngest," said Bridget.

"Not by several years," said Daddy. "Ah, thank you, Miss Powell. . . ."

Miss Powell had come in and set a huge dish with a cover on it before Commander Walker. She lifted the cover and the little room was full of the smell of fried bacon. There was a busy minute or two while people were burning their fingers passing round hot loaded plates.

"No more talking," said Daddy. "Finish up your breakfasts. No seaman lets hot bacon and toast get cool if he can help it. And there's no time to waste. High tide to-day about a quarter past two. We've got to be at the islands before then. All that stuff to be put aboard and we'll have to be sailing by twelve."

"Gosh!" said Roger. "To-day. . . ."

He was too busy to say more, and after that there was silence except for the crunching noise natural to toast when being eaten.

*

Four men were carrying a sailing dinghy down the hard to put her in the water. Four explorers, who only an hour before had thought that for this summer at least their exploring days were over, raced down the hard in pursuit. Daddy followed in less of a hurry. Bridget had stayed behind to help Mother to turn a thick woollen blanket into an explorer's first sleeping bag.

"She's as big as *Swallow*," said John.

"She's called *Wizard*," said Titty, looking at the name on the boat's stern.

"Because she whizzes, I expect," said Roger.

The men slid her into the water. Daddy had a look at her gear and hoisted her brown sail. John and Daddy went off to try her while the others waited. Then John came ashore and Susan took his place. Then Daddy sailed with Roger and Titty together and watched them handle her in turns. Everybody got full marks, including *Wizard*.

"Now then," said Daddy. "We'd better borrow a wheel-barrow. We've got our work cut out to get all that stuff aboard."

The boatbuilder lent them a wheelbarrow and they took it to the steps below Miss Powell's cottage. Mother was sitting on the wooden seat at the top of the steps, sewing away at Bridget's sleeping bag. Bridget was telling Sinbad he was going to sea. Miss Powell was cutting an enormous pile of sandwiches to be eaten on their way down the river. Daddy had hurried up the hill to buy all the chops in the village so that they could take them ready-cooked to make things easier for their first meals on the island.

"I don't believe you'll ever get all that stuff into the *Goblin*," said Mother.

"There's a lot of room in her," said John, but that inner room at Miss Powell's looked pretty full.

"Come on," said Titty. "Let's everybody carry something."

Journey after journey was made from Alma Cottage to the dinghy floating by the hard. John, or Daddy after he had come back with the chops, pushed the wheelbarrow at the run, while others ran alongside keeping things from falling off. Voyage after voyage was made from the hard to the *Goblin*. Bit by bit that inner room began to look more like a room in somebody's house and less like a general store. It was extraordinary how different everybody felt. Yesterday it had seemed that adventure was over at least for these holidays. To-day, adventure was ahead . . . just round the corner. Real exploration. . . . Islands, and islands of a kind they had never seen . . . an empty map to be filled with the discoveries they would make themselves. A little way upstream among the other yachts they saw the big yellow cutter with the three sailing dinghies clustered round her, and a boat from the shipwright's lying astern of her. Men were working aboard her. That girl and the two boys dropped into the dinghies and went off for a sail up the river. But to-day it never occurred even to Roger to call them pudding faces. There was no need to envy them. *They* were not going to sleep that night on an unknown island. *They* were not going to be marooned. *They* would not watch a ship sail away into the distance leaving them to pitch their camp and face the world alone. Roger looked at them with pity. "Those children again," he said.

"I do believe that's all," said Susan, back at the cottage looking round the room. The table had been cleared. Chairs that had been piled high were fit to sit upon once more. Everything left in the room belonged to it and not to an exploring expedition. Susan looked carefully round, straightened the tablecloth, and put a chair (that had somehow strayed) neatly in its place against the wall. "I don't believe we've forgotten anything."

"*Swallow's* flag," said Titty, and darted upstairs to fetch it.

"Will it be all right to fly it on *Wizard*?" asked Roger, as she came down with it.

"We must fly it over the camp," said Titty.

Mother's voice came from outside. "A glass of milk for everybody," she said. "You've earned it after all that racing up and down."

"Pretty good work," said Captain Walker, pulling at his pipe. "Well done the Able Seamen."

"How soon will I be counted Able Seaman?" asked Bridget.

"Not till you can swim," said John.

"And she mustn't try swimming this time," said Mother, "because of the tides."

"And the mud," said Daddy.

"And the sharks," said Roger.

And then Daddy asked how many of the others had got their life-saving certificates, and handed out half a crown to each of

34

"NO NEED TO ENVY THEM NOW"

them, on hearing that Roger and Titty had got theirs in the summer term at school, and that John and Susan had got theirs the year before.

'Penny for your thoughts, John," said Mother, after John had been silent for a minute or two.

"No good offering him a penny when I've just made him a rich man," said Daddy. "Out with it, John, all the same."

"I was only thinking what a pity it is that Nancy and Peggy can't come too."

Daddy and Mother looked at each other but said nothing.

"Captain Nancy'd just love being marooned," said Titty. "But I expect they're doing something too. Sure to be. They'll probably write and tell us about it. She wouldn't have sent three million cheers unless they were up to something pretty larky."

"They won't be doing anything as good as this," said Roger.

Captain Walker looked at his watch.

"Are you ready, Mary?" he said. "All aboard. Hurry up and say good-bye to Miss Powell. We'll have to start at once to make sure of having the tide with us going in."

PIN MILL

CHAPTER III

INTO THE UNKNOWN

THE *Goblin* was floating well below her usual water line as she left Pin Mill to sail down the river into the unknown. She had never been so laden before. Inside her there was hardly room to move. Stuffed knapsacks, cases of ginger beer, tin boxes and bundles were piled on the cabin floor and in the bunks. Huge rolls of oilskins and ground sheets had been lashed down on the cabin top. A bundle of long bamboos for surveying was made fast on one of the side decks. And beside their gear there were all the members of the expedition. John, Susan, Bridget (on her first sea voyage) and the kitten, Sinbad, were in the cockpit. Titty and Roger were on the foredeck. Down below in the saloon, Commander Walker was ticking things off on a list and telling Mother that everything was really quite all right and that there was nothing about which to worry.

"It isn't as if there wasn't Susan," he said, "and it isn't as if John had no sense. I say, John. You keep straight down the middle of the river. I'm going to turn the engine on to get us quickly down over the tide."

"Aye, aye, sir," said John seriously. He, like Susan, had heard that their father was depending on them.

The engine started chug, chugging beneath them. Roger scrambled aft in a hurry, to be allowed to push the lever forward and put it into gear. The *Goblin's* wake lengthened, and the water creamed under the bows of *Wizard*, the sailing dinghy, towing astern.

In the cockpit, they had to shout to each other to make

themselves heard over the noise of the engine, and could no longer hear what was being said by the friendly natives in the cabin. But there was little need for talk while everybody, even John the steersman, was busy with sandwiches and ginger beer.

They passed boats not in a hurry going slowly down under sail alone. They met boats coming up fast with the tide. They were interested in all of them, but the *Goblin*, they knew, was the only boat that was on her way to maroon a party of explorers on an island. The wooded banks slipped by and were left behind. The river opened into the wide harbour. They looked up the Stour and pointed out to Bridget where they had spent their first night in the *Goblin* anchored off Shotley pier. They drove down past the dock where (how long ago it seemed!) they had seen Jim Brading row in for petrol before the fog had come down on them like a blanket. Ahead of them once more was the Beach End buoy.

"Listen!" said Titty at the top of her voice.

"I can hear it," shouted Roger.

"Clang! . . . Clang! . . . Clang . . . ."

It was very different, hearing the bell buoy now with Mother and Daddy aboard, and bright sunshine everywhere, from what it had been, hearing that 'Clang . . . Clang . . .' coming blindly nearer in the fog.

"We're nearly out at sea," said John.

"John says we're nearly out," Bridget called down into the cabin.

Commander Walker put his head out, looked round and went down again. The chug, chug of the engine came to an end.

"We shan't want that now," said Daddy, coming on deck again and talking quietly in the sudden silence made by the stopping of the engine.

They made as much room for him as they could and he sat on the after deck looking at Jim's chart.

ON THE WAY TO THE ISLANDS

"I'll take over now," he said. "John, you've got the best eyes. Get forward by the mast and keep them skinned. Look out for a small black buoy with a square topmark." He changed the *Goblin's* course, and looked at the compass. "We ought to be heading for it now."

John scrambled forward. The sea was smooth, the wind light, but the *Goblin* seemed to be moving faster than when she had been coming down the harbour with her engine going. The tide was with her now instead of against her and they could see by the buildings ashore how fast they were moving. Nobody even felt like being seasick.

Away to the south was a bit of a hill with a tall narrow tower. Ahead of them was a wide deep bay with a low straight coast-line far away in the distance. John, standing by the mast searched for the buoy. Suddenly he saw a black speck dancing on the water.

"Small black buoy almost dead ahead," called John.

"Piccaninny," said Roger.

"It's got something on the top of it," said Titty who, looking where John was looking, had managed to bring her telescope to bear.

"That's the fellow," said Daddy. "See any others?"

"There's another beyond it."

"Good."

Soon they were sailing close past it, a black tarred barrel, with a stick and a sort of squarish box on the top of it. Ahead of them was another black barrel, and far ahead of that was a red one with a pointed top.

"In the channel now," said Daddy, and Mother came up the companion ladder and put her head out and looked away over the water which seemed to stretch for miles on either side of them.

"Pretty narrow just here," said Daddy.

"It doesn't look it," said Mother.

"It is, all the same. There's hard sand just below water on that side, and rocky flats on the other. At low tide we wouldn't be able to get in."

"What would happen if we went over there?" said Roger, "so that we could have a better look at that tower."

"A good old bump," said Daddy, "and no more *Goblin* if we weren't lucky. Lots of boats have been smashed up on that."

"Are you sure it's deep enough for us here?" asked Susan.

"Plenty," said Daddy.

"I don't see any islands," said Bridget.

"Right ahead of us," said Daddy.

Ahead of them the land seemed hardly above the level of the sea, just a long low line above the water, with higher ground far away behind it. But that low line of coast seemed to have no gaps in it. It looked as if it stretched the whole way round across the head of the bay. Even John began to doubt if there could be islands ahead. But Daddy was ticking off one buoy after another on Jim's chart and seemed quite sure of his way. A couple of men were hauling a trawl net in a small boat and a cloud of gulls hovered above them. A motor boat appeared ahead, came to meet them and passed them in a flurry of foam.

"She must have come out from somewhere," said Titty, but still could see no gap in the coast line.

"We're nearly there," said Daddy at last. "Look out for a round buoy with a cross on a stick above it."

"There it is," called John. "Close to the shore."

Almost at the same moment, everybody saw a break in the line of sand away to the south, and a thread of water going in there, and one or two tall masts showing above sand dunes. And, as they came nearer to that round buoy with the cross they saw that a much wider channel was opening before them with smooth shining water stretching to the west and low banks on either side.

"There you are," said Daddy. "That buoy marks the cross

roads. Turn left, follow that creek in there, past those masts, and you'll come to a town."

"I can see houses now," said Roger, "and lots more boats."

"You can get right up to the town at high water in a dinghy. But if you go, don't wait there too long, or there won't be water to take you back."

"But we're going to an island aren't we?" said Titty. "Not a town."

"We are," said Daddy. "We leave that buoy to port and carry straight on."

"Crossroads buoy," said Roger as they passed it.

A minute or two later they had left the open bay and the *Goblin* was slipping easily along in the quiet water of an inland sea. A low spit of land with a dyke along it already hid the creek that led to the town, though they could still see the tops of distant masts. Far away, on the opposite side, was another low dyke. Standing on the deck and in the cockpit they could see bushes here and there. Ahead of them the inland sea seemed to stretch on for ever.

"What's it called?" asked Titty, from the foredeck.

Daddy smiled. "Do you want the name on Jim's chart? I thought you'd give it a name yourselves."

"It's a very secret place," said Roger. "You don't see it until you're almost inside."

"Secret Water," said Titty. "Let's call it that."

"Why not?" said Daddy and Titty scrambled back into the cockpit and pencilled in the first name on Daddy's blank map.

"How far does it go?" asked John.

"Good long way at high tide," said Daddy.

"It's like a lake with no mountains," said Titty.

"But where are the islands?" asked Roger.

"All round us," said Daddy. He looked at his chart. "That's one, right ahead. And that's another, over there. And this is the island you're going to be marooned on." He pointed to port. "At high water you'll be able to sail right round it through an inland sea wider than this, and get into the creek going to the town. At low water that's probably all mud. Jim's chart shows a track across it. ... My blank map'll give you a general idea, but you'll find it all out for yourselves."

"Unexplored," said Titty, "until we've explored it."

"Just so," said Daddy.

"Gosh!" said Roger. "This is the real thing. Hullo! There's another creek over on that side. And another on this. ..."

"That's ours, I think," said Daddy.

The *Goblin* slipped on. A wide creek opened to starboard. But Daddy was taking no notice of it. He was watching a smaller creek that was gradually opening on the other side, and glancing now and then at Jim's chart.

"That must be the place," he said. "I think we can run in now. Roll that jib up, John."

"Aye, aye, Sir."

"Ready? Haul away. Make fast. Now come aft and take her."

John hauled on the line that made the jib roll neatly up on itself, made fast so that it should not unroll again, and clambered back into the crowded cockpit. Already the *Goblin* had left the Secret Water and was in the creek, moving more slowly now, under mainsail only, between green shores.

"Keep her as she's going," said Daddy, and went forward to deal with the anchor. There was the grumble and rattle of chain being hauled up and ranged on deck. Then Daddy was busy at the mast. The green banks slipped by. A heron got up and flapped slowly across the creek. A curlew cried. Daddy stood up on the foredeck watching the eastern bank, looking for something. Suddenly he flung out his right arm.

"Starboard," he said quietly, and John steered towards the western bank.

"Now. Right round into the wind. Helm hard over."
John swung her round and the sail spilt the wind and flapped
heavily as the *Goblin* headed back across the creek.

Splash!

The anchor was down, and Daddy was paying out chain.
He was at the mast again. The boom lifted over their heads
in the cockpit, and the sail came down with a run.

"Two tiers," said Daddy. "We shan't need more."

In a minute or two, he had bundled the sail along the boom
and put a couple of tiers to hold it there.

"We'll call this Goblin Creek," said Titty, pencil in one
hand and the blank map in the other.

"Good name," said Daddy. "Now then, John, haul in that
dinghy. Will you put your Mother and me ashore?"

"What about us?" said Roger.

"Your turn'll come," said Daddy. "We've got to visit that
kraal and make sure the natives won't want to tell you to clear
out after we've sailed away."

CHAPTER IV

THE EXPEDITION GOES ASHORE

"Y ou can see it's an island now," said Titty. "Look at all
that water behind it. And, I say, Daddy's blank map's wrong.
That lump isn't a peninsula. It's another little island."

"Rum islands, aren't they?" said Roger. "No rocks."

"They're landing," cried Bridget.

John was rowing Daddy and Mummy ashore. They were
close to a sort of gap in the green bank, where the tops of
some piles showed above the water. Daddy was pointing.
John looked over his shoulder and took a stroke or two. The
Wizard grounded. Daddy had taken an oar from John and
was prodding over the side. He was feeling for foothold. He
was stepping out into the water.

"Daddy's landed," said Bridget.

They saw him pull the boat a little further up. Mother was
getting out, then John, carrying the anchor. They saw all
three, splashing a little, lifting their feet high and putting
them down carefully, walking one behind the other, as if in a
narrow path, towards the dyke. They were on the dyke, clear
against the sky. They had stopped by a row of bushes and
small trees. Daddy was pointing this way and that. John was
stamping about, as if trying the hardness of the ground.

"Come on, the Able Seamen," said Susan. "All hands to
untying those knots. They'll be wanting those groundsheets off the cabin roof first of all."

"Daddy and Mother have gone," said Bridget. "John's
coming back. No he isn't. He's taking the mast and sail out
of the *Wizard*. He's carrying them ashore. He nearly fell

down. He's going to fall down. No he isn't. . . . I say, can't I go ashore and help?"

"You can't till he comes back," said Susan.

"Why's he taking the mast and sail out?" said Roger.

"To make room for the stores, of course," said Susan. Presently they saw John back at the *Wizard*, sitting on the gunwale and washing his boots in the water. Then he came rowing off to the *Goblin*.

"Groundsheets first," he said as he came near. "You'll have to get them unlashed."

"They're all ready," said Susan.

"Well done. Can you heave them down?"

"Have you got a good place for the camp?" asked Titty.

"Gorgeous," said John. "But it's going to be an awful job getting the things ashore without covering them with mud."

"Hadn't you better wash your hands?" said Susan.

"I've done it once already," said John, but glancing down at his hands he dipped them again over the side of the dinghy.

"He can do his face afterwards," said Roger.

"You shut up," said John. "Just wait till you've tried it. It's all right once you're on the dyke, but getting across the saltings the mud splashes up over everything."

"What are saltings?" asked Titty.

"That's what Daddy called it . . . sort of marshy ground between the creek and the dyke. He says it goes under water at very high tides. Good, Susan. Hang on just a moment. Now let it come. . . ."

The first bundle of groundsheets was lowered into the dinghy. It was followed by another and yet another.

"Can't we come ashore too?" said Bridget.

"Susan had better," said John. "To help carry the things up. You can come too."

"And Sinbad?"

"All right. The Able Seamen had better stay in the *Goblin*

LANDING THE GEAR

to pass the things down. We don't want to bring more mud aboard than we can help. Come on. Room for a couple of tent-rolls. . . . Now Susan."

Susan slipped down into the dinghy.

"Bridget next. . . ."

"Give me Sinbad," said Susan. "You'll want both hands."

"I'll never manage," said Bridget looking down from *Goblin's* deck into the loaded dinghy.

"You will," said John. "Sit on the edge . . . right at the edge. Now let yourself go."

Bridget found herself in a heap on the groundsheets.

"I did it all right," she said and her face which had for a moment been serious broke into a pleased smile.

"Fend off, Susan," said John, and the *Wizard* started on her second voyage to the shore.

There was not far to go, but the loaded boat grounded a little further out than she had last time.

"The water'll be over Bridget's boots," said Susan.

"I'll carry her," said John. 'She'll have to get on my back."

"What about Sinbad?" said Bridget. "Can you manage two people at once?"

"I'll take Sinbad," said Susan. "You'll want both arms to hang on to John."

John, after taking the anchor ashore, came back and, standing in the water stooped with his back to the dinghy till he was almost sitting on the gunwale.

"Up you come, Bridgie," he said.

Bridget stood on the thwart, let herself fall forward and got John firmly round the neck. John felt behind him and took hold of her legs. He lifted, and choked.

"Don't throttle him, Bridget," said Susan.

John gave a good jerk that jolted Bridget higher on his back, and took a step towards the shore. Down went his foot through a patch of soft mud and he all but fell. The next foot was luckier, finding a stone. Step by step he staggered up the path through the saltings till he came to harder ground where he dumped his passenger and took a long breath.

"You must have eaten ten times your share of those sandwiches," he said.

Susan, taking now a long stride, now a short, now sliding back, now slipping forward, came after them with Sinbad. Then, while Susan and John went back to bring the things up from the boat, Bridget and Sinbad climbed up the dyke, and were presently standing guard over a growing pile, as the Captain and the Mate staggered to and fro across the saltings as fast as the mud and their loads would let them.

Meanwhile, aboard the *Goblin*, the Able Seamen were busy lugging things up from below and stacking them on the decks and on the cabin roof ready for ferrying ashore. Presently John came back for another cargo, and then again for another.

"I do believe that's the lot," said Titty at last.

"Nothing left down below," said Roger.

"Hop in then," said John. "But jolly well sit steady, or we'll have the water over the gunwales."

The Goblin lay deserted and the last of the explorers landed on the island. The last boatload, with four porters instead of only two, did not take long to carry up across the saltings to the dyke.

The dyke for the most part was narrow, just wide enough for a path along the top of it, but at the place where the explorers had dumped their stores it widened, giving plenty of room for a camp well above the level of the marshes. On the inner side it sloped steeply down to meadowland, with a drain running along the foot of it, and close to the camp there was a small pond. Just here there were a row of little stunted trees and bushes, and beyond them they could see cattle grazing in the distance, and the roof and chimneys of a farmhouse. Looking northward they could see where Goblin Creek opened into the Secret Water, and to the south they could see the creek again, curving round and opening into another inland sea.

"It's a lovely place for a base camp," said Titty. "And luckily the native kraal's a good long way off."

"What's in this box?" said Roger. "Can I start unpacking?"

"Not yet," said John. "All hands to pitching tents. Let's have it looking like a camp before Daddy and Mother come back."

"Lay the groundsheets first to see how they go," said Susan. "We can have the little ones facing the creek, but the big one'll have to go between these two trees. Let's get that one done first, so that in case Mother comes back too soon she'll be able to see where Bridget's going to sleep."

The big tent was one of the two they had used on their first visit to Wild Cat Island. It had to be slung on a rope between trees, not like the little tents, which had their own poles, and could be pitched anywhere. It was always rather a job to get it up, because of the difficulty of getting the rope high enough and taut enough. With these little trees it was worse than usual, but John and Susan managed it at last, and Bridget found her way inside it even before its walls were properly pegged down. They looked round to see that Roger's and Titty's tents were already pitched. Titty was unrolling Susan's own tent, which, as she was not going to sleep in it, was to be used for a storehouse.

"Where's Roger?" said Susan.

But just then Roger came running along the dyke.

"I've been to the corner to look at the other island," he said. "Daddy and Mother are in sight, coming from the kraal. They'll be here in a minute."

There was frenzied work in the camp. Boxes and knapsacks were bundled out of sight. The last two tents went up in record time. Titty had pulled one of the surveying poles from among the others and was hurriedly fastening *Swallow's* flag to it. The moment it was done John drove it into the ground, and Daddy and Mother came back to find all five tents up, and the *Swallow* flag on a bamboo flagstaff fluttering in the breeze.

"Good work," said Daddy.

"Everything's ashore," said John.

"Not properly stowed," said Susan. "We've pushed things in anyhow, just so that you could see the camp."

"Good camp, too," said Daddy. "Well, you're lucky. There's a very decent chap at the farm and he says any friend of Jim Brading's a friend of his, so that's all right. But he says you mustn't drink from the pond. Salt water got into it and spoilt it. All right for washing but keep it out of your mouths. I'll put ashore two full water carriers from the *Goblin*, and when you want more you'll have to get it from the well at the farm. I'll bring them ashore now, and then we'll have to be starting. The tide's going down fast."

"What about your fireplace, Susan?" said Mother, as Daddy hurried down to the landing place.

"There's a good place on dry ground just below the tents," said Susan.

"No stones here to build it with," said Mother.

"Plenty of earth," said Susan, "and we've got a spade."

"There's no post on the island," said Mother, "but you can send messages through the man at the farm. He goes to the mainland nearly every day. And you've got Miss Powell's telephone number."

"But is there a telephone?" said Roger.

"No there isn't. Not on the island. But the farmer'll telephone for you if you want anything, or you can if you go to the mainland yourselves. And we've got the number of his dairy in the town, so that we can get a message to you through him. What's become of Bridget?"

Susan pointed quietly to the big tent. Mother looked into

it. Susan had already made up her bed and Bridget's with rugs and sleeping bags. From the smaller of the sleeping bags came a loud snore.

"Sure you wouldn't rather sleep comfortably in a bed at Miss Powell's?" said Mother.

Bridget sat up suddenly. "Oh, Mummy!" she said.

"Oh well," said Mother. "I suppose you have to grow up some time."

"Sinbad's the youngest now," said Bridget.

Aboard the *Goblin*, Daddy had already lowered the two big galvanized water carriers into *Wizard* lying alongside. He was busy at the foot of the mast.

"Look," said Titty. "He's hoisting a flag."

A blue flag with a white square in the middle of it fluttered up to the *Goblin's* cross-trees.

"It's the Blue Peter," said Mother. "He's ready to sail."

In another few minutes Daddy had rowed ashore and brought the water carriers up to the camp.

"Here you are," he said. "And a good weight too, as you'll find when you take them to be refilled. You'll be treating water like liquid gold when you have to carry every drop of it."

"That's what Jim said, when we were with him in the *Goblin*," laughed Roger.

"Sensible chap," said Daddy. "Now then, Mary, we've got to be off. The heartless skipper and his cruel mate will now sail away leaving their victims on the unknown shore. Come along, Mary. You're the cruel mate. Good-bye all of you. Use sense. Watch the tides. John and Susan in charge."

"You will be careful, won't you?" said Mother, kissing the explorers good-bye.

"You aren't going away altogether," said Bridget.

"Sure you wouldn't like to come too?" said Mother.

Bridget wavered for a moment.

"No thank you," she said.

Daddy laughed. "Well done, Biddy," he said.

Mother got very muddy kissing John, who had forgot to rub the splashes off his face.

"John," she said, "You look like Ben Gunn already."

BLUE PETER AT THE CROSSTREES

"He'll have a matted beard by the time we come back," said Daddy. "Come on John and get some more mud on you putting us aboard."

John rowed Daddy and Mother back to the ship. For a moment or two he waited, watching Daddy hoist the mainsail. Then, remembering that he was in charge of the expedition, he rowed back and joined the others who were watching by the camp.

Already Mother was at the tiller of the *Goblin* and Daddy was hauling up the anchor hand over hand. The jib unrolled and filled with wind. Daddy was getting the anchor over the bows and sloshing the mud off with a mop. The *Goblin* swung round and headed out of the creek.

"Good-bye ... Good-bye. ..." The marooned explorers shouted from the camp.

"Good-bye and good luck," an answering call came from the *Goblin*. The Blue Peter fluttered down. Daddy went aft and took the tiller. Mother waved a handkerchief. The *Goblin*, leaving the shelter of the creek, heeled over and moved faster. She was gone. Only her red sails showed above the long line of the dyke as with the ebb to help her she hurried to the sea.

Everybody felt a sudden emptiness.

"Marooned," said Titty.

"We're in for it now," said John.

"Come on," said Susan. "We've got an awful lot to do."

"What about unpacking those boxes?" said Roger.

Bridget had taken Sinbad from Titty. For a few minutes she watched the red triangle of *Goblin's* mainsail moving above the dyke.

'It's all right, Sinbad," she said. "They'll come back for you."

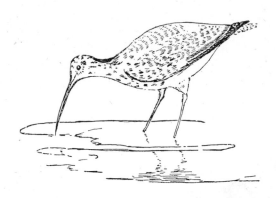

CHAPTER V

MAROONED

U NPACKING had begun in earnest. The explorers were taking stock. Susan with pencil and paper was making a list as they dug into the three boxes that Daddy had had sent down to Pin Mill from the Army and Navy Stores. Bridget and Roger were trying to count the apples and oranges they could see through the open slats of a crate. Titty and John were going through the contents of a large parcel with all the things Daddy had put together for map-making, a drawing board, lots of paper, pencils, a bottle of Indian ink, parallel rulers, drawing compasses, a protractor, a box of drawing pins.

"Daddy was going to do it really properly," said Titty.

"So are we," said John. "He'd be awfully pleased if we manage to go everywhere and get the whole thing mapped."

"Secret Archipelago Expedition," said Titty.

"What's Archipelago?" said Bridget.

"Lots of islands," said Roger. "Look here, Bridgie, you haven't counted that apple showing through the paper."

"Two dozen tins of milk," said Susan. "Eleven . . . No . . . twelve tins of soup."

"Monsters," said Roger.

"Three big tins of steak and kidney pie. . . . Three tongues."

"Oh good!"

"Three tins of pemmican. . . . Six tins of sardines. . . . One tin of golden syrup. . . . One stone jar of marmalade. . . . Six boxes of eggs. . . . One dozen in each box."

"Why such a lot of eggs?" said Roger.

"You and John always have two for breakfast and one each for the rest of us. . . . That's seven at a single meal. . . . And what about scrambled egg suppers? Come on ... Roger, it's no good counting apples in their crate. You can't see through them. You be putting the tins in the store tent. Four packets of cornflakes. Six loaves of bread. The bread and the corn-flakes'll have to be kept in one of the boxes. One tin of ginger nuts. ... One tin of biscuits. ..."

"Can I tear the paper off?" said Roger. "Good. Garibaldi. That's squashed flies. What about opening this box? We're bound to want to ..."

"Shut up just a minute. One bag of potatoes. ... What's that other bag?"

"Beans," said Bridget.

"Three slabs of sticky cake. ..."

"A whole box of chocolate," said Roger. "Nut and raisin kind, in slabs. Let's ..."

"Leave them alone," said Susan. "Six pounds of butter. ... Two boxes of lump sugar. Two of soft. One tin of salt. ... One bar of cheese. ... Good. ... That's the crustless kind in silver paper."

"First rate for marching rations," said John.

"I say," cried Bridget suddenly. "This box has got Sinbad on it."

It was a cardboard box, and in it was a packet of cat's biscuits, a small bottle of Bovril and half a dozen very small tins of salmon.

"He'll love the salmon," said Roger. "But what's the Bovril for?"

"It's to put with the hot water you have to pour over the biscuits," said Susan. "What's the label on that basket?"

"To-night's supper," read Titty. "And there's a parcel labelled 'To-morrow's Dinner'."

"We won't open that till we want it," said Susan. "Look here, Roger. Fishing lines and fish hooks. You'd better look after them."

"Shall I take the spade, too? For digging worms."

"No need to put the spade in your tent. But do put those fish hooks where Sinbad won't tread on them. I'll want the spade in a minute to make a fireplace. I'll tell you one thing we are going to be hard up for and that's firewood. It's not like Wild Cat, with dead branches everywhere. . . ."

"Come on," said John. "Let's see who gets most. High-water-mark's the likeliest place."

Exploration in a small way began at once. While Susan was busy making a fireplace exactly as she wanted it, cutting slabs of earth and arranging them in a circle, the others soon found out that every bit of burnable wood took some finding. They worked along the side of the dyke nearest to the creek, picking up here and there small pieces of driftwood. All along the foot of the dyke, marking the highest tides was a wide belt of old weed-stalks like reeds that had been washed up there and left.

"I expect they'll burn all right," said Titty.

"Too fast, probably," said John. "We want every scrap of real wood we can get."

"What about the dead crabs?" said Roger. "There are hundreds of them in among the reeds."

"They won't be much good," said John. "I say, we'll have to make a rule that nobody leaves the camp without bringing back a bit of wood."

Gleaning carefully along the dyke, John and Titty got together two bundles of scraps of wood and a few bigger bits that looked as if they might have come from an old railing.

"Enough to boil a kettle on anyway," said John. "Let's take it along and something to carry reeds in. Where's Roger?"

"Somewhere round the corner," said Titty.

They found Susan sharpening the ends of two forked sticks she had cut from a willow. A long piece to carry the kettle was already lying on the ground beside her round fireplace.

"Is that all you've got?" said Susan. "I thought it was going to be difficult. There's hardly any dead wood under these bushes. I've got a little, but not much."

"There's lots of that reed rubbish. We'll take a basket . . . No . . . oilskins'll be better. Lay them flat and pile the reeds on them, and bundle them up for carrying. Hullo! What's the matter?"

Roger, who had not, like Titty and John, been able to put wood-gathering before everything else, came running into the camp.

"I say, John," he cried. "I've been down to the landing. The island's growing like anything. *Wizard* 's high and dry."

"Tide's going down," said John. "I'll come and have a look. Haven't you got any wood?"

"One bit," said Roger. "There simply wasn't any where I was looking."

"One bit," said Susan. "Oh Roger."

"Well it's a jolly good one," said Roger.

"You take your oilskin and fill it with as much of that reed stuff as you can carry," said John.

"All right," said Roger. "Dead crabs and all."

John and Titty took their oilskins too and went down over the saltings to look at *Wizard*. A few hours had made an enormous difference. They had brought the things ashore from the *Goblin* almost to the edge of the saltings. Now the saltings were far above the water level. There was a widening strip of mud beneath them. The narrow pathway between the heads of old rotting piles stretched down over the mud, and into the water.

"Good," said John at the sight of it. "Jim said it was a proper hard. We'll be able to get afloat even at low tide. But we won't shift *Wizard* now. We'll be able to slide her down over the mud if we want her."

THE MAP BEGUN

"What's happening to Bridget Island?" said Roger. "The little one . . . It's almost not an island any more."

They went floundering along the saltings to look at it. That little island that had been divided from the big one by a wide channel was an island no longer. The channel had narrowed and broken up, into little streams trickling down both sides of a mudbank. Roger tried to get across, but soon stuck and struggled back to firmer ground.

"Gosh!" he said. "It'll be easier to get to it when it's cut off at high water than when it's part of our island. This is a rum place."

"We'll have to mark that channel, 'Mud at low water'," said Titty.

On the way back to the camp they piled armfuls of dead reeds on their oilskins, bundled them up, staggered into camp with the bundles over their shoulders, and emptied them into a heap, beside the fire that was already burning.

"What's the time, John?" asked Susan.

"Haven't got a watch," said John. "Mine's still in Ipswich being mended."

"I thought it was," said Susan. "I've done the most awful thing. I've gone and left my alarm clock in the *Goblin*."

"Good," said Roger. "We'll be able to go to bed just when we like."

"Will you?" said Susan. "We'll see. But I won't know when it's time for meals. . . ."

"We'll tell you," said Roger. "It's about time for supper now."

John looked at the sun, that was already sinking low towards the western marshes.

"We'll manage all right about time," he said. "Where's a straight stick?"

"I've got one," said Titty. "I was just going to break it up for the fire."

"Fine," said John. He stuck it carefully upright. The sun threw its shadow along the ground. He cut a twig from one of the bushes behind the tents, sharpened one end of it and cut a deep notch in the other. Then he took a piece of paper from the pad on which Susan had been writing her list of stores, folded it, wrote "SUPPER" on it in large letters, fixed it in the notch, and then pushed the pointed end of the twig into the ground exactly in the thin line of shadow cast by the upright stick.

"Gosh!" said Roger. "A meal-dial."

"It'll have to do," said John. "We can't be far wrong now. It must be about supper time. We'll have supper each day when the shadow falls on the supper stick. We'll watch for midday to-morrow when the sun's highest and the shadow's shortest, and we'll shove in a dinner stick too."

"Regular meals is what matters most," said Susan.

"Well, the sun's regular enough," said John.

"What if it's cloudy?" said Roger. "And it might rain. Don't we get anything to eat unless the sun's shining?"

"We'll just have to guess," said John. "But tides are going to be a bother. Daddy gave me a tide-table, but it won't be much good if we don't know the time. The tides keep shifting round. We can't keep track of them without a clock."

"I say," said Titty. "We ought to count days, like Robinson Crusoe."

John bent down and cut a notch in the flagstaff. "That's for to-day," he said. "Every day we'll cut another notch until the *Goblin* comes back. . . ."

"And then when we lie exhausted on the sand . . .' said Titty.

"Jolly wet mud," said Roger.

"We'll see a sail far away. And it'll come nearer and nearer. And the captain will say, 'Clap your eye to a spyglass, Mister Mate.' And the mate (that's Mother) will say, 'There's something moving on the shore. They're still alive.' And we will wave and try to shout, but our parched throats won't let us. And they'll sail in, and we'll hear the anchor chain go rattling out. And then we'll all sail away together and see the island disappear into the sunset."

"It may be morning," said Roger.

"The tops of the palm trees will show like feathers above the sea, and then even they will be gone, and we shall be telling the people on the ship about the discoveries we've made and the long years we've spent here."

"Not years," said Bridget.

"Ages anyhow," said Titty.

"We'll have to get the palm trees from somewhere and plant them," said Roger. "Susan. Do look at the meal-dial."

"Well," said Susan.

"The shadow's left the supper stick already."

"Supper's ready," said Susan.

"But where?" said Roger.

"Mother's done the whole thing," said Susan. She went to the store tent and came back with the basket with a label on it, "To-night's supper". Out of it came a parcel of chops, ready-cooked, a bag of tomatoes, two lettuces with a bit of paper on which was written "The lettuces have been washed", and a bag of rock buns. At the bottom of the basket was another bit of paper with a message. "Fill up with bananas".

"There's nothing to do but to make the tea," said Susan, "and the kettle'll be boiling in a minute."

"What about Sinbad?" said Bridget.

"He shall have cold salmon and a drink of milk," said Susan.

"Jolly good supper," said Roger.

It lasted a long time, and when it was finished, there were only five mugs, five plates and one saucer to wash up. Then the explorers made ready for bed, after planning to begin work in earnest first thing in the morning. The sun had set and the wind had dropped. John, Titty and Roger brought into the camp fresh armfuls of the dead weed-stalks, which smoked for a moment and then blazed up on the fire. Bridget, already in her pyjamas, crouched at the door of the big tent looking out at her first camp-fire and at the figures of her elders moving in the dusk.

"Off you go, Roger," said Susan.

"I'm going to bed now," said Titty. "Wake me in the morning, whoever wakes first."

"Everybody got their own torches?" asked John.

"Have you filled the hurricane lantern?" asked Susan.

"Just doing it," said John. "We'll have it burning in the camp all night."

"Like a riding light," said Roger.

"To frighten away wild beasts," said Titty. "But we've got one tiger of our own. Come on, Sinbad. You're going to sleep in my tent. Bridget's got Susan."

The stars came out all over the enormous sky that came right down to the flat marshes and the open sea, a sky much bigger than the sky of the mountain country of the north. John lit the hurricane lantern and stood it on the ground outside the big tent.

"No good trying to bank up a reed fire," he said. "Not even charcoal burners could do it. . . ."

"Damp reeds would keep it going," said Susan.

"They'd only get dry and then blaze," said John. "Better not. We'll look for more driftwood in the morning."

"You get quickly into bed while you're still warm," said Susan to Bridget.

"I'm in," said Roger.

"So am I," said Titty . . . "Hullo. Sinbad's out. No, pussy. Oh all right. He's trying to curl up on my bed like he did in the boat."

"Why don't the curlews go to bed too?" said Roger. "And the gulls."

"Duck, too," said John.

"I say, was that splash a fish?"

"Aren't you going to bed, John?" said Susan.

"In a minute."

Roger, in the middle of asking questions about the noises of the birds, chattering along the edge of the mud, had fallen suddenly asleep. Bridget thought of last night. She had been in bed long before this, in a real bed, in a room with dark curtains. For the first time in her life she was sleeping, just like the others, in a tent. She wriggled a little. It was not so comfortable as a bed, but the others had always seemed to like it. So would she. She wriggled again. That must be a crease in the rug with the hard ground sheet and the ground underneath. That was better. A faint whiff of burnt reeds drifted in through the open mouth of the tent. A curlew called. Again there was a sudden chatteration of gulls. Yes. They were alone, on an island. And she was old enough to be with them at last. She put out a hand to feel for Susan.

"That you, Bridget?" said Susan. "Are you all right?"

"Very all right," said Bridget. "I was only making sure you were there."

John was last into his tent. Standing outside it he listened. Dimly, from far away, he could hear the slow murmur of the sea on the sands on the other side of the island. . . . No. . . . that must be farther still, where the open sea came in beyond that other creek. He listened to the birds. Far away, as the dark closed down, he saw a bright line of lights on the mainland to the north. He half thought he ought to keep awake this first night. Just in case. But, after all, there was nothing against getting into his sleeping bag. He could lie awake in it, ready to jump up. To-morrow they must explore the island. . . . Hullo. That was Titty whispering.

"John."

"Yes."

"It's about Nancy's message. We never answered it."

"We couldn't," said John. "It'd be rather beastly to tell them we've started another adventure already, when they're all by themselves without even the D's."

"Whatever Nancy's doing can't be as good as this," said Titty. "I wish they were here."

"So do I," said John. "But we can't help it. Good night."

"Good night."

An hour later John woke. The fire had gone out. The hurricane lantern was burning. He could see the light of it through the thin canvas of his tent. He remembered that he was in charge, in charge of a party of explorers marooned on a strange and desert island. He wriggled out of his sleeping bag, crept out and stood up outside, in the cool night. The camp was silent. The birds had quietened down. He heard an owl somewhere on the mainland. . . . If that *was* the mainland over there. He crawled back into his tent, wriggled into his sleeping bag, and, with the torch, looked at the blank map Daddy had made. There seemed to be water almost everywhere. He found his eyes closed and the torch still lit. How long had he been using the battery all for nothing? He put it out and was asleep once more.

THE NATIVE KRAAL

CHAPTER VI

FIRST HINT OF SAVAGES

B<small>RIDGET</small> stirred in her sleeping bag.

"Mummy," she began, and suddenly remembered that Mummy was far away, and that she was really ship's baby for the first time, sharing adventure with the others. She rolled over, sleeping bag and all. One side of the tent was pale with sunlight. She looked out through the open door. Wisps of white smoke were drifting past and there was a sharp smell of burning reeds. She wriggled out of her bag and crawled to the door. Smoke was pouring from the fire. A kettle hung in the smoke, and Susan was stooping beside the fire, poking sticks under the kettle. Flames licked up round the kettle and the smoke blew away. Titty and John were not to be seen, but Roger was hopping about at the edge of the little pond, first on one leg and then on the other, scrubbing himself with a towel, and saying "Grrrrrrr. Grrrrrr. . . . Jolly co . . . old."

"Well, you needn't have gone right in," she heard Susan say. "I only told you to get washed. There's boiled water for your teeth in that mug."

"They're chattering too fast to be brushed," said Roger.

"If they're chattering as fast as that you won't be able to eat any breakfast."

"Where's John, and Titty?" asked Bridget.

"Hullo, Bridgie. They've been up ages. They've gone off to get more wood. Hurry up now and get dressed. Breakfast's nearly ready. Water in that bucket. And soap."

"Don't forget to wash behind your ears," said Roger.

"Used they to say that to you?" said Bridget earnestly,

and wondered why Roger grinned a little sheepishly and Susan laughed.

Five minutes later Bridget, more or less washed and fully dressed, was explaining to Sinbad that he would have to wait till his soaked biscuits had cooled. Roger was watching the shadow of the meal-dial, with one eye on Susan, and a cleft stick with a "BREAKFAST" label all ready. Susan had opened a tin of condensed milk and mixed it with the right amount of water in a jug. Five plates heaped with cornflakes lay in a row. She had filled up the kettle with water and had begun to scramble seven eggs in the frying pan. She put the pan down for a moment.

"Hold tight, Bridgie," she said. "I'm just going to blow it."

She blew a piercing blast on her mate's whistle, and Roger drove the "BREAKFAST" twig into the ground exactly in the shadow of the upright stick. "That's two meals marked on the dial anyway," he said.

"Coming, coming," sounded in the distance, and presently John and Titty, each with an armful of sticks, came into the camp.

"I've put the breakfast peg in," said Roger.

"Good," said John, and cut a notch in the flagstaff to mark the expedition's second day.

"The inland sea's nearly dry," said Titty. "We saw some-one coming across in a horse and cart."

"The tide's right out," said John. "We've found why Daddy's map makes Bridget Island look as if it was part of this. The line he's drawn goes round outside the saltings. So it makes everything that's joined at low water look like one."

"Our map's going to show them separately," said Titty. "We're going to put in all the channels we can sail through when the tide's up."

"We're going to survey the dyke first," said John. "Everything inside that's always dry. And we're going to make a good lot of copies of Daddy's map, so that it won't matter if we make a mess of them. We'll keep Daddy's own map in the camp, and mark in each bit as we do it. Titty's going to do the explored bits in ink. Daddy's done his blank map in pencil so that we can rub the lines out and our map'll spread day by day till there are no unexplored parts left."

"Where do we begin?" asked Roger.

"With breakfast," said Susan.

*

"Morning!"

Everybody jumped. The mixture of breakfast and plans had made them deaf and blind to everything else, and here, standing close above them, smiling down at them, was a tall man in corduroy breeches, muddy sea-boots and a rough tweed coat.

"Good morning."

"Hostile or friendly?" whispered Roger, hoping Titty would hear him.

The man held out a large bottle.

"When your dad and mam were over to mine," he said, "I tell'em there'd be milk to spare some days. This any good to you?"

"Thank you very much," said Susan. "We didn't mean to bother you. We've brought lots of milk in tins. But this'll be ever so much nicer. Would you like a cup of tea?"

"I won't say 'No'," said the man. "Up early this morning and over to the town. Just come back across the Wade."

"We saw your cart in the distance," said Titty.

"But isn't it an island?" said Roger.

"Not at low water it isn't."

Susan had filled a mug and handed it up to him. She offered him the tin of lump sugar and his own bottle of milk. "You won't like ours after the real milk," she said.

"Do you mean it's really just part of the mainland?" said Roger. What was the good of an island, he was thinking, if people could get to it in carts?

"Oh no. It's an island all right. But when the tide's out, there's just one way you can get across if you follow the track over the mud. When the tide's in you can't get nowhere without no boat."

"That's all right," said Roger.

The man emptied the mug down his throat. "If you keep to the dyke you'll be all right," he said. "But the saltings is treacherous. You might easy get in soft and not get out in a hurry. I've lost more'n one pair of boots myself. Friends of young Brading's aren't you? Well, if there's anything I can do for you, let me know. But you'll find it a dull place, I reckon. No life, if you know what I mean. Nobody about. Only you and them savages. And as for them savages . . ."

"What savages?" asked Titty and Roger together.

"Savages?" said Bridget.

Susan stared. John opened his mouth to speak but said nothing.

"I tell your dad about 'em, and he say you'd deal with 'em all right."

"But what savages?" said Roger. "Where are they?"

"Ain't seen 'em for a few days," said the man chuckling. "Not more'n one of 'em. But they might be back any day now. You'll know 'em when you meet 'em. Well, so long." He turned to go, and then, over his shoulder, he asked, "You ain't got no dog? I meant to ask your dad."

"We've got a kitten," said Bridget.

"That's all right," said the man. "He won't take to chasing buffaloes. . . . That's what they called it. We had to make 'em send their dog away." He waved his hand in a friendly manner and was gone, striding along the top of the dyke.

"Gosh!" said Roger.

"Savages!" said Titty.

Bridget moved a little closer to Susan.

"Well that settles it," said John.

"Settles what?" said Roger.

"What we do this morning. You heard what he said about savages. The first thing we've got to do is to make sure the island's clear of them. We'll do the survey at the same time."

"Let's start," said Roger.

But there was a good deal to be done first, while Susan was washing up and Titty and Roger were doing the wiping and Bridget was keeping Sinbad from licking the cleaned plates. "He's trying to help, really," she said, but Susan thought he'd be more use if he didn't. John, putting a piece of paper on the top of Daddy's blank map and then holding it up to the light was making a careful tracing. "We want about a dozen of them," he said. "We're sure to spoil a good many. And we ought each to have one to put down anything we discover." Then, for the purpose of the survey, he made on a larger scale a copy of the big blob that on Daddy's map showed the island on which they had landed. In the corner of it he made a copy of the compass rose that Daddy had drawn, using the parallel rulers to make sure it was pointing in the same direction. North, South, East and West were easy to mark, and then with a pair of dividers, he cut each half circle in half, and marked North-East, South-East, North-West and South-West. There really was some use in some of the things they taught at school. Then the quarter circles had to be cut in half in the same way, to get North-North-East, East-North-East and the rest of them.

Then, when the washing up was finished, Roger was sent off to plant one of the bamboo surveying poles at the corner of the dyke to the south of the camp, while John and Titty went off with the map, the compass, a note-book and another bamboo to the corner north of the camp, where the dyke turned sharply eastwards near the mouth of Goblin Creek. Titty planted the post, and John took a bearing from one post to the other, which was easily seen with Roger standing beside it.

"This bit of dyke's about north by east. It'll do for a base line. Now for the kraal." He turned and faced inland towards the clump of small trees and the farm chimneys. "South-east. Got the parallel rulers?"

Kneeling on the ground, he ruled a line between the two posts, and then ruled another across the middle of the island from the dot on the map that marked the northern post.

"It's somewhere on that line," he said. "Come on. Now we'll take a bearing of it from the other post."

The two surveyors hurried along the dyke to join Roger, who was getting a little tired of holding up his post, because he had not been able to drive it far enough in to make it stand by itself.

John jammed it in, and then, compass in hand, looked across at the distant chimney of the farmhouse. "Bit south of east," he said.

"Let me try," said Roger, put the compass on the ground for steadiness and straddled above it. "Jolly nearly east-south-east."

Titty tried. "It looks to me just between the two."

John looked carefully across the compass at the farm, agreed.

"All right," he said. "We'll call it east by south. Now let's try." He made a mark on the compass rose half way between east and east-south-east, and putting one edge of the rulers on the centre of the rose and on this mark, he used the other edge to draw a line east by south through the dot that marked the position of the southern post.

"It's all right," he said. "Look."

The two lines crossed each other just about in the middle

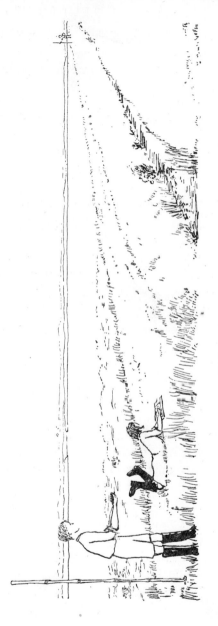

TAKING BEARINGS

of the blob where Daddy had put a little square to mark the farm.

"Well, that's the kraal done anyway," he said.

They went back to the camp and showed Susan what they had done.

"It's going to take an awful long time to map each island," said Susan.

"We needn't do it all like that," said John.

"How are you going to do the marshes?"

"Put them in afterwards," said John. "But we've got to get the solid land done first. We'll go along the dyke right round the island, taking a bearing wherever it turns a corner. It's sure to be all dry land inside it."

"Any savages," said Roger, "are bound to be on the dry."

"Have you seen any?" asked Bridget.

"Not yet," said Roger.

"Ready to start?" asked John. "We'll each take a bamboo."

"I'd better make some more copies of the blank map first," said Titty.

"Somebody ought to look after the camp," said Susan, "if there really are people about."

There was a moment's debate, and then it was decided that the main body of surveyors would follow the dyke north-about round the island and that Bridget, Sinbad and Titty would go the other way, not hurrying and giving Titty time to make some copies of the map before they started. With the whole island flat and open between the two parties, it was felt that prowling savages, if there were any, would stand a poor chance of not being seen.

"If we see any savages near the camp," said Bridget, "we'll . . ."

"Blow the mate's whistle for us," said Roger.

"We won't," said Bridget. "We'll send Sinbad at them like a tiger."

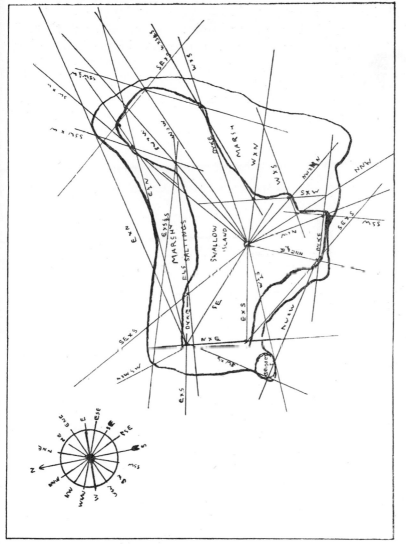

ROUGH MAP WITH BEARINGS

"His claws are pretty sharp," said Roger. "But he'll probably only purr at them."

"There won't be anybody," said Bridget. "Or will there?"

"There can't be anyone at this end of the island," said John, "or we'd have seen them already. Do let's get started."

The surveying party, with bamboo poles, compass, drawing board and instruments was on its way.

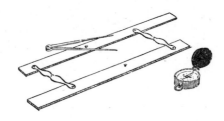

CHAPTER VII

HOOFMARKS IN THE MUD

Titty forgot about savages while, one after another, she made a dozen copies of the blank map. It was not difficult, but it needed careful doing, and she enjoyed doing it, and, as usual when she had a pencil in her hand, could think of nothing else. But when eleven of those copies were piled in John's tent, with his barometer for a paperweight, and she had taken the twelfth and had set out with Bridget and Sinbad to follow the dyke along the southern side of the island, she remembered the savages once more. Bridget, who had been keeping a look out, had not forgotten them for a moment.

They had left the camp and were moving along the dyke very slowly at first, because Sinbad was not a quick explorer. He trotted this way and that in the short grass, wrinkling his nose and sniffing at things, and then going back and sniffing again. The only way to get him to come on was to walk backwards in front of him. "We'll have to carry him if we're going to get anywhere," Titty said at last and hove him up in her arms.

That was better. The able seaman and the ship's baby were able to get going at human instead of at kitten speed. They stopped now and then, and Bridget took the kitten for a minute or two while Titty, who found she could do quite well without surveying poles or the compass, dotted in the line of the dyke on the blank map, and with little scrabblings of her pencil showed the marshy saltings between the dyke and the channel that joined Goblin Creek to the inland sea. The tide was still too low to let her see the water in the channel, but she could see where it was and dotted it in, to be marked properly when they were able to sail through it in the *Wizard*.

"No savages yet?" said Bridget, when they had moved on and Titty, with the kitten on her shoulder, was looking across the island through the telescope.

"No," said Titty.

"Where have the others got to by now?"

"There's somebody. Right away on the other side. They've got on jolly fast."

"May I look?"

Titty handed over the telescope. It had not been easy to use it with the ship's kitten thinking he would like to get down and do some more exploring on his own. Bridget put the telescope to her eye, and pushed it in and pulled it out.

"It's all blurry," she said. "I can see better without it."

Far away on the skyline on the other side of the island small figures were moving, figures so small that it was hard to tell who was who.

"If we wanted help, they're too far to come," said Bridget, looking at Titty's face to see how she took this bit of news.

"We shan't want help," said Titty. "Not three of us." But she lowered her voice a little and looked warily round. Not a savage was in sight.

They went on. Below the dyke the saltings were narrowing. Wide mudflats stretched beyond them, divided by a ribbon of water. On the landward side they could see the farm, sheltering among its trees, green meadowland and grazing cattle.

"Well, there are plenty of buffaloes," said Titty.

"But no savages," said Bridget. "Couldn't we let Sinbad explore for a bit?"

For some time now Sinbad had been more difficult to hold. He was down in a moment, crawling through the grass, pretending to pounce on a dry bit of reed that was lifted by the wind, and then shaking a paw almost angrily after stepping in the damp mud of the footpath.

"Come along," said Bridget. "Puss, puss, puss!" And Sinbad, in his own good time, moved slowly after her.

"Try with a bit of string," said Titty, and took a coiled up bit from her pocket, tied a small handful of dry grass at one end of it and gave it to Bridget. Bridget walked backwards, jerking the little bundle of grass along the ground. Sinbad crouched, leapt after it, rolled over, crouched and leapt again. "He likes that kind of exploring," said Bridget.

"Good," said Titty. "Keep him going."

She walked slowly on. The saltings below the dyke grew narrower, and were now no more than a fringe to the wide expanse of mud that stretched across from the island to the mainland instead of the bright, shimmering sea that they had seen from the deck of the *Goblin* when they had sailed into the Creek. A ribbon of water was spreading in the middle of the mud. Tide was coming up. Soon the mud would be a sea once more.

In the saltings, close below the dyke, was a narrow ditch, leading out towards the mud. At the side of the ditch was a landing stage made of a few planks, and a big heavy rowing boat lay beside it. Titty carefully marked it on her map and wrote "Native Harbour". That, she decided, must be the boat the native from the kraal used when he could not use his cart.

She was walking on, looking far out over the mud. Suddenly she stopped. On the edge of the ribbon of water out there were wading birds. But the water, slowly rising, was lapping at something that no birds could have made. If it had been sand, she might have thought that someone had been playing there with a spade and bucket. But no one builds castles in the mud.

She pulled out the telescope. Yes. She could see that the

mud had been freshly turned, as if with a spade. Savages after all? It was not piled high enough for even the smallest savage to hide behind it. But someone had certainly been digging. With the telescope she followed a long line of diggings, here quite a big heap of mud, there only a few spadefuls turned over. There were marks in the mud going from one digging to the next. The line of marks curved in over the mud towards the island. It looked as if it ended by a sort of promontory, where there were no saltings, and the mud came close up to the foot of the dyke. Whoever had done that digging might have come ashore there. He might be behind the promontory. Or he might have crossed the dyke and be on the island itself, hiding, perhaps, on the landward side of the dyke.

Titty looked back. Bridget, stooping down, was coming slowly along, enticing Sinbad as she went. There was no sign of anybody moving on the meadows. John, Susan and Roger were not in sight. By now, she thought they must be at the other end of the island, somewhere beyond the part she had already called the "prairie", where a large herd of cows were calmly grazing, not suspecting for a moment that they had been promoted to be buffaloes. The other party of explorers would be coming round behind them. Whoever had done those diggings might be between the two parties, or somewhere in the middle of the island. She turned her telescope on the buffaloes. Yes, some of them had stopped grazing, but they were looking all in the same direction, not towards the middle of the island but the other way. They must have sighted the surveying party. Not a single buffalo seemed to be interested in anything between them and herself. It was safe to go forward.

"Bridget," she called, not very loud, "Pick up Sinbad and come along."

"Wait for us," called Bridget.

"Hurry up."

Titty looked first one way and then the other along the green dyke. She looked across the wide flat meadowland. There was not a moving thing to be seen. No. Yes. Those were rabbits close to the railing that enclosed the native kraal. But the rabbits were peaceably feeding. And the birds, too, all seemed busy about their own affairs. Those must be pigeons near the kraal. Those were peewits on the meadows. Well, there are no fussier birds than peewits when human beings are about, but these seemed not to have a care in the world. No. They were quite safe in moving on. There was no danger of any savages cutting them off from the camp. And John, Susan and Roger must be much more than half way round by now. It ought to be safe to go as far as the promontory.

"Come on, Bridget. . . . There's something we've got to go and look at."

"Where?" asked Bridget. "Those birds?" She looked out over the mud, following Titty's pointing finger.

"Don't hold your arm out," said Titty. "Just in case somebody might be watching us. Point like this, if you have to." She crooked her wrist, and pointed with a finger, her hand held close in against her body. "Not the birds. Someone's been out there on the mud."

Already she was moving on, along the top of the grass dyke, that divided the meadowland from the reedy saltings and the shining mud beyond them. She could see that line of diggings leading over the mud towards the point. From there she would be able to see just what those marks were like, that made a trail from digging to digging. Would they be the prints of naked feet? Or did these savages wear boots?

As she came nearer to the point, she noticed something else. At long intervals a withy, a thin, leafless sapling, was stuck upright in the mud. There was one, and then another beyond that, a long line of them leading away over the mud

F   81

towards the mainland. As she came nearer she saw that they marked a cart track.

"That's how the native from the farm gets to the town to do his shopping," she said to Bridget. "He gets across at low water, when the tide's out like this. And then when the tide comes up if it isn't too deep he comes splashing across in his horse and cart, and those little trees show him where the road is. That's what he meant when he said he'd come across the Wade."

"Oh," said Bridget. "Was it him that was digging in the mud?"

"We'll soon know," said Titty. "We'll look at those footmarks. The native was wearing seaboots, just like ours. But . . . I say . . . Giminy. . . . The native never made tracks like those."

She waited for Bridget no longer, but ran forward. There was something very funny about those footmarks. They seemed . . . She hardly knew what they seemed. The boots of the native had certainly been big, but she did not think a boot had ever been made to make prints as big as these.

Bridget, clutching the unwilling Sinbad, panted up to find Titty staring at huge round marks in the mud. Yes. They were a track all right, but what native could leave huge round footprints nearly two feet wide. Two lines of these enormous prints, two double lines, lay on the mud stretching far away till they disappeared at the edge of the incoming tide.

'Giminy,' said Titty. "They aren't human footprints at all. They're the hoofmarks of a mastodon." She looked across towards the mainland. Those marshes might stretch for miles. Anything might live in them and nobody would know.

"What's a mastodon?" said Bridget. "A sort of savage?"

"No. A sort of elephant."

"With a trunk?"

"Yes. Hairy all over."

"THE NATIVE NEVER MADE TRACKS LIKE THOSE..."

"Horrible?" Bridget looked at the huge prints on the mud and then anxiously over her shoulder.

"No. Gorgeous," said Titty hurriedly.

"Oh. Then it's all right," said Bridget.

"Quite all right," said Titty, though she did not think so. "Hullo!"

They had gone down to the edge of the mud to have a closer look at the hoofmarks, but at that shout Titty ran up again to the top of the dyke. Yes. There they were, John, Susan and Roger, coming along on the other side of the point. She beckoned eagerly.

In another two minutes they joined her. Roger was telling her their news long before they arrived. "We've been all round," he shouted. "We've been to the kraal. We've been to the edge of the sea. We've seen those anchored dhows. And there are islands. Lots of them. Some all sand. Some just marshy, with bushes on them. And there's a huge lot of blackberries close to our camp. What's the matter?"

John as he came was looking at his map. "We've got all the bearings clear," he called out. "We've just got to work them out with the rulers. I say, what is it?"

"Come and look," said Titty.

John and Roger dumped surveying instruments and bamboo poles on the top of the dyke, and ran down to the edge of the mud. The others followed.

"What on earth are they?" said John.

"It's a sort of elephant," said Bridget. "Titty says it's quite all right."

"The hoofmarks of a mastodon," said Titty. "At first I thought they were the footprints of a savage, but they can't be."

"Too big," said John, peering about on the ground. "It's by itself, whatever it is. There's no sign of a human being."

"Perhaps there was a human being on its back," said Roger.

He ran out on the mud to have a nearer look, and instantly sank to the top of his boots. He floundered, trying to pull out first one foot and then the other. He fell forward on his hands and lifted them, black to the elbow, dripping and shiny.

"Oh, Roger!" cried Susan.

"Black gloves," said Bridget.

"Come out, Roger!" said Susan.

"I'm coming," said Roger. He tugged mightily, left one boot in the mud, then the other, sank to his knees, lost both socks, and staggered ashore. He put up a dripping black hand to brush the hair out of his eyes, and grinned at them, a sort of piebald negro.

John, stepping with great care, sinking deep but keeping his balance, rescued Roger's boots and threw them to the foot of the sea wall. It was no use even trying to rescue the socks. John, balancing himself with his arms, had a good look at those enormous prints. Then, slowly, using his hands to keep his boots on, he rejoined the others.

"It's very rum," he said. "The thing can't be a mastodon or any kind of elephant, or it would have sunk in deeper than Roger or me. Those hoofmarks hardly go in at all."

"Whatever it is, it's alive," said Titty.

"I've got most of the mud out of the inside," said Roger, who had been wiping out his boots with a handful of grass.

"We'll never get them properly dry," said Susan. "Come along. Let's get back to the camp."

"It must be nearly time to put another mealstick in the dial," said Roger.

"And Sinbad's thinking about that milk," said Bridget.

Titty felt a little disappointed. Nobody seemed to take those hoofmarks seriously.

She showed John her map.

"Jolly good," said John. "We can check it by taking bearings from that place where the dyke turns round at right angles. Half a minute. We want a bearing to see how that road to the mainland lies over the mud."

"I'm going to put in the buffaloes," said Titty. "And we'll have to call all this the Red Sea." She waved her hand towards the muddy plain with the cart road across it with withies sticking up. Already the water was creeping over the mud towards the road, a tongue of water from the east moving slowly on to meet another tongue of water from the west.

"Why?" said Roger.

"Pharaoh and the Israelites," said Titty. "Just the place for them. The waters divide when the tide goes down and they can rush across where those sticks mark the road, and then the water comes back from both ends and joins and sweeps them away, chariots and all."

"Right you are," said John. "Red Sea. I've put down the ford. That's what he means by the Wade. At high water we'll take *Wizard* and sail across it."

"If it's safe to leave the island," said Titty. "We haven't seen any savages yet. But what about those mastodon marks? They must have been made by something."

"Not a mastodon anyway," said John.

"Well, if it isn't a mastodon, what is it?"

"We'll keep a look out," said John, "and see if we can find any more. But I think the native was just rotting. I don't believe there's a single savage about. I say, come on. Susan and Bridget are miles ahead."

Susan, thinking more of the explorers' dinner than of strange hoofprints, had picked up Sinbad and was hurrying back to the camp with Bridget close behind her, keeping up with two steps and a run. The others followed.

"Don't go so fast," said Roger. "It's awful with bare feet."

Ten minutes later he had forgotten they were bare. Susan had hardly reached the camp before they heard the frantic blast of the mate's whistle, and saw her beckoning, looking first one way and then the other and then waving again. She was not making proper signals. But anybody could see that what she meant was "Come as quick as you jolly well can." Something serious had happened. John, Titty and even Roger, covered with mud and carrying boots as well as a bamboo pole, broke into a run.

Susan was standing by the fireplace, pointing. Bridget was close to her, as close as she could get.

Susan had a finger to her lips. "Sorry," she whispered. "I oughtn't to have whistled. Someone's been in the camp. Look at that!"

A stick, painted red and green and blue, and carved so that it looked like a snake, with a long narrow head, was stuck upright in the ground. Round the neck of the snake were hung four small yellow shells.

"Gosh!" said John. "What about our boat?"

He put down compass and drawing board and bamboo poles, and raced down to the edge of the saltings, Titty, Roger, and Susan close behind.

"I'm coming too," shouted Bridget, and Susan waited for her.

The tide was rising in Goblin Creek. The *Wizard* was as they had left her, with her anchor well up on the saltings. There was still a strip of mud between her and the water.

"The mastodon," cried Titty. "It's been here too."

From the edge of the saltings, close by the *Wizard*, a double line of those same enormous prints crossed the mud.

"Look, look," shouted Roger. "Too late. . . ."

"What? Where?"

Roger was pointing. "A boat. I saw it. It was just going behind the other island."

The others looked up the Creek where Roger was pointing.

"We can't see it now," said Roger. "It simply disappeared into the land."

"Are you sure?" said John.

"As eggs is eggs," said Roger.

"Who was in the boat?"

"I didn't see that," said Roger. "I just saw the stern of the boat disappear. We'd be seeing it now if it wasn't for the land being in the way."

"Come on," said John. "We've got to get *Wizard* down to the water."

In another minute he had coiled the muddy anchor rope in the bows, and Roger, barefooted, and Titty and he were hauling *Wizard* down along the edge of the little hard where the tops of the old piles showed above the mud and there was ground firm enough to let people move without getting stuck.

"Look here, John," said Susan. "Are you sure we ought?"

"We must," said John. "If it's just a native, it won't matter. But if it's savages, we've simply got to know where we are. That snake wasn't stuck in our camp for nothing."

"And we *must* find out what makes those marks," said Titty.

John stopped. "There may be more of them about," he said. "Look here, Susan. Will you and Bridget guard the camp. . . . ?"

"Susan," said Bridget. "We've left Sinbad all alone there."

"And do look at the shadow on the meal-dial," said Roger. "I bet it's short enough for dinner time. Put a stick to mark the place. We'll be extra hungry after hunting mastodons."

John and Titty were already in the boat.

"Sit on the bows, Roger," said John, "and wash your hoofs over the side. We've got enough mud in already."

The *Wizard* slid off into deep water. John spun her round, and with quick strong strokes of his oars and no splashes,

WHAT SUSAN FOUND IN THE CAMP

rowed up the creek. Roger splashed first with one foot and then with the other, and his legs showed white again, as if he had been tearing black stockings off them.

"Quiet, Roger," said Titty. "What's the good of John being quiet if you make such a row."

"Keep a good look out," said John. "Don't talk. Titty, you make a compass of your hand, pointing which way the boat's nose ought to go. They may be close round the corner. If they hear somebody shouting 'Pull right' and 'Pull left' they'll know we're after them and get away altogether."

CHAPTER VIII

THE MASTODON'S LAIR

Titty sat in the stern of *Wizard*, holding one hand just above her knees, pointing, now a little to the right, now a little to the left, so that John, watching it, need not look over his shoulder to see where he was going, and could give his whole mind to driving the boat along and getting his oars in and out of the water without a splash. The tide had still a long way to rise, and they could see nothing on either side but brown mud and the green line of grass and weeds against the sky.

The small island was still joined to their own by mud. The creek bent round it on its way to the Red Sea. Nothing seemed to be moving on the water.

"Over there. Over there," whispered Roger. "That's where it must have gone."

Titty's hand pointed suddenly sharp to the right. John backwatered with his left oar and the boat spun half round. Now, for the first time, he looked over his shoulder.

In the bend of the creek, opposite the little island, was an opening. John rowed straight for it and they shot into a narrow gully far below the level of the marshes.

"There's hardly room to row," whispered Roger.

"Look out, Titty, I'll have to scull over the stern."

Titty and John changed places, and John with quick twisting strokes, drove the boat on into the gully. There was mud close on either side of them, and beyond the mud, steep banks with great holes where lumps had fallen away.

"It's pretty shallow," whispered John. "I was on the bottom just then. There it is again."

They turned another corner.

"There's the boat," whispered Roger. "But there's nobody in it."

John gave up sculling and poled the *Wizard* forward as well as he could, though the oar stuck in the mud when he pushed at it. The *Wizard* touched the mud, and stopped, only a few feet from a small brown rowing boat. Beyond the rowing boat was mud only. A rope ran from the boat to the side of the gully, and at the end of it they could see a small anchor, high on the bank. Whoever or whatever had been in that boat had made it fast before leaving it. But he or it had not landed, at least, not here. Again they saw those huge prints, a plain trail of them, two lines of enormous round hoofmarks leading from the water towards the anchor, and then away from the bank and on round another corner, along the muddy bottom of the gully.

"We'd better get ashore," said Roger.

John prodded downwards with his oar, and brought it up black and dripping. "We can't land here," he said. "We'd only sink. We've got to get back. I saw a place where I think we could, just after we left our creek."

Titty with an oar at the bows, John with an oar at the stern, drove the *Wizard* back along the gully, till the water was wide enough to turn in. Near the mouth of the gully they came to the place John had seen, where some of the bank had fallen down. They prodded the fallen earth. It was a good deal harder than the mud. One by one they scrambled ashore. John took the anchor with him and planted it in the top of the bank. They found themselves on a dyke like the one that ran all round their own island.

"She'll be all right here," said John looking down at the *Wizard*. "The tide's coming in the whole time. It won't be so hard getting back into her."

"We haven't got any weapons," said Titty.

"Shan't want any," said John. "We're not attacking. Only scouting. We've just got to find out."

From the top of the high bank he looked back across Goblin Creek to the island they had left. There were the tents and smoke from the fire. Everything looked peaceful. He could even see that Bridget was walking backwards, probably pulling something along the ground for Sinbad. War, even awkwardness with strangers, was the last thing he wanted. But that carved snake in the camp meant something. Strangers had been there. And there was that boat and those enormous hoofmarks. There was nothing for it but to go on.

"It'll get away if we're not quick," said Titty.

"Come on," said John, and they hurried along the top of the dyke looking down into the gully. They passed the anchored rowing boat, and hurried on, their eyes on the trail of huge hoofmarks in the mud below them.

"I say," said Titty. "Look at that. It's the wreck of a ship."

The gully was bending round, and ahead of them a lot of gaunt black timbers were sticking up above the mud.

"An old barge," said John.

"She must have been here hundreds of years," said Titty. "Just bones of her left."

Then, as they came nearer, they saw that though the stern part of the barge and the middle had all been broken or rotted away, the bows, close under the bank, still looked like the bows of a seagoing ship. The forepart was still decked. There was a rusty windlass, and a hatch, and the heavy tabernacle that once had held the mast. A rusty chain ran through a hawsehole in the bulwarks, over the dyke, to a rusty anchor bedded in the meadow. The sides of the old barge had fallen away aft, but forward they had been newly tarred. There was a small square window below the bulwarks. And someone had put new paint, blue, and yellow, on the scrollwork round the barge's name, the bright red letters of which looked as if they were hardly dry.

"*Speedy*," said Roger. "She won't go very fast now."

"Never again," said Titty, thinking of water foaming under those old black bows now wedged into the mud.

"They must have just shoved her out of the way here, and left her to rot," said John.

"But why have they bothered to put new paint on her name?"

"Both sides," said Titty, who had walked on till she could see the other side of the barge's stem. "I say, John. There are no more hoofmarks on this side." She lowered her voice. "Perhaps it's lurking in the wreck."

"There's a regular path on the marshes over there," said John. "He's probably got away ... What's that? Listen."

There was a noise of splitting wood.

"It's inside," said Roger.

"Keep quiet," said John.

"If it's natives," said Titty, "we could just ask if they've seen it.'

"Seen what?"

"A mastodon," said Titty, "or whatever it is that makes those hoofmarks."

"Hullo," said Roger. "Somebody must be living here. Look at that."

A thick cloud of yellow smoke had poured suddenly out from the top of a rusty iron pipe that stuck up through the deck close by the ancient windlass. Knee deep in the rank grass of the dyke, they stood and stared and sniffed the pungent smell. There could be no doubt about it. One end of the wreck was derelict, but the other end was still in use. That new tar on the bows, the new paint on the name, and now this smoke from the chimney, showed that, even if the *Speedy* would never sail again, even if it was only a matter of time before most of

SPEEDY

her would fall apart and disappear in the mud, someone still had a use for part of her. One end of her was wholly dead, but the other was very much alive. It was as if they had come across a skeleton and on looking at the skull had been greeted with a wink.

They stood there, looking up and down the narrow winding gully, across it to the marshes of the mainland, to distant fields, trees, and farms, back towards the Secret Water, and Goblin Creek, and their own camp on the other side of it. They could see flashes of white, the tops of their tents along the dyke. But near by everything was wild and desolate, marshes, the creek that was more like a ditch than a creek, mud, and the derelict old barge. And here, with not a human being in sight except themselves, there was smoke pouring from that rusty chimney, and the noise of splitting wood had changed to the crackle of a new lit fire.

"Someone's looking at us," whispered Roger. "I saw a face . . . it's gone now . . . someone was looking at us through that window."

"We'd better clear out," said John. "It isn't our island."

"Couldn't we just ask?" said Roger.

But John had turned and was walking back along the top of the dyke. "It'd be all right if we were afloat," he said to Titty. "We could row up here at high water, and try to get out the other side, to see if it's really an island. Whoever it is may be on deck then, swabbing down or something. . . ."

"I say!"

A boy had come up through the *Speedy's* fore (and only) hatch. Bigger than Roger though not as tall as John, he was dressed in a rather ragged grey jersey and his muddy grey trousers were tucked into socks. He had a mop of stiff sandy hair. His eyes shone bright blue in a face burnt brick red by the sun.

"Where are his boots?" said Roger. "Has he got stuck too?"

96

"Hullo," said John.

"I say," said the boy. "Is that your camp over there? Sorry I barged in. I thought you were somebody else. As soon as I saw you coming I tried to clear out. I thought you hadn't seen me."

"We didn't," said Roger. "But we saw your boat."

"We wanted to know what made those hoofmarks on the mud," said Titty. "Do you keep it in the barge?"

The boy laughed and then was serious again.

"I left something behind in your camp," he said.

"I know," said John.

"I meant to come and take it away again after dark."

"Oh! He mustn't do that," exclaimed Titty. "He'd only frighten Bridget."

"We'll give it back," said John.

"We wondered what it was," said Titty.

The boy opened his mouth to speak and shut it again. "Just a game," he said after a pause.

For some moments nobody said anything. Then the boy spoke again.

"Look here," he said. "Do you know the Lapwings?"

"I saw lots this morning," said Roger, "when we were walking round the island."

"Not those," said the boy. "*Lapwing*'s a yacht. Look here. How did you get here? I never saw you come. I wasn't here yesterday."

"We came in a boat," said John.

"You didn't know about the Lapwings?"

"No. We've never been here before."

"I thought it was rum," said the boy. "Because they said they were going to camp on Flint Island as usual. But when I saw your camp I was sure they'd changed their minds. I didn't think anybody else knew about this place."

"We didn't," said Titty. "We're exploring. We aren't

exactly shipwrecked. But we can't get away till our ship comes back. We're marooned."

"Marooned," said the boy, considering. "Do they know at the farm?" He looked far away across Goblin Creek, to the island beyond it.

"In the Native Kraal?" said Titty. "They know. One of them brought us some milk this morning, but that was just to see what we were like. We've got our own milk, in tins."

"Kraal's a good word," said the boy. "My father's got a Kraal, too. Over there." He pointed south over the marshes. "You can't see it. Hidden by the trees. So it's just as good as if it wasn't there. There's nobody here except just them. . . ." Again he looked away towards the distant farm, a bit of tiled roof showing above the little trees. "Only the Lapwings and me . . . until you came."

John said, "Look here, I'll go and bring that thing if you put it up in our camp by mistake."

"Never mind," said the boy. "I'll come across and fetch it."

"Do you live here?" asked Roger.

The boy considered.

"Like to come and see?" he said at last.

"Very much," said John.

"It's too far to jump," said Roger.

But the boy stooped and from below the bulwarks lifted a broad plank and stood it on end, and then let it fall forward so that it made a bridge between the wreck and the dyke.

"Make sure that end's firm," he said.

Roger was first on the plank. Titty had taken a step or two after him when he stopped dead.

"Look out, Titty," he said. "If two of us are on it, it'll jump and Susan'll be in an awful stew if I go in the mud again."

"It'd be a job to get you out," said the boy.

One by one they crossed the plank and stepped down on the wreck. It was like standing on the deck of a ship of which nothing was left but the bows. Looking aft, there were gaunt ribs sticking up out of the mud, and the remains of the stern. But where they were standing, everything was solid. The deck was scrubbed and clean and there was new paint on the bulwarks that ended in mid air.

"I began looking after her just in time," said the boy. "Look here. I'd better go first, just to clear things out of the way down below."

He slid out of sight, backwards, down the steep ladder in the hatchway. The others followed him, one by one, and, for a moment stood blinking at the foot of the ladder. A lot of light came down through the hatch, and a little from each of the two small square windows that had been cut high up in the sides. But all the woodwork was black with age, and it was a minute or two before they could see what sort of living place this was that the boy had made for himself in the bows of the old wreck. There was a rusty little stove, into which the boy was pushing some scraps of wood. There was a sort of bunk, built into the side with rugs in it. There was a table made of thick black wood, roughly nailed together. "Made that out of some of the old planking," said the boy proudly, and John thought, though he did not say, that it might very well have been rather better made. There was a good solid seat that had clearly once been the thwart of a boat. There were shelves, very rough, along the walls. An old hurricane lantern, not lit, hung from a beam. There were nails driven into the beams, and into the walls, and from these nails hung all kinds of things, fishing lines on wooden winders, a net of some kind, begun but not finished, with a big wooden needle, half full of string, stuck in among the meshes. In one corner were some fishing rods, and beside them, leaning against the wall of the cabin, were three more carved sticks, like the one they had found stuck in the ground by Susan's fireplace. Roger saw them first.

"More snakes?" he said.

"Eels really," said the boy. "Snakes don't have a fin down their backs."

"I thought there was something funny about it for a snake," said Titty.

"What are they for?" asked John.

"They're . . ." and then the boy pulled himself up. He had just been going to say something, but changed his mind.

"Don't tell us if it's a secret," said Titty. "Is the thing that makes those hoofmarks secret too?"

The boy threw back his head and laughed. "Don't you know splatchers?" he said.

"Splatchers?" said Roger.

"Splatchers," said the boy. "For walking on the mud."

"Gosh!" said Roger. "Like snowshoes?"

"I'll show you," said the boy. "I always leave them outside so as not to get mud all over old *Speedy*. It's only at high tide the water comes up here, and I couldn't get home without them, or get to my boat, or anything."

"They make marks just like a mastodon," said Titty.

"I've never seen one," said the boy.

"Neither have I," said Titty. "But like an elephant anyway."

The boy busied himself with his fire, took a saucepan from its hook on the wall, and opened a parcel with bacon in it. They watched him. "Susan's cooking our dinner," Roger said absently.

Titty looked at John.

"I say," said John. "Why not come back with us now to get your eel and have dinner. Unless you *want* to cook. We've got an enormous lot of grub."

SPLATCHERS

"I don't mind," said the boy. "And if you want to see those splatchers. . . ."

They climbed on deck once more. The boy went to the edge of the deck furthest from the bank. A rope ladder hung there, and beside it, on hooks, were the splatchers, two large oval boards, with rope grips in the middle of them for heel and toe, and stout leather straps for fasteners. The boy unhooked them and dropped them neatly so that they fell flat on the mud with their fastenings uppermost. He hauled on a pair of sea-boots and went down the rope ladder.

"Mud's very soft here," he said. "If I didn't drop them first I wouldn't be able to stand to get them on."

With his weight on one of the splatchers, he put his foot in the right place on the other and made it fast. Then with his weight on that splatcher he strapped the other on the other foot.

"Now," he said, and was off, swinging each leg in a wide circle so as not to trip himself with the big oval boards on his feet. Off he went, with a loud sucking noise, as he lifted the splatchers from the mud, one two, one two, one two, one two, leaving behind him the mastodon track of enormous hoof-marks. Off he went, swinging his legs, running easily along the muddy bottom of the creek where they knew the mud was so soft that in ordinary seaboots he could not have taken a step without being bogged.

He turned and came running back, left his splatchers on the mud, climbed up his rope ladder and, a little out of breath, was once more beside them on the deck of the old barge.

"Gosh!" said Roger. "Can anybody do it?"

"It needs a bit of practice," said the boy. "I'll get the plank in, if you'll go ashore. I never leave it up when I'm not here."

"Are there other savages?" said Titty.

"I say. Did he tell you?"

"Who?"

"The man from the farm . . . the Kraal."

"He said there was one of them about," said Titty. "Is it you?"

"Oh well," said the boy. "If you know that. . . . He oughtn't to have told you really."

"Sorry," said Titty. "We didn't know the savages were a secret. We'll pretend we don't know. We'll just call you the Mastodon."

"My name's Don," said the boy.

"Short for Mastodon," said Titty.

The boy laughed. "It doesn't matter your knowing about savages," he said. "At least I don't think so. If you've been marooned, it's really right for you to know."

A shrill whistle sounded in the distance.

"Grub," said Roger, hurrying across the plank. "That's the mate's whistle."

"I'll catch you up," said the boy. "Where's your boat?"

"Close to yours."

Titty and John followed Roger ashore and along the high bank above the gully. The boy pulled in the plank, slipped down the other side of the wreck, and, hardly a moment later, they saw him running below them on the mud with that queer swinging run, leaving behind him a beautiful trail of mastodon hoofmarks. By the time they reached their boat, he was already in his, and they pulled out into Goblin Creek close together.

Roger was first ashore on the other side, and ran up to the camp.

"Extra plate, Susan," he shouted. "Extra plate. The Mastodon's coming to dinner."

CHAPTER IX

MAKING A FRIEND OF A SAVAGE

"OH bother!" said Susan, but not very loud.

"What's it like?" said Bridget.

But Susan had darted to the stores tent and was digging out another soup plate. The trouble was that she had already poured out the soup into five plates and there was none left in the saucepan. Roger had said enough to let her know that whatever the Mastodon might be, it ate like ordinary people, and she had to spoon a little soup from each of the five full plates into the sixth before the guest arrived. To see this being done would make any guest wish he had not come.

She was just in time. Six plates, each practically full of soup, lay in a row by the fire when John, Titty and the Mastodon followed Roger across the saltings and came to the dyke and the camp.

"Titty," said Bridget, "it isn't true."

"What isn't?"

The Mastodon was shaking hands with Susan and did not hear her answer: "You said he had a trunk."

But the next minute she had decided that he had a nice grin, and was shaking hands with him herself, though, looking closely at him, she saw that he was not very hairy either.

"Do sit down," said Susan.

The Mastodon looked uneasily at the carved stick which was still in the ground where he had stuck it.

"I say," he said. "You know I'm awfully sorry for butting

into your camp. I thought it was somebody else's. I'll take the totem away."

"Is that what it is?" said Titty. "Is it the totem of a whole tribe?"

"Four of us, really," said the Mastodon. "We count their grown-ups missionaries."

"He can run over the mud like a duck," said Roger, and after taking his first mouthful of soup, put his plate down and jumped to his feet. "I say, Susan, you forgot," he said. The sun was high overhead, and the stick in the middle of the meal-dial cast a very short shadow. In that short shadow Roger planted the cleft stick that had already been made for the purpose, wrote "DINNER" on a bit of paper and wedged it in the cleft.

"We haven't got a clock with us," said John.

"It's so that we get regular meals," said Roger.

"It's a fine idea," said the Mastodon.

"Why is your totem an eel?" said Titty.

"Mud everywhere," said the Mastodon. "Eels like it, and so do we. And we catch eels and eat them and get eelier and eelier. There's nothing much else you can catch except flatfish and they're dull. But eels can wriggle through anything and out of anything. An eel's a jolly good totem to have when you don't want to get into trouble with the missionaries. . . . Not that they're half bad," he added.

"To eat?" asked Roger.

"Not the missionaries," grinned the Mastodon. "We've never tried. No. I meant the missionaries aren't bad. They come round from Colnsea in a yacht and anchor by Flint Island and they put the rest of the tribe ashore in tents. And the Eels have each got a boat.'

"Sailing boats?" said Titty.

"Little ones," said the Mastodon. "Dinghies."

"We've seen them," said Roger.

"What rot," said John. "Of course we haven't."

"Yes we have. Pudding faces," he added half under his breath.

"What's their yacht like?" asked John.

"Square sterned cutter. Painted yellow. White sails. *Lapwing*'s her name. They've taken her to Pin Mill to have something done to her deck."

"We *have* seen them," said John. "They were at Pin Mill yesterday and the day before. We saw the three dinghies go alongside."

"What did you call them?" the Mastodon asked Roger.

"Well," said Roger, "I called them pudding faces. But that was only because they had boats and we hadn't. Not then. I wasn't near enough to see what their faces were like."

"Good name for savages," said the Mastodon, "but they're Eels really. I thought they were still at Pin Mill, and then, when I saw your camp, I thought they must have come in yesterday while I was away."

"Why do you say they're eels?" said Roger.

The Mastodon hesitated. Then the words came with a rush. "Oh look here," he said. "If you're marooned it won't matter a bit your knowing. Your being explorers makes it right too. They always shove a bit in their books about savage rites and so on. That's how we got the idea. The others won't mind. I'll explain to them. You see the eel is the totem of the Children of the Eel. That's the name of the tribe. But it's an awful secret. Even the missionaries don't know. You see if they did they might feel they ought to stop us having human sacrifices."

"What?" Even Susan was startled at this.

"We do it every summer holidays," said the Mastodon. "You know, a good big fire, and necklaces dangling from the totems, and tomtoms going, and a corroboree and everyone dancing like mad and the victim waiting to be sacrificed."

"Who's the victim?" said Roger.

"Daisy," said the Mastodon. "She's a bit skinny," he added, "to make a really good victim. But she's the best we've got. . . ."

He was looking almost enviously at the plump Bridget as he spoke. Everybody noticed it. His words faded off into silence.

"Bridget's not going to be a sacrifice," said Susan hurriedly.

"She'd make a perfect beauty," said the boy. "She's much smaller than Daisy and much . . . well, you know what I mean. Some people can't help being thin. It doesn't matter generally but savages stuff their victims like anything. And of course if we were a different tribe it wouldn't matter. . . . With Herons for instance, scragginess would be all right . . . but the Eels' victim ought to be fat. Of course I should have to ask the others, but I don't believe Daisy would mind. The savages would come charging down on the explorers' camp, pick the plumpest. . . .'

"Oh no, you can't have Bridget," said Roger.

"If you did want one of us for a victim," said Susan, "you'd better take me or John."

"I wouldn't mind," said Roger.

"Anybody but Bridget," said Titty. "All right, Bridget. Don't go and cry. Nobody's going to make you a human sacrifice."

"I think you're beasts," said Bridget. "You always make out I'm too young for everything. And now Daddy and Mummy have let me come. They think I'm old enough. And you won't let me be a human sacrifice when somebody wants me. . . ."

"Do you really want to?" asked Susan.

"Oh do let her," said Titty. "She'll be all right."

"Why shouldn't she if she wants to?" said Roger.

"All right, Bridget," said John. "If you're jolly good, and always do what the mate tells you. . . ."

"And never forget to say 'Aye, aye, Sir'," put in Roger.

Bridget cheered up and looked hopefully at the Mastodon.

"I think it'll be all right," he said. "But I'll have to ask the others first."

"Chops in the same plates," said Susan. "We always do if we can to save washing up," she added, remembering that the Mastodon was a visitor and not one of the crew.

By the time bananas had followed the chops the explorers and the savage knew a good deal about each other. He had heard something, not much, about their North Sea adventure. He was very pleased. "That makes it much better," he said. "They can't object when they know you've come from Holland quite lately. Coming across the sea makes you properly explorers." He was thinking all the time of the other savages. "You see," he said. "We've all promised to keep it secret. They're awfully keen not to have crowds of people coming in and spoiling everything."

"That's just what we felt when we thought strangers had been camping on Wild Cat," said Titty.

"Wild Cat?" said the Mastodon, and they told him of the lake in the north, and the camp on that rocky, wooded little island, and the alliance with the Amazon Pirates.

"Do you do signalling too?" asked Roger.

"Rockets," said the Mastodon.

"Morse?" said Roger. "And semaphore, with flags?"

"Savages don't."

"We do," said Roger.

"It's all right for explorers," said the Mastodon. "Not for savages. We've got our own way."

"Awfully useful for secret messages," said Titty. She dived into her tent, and brought out Nancy's message, with the skull and crossbones in one corner, and the row of dancing figures. She showed it to the boy, keeping her finger over the letters that John had written under each of the dancing figures.

"Looks like a corroboree," said the boy.

"It's a message," said Titty. She took her finger away, and showed the letters. "It says 'Three million cheers'."

"What does it mean?" said the boy.

"Well," said Titty. "We don't know. Something they've done, probably. Nancy couldn't have known what was going to happen here."

"She couldn't have guessed we were going to have a Mastodon to dinner," said Roger. "We didn't know it ourselves."

John showed the boy Daddy's rough pencilled map of the islands and the Secret Water.

The Mastodon looked at it with care.

"But it's wrong," he said pointing with a finger. "There's a way through there at high water. That's an island, not just a cape. And you can get miles inland if you go on past the mouth of this creek. And there are two islands there, not one. . . . And . . .'

"That's just it," said John. "We're going to get it all properly mapped before they come back to take us away."

"It'll take a long time," said the Mastodon. "With only one boat."

John showed him the work done that morning, the rough map of the island they were on, with bearings laid down from point to point all round the sea wall.

The Mastodon considered. "Jolly good," he said. "But what about the channel between the island and the mainland?"

"We were going to sail round," said John. "You couldn't see it properly from the dyke."

"You'd have a job to find it anyway," said the Mastodon. "And you ought to put in two channels not one. Three really. Look here. Let me help. Tide's up now. Let's go. We ought just to be able to get round and back over the Wade before the tide drops again."

"What's the Wade?" asked Roger.

"Road to the mainland," said the Mastodon. "Under water when the tide's up."

"How long will it take?" said Susan.

"Ought to do it in an hour," said the Mastodon. "If we go north about. That'll mean we're going against the tide to the point, and we ought to have it with us nearly to the Wade and then we'll have the ebb this side of the watershed to bring us home." He pointed on the map to the place where they had seen the road over the mud, and explained that the tide came up from both sides to meet there, and poured back both ways when the ebb began.

Titty and Roger were already on their feet.

"What about Sinbad?" said Bridget, and a moment later, "Where *is* Sinbad?"

"'Sh," said Titty at the door of her tent. "He's gone to sleep."

Sinbad, his stomach round and full after his dinner, had gone into Titty's tent and curled himself on her sleeping bag. His round fat stomach rose and fell. Titty crawled in and without waking him, lifted the blankets and pulled them together to make a sheltering wall about the sleeping kitten.

"He'll be all right for an hour or two," said Susan.

"Tired, probably," said Titty. "He's done enough exploring for one day."

They crossed the saltings and went down to the boats. Already much of the old piling that marked the landing place was under water. But bubbles and foam, slipping slowly along the edge of the mud showed that the water was still rising.

"We'll do it all right," said the Mastodon. "Who's coming in my boat?"

"I will," said Roger.

John and Susan looked at each other.

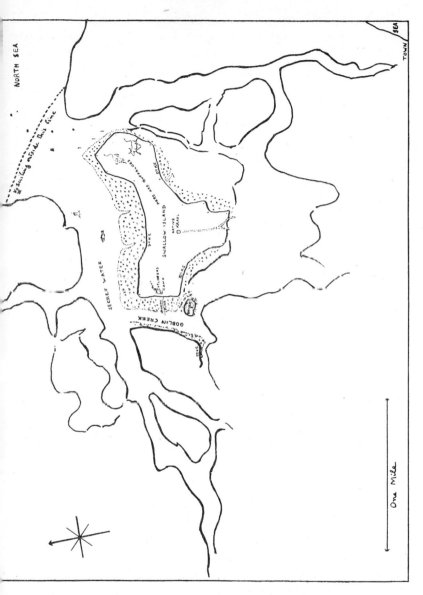

THE MAP: WITH SWALLOW ISLAND

"It's the first time we've sailed this boat by ourselves," said Susan. "Bridget and I'll go with John, if you'll take Titty and Roger."

"Look here, Titty," said John. "You'd better take another copy of the map, to stick things down on, and we'll compare afterwards."

"You can give me a tow when we're going with the wind," said the Mastodon. "And I'll tow you through the narrow places when the wind's the other way."

*

They were off. The Mastodon was away first, with Roger in the bows and Titty sitting in the stern. His was a small, tarred rowing boat. His splatchers, clear of mud which he had washed off before putting them in the boat, lay at Roger's feet. Under the middle thwart, where he sat rowing, was a shallow wooden box, with another shallow box fixed in the middle of it. A coil of line lay round the outside of the inner box, and from this coil dozens of short lengths of line with hooks on them lay in notches in the sides of the inner box, so that all the hooks were in the middle, not touching each other and safe from getting tangled up with the main coil.

"What's that?" asked Titty.

"Eel line," said the Mastodon.

"Do you fish with minnows?" asked Titty, remembering fishing for perch on the lake.

"No," said the Mastodon. "Lugworms. If you lift that bit of sacking, you'll see them. Just behind your feet."

Titty stooped down. Under the seat in the stern was another shallow box, and her heel was just touching a piece of wet coarse canvas, that lay in the box like a blanket in a bed. She lifted a corner of it. Underneath it, on another layer of wet canvas lay a squirming mass of the most horrible looking worms she had ever seen. Each worm seemed to be in two parts, one thin, tapering and shining, the other bloated and hairy.

Titty held the canvas for a moment, staring at them, and then, hurriedly, closed it down again.

"Do eels like them?" she asked.

"Don't they just? Flatfish, too, and whiting when they come up. It's harder work getting worms than catching fish when you've got them. I was digging two hours this morning to get that lot."

"Oh ... I see." Titty saw once more those mastodon tracks across the mud and the little heaps that had looked as if someone were making mud castles.

"We've got fishing things," said Roger.

"There's a good place at the mouth of the creek," said the Mastodon. "Specially at low tide."

Meanwhile John was getting up the *Wizard's* sail, not too easily. They could see from the Mastodon's boat that things were not going quite right. Susan was lifting the boom clear and holding it up while John was pulling at something. They had made the ship's baby sit in the bottom of the boat.

"He's never set it before," said Titty, thinking that the Mastodon might be getting a poor idea of the explorer's seamanship. "Daddy set it for us yesterday. He's got it now." The sail was up, John was tidying ropes at the foot of the mast, Susan was steering, the *Wizard* was moving through the water and the head of the ship's baby showed above the gunwale. "That's all right."

The Mastodon laid to his oars, and they were soon out of the creek, and rowing along close to the northern shore of the island.

"Less tide close in," he said.

A narrow opening showed in the saltings. Titty with a pencil marked it on her map.

"Only a drain," said the Mastodon. "But you can't tell

unless you go in and have a look. Even at high water you can't get more than a few yards up there. But the other place I told you about, on the other side of the island, doesn't look any bigger, and we've gone right through with the whole fleet, the Eels, I mean, and come out in the main channel on the other side.

"Do let's do it," said Titty.

"John's gone aground," said Roger.

The *Wizard*, following close behind them, was also dodging the tide, but John had forgotten that with her centreboard down she needed more water than the Mastodon's rowing boat. They saw him hauling the centreboard up a little way, and sheering out into the channel.

"Good enough wind," said the Mastodon. "She'll beat the tide easily."

"I say," said Roger. "Are we going right out to sea? It's out of bounds."

It did look like it. At the mouth of the Secret Water there was nothing to be seen but rippled blue water. The sands were covered, and far away on the horizon, they could see the tall brown sails of barges, and the smoke of a steamship.

"Only round the corner," said the Mastodon between strokes of his oars.

"Can't we pull for a bit?" said Titty.

"I'll stick to it till we get round into the other channel. Then we'll have the tide with us. Want to save every minute here."

Titty marked down the opening of another tiny creek or ditch running up into the saltings.

They came at last to the end of the island and cut across inside the crossroads buoy. Ahead of them was the island of shingle and bright yellow sand and the two or three yachts at anchor they had seen the day before. They were turning into the channel to the town.

"There are the dhows we saw yesterday," said Titty.

The Mastodon looked over his shoulder. "Traders," he said. "Probably slavers. But they haven't caught any of us yet. *Lapwing*'s not there. She usually anchors just in there and they make a camp close by. The sand dunes give them good shelter. The real reason they camp there," he added, "is because there's no chance of setting anything on fire. Good bathing too. It's the only sandy bit of beach for miles."

"We never set things on fire," said Roger. "We nearly got burnt once," he went on, but caught Titty's eye and stopped. Oh well, perhaps she was right. The Mastodon might think it was showing off.

The *Wizard* turned the corner and came after them, rapidly catching them up.

"Can you throw them our painter?" asked the Mastodon.

Roger coiled the painter and threw it. Susan grabbed it, the panting Mastodon rested on his oars, and the *Wizard* took on the extra load.

"Did you see those two creeks?" called John.

"I marked them," called Titty. "But they don't go anywhere."

"They couldn't go far anyway," said John. "Because of the seawall. There isn't a gap in it. I say, is that the place you call Flint Island?"

"Yes," said the Mastodon.

"Why Flint?" asked Roger.

"Because if you land and go along the shore when the tide's out you've got a good chance of finding flint arrowheads and things. The missionaries collect them."

"Gosh!" said Titty. "Prehistoric?"

"Yes. We swop most of the ones we find for stores."

They passed the anchored yachts. The dyke on their right curved suddenly away and a creek opened into low weedy marshland.

"Is this the channel?" shouted John turning towards it.

"Not the main one," shouted the savage guide. "Look here. We'll do them both at once. You go straight on, and you'll find another opening, with a few more traders moored in it. Not the next one. The first one you come to with boats in it. Go in there and keep in the middle. We'll go through this one and meet you. Tide's still flowing. We'll just be able to do it."

"Right. Cast off the tow rope Mister Mate."

"Good-bye," shouted the ship's baby.

"Good-bye," shouted the able seamen.

The Mastodon was already rowing. They shot in between marshy banks and weeds, and a moment later could see nothing of the *Wizard* but the top of her sail. Presently that too disappeared. The able seamen were alone in his boat with the savage.

Roger looked a little anxiously at Titty, but remembered that after all, they were two to one, even if the Mastodon did look as if he would be pretty tough to fight if he happened to turn hostile to explorers. But the Mastodon seemed to have no such thoughts in his head. He was rowing as hard as he could between banks that were growing narrower and narrower.

"This tide isn't as high as it might be," he said. "We're going to have a job getting through."

CHAPTER X

THE STRAITS OF MAGELLAN

Just for a moment, in the sudden loneliness that came when she realized that she could not see *Wizard's* sail any more, Titty almost felt like saying that she thought it would be better if they all kept together. Suppose the savage were to live up to his totem. Eels. Slippery eels. You never knew where you had them. Supposing it was all a trick and the Mastodon, rowing as hard as he could along this narrow winding ditch where you could see nothing but reeds and mud, had planned an ambush. . . . Supposing round one of these corners they came upon a whole tribe. . . . Suppose others were lurking in these sodden patches of mud and reeds.

But the Mastodon, rowing fit to bust, did not look as if he were thinking of plots. Titty remembered that she was an explorer. She marked on her map the place where they had left the main channel and begun this queer voyage through the marshes. She could not measure the distances, and she had no compass to take bearings, so she turned the map over and, as the ditch twisted and turned, she drew a single line, now bending one way now the other, with every curve and wriggle of the ditch. It would be easy to fit it in afterwards.

"Which way do we go?" said Roger. "It divides in two."

The Mastodon stopped rowing, and his boat ran instantly aground. Just ahead of them the ditch turned into two ditches, one twisting to the right, the other to the left. Both seemed about the same size.

"Right I think," said the Mastodon. "But it's a long time since I've been through."

He pushed off from one side of the ditch with an oar, ran on the mud on the opposite side, pushed off from that, and rowed on. Titty marked on the back of the map the place where the ditch forked. Her line began to look as if she were making a drawing of zigzag lightning.

The ditch bent round to the right, and forked.

"Right again," said the Mastodon.

His oars almost touched the sides of the ditch as they passed through a narrow place.

A heron got up from close in front of them. Three wing flaps took it out of sight.

"I say," said Roger. "Isn't that the dyke?"

Ahead of them, above the reeds, was the straight line of a high grass-covered bank.

"Must have gone wrong at the last divide," said the Mastodon.

There was hardly room to turn, and Roger hopped out on a tussock of mud and weeds to pull the bows of the boat round.

The Mastodon rowed back to the last place where the ditch forked and this time took the turn to the left.

"Got to hurry," he said grimly. "Tide's stopped rising. We may be too late to get through."

"Hadn't we better go back to the main channel?" said Titty.

"Oh no," said the Mastodon. "We'll do it yet. We're all right this time."

"Hullo," said Roger a few minutes later. "It's come to an end."

The boat slid into a little pool and stopped. There was nothing ahead of them but mud and weeds, and no way out but the way by which they had come.

"Sorry," said the Mastodon, worked the boat round and started back. "We'll have to go right back to that first place where we ought to have gone left."

This time worry showed clearly on the face of the savage guide. Titty knew he was badly bothered.

"It's the tide," he said at last. "Going down. We don't want to get stuck."

"Hullo," said Titty. "Isn't there water through there?"

They had just passed a narrow drain, and Titty looking through the gap had seen something very like open water.

The Mastodon backed with both oars.

"It's worth trying," he said. "We could do it yet, if only we were in the right channel now."

He edged up to the muddy bank and scrambled out.

"Come on," he shouted. "It's the other channel. Quite near, if only we can get her through."

He jumped back, all muddy, into the boat, and tried to pole her into the gap. She moved in a few yards and stuck.

"She's aground," he said. "Look here. Could you get out, both of you, and I'll try to lug her through?"

Roger, for the second time that day, got mud over his knees. Titty was luckier. They found themselves on a bit of soft boggy ground, and for the first time, were able to look round them and see what sort of place this was. Away to the right of them they could see the long dyke, curving round the island. Behind them, to the left of them and in front of them were saltings, reedy marshland, cut up into islands by narrow channels now, soon after high tide, full of water. Twenty yards away was a wider channel, and they could see that it wound its way towards water that was really open.

"Quick, quick," said Roger, jumping from one tussock of rank grass to another.

Titty followed him, and waited where the narrow drain widened into a bay at the side of the channel they had missed by taking the wrong turn.

"Here's a good place for getting in again," she said, "if only he can get the boat through."

"She's moving all right," said Roger.

They could not see her, but they could see the Mastodon, poling her along.

"Stuck again," said Roger. "Gosh! He's gone in."

The Mastodon had stepped out over the stern, and was pushing the boat before him.

"Why doesn't he sink?" said Roger. "He's got his splatchers on. Good old Mastodon. He's done it. Here she comes."

The boat slipped suddenly forward, and the Mastodon nearly fell. In a moment, he had his splatchers off and was in his boat again, poling with an oar. A moment after that she slid out from the drain, and the explorers were getting aboard once more.

"Never mind the mud," said the Mastodon. "I can wash her out afterwards. If only we manage to get through."

"Let me take an oar," said Titty.

"I can row," said Roger.

"I know her ways," said the Mastodon. "Better let me. There isn't a minute to lose."

The weedy banks flew past them on either side, but presently flew not so fast, though the Mastodon was rowing just as hard, and the water was foaming under the bows of his little boat.

"Tide's going out," he said between his teeth.

"There's *Wizard*," shouted Roger.

"That's mud," said the Mastodon. "There it is again. We've got jolly little water under us."

"What would we do if we got properly stuck?" asked Roger.

"Have to wait till the tide's gone out and come up again enough to float us."

"After dark?" said Roger.

"Long after," said the Mastodon. "About three o'clock in the morning. Good, good. Deeper water already. But the others oughtn't to have waited for us. They've got to get across the Wade. And your boat's deeper than mine."

The *Wizard* was sailing slowly towards them in the main channel, a wide stretch of water between the reeds. Bridget was waving.

The Mastodon waved them on. John understood, and swung round. The wind had dropped and the *Wizard* was sailing no faster than the Mastodon could row. Titty was hurriedly marking on the back of her map the channel through which they had come. "I'll just have to guess that bit where we went wrong," she said.

"Make it clear we ought to have turned left when I turned right," said the Mastodon. "Well," he said more cheerfully. "You see there are two ways through. Three really. The main channel's the way they went, but there's this other way inside it."

"Like Cape Horn and the Straits of Magellan," said Titty. "*Wizard*'s gone round the Horn, and we've come through the Straits."

"What happened?" asked John, as the two boats came nearer together.

"We got mixed up with Terra del Fuego," said Titty.

"We had a beautifully narrow squeak getting through," said Roger.

"Took a wrong turn," said the savage guide. "Look here, you oughtn't to have waited. It's going to be a squeak getting home across the Wade. You see it's a watershed, and the tide's going down."

"Had we better go back the way we came?" suggested Susan.

"Oh let's go right round," said Roger.

The Mastodon showed what he thought by laying to his oars and rowing on. The shores were widening on either side, and they were coming out into a broad lake of shimmering water which covered the sea of mud that they had seen in the morning. Here and there, ahead of them, a withy waved gently in the tide.

"Leave all those withies to starboard," called the Mastodon. "They mark the edge of the shallows on this side. Keep fairly near them."

The weed banks were further and further away and it was hard to believe that there was only a narrow channel of water deep enough for sailing. It looked as though they could sail for as far as they wanted in any direction.

"What are those other withies?" called John, pointing to some far away towards the mainland.

"They mark the road over the Wade," said the Mastodon. "There you are, right ahead. Those four posts that you can see above the water. That's the shallowest place. Deeper water either side of them. Hard bottom. Causeway right across."

They came nearer to the four posts, black posts, with a high water mark showing near the top of them. They came level with the posts. They passed them.

"That's that," said the Mastodon. "We'll have the tide with us now...." His voice changed. "He's gone between the posts.... He's touched!"

They saw the *Wizard* stop dead. They saw John's face suddenly worried. They saw Susan jump to pull up the centreboard, as the *Wizard* swung round broadside and began to heel. Then the *Wizard* began to move again, came back on her course, and was presently gliding beside them.

"Narrow thing," said the Mastodon. "He oughtn't to have gone between the posts."

"I ought to have pulled the centreboard up before we got there," said John. "But she doesn't sail well without it unless the wind's dead aft."

They had no more trouble, but slipped slowly homewards,

watching the shore from which in the morning they had seen the hoofmarks of the Mastodon on the mud over which they were now sailing. There was the landing place belonging to the native kraal, there the cart track from the kraal coming over the seawall and down to the causeway the end of which was already beginning to show above water. Far away on the other side the Mastodon pointed out other withies marking a channel that at high water would let them reach the mainland.

They slipped slowly on. The weedbeds were coming nearer again. They were passing the little Bridget Island that at low water was part of their own. They were passing the opening of the channel that led to the old barge hulk, the Mastodon's private lair. They came round into Goblin Creek and back to the landing place below the camp from which they had started.

"Well," said John. "We've circumnavigated it. I've got an awful lot to put on the map. I say, there are several bits I want to ask you about."

"I've got a rough sketch of Magellan Straits," said Titty. John looked at her.

"You went round Cape Horn," she said. "You'll see when we put it all in."

"I wonder if Sinbad'll be pleased to see us," said Bridget. "Coming back from a voyage."

They went up to the camp. Bridget peeped into Titty's tent.

"'Sh!" she said. "He's still asleep."

"Not much good as a watch cat," said Roger.

But just then the kitten stirred, got up, and walked slowly out, stretching its hind legs and the whole of its body as it came out of the tent.

"Are you a good watch cat?" said Titty.

The kitten rubbed against her leg, opened its mouth and mewed. "He wants some milk," said Bridget.

"All right, Sinbad," said Susan. "You shall have some. But you haven't really earned it."

John, Titty and the Mastodon flung themselves on the ground to compare maps, fitting the wriggling line of the Magellan Straits into the space east of the dyke that John had marked in the morning. An enormous lot of the big blob that in Daddy's rough map had seemed to be all one island had turned out to be marshes. "That's quite right," said the native guide. "That's where we ran up against the dyke and had to turn back. And that bit's another island. And so's that. And there's another way in between the two of them."

"Don't put it in," said Titty. "Not till we've sailed through it."

"I'll leave it just dotted," said John. "Between Magellan Straits and the Horn."

"What are we going to explore to-morrow?" asked Roger, who liked exploration better than mapping its results.

"Is that an island where we landed when we came to *Speedy*?" asked Titty. "You can't tell from Daddy's map whether it is or not."

"Yes," said the Mastodon. "And there are more further up. And islands on the northern shore. You can see the way in if you walk along the dyke."

"Let's go and look," said John. "Just half a minute while I copy this bit from my map into Daddy's. There'll be a good lot ready for Titty to ink."

"Get some more wood if you can," said Susan. "Bridget and I are going to start the fire."

The savage guide and three explorers left the camp and strolled along the dyke, now and then going down to the foot of it to pick up bits of driftwood. The savage was full of plans for the further exploration of his native wilds. "You ought to do the channel to the town when the tide's up," he was saying. "And then you ought to walk across the Wade at low tide. And

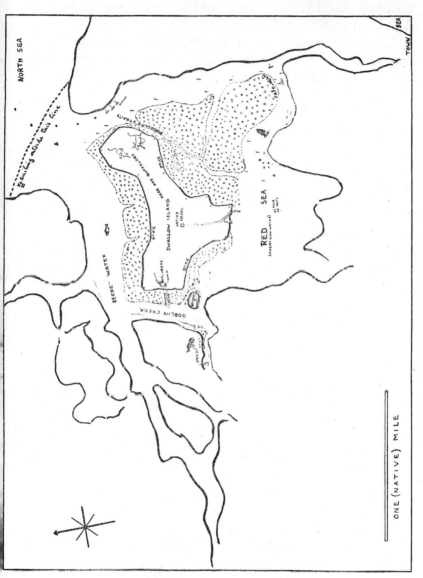

NORTH SEA

RED SEA I.
(MOSTLY LOW WATER)

SWALLOW ISLAND

SECRET WATER

GOBLIN CREEK

NORTH SEA

ONE (NATIVE) MILE

THE MAP WITH MAGELLAN STRAITS AND CAPE HORN

then you ought to sail round my island and map it like yours. And then there's the islands up at the top."

They were walking along the dyke, above the marshes that fringed the Secret Water, looking across it to shores full of promise on the further side, when Roger suddenly pointed out to sea.

"A sail! A sail!" he shouted. "At least it's not got a sail. It's a motor boat."

Far away out they could see it, throwing the water in white splashes from its bows, coming in, heading for the cross-roads buoy.

"I thought you could only get in at high water," said John. "And the mud's showing below the saltings. The tide's gone down a long way."

"Fishing boat," said the Mastodon. "They draw nothing. Get in and out any time. She'll be turning into the channel by Flint Island. They never come up here."

He turned away and pointed up the Secret Water. "You ought to go right up as far as ever you can go," he said. "We go up there sometimes to visit a trading post."

"Trading post?" said Roger, his eyes still on the distant motor boat.

"Ginger beer and chocolate," said the Mastodon. "But that other place I showed you was better."

"I say. They're coming straight on," said Roger. "They haven't turned."

"That's rum," said the Mastodon. "Not a local boat either. Strangers. They've mistaken the channel."

"Towing a sailing boat," said John.

"They're stopping," said Roger.

Foam was no longer flying from the bows of the motor boat that was now well inside the Secret Water. She was slowing down.

"Green," said Titty. "Like the one at Pin Mill."

"Hullo," said the Mastodon. "Somebody's getting into the sailing boat. Girl. Or is it a boy? There's another. I say, I do believe it's the Eels. Something's happened to *Lapwing* and they've come along to say so."

Titty remembered that the Mastodon was a savage, and that he had said he would have to explain to the others about them. It would never do, before he had explained, for the rest of the tribe to find him hob-nobbing with a lot of explorers.

"Won't they be going straight to the *Speedy*?" she said.

But the Mastodon did not answer.

"I don't know who else it can be," he said. "And yet . . ."

"They're dumping stuff into the boat," said Roger.

The green motor boat was slipping slowly through the water with the sailing boat pulled up alongside, so that the explorers could see only the mast of it nodding beyond the green gunwale. People seemed to be in a hurry about something.

"There goes another bag," said Roger. "And what's that long bundle?"

"How many of them are there in the sailing boat?" said the Mastodon. "I only saw two. Red caps."

"Two," said Roger, "and two men in the big boat. Hullo. They're letting them go astern. We'll see better in a minute."

One of the men in the motor boat was walking to the stern with the painter of the sailing boat. The little nodding mast slipped back. A little brown sailing boat slid into sight. The people in it were struggling with a white sail.

"He's cast off," said Roger.

"They're turning round," said John.

The motor boat began to move ahead. The men in it pointed towards Goblin Creek. Someone waved from the sailing boat. The motor boat swung slowly round, and then, suddenly picking up speed, shot away towards the mouth of Secret Water and the open sea.

A white sail was being hoisted in the little boat. Up it went, stopped fluttering and filled with wind. Someone in a red stocking cap was steering. Someone else in a red stocking cap was busy by the mast.

"Hoisting a flag," said Roger. "Do their flags have eels on them?"

But there were no eels on the flag that suddenly fluttered from the mast head. The flag was black, with something white on it.

"Skull and crossbones," said the Mastodon. "Well I'm blowed. Whoever can it be?"

"Hey!" Titty was shouting at the top of her voice. "Hey!"

"Ahoy!" shouted John.

"Ahoy!" yelled Roger.

"Do you know them?" said the Mastodon.

"It's Nancy and Peggy," said Titty. "It's the Amazon pirates. Hey! Hey! Ahoy!"

"Three million cheers!" said John.

"Gosh!" exclaimed Titty. "That's what Nancy meant. She knew they were coming. And Daddy and Mother never said a word."

"Swallows ahoy! Swallows ahoy!" A hail came over the water.

They saw Peggy standing up and waving. They saw Nancy pull her firmly down, as the little boat heeled to a sudden puff and came sailing in towards the mouth of Goblin Creek.

CHAPTER XI

WAR OR EXPLORATION?

"AHOY!" shouted John, as he saw the Amazons turning towards the shore. "You can't land there. All swamp. Further in. Land where you see our boat."

"Aye, aye," shouted Nancy.

John, Titty and Roger set off at a run, and the Mastodon followed them, doubtfully, lagging a little behind.

"Susan," shouted John. "It's the Amazons!"

"They're here," yelled Roger.

"They're only ragging," said Susan. And then, looking over the saltings, she saw the sail of a boat, and then the red caps of the Amazons. "No, they really are. Come on, Bridget."

"Sinbad too," said Bridget, and grabbed the startled kitten and ran after Susan to the landing place.

"This side. Close along the piling. Step out between the piles. Soft mud everywhere else."

"All right, Peggy. Let the sail flap till we get unloaded. We'll never get the tent and things out if we have the sail down on the top of the lot."

"Keep that bag out of the mud, Roger."

"Hullo, Ship's baby! Hullo, kitten!"

"We just couldn't believe it was you," said Titty.

"Well it jolly well is. Didn't you get our message? Look out, John. I've stuffed our compass into that."

"Good," said John. "We've only got one. Another'll make all the difference."

"It's *Firefly*," said Roger, who had worked himself out

along the little hard till, standing in the water, he could read the name on the stern of the boat. "I saw her at Pin Mill."

"Captain Walker borrowed her," said Peggy.

"Gosh, it has been a rush," said Nancy . . . and stopped, looking at the Mastodon, who was waiting, not knowing whether to go or stay.

"He's a savage," said Titty. "We thought he was a Mastodon, because of his hoofmarks in the mud."

"Big as teatrays," said Roger. "He can run on the mud, and he lives in a barge over there. You can't quite see it from here."

"He's got a tribe, but they're not here yet," said Titty. "He came with us as a guide through the Straits of Magellan. You know we're doing real exploring."

"Greeting," said Nancy in the grand manner.

"Titty and I call him Mastodon," said Roger. "He doesn't mind. But he's a chief of the Eels."

Nancy held out her hand, and the Mastodon shook it, and then shook hands with Peggy.

"My Mate," said Nancy.

"Well, I'd better be going," said the Mastodon shyly.

"Jibbooms and bobstays . . . why on earth?" said Nancy.

"Oh I say," said John. "There's no need. Aren't you going to help with the map? There's lots more to do."

"What map?" asked Nancy.

"You'll see," said John.

"Come on, noble savage," said Nancy firmly. "You take the other end of the tent and go first." And the Mastodon, carrying one end of the long roll of the Amazon's big tent, followed by Nancy with the other end on her shoulder, found himself leading the way up to the camp.

Everybody carried something. Roger lowered the black flag with the skull and crossbones on it, ran, splashing, across the saltings, fastened it to a surveying pole, and planted it

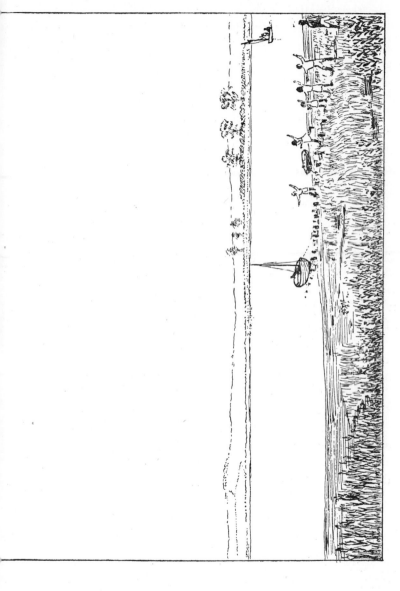

ARRIVAL OF THE AMAZONS

beside the Swallow flag in the middle of the camp. Even
Bridget, with Sinbad in her arms, managed to carry a pair
of Peggy's shoes, that she had taken off in the boat in order
to get into seaboots for landing.

"Plenty of room for another tent," said Susan. "There's
a good flat place just this side of that willowbush."

"Gosh," said Roger. "Things'll happen now."

"Looks to me as if they've begun," said Nancy. "The
one thing we hadn't got at home was savages. Hi, Mastodon,
just lug at that end of the bag and the tent'll come out poles and
all."

"Dump the bags on the groundsheet," said Peggy. "I say,
this is a gorgeous place."

"You don't know how gorgeous," said Titty. "It's real
exploring this time. Miles of it. Islands and straits and everything changing all the time because of the tide. There's a Red
Sea with a track across it at low water and at high water you
can sail. We saw the tracks of Pharaoh's chariots this morning,
and we sailed over it this afternoon."

"When did you leave Beckfoot?" asked Susan when the
Amazons' tent was pitched, and Nancy and Peggy were
tightening their guy ropes.

"Yesterday morning," said Peggy.

"It was one long stupendous rush," said Nancy. "Where's
my knapsack?" She rummaged in it and brought out a sheaf
of telegrams. "We didn't know for certain till the day before
yesterday. The D's had gone, and Captain Flint and Timothy
couldn't talk about anything but copper, and then Mother got
a letter from your Mother asking us to come and Mother wrote
and asked which day, and after that we were all of a dither.
We didn't think there'd be an answer for at least two days.
Then came the first telegram and our spirits shot up like
rockets. Your Mother couldn't have sent a lovelier telegram.

"What did she say?" asked Titty.

Nancy showed the first telegram:

MRS. BLACKETT BECKFOOT

EXPECT NO COMFORTS BUZZ THEM ALONG

MARY WALKER

"Doesn't sound a bit like Mother," said John.

"Daddy said he'd sent a telegram for her," said Titty.

"Good one anyway," said Nancy. "Well, we began getting ready at once, and then Captain Flint and Timothy came in, and the telephone rang again and there was another.

BLACKETT BECKFOOT

BRING TENTS

WALKER

We thought that couldn't be your mother because she knows we've only got one. And we were packing the tent up in the garden when the next telegram came.

BLACKETT BECKFOOT

BRING COMPASS

WALKER

By that time we knew something was really up, and Captain Flint and Timothy got interested too, and said it must be some more prospecting. But Timothy said there were no minerals in these parts. Captain Flint said you must have found something or other.

And they lent a hand with the tent and I was packing the compass and Mother was scurrying round with clothes and then another telegram came.

BLACKETT BECKFOOT

GUMBOOTS AND OILIES PUT THEM IN FIRST POSSIBLE TRAIN

WALKER

After that everybody was fairly whirling, and nobody really slept, and Captain Flint and Timothy rushed us round to the station in Rattletrap first thing in the morning, and we spent the night in London with Aunt Helen. . . ."

"Not the Great Aunt?" said Roger.

"No. A good one," said Nancy. "And then your friendly natives met us at Ipswich and rushed us to Pin Mill. We just saw Miss Powell's and had one look at the *Goblin* and then we were dumped into that motor boat and your natives said Good luck and were off for London and we were off for here. Buzz was the right word from the beginning."

"I knew Daddy was up to something," said Titty.

"They never said a single word," said Roger.

"I know now why Mother put in too many mugs and plates," said Susan.

At that moment, Peggy, admiring the flags, tripped over the supper peg of the meal-dial and kicked it out of the ground.

Roger darted to put it back. "Look out," he said, "or there won't be any supper."

"What's that?" said Nancy.

"Meal-dial," said Roger.

"I say, have you got a watch?" exclaimed Susan. "Thank goodness you have. I went and forgot my alarm clock in *Goblin.*"

"Here you are," said Nancy. "But a meal-dial's even better. Wouldn't Dick have liked it?"

"Oh good," said John. "We'll be all right about tides now. A meal-dial's only good for meals."

"It's no good even for meals," said Roger, "unless the sun's shining. No sun no shadow and we'd all starve."

"Bet *you* wouldn't," said Nancy.

Roger disappeared into his tent. A moment later everybody was startled by the noise of a penny whistle.

"It's only Roger," said Bridget.

"Come out of that," said Nancy, "and let's see the horrid instrument."

"Can't," said Roger. "The wind sends all the notes wrong. I'm playing welcoming music in spite of Nancy being so beastly rude. What tune would you like?"

Suddenly the Mastodon, who had been listening in silence, spoke to John. "I say," he said. "I really have got to go. I forgot those worms. I've a night line to set."

The music ended in the middle of a bar.

"Can I come too?" asked Roger.

"You can lend a hand with the oars," said the Mastodon. "It's much easier with two."

"Come back to supper," said Susan.

"Oh I say," said the Mastodon. "I was here to dinner."

"There's lots of grub," said Susan.

"Of course you'll come back," said Nancy.

"We've got an enormous cake," said Peggy.

The Mastodon hesitated. "I'd love to come," he said. "Look here, will all of you come to supper in *Speedy* to-morrow?"

"I should think we jolly well will," said Roger.

"In your lair?" said Nancy. "Of course we'll come."

The fishermen went off to the landing place.

"What about inking some of it in?" said John, and Titty went into her tent and came out with the map on a drawing-board and her case of drawing things.

"What on earth are you doing?" asked Nancy.

"Mapping?" said Peggy.

"You show them what we've done," said John, watching the Amazons anxiously.

"It was Daddy's idea first," said Titty. "He was coming, too, and Mother, and we were going to make a proper map of this place. This is what he did for us to start with. All un-explored. And this bit in the middle is the bit we've done. I'll put it on the ground so that you can see better. That's this island. This is where the Mastodon lives in a wreck. The idea is to get the whole map explored before the relief ship comes to take us away again."

"We'll get on faster now you've come," said John.

Nancy went down on her knees beside the map. "Let's have a look," she said. The true lines of the island had been drawn. A thick pencil line marked the dyke, and outside it, not so thick, a wavering line showed the edge of the marshes. The straight lines of the compass bearings, going from point to point, looked like a net holding the island to the paper.

"All those straight lines'll be rubbed out when Titty's done the inking," said John.

"I've only got black ink here," said Titty. "But when we get home we'll put each journey in with dotted lines, different sorts of dots. Explorers always do."

She filled her pen with ink, and began her work, while Nancy and Peggy looked over her shoulders.

"It's a grand place for a war," said Nancy. "Better than Wild Cat and our river. Surprise attacks from all sides. And savages too."

John and Titty looked at each other in horror.

"We've sailed all round this island," said Titty. "We had to begin with that. We're going to do a new bit every day. And gradually the explored part, properly mapped, will come spreading out till the whole thing's done."

"What a place for war," said Nancy again. "Specially with savages. Think of an attack . . . war canoes coming through there . . . and savages creeping through the reeds. . . ."

"But there won't be time for any war," said John.

"And the Mastodon's a friend," said Titty.

For some time the Amazons watched in silence.

"You'll get a medal from the Royal Geographical Society," said Nancy at last. . . . "The Walker Expedition."

Both John and Titty noticed that she said "you" instead of "we".

"You're in it too," said John.

"It isn't Walkers anyway," said Titty, taking her pen from the paper and holding it well away from the side of the drawing-board for fear of a blot. "It's Swallows and Amazons as usual. The Swallows and Amazons Expedition."

"But we haven't got *Swallow* or *Amazon*," said Peggy.

There was silence while Titty dipped her pen and drew another careful line. Then she spoke again. "Archipelago Expedition . . . Secret Archipelago Expedition . . . S.A.E. . . . The S. and the A. will do for Swallows and Amazons as well. We've got their flags. And we've called this island Swallow Island . . . unless you'd rather not. . . ."

"No, that's all right," said Nancy. "Secret Archipelago Expedition it is. At least I vote for that."

"So do I," said John.

"Can I ink in the kraal?" said Titty.

"It's in the right place," said John. "I got a bearing of it from three different posts."

Titty inked it in and in small capital letters wrote "NATIVE KRAAL" and away towards the eastern end of the island she wrote "HERE ARE BUFFALOES". Then, drawing tiny clumps of reeds, just three short thin strokes in a bunch, she began putting in the marshes outside the dyke.

"Giminy," said Nancy. "If it's going to be all like that it's going to be jolly fine. We'll discover an Amazon Island too."

"Wait till we've rubbed out the pencil marks," said Titty much relieved. It would have been too awful if the Amazons had set their hearts on war.

The inking went steadily on.

"How many savages are there?" asked Nancy suddenly.

"He's the only one so far," said John. "But he says three more are coming."

"You can't have much of a war," said Nancy regretfully, "with only one savage against six of us."

"Seven," interrupted Bridget, "and eight counting Sinbad."

"Sorry, Ship's Baby," said Nancy. "Well, seven to one's no good. It ought to be a handful of explorers holding a stockade against a howling horde. Look here. Peggy and I are sick of being pirates."

"Oh I say," burst out John. "There simply isn't time. We've cut two notches already. Two days gone. If we go and start a war now we'll have 'unexplored' sprawling all over the map. And the Mastodon won't be much good as a guide if he's got to think of ambushes. He's going to be jolly useful as it is, and anyway we've promised him Bridget for a human sacrifice when the others come. It's no good having battles and massacres as well."

"They thought I wasn't old enough but I am," said Bridget.

Nancy considered, looking round from the camp over Goblin Creek and the marshes and island beyond them, and the wide Secret Water with the low-lying coast beyond it. It certainly did seem waste, but you couldn't have much of a war with a solitary savage and all the Swallows set on peace. She glanced down at Titty, who was crouched over the drawing-board working away with her pen. Of course it was different from the lake in the north where, even when in bed with mumps, she had always set the tune for everybody.

"Exploring's going to be jolly good fun," said Peggy.

"Galoot," said Nancy. "Of course it is. I'm only thinking. When's Bridget going to be a human sacrifice?"

"When we've done the map," said John.

"If the other savages agree," said Susan. "He said he'd have to ask them, so you mustn't count on it, Bridgie."

"He said their sacrifice was too skinny," said Bridget.

"Right," said Nancy. "Exploration first."

"Good," said John.

"And it's all right being friends with the Mastodon?" asked

Titty, looking up from the map before taking another dip of ink.

"Why not?" said Nancy. "Explorers meet savage chief. They make him presents. I only wish I'd thought of bringing some beads."

"Can't do any more to-night," said Titty at last, wiping her pen and putting it away.

"Let's rub out the pencil marks and have a look," said John.

"Ink's not dry," said Titty, and put the drawing-board in her tent, safe from explorers' wandering feet.

"Supper's ready," said Susan, who had for some time been busy at the fire. "Scrambled eggs."

"Good," said Nancy, jumping up. "Shall I go and yell to Roger and the savage?"

"I'll whistle," said Susan, but before the first blast of her whistle had died away they saw the fishermen coming up from the landing place.

"I say," called Roger. "We've put out a line with twenty hooks. He's going to bring us some of the fish when he takes it up in the morning."

Seven explorers and a savage shared their scrambled eggs, after which Peggy dealt out huge slices from the cake they had brought from Beckfoot.

Towards the end of the meal, Nancy fell oddly silent. It was Peggy who was telling the others about what had happened at High Topps after the Swallows had gone south, and how the D's, also, had been called away to join their parents. Nancy did not interrupt her, even to say "Galoot". Titty could see from her face that she was turning something over in her mind. John, looking at her anxiously, began to fear that she was relapsing into thoughts of war. More than once the others laughed at things in Peggy's story of what had in the end been done to Timothy, and Nancy did not laugh with them. More than once she laughed to herself when the others were perfectly serious. She did her share of washing up without a word.

"What's the matter?" said John at last when Nancy suddenly broke into a cheerful chuckle.

"Nothing's the matter," said Nancy. "Jibbooms and bobstays! Everything's just right. I'm only thinking about the savage chief. We ought to do things properly. Look here, Mastodon."

The Mastodon looked at her gravely.

"Look here," she said again. "We're explorers. You're a savage chief. We ought to load you with presents, but we haven't got a single bead."

"I've promised him some of our fish-hooks," said Roger.

"Good," said Nancy. "Why not?"

"I say," said the Mastodon. "I don't want to take any unless you've got plenty."

"We've got a whole packet," said John.

"Barbecued billygoats!" said Nancy. "Bother the fish-hooks. Do let me talk. Look here. We're explorers and we've met you and made friends. . . . Haven't we?"

The Mastodon stared at her. "Yes," he said.

"Then the next thing to do is to prick our fingers, all of us, and rub the blood in each other's wounds, so that we're blood brothers. . . ."

The Mastodon grinned. "That's what we did, when we first made our tribe, and the others got in a row with their missionaries about it. Daisy went and had a sore finger for about a week."

"We won't get into a row," said Nancy. "There's nobody to make one. And then, if we're blood brothers it'll be all right for you to help in the exploring. And if there was your blood in us, you could borrow one or two of us if you happened to be short of savages. Let's do it at once. Who's got any needles? Come on, Susan. You'd better prick Bridget's finger for her and I'll do Peggy's. She'll never prick it herself."

"I don't want to have my finger pricked," said Bridget.

"You shan't," said Susan.

"I'll prick my own," said Peggy. "If you don't go and hurry me."

"Good," said Nancy. "Where's a needle? It won't really matter about Bridget if she doesn't want to. . . ."

"But then I'll be left out," said Bridget. "All because I'm too young."

"It isn't because you're too young," said Nancy. "It's only because you don't want to have your finger pricked."

"Well, I don't," said Bridget.

"Come on, Bridget," said Roger.

Bridget's lip quivered, and for the second time that day, Susan, who was an expert in Bridget, knew that something had to be done about it at once.

"No one's going to prick your finger," she said. "And there's no need for anyone else to prick theirs. We can make an alliance with the savages without any blood at all."

"It's all right," said Titty. "There was bread at supper, and lots of salt in the scrambled eggs. He's eaten our bread and salt and we're going to eat his to-morrow. That's all that really matters."

"I don't mind doing it," said the Mastodon, choosing a finger to be pricked.

"No need," said Susan, and then, privately to Nancy. "Look out. It's after Bridget's bed time."

"All right," said Nancy. "Bread and salt counts. Pity about the blood all the same. What time are you coming in the morning, Mastodon?"

"I'll come over as soon as I take up the night line," said the Mastodon. "But it's low tide about ten. We shan't be able to do much till the afternoon. Not in boats anyway. And I've simply got to go now. I left old *Speedy* in an awful mess."

"Come on, Bridgie," said Susan. "Bed, and quick too, if

we're going to be up early enough to go blackberrying before we start exploring."

*

The Mastodon rowed away in the dusk. The explorers watched his boat until it disappeared.

"Mastodon Island?" said Titty, looking across the creek.

"All right," said John. "If he doesn't mind."

"He's a first rate savage," said Nancy. "I wonder what the others are like."

Back at the camp, Susan met them with a finger to her lips.

"Human sacrifice asleep," whispered Roger.

"So's Sinbad," said Titty, looking into her tent and bringing drawing-board and indiarubber to the light of the fire. She looked sideways across the map. "Ink's dry now," she said. For a moment she used the indiarubber, and then, blowing at the map, and dusting it lightly with her fingers, she handed it over to Nancy, to take her mind off savages and war.

"You've done a jolly good lot already," said Nancy, looking at the island, its seawall, its landing place, the native kraal, the camp, the Straits of Magellan and Cape Horn, all neatly inked in the middle of the map with Commander Walker's blobs and wide blank spaces lying unexplored all round it.

"But just look what a lot there is to do," said John.

"Don't let's put any more on the fire," said Susan. "It isn't like Wild Cat where we always had plenty of wood."

"It's a pity about that blood business," said Nancy, handing the map to John. "It would make things a lot better."

"Bridget does get so upset if she thinks she's being left out," said Susan. "And it doesn't really make any difference."

There was an odd smile on Nancy's face, lit by a flame as she stirred the dying fire.

"You never know," she said. "It might make quite a lot."

CHAPTER XII

BLOOD AND IODINE

Nancy woke the camp with a war cry long before the shadow on the meal-dial was anywhere near the breakfast peg. Susan, who had Nancy's watch in her tent, saw that it was terribly early, but knew that there was no hope of getting anybody to sleep again with the sunshine pouring through the walls of the tents. Everybody but Bridget went down to the landing place and had a morning wallow, getting so muddy on their way up again that it took another wallow in the pond to get them clean. Bridget, who could not swim, did the next best thing in standing by the pond and letting the others empty bucketfuls of water over her head. John cut the day's notch in the flagstaff. There was no sign of the Mastodon. They had breakfast. They wrote the first Report of the Secret Archipelago Expedition. Everybody signed it, and Susan put it in a stamped envelope, meaning to ask the farmer to post it next time he went to the mainland. Roger went twice to his look-out post to see if the Mastodon had come out to take up his night-line. John and Nancy were looking at the map considering what to explore next. "He said we couldn't do much boatwork until the afternoon," said John, looking at his tide-table. "High tide's not till 3.36."

"Don't let's decide till he comes," said Titty, wiping the last of the breakfast mugs.

"He's going to bring us some fish," said Roger.

"He probably won't turn up at all," said Nancy. "Now, if only we'd done the blood business he'd have had to."

Bridget changed that subject. "Aren't we going to get some blackberries?" she said. "Susan promised."

"All right, Bridgie," said Susan. "Foraging party. We're going blackberrying while you make up your minds. We can't live off the land altogether, but that hedge is black with blackberries."

"Good against scurvy," said Titty.

"Give a yell when you're ready," said Susan. "Come on, Bridgie. There's your basket."

"I'll come too," said Peggy.

"More hands the better," said Susan.

"So'll I," said Roger.

"Not your hands," said Susan. "We only want hands that know their way to the baskets. Yours always go somewhere else by mistake."

"Oh look here," said Roger. "That was when I was as young as Bridget. I promise I won't eat a single one."

"Come on then," said Susan. "You can eat every tenth blackberry. But all the others go into the basket. It's no good picking them if there isn't enough to go round."

The blackberrying party, of Susan, Peggy, Roger and Bridget, went off along the dyke and inland towards the hedge that Susan had noticed when she had been too busy surveying to do more than taste the ripeness of a blackberry or two. John, Nancy and Titty crouched more closely round the map.

"The trouble is," said John, "that it isn't only boatwork that's no good except when the tide's up. The mud runs so far out that there are jolly few places where we can land."

"We could get ashore on Mastodon Island, like we did yesterday," said Titty.

"Bother that Mastodon," said Nancy. "We ought to have told him to turn up early."

"We don't really know him well enough," said Titty. "It isn't as if he was one of us."

"That's just what I mean," said Nancy. "We ought to have

Secret Archipelago Expedition

Report to Geographical Society's
Headquarters:~ Pin Mill

All well Reinforcements arrived (Thats
what the three million were cheering about)
Swallow Island circumnxavigated, via
Magellan Straits and via Cape Horn.
Savage Chief tracked to his _Lair_ by hoof—
—marks as big as teatrays. He is our
native guide and faithful friend. More
of his tribe coming.

Signed :-	Wizard	Firefly
Captains	John	Nancy
Mates	Susan	Peggy
Able Seamen	Titty ₊ Roger	
Ships Baby	BRIDGET	
Ships Kitten	X sinbad his mark	

(Beckfoot Papers Please Copy)

THE REPORT[1]

[1] See page 263 for Semaphore Alphabet.

K

grabbed our chance last night. A drop of blood all round would have done it."

"We couldn't," said John. "There'd have been awful trouble with Bridgie. Whether we pricked her finger, or didn't and left her out."

"There's another thing," said Titty. "We don't know what the rest of the Eels are like."

"They must be all right," said Nancy. "Or they wouldn't be Eels. It's as good as anything we've thought of ourselves."

"But perhaps he wouldn't have wanted to," said Titty. "He took his totem away."

"Galoot!" said Nancy. "Oh. Sorry. I was forgetting you weren't my mate. But don't you see he had to? How could he leave it in a camp of white explorers? It's a totem of the Eels, and we're not Eels. One drop of Eel blood in our veins and it would have been all right."

"What about rowing across now and digging him out?" said John. "You haven't seen his lair yet."

"Let's," said Nancy.

The three of them walked down to the landing-place, but went no further, for out on the creek was the Mastodon himself hauling in his night line and coiling it in the bottom of his boat.

"Coming in a minute," he shouted.

They watched the dripping line coming in, the Mastodon stopping at each hook, putting it in its place and then hauling in afresh.

"There's a fish," said Titty. Something white and splashing came up out of the water, and the Mastodon held it up for them to see.

"Flatfish," said John, "by the look of it."

"There's another," said Titty.

But after that they saw no more. The line came in hand over hand, and the boat moved slowly across the creek, but hook after hook came in bare, and presently the Mastodon was hauling up the weight to which the end of his line was made fast. He stowed that with the rest of his tackle, and then, bending to his oars pulled hurriedly towards them.

"Karabad . . .' he said cheerfully as he landed, and cut himself short. "I was forgetting you weren't Eels," he said. "Good morning."

"Good morning . . . I say, was that Eel language?" said Titty.

The Mastodon turned rather red. "It was a mistake," he said.

"Secret password?" said Nancy.

"It just began to slip out," said the Mastodon.

"If only we'd blooded each other," said Nancy.

"Come along to the camp," said John. "We're just deciding where to explore next."

"Well just for a minute," said the Mastodon. "But I can't stop this morning. You're coming to supper in *Speedy*, and I've got to go to the main first. I say, will you bring your own mugs? I've only got four, just enough for the Eels." He looked at two flounders in a bucket in the stern of his boat. "Look here, it's no good giving you these. Little miseries. Not worth eating. And every bait gone. I bet all the others were eels. There's nothing like them for not getting hooked." He emptied the bucket into the creek, and the two little flounders flapped away, like pancakes come to life.

"Mastodon," said Nancy suddenly. "Did you mean it last night? Would you have blooded with the rest of us?"

"It was you people who didn't want to," said the Mastodon.

"If only Bridget was a little older," said Titty.

"It'll be low water pretty soon," said the Mastodon. "You can't do much in the boats. But what about this afternoon? Tide won't be high till half past three. I've got to go home to get some things, and I want some more netting string from the town. Run right out. And there may be a letter from the tribe. . . ."

"Do they use native post?" asked Titty.

"Have to when there's no other way," said the Mastodon. "They're almost sure to send a letter before they leave Pin Mill. . . . I've got a pretty good plan for to-day," he went on. "I'm going straight over the marshes from *Speedy*, easy enough with nothing to carry. But I'll be loaded up when I come back. You know when we passed the Wade on the way home yesterday I showed you where the withies mark a channel going right in to a landing place on the mainland. You ought to have that in the map. Couldn't you explore that while the tide's coming up? Start from here about half past two. There's a channel all the way in. We've marked a lot of it. It twists about a bit, and we've put marks at the bends, secret ones. You'll see them when you're close to them, but not from the shore. If you work your way up there, there's a fine landing place. It's an old barge quay really. I'll get all my stuff there by high water and meet you there. And then we'll load it into your boats and dump it in *Speedy*, and there might be just time to sail round my island before you come to supper."

"Good idea," said John. "And this morning we could be mapping it. We could get ashore at the corner even at low water and do all the land part without a guide. Then we'll have both sides of the creek done. And the Amazons have never seen *Speedy*."

"Shall I leave the plank up?" said the Mastodon doubtfully.

"Oh no," said Nancy at once. "We won't go aboard if you're not there. We'll be seeing *Speedy* when we come to supper."

They came up to the camp and explained that the others had gone to get blackberries. They gave him the Report in its stamped envelope, to be sent off, by native post, in the town. They showed him the map with the work of the day before all neatly inked and the pencil markings rubbed out.

He pointed out on it the place on the mainland where he wanted them to meet him.

"Your island'll be done next," said Titty. "Do you mind if we call it Mastodon Island?"

"Not a bit," said the Mastodon. "But, look here, I mustn't stop another minute. It's a fearful trek overland, and if I'm not at the landing place at high water you'll have to start back without me, or you'll get stuck. And I may be held up at home . . . at the kraal. . . ."

"We know," said Nancy. "Native business."

"There's nearly always something," said the Mastodon. "If it isn't clean shirts it's something else."

He turned to go back to his boat.

The quiet of the island was broken by a sudden loud wail.

"Bridget," said John. "She's hurt herself."

They stood still and listened. There was another wail, as if Bridget had taken a long breath and was using it.

Then came Susan's voice, very angry, "Roger!" a gasping howl cut off short from Bridget, and a very cheerful shout from Roger, "Hurry up, Susan. Hurry up!"

A moment later Roger and Bridget appeared on the top of the dyke. Roger had Bridget by the elbow and was running her along. Bridget, perhaps because she had no breath to howl with, had stopped wailing. Roger was waving frantically with his free hand, and at the same time stooping to encourage Bridget.

"Hi!" he shouted. "Hi!"

"Roger!" shouted Susan again, and presently her bobbing head showed behind the dyke, and then they saw her running in pursuit.

John and Titty ran to meet them.

"Hi," shouted Roger again. "Somebody must fetch the Mastodon. Oh good," he shouted. "Come on, Susan. He's here."

"What's happened?" called Titty.

"Quick. Quick," shouted Roger. "Bridget's scratched herself. She's bleeding beautifully. All right Bridget, it's stopped hurting. Don't suck it. Don't waste it. Come on. Where's a bucket?"

"Jibbooms and bobstays!" cried Nancy. "We're saved. Well done Bridget! Good for you Roger!"

She grabbed the Mastodon by the hand and hurried him towards the others.

Susan came panting up. "Roger," she cried. "What did you make her run like that for? Poor old Bridgie. Everybody gets scratched blackberrying. Wait a minute and I'll put a drop of iodine on it and a bit of sticky plaster."

Peggy came up. "Poor old Bridget!" she said.

Nancy took charge. "Good old Bridget!" she said. "Here's a clean plate. Let it drip. Titty, get hold of a needle for the rest of us."

Bridget, looking from one to another, had stopped crying, though a tear was still wet on her cheek. She looked at her finger and, at the sight of the blood on it, opened her mouth to wail again.

"Well done, Bridget," said Nancy. "You've saved the whole show. Don't suck it. Save that drop."

Susan came out from her tent with her First Aid Box already open and the iodine bottle in her hand.

"Let's see it, Bridget," she said. "It'll be all right in a minute."

"It's all the better for it to bleed," said Nancy, carefully catching a drop that was just falling from the tip of Bridget's finger. Don't put the iodine on it yet. Good for you, Titty. Take a needle, Mastodon. What's the colour of Eel's blood?"

Titty was handing round a packet of needles.

"What are you doing, Nancy?" said Susan. "Turn round, Bridget. I can't get at it if you stand like that."

THE BLOODING

151

Roger, who had already taken a needle, was standing with his back to the others. He turned suddenly round. "I've done mine," he said, squeezing the first finger of his left hand. Where's the plate?"

"Oh, Roger!" said Susan. "Put some iodine on it at once. How do you know the needle was clean?"

"New one," said Roger. "It didn't hurt. At least only for a moment. Here's another drop."

"Titty!" exclaimed Susan. "Don't be such a donkey. John!"

"Oh look here, Susan," said Nancy. "We can't miss a chance like this. Bridget may never scratch herself again."

Susan hesitated. "You ought to dip the needle in iodine," she said. "And you'll all get blood poisoning anyway. What are you going to do next?"

"Mix all the blood together and rub it in. Come on Susan. Perhaps you're right about the iodine. Dip your needle, Titty. You too, Peggy."

"Ouch!" said Titty.

"You haven't got as much as I did," said Roger. "You'll have to pinch it pretty hard. Gosh! The Mastodon's fairly jabbed himself. But nobody's got as much as Bridgie. Wasn't it a good thing I thought of it?"

"Now then, Susan," said Nancy. "Come on, ship's doctor. You ought to do it better than anybody."

Susan chose a spot on her finger with great care. "All right," she said . . . "I've done it. But I'm sure we ought to mix some iodine with it before rubbing it in, and I'm going to."

"Good idea," said Nancy. "It'll make the blood go further anyway. Who hasn't done it? Oh well done, John. Let me have the plate. Here's another drop. Peggy!"

"I can't."

"Barbecued billygoats! You can."

"It won't go in."

"Give me your hand," said Nancy. "I'll do it. No don't go and pull like that. Hold your hand still. Turn the other way. Talk to her, Roger!"

"PEGGY!" shouted Roger at the top of his voice. She looked round.

"All over," said Nancy. "It went in all right. That finger's as soft as butter. No, don't suck it. We want every drop."

There was now a small, a very small puddle of mixed blood in the middle of the plate, which Roger was greedily offering to anyone who seemed to have a drop ready to add to the rest. Susan poured a little iodine from the bottle and stirred it with the tip of her finger.

"What do we say?" asked Titty.

'Swallows and Amazons and Eels for ever!"

"Nothing about blood brothers?" said Titty.

"Blood brothers . . . and sisters till death do us part. That ought to do."

"Hurry up," said Susan. "I must put something on Bridget's finger to keep the dirt out."

"Say it all together," said Nancy. "Can you say it, Bridgie? You're the most important. We couldn't have done it if it hadn't been for you. Swallows and Amazons and Eels for ever. Blood brothers and sisters till death do us part. Now then."

"Swallows and Amazons and Eels for ever. Blood brothers and sisters till death do us part."

Even Bridget got it right first time.

"Now everybody rubs her wound in the blood . . . or his," said Nancy.

"Gosh!" said Roger. "It stung worse than the needle."

"Ow," said Bridget.

"Good," said Nancy. "That shows it's really got in. Vaccination's never any good unless it hurts. You only have to be done twice over. Come on, Mastodon, don't hang back."

The Mastodon obediently rubbed his finger in the now drying puddle. "It's a pity the tribe isn't here," he said. "But I don't believe Daisy would have done it again."

"I did," said Bridget, and everybody laughed.

"Well, didn't I?"

"You gave more than anybody else," said Roger.

"Everybody's going to put some more iodine on now whether they like it or not," said Susan.

Everybody did, and Susan put a neat bandage round Bridget's scratched finger.

"I've simply got to bolt," said the Mastodon, "or I'll never be back at the quay by high water." He started for the landing place, followed by his new brothers and sisters.

"Well, it's all right now," said Nancy. "We've all got Eel blood in us, and you've got some of all of ours."

"I say," said Titty. "Is it all right now for us to know that word you were going to say?"

"Oh yes," said the Mastodon. "It's the word to say when you meet another Eel or are saying Good-bye. It's Karabadangbaraka. And the answer's the same word backwards. Akarabgnadabarak."

"Half a minute while I write it down," said Titty. "Say it again."

The Mastodon said it slowly. "The countersign's the difficult one. Daisy always gets wrong with the gnad. She keeps on saying 'gand' instead."

"Akarabgnadabarak," said Titty, writing it as she spoke.

"Don't let anybody else see that," said the Mastodon.

"I'll burn it as soon as we know it by heart," said Titty.

"And what about that totem?" said Nancy. "Now we've all got Eel blood in us."

"All right," said the Mastodon. "I've got to nip across to *Speedy* before starting home. If you come across right away I'll give it you now."

"Let's all go," said Bridget, who was looking proudly at her bandaged finger.

"Are there any blackberries on your island?" asked Susan.

"Lots."

"We'll catch you up," said John. "Just half a second while we get our compasses and things."

The Mastodon pushed off his boat.

"Karabadangbaraka!" Titty called after him.

"Akarabgnadabarak," he shouted back.

"Great Congers!" said Nancy gleefully to herself.

"What?" said John.

"Oh nothing," said Nancy. "It's only the Eel's blood beginning to work."

CHAPTER XIII

MASTODON ISLAND

THERE was a hurried rush to the camp and back, for baskets, surveying poles, compasses and blank copies of the map. The ship's kitten, who was having a nap after his breakfast, was left in charge. The explorers were on their way only a few minutes after the Mastodon. They found his boat at the mouth of the small creek that ran in behind Mastodon Island, and they went ashore close beside it, carrying their anchors to the top of the bank. The little creek was dry almost to the mouth.

"It won't be high water till half past three," said John. "He says we ought to start about half past two to meet him at that place."

"Lots of time to do the island first," said Susan. "And then we'll have dinner, and while you're meeting him, Peggy and I and Bridget are going to make a blackberry and banana mash. I bet the Eels don't know it. We'll take it to *Speedy* to add to the feast."

When they came along the dyke to the old barge, they were just in time to see the Mastodon drop down her side and get his feet fixed on his splatchers.

The totem in its blue, red and green paint gleamed in the sunshine on the top of the dyke where the Mastodon had planted it.

"Thank you very much," they called down to him.

"I'm awfully late," shouted the Mastodon. "Can't stop another minute. You'll find the best blackberries close to the heronry."

"Where's the heronry?" called John.

"Those high trees," shouted the Mastodon. "The tops are full of nests. We very nearly decided to be herons instead of eels. But Daisy decided eels were best. I say, I've thought of a whole lot of things we can do when the rest of the Eels come. Four's nothing. But with seven of you as well."

"Eels for ever!" shouted Nancy, and added, to John, "I told you it would make all the difference."

"There may be news from the others at home," shouted the Mastodon. "Anyhow . . . No time now. We'll talk to-night."

"Grand Council," called Nancy. "Eels for ever!"

"Karabadangbaraka!" shouted the Mastodon joyfully.

"Akarabgnadabarak," shouted seven explorers from the top of the dyke, as they watched the Mastodon, with a flapping empty knapsack in one hand, run, with that queer swinging gait of his, so that his splatchers should not catch each other, across the soft mud at the bottom of the creek. They watched him struggle up the bank on the further side, hang his splatchers on a bush, and race off over the marshes.

"I don't wonder you thought he was a mastodon," said Nancy, looking down from the dyke at those huge round hoof-marks on the mud of the creek. "And what a place he's got to live in."

"Wait till you've seen the inside," said Roger. "Susan and Bridget haven't seen it either."

"How do you get into it?" asked Bridget, looking at the wide gap that separated the bows of *Speedy* from the bank.

"He's got a drawbridge," said Roger. "Jolly springy too. You and Sinbad'll both have to cross it on all fours. There'll be water all round it. It'll be as good as the houseboat, only we won't be making the Mastodon walk the plank."

"Why not?" said Bridget.

"Because you scratched your finger," said Roger.

"Oh," said Bridget. "Because he's a blood brother and sister. I said it right first time."

"Look here," said John. "Let's begin. This island looks just like ours and we'll do it the same way. It looks as if there's a dyke all round, with marshes outside it and dry ground inside. That heronry'll be jolly useful, too. We'll be able to see the tallest of the trees from anywhere."

"Why do you want to see it?" asked Peggy.

"Not to get lost," said Nancy. "But I don't see how you could on an island."

"It's like this . . ." said John.

Nancy and Peggy, for once, had something to learn. The others, now experienced surveyors after their work on Swallow Island, showed them how to plant a bamboo at a corner of the twisting dyke, and how to take bearings from that bamboo to another on another corner, and to the tallest tree in the heronry which served as a bamboo pole without having to be planted. Bit by bit, they worked all round the island, and though, perhaps, the resulting map was not up to the standard of the ordnance survey, it gave a much better idea of the island than the mere blob that Daddy had roughed out in pencil.

Their map showed all the really important things. There was the line of the dyke, with its fringe of saltings. There was the heronry shown by drawings of trees. Though it was not the nesting season they had been lucky enough to see a heron alight on the top of a tree, "backwatering" (Titty's word) with its wings, as it brought its feet forward to take hold. Most important of all, there was the old barge, *Speedy*, resting in the mud of the narrow channel that divided Mastodon Island from the mainland.

They had done a good morning's work when, at last, they worked round to *Speedy* again. John and Titty were very much relieved. They had been rather bothered by all that talk of war. They had been a little afraid that the Amazons would not see how important it was, when exploring, to explore, and to make a map as nearly as possible as good as the one they would have made if Daddy had been there to help them. But, though Nancy had all the time been trying new eelish swear words on her tongue, she had worked as hard as any of them. The Secret Archipelago Expedition was going to be the most successful they had ever made.

From the far side of Mastodon Island, they had seen other islands, far more than Daddy's map had promised. And now with two boats of their own, and Nancy no longer hankering after war, and the Mastodon an ally, a friend and a blood brother, and more friendly savages to come, they felt there really was a chance of carrying their explorations, north, south, east and west to every bay and island of these inland seas.

It had been a successful morning in another way. They had found a lot of dead wood and sticks under the heronry, and every stick was worth having in this place where good fuel was so rare. It was lucky, as Roger pointed out, that the herons had not wanted them all for their nests. Everybody but Bridget was carrying something for the fire. Bridget, because she was going to be a human sacrifice, was allowed to carry the totem in the hand that was not bandaged. She sat in the bows of *Wizard*, holding the totem as a figurehead, when they left Mastodon Island and rowed across to the landing place below the camp.

Back in the camp, the totem was planted in its old place by the meal-dial.

"He's taken away the four shells," said Roger.

"Of course," said Titty. "Those were meant for the four savages of the tribe."

"We'll give it something better," said Susan. "Let's give it Nancy's watch. You don't mind, do you?"

"Good idea," said Nancy, and unstrapped her wrist watch and then, fastening the buckle, slipped it over the eel's head of the totem, and let it hang there.

"Totem and clock-tower," said Roger. "One o'clock, too. Look at the dinner stick. We'd got it in just the right place. The shadow's going to touch it in a minute."

"Dinner in half an hour," said Susan. "No chops left. We'll hot up a steak and kidney pudding. And what about tinned pears?"

"I'll be opening them," said Peggy.

"Wriggling Elvers!" said Nancy. "My throat's as rough as the inside of a seaboot."

"I'm jolly thirsty, too," said Roger.

"Ration of grog," said John. "We've earned it."

"Splice the mainbrace," said Nancy.

Bottles of ginger beer were dealt out, with a warning not to gollop them and have nothing to drink at dinner. The explorers wetted their throats while the survey of Mastodon Island was added to the map. Nancy and John compared the rough maps they had made and pencilled in darkly the outline on which they finally agreed. John, working carefully with the parallel rulers to check the important bearings, copied the result. Daddy's map began to look more and more like a real map instead of like a lot of lines that might be water or earth or anything else. The beginning, with Swallow Island, Cape Horn, the southern part of the Secret Water and the northern part of the Red Sea, by taking in Mastodon Island had made a notable push into the west.

"I do believe we're going to get it all done," said John. "If the rest of the Eels are half as good as the Mastodon, we'll have six boats for doing all the rest."

It was a very cheerful dinner, though John was in rather a hurry to get it over, and kept looking at the totem clock-tower.

"We've got to meet him at high water," he said. "He says you can't get to the place except then, and we've got to find the way ourselves. The sooner we start the better."

"We mustn't miss him," said Roger. "I expect he's bringing grub for to-night."

"Peggy and I've been thinking about that," said Susan. "He's all by himself and there's such an awful lot of us. There'll be the banana blackberry mash to take. We'll want a few more blackberries, and we've thought of something else to help in case of need. We're not coming with you. Bridget's done enough exploring for one day. We're going hunting for the pot."

"Hunting what?" said Roger.

"Mushrooms," said Susan. "I spotted some yesterday on the buffalo grazing grounds."

"We thought we'd take some stewed mushrooms with us," said Peggy. "Ready done, so he won't have to cook them."

"And a tin of pemmican," said Susan. "Living alone, he probably doesn't know what a lot seven explorers can eat. It'd be awful if at the last minute he hadn't got enough to go round."

"We needn't say anything about the pemmican," said Titty. "We could just keep it hidden in the boat and remember it was there if it was wanted."

"Let's get started anyway," said John.

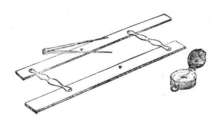

CHAPTER XIV

WITCH'S QUAY

THERE was little more than enough wind to fill the sails as the two boats of the explorers drifted up Goblin Creek and round the island into the Red Sea. John and Roger were in *Wizard*. Titty had joined Nancy in *Firefly*.

With one of the rough copies of Commander Walker's map in each boat, they were off to chart the winding channel to the old quay of which the Mastodon had told them, and, if possible, to get there at high water and to meet the Mastodon on his return from civilization. Civilization, houses, railways, motor cars, and all the rest of it, seemed very far away as the two boats drifted along with the tide. Only, in the distance a thin tower, like the stump of a pencil, and a few white houses and the top sail of a barge moving beyond them out at sea, reminded them that there was anything outside this secret world of mud and weeds and gently moving water.

The narrow channel widened and the Red Sea lay before them.

"If only it was always like this," said Nancy. "So that we could sail anywhere, any time. I don't see the good of tides. What's the good of a sea if it's all going to be mud in a few hours."

"It's like breathing," said Titty. "Up and down. Up and down. It makes everything alive."

"Um," said Nancy. "When the tide's out everything goes dead. Hullo. We touched then. I'll get the centre-board half up."

The two boats sailed slowly on, side by side.

Wider and wider the Red Sea opened before them. To port was the long low dyke of the island, and shimmering water over the mudflats where Titty and Bridget had seen the long trail of the Mastodon's hoofmarks. To starboard all was new. The bank on that side was further and further away. Little clumps of weeds standing in the water hinted of shallows, but beyond them water stretched into a misty distance. Somewhere over there they were to meet the Mastodon. An old barge quay, he had said, but there was no sign of anything but sunlit water and small islands of weeds.

John was sitting on the middle thwart of *Wizard* searching for signs of a marked channel. Nancy in *Firefly* was doing the same. Roger and Titty were steering.

"Starboard a bit," said John, and Roger altered course.

Titty, catching Nancy's eye, did the same.

"There's one of those little trees, sticking up out of the water on the port bow," said Roger.

"We can't go wrong if we make for that," said John. "It's a withy. We passed that on the way home when we sailed round the island. We'll go to it, and then we may be able to see something else."

"We haven't really begun the unexplored part yet," said Titty.

"How do you know there really is a channel over there?" said Nancy.

"There's a good wide opening shown on Daddy's map," said John. "And the Mastodon said we'd find the marks in it as we went along."

"More withies ahead," said Nancy.

Far ahead of them were a line of withies, bending in the tide, perhaps a hundred yards or two hundred yards one from another.

"That's where the road goes," said John. "We saw them yesterday, and you see those posts, just showing? That's the place we bumped on coming home ... the high bit half way across the Wade. We've got to turn south before coming to them or we'll miss the way altogether."

"What's that away to starboard?" said Titty.

"It's a stick, it's a stick," cried Roger.

"Steer for it," said John. "Pretty well south from here. That's all right. It'll mark the beginning of the channel."

Both little boats swung round. Roger and Titty hauled in their main sheets, and steered for the little branch of leafless twigs far away over the water. John and Nancy were busy with their compasses.

"It can't be anything else," said Nancy.

"Better have the centreboards nearly up," said John. "The wind's free, and anything's better than getting stuck in the mud with the boards down."

Titty, just nipping the end of her tongue between her teeth, kept a straight wake as she steered.

"That clump of weeds is pretty close," she said. "Is it all right?"

Nancy watched the weeds coming nearer and nearer. There was clear water all round them. She took an oar and prodded over the side.

"Keep as you're going," she said.

"Aye, aye, Sir," said Titty.

The weeds slid by and were left astern.

"What about the other withy?" asked John. 'It looks a long way to port." He pointed to another thin sapling with twigs on the top of it, far to the left of the one they were now coming near.

"Can't be anything to do with us," said Nancy. Everything looks clear ahead."

"Keep her as she goes," said John.

"Aye, aye, Sir," said Roger.

"Get bearings from this withy to the posts on the Wade and to the native's landing-place."

"Moving too fast," said Nancy. "You do the one to the Wade and I'll do the other."

"She's steering funnily," said Titty.

"What's happening?" said Roger. "I say, John! I thought it looked a bit shallow."

Side by side, *Wizard* and *Firefly* lost speed and came to rest. They were aground, yet clear water stretched far away on every side of them.

"Suffering Lampreys!" cried Nancy. "Let go your sheet."

Roger had already let go of his, and for a minute or two both skippers wrestled with the oars, making their able seamen move now forwards now aft as they worked to get their ships afloat again. The mud was so soft that prodding at it was very little good.

"I say," said Roger. "What'll happen if we can't get off, and the tide goes down and leaves us here? We can't walk over it like the Mastodon. And we haven't even a bit of chocolate."

"Even he couldn't walk over mud as soft as this," said John. "She's coming. Nancy's off too. We ought to have gone for that other withy after all. He did say the channel twisted a lot, but I never thought it'd turn right across like that."

Again the little boats were sailing, this time in a new direction, almost at right angles to their old course. John took a bearing from one withy to the other. Nancy tried the depth and washed the mud off the blade of an oar at the same time.

"We're in the channel now all right," she said.

"This is much worse than the Magellan Straits," said Titty. "There we only had to find the right ditch and keep to it, and here there are no banks to show where the ditch is and where it isn't."

When they came to the next stick, John lowered *Wizard's* sail.

"Don't want to get stuck again," he said. "I can't see another mark anywhere."

Nancy brought down the sail in *Firefly*. "Sit in the bottom of the boat, just for a minute," she said. "I'm going to stand on the thwart to have a look round."

"Don't have her over," said John.

"I won't," said Nancy.

"He said some of the marks were secret ones," said John.

"Well there just aren't any," said Nancy. "And it looks pretty shallow everywhere. Weeds showing all over the place. Hullo!"

"Seen anything?"

"There's something floating over there. Not moving. Must be anchored whatever it is."

"I can't see anything," said John.

Nancy hopped down and took the oars.

"Plenty of water," she said. "I'll paddle gently in case of it getting too shallow."

"There *is* something," cried Titty. "It looks like a necklace."

"Galoot . . ." said Nancy. "It can't be."

"It is," said Titty.

"Sorry," said Nancy. "So it is."

Nancy stopped rowing, and *Firefly* slid slowly through the water towards a floating ring of old corks threaded on a string. Titty reached over the side as they drifted by.

"It's tethered to something," she said. "Shall I lift it up?"

"No. No," shouted Nancy. "We don't want to move it if it's a mark. Come on John. We're all right so far."

"Where do we go next?" asked Roger.

"Let's get this put down first," said John, and then, standing up in the boat, looked anxiously round over a waste of water. Some duck swimming along the edge of a clump of weeds, began to swim faster, and suddenly splashed up into the air and flew away.

"One of them's left behind," said Roger.

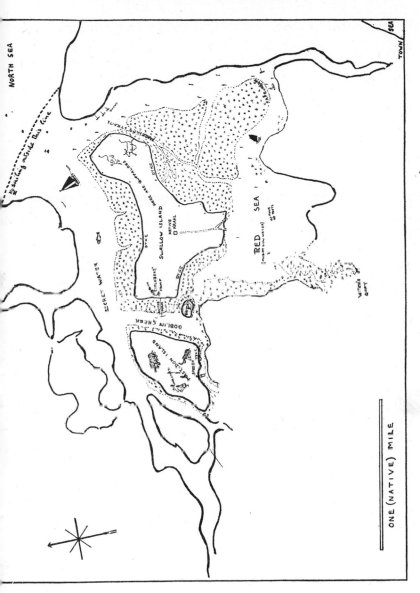

THE MAP WITH MASTODON ISLAND AND WITCH'S QUAY

ONE (NATIVE) MILE

"Perhaps it's hurt," said Titty, and looked at it through the telescope. "Oh, it's only a bottle . . . floating."

"Why doesn't it move?" said Roger. "It must be swimming against the tide. Or is it high tide already?"

Titty looked at it again. "It's the wrong way up," she said.

"Come on," said Nancy. "Good for you, Titty. I ought to have spotted it. Bottles always float neck upwards when they're just bobbing about. That one's anchored. Come on, John. We've found the next mark."

From near the bottle, an old lemonade bottle, anchored to something on the bottom, they saw a withy, a stick with a bunch of twigs, like those that marked the channel outside, though not so big. John saw it first, rowed straight for it and, a moment later, stuck fast. Nancy backwatered in *Firefly* just in time to save herself from joining John on the mud.

"There must be another mark to go for first," said John. "You know if we go on getting stuck like this we won't be there before the tide turns, and then we may not get there at all."

"Let's go back at once," said Roger. "I say, will we ever find the way?"

"I've got it all down all right so far," said John.

"Look there," said Nancy. "There's another lot of corks. Probably we ought to go round them before going for the stick."

She pulled away, went back to the floating bottle, and from there rowed to the ring of floating corks.

"Come on," she said. "It's all right. Deep water all the way. Now for the stick."

"We can't go straight for the stick from here. There's a tuft of reeds right ahead. She's touching. Look out, John. We're stuck again."

"There's another bottle over there," said John, who had got *Wizard* free of the mud and had just arrived at the second ring of corks. "Gosh!" he cried. "I've got it. Port and star-board buoys. We've got to leave all bottles to starboard and all corks to port. Why on earth didn't he tell us?"

"Then what does the stick mean?" said Roger.

When they came to the stick, they knew. From beside it they could see another anchored bottle away to the south, and to the west two more sticks, the further of them close to the shore.

"There must be a landing-place in there. There's a fishing boat pulled up there. The stick just marks where the channels divide. Half a minute while I jam that down."

"Is that where we're going?" said Titty.

"Can't be," said Nancy, who was down in the bottom of *Firefly* with compass and map. "Almost due west, and we ought to be going almost south."

"There's nothing like a quay in there," said John. "Come on. Next bottle."

This way and that the channel wound, each turn of it marked by a ring of corks or an old bottle, corked and anchored by its neck.

"It doesn't look as if we're going anywhere," said Roger.

"It's getting narrower anyway," said Titty. "We must be getting to the end."

Ahead of them long low banks of weeds pushed out into the water, and were closing in on either side. Nobody who did not know could have guessed that there was a way through. Even John began to feel doubtful, watching his compass, and noting the course from secret mark to secret mark.

And then, suddenly, they saw it. Paddling carefully, *Firefly* close astern of *Wizard*, they were making for a ring of corks close to a bank of mud and weeds. As they reached the corks they could see round the bank, and ahead of them, only a few hundred yards away was an old wooden quay, with a house on it, and a couple of boats pulled up on dry land.

"Hurrah!" cried John and ran aground again.

Even here, within sight of the quay, they had to follow the channel and feel their way along. They could find no more marks to guide them, and had to sound their way in with an oar.

"Well, we've done it," said John, as the two boats ran alongside the quay, and they climbed ashore. From the top of the quay they looked back and, far away over the water, could see the roof of the native kraal on Swallow Island. "Gosh!" said Nancy. "It looks simple enough from up here."

"It jolly well isn't," said John, "when you're down on the level of the water."

"But where's the Mastodon?" said Roger.

"It isn't high water yet," said John.

The two skippers settled down on the top of the quay where the old storehouse sheltered them from the wind, and began comparing their maps. For a minute or two Titty and Roger looked over their shoulders and listened to argument about the right place for this mark and that.

"Come on, Rogie," said Titty at last. "Let's go and explore."

"Don't go too far," said John. "We'll want to start the moment he turns up."

"Perhaps we'll meet him," said Titty.

Long years ago there must have been busy barge traffic in and out from this old quay when there were no railways and poor roads and everything that could be was carried by water. They could see that the quay had once been bigger. They found the remains of an old crane, and heavy rings, now almost rusted through, to which in old times the barges had made fast. But now the wood of the quay was rotting, and water was working in and out through gaps in the piling. The storehouse was empty. Beside the quay was an open space, big enough for a wagon to turn round in. But there were no cart tracks, and grass and thistles were growing through the sand.

There were footmarks in the sandy ground.

"Natives," said Titty. "We'd better go carefully."

"What are these squiggles?" said Roger. "Somebody's been drawing snakes."

"Eels!" cried Titty. "You can tell by the head and the fins. Hey! John! The Mastodon's been and gone."

John and Nancy came running along the quay and looked at the squiggles in the sand.

"Eels all right," said John.

"Why on earth couldn't he wait?" said Nancy. "The tide's still coming in."

"They're all pointing the same way," said John.

"Patterans," said Titty. "I bet he drew them to show us which way he's gone."

"Here's another," said Roger, who had already left the edge of the quay and was moving in the way the eels were pointing, stooping and looking at the ground.

"And another," said John.

"He must think us galoots, to draw such a lot," said Nancy.

Eel after eel drawn in the sand and all wriggling in the same direction led them across the open space towards the mouth of a green lane. Titty ran ahead into the lane, and searched the ground. The others followed her.

"He couldn't draw eels in the grass," said Nancy.

John went back to the last of the eels they had seen. It was not as straight as the others. All were wriggly lines, but it was easy to see which way they were going. This last one had a decided kink to the left.

"He's turned off here. Or hasn't he?"

Away to the left was a broken down wooden fence, with a wicket gate in it, and beyond it a thatched cottage, a very small cottage of tarred black wood standing in a small potato patch.

John went to the wicket gate, which stood half open, and

there, on the ground between the gateposts, was a wriggly line. There was another on the path across the potato patch.

"He went in here," said Titty.

"Come on," said Nancy. "I'm going in too."

One of the windows of the cottage was broken, but there was a bit of paper stuck over it, and a geranium on the sill inside.

"Somebody's living here," said John doubting whether to go or not.

Somebody tapped at the window. The door of the cottage opened and a bent old woman stood on the threshold, leaning on a stick.

"Looking for young Don?" she whispered, and coughed. "Lost me voice, I have. He've put his bag in the shed."

She pointed to a lean-to shed at the end of the cottage.

"Thank you very much," said John.

The old woman stood there, watching them.

"New friends for him," she cackled. "Not seen you before."

"May we go to the shed?" asked John.

The old woman did not answer. She began to cough, and her cough turned into a laugh and then into a cough again. She went back into her cottage.

John led the way to the shed. Just inside it was a sack, with a bit of rope round the mouth of it. A bit of paper lay on it, skewered to the sack with a splinter of wood. They read it together.

"Please take this lot in your boat. Bringing the rest. Don't wait for me after the tide turns or you won't get back. If I don't get back in time I'll go overland." There was no signature except a drawing of a wriggling eel.

"What are those words crossed out?" said Nancy.

"Bad something," said John. "Bad news."

They looked at each other. What bad news could there be?

"Oh well," said Nancy. "He's crossed them out anyway. You get hold of one end, John, and I'll take the other."

"They hove up the sack, which was very heavy, and carried it past the cottage and out by the wicket gate. The cottage door was closed, but they could see the face of the old woman, coughing and laughing, looking at them through the broken pane by the geranium.

"I bet she's a witch," said Titty, remembering her mother's story of the Obeah Woman. "Wrinkles deep as ditches on her brown face. A native witch. I wonder if she's got eel blood in her too."

They took the sack to the quay, and lowered it down into *Wizard*.

"Tide's still rising," said John. "But it must be nearly high water."

Roger worked his way down by the side of the quay, and stuck a bit of wood into the mud, and crouched on the bank to watch it. John looked out over the Red Sea, at the distant line of their island.

"Sing out the moment it stops rising," he said. "Come on, Nancy. Let's get on with the chart. It's that bit where the other channel starts that looks wrong."

Titty crouched on the bank by Roger.

"Something must have happened to make him write 'Bad News'," she said. "And then something else must have made him cross it out."

THE NATIVE KRAAL

CHAPTER XV

THE MASTODON WISHES HE HADN'T

"It's begun to go down." Roger's shout disturbed the map-makers on the quay. Titty had joined them, to see the two maps which now more or less agreed with each other, though it was hard to tell which of the pencilled lines were meant to count and which would have been rubbed out if only the surveyors had not forgotten to bring an indiarubber from the camp.

"Come on then," said John.

"What about the Mastodon?" said Nancy.

"He said we weren't to wait for him. There's jolly little water anyway, and you know how it runs out once it starts. We can't wait. If we don't get out before the water goes, it means not getting home till to-morrow morning."

"And we haven't even iron rations," said Roger, coming up and untying *Wizard's* painter.

"He said he was going to do his best to get here," said Nancy.

"I'll run to the lane and see if he's in sight," said Titty.

"Go on, Able Seaman," said Nancy.

"But buck up," said John, dropping down the side of the quay and reaching with a foot for *Wizard's* middle thwart. "All aboard!"

"Aye, aye, Sir," said Roger.

The *Wizard* drifted slowly from the quayside.

Nancy, standing up in *Firefly*, hung on to the piling.

Titty came running back. "Not a sign of him. I say, hadn't one of us better wait? I will. I'll come back with him over-land."

"We can't leave you," said John. "Susan would only get worried."

"Half a minute then," said Titty, and went to the place where they had found the first eel drawn in the sand, scratched it out and drew another heading out towards the creek. "Just to show him we've been and gone."

"Look here, we must start," said John. "It's dropped inches already." He began to row. "Come on Nancy. With the wind like this we'll be able to sail, once we're clear of those weeds."

"Buck up, Able Seaman," said Nancy. But, even after Titty had dropped into the boat, and she was rowing after *Wizard*, Nancy did not row as hard as she could. Her eyes were still on the quay and the open space behind it. The thought of getting stuck on the mud bothered Nancy a good deal less than it did John and, while he was thinking mainly of Susan and the camp, she was still hoping against hope that the Mastodon would come running out of the green lane before it was too late.

"Oh well," she said at last. "It's no good waiting any longer," and bent seriously to her oars. She gave one hard pull and then backwatered so suddenly that Titty nearly shot forward off her seat in the stern.

"Coming!" she shouted. "Coming!" spun the boat round and headed for the quay. John stopped rowing and waited for them. The Mastodon with an enormous knapsack on his back, a parcel in one hand and a big milk can in the other was staggering to the quayside.

"Karabadangbaraka," said Nancy as she brought *Firefly* back to the to the quay.

"Akarabgnadabarak," panted the Mastodon, but Titty had a queer feeling that he had not wanted to say it. She looked round, wondering if some native was within earshot, someone who ought not to be allowed to hear password and countersign.

There was nobody. Perhaps it was not that he had not wanted to say it, but only that he was out of breath.

"Sorry I was late," said the Mastodon. "I had to wait in the town till the last possible minute."

"Lucky we hadn't started," said Nancy. "If we'd got round the corner of those weed banks we shouldn't have seen you."

"Jolly glad you waited," said the Mastodon. "It would have been an awful job humping this lot overland. I say, you did get the sack, didn't you, from the hut?"

"We got it all right," said Nancy.

"Did you have much trouble in getting in?" asked the Mastodon.

"Show him our sketch map, Titty," said Nancy. "We went aground once or twice at the bends."

The Mastodon stared at the map, which looked like a tangled spider's web to anyone who did not know that the little circles meant rings of corks and the black spots bottles and the letters noted down at the side of each one of the maze of straight lines was a compass bearing.

"I say, Nancy, John's putting up his sail."

"We'll do the same," said Nancy. "And the Mastodon'll steer. Do you think you'll be able to read the map?"

"I'll manage better without," said the Mastodon, and grinned, for the first time since he had come aboard. "But you'd better do the steering."

"All right," said Nancy. "Titty, you steer, and the Mastodon'll be pilot, and I'll check the marks as we go past them. Hi! John! Wait for us. The Mastodon's going to pilot, so that we shan't waste time running aground."

"All right," shouted John, with relief in his voice. "I'll follow you close astern." He kept *Wizard*'s sail flapping loose in the wind till *Firefly*, with Titty at the helm, the Mastodon sitting on the middle thwart and Nancy, map in hand, sitting on the bottom boards, sailed past with the water bubbling under her bows. Titty, glancing over her shoulder, saw him haul in his sheet. The sail filled, and *Wizard* came foaming after *Firefly* a couple of boat's lengths astern.

"Sorry we started," called John. "But I got in a bit of stew about not being able to get out. The water's going down like anything."

"Quite all right," said the Mastodon. "You wouldn't have had any time to spare if you'd made any mistakes, and if you did go aground you might be high and dry before you could get off again. Starboard a bit. . . ." He pointed with his right hand. "There's a shallow patch here. . . . That's right. . . . Port again. . . . Now starboard. . . . Straight for those corks. . . ."

John gave Roger the tiller and settled himself in the bottom of the boat with the compass, checking the courses from mark to mark, and now and then making small corrections on his map. Nancy was doing the same. The Mastodon just waved the map away when she wanted to point something out to him. He was a pilot on his own ground, and had no need for maps. Also the tide was pouring out, and the boats were sailing fast and he had no time to spare to look at anything but the marks he knew. First one hand lifted, then the other. "Port. . . . Starboard again. . . . Straight for the withy. . . . Not too close. . . . Now for that bottle. . . ." This was very different from the slow careful way in which John and Nancy had felt their way up the winding channel. The Mastodon never even bothered to test the depth with an oar. He knew. As they came to one mark he had already got his eyes on the next. He never had to look for it.

"Giminy," said Nancy, when, at last, they reached the open water of the Red Sea, and could see the withies marking the road that still lay under water, and the four posts just showing in the middle. "You must know it pretty well."

"I was born here," said the Mastodon.

"What about the Eels?" asked Titty, and it was as if a shadow crossed his face.

"Oh yes. They know it too."

"Really well?"

"Daisy did it in the dark once."

"Great Congers!" said Nancy, looking back at that puzzling maze of water and weed patches.

"What?" said the Mastodon.

"Jolly good work," said Nancy.

"But what was it you said? Something about congers?"

"She's been getting eelier and eelier," said Titty. "Ever since last night."

"What's the matter?" exclaimed Nancy, looking at him.

"Keep her as she's going," said the Mastodon. "Don't turn yet. It looks deep there but it isn't."

"The map's pretty well right," called John. "There was just that one place where I'd got muddled. Did you tick off all the marks?"

"Yes. But it's going to be an awful job getting it clear for the final copy."

"We'll do it in *Speedy* after supper," said John.

"He's got a grand lantern," said Roger.

Again Titty saw that odd unhappy look on the Mastodon's face.

"What do you call that place where we met you?" she asked.

"Witch ..." The Mastodon stopped short. ... "It's got two names, really."

"What's its Eel name?" asked Titty. "Never mind about the other one."

"Witch's Quay," said the Mastodon, and then, "I don't see how it can matter your knowing that."

"Of course it doesn't now we're Eels," said Nancy, and again that queer shadow crossed the Mastodon's face. Titty saw it but Nancy was busy writing "Witch's Quay" on her map.

It was not until they were already in the narrows coming round the island into Goblin Creek that anybody mentioned the Eels again.

"No news of the rest of the tribe?" asked Nancy.

"Well there is, really," said the Mastodon. "They may be here any time. They may be here now. That's why I was so long. I thought they might be coming to the town for stores at high water. But they hadn't got there when I left."

"Three cheers," said Nancy. "An extra three savages'll make a lot of difference. Specially as each of them's got a boat."

The Mastodon did not answer

"I say," said Titty. "There isn't really any bad news, is there?"

The Mastodon looked at her, and even the cheerful Nancy saw that he was worried.

"It's my fault if there is," said the Mastodon.

"Native trouble?" said Nancy consolingly. "We know. It's often practically impossible to keep clear of it."

John hailed from the other boat. "What about landing?" he called. "Will there be enough water for us to bring the boats round to *Speedy*, or shall we have to put the things ashore at the mouth of your creek?"

"We'll get to *Speedy* all right," shouted the Mastodon, "if you're sure you don't mind?"

"Eels for ever!" said Nancy. "Don't be so polite."

Sails were lowered, and John and the Mastodon rowed *Wizard* and *Firefly* up the narrow winding little creek that led behind Mastodon Island to the old barge. The tide had gone down a long way, but there was still water for them to come alongside.

"Too late to get right round," said John, seeing mud ahead further up the creek.

"Never mind," said Nancy. "We've got a fearful lot for the map already."

The Mastodon climbed up his ladder, and they hoisted up his knapsack and the big bag and, more carefully, his parcel and the milk can.

"Coming aboard!" said Nancy, without waiting to be asked. She swung herself up and over the rail to the deck. Roger was beside her in a moment, then John.

"Come on Titty," Nancy called down. "I've made fast. I say, Mastodon, what a lovely place to have."

"You haven't seen what it's like down below," said Roger. "It's as good as a real ship."

"Shall I go down first?" said Nancy, lifting the knapsack. "Or will you go and we'll pass the things down?"

The Mastodon dropped his parcel down the hatch, and then went backwards down the ladder, holding on with one hand, and carrying the milk can in the other. Nancy lowered the knapsack after him. Roger lugged the sack across the deck. John and Nancy lowered it between them.

"Got it?" called Nancy.

"Got it," said the Mastodon.

"All clear?" said Nancy, and came down the steps, followed by the others.

"Pretty good, isn't it?" said Roger.

"Giminy," said Nancy. "I don't wonder you don't bother about a tent."

The Mastodon stood there silent, looking oddly bothered and unhappy.

"Aren't you going to unpack?" said Nancy.

"Only provisions," said the Mastodon glumly.

"Do let's see," said Roger.

"Never mind if you don't want to," said Nancy. "And

don't you worry about native trouble whatever it is. You've only got to give them time. We've got a Great Aunt who makes things fairly awful but we always bounce up again somehow, and we manage to do things right under her very nose. . . ."

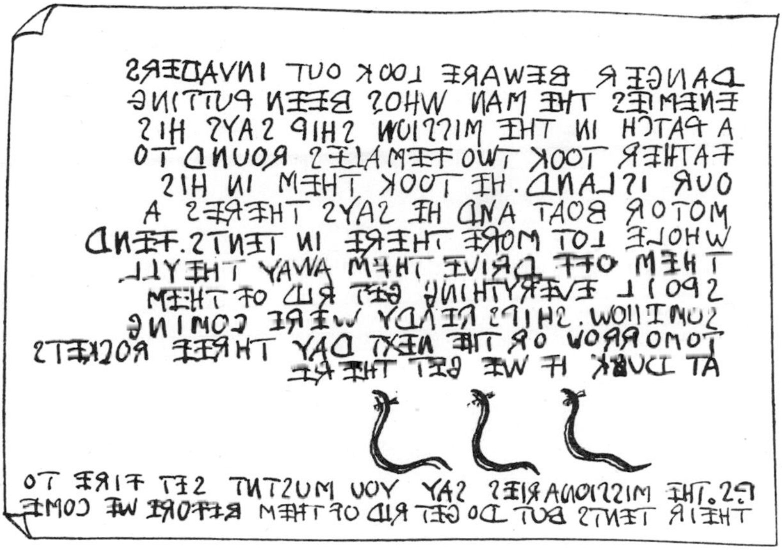

(Note written in mirror-reversed handwriting; decoded it reads:)

DANGER BEWARE LOOK OUT INVADERS ENEMIES THE MAN WHO'S BEEN PUTTING A PATCH IN THE MISSION SHIP SAYS HIS FATHER TOOK TWO FEMALES ROUND TO OUR ISLAND. HE TOOK THEM IN HIS MOTOR BOAT AND SAYS HE THERES A WHOLE LOT MORE THERE IN TENTS. SEND THEM OFF DRIVE THEM AWAY THEY'LL SPOIL EVERYTHING GET RID OF THEM SHILLION. SIRS? LADY SAYS WERE COMING TOMORROW OR THE NEXT DAY THREE ROCKETS AT DUSK IF WE GET THE RATE

P.S. THE MISSIONARIES SAY YOU MUSTNT SET FIRE TO THEIR TENTS BUT DO GET RID OF THEM BEFORE WE COME

"It isn't that sort of trouble," said the Mastodon. "Look here, you'll have to know. I ought never to have let out about the Eels. I got a letter from the rest of them this morning. And it's all about you."

"But we don't know them yet," exclaimed Titty.

The Mastodon was fumbling in his pocket. He pulled out an envelope.

"Hullo," said Nancy. "Are those eels in the corner? We always put a skull and crossbones."

The Mastodon did not answer. He took a folded sheet of paper from the envelope. "You'd better read it," he said.

"But I can't," said Nancy, staring at meaningless letters and words in an unknown language. "I say, have the Eels got a language of their own?"

"It takes a bit of practice," said the Mastodon. "It's easy really when you're accustomed to it. There's a looking glass on that wall. You hold it up to that."

Nancy held the bit of paper up and, in the looking glass, it turned into ordinary English. They could all read it.

"DANGER BEWARE LOOK OUT INVADERS ENEMIES THE MAN WHOS BEEN PUTTING A PATCH IN THE MISSION SHIP SAYS HIS FATHER TOOK TWO FEMALES ROUND TO OUR ISLAND. HE TOOK THEM IN HIS MOTOR BOAT AND HE SAYS THERES A WHOLE LOT MORE THERE IN TENTS. FEND THEM OFF DRIVE THEM AWAY THEYLL SPOIL EVERYTHING GET RID OF THEM SOMEHOW. SHIPS READY WERE COMING TO-MORROW OR THE NEXT DAY THREE ROCKETS AT DUSK IF WE GET THERE."

There was no signature, except a lively drawing of three eels. Underneath the eels there were another two lines of writing:

PS. THE MISSIONARIES SAY YOU MUSTN'T SET FIRE TO THEIR TENTS BUT DO GET RID OF THEM BEFORE WE COME."

They read it and read it again with lengthening faces.

"But who are the two females?" said Nancy. "We haven't seen any grown-ups about at all."

"They mean you and Peggy," said Titty.

Nancy turned suddenly red. She was just going to burst out with something, but stopped herself and swallowed indignantly.

"Two females indeed!" she said at last, under her breath.

The Mastodon was looking at them miserably.

"It's going to be awful," he said. "They'll never understand. If only they'd been here it might have been all right. But now they'll come and I've gone and spoilt everything. Nothing's secret any longer. I've gone and told you everything . . . even the passwords. And I've been helping instead of driving you away. I don't know how it all happened. They'll think it was simply treachery."

"Oh look here," said Nancy. "It doesn't matter. When they come you can just try to turn us out. We'll put up a stockade and defend ourselves. It'll be as good a war as anybody could want. If there aren't enough of you, some of us'll help on your side."

"It's not that," said the Mastodon. "Daisy won't want anybody here at all. I ought to have kept right away. I would have done if I hadn't gone and thought you were them, and then coming to your camp, and letting out one thing after another, and what can I tell her about the blood brotherhood business?"

"Great Congers and Lampreys," burst out Nancy. "We can't deblood ourselves now."

"I can't either," said the Mastodon. "That's just it."

John had listened in silence.

"Look here," he said at last. "If you think they wouldn't like it, you'd better not let us come here for supper."

The Mastodon looked at him gratefully.

"If I could only have explained to them," he said.

"Let's put it off," said John. "We'd better go and tell Susan now."

"I'm most awfully sorry," said the Mastodon. "I'd got everything ready. Mother gave me a ham when I told her how many you were. And she's put in an extra lot of stores."

"I thought that sack was pretty heavy," said Roger.

"It'll keep," said Nancy.

"It's all my fault," said the Mastodon. "I don't know how it all happened. Everything just slipped out. . . . Of course, Daisy doesn't know you were marooned," he added hopefully.

"Cheer up, Mastodon," said Nancy. "We won't come.

But I don't see why you shouldn't come to supper with us instead. Savage spy in paleface camp. Nobody could object to that."

"Better not," said the Mastodon. "Look here. You take the ham. . . ."

"Oh we can't do that," said Titty.

Silently they climbed up through the hatch and came on deck. Silently they went down into their boats.

"You'll explain to the others," said the Mastodon, looking down from *Speedy's* deck.

"Come on, Mastodon," said John suddenly. "You come to supper with us, even if it's the last time."

"I'd really better not," said the Mastodon. "I say, you know I am most awfully sorry."

"It's not your fault at all," said Titty.

"Anyway, thank you very much for all you've done," said John. "Showing us channels and things."

"I oughtn't to have done it," said the Mastodon.

They rowed silently away. The Mastodon stood for a moment watching them from the deck of the old barge. The bright colours of her name, *Speedy*, in the painted scroll-work on her rail, seemed almost to mock them. That gaudy bit of painting looked so much more cheerful than they felt.

Nancy stopped rowing to give the Mastodon a parting wave. The others waved too. The Mastodon waved back and then turned sharply round and went below. For a few minutes they could see the old barge, a wreck, with nothing to show that it was the lair of a savage. Then, as the creek twisted, it was hidden by the high banks.

*

Not a word was said by anybody as they rowed down Goblin Creek to the landing place.

Bridget came running to meet them as they walked up the

path across the saltings. "Hullo!" she said. "We're all ready."

Peggy was close behind her. "Is it time to start?" she said. "We've made a huge lot of blackberry and banana mash. My wrist's nearly bust with mashing them. And Susan's got a saucepan full of mushrooms stewing now. We went to the kraal and she got a jug of cream."

"I'm going to carry my own mug," said Bridget.

"We're not going," said Roger.

"I wish we could fry every eel in the world except him," said Nancy. "It isn't only your wrist that's bust."

"Not going?" said Bridget.

"What on earth's happened?" said Susan the moment she saw them.

"It's the rest of the Eels," said John. "They're coming, and they've got to know about our being here, and they've sent him a letter telling him to clear us out. And he doesn't know what to do because he's made friends with us first."

"He wishes he hadn't blooded," said Titty.

"He showed us the letter," said Nancy. "Jolly clever. All the letters inside out and the words the wrong way round. They knew about me and Peggy coming in the motor boat...."

"Two females," said Roger with a grin.

Nancy scowled at him. "They know about the camp. They told him to chivvy us out. They told him to do anything short of setting our tents on fire. So he couldn't very well have us to supper. Those beasts may be here already. And he thinks they'll think he's a traitor. He'll never come with us again."

"They're going to send up rockets at dusk," said Roger.

"Why didn't you bring him along here?" said Susan.

"Wouldn't come," said John.

"Oh, I say!" said Bridget. "Does it mean they won't let me be a human sacrifice? I think they're horrid. And I bled more than anybody."

"He blooded with them before he did it with us," said Titty.

"They want the whole place to themselves," said Nancy.

"Cheer up, Bridgie," said John. "We'll sacrifice you ourselves."

"But I've never even seen *Speedy*," said Bridget.

"We've done a huge lot of blackberry mash," said Susan, "and the mushrooms are just ready to take across."

"They won't be altogether wasted," said Roger. "We can eat them here."

"We'd better have supper right away," said Susan. "I'll open a tin of pemmican."

"He had a ham," said Roger. "And simply tons of grub."

"Well we've got tons too," said Susan. "Bother those Eels."

What with pemmican and stewed mushrooms, a mash of blackberries and bananas, and a bottle of grog to each explorer, it was too good a supper to allow much talking. It was so good a supper that even Nancy, though still fierce at being called a female and having her most private plans upset, cheered up a little.

"Well," she said, "if it's going to be war. . . ."

"But it isn't," said John. "They won't have anything to do with us. And the worst of it is, we shan't have a guide any longer. But we didn't count on having one. And anyway we've done a tremendous lot before we've lost him. Come on Nancy, let's get at those maps. I'll just fetch the parallel rulers."

No inking was done that evening. There was the survey of Mastodon Island to work out, in which everybody had taken a hand, besides the mapping of that corkscrew channel going in to Witch's Quay. The explored part of the map had spread that day both east and south, and they were hard at it with pencils and rulers until Bridget had long gone to bed and it was too dark to see. Dusk fell, and dark.

"Where's Roger?" said Susan suddenly. "And Titty?"

There was the flicker of a torch along the dyke. Roger and Titty came back into the camp.

"Well, they aren't here yet," said Titty.

"How do you know?" said Nancy.

"No rockets," said Roger. "We've been watching for them."

CHAPTER XVI

ENEMY'S COUNTRY

"NOT a sign of the Mastodon," said Roger.

"He won't be coming here anyway," said Titty.

They had gone down to the landing place after breakfast and, barefooted, black to the knees with mud, were working *Wizard* down towards the water.

Peggy came down to join them, left her boots on the saltings, and began pulling at *Firefly*.

"You push at *Wizard's* nose," said Roger, "and then we'll come and help to get *Firefly* out. The mud's most beastly sticky."

"Have they decided yet?" asked Titty.

"Still at it," said Peggy. "But one thing's settled. We're all coming. John says the Mastodon won't do anything to our tents. He knows we're marooned and can't get away. Besides, he's a blood brother even if he wishes he wasn't. But once the others come we'll have to leave a guard all the time. To-day'll be the last chance of exploring with the whole expedition. Susan's packing the grub now."

"Bother the beastly Eels," said Titty. "Roger, don't splash!"

"Eels," said Roger. "I felt one wriggling round my toes."

"Well, you needn't send the mud flying all over the place."

"Where are we going?" said Roger.

"Don't know," said Peggy. "Nancy wanted an attack on the Mastodon. She said that if we captured him and held him prisoner we could tell the other Eels that if they weren't decent we'd never let him go."

"Good idea," said Roger. "We could take his worms too, and do some fishing. I say, we could make him fish and be a prisoner at the same time . . . a sort of tame cormorant."

"John and Susan said 'No'. Susan said we can't have him a prisoner in our camp because there isn't a spare tent. Nancy said it was quite warm at nights and we could tether him like a goat. John said it wasn't as if he was an enemy. It's not the Mastodon's fault that the other Eels want the whole place to themselves. And somebody'd have to guard him all day, and he's too strong for anybody except John, and that would mean that the map would never get done. So we're just going exploring without him."

"He was fine as a native guide," said Titty.

"But if he doesn't want to be one any longer," said Peggy.

They worked first *Wizard* and then *Firefly* down to the edge of the water. They had just got *Firefly* afloat when they saw the rest of the expedition coming down the path across the saltings, everybody carrying something, Bridget carrying Sinbad, John with the compass and a knapsack, Nancy with a compass and a bundle of surveying poles, and Susan with a kettle of drinking water.

"Where are we going?" asked Roger.

Nancy answered. "We're going to explore Flint Island while we can. We shan't be able to do it when they're camped there so if we don't get it done now there'll be all that lump left unexplored."

"I say," said Roger. "What if they come while we're on their island?"

"We'll see their ship in plenty of time to clear off," said John.

"It'll be six to three anyway," said Nancy.

"Four with the Mastodon," said Titty.

"They'll be six too," said Roger.

"They won't make their missionaries fight," said Nancy. "And who cares if they do?"

"You always leave me out," said Bridget.

"We'll be seven," said Nancy.

"And Sinbad."

"Jibbooms and bobstays. Eight if you like," said Nancy. "Who's coming in our boat? Hop in Bridget. You and Sinbad'll fit in fine before the mast. We've got room for one more, or a lot of baggage. All right, Roger."

Titty looked at Nancy but said nothing. She knew very well why Nancy had stopped swearing like an Eel.

"We don't want a row if we can help it," said John.

"I suppose it's no good even trying to collect the Mastodon?" said Peggy.

"Bob-tailed galoot," said Nancy. "Can't you understand he's wishing he'd never met us?"

The two little boats were loaded up. The explorers, sitting on the gunwales, washed their feet or their boots over the side so as not to fill the boats with mud. Sails were hoisted and a good south-west wind soon blew them out of the creek into the Secret Water. Everybody just glanced up the creek as they left it, but there was still no sign of the Mastodon. They had only known the Mastodon a couple of days, but, after all, they had made a blood brother of him and it was as if they had lost an old friend, besides having pricked their fingers for nothing.

But out in the sunshine on the Secret Water, with the sails pulling, and the cheerful lap-lap under the forefoot, nobody could feel grim for long. Just to look at the other boat, foaming along, made each crew feel how fast they were going.

"Ahoy, Admiral," said Captain Nancy. "Race you to the point."

"All right. Whoever's first to the buoy with a cross on it. We've got to go round that to get into the other channel."

"Shift your weight up a bit, Peggy," said Nancy. "Giminy, they're gaining on us already. Is anything wrong with our sail?"

"I could get the boom down a little by the mast," said Roger.

"Go ahead. That's better. Cock the peak up all you can."

First one and then the other boat shot ahead as their crews tried different dodges to get the most out of their sails. The shores of their island, already mapped, slipped by. Before them the Secret Water opened to the sea. Far away, brown sailed barges were coming out of harbour with the last of the ebb to get the whole six hours of the flood tide to help them on their way to London.

"Bother the sun," said John. "I say Susan. Is that the cross-roads buoy?"

"Sun's in my eyes too," said Susan, "but I think it is. Yes, there's the cross on the top of it."

"Roger's spotted it," said Titty, looking across at *Firefly*. "They're going to win."

"They're too near the shore," said John. "Nancy doesn't know about tides. More tide here. We're going faster than they are because we're out in the stream."

But, out in the middle, while the shore was still hiding it from *Firefly's* crew, the explorers in *Wizard* were the first to catch a glimpse of the golden hummocks of Flint Island. It lost them the race.

"Gosh," said John. "Look at those masts. Is that *Lapwing* there or not?"

"It's only the dhows," said Titty. "Three of them. They've been there all the time."

"John," cried Susan. "Look out for your steering."

Wizard had swung right round into the wind. Her sail was flapping, and though John got her going again in a moment and back on her course, he passed the buoy a boat's length astern of *Firefly*.

"We won," cried Bridget.

"Nothing much in it," said Nancy. "It's as good as old *Amazon* and *Swallow*. Where now?"

"Starboard," called John. "Look here. You follow us. We've been through here with the Mastodon and I've got it on my map. Leave those black buoys to port, and keep clear of the withies on this side."

The channel suddenly narrowed. There was a sandy bank between it and the open sea. Ahead it stretched inland, a shining lane of water.

"What is there up there?" called Nancy.

"Town," said John.

"Native Settlement," said Titty. "And Cape Horn and Magellan Straits where we nearly got stuck with the Mastodon."

"Bother the Mastodon," said Nancy. "Where are we going to land?"

"There's a sort of bay just before we come to those yachts," said John. "That looks good enough. Up with the centreboard, Mister Mate. We don't want to bust it. Good. Stand by to lower sail. . . . Now. . . ."

There was a gentle scrunch and then another, as the two ships of the explorers touched the steep, sandy beach.

*

For some minutes after landing, the explorers kept together. They felt a little as if they had broken into someone else's house. The *Lapwing* was not in the anchorage; there were no tents among those sandy hillocks; the island was deserted; but they felt as if they might at any moment come face to face with the rightful owners.

Susan was the first to find the savage camping place. Close

behind the steep rise of the beach there was a hollow in the sand. A small circle of charred stones was in the middle of it. "Here's where they camp," said Susan. "Lucky beasts. They've found stones to make a proper fireplace. And look at those logs. Much better than we get."

"Open sea on the other side of the island," said John. "They'll get real driftwood."

"Let's bag some," said Roger.

"No," said Susan.

"We'll get lots of our own," said Titty.

They looked round the hollow and found the marks of tent pegs.

"Pretty good place, they've got," said Nancy.

"Wouldn't it be awful if they came while we were here," said Titty.

"They won't," said John. "We'd see them coming across from Harwich long before they were anywhere near. And anyway they won't come till high water. Come on, Nancy. Let's start. Skip along to the point, Roger, and plant a pole. And we'll have one at the other side of the bay, and then one in the middle."

"Have you been right up the channel?" asked Nancy, standing on the edge of the hollow and looking at the ribbon of water winding inland. "Ow! I say, Bridget, look out for this sea-holly. It's as prickly as the land kind. You'll be losing some more blood for nothing."

"Not as far as the town," said John. "We turned off round Cape Horn."

Nancy was looking at her copy of the map. "Hadn't we better get that done too while we can? And what's this gap between Magellan Straits and Cape Horn?"

"We've got to keep a look out to sea," said John. "So as to spot them coming."

"Peggy and I'll do it on our own," said Nancy. "Or we'll

toss you for it. One lot works up to the town and the other does the island and keeps a look out."

John hesitated. "Go ahead," he said. "Work up with the tide. It's just turning. It won't be high water till about half past four. That's when they'll be coming if they do come. But we'll have to clear out as soon as we see them."

"That's all right," said Nancy. "If we see your boat's gone we'll know what's happened and nip back home through the Red Sea."

"Look here," said Susan. "If you do get to the town, could you telephone to Miss Powell's to say we're all right? Mother'll have got that Report this morning, but I promised we'd ring up if we got a chance. Woolverstone 30."

Nancy scribbled the number on the back of her map. "Right," she said. "Lots of things have happened since we sent the Report. I'll tell her. Enemies on every side. Hostile savages threatening massacre. All well and love from everybody."

"All well's what matters," said Susan.

"Don't go off without your share of grub," said Roger.

"Jolly good idea of Nancy's," said John, as the *Firefly* sailed away. "Once the savages are here it'll never be safe to go out of sight of the camp. We've got to get every scrap done that we can do before they come."

"And then just write 'Cannibal Tribes' over all the rest," said Titty.

*

Steady work with compass and surveying poles went on through the rest of the morning. They mapped the channel which, dry at low water, made Flint Island really an island when the tide came up and not just the nose of a promontory as it was shown on Daddy's rough sketch. Before the tide came up and filled it, they made a hurried expedition along the sands beyond it, where Bridget found shells and Sinbad played with them, and they picked up good bits of driftwood for a midday fire on which to boil their kettle. There was a moment's horror at the thought that the two explorers in *Firefly* would get none of the tea, but it was remembered that if they did indeed get to the town, they would be able to have something else instead. "Lapping up grog like anything," said Roger. "I bet Nancy thought of that before she started."

Susan made a new fireplace of her own, down on the seashore, well away from the fireplace of the Eels. And all the time, no matter what they were doing, surveying, exploring, marking things down on the map, or eating their well earned meal on the shingle beach, their eyes kept turning seawards watching for the *Lapwing* with her fleet of little boats and the savages who had sent orders that they were to be driven away at all costs. After dinner, when the tide had cut off Flint Island from the main and was pouring in through the channel, they saw that they were not the only watchers.

Out near the mouth of the Secret Water the Mastodon was fishing from his anchored boat. He too was watching for a cutter, with three dinghies astern, coming in from the sea, ready to meet them when they arrived and, no doubt, to confess that instead of driving the explorers away, he had made friends with them, swopped blood with them, and given away to them the secrets of the Eels.

"Gosh!" said Roger. "I wish he'd come in for me. I bet he's got a spare line in the boat. I wonder if he's seen us."

"Of course he has," said Titty.

"Shall I wave?"

"No good," said John. "Much better leave him alone."

An hour before high water, mapping came to an end. They had done as much as they could do and, for the time, turned into coastguards, looking out to sea for an enemy vessel, and keeping an eye also on that other watcher who still

lay out there alone in his boat. The tide turned. The ebb
began, and they saw that the Mastodon was getting up his
anchor. Nothing was moving out at sea, except the big mainsail and tiny mizen of a barge so far away that they could not
see her hull. The Mastodon stowed his anchor, took to his
oars, and presently disappeared.

"Going home," said John. "Well, they won't be coming
in now."

"He'll be alone again to-night," said Titty. "Isn't it
beastly not being able to talk to him?"

"It isn't our fault," said John.

The Mastodon was hardly out of sight before, looking the
other way, up the channel leading to the town, they saw
Firefly coming back. The wind had dropped and, though the
sail was set, somebody was using oars, and rowing as hard as
she could.

"Ahoy!" shouted Nancy as soon as she was near enough.
"Ahoy! Buck up. Get afloat!"

"It's all right," shouted Roger. "They aren't even in
sight."

"They won't be coming now. It's after high water," called
John. "There's no hurry."

Peggy, steering, brought *Firefly* in to the beach.

"Barbecued billygoats!" cried Nancy, jumping out. "No
hurry! Get afloat as quick as you can. They're not coming
from the sea. They're coming the other way. We've seen
them. They're anchored up there close to the town. They'll
be here any minute. They must have got in at high water
yesterday. If the Mastodon had waited a bit longer instead of
meeting us at that quay he'd have seen them."

In two minutes the explorers were all afloat, and Flint
Island deserted once more, was ready for its savage owners.

"Did you get right up to the town?" asked John, as the
boats moved out into the creek.

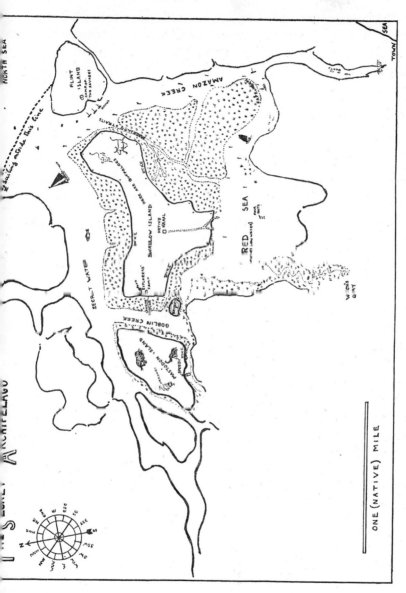

THE MAP: WITH FLINT ISLAND AND AMAZON CREEK

ONE (NATIVE) MILE

"Of course we did," said Nancy. "We worked slowly up with the tide like you said. We've mapped the whole channel. ... Amazon Creek it's going to be. ... You've got Swallow Island. ... And we had a good look at the gap between Magellan Straits and Cape Horn. It runs straight in towards the dyke and joins the Straits."

"The Mastodon said it did," said John.

"We landed twice," said Peggy. "Two good places. We had our grub on a sort of landing stage, and we got lemonade from a shop."

"I told you they would," said Roger.

"Did you telephone?" asked Susan.

"Rather," said Nancy. "Your mother was there. She'd just got back from London, but she's going up there again to-morrow. She said the Report was a beauty, and she sent her love, and she said you were to be sure not to starve Roger."

"Oh look here," said Roger. "You made that up."

"Are you sure it was the Eels?" said John, looking back up the channel towards the town.

"Couldn't be anybody else. We passed a yellow cutter at anchor on our way in, and then we saw three dinghies close to the town and when we were coming back just now the dinghies were by the cutter, and we read *Lapwing* on her stern, and we heard one of the missionaries tell them to hurry up and help make sail."

"We shan't be able to do much exploring once they've come," said John. "There won't be a hope of getting the map properly finished."

"The Mastodon did say I could be a human sacrifice," said Bridget.

"They don't want one," said Titty.

With the ebb running out and the wind light and ahead, sailing was useless, and the two boats rowed side by side up

THE SECOND ROCKET

Secret Water and into Goblin Creek. For all that they could see, nothing had changed. Yet everything had.

"Better fill our water-cans to-night," said Susan. "We don't want to run into them at the kraal."

John and Susan, Nancy and Peggy, carried the two water-cans to the farm, each water-can slung from an oar. Even at the kraal they were not allowed to forget that things had changed. "Seen anything of them savages yet?" laughed the man as he filled their cans for them. "Only one? The others'll be all over the place to-morrow. I met their dad when I was across in the town. He bring the yacht in yesterday, and they'll be camping down at the mouth to-night."

Back at the camp they had a rather silent supper.

*

Dusk fell.

The explorers sat round the dying embers of their fire. Bridget was in bed. Sinbad was asleep. Nancy was holding a torch to light the map on which John was tracing the outlines of Flint Island and the channel to the town. Titty was sharpening a pencil. Peggy was yawning. Susan was polishing a grease spot off a plate. Roger had slipped away to his look out point at the corner of the dyke.

Suddenly there was a shout, a distant bang, and the sound of running feet. Roger charged into the camp.

"Didn't you see it?" he shouted.

No one had seen anything. Roger was pointing away into the darkness over the island.

A thin line of white light streaked up into the evening sky. There was another of those distant bangs, and high in the darkness half a dozen stars shot in different directions. A rocket.

"That's the second."

They were all on their feet now.

"There goes the third," said Titty, as yet again a spark

flew up into the sky, seemed to hang there for a moment and, before falling, burst into shooting stars.

"I wonder if he's seen them," said Titty.

They turned and looked across the dim creek at the dark line of Mastodon Island on the other side.

"He won't have seen them if he wasn't watching," said Roger.

But a minute later they saw the glimmer of a light. There was a bang at the other side of the creek. A rocket hissed up into the sky and burst. Three red stars curved from it, fell slowly and died as they fell. All was dark once more.

"Fireworks?" said Bridget, who had crawled to the mouth of her tent on hearing the stir outside.

"You ought to be asleep," said Susan.

"They've come," said Nancy.

"I wonder if I ought to stay awake," said John.

"Shouldn't think they'd try to do anything till to-morrow," said Nancy. "But I bet it's war now whether you like it or not."

That night not one of the explorers slept without waking. First one, then another, stirred in sleep, woke, and listened, now to the stir of wind in the reeds, now to an owl hawking over the marshes, now to the noise of a train on the mainland far away, now to the distant hooting of a ship coming into harbour. First one of the explorers and then another stirred, listened wide-eyed, and slept again.

CHAPTER XVII

A STATE OF WAR

THE explorers woke into a new, unfriendly world. Everything about the camp was the same as usual. The boats (John and Nancy ran down to see before breakfast) were just as they had left them. The same curlew was whistling over the marshes. The same gulls and oxbirds were busy on the edges of the mud. The same sun had risen in the east and the same shadow was darkening the breakfast peg of the meal-dial. But the whole feeling of the place was different. Last night they had seen the rockets that announced the coming of the savages. And the savages, even before they had arrived, had made the Mastodon ashamed of his blood brotherhood, and sorry for his friendliness.

John and Nancy, after looking at the boats, separated and went north and south along the dyke, eyes and ears alert.

"Nothing moving on Secret Water," said John as they met again at the camp, to find the others half way through breakfast and Sinbad licking an already empty saucer.

"Red Sea's nearly dry," said Nancy. "And tide still going out. They won't come that way for a bit."

"What about the Mastodon?" asked Titty.

"No signs of him."

"Do you think they'll come at all?" said Susan. "Won't they just pretend we aren't here?"

"The letter the Mastodon got said 'Drive them out. Fend them off'," said Titty. "And then it said he wasn't to set fire to our tents. I should think they'll probably try something."

"Of course they will," said Nancy. "And we'll jolly well smash them if they do."

"Let's burn their beastly totem," said Roger.

"Jibbooms and bobstays! Why on earth?" said Nancy. "We've bought it with our blood."

"I bled more than anybody," said Bridget.

"Won't it make them mad to see it there?" said Titty.

"Who cares?" said Nancy. "It's ours now. We're Eels just as much as they are."

"Somebody'll have to stay in the camp," said John.

"I've got to anyway," said Titty, "to catch up with the map. There's simply masses to ink in."

"There won't be much more," said John sadly. "We'll have to keep within signalling distance all the time. We'll have to go back with half the map unexplored."

"You'll want a sentinel," said Nancy. "You know what it's like when you're drawing. They could come and take the tents away and you wouldn't notice."

"I'll be sentinel," said Roger.

"You'll be wanted for surveying," said John. "Specially if Titty's staying in camp."

"Can't I be sentinel?" said Bridget.

Nancy laughed.

"I'm old enough," said Bridget.

"I don't see why not," said John. "We'll be within sight all the time. Got to be. All they've got to guard against is a surprise. If they keep watch on the dyke they'll see the enemy coming even if we don't. If they see anybody they lower the flags. We'll keep on looking, and the moment the flags go down we'll come racing back. It isn't as if there was a real horde of savages so that they could attack from all sides."

*

An hour later the exploring party with the two boats sailed out from the creek. Bridget, Sinbad and Titty were at the landing place to see them go.

"Down the flags at the least sign of danger," said John as he pushed off. "And get as much of the map done as you can."

"Aye, aye, Sir," said Titty.

"Aye, aye, Sir," said Bridget, and then a moment later, "Couldn't you hear him? Sinbad said it too."

"Good for him," said John.

*

"I suppose they will be all right," said Susan, as the *Wizard*, close behind the *Firefly*, slipped across the Secret Water.

John looked back. The tents were already hard to see, but the flags were fluttering in the sunlight, and on the skyline a small bright blue figure was walking solemnly along the top of the dyke.

"Bridget on sentry go," said Roger.

"They'll be all right," said John.

*

"What am I to steer for?" asked Peggy.

Nancy, who was sitting scowling in the bottom of *Firefly*, looked over her shoulder.

"Straight for the creek on the other side," she said.

For a time neither of them spoke.

"If it was only us," said Nancy at last. "We'd go straight for their camp, bang an arrow into the middle of their fire and see what happened."

"We haven't got a bow with us," said Peggy.

"It's not that, you blessed gummock. It's John and Susan. Titty too. They don't want a war if they can help it. They want to do their map. And the savages are just as bad. If only they'd been decent we'd have had six boats to work with,

and four native guides, and we'd have got the whole thing done
and had time for a bit of war as well. And to-morrow it'll be
our turn to stick in the camp all day with nothing to do and
nothing happening. It was all waste jabbing our fingers."

"I wish we hadn't," said Peggy.

"Too late now," said Nancy. "If I could I'd suck the Eel
blood out and spit it away."

*

The other boat was closing in on them as they came to
the wide mouth of the inlet for which they were making.
There was mud on either side, and green topped muddy banks.
The water, narrowing between the mud flats, stretched far
ahead.

"We're going to have a job to get ashore," said John.
The Mastodon said there's a landing on each side. But it
may be only when the tide's up. Gosh, I wish he was here."

"There he is," said Nancy.

Far away on the other side of Secret Water a little rowing
boat was coming out of Goblin Creek. A spot of bright
blue on the dyke showed where the sentinel, Bridget, was
keeping an eye on it.

"He isn't coming this way," said Roger.

"He's going to see his horrid little friends," said Nancy.

The Mastodon, shaving close round the mud spit at the
mouth of Goblin Creek, turned east, and they watched him
for a long time steadily rowing away.

"Well, it's no good watching him," said Nancy. "Let's get
ashore."

*

With the Mastodon rowing away down the Secret Water
to meet the Eels, it did not seem likely that anything much was
going to happen. He, no doubt, was going to get into trouble
for having been too friendly with the explorers, but they

could do nothing about it. They settled down to their work. Nancy and Peggy, black to the knees, struggled ashore on the eastern side of the inlet. John, Susan and Roger landed fairly dry at the remains of an old hard on the western side, like the one by their camp in Goblin Creek. Poles were set up as landmarks, and both parties did the best they could, taking bearings from one pole to another and to the promontories, the kraal and the other landmarks on the islands they had already surveyed. Every now and then they kept looking for the sails of the savages or glancing across the Secret Water to see the flags still fluttering above the camp, a sign that all was well.

But, though the flags flew above the camp, the savages, without even showing themselves, had made the work of the explorers very difficult. They could not do things properly when they had to stay within sight of those flags and within reach of their boats, ready to row across if Titty and Bridget signalled a warning. They did their best with the coastline but were not able to settle the most important question of all. Were they on islands or just on odd-shaped promontories? They could not go far enough away from their landing places to make sure. Neither of the exploring parties were pleased with their work. At last Roger complained that the sun could not get any higher, that the shadows of the surveying poles were growing longer again, and that if they were in the camp the meal-dial would be showing that it was after dinner-time. Nancy and Peggy came rowing across to join the others, scraped the mud off their legs with handfuls of grass and agreed with Roger that it was time for grub.

"What's your bit like?" asked John. "Is it an island or not?"

"I don't know," said Nancy. "There's a sort of creek that looks as if it might join this but we couldn't go far enough to see. Dry at low water. We wallowed across it. Mud to our ears. One little bit's an island. We've put it on our map.

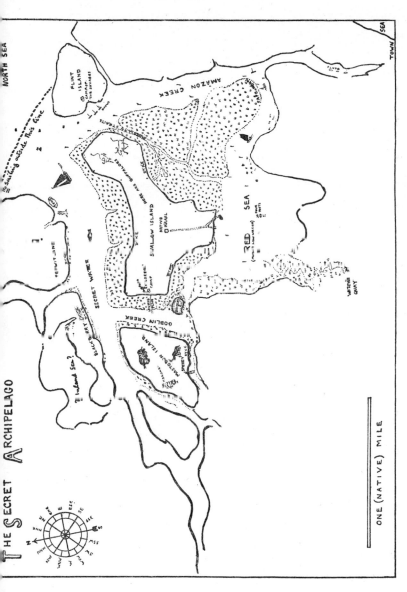

THE MAP: WITH BLACKBERRY COAST AND PEEWITLAND

ONE (NATIVE) MILE

What are those birds that keep on fluttering and diving . . .
white with black hoods. . . ?'

"Terns," said Roger.

"Tern Island. . . . They're diving all round it." She
scribbled in the name and gave John her map, on which was
a spider's web of lines and bearings. "Poor old Titty," she
said, looking at the work of John, Susan and Roger.

"It won't look as bad as this when we've worked it out
with the rulers, and copied it ready for her to ink it in."

"What about Peewitland for the rest of it?" said Peggy.

"Ours is the Blackberry Coast," said Roger. "Susan's
found a better lot here than anywhere."

"We won't put 'Coast' in till we're sure it isn't an island,"
said John. "Just look over there. All that mud and water.
Nearly as big as the Red Sea. Either it's a lake or it comes into
this creek. And if there's a way through further up Secret
Water, a North West Passage, that'll be a sort of Arctic Sea
and Blackberry's an island not a coast. We found two ditches,
but they don't go right across. But there may jolly easily be a
passage further along."

Half an hour later, when they had drunk their pop and
eaten their sandwiches and a few of the fruits of the Blackberry Coast, John and Nancy stood looking across Secret
Water to the distant fluttering specks above the camp.

"They're all right over there," said John, "and the tide's
rising fast. Let's just go a little way up and see what it looks
like."

"I'm coming too," said Roger, who was heartily sick of
surveying poles.

"Peggy and Susan'll keep a look out," said Nancy. "Come
on."

They paddled down the mud of the old hard and got afloat
in *Firefly*, but they had not gone very far before they heard
behind them a bad imitation of an owl.

"Owl at midday," said John, grinning, remembering something that had happened long ago. "Something's up."

There was Peggy on the dyke near the mouth of the creek, earnestly signalling.

"What's she saying?" asked Roger. "Gosh, she does go at a lick." Peggy's arms had hardly shown one letter before they were in a new position showing another. "M . . . A . . . S . . . T . . ."

"Mastodon," said Nancy, without waiting for any more. She pulled back as hard as she could.

"He's coming back," called Peggy.

"Alone?"

"Yes."

They hurried ashore and joined Susan, who was lying on a dry patch of ground, watching the little rowing boat coming fast up Secret Water with the tide. The Mastodon stopped rowing just before turning into Goblin Creek. Suddenly he turned his boat and rowed across towards the watchers.

"Good," said Nancy. "He's talked them over. He's coming to say it's all right."

But, as the Mastodon stopped rowing and turned round within shouting distance of the Blackberry Coast, they could see that he was not looking very cheerful.

"Shall I give the password?" said Roger. "Karabadang and the rest of it."

"Shut up," said John. "Wait till he does it himself."

But the Mastodon gave no password. He might have been just anybody inquiring from a passer-by. "You haven't seen three boats?" he called.

"Only one," said Roger.

"With a sail?"

"No. Yours."

"Oh," said the Mastodon, and then, "You didn't see them earlier, before I started?"

"We haven't seen anybody but you," called Nancy.

"We saw the rockets last night," said Roger.

"Shut up," said John again.

The Mastodon waited a moment, with his oars out of the water, looking far away to the west along the Secret Water, and then away to the east once more.

"They must come this way," he said. "Not enough water yet to come through behind the island."

"Lost them?" called Nancy. "Eels *are* a bit slippery."

Both John and Susan looked at her rather doubtfully. They knew very well that the Mastodon was wishing he had never told them anything about the Eels."

"My fault," said the Mastodon. "I ought to have gone first thing in the morning, but I thought they'd be coming to *Speedy*."

"Poor beast, he'd awfully like to be friendly," said Nancy under her breath. "We haven't seen them. Not to-day," she called aloud. "And we've been on the look out."

"May as well let him know we've got our eyes open," she added quietly.

"I've been to their camp and there's nobody in it," called the Mastodon, "*Lapwing*'s there. And they've put up their tents. Perhaps I ought to have asked the missionaries. I'd better go back. They must have been sent to the town for something."

He spun his boat round and pulled away, back once more towards the mouth of the Secret Water.

The explorers watched him out of sight. Suddenly Peggy said, "Supposing he's wrong and they didn't go to the town. . . ."

"What else could they have done?" said Nancy. "It's been low water. They couldn't have come round through the Red Sea."

"Not the whole way," said Peggy. "But suppose they got

across and landed early, before the tide went down too far."

"Barbecued billygoats," said Nancy, who seemed to have shaken off the effects of the Eel's blood. "They may be on the island now."

"But they aren't," said John. "They couldn't have kept hidden all this time. Titty and Bridget would have seen them and signalled."

"You've got to remember they're Eels," said Nancy.

"They aren't invisible," said John. "Look here, the water's coming up well. We ought to be able to take a boat and find out if there is a way round behind all this. I'm pretty sure there must be. It ought to be all right if we go full tilt. They'll be a long time if they've gone to the town."

But Peggy's idea was bothering Susan now.

"It's no good taking the boats away," she said "What if Titty signals and we want to get back? If you go up the creek you may be right out of reach. And look here, John, we ought to be on our own island long before high tide."

"She's right," said Nancy. "No good our being here keeping a look out on the Secret Water when they can bring their whole fleet sailing up the Red Sea."

"They can't yet," said John.

"They'll be able to soon," said Nancy.

"I'm going back," said Susan.

*

It was almost a calm, and it was not worth while to hoist the sails. They rowed grimly home. To-day's surveying had amounted to next to nothing compared with the big areas explored on other days.

For a moment the flags at the camp were hidden from them as they rowed across, but they saw them again as they came to the mouth of Goblin Creek.

"That's all right," said Susan. "Just for one awful moment I thought they'd gone."

"John," said Nancy. "I've been thinking. I was wrong about that totem. What about yanking it up and taking it across and leaving it on *Speedy*. If they don't want us, we don't want them or their beastly totems. Let them find it there."

"Perhaps we'd better," said John. "He probably wishes he'd never given it to us."

"Of course we could burn it," said Nancy.

"Better just take it back," said John.

"I'd like to fry the lot of them," said Nancy.

"And eat them," said Roger.

*

No one met them at the landing place.

"Rotten sentries," said Roger.

"Don't pull our boat up, Peggy," said Nancy. "We'll want it in a minute to take that totem back."

She led the way up the track to the camp.

"Hullo," she said. "Titty's thought of it too. She's taken the totem down."

Titty, hard at work, did not hear them coming.

"What have you done with the totem?" asked Nancy.

Titty, pen in hand, started violently.

"Gosh!" she said. "Lucky I didn't blot. I've nearly done."

"Where's the totem?" said Nancy. "We're going to hurl it back."

Titty stretched her cramped arms and rolled over.

"Isn't it there?" she said.

"No it isn't," said Nancy. "There's the hole where it was and there's my watch."

"Where's Bridget?" said Susan.

"Sentry-go on the dyke," said Titty.

"Oh look here, Titty, you must have pulled it up. It was here when we left."

"But I haven't touched it," said Titty. "Perhaps Bridget . . .'

"Bridget!" called Susan. "Run along the dyke and fetch her, Roger."

"She was here not long ago," said Titty. "Then she went off with Sinbad."

"She'd never have taken the totem," said Nancy.

"Well, I haven't touched it," said Titty.

"Gosh," said John, "You've made a lovely job of the map."

"Bridget! Ship's Brat! Bridget!" They heard Roger calling along the dyke.

Susan, packing away the knapsack and the empty bottles, heard a sudden doubt in his voice. She started up. Roger was coming back along the dyke, calling now and again, and looking far away over the meadows.

"I can't see her anywhere," he said, as he came back into the camp. She's been at the corner by the little island, I found her hair ribbon on the path.

"Blow your whistle for her," said John.

Susan blew the mate's whistle that was usually enough to bring Bridget on the run. There was no answer.

"All shout together," said Roger.

"Bridget! BRIDGET!" Six explorers shouted at the top of their voices, standing on the dyke by the tents and looking in all directions over the island.

There was no answer.

"She can't have gone far," said Titty. "She had Sinbad with her. She was just walking up and down on the dyke."

"She's gone down to the water and tumbled in," said Susan.

"Oh no . . . no . . . no . . ." said Titty.

"It's nothing like that," said Nancy, and they turned

to see a surprising glitter in her eyes, "Can't you see? The totem's gone too."

They stared at her.

"She's a prisoner. She's been taken by the Eels. They've grabbed Bridget and they've grabbed the totem too. Come on Roger. Where did you find that ribbon?"

"It's my fault," said Titty, "trying to get the map done. I ought never to have let her go out of sight."

Nancy, with Roger trying to keep up with her, was already racing along the top of the dyke.

CHAPTER XVIII

EAGER PRISONER

It had been a dull morning for Bridget after the others had sailed away leaving her and Titty to look after the camp. Titty was so far behind with the map-making that she could think of nothing else. There were the separate maps and charts of the channel to Witch's Quay to compare and to transfer in pencil to Daddy's map, together with the work done on Mastodon Island, and Nancy's map of the channel to the town, besides the map of Flint Island, and the marshes between Magellan Straits and Cape Horn. And the pencilled outline was only the beginning. All had to be done in ink. The marshes had to be shown by dozens of tiny tufts of reeds, a boat or two or a fish had to be put in to distinguish the water from the land, and if there was room without making things too much of a muddle, she meant to mark with dotted lines the actual journeys of the explorers. Titty had been much too busy to talk. Bridget had begun by being an active sentinel marching up and down the dyke. She had seen the Mastodon row away. Then, needing company, she had helped for a time by keeping the separate maps from blowing away, but stones made better paperweights than Bridget's fingers. For a time she had held the little bottle of Indian ink, but from the point of view of the person who had to dip a pen in it the bottle was really much better on the ground where it was not so likely to move about. Then, as sentinel again, she had walked to and fro, looking far away at the explorers on the other side of the Secret Water and watching for signs of the savages. She had seen the shadow of the meal-dial creep slowly round, shortening as it crept, until at last it had darkened the paper label marked "Dinner". She had waited to disturb Titty till the shadow touched the paper. Then she had brought out the sandwiches, the oranges, the two bottles of ginger beer that Susan had left for their dinner. Titty was still drawing, lying on her stomach with her nose in the map. "Dinner's ready," said Bridget. "All but Sinbad's."

Titty put down her pen, corked the ink bottle and rolled stiffly over, stretching her cramped arms.

"Not half done," she said. "All right, Ship's Baby. I'll open Sinbad's tin."

"He's been squeaking for it like anything," said Bridget.

Even dinner had been rather melancholy after the first cheerful moments when Sinbad had been lapping up his milk and Titty and Bridget had been biting into their sandwiches, three explorers feeding together in their camp. They were at the orange stage when Bridget asked, "I say, Titty, tell me about human sacrifices. Have you ever been one?"

"No," said Titty, "but don't you go thinking about that. It isn't going to happen. They aren't going to have anything to do with us and the Mastodon isn't either any more."

"But what about all the blood."

"They don't know about that," said Titty, "but it wouldn't make any difference if they did. They've made him wish he'd never even talked to us."

"I think it's beastly," said Bridget.

"It jolly well is," said Titty, "but the map's the main thing. We're going to get it done even without the Mastodon."

*

After dinner when Titty settled down to work again, Bridget and Sinbad wandered off along the top of the dyke. Just at the corner where the dyke turned east was a good place for a sentinel. From that point you could see all along the dyke to the camp and beyond it. You could look the other way and see the patch of marsh at the corner that turned into a tiny island at high tide. You could see the creek curling towards the Red Sea. You could look out eastwards over the whole island to the distant prairie and its grazing buffaloes.

Bridget sat down. Yes, this was a very good place for a sentinel. You could see without being seen, because of the tall grass on either side of the trodden path along the top of the dyke. She looked at the camp, the row of white tents, where Titty, hard at work again, was deaf and blind to everything except the following of pencilled lines with a careful pen. Bridget felt sleepy. She played with Sinbad for a minute or two, but Sinbad also had just had dinner and was inclined to sleep.

The sentinel lay down and tickled Sinbad behind his ears.

It was very hot.

The sentinel rested her head on her arm and looked at Sinbad on Sinbad's own level.

The sentinel dozed.

*

Titty, Able Seaman and draughtsman to the expedition, scratched in tuft after tuft of reeds, three little upward strokes with a fine mapping pen for each tuft. The blank map, that might have been anything, was coming alive inch by inch. The explored part was slowly spreading over it. Water, dykes, marshland, channels were beginning to look like what they were, very different from Daddy's rough pencilled scrawls and the plain white spaces of the unknown. One, two, three strokes to a tuft, and each tuft the same distance from the next one, made marshland really look like marshland. That cow in the buffalo country really was not bad. Better perhaps if its horns were a wee bit longer. Anyhow anybody would know that was a ship marking the Secret Water. But never

mind that. More tufts. She must get all this lot done before
John and Nancy and the others came back with a new lot of
explored country to put in. One, two, three. One, two,
three. Ow, that tuft was a bit too near the one before. What
was that noise by the tents? Bridget of course. Poor old
Bridgie, not going to be a human sacrifice after all. One, two,
three. One, two, three. Titty never turned her head.

*

From the further side of the dyke a savage watched her.
He lay on the slope of the dyke between the row of the tents
and the little pond. Between two tents he could see her.
He looked along the dyke to the north. A black hand and arm
waved in the grass. All clear. Inch by inch he crawled up
over the edge of the dyke, and between two of those white
tents. Yes. There it was, only half a dozen yards from that
girl. What had those palefaces hung round its sacred neck?
A watch? Eel-like he wriggled forward. Titty moved and he
lay still. She dipped her pen and went on working. Flat to
the ground he wriggled on. His hand was on the thing he had
come to take when she moved again, but it was only to stretch
her fingers cramped from holding the pen. She never turned.
A moment later the watch lay on the ground where the totem
had been and the savage, clutching his prize, was slipping
back into hiding on the further side of the dyke.

*

Bridget woke slowly. It was as if a scarlet curtain hung
before her eyes, the sun through her closed eyelids. She
opened them and blinked, still more than half asleep. She
had a queer feeling that she was not alone. She rolled over
and saw Sinbad. Of course it was Sinbad. He had been there
all the time. How long had she been asleep? He must have
been very lonely to have started playing by himself. She saw

A SAVAGE WATCHED HER

the kitten crouching to the ground, his tail switching slowly from side to side. The kitten pounced. He had pounced on the tufted end of a weed that was lying on the path. Sleepily, Bridget watched him. He was crouching again, and that same weed seemed to be a little further from him. He pounced and as he pounced the flowery tuft slipped out of reach. The kitten waited, puzzled, close to Bridget's head. The weed began to twist as if someone were twiddling the other end of it. Bridget's eyes followed it into the grass. The grass parted and Bridget found herself looking straight into another pair of eyes, dark, sparkling, smiling at her through the stalks.

"Sh!" said a voice, just as Bridget was going to jump up.

The grasses opened wider, and Bridget saw that she was looking into the face of a girl who was lying on the sloping side of the dyke, just high enough to bring her head to the level of the footpath on the top.

"Who are you?" said Bridget whispering, though there was no one else to hear, and then, suddenly, she guessed.

"Kara . . . kara . . . karabadangbaraka," she stuttered.

"Akarabgandabarak," said the girl instantly.

"Gnad," said Bridget. "Gnad . . . You're Daisy. He said you always said 'Gand' by mistake."

"He's said lots too much," said Daisy. "Who are you?"

"I'm Bridget, and . . ."

"Sh!" said Daisy. "Just a minute . . . All right. What?" She was talking to someone else, whom Bridget could not see.

"Stuck in the middle of their camp," said a boy's voice. "Beastly cheek. They must have swiped it from Don. They'd even hung a watch on it. So Dee kept *cave* and I eeled it out. One of them was there too, but she didn't spot me."

"Where's Dee?"

"Coming."

There was a stir in the grass on the island side of the dyke and someone shot over the dyke and into hiding again.

"Good," said the voice of Daisy.

"Dum did a lovely bit of eeling," said a third voice. "The paleface never stirred. How do you think they got it?"

"They've got the password too." That was Daisy's voice. Her face showed again through the grasses.

"Hi, you!" she said.

"Yes," said Bridget.

"Don't get up. . . . Wriggle down on this side."

Bridget did as she was told, and crawled through the grass down the steep side of the dyke.

Two boys and a girl, crouching below the dyke where they could not be seen by anybody on the island, watched her arrive. For one moment even Bridget was a little startled. Except for their faces all three were shiny and black. All three were in bathing things, but it was hard to see where bathing things ended and mud began. The savages. There was no doubt about it. Bridget had her chance and knew it.

"Karabadangbaraka," she said.

"I told you so," said Daisy.

"Akarabgnadabarak," said the two boys together.

"Has he asked you yet?" said Bridget.

"Asked us what?" said Daisy.

"He said he'd have to ask you. But I really am old enough. Even John and Susan said so. So it all depends on you."

"What does?"

"Well, I'm quite old enough to be a human sacrifice, and not a bit skinny. . . ." She looked at Daisy whose mouth had fallen open. . . ." And he said I'd do very well, only he'd have to ask you first. . . ."

"Tide's high enough to get through to *Speedy*," said one of the boys. "Better go and see what he's been up to."

The girl seemed to think for a minute. "No," she said at

last. "Let him come and find us." She whispered to the boys, and then turned to Bridget.

"You'll have to be captured first," she said.

"Then you will let me," said Bridget.

"Come along," said Daisy.

"Can I bring Sinbad?"

"Who?"

"Our kitten. They rescued him at sea. . . ."

"Really at sea?" said the boy called Dee.

"On the way to Holland," said Bridget.

"Can you catch him?" said Daisy. "He can be a prisoner too."

"But not a sacrifice," said Bridget. "They all promised I could. Come on, Sinbad. Quick."

Sinbad himself seemed anxious to join them. He pushed through the grass. Bridget picked him up.

Daisy, the female savage, was talking earnestly to the other two. "Well, if we can't, we can't," she said. "But we're going to try." She turned to Bridget. "Now then. You keep close to me. Pity your dress is so clean. That blue can be seen for miles."

"It was much cleaner before I slipped," said Bridget.

"You could roll in the mud," said Daisy.

"Susan wouldn't like it."

"Who's Susan? Missionary?"

"Mate," said Bridget.

"All right," said Daisy. "So long as you don't get seen. We shan't because of the mud. That's why we do it. But a dress as bright as that. Well, if anybody does see you we'll just have to bolt for it and leave you behind."

"Oh no," begged Bridget. "They said I could if you'd let me."

"On the trail," said Daisy, who seemed to be in command, though the boys were bigger in size. "Dum leads, Dee at the rear. Nobody shows a head above the dyke. If we see anybody we'll all go down in the mud, Susan or no Susan. . . ."

"I mustn't really," said Bridget.

"Let's hope you won't have to. Come on, prisoner!"

"And you'll let me be the human sacrifice?"

Already the savages were on the move. The one whom Daisy called Dum galloped ahead, keeping well below the top of the dyke, looking keenly about him, a stooping, running figure the colour of the mud. Daisy followed him with Bridget, who was carrying the kitten. The other savage, whose name seemed to be Dee, came after them, looking behind him every now and then as if to see that they were not pursued.

Bridget in her blue shirt trotted cheerfully along with the mud-coated savages. John and Susan and Titty had been wrong after all. Even Nancy had been wrong. They had all said that the savages would have nothing to do with them, and that even the Mastodon would not be able to keep his promise. Well, they were wrong. Bridget was extremely happy. She was going to be a human sacrifice after all.

They hurried along the foot of the curving dyke close to the mud of the Red Sea. Bridget wanted an answer to her question, but was soon too short of breath to speak, and anyhow the answer must be Yes or they would never be taking her with them. How wrong the others had been.

"I'll carry the kitten for a bit," said the female savage.

Bridget handed Sinbad over and they ran on.

Suddenly the foremost savage stopped dead, took three or four quick steps to one side, stooping low, and threw himself full length in the mud. Bridget suddenly found herself flat in the grass. The female savage had pulled her down, put the kitten into her hands, and rolled sideways off the dyke. Bridget looked round. The third savage had disappeared. If she had not known exactly where to look for Daisy, Bridget could have thought she was alone.

"Flat as you can," came a whisper from Daisy lying in the mud. "It's the farmer. Bother your dress being so bright.'

"I've got a lot more mud on it now," said Bridget breathlessly.

"Good."

Some distance ahead of them a man was standing on the top of the dyke, watching the rising tide spread over the mud of the inland sea. He had not seen them. Bridget lay still. For a moment the man seemed to be looking directly towards them.

"It's the man from the kraal," whispered Bridget. "He's a friend."

"Don't move. He's a paleface." The answering whisper came from the mud.

The man seemed to look right round the horizon. He turned, strode off the dyke and was gone.

The savages gave him a minute or two.

Then, glistening with fresh mud, they were up and on the move once more. Just before they came to the place where the road from the farm came over the dyke they stopped, and the foremost savage signalled to them to wait while he scouted. Bridget lost sight of him again and again while he wormed himself through the grass.

Then she saw a black arm flung up in the air.

"Coast clear," whispered the female savage, and they ran on, crossed the road, and, still keeping well below the top of the dyke, turned a corner. Here the water ran close in to the land. Three small sailing dinghies lay some distance away among the weeds. The foremost savage was already plucking at an anchor hidden in a tussock. A long painter slapped and dripped as he tugged, and a dinghy left the weeds and shot in towards the shore. Daisy and the other savage did the same and three little boats were dragged in and grounded at their feet.

"Hop in," said Daisy.

"My boots are awfully muddy," said Bridget.

"Not as muddy as we are. We'll wash the boats out afterwards."

Bridget scrambled in, Daisy after her. The other two savages pushed off in their boats. All three rowed out and away into the channel. Presently mud banks and weedy marshes hid the island.

They stopped rowing and let the boats drift.

Bridget wondered what was going to happen next. There was a splash, and then another. Two savages had gone overboard, bobbed up again and were hanging to their boats with one arm while they washed the mud off with the other.

"Won't be a minute," said Daisy. "We've got to think of the missionaries." The next moment she too was over the side, and rapidly changing colour.

Presently the three savages climbed in again over the sterns of their boats, not exactly white, for they were very sunburnt, but looking almost as if they were explorers and not savages at all.

"No wind," said Daisy. "Tide coming in. We'll have to row like smoke."

The three savages bent to their oars. The three little boats foamed through the water. The marshes closed in on either side as the channel narrowed, and presently opened again.

"We've done it all right," said Daisy.

"Where are we going?" asked Bridget.

"Our camp," said Daisy.

"I knew I was old enough," said Bridget.

CHAPTER XIX

HOT ON THE TRAIL

Hᴇʀᴇ's where I found it," said Roger.

"Here's where they got her," said Nancy. "Look at the way the grass is all broken. Someone's been lying here on the side of the dyke."

"But look at all the mud on the grass."

"She's fallen in the mud," said Susan. "Anything may have happened."

"Well if she's been in the mud she's got out again," said John. "She couldn't have got all that mud on the grass before she went in."

"I say, look here," said Roger. "Someone's been fairly wallowing." He had gone down the side of the dyke and was looking at the muddy ditch that at high water cut off the marshy point and made an island of it. "Looks as if it was a young hippo. It couldn't be the Mastodon?"

"He's been away all day. We've seen him," said John.

"Those aren't Bridget's footmarks," said Peggy, who had also gone down to the edge of the ditch. "They're longer. Besides, if she'd taken her boots off we'd have found them. Whoever made these had bare feet."

"Somebody's been lying down here," said Roger. "And here's another lot of mud."

Nancy, stooping low, was moving along the foot of the dyke. Suddenly she straightened herself. "Susan," she said. "Have a look at this."

In the soft ground at the edge of the mud was a group of

clear footprints. Some showed toes, but there were a few smaller ones without.

"Those are Bridget's," said Susan. "I'd know them anywhere."

"She stood here," said Nancy, "and somebody else with no shoes on was talking to her. Two other people. That bare foot's bigger than the other one. Eels, I bet you anything."

"But why didn't she yell?" said Titty. "I'd have heard her."

"Not if you were drawing," said Roger. "When you're drawing you have to be prodded."

"Perhaps she didn't yell," said Nancy. "Perhaps she couldn't. Gagged. Bound hand and foot." She pulled up short on seeing Susan's face.

"Come on," shouted Peggy. "This is the way they went." She had gone on along the foot of the dyke, and was pointing to a trail of broken and bent grass, and to another lot of footprints on a soft patch of ground.

"They couldn't have got ashore here," said John, looking out over the marshes, "or got afloat again. They may be still on the island."

"Come on. A rescue. A rescue." cried Nancy. "Catch them before they get to their boats."

The explorers, like a pack of hounds, nose to the scent, hurried along the foot of the dyke. Bent and trodden grass showed the way the savages and their prisoner had made off.

"Hullo," Roger who was galloping ahead, suddenly stopped. "Here are footprints going the other way."

" Well," said Nancy. "They had to get here first. The Red Sea's been dry most of the day." She hurried on.

"Cheer up, Susan," said John. "We'll get her again."

"She'll have been awfully frightened," said Susan. "I ought never to have left her. It isn't Titty's fault. You know what it's like when she's doing something."

"Can't think how they managed it," said John.

"Good Eels," said Nancy.

"Beasts," said Titty.

They hurried on below the dyke towards the place where the cart track from the farm came over it and down to the Red Sea, where, already, the waters had met over the Wade and the mudflats were narrowing as the tide crept over them.

Roger, who was again running ahead, stopped once more. "Someone fell down," he said. "You can see where they lay on the grass."

"But look here," said Nancy. "This is mad. More wallowing. Look at this. What on earth were they doing, going off the bank and rolling in the mud?"

"Don't wait," said Susan. She hurried on, following the track clearly marked in the grass. "It doesn't matter what they did. We've got to find her. I do wish I'd stayed in the camp with her."

Where the cart track came down to the Red Sea there was damp ground for a few yards and no grass on it.

"It *is* Eels," said Roger. "Two running barefoot, and Bridget."

"Three of them," said John. "That pair's different from this, and these are smaller than either. Three barefoot and Bridget."

"Oh don't wait to look at them," said Susan.

They ran on, and suddenly found they were running through grass that had never been trodden. The trackers spread out up and over the dyke, like hounds that have lost the scent. Away to the right were the marshy islands of the Magellan Straits. Away to the left were quiet fields with grazing cattle. The sun shone warm on the red brick of the native kraal in the middle of the island. Far ahead of them was the line of the open sea, and the golden sand dunes of Flint Island. But there was never a sign of savages or prisoner.

Peggy was the first to turn back, and within a minute she was calling to them.

"Got something, Peggy?" called Nancy, and added, "She's a galoot on some things but pretty good on tracks."

Peggy was pointing at the ground. The tide was lapping near the bank, and by a tuft of grass she had found heavy footprints, and three deep holes with torn edges. From this tuft it was as if lines had been lightly scratched on the mud. People had been trampling there. People had jumped from one soft tussock to another.

"Boats," said John. "They had their anchors here. They've gone."

Titty was already on the top of the dyke, racing back as fast as she could run.

"That's it," cried Nancy. "Come on. They've taken her with them to their camp. We can't get after them without boats. Come on. Back to our landing place," John, Susan, Peggy and Roger pelted after her, with Titty already far ahead of them.

Breathlessly they reached the camp. Breathlessly they splashed down the marshy path to the landing place. Nobody bothered to wash the mud off, as they tumbled into the boats and pushed off, six of them, three to a boat.

"You steer, Roger," said Susan. "John and I'll take an oar each."

"I'll manage all right," said John.

"No," said Susan, who felt that every moment counted, and could not bear the thought of sitting there doing nothing while someone else rowed.

"I'll keep time with you," said John.

Nancy saw what they were doing, and for different reasons did the same. "Titty'll keep us straight," she said. "Can't let them beat us. Go it, Peggy. One. Two. One. Two. Lift her along."

The two boats shot out of Goblin Creek and began the long pull down the Secret Water.

*

"What are we going to do?" asked Roger.
"Get her back," panted John.

*

"What are we going to do?" asked Titty.
"Bust those Eels," jerked Nancy, as she swung forward with her oar.

*

It was hard rowing against the tide, but they came at last to the buoy with a cross on it and the channel leading between their island and the sandy dunes of Flint Island. Both boats swung round to the right as if going up to the town. There were the yachts they had seen at anchor, three of them . . . no . . . four. Another had come in since yesterday and was lying in the bay nearer the mouth of the channel than the other three. The fourth was the yellow cutter.

"There's their ship," said Roger.

"Better go straight to it and ask for her," said Susan.

John wiped his forehead. "We can't do that," he said. "We don't want to get them in a row with their missionaries."

"But if they've got her aboard," said Susan. "They ought never to have taken her."

"There's only a little punt lying astern," said John. "They won't have taken her there. Hullo. Nancy's seen something."

Nancy and Peggy had stopped rowing. Their boat was a little way ahead and Nancy was pointing in towards the shore.

John and Susan pulled on, Susan watching the yacht all the time, looking for any sign of a prisoner.

"Their boats," said Roger.

Three small sailing dinghies lay in a row, pulled well up

230

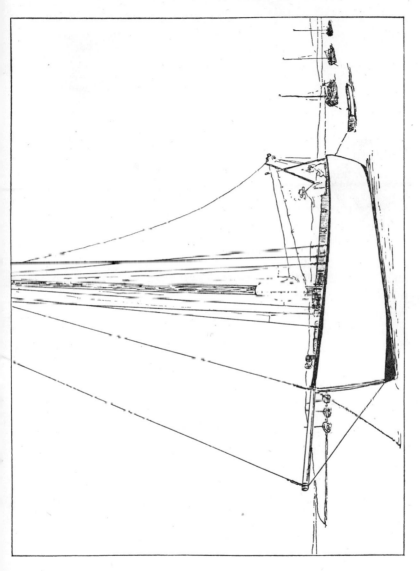

THE MISSION SHIP OFF FLINT ISLAND

on the bright golden beach of Flint Island. There were no tents to be seen, but plenty of footmarks going up from the shore.

"They've landed," said Nancy quietly. "What do we do? Go in quietly, grab their boats and then rush the camp?"

"Where are their tents?" said Peggy.

"They'll be in the hollow where we found that fireplace."

"Funny they've left no one on guard," said John. He looked doubtfully towards the yacht lying off the shore. A man in a white sweater had come up into the cockpit and was shaking his pipe out over the side. "I suppose they think they're safe with the missionaries out there."

"Do hurry up," said Susan. "Bridget's probably frightened out of her life."

They rowed in and grounded their boats beside the three small sailing dinghies they had last seen at Pin Mill. Nancy and John took the anchors well up the steep sandy beach.

"Somebody stand guard over the boats," said Nancy.

"Never mind the boats," said Susan, and ran towards the dunes.

At the top of the steep beach she stopped, and the others, who had been close behind, stopped with her. No wonder now that, on the morning after their arrival, the Mastodon had mistaken their camp for the camp of the friends he was expecting. The Swallows looked down into the sandy hollow between the dunes to see three tents exactly like their own, and a fourth a little larger. It was as if somebody had taken their tents and planted them in a new place. But it did not seem that anybody was there. They had expected to come upon the Eels and their prisoner, not upon a deserted camp.

"They must have known we were after them," said Nancy.

"Bridget! Bridget!" Susan called again.

"No good shouting if they've got her gagged and bound," said Nancy.

But at that moment, Bridget herself, neither bound nor gagged, crawled out of the larger tent.

"Hullo, Susan," she called. "They've agreed. They say I'm quite old enough and I'm going to be a human sacrifice after all."

"Oh, Bridget," cried Susan. "Are you all right?"

"What happened?" said John.

But others were coming out of the tent. Two boys and a girl, all in black bathing things.

"Karabadangbaraka!" All three spoke together.

For a moment nobody answered.

"I remembered it," said Bridget. "And she did say 'gand' instead of 'gnad'."

"They didn't hurt you?" asked Roger fiercely.

"Of course not," said Bridget. "And they're going to tell him it's all right."

"Karabadangbaraka," said the girl earnestly, and then stamped her foot. "Aren't you Eels?"

"Look here," said John. "There's absolutely no need for you to be friends with us if you don't want to. But it's no good trying to make us clear out, because we can't. We're marooned. We can't go till the ship comes to take us. And anyway I don't see why we should. There's plenty of room."

"It was all a mistake," said the girl. "We didn't know what you were like till we caught Bridget. We had no idea you were blood brothers."

"You oughtn't to have taken Bridget," said Susan.

"It was too good a chance to miss," said the girl. "And here's something else of yours. We thought you'd bagged it." She darted back into the tent and came back with the painted totem pole.

"But how did you get it?" said Titty. "I never left the camp all day."

A slow grin spread over the face of the larger of the two boys.

The girl looked at Susan. "Are you Eels or are you not?" she said. "You've never given the countersign."

"Congers and Lampreys," said Nancy, and gave Susan a look as powerful as a battering ram. "Try us again."

"Karabadangbaraka," said the three savages.

"Akarabgnadabarak" burst from the seven explorers.

"That's all right," said the girl. "I'm Daisy. These are my brothers. We're all Eels. They're not twins, but everybody thinks they are. I call them Dum and Dee, you know, Tweedledum and Tweedledee, and you can too as you're blood brothers. You must be John and you're Susan. And that's Roger. Which is the one with the funny name?"

"Oh no," said Bridget. "This is Susan. That's Peggy. This is Titty. And that's Captain Nancy. I told you. She and Peggy are pirates when they're at home."

"Not here," said Nancy quickly. "It's a much better place for savages than pirates. And with Eel blood in us. . . ."

"Oh but look here, Nancy," said John, who saw her turning savage before his eyes. "We've simply got to finish the map. The last two days we've done hardly anything."

"What about the map?" said Daisy. "What's it for? I couldn't make head or tail of what our prisoner was saying."

"Exploring," said Titty. "And the Mastodon was helping. That's why we did all the blooding. And then your letter upset everything and he wished he hadn't."

"We'll all help," said Daisy. "It's the best thing he ever did. And Mastodon's a lovely name for Don. I wish we'd thought of it ourselves."

"Where is he?" asked Nancy.

"He's been looking for you," said John.

"We haven't seen him," said Daisy.

"He's pretty miserable," said Nancy.

234

CHAPTER XX

ALL'S WELL

THE Mastodon, low in spirits, was rowing down the channel from the town. Twice already that day he had been to Flint Island and seen only the missionaries' ship, no savage boats at their usual landing place and empty tents in the camp of the Eels. He had seen the signals last night and they must have seen his answer. All morning he had been expecting them. They could not have sailed through the Red Sea, because until late in the afternoon there had been no water to let them. He had been sure they would come sailing up the Secret Water, three little boats, as they had come sailing many times before. But they had never come. Again and again he turned over in his mind what he was to say to them, to explain how and why instead of fending off the explorers he had made friends with them and even made them blood brothers of the Eels. Would they understand or would they not? Would Daisy ever forgive him for letting out the secrets they kept even from their own missionaries?

Almost he hated the explorers. Somehow they had swept him off his feet, and he had found himself eagerly telling them things he had no right to tell unless after a council of the tribe. Get rid of them? Why, they had made him welcome them instead. And then for the hundredth time he began to find excuses for them and for himself. They were not just invaders. They had been marooned. They could not get away until a ship came to take them off. And it wasn't as if they were just camping. They were explorers, and what could be more natural than that they should meet savages and that the savages, in return for beads and things (Oh bother! He hadn't even got the fishhooks to show Daisy what had happened) should act as guides? And then that map business. They'd never get it decently done without someone who really did know something about mud. A poor show they would make of it. And then he began to feel a traitor to the explorers as well as to the Eels. It had been pretty awful rowing past and seeing them at work without him when he had promised to help. And they had been jolly decent about it. Not one of them had reproached him with a single word. They had just watched him row by, and to-day, when he had spoken to them from a distance and asked if they had seen the Eels, they had answered him just as if he had not let them down.

And now the Eels would be thinking. ... Well, what would they be thinking? They must have been expecting him to come to Flint Island? And he had been expecting them to come to *Speedy*. It had never happened before that they had not got in touch with each other almost as soon as they arrived. Perhaps they had thought he would come rowing round in the dark last night. Perhaps they had wanted a council round the camp fire. And he had just sat tight in *Speedy*, carving a new totem to take the place of the one he had given to the explorers. Pretty good totem, too, he could not help thinking, as he looked at it propped in the stern of his boat . . . though, of course, it was a pity that the paint wasn't dry. But what would Daisy say when he had to tell her that he had given another totem just as good to the strangers she had told him to drive into the sea?

And where were the Eels anyhow? He had been sure they had gone up to the town in the morning, been held there by the falling tide and had waited for the afternoon flood. And now he had rowed the whole way up to the Yacht Club Hard. And no one had seen them that day. He had just missed them the day before. He was rowing disconsolately back. He knew where *Lapwing* was anyhow, and there was only one thing to do, though it was rather humiliating to a savage. He would have to ask the missionaries. Daisy would have something to say about that too. If savages could not find out about each other without inquiring from paleface missionaries, they were pretty poor savages.

He rowed steadily on, down the middle of the channel. He passed the first of the three anchored boats. What was it Titty had called them? Arab dhows? Not bad. Even Daisy would like that. He passed the second, and the third. Now for *Lapwing*. He must be close to her. He lifted his oars and turned round. There she was and . . . No need to ask the missionaries after all. There were the three little boats of the Eel drawn up on the beach. And two other boats, most awfully like. . . . What on earth had happened? Had the explorers attacked them? Seven to three. And he had not been there to help. Every single thing in the world was going wrong. His oars bit the water with a splash.

"Hullo, Don!"

He looked up. This was no moment in which to talk to missionaries. But there was the he-missionary looking out from *Lapwing's* forehatch.

"Hullo," said Don.

"We've got the kettle on here," said the he-missionary. "If you're going across to the camp, will you tell them to come when we ring the fog-bell? Tell them they can bring their friends. You too, of course."

"Thank you very much," said Don, dipped his oars again and rowed as if in a boat-race for the beach. Friends! FRIENDS! Why there might be no camp left. He had told the explorers that Daisy had ordered him to get rid of them and do anything short of burning their tents. The explorers might well have decided that attack was the best part of defence. Seven to three. What could the Eels have done against them? Don rowed as hard as he could, drove the bow of his boat up the shingle, jumped from it, threw the anchor out and charged to the rescue up the steep slope of the shore.

"Hullo, Mastodon!"

Dum, or was it Dee? greeted him before he had gone more than a couple of yards.

"What's happened?" panted Don, and gasped. "Mastodon" the Eel had called him. But that was the explorers' name for him. What, indeed, had happened? He ran up to the top of the slope and looked down into the sandy hollow of the camp. A whole crowd of people were eagerly talking by the tents.

"Karabadangbaraka!" called Daisy with a laugh.

"Karabadangbaraka!" they all shouted together.

The Mastodon could hardly believe his ears. All was peace. Eels and explorers were together, and Daisy, Daisy herself, had been the first to give the secret password in the presence of the people she had said were to be driven off at all costs.

"Akarabgnadabarak," the Mastodon answered at last in a very puzzled voice.

Then, stuck in the sand in the middle of the camp of the Eels, he saw the totem that he himself had planted in the camp of the explorers.

"It's a beauty," said Daisy. "We thought they'd grabbed it so we took it away without their knowing. We got a prisoner too. We'd no idea they were Eels, till Bridget told us. It's the best thing you've ever done. And we're all going to call you Mastodon. Don's as good a short for Mastodon as it is for Donald. Just the name for a savage. You'll have to make another totem for us."

"It's in my boat, but the paint's still wet. . . ." said the Mastodon. "You see I'd made this one for you, and put it in their camp by mistake. . . ."

"They've told us all about it," said Daisy. "Best mistake you've ever made. And now they're going to let us help with the exploring, and four's not many for a corroboree, but we can have as many of them as we want. . . ."

"Daisy says it's all right about me," said Bridget. "I asked her."

"We're going to take them to the upper waters to-morrow. . . . All six boats. . . ."

The Mastodon looked from face to face, and saw not a hint of blame on any of them. Daisy must have forgotten the orders she had sent. The explorers must have forgotten that for two days their blood brother had held himself aloof. The same thing must have happened to Daisy that had happened to himself and everything was very much all right.

"But how did you get their totem?" he asked.

"Good eeling," said Daisy.

"They got it and got away again without my noticing anything," said Titty ruefully. "I was in the camp all the time and never knew."

"Not your fault," said Daisy. "Dum's our best Eel. He could scalp a whole camp full and the victims wouldn't know till they saw their own scalps hanging round his waist. . . ."

CLING, CLANG . . . CLING, CLANG . . . CLING, CLANG! . . .

What's that?" said Nancy.

"It's the missionaries," said the Mastodon. "They said I was to tell you to come to *Lapwing* for tea. The others are to come too. . . ."

"Oh, we can't," said Susan.

"You must," said Daisy. "It'll be a bit sardiny in the cabin. I wonder if they know how many. Come on. They'll be awfully sick if you don't . . . COMING!" she yelled at the top of a shrill voice. . . . Then, almost whispering, she added "No Eels. You've never heard of them. Nothing about prisoners. . . . Nothing. . . . Eels. What are eels? Fish, I think, or are they reptiles? Anyway, just part of natural history. . . ."

The Mastodon ran back to his boat and brought the new

totem and set it up beside the other. "Look out for the wet paint," he said.

"You can collect yours when we come back after tea," said Daisy to the explorers. "Come on. Everybody ready? ... Prunes and prisms. ... Come on. ...."

"Suffering Lampreys!" exclaimed Nancy. "However do you do it? You even look quite different."

" 'Sh!" said Daisy. "What a quaint expression. I wonder where you picked that up. ... I think, perhaps, we had better come in your boats, so as not to have too many clustering round the *Lapwing*."

Wizard and *Firefly*, heavily laden, six in one, five and a kitten in the other, were ferried across to the *Lapwing*. Eels and explorers had somehow vanished. Anybody might have taken them for members of a picnic party.

The missionary and his wife, who looked just an ordinary pleasant couple of grown-ups, were waiting to receive them, with fenders handy, but unnecessary, as both John and Nancy showed that they could bring boats alongside a ship without damaging the paint.

"Well, this is delightful," said the she-missionary. "So you have found friends already."

"I am afraid there are an awful lot of us," said Susan.

"The more the merrier," said the he-missionary. "We've a big kettle, but not quite enough cups. But I daresay some of you won't mind drinking out of saucers."

"Sinbad'll like it," said Bridget.

"So'll I," said Titty hurriedly.

"And me," said Roger.

*

It was a very pleasant tea party of the sedater sort. Polite questions were asked and answered. The missionaries had heard at Pin Mill about the adventures of the *Goblin* and how she had got to Holland, and Susan earnestly explained that they had not meant to go to sea. Nancy and Peggy wondered whether the *Lapwing* was as big as the *Goblin*, and learnt that she was bigger. The explorers were shown all over her, and, with a good deal of squeezing, it was found that only four need have tea on deck if the he-missionary sat on the companion steps to pass up cups of tea and buns when wanted, and the she-missionary sat in the doorway between the saloon and the forecabin, which she said was the best arrangement as she had to keep within reach of the kettle. "In *Goblin*, the cooking place is aft," said Roger, and added, "I think this way, with the galley forward, is almost cosier." The he-missionary showed John round the decks, and Roger bolted out to join him, because, as he explained afterwards, it was too much for him to hear Nancy solemnly talking about gardening. Daisy was sitting in the cockpit, entertaining Susan and Titty with a few words about School Certificates. He caught her sparkling eye and nearly darted back again, but blew his nose instead (lucky that time he had a handkerchief) and hurried forward over the deck to ask an intelligent question about the working of the winch.

The missionaries seemed very pleased that their children had found companions. "That will be very pleasant," said the she-missionary, when she heard that they were all going to spend next day together. "Going to the upper waters is always one of our favourite picnics. Of course there is not much to do there, but it is a lovely place. Only you'll have to be careful about your tides. You have to get there as soon as the tide will let you, and start back the moment it begins to fall. But the boys know all about that."

Susan, at the right moment, rose to go. Daisy and her brothers asked if John and Nancy would mind putting them ashore, and the whole party left the *Lapwing* after thanking the missionaries for letting them come aboard.

"They're the politest children I've ever met," they heard the she-missionary say as they were rowing off.

"Too polite to be good," said the he-missionary. "Daisy's up to one of her games. I know that look in her eye." But fortunately this sentence was not heard by the departing guests.

"You did awfully well," said Daisy, as she landed.

"Jolly nice missionaries," said Roger.

"They are," said Daisy. "But missionaries are missionaries. It's no good being Eels if you don't remember that. What the eye doesn't see. . . . You know what I mean. Well, it's much better not to give them things to grieve over. Aren't you coming ashore?"

"We've simply got to get back," said John. "We've got things to put on the map. And supper to cook. And there's a speck of wind too."

"Quick," said Daisy. "Don, you get it. You mustn't go without your totem. We'll come to the mouth of the channel with you. . . ."

"Bridget held the totem as she sat in the bottom of *Wizard* with Sinbad on her lap. John steered. Susan sat on the middle thwart, when she had hoisted the sail. Close beside them Titty was steering *Firefly*, and a convoy of four savage boats rowed hard to keep up.

At the mouth of the Secret Water the wind freshened, and the two boats of the explorers drew away. The savages turned back.

"To-morrow early," called Daisy.

"We'll be ready," John called back.

"Karabadangbaraka," called Nancy.

"Akarabgnadabarak," came from Dum, Dee, and the Mastodon.

From Daisy came something slightly different.

"Gnad . . . gnad," shouted Bridget. "Did you hear, Susan?

She said 'Gand' again. That's how I knew it was her when I met her in the grass."

"Well, I'm glad it's all right," said Susan. "But you did give me an awful fright when I thought you'd fallen in."

"Dum and Dee," said Roger. "The silent brothers. They both ought to be called Dumb."

"They're grand savages," said John. "And with six boats we'll be able to explore a hundred miles a day."

"We mustn't waste them," said Nancy. "Great Wriggling Congers, Titty! Look out how you're steering. We don't want to bump the other boat. Eels for ever! Suffering Lampreys! What a time we are going to have!"

Late that night, after dusk, when Bridget was already in bed and the others were turning in, Peggy heard the noise of oars in the creek. "What's that?" she said. "They aren't going to attack again?"

They listened.

The Mastodon's voice, extraordinarily happy, sounded across the water. "I say. I'll bring my splatchers across in the morning."

"Good," cried John.

"Karabadangbaraka," called Nancy.

"Akarabgnadabarak!" a joyful reply came out of the darkness, and the sound of oars drew rapidly away, as the Mastodon rowed up the creek to make his way to *Speedy* and his lair.

CHAPTER XXI

SIX BOATS EXPLORE

Fɪʀsᴛ thing in the morning, even before the breakfast things had been washed up and put away, the Mastodon arrived in the camp, bringing his splatchers with him.

"Karabadangbaraka!" he greeted them joyfully, and, almost before they had time to give the countersign, went on. "Everybody's coming to supper in *Speedy* to-night. I've still got that ham and all the grub Mother gave me when I told her I'd asked you the other day."

"Three cheers!" said Roger.

"We'd love to come," said Susan. "But we've gone and eaten the mushrooms and the blackberry mash we'd meant to bring."

"There's simply tons of grub," said the Mastodon. "The only thing I'm short of is mugs and plates."

"We'll bring our own," said Susan.

"And could Roger bring his whistle?" said the Mastodon.

"I'll begin practising at once," said Roger.

"You jolly well won't," said John. "One go a day's enough for anybody."

"All right," said Roger. "I won't. But it'll be John's fault if I play false notes to-night."

"I say," said John. "Do just look at the map. Is there a way through round the place where we were yesterday?"

"I don't know," said the Mastodon. "There is a sort of gap, but it doesn't look as if it went right through. Anyway there's nothing but mud the other side."

"It's awfully important," said John. "You see, if there's a

North West Passage then where we were yesterday's an island. If there isn't it's only a promontory. You can't tell from Daddy's map. What about going to have a look?"

"No good with a falling tide," said the Mastodon. "It's gone down a long way. Didn't you say you wanted to try my splatchers? Now's the time. No good starting for the Upper Waters till the tide turns again."

"Can I have a shot, too?" said Nancy.

"And me?" said Roger. "Hullo! Here are the others."

"Karabadangbaraka!" Daisy and her brothers were rowing up Goblin Creek.

"Akarabgnadabarak!" The Mastodon and the explorers went down to the landing place to meet them.

"It's all fixed," cried Daisy as she splashed ashore. "Corroboree to-morrow night. And the missionaries are going to let us stay till after dark. And high water's pretty late. Everything's just right."

"But you'll come to supper in *Speedy* to-night," said the Mastodon. "I've got a feast all ready."

"That's all right too," said Daisy. "Only we'll have to clear off pretty early. We'll have to be up at dawn to-morrow." She whispered in the Mastodon's ear.

"We're just going splatchering," said Roger.

"Ever done it before?" asked Daisy.

"No," said Roger. "But we've seen him do it."

The two silent brothers, Dum and Dee, looked at each other.

"We'll watch," said Daisy. "Who's going first?"

"I am," said Nancy, and stood on the splatchers while the Mastodon fastened the straps over her insteps.

Slowly, inch by inch, she moved the splatchers along the mud, grabbing at the gunwale of a boat to keep her balance.

"That's not the way," said Roger. "You ought to swing them round and fairly gallop."

"Let him try," laughed Daisy.

Nancy looked oddly worried, let go of the boat and took a few steps. "Come on John. You have a go," she said. She sat on the gunwale of the boat while the Mastodon freed her feet.

John stood on the splatchers and made the straps fast. He moved slowly off. "It's not as easy as it looks," he said. One foot slid from under him on the sloping mud. He tried to balance on the other. That splatcher also began to move like a toboggan. The next moment John was sitting in the mud. He tried in vain to bring a splatcher under him. It was no good. He rolled over and struggled back to the hard on all fours.

"That's quite enough," said Susan. "You'll have to take everything off."

"He ought to have moved much faster," said Roger. "And he ought to have leant forward."

"Let's see you try it," said John.

"One all mud's quite enough," said Susan.

"Oh let him try," said Daisy.

The Mastodon fastened the splatchers for Roger. "Now you watch," said Roger. "You ought to lean forward and swing your legs . . . like this. . . ." He stood for a moment. A queer look of uncertainty came into his face. Then, remembering how he had seen the Mastodon go running along the bottom of his creek, he threw himself forward. The first step was all right. So was the second. At the third he caught one splatcher on the other and fell on his nose.

Dum and Dee said not a word but looked at each other and rocked with silent laughter.

"It takes practice to be a Mastodon," said Daisy.

After that, the Eels were taken up to the camp, to visit it this time as friends not enemies. John and Roger spread their clothes on bushes, decided that for the rest of the day they would wear bathing things, like the savages, and had a wallow in the pond to get rid of the mud that they had not taken off with their clothes. Susan and Peggy set to work to make packets of sandwiches for the expedition to the Upper Waters. John and Titty made copies of the blank map showing just the part west of Goblin Creek, so that there would be one for each of the six boats. The Mastodon, squatting beside them, was admiring the work that had been done, and pointing out one or two places where he thought the surveyors had gone a little wrong. A little way along the dyke shouts of laughter told where Nancy, Daisy and the Eel brothers were holding a private conference. Bridget, rather cross at having been shoo'd away by them, was playing with Sinbad. Roger, chivvied from the camp, was practising "The Keel Row" on his whistle down by the boats, and watching for the turning of the tide. Slowly the water went down, and at last began to creep up again over the mud.

Roger came running with the news.

"It's started coming up," he said.

"Give it at least an hour," said the Mastodon. "No good going before there's water in the channels."

Final preparations were made. Bridget unwillingly agreed that Sinbad should stay in camp. "He'll be miserable in a little boat all day," said Susan, and promised that he should come on the next expedition by land. The Mastodon pointed out that the bigger boats would have to keep to the main channels.

"The little channels'll be the hardest to map," said John. "Look here. Titty and I'll have to go in the Eel's boats. They're shallower than ours."

"I'm going with Daisy," said Nancy.

"In some of the places we may have to get out and push," said the Mastodon cheerfully.

"Do let's start," said Titty at last.

"What about having dinner first?" said Susan.

"Better eat under way," said the Mastodon. "We might just as well be drifting up with the flood."

*

Half an hour later the camp was deserted. Goblin Creek was deserted, too, but, if anybody had been looking from an aeroplane they would have seen something like a floating island moving slowly with the tide in the middle of the Secret Water. It was a smooth, oily calm, without a breath of wind. *Wizard* had tied alongside *Firefly*. Nancy and Daisy, John and Dee, Titty and Dum, each couple in one of the tiny dinghies of the Eels had thrown painters aboard one of the larger boats. The Mastodon with Roger had rowed round them all, and ended by coming up close under *Wizard's* stern. All six boats were close together. Food was being passed from boat to boat, and everybody was busy eating.

Slowly the tide carried the floating island of boats up the middle of the wide channel. On either side there were low green shores, and wide stretches of shining mud. Ahead the glassy water lost itself in the distance. There, too, were green shores. The roof of a house showed far away and low green islands fringed with mud.

"Oughtn't we to be rowing?" said John at last.

"No good hurrying till the tide's a bit higher," said the Mastodon.

"I've started filling in my map," said Roger.

"But there's nothing to put in yet," said John.

"We've put it in," said Roger. "That's just it. And jolly good, too. Specially the bananas."

"But what's that got to do with the map?" said John.

"It's all right," said Roger. "I've just put in 'Here the fleet hogged', and so we have."

A little patch of ripples showed on the glassy water, and then another.

"Cat's paws," said Daisy.

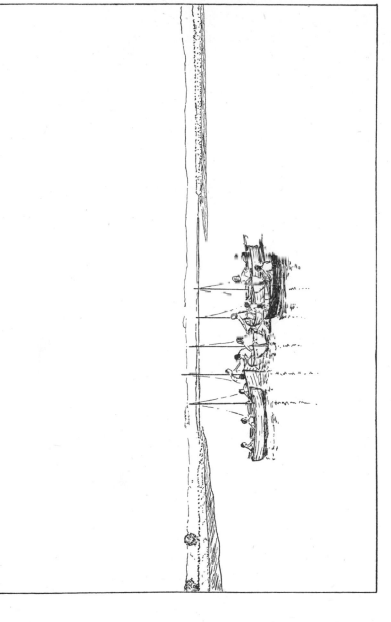

DRIFTING UP WITH THE TIDE

"Wind coming," said John.

"Cast off," said the Mastodon. "Come on Roger. If they're going to be able to sail, we'd better start rowing."

In a moment the floating island began to break up into half a dozen little boats. Roger and the Mastodon shot out ahead. In all the other boats people were getting up sails.

"Eels' wind," said Daisy, hauling her little sail up while Nancy, for once an idle passenger, sat on the bottom of the boat with a pencil and her copy of the map.

"Why Eels'?" she asked.

"It's just the wind we want," panted Daisy swigging on her halyard. "It's just a perfect wind. We'll be able to sail both ways without tacking."

Susan, in command of *Wizard*, had fixed her rudder, and put Bridget, for once promoted able seaman, at the tiller while she hoisted sail.

Peggy, alone in *Firefly*, was having slight difficulties but when John offered to come and help she answered, as if she was Nancy, "Jibbooms and bobstays! Shiver my timbers! It's only stuck. Barbecued billygoats! Up she goes."

Dum and Dee, anxious to show their passengers what savages could do, had their sails set and drawing almost before their passengers knew what was happening.

"I say," said Titty. "That was jolly good."

"Dead heat," said Dum. "Sometimes Dee's quicker than me, and sometimes not."

"What do we do now, White Chief?" asked Dee, grabbing the tiller and stepping over John's legs.

"Let's all go on together to where the channels divide," said John, curling round in the bottom of the boat, so that he could keep his chart on the middle thwart. "But let's keep near the northern shore. I haven't been along this bit. You see when we were doing that part we thought you were enemies and we had to keep within sight of the camp."

Dee chuckled. "You didn't keep quite near enough."

"You wouldn't have done it if Titty hadn't been so busy with the map," said John. "Anyway, it's a good thing you did. But it's a pity that we haven't properly done that northern shore. I say, is that an island ahead?"

"One of them," said the savage guide.

"Look here," exclaimed John a few minutes later. "What's that gap? Is there a way through? If there is, all that part where we were exploring may be an island."

Dee looked where John was pointing. There was a break in the long line of the dyke to the north of them.

"There may be," he said.

"Hi! Mastodon!" shouted John.

The Mastodon stopped rowing, and looked back. In this light wind, he was ahead of the sailing boats. "What is it?" he shouted.

John pointed. "Is that the gap you were talking about?"

"Yes," shouted the Mastodon.

The tide was carrying them past.

"I say, let's try it," said John.

It was at that moment that Bridget saw the seal. Ahead of them where the Secret Water seemed to lose itself in low green shores, there was a spit of mud or sand and on it something had moved. "Look," said Bridget. "Somebody bathing and wallowing. Just like Dum and Dee."

Everybody looked that way in a hurry, bristling at the thought of a stranger.

"It's a seal!" cried Titty, looking through the telescope.

"It's the seal," said Daisy.

"It's George," said the Mastodon, and swiftly and quietly rowed towards it.

The seal, idly sunning itself after a bathe, might have been a sort of magnet. The whole fleet turned towards it. Even John for a moment or two had eyes for nothing else. After all, islands do not move and seals do. And anyhow, Dee had the tiller, not John, and Dee altered course with the rest.

"First time we've seen it this year," said Dee. "Don says it's been here again and again. But we've always been somewhere else."

"Why does he call it George?" asked John, and the same question was being asked in every boat.

"Why not?" said Dee, and his answer was as good as any.

It might have been a regatta, with George, the seal, as the finishing mark. All six boats drew nearer and nearer to each other. Even the quietest talk could be heard from boat to boat. "Don't splash so," hissed Daisy at the Mastodon. "Don't talk," said the Mastodon to Roger. "What'll we do when we catch him?" Bridget asked Susan. "Peggy, you've taken our wind," said Titty. "Well, don't come so near," said Peggy. "He's seen us," whispered Dee.

The seal, lying flat on the mud, suddenly lifted a round grey head. Slowly, with no sort of hurry, he raised himself on his flippers and waddled towards the water. In the water, he lay awash for a moment, and was gone.

The fleet sailed on towards the place where he had been.

"He'll come up again," said the Mastodon.

"But where?" said Roger.

"There he is," said Daisy, and the whole fleet altered course together. George had come up a hundred yards away and more. His head and shoulders were above water. He was as interested in the fleet as the fleet was interested in him.

"Do let's get near enough to draw him," said Titty. "We ought to put him in the map."

But George had had enough of them. He dived, and though they sailed over the place where he had been they did not see him again.

John turned round to look for the gap once more. "I say, Mastodon, I ought to go and try that gap," he called. "It may really be a North West Passage."

"To-morrow," called the Mastodon. "You couldn't do it now, not if you're coming along with the rest of us. Even if it does go through you'd have to wait for water. And if you went right round you'd be too late for all this." He pointed at the low marshy islands ahead of them.

John marked the gap with a big question mark. If that was a way through to the Northern Sea, it was certainly worth an expedition for itself alone. That opening looked as if it ran in a long way. North West Passage. And there might be a North East as well. He would do one and Nancy would do the other. But now, with the tide sweeping them on, they must follow the savage guides.

"Who'd better go which way?" shouted Daisy.

"Two main channels," shouted the Mastodon. "And there's a creek to the south, and channels through the saltings in the middle. I'll go up the creek with Roger, because my boat draws less than any, and I'll be able to get to the top and back before there's water for any of the others. Then we'll work through the saltings and join you."

"Right," called Daisy. "There you are, White Chief. You take that one." She pointed to the opening of a channel. "Take him through there, Dee. Wait for us at the other side, if you get through first."

"Better get the sail down," said Dee. "There won't be room for sailing."

John lowered the little sail, watching the five other boats moving in a bunch along the edge of the marshes.

"Better let me row," said Dee. "You'll be busy with the map."

"Good," said John. "Hullo. Somebody else lowering sail."

"That's my brother," said Dee. "He'll have a time of it, getting through there. It's only about four feet wide."

"Down go two more."

In another moment all the other boats were hidden by land, and John, watching his compass, had no time to look at them even if he could have seen them. This mapping on the move was no sort of joke, and he wondered what some of the others were making of it. Due east to that point on Mastodon Island. He jammed that down, and then every few minutes had to put down a new compass course, as Dee, rowing now in water, now with his oars scraping the mud, worked his way between the banks.

"It's a much better channel than some of them," said Dee, watching John feverishly at work.

"Good thing we're going through with the tide rising," said John, "and before the mud's all covered."

"There's one of them," said Dee when, at last, they sighted clear water ahead, and, almost at the some moment, saw the mast of a small boat apparently moving on dry land to the south of them.

"There's another," said John.

"And another. That's the lot. No. There's one missing. Who is it?"

Five small boats met where the channels between the islands joined. *Wizard*, *Firefly*, the Mastodon's rowing boat, and two of the savage sailing dinghies. One, with Nancy and Daisy aboard, had not arrived.

"They've got stuck," said the Mastodon, standing in his boat and looking back.

"We got stuck three times ourselves," said Roger. "And once the Mastodon had to put on his splatchers and get out and push."

"We got stuck at least twice," said Titty.

"We got stuck a hundred times," said Bridget. "Didn't we Susan?"

"Daisy ought to have got through all right," said the Mastodon.

Dee and Don both turned their boats round to go back to the rescue. But there was no need. The top of a mast showed, moving through the marshes, and a few minutes later they saw the boat itself, being poled along by the savage Daisy on one side and an explorer with a red cap on the other.

"Hullo! What happened?"

"Stuck really hard," said Daisy. "We just had to wait for the tide. It didn't matter. There was a lot to talk about."

Both of them were smiling. It seemed to John almost as if they had been glad of the delay.

"What now?" said Roger.

"Better swop channels and go through again," said John.

Back they went, each boat taking a different channel from the one through which it had come. Already the water was higher, and this time nobody got stuck for more than a minute or two. Then back again, explorers in each boat plotting their tracks as best they could.

"Mango Islands," said Titty. "All swamp. Nowhere to land."

"There were two good landings up the creek," said Roger.

"We could land over there," said Bridget.

"Let's," said Titty. "It's a settlement. People in native costumes."

They rowed on through a bit of open water, with patches of mud still showing here and there. On one side of it was an old quay, with some native boats pulled up beside it. Behind the quay were cottages, and a field in which horses were grazing, flicking at flies with their tails. Under the quay, some men in shirt sleeves and trousers (native costume) were painting a boat. The explorers landed on a bit of gravel beside the quay, and climbed up it to have a look round from above over the Mango Islands and the channels through which they had come.

"That's where we go next," said the Mastodon, pointing across the open water to a gap in the bank on the other side. It's a canal. But the water's not quite high enough yet."

John and Titty hurried off along the high bank of a creek and found that this bit of Daddy's map needed little change, though it did not show the canal, and did not mark the native settlement. By the time they got back the water had risen another foot, and the others were already in their boats ready for the last stage.

"Come along," said the Mastodon. "Roger and I'll go first. There won't be room for two boats side by side."

Six boats, one after another, left the open water and pulled into the narrow mouth of the canal. This was the queerest bit of exploration they had yet done, but easy to put on their maps, for the canal was almost straight. They stopped when the water ended and they could go no farther, close under some old, tarred piling that had once been a staithe for barges. The water was so shallow that they had to pole the last few yards.

"We haven't been here for ages," said Daisy, as, each taking an arm, she and Nancy hoisted Bridget to dry land. "Let's go and see if the cowman's still here."

Close to the staithe were some houses with an inscription on them to say that they had been built with stones from old London Bridge. Savages and explorers wandered round them, as if in a foreign country, and came to a farmyard, where cows were being milked in a wooden cowshed.

"Come for some milk, have you?" said the cowman, and

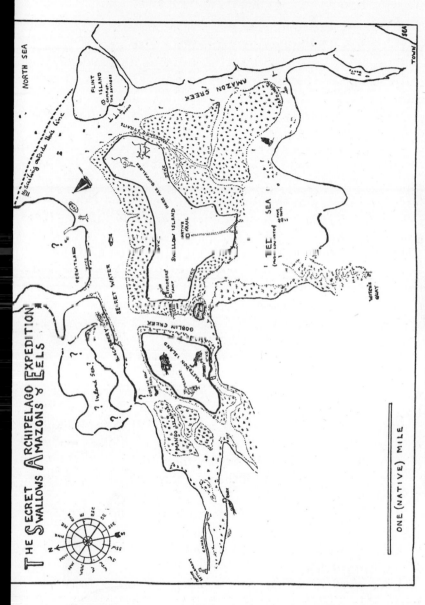

THE MAP: WITH THE UPPER WATERS AND THE MANGO ISLANDS

ONE (NATIVE) MILE

sent his son for some glasses. "I remember you ... and you ..." he said, "but you're a stranger and so are you. ..."

There were hurried whisperings among the savages, and Daisy said, "We haven't a penny among us. We don't really want any milk."

"We've got plenty," said John. "Susan's got the expedition's purse. We won't have any unless you will too."

"Of course you must have some," said Susan.

"Well, we are jolly thirsty," said Daisy. "Thank you very much."

"Drink up," said the cowman, and the seven of them took turns with the glasses, because there were only three of them among the lot.

"Loving cups," said Nancy. "Troll them round."

"I say," said Roger, as they turned to go back to their boats. "He only charged twopence a pint. That's a penny less than at home. I mean, in our own country."

"Come overseas, you have," said the cowman, laughing.

"Well, we have," said Roger.

The cowman laughed again, as if Roger had made a joke, and no one explained that Roger had been telling the exact truth. The water was still coming in when they went back to their boats.

"Hop in, Roger," said the Mastodon. "The wind's blowing straight down the canal. They'll be able to sail back, and we'll have a job to get to *Speedy* before them."

"Dee," said John. "Will there be time to look at that North West Passage?"

"No," said Dee. "Not unless we give up going to *Speedy* for supper."

"Hurry up," called the Mastodon. "Set your sails and see if you can catch us."

John gave in. First that seal and now the Mastodon's party. He badly wanted to make sure of that passage, but it would be pretty beastly to go off and take Dee with him. "We'll catch you all right," he shouted.

One after another the little sailing boats hoisted sail and blew down the canal. They shot out, to see the Mastodon, rowing hard, disappear into the channel south of the Mango Islands. They were close behind him, close enough to hear Roger encouraging him as if he were a horse, when they came out again into open water, saw Mastodon Island ahead of them and the tall trees of the heronry, and presently had to lower sails and take to oars to follow him through the winding western end of Speedy Creek.

CHAPTER XXII

THE MASTODON GIVES A PARTY

Round a bend in the channel, six boats swept in a bunch towards the ancient wreck in which the Mastodon had made his lair. Water was washing through the upright timbers, but the bows, newly tarred and painted by the Mastodon himself, looked, with the water lapping round them, as if they belonged to a barge still ready to put to sea. It was a close thing, but the Mastodon had got a fresh start while the other boats were downing sails, and he had just time to climb aboard with Roger before the rest of his visitors came alongside.

The Mastodon helped them over the rail when they had climbed the ladder much as if he was welcoming them aboard a private yacht. "Never mind about the mud," he said. "It'll wash off afterwards. No trouble at all. I always do wash down every morning. Oh well, if you do want to get it off, here's a bucket." He dropped it over the side and brought it up full of water. Those of his visitors whose feet were bare, washed the worst of the mud off. Those who had boots, followed the Mastodon's own example, got out of them, and stood them in a row in the scuppers. He was assisted as host by Roger, who showed Peggy, Susan and Bridget round the deck as if he owned the barge. "This is the windlass," said Roger. "You've seen the anchor up on the bank. This is where the mast used to be. That's the chimney. ... He's got a real stove. ... That's the way down to the cabin. ..."

"Let's go down," said the Mastodon. "It'll take a minute or two getting things ready. Thank you for bringing those mugs and plates. I'll take them down. You'll want two hands for the ladder."

Somehow or other eleven people crowded into the Mastodon's cabin. For some moments people could hardly move until the Mastodon begged them to sit down, when they found places for themselves on boxes, on his bunk, on his bench and on the floor, while the Mastodon lit his stove, put a kettle on and began to hack at a ham with a carving knife.

Susan watched him for a minute or two with increasing pain. "Do let me cut the ham," she said, when she could bear the sight no longer.

"She's a dab at it," said Roger, and the Mastodon thankfully handed over and turned to other things.

Roger was pointing out the fishing lines, the nets that were being made, the cupboards, the hooks for hanging clothes, when Nancy caught sight of the looking-glass message that had caused all the trouble, spiked on a nail on the wall.

"There it is," she cried. "There's their secret message with the words all inside out. Jolly clever. Have a look at it, Susan. It's as good as any of ours."

The Mastodon's happy smile faded from his face.

"Don," exclaimed Daisy. "It was all a mistake. You oughtn't to have kept it." She jumped up, grabbed the message, scrumpled it up and poked it into the stove. "There you are. It's gone. Peace for ever!"

The Mastodon smiled again and went on digging tins of stewed peaches out of a sack.

"Until to-morrow night!" said Nancy.

"Of course," said Daisy. "And then corroboree and human sacrifice and peace for ever and ever. We're awfully glad you people came. The tribe's never been big enough for a proper war dance. . . . And, I say, you've seen ours. Do show us how you do your messages."

"You have to know semaphore," said Nancy. "It's like

this." She took a piece of paper that had been wrapped round a loaf of bread. " 'Peace for ever,' you said. Well look here. Those are the signals for it. Now put legs on them . . . like this. . . .'

"It looks like a war dance," said Daisy.

"That's just it," said Nancy. "Nobody who saw it would think it had anything to do with peace. Look here. I'll draw you the whole alphabet. It's the arms that matter. You can make the legs do anything you like."

Susan, cutting slices of ham, took up one end of the table. John, who had collected all the maps, spread them at the other end, comparing them side by side, and sometimes putting one on the top of another and holding them up against the light that came down through the hatch. It was going to be a tremendous job, making one map out of the lot of them and getting all those channels in their right places. He borrowed a sheet of paper from the Mastodon, who was busy with a tin-opener, and began to see what he could make of it. A creek down there. Yes. Roger had done that pretty well, and then the southern channel, and the ways through the Mango Islands. . . . It would pan out all right in the end, but it was going to take time.

At first, while he worked, he hardly heard the talk that was going on around him, but later, when he came to rubbing out lines that had gone wrong in his sketch and darkening others that were there to stay, he heard sentence after sentence that showed that other people were thinking of anything but mapping. "Barbecued Billygoats. . . . I mean Great Congers. . . . It'll be the best ever." That was Nancy's voice, urging something, and he knew that the explorer in Nancy was only skin deep. That was the pirate coming through. Or had the pirate got somehow mixed up with the Eel? Oh well, it didn't matter, so long as the map got done. Then he heard Bridget: "And you have promised, haven't you? Even Susan says I'm old enough."

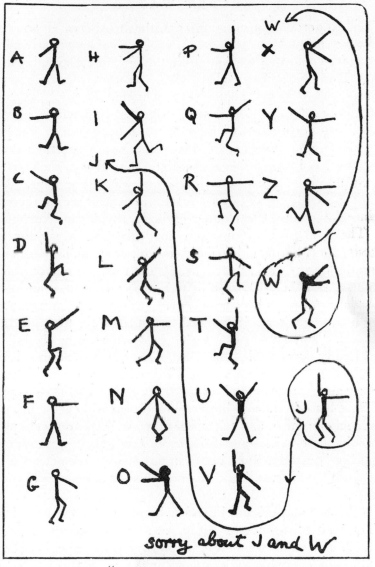

SEMAPHORE ABC. "YOU CAN MAKE THE LEGS DO ANYTHING YOU
LIKE"

Then Roger, in consultation with the brothers: "I don't see how we can make a really good one. We've used nearly all the wood we could find for boiling kettles." Then Daisy, breaking in: "Don't you worry about that. You wait till to-morrow morning." "What about your whistle, Roger?" said the Mastodon. "Oh Gosh!" said Roger. "I've left it in your boat." Roger hurried up the ladder, and presently "The Keel Row" sounded on deck, and Daisy and Nancy and then Peggy and the Eel brothers began stamping their feet in time with it.

Susan said, "Look here, John, put away those maps. We'll want the table to lay out the feast. . . . And there's no room to dance down here. Clear out, everybody, if you can't keep still."

The final preparations were made by the Mastodon and Susan alone, hardly able to hear each other speak because of the thunder on the decks overhead. There was still plenty of light outside, but the Mastodon lit the hurricane lantern and hung it from a hook. Then, with a grin at Susan, he unwrapped a big box of crackers. "Mother had got them for my birthday," he said. "But I told her it would be waste to keep them."

"Ready now," called the Mastodon, but no one heard him. "READY!" he shouted. The music of the whistle was cut off short, and musician and dancers came down to their supper.

Tea, ham, bread and butter, tinned peaches, cheese biscuits, chocolate biscuits, and cake went down well. There were paper caps in the crackers and Bridget looked well in a pink crown and the Mastodon even better in a pale blue bonnet.

"Jolly good feast," said Roger, when at last he could eat no more.

"Bridget and eel will be much better," said the Mastodon. "You wait till to-morrow night. . . . If only I catch a decent lot. . . . You won't want me for exploring to-morrow," he added. "You won't be able to do much anyway."

John looked at his map. "There isn't an awful lot left to do," he said. "The most important bit's that northern shore we didn't finish. We've got to settle whether there's a North West Passage or not round behind the Blackberry Coast. And we've got to find out if there's a North East Passage to make Peewit-land an island. And then there's the road across the Red Sea."

The Mastodon looked up at the tide-table nailed to the wall. "High water before eight," he said. "That means low water about two. No good in boats with a falling tide. All through the middle of the day there won't be any water except in the main channels. Just right for doing the Wade."

"We'll do the road while the tide's out," said John. "And we might have a go at the Northern Coast while it's coming in again. The road won't take long. Couldn't you come then, to try that gap?"

"What about the ceremonial stew?" said the Mastodon. "Eels are awful to catch. I may have to keep at it all day as soon as I've got a good lot of worms."

"And we've got to get ready for the corroboree," said Daisy, looking at Nancy.

"We shan't want guides for mapping the road," said John. "And when that's done there'll be only that northern part left. But it's the most important bit of all."

"We'll get the whole thing done," said Nancy. "But don't you start thinking of going off on a voyage to-morrow after-noon. It's waste of good savages not to be attacked by them. And if you're all away somewhere else, they'll have nobody to attack. And you can't have a decent war dance without a bit of war."

"We'll be ready for them," said John. "Four of them against seven. They won't have much of a chance."

Nancy grinned. "You wait and see. The Swallows'll be up against a horde."

The tide had begun to fall again when they went up the ladder and looked round from the deck. The explorers hurried down into their boats to get away before the water left them. Daisy and her brothers, with smaller, shallower boats, waited for a last private word or two with *Speedy's* skipper.

"It was a grand feast," Roger called out.

"Thank you very much," shouted the others.

"Three cheers for the Mastodon," shouted Roger.

"Jolly good thing we didn't have it the other night," said Nancy. "Much more fun with the cabin busting full."

They rowed away.

"Race you home," said Nancy. "Starting now with sails down."

There was frantic bustle in both boats. Yards were yanked to mast heads, tacks hauled down, rudders hurriedly shipped. Every second mattered with only such a little way to go.

"Whoever gets a foot ashore first," cried Nancy, as the two boats, almost touching, shot out into Goblin Creek.

"Our rudder's a bit stiff," said Susan, who was steering *Wizard*. "I say, Titty, are you sure you got it properly shipped?"

"Let's have another shot," said Titty. "I jammed it in in an awful hurry."

"It's sometimes wobbly and sometimes stiff," said Susan. "There's something awfully wrong with it."

"Carry on as it is," said John. "You're steering all right. We won't have a chance if we stop. Bring your weight a wee bit forward Titty. Good. We're gaining. Gosh, it's going to be pretty close."

"Wind's on our shore," said Susan. "Will you lower sail before we come in?"

"Lose if we do," said John. "Nancy won't. I've got the centreboard up. Steer for the mud just this side of the piles, and let your sheet go as you touch. Roger, are you ready to jump for it? She said 'First one ashore'."

"Aye, aye, Sir," said Roger.

The two boats headed for the shore together. Peggy was scrambling forward in *Firefly*, ready to jump.

"Look out, Nancy," called John suddenly. "Give us room. Lots of piles under water. . . ."

He was too late.

"Bring her in the other side of the hard," he shouted to Susan. "Now . . . Let go your sheet. Jump, Roger. . . . Jump. . . ."

There was a simultaneous splash, as Roger and Peggy, from opposite sides, landed in the mud on the narrow pathway, and grabbed each other to save themselves from falling.

"Dead heat," said Peggy.

"Something's happened," said Susan. "We're stuck. It's the rudder. I can't move it at all."

Everybody in *Wizard*, except Roger who was in mid air at the time, had felt a sudden jar. *Firefly* had slid easily up the mud beside the hard and come to rest. *Wizard* had stopped as if she had hit a wall, her bows still afloat.

"She's on the piles," said John. "Everybody get ashore. I'll lower sail afterwards."

They scrambled out into the water. Bridget splashed up the pathway and ran to the camp to tell Sinbad he should have his supper in a minute.

John pulled gently at the boat. She moved a little from one side to the other but not forward. John waded to her stern and felt under water.

"Rudder's caught between two of those beastly piles," he said. "I'll have it out in a minute."

"I say," said Nancy. "I'm awfully sorry. I thought you were coming in on the other side."

"Well, so we have," said John. "But some of those piles stick up a long way. . . . Look here. You hang on to her."

John got hold of the slim wooden rudder with both hands,

reaching down under water. He gave a tremendous tug and freed it.

"Fairly jammed between them," he said. "Oh gosh! Look at this."

The rudder, in the ordinary way, swung on two pintles which dropped into gudgeons. Titty, hurriedly shipping it, had slipped the upper pintle into place, but had missed the gudgeon with the lower one, so that it was no wonder that Susan had found steering difficult. And now, the upper pintle itself had been bent sideways when the rudder caught in the piles.

"We'll bend it straight again," said Nancy. But John had already tried.

"No good," he said. "They've both got to be in a dead straight line. And she's not our boat. I'll have to take it to a boat builder."

"Karabadangbaraka!"

The three Eels were passing on their way home.

"Akarabgnadabarak!" replied the explorers.

"What's happened?" said Daisy.

"Bust a rudder," said Nancy.

"Where's the nearest boatbuilder?" called John.

"Up the town creek," shouted one of the Eels. "A good one close to the Yacht Club!"

The little boats were moving fast, they too racing on their homeward way.

"Palefaces!" Daisy's voice shrilled over the water. "Hi! White Chiefs!"

"Hullo!"

"You'd better wear hats to-morrow night."

"Why?"

"And stick them on with glue."

"What for?" shouted Roger.

"To save your scalps!"

With tide and wind to help them, the savages were already nearing the mouth of Goblin Creek, and out of shouting distance, before even Roger had thought of what to say to them.

The explorers went up to their camp. John carried the damaged rudder. The iron of the pintle was too strong to be bent by either of the captains. "It's a boatbuilder's job," said John. "We've got to have it put exactly right."

"Well, there's one thing about it," said Nancy. "You were going to do the road over the Red Sea to-morrow anyway. You could just as well go on into the town. It won't really be waste of time, you haven't been there yet."

"And we can telephone," said Susan.

CHAPTER XXIII

RED SEA CROSSING: ISRAELITES

IT was a broiling hot day. The hard sharp shadow of the meal-dial was moving towards the dinner peg. Nancy's watch, hanging on the totem, said that it was getting on for twelve o'clock, when the Wade would be dry, and the explorers would be able to cross the Red Sea, survey the road, and take the damaged rudder to the town. They were all going, except for Nancy and Peggy who had been to the town before and, full of plans for the evening, had almost turned into Eels already. Everybody wanted to see what the town was like, and it was the first chance they had had of talking to Mother on the telephone. Since breakfast they had been busy on the map. Yesterday's work with the six boats, had given them a lot to do, John fitting six sketch maps into one, Titty copying and inking, and the others explaining what those squiggles meant which nobody but the one who had drawn them could understand.

The map was looking really like a map. Almost everywhere Daddy's broad pencil outlines had been rubbed out. Land and sea no longer looked the same. The huge unexplored areas had shrunk almost to nothing, except to the north of the Secret Water where, on the day that they had spent there, fear of hostile savages had made exploring almost impossible.

"It's getting on now," said Titty, lifting herself on her elbows to look at her work from a distance.

"I do believe Daddy'll say 'Not bad'," said John.

"Meaning 'Jolly good'," said Roger.

"Just those two passages to make sure of," said John. "I say, Nancy. . . . Where is she?"

There was a noise of singing. Nancy, who had wandered off to look out over the Secret Water, was coming back along the dyke and lifting up her voice in a tune that everybody knew. Everybody knew the tune, but something had happened to the words.

> "The Congers are coming, Hurrah! Hurrah! . . .
> With a tumty ti tiddley la la la . . ."

She broke off short and started again.

"She's making a song for to-night," said Peggy. "She began this morning as soon as she woke up."

John beckoned. Nancy looked over her shoulder, waved and tried another tune.

> "The mud's all a-shiver
> With fins all a-quiver.
> Big eels and little eels snaking along.
>
> "Squirming and squiggling,
> Worming and wriggling
> Answer the call of the savages' gong. . . .

"They're in sight," she said, as she came into the camp.

"It's about Peewitland," said John. "Couldn't you . . .?" He got no further.

"There they are," cried Roger. "Why aren't they sailing?" The three little boats of the savages were coming in at the mouth of Goblin Creek.

"Boats jolly low in the water," said Roger. "They've got a cargo." He set off at a run to the landing place, followed by the others.

"Karabadangbaraka!" Three joyful hails came over the water.

"Come on," said Nancy quietly. "Let them have it. All together!"

A combined roar of "Akarabgnadabarak!" came from the seven explorers.

"No wonder they aren't sailing," said Roger. "They've hardly got room for themselves. That's for the fire. I told them we hadn't much wood."

Sticks and logs and bits of broken boxes stuck up above the gunwale of each boat. Each boat was loaded as full as she could be.

"Look at that," said Nancy. "Good old Eels."

"We've been up since five," said Daisy, as she pulled in to the landing-place. "And just look at the result."

"It'll make a gorgeous fire," said Roger. "Enough to roast an ox."

"Just right to roast a sacrifice," said Daisy.

"Roast?" said Bridget rather doubtfully.

"All right, Bridgie," whispered Titty. "Human sacrifices always get rescued at the last minute."

"Has the Mastodon caught the stew?" asked Daisy.

"I saw him digging worms," said Roger. "He said low water's the time to start fishing. But I'm not going to be able to help him. We're all going to the town."

"That's all right," said Daisy. "So long as you get back in time for the Corroboree. And you'll have to because the Wade'll be covered again by four. I say, it's an awful pity about that rudder. . . ."

"The boatbuilder's close to the Yacht Club," said Dum.

"All hands to discharge cargo!" said John.

Daisy looked at Nancy, and got an answering wink.

"We'll do all that," she said. "The sooner you go the sooner you'll get back."

"The Wade must be pretty nearly dry," said Dee.

"You've all got boots," said Daisy.

It was clear that the Eels were anxious to see the explorers on their way.

"Well, I'm ready," said Susan. "Peggy's got one lot of sand-wiches, and ours are in my knapsack. I haven't made a shop-ping list. But we'll do that on the way. Can anybody think of anything we want?"

"We ate the last bit of chocolate yesterday," said Roger.

"Can't you think of anything but chocolate?" said John.

"Of course I can," said Roger. "But chocolate's jolly im-portant. All explorers have it. Scott and Nansen and Colum-bus. . . ."

"Not Columbus," said Titty. "It wasn't invented then."

"Well, I bet he'd have fairly hogged it if he'd had a chance."

"I've just got to catch Sinbad," said Bridget.

"Oh, look here, Bridget, we simply can't take him," said Susan.

"Not without sea-boots," said Roger.

"With or without," said Susan.

"But you didn't let me take him yesterday," said Bridget. "You promised I could take him next time. And we're going to be on land, not in a boat."

"Why not leave him with us?" said Daisy.

"Great Congers!" said Nancy. "We can't have him. Just remember all we've got to do."

"He's coming with me," said Bridget. "He loves walking."

"In circles," said Roger.

And then, seeing danger signals in Bridget's face, Susan gave in and said Sinbad could come if he came in a basket."

"You'll have to carry him all the way," said John. "We've got to go like hares, and we can't have Sinbad holding us up while he's chasing his tail."

"Turning us into tortoises," said Roger.

"All right, Bridgie," said Titty. "Sinbad'll cross the Red Sea in a palanquin."

The Eels, leaving their laden vessels at the landing place, came up to the camp to see the explorers start.

"Get back as quick as you can," said Nancy. "And set out your sentinels. I bet you can't stop us. And don't go thinking the whites'll have it all their own way. Six full-blooded Eels, counting Peggy and me. One awful rush and the camp'll be full of a howling horde."

"We'll be ready for you," said John. "But look here, Nancy. Do get Peewitland mapped. No need to keep in sight of the camp now. If you get ashore there you could finish it up and find out if it's an island or not, even if you can't sail round it with the tide out. Then there'll only be the North West Passage left . . . if there is one."

"Aye, aye, White Chief," said Nancy.

"You can't have the sacrifice till I come back," said Bridget.

"Don't you worry," said Nancy.

"Give her lots of those cream buns in the town," said Daisy. "The ones grown-ups won't eat because of their figures."

*

They were off, hurrying in single file along the narrow pathway on the top of the dyke. Susan had an empty knapsack on her back. They had run short of cornflakes and sugar and with all the savages coming that night there were several other things that Susan meant to get. John was carrying the damaged rudder and a bulging pocket showed that he had not forgotten his compass. Titty had brought the telescope. Both she and John had brought copies of the map. Roger was carrying Sinbad's basket, and Bridget, close behind him, was putting a hand in now and then to tickle Sinbad and to make him feel he was part of the expedition and not a mere parcel.

Already the marshes below the dyke were clear of water. Where at high tide patches of weed showed above the surface, there were now lumps of weed-covered mud, with ditches running winding this way and that among them. And beyond the marshes was a wide smooth sheet of mud. The Red Sea was sea no longer, but mud with narrow rivers winding through the middle of it.

Titty had been looking forward to the crossing of the Red Sea ever since that first day when in the morning she had seen it a muddy desert with the strange tracks and diggings of the Mastodon straggling across it, and in the afternoon had been rowed over that same desert when circumnavigating the island. At low tide she had seen the road, with its cart track, and the withies here and there to mark where it lay. At high water she had crossed that line of withies in a boat, knowing that the road lay somewhere under her keel. But she had never walked along it. The Red Sea was the very name for that strange place. Israelites and Egyptians. A tidal wave, rolling in unexpectedly from the sea just when the Israelites were half way across, would turn them suddenly into Egyptians, drowning them and their camels and baggage trains and sacred cats. Titty just glanced back at the basket Roger was carrying. Sinbad. Some people might almost think it was an omen. The sacred cat in his palanquin. And then she remembered how very different was the sheltered life of a sacred cat from the short and far from sheltered life of Sinbad, who had already had all kinds of adventures and been rescued from a chicken coop floating in the North Sea. She laughed.

"What is it?" asked John.

"I was just thinking about sacred cats," said Titty.

"What?"

"And the Egyptians. ... You know. ..." And she stopped. She remembered Bridget. No good talking to Bridget about the sea swallowing up the Egyptians, just when they were going to leave the island and walk out over the mud on that narrow road with salt water still in its ruts, and the land on the further side still so very far away.

"Go on," said Roger. "Spit it out, Titty. What made you laugh?"

"Oh nothing," said Titty. "Just thinking about sacred cats and Sinbad. He's so very different," she finished lamely.

"Just as heavy," said Roger, and Titty snatched gratefully at the change of subject.

"I'll carry him for a bit," she said. "Of course, to make his basket a real palanquin we ought to sling it from a pole, but he'd probably be seasick, swinging about."

"It's a beastly awkward basket," said Roger. "And he will move about in it, so it's his own fault when it bumps against my knee."

At the point where the road from the farm lifted over the dyke and dropped down, a narrow strip of hard gravel, to the level of the sea, John stopped, put the rudder on the ground and had a look at his compass, squinting over it first at the farm, and then at the line of the road over the mud.

"We've got that all right," he said. "The kraal bears due north from here, and the road lies just about south by west. I'll take another couple of bearings from the place with the four posts out in the middle." He scribbled the bearings on his copy of the map, and set out to follow Susan, who had not waited but was already on the way out over the mud.

"We'd better get there as soon as we can," she said as the others caught up with her.

"It doesn't take a moment just getting the bearings," said John, "and we may be in even more of a hurry on the way back."

"Before the tide comes in again," said Roger. "It'd be a jolly long way to swim."

"There isn't going to be any swimming," said Susan.

"We couldn't anyhow," said Roger. "Not with Bridget and Sinbad."

"You weren't able to swim once," said Bridget.

"He used to swim with one foot on the bottom," laughed Susan.

"I can do that," said Bridget.

"Sinbad can't," said Roger.

The road was much better than they had expected. There were deep puddles in it, left by the tide. There was a layer of soft mud over it, but never deep enough to cover their ankles. Under the mud there was good hard gravel, and it was easy walking, though they found it best not to walk too near together, because nobody could help splashing the mud about. There was nothing but mud on each side of the road and Roger, just trying whether it was hard or soft, very nearly lost a boot in it.

"Gosh!" he said as he struggled back on the hard track, with one boot muddy almost to his knee. "It wouldn't be much fun crossing in the dark."

"Oh, look here," said Susan. "You can't go into the town with one boot as filthy as that."

"It'll be all right in a minute," said Roger. "There's still water across the road just ahead. We'll have to paddle and I'll wash it all off."

"We'd better wait till it's gone down a little more," said Susan, seeing a thin ribbon of water crossing the road and joining the channels on either side.

"It's only a few inches deep," said John. "I'll go first and try."

A minute later he was splashing through. "All right," he said. "Come on. Keep in the middle of the road. It isn't up to my ankles. There's another wet bit ahead. There must be two channels, not one. Here are the posts we sailed through. We'd have found deeper water on either side of them. Half a second, Roger. Make a desk of your back. I say, Titty. Hang on to the rudder a minute."

Roger set his legs apart and steadied himself, while John made pencil notes on the map which he put between Roger's shoulders.

"Don't wriggle," he said. "East by south to the point. North half east to the kraal."

"Don't tickle with the pencil," said Roger, trying to look upwards while still being a desk. "What is it? What is it, Titty? Hawk? I can't see anything."

Titty did not answer. She did not hear him. She was standing between the four tall posts, the tops of which had been awash when they had sailed through. She was looking straight above her and seeing not hawks or larks or infinite blue sky, but a few feet of swirling water over her head and the red painted bottom and centreboard of a little boat.

Bridget wriggled a hand into the basket to stroke Sinbad. Roger pulled at Titty's elbow. "I can't see anything," he said again.

"Neither can I," said Titty, "not really." She looked back towards the island and then forward towards the distant shore. When she had crossed the Wade in the Mastodon's boat, there had been water from shore to shore and the posts had been awash, with here and there just the top of a withy swaying in the current. And now, here they were, standing in the middle of what had been a sea, with drying mud everywhere, the tall posts standing up above their heads, and the withies sticking up out of the mud like sapling trees on land.

"In a few hours it'll all be water again," said Roger slowly.

"Hurry up, John," said Susan. "We've got to get to the town and back before that. And you don't know how long they'll take to mend the rudder."

They went on. The water was only an inch deep at the second place where it crossed the road. In a few more minutes there would have been none at all. But now, in all their minds except Bridget's, there was that odd thought that presently the water would come back, meet over the road, widen and widen, till once more it stretched from the island to the main, a real sea, impassable unless in a boat. It would be hours yet before

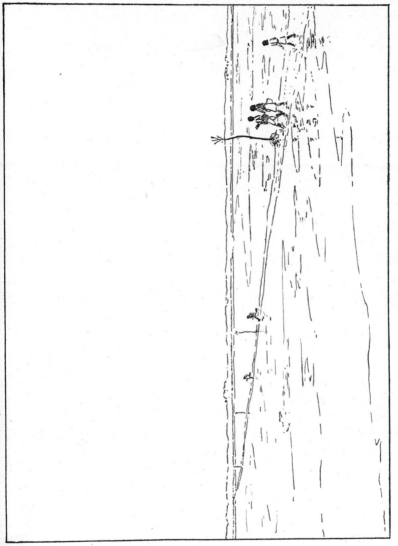

CROSSING THE WADE

that could happen, but Bridget, who was thinking of quite other things, was the only one not to feel that the sooner the crossing was over the better.

"I bet the Israelites went at a good lick," said Roger. "They would be wondering all the time how soon the water would close up again."

"I'll take Sinbad now," said Susan. "Roger, you give Bridgie a bit of start and race her to the end of the road."

"Don't let him start till I say 'When'," said Bridget, and splashed off ahead of them.

"Winning post's the top of that dyke where the road goes over," said Roger.

Bridget, far ahead, looked over her shoulder. She ran on and looked over her shoulder again.

"Now," she cried, and galloped on, splashing through puddles and thin mud. Roger was off, after her. Susan, Titty and even John, though they did not run, walked pretty fast. Of course it was all right really. The tide had still some way to fall, and would be a long time coming back again, but everybody found it very pleasant when the road rose steeply towards the land, and there was no more mud on the gravel, and the gravel turned to sand, and the sand was dry enough to stir and lift in little clouds about their feet as they joined Bridget and Roger who, after the usual dead heat, were lying in the hot sun on the top of the dyke getting back their breath. It somehow felt quite different to be on dry land again, instead of on a road that was under water for a good part of every day.

Again John took bearings, to make sure of getting the end of the road marked in the right place on his map. Susan dealt out sandwiches, and Sinbad was let out of his palanquin, to see what he thought of the new country and to get a bit of exercise.

"The mainland's quite different from any of the islands," said Titty. "More like a continent. You can see by the trees the salt water's been kept off it for ages."

Indeed, it was hard to believe that the country before them was not a thousand miles from the islands, creeks and marshes they had left behind. The bare cart track over the Red Sea turned beyond the dyke into a country lane, with high hawthorn hedges and here and there hollies, oaks and ashes meeting overhead. Away in the distance were woods and stubble fields, the thatched roofs of cottages and a line of tall telegraph posts marking the main road leading into the town. They could see motor cars flashing along it.

"Civilization," said Titty. "I don't suppose the people in the town ever dream they're so near the Secret Water and the Country of the Eels."

"What is civilization?" asked Bridget.

"Ices," said Roger, "and all that sort of thing." He looked hopefully at a cloud of thin blue smoke that, in the windless air, hung lazily above the town.

"Come on," said Susan. "We'll see if they've got any. Remember we've got to get back before the tide comes in again. Finish the sandwiches on the march. Catch that kitten Puss! Puss! Come on Sinbad. We'll get you a lick of cream."

CHAPTER XXIV

CIVILIZATION

After walking for half a mile along the lane without meeting even a cart, they came out into the busy traffic of a main road. They stopped at the corner just long enough for John to do a little compass work. The lane ran due north and south, the main road a little south of east. Daddy's map showed where the town was, down in the right hand corner, so John and Titty were able to pencil in both lane and road and to get them very nearly right. They went on, Bridget doing her best, and the others keeping pace with her. It was a longer walk than they had expected; sea-boots made hard work of it on the tarred road; and motor cars, roaring past, made them feel that even Bridget's best was very slow. Still, if you want to get anywhere you have only to keep moving, and presently fields and thatched cottages came to an end, there were houses on both sides of the road and they found themselves in the outskirts of a little seaside town.

Quite suddenly they felt that they were indeed explorers from the wilds visiting for a moment the haunts of the sedate and stay-at-home. The pavements were crowded with people dressed for a seaside holiday. Some of the younger ones carried spades and buckets. Others had model boats. Others had shrimping nets and fishing rods. Some were in bathing things, and were very sunburnt in the arms and legs, others were evidently new-comers, proper pale faces, with their skins a dismal white. But not one of them had a spot of mud. Sand? Yes. More than once they saw someone slip off a shoe and pour the sand out of it. But no mud, none at all. And the explorers, who had splashed across the Wade, were spotted with mud all over and were suddenly conscious of their muddy sea-boots. They strode sturdily on. What did it matter if these people did stare, these people with their buckets and toy boats? What did these people know of the real thing, of islands unexplored, of savages who that very night would be dancing in corroboree?

John stopped a postman and asked him the way to the Yacht Club and was told to turn left in the middle of the town.

They hurried on, looking for the signboard the postman had said they would see.

"Keep a look-out for a shop where it says you can telephone," said Susan.

They were near the middle of the town before Roger pointed to a blue and white notice hung outside a grocer's shop. It said, "You may telephone from here."

"We'll telephone to Mother right away," said Susan. "And we can do our shopping at the same time."

John pointed to a clock hanging out over the street. "Gosh," he said. "Just look at that. Nearly two o'clock. The Mastodon said the Wade's dry for about four hours. The tide'll be up to it again by four, and I don't know how long the man'll take to mend the rudder. We've got to get him started first. We'll telephone while he's doing it."

They hurried on, saw at a street corner a signboard pointing "To the Yacht Club", turned down that street, passed a pond where people were sailing toy-boats, found the Yacht Club, and two minutes later were talking to the boatbuilder.

"And when do you want it?" said the boatbuilder, looking at the rudder and fingering the bent pintle and the twisted screws that held it to the wood. "Day after to-morrow do you?"

There was a moment of horror. "We wanted to take it back with us," said John. "And we've got to get across the Wade to the island."

The man looked at an enormous watch. "I've another job on hand," he said, "and my man's away. . . ."

"I'll help," said John, "If you think I'd be any good."

The man laughed and looked at his watch again. "We'll do the best we can," he said. "What time was it when you came across? You won't have much time to spare."

It was arranged that John should stay with the boatbuilder, while Susan and the others went to the telephone.

Things began to go wrong almost at once.

To begin with, when they came into the grocer's shop, he was busy serving a customer, wrapping up parcels and talking about the weather. "Beautiful and warm for the time of year," he told her. "Hotter than in July. Good for the town now, weather like this. Brings the visitors and keeps them happy. A spell of rain would send them all away giving the town a bad name. Dependent on the weather we are here. As I always say, we ought to make the clerk of the weather a member of the town council. Then it would be up to him to do his best for us."

It was a long time before Susan caught his eye, and was able to ask the way to the telephone.

"Straight through that door, Miss," said the old grocer, and the whole four of them went through the door and found the telephone in the passage.

Then, as always happens when people are in a particular hurry, there was difficulty in getting the right number. And when at last she had got it, and Miss Powell came to the telephone and Susan asked if she could speak to Mother, the others saw her face change. "Not till three o'clock?" she said. "Don't let her go out again when she comes. We'll telephone again."

"What's happened?" said Titty.

"Daddy and Mummy aren't going to be at Miss Powell's till three o'clock. Oh dear? What time did John say we had to be back at the Wade?"

"Before four," said Roger. "And the boatbuilder said there wouldn't be much time to spare."

"Well, we'd better get the shopping done anyway," said Susan, "and then we'll go back to the boatbuilder's."

They left the telephone and went into the shop. Another customer was at the counter. They heard the old grocer talking. "Rain would send them all away giving the town a bad name. Dependent on the weather we are here. As I always say, we ought to make the clerk of the weather a member of the town council. . . ."

"I say," whispered Roger. "He's saying all the same things".

"But it's a different customer," whispered Titty.

Susan did her shopping, in a very worried manner. She had never made her list of the things she wanted and she was bothered at not finding Mother at the other end of the telephone. She bought a lot of cream buns of the kind Daisy had thought would do for fattening the human sacrifice. She bought a packet of cornflakes, a pound of lump sugar and a pound of soft sugar. She bought a tin of milk for Sinbad. She bought a tin of cocoa complete with milk ("It'll only want hot water and it'll be just the thing to have after the feast to-night.") She bought a fresh supply of chocolate and several other things, and the old grocer wrapped them up in separate parcels and began to talk.

"Beautiful and warm for the time of year, Miss. . . . Dependent on the weather we are here. As I always say . . ."

Susan, out of the corner of her eye, saw Roger bolt out of the shop.

"What's the matter with Roger?" she said.

"I'll go and see," said Titty hurriedly and followed Roger.

It was very odd that once safely outside the shop they no longer felt that they must laugh out loud or die.

Susan, with all the parcels dumped in her knapsack, came out of the shop with Bridget. They went back to the boatbuilder's and found he had already taken all the metal work off the rudder.

"John," said Susan. "Daddy and Mother aren't there. They won't be there till three o'clock. We'll have to telephone again. How much time are we going to have?"

"Not much," said John. "We'll probably have to run like hares. You know what telephoning is."

Susan looked at Bridget, who was carrying Sinbad's basket.

"We can't really do any running," she said. "You'll have to telephone and catch us up."

"There may not be time after the rudder's done," said John.

"Well, somebody must telephone," said Susan. "Mother'll be awfully disappointed if Miss Powell tells her we've been here and she doesn't have a word with any of us."

"Send the able seamen and the ship's baby on ahead," said John. "Then they won't have to hurry, and we'll bolt after them and catch them up as soon as we can."

"Aren't we going to telephone too?" said Bridget.

"You can't," said Susan. "You know what it's like running. Joggling poor old Sinbad. John and I may really have to run for all we're worth. I'll tell Mother you couldn't help it."

"They'd better start now," said John. "Go ahead. Able Seaman Titty in charge. Just get along back. It's no good risking their having to run all the way at the last minute."

"All right," said Titty. "We'll take the knapsack too. It's no bother going slow, but awful if you're in a hurry."

"What about a bit of civilization before we start?" said Roger.

"Give them an ice apiece and get them going," said John.

They had their ices near the Yacht Club and then Susan walked back into the town with them, said "Good-bye" to them under the clock by the grocer's, and sent them on their way.

"Starting now, you've got lots of time," she said. "No need to hurry. We'll probably catch you up before you get across the Wade."

*

"I think they might have let us wait to telephone," said Bridget, as they left the shops behind them.

"They couldn't," said Titty. "By the time John's got the rudder and Susan's been able to telephone they may have to run like anything."

"I'm old enough to run too," said Bridget.

"Sinbad isn't," said Titty. "And you don't want him to be joggled to death."

"If they could have sent Sinbad on alone," said Roger, "they would. But somebody has to be with him. We're not sent on because we're too young. It's so that we don't have to hurry with the ship's kitten."

"It isn't only the ship's kitten who mustn't be hurried," said Titty. "Running makes people thin in no time."

"Like Daisy," said Bridget. "I never thought of that. What about those cream buns she said I ought to eat?"

"In the knapsack," said Titty. "We'll fatten you up a bit when we get near the Red Sea."

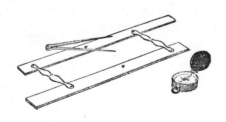

CHAPTER XXV

SINBAD'S CREEK

"No more motor cars and stink of exhaust," said Roger, as they left the main road and, no longer having to keep to the side for fear of the traffic, strolled comfortably down the middle of the green lane between high hedges that shut out the rest of the world.

There was a mew from Sinbad's basket, which, at the moment, Bridget was carrying herself.

"He wants to get out," said Bridget.

"We must get a bit further first," said Titty. "Then you can let him have a run."

"Good for him," said Bridget. "It isn't as if he had to be fattened up like me."

"Why good for him?" said Roger.

"I didn't say 'Good for him'," said Bridget. "I said 'Good *for* him.' Ship's kittens ought to have exercise."

"All right," said Titty. "He shall have a run in a minute."

They went on down the green lane, being lucky with black-berries here and there. All was well. No need to hurry now. Even if the others caught them up, they were already close to the Wade. Titty, in charge of the party, looked about for a good place to stop. She knew just what to look for . . . a place where people could properly make a halt when on the march, a place good to sit down in, a place with a bit of secrecy about it, a place where explorers resting tired limbs would not have suddenly to turn into children and get out of the way of some farm cart or other.

Roger found it. He had run on ahead to a likely looking bramble thicket. He had picked two really juicy ones for himself, good ones that dropped off as soon as he touched them, not the kind that have to be pulled and are sour even if black, and two more just as good for Bridget. He stopped short, with his mouth already open to call to her. Behind the brambles was the opening into a footpath, a footpath too narrow for carts, but with a hedge on each side of it.

"Roger's disappeared," said Bridget.

"Ahoy, Roger!" called Titty.

"Ahoy!" The voice came from behind the thicket. "Ahoy! Come on. Here's a good place for a halt. Come on. There's even a tree to sit on."

"Don't go and get scratched, Bridgie," said Titty. "Do take care. We don't want any more blood, and Susan isn't here with the iodine."

"I've only torn my dress a little," said Bridget. "Come on, Titty. It's a lovely place."

Titty worked her way through the brambles, had one look, and went back into the lane. "It'll do all right," she said. "Half a minute while I lay a patteran, so that the others'll know where we are." She took a long stick and a short one, and laid them on the ground, one across the other in the middle of the lane, with the long stick pointing towards the blackberry bush. She went back into the footpath, twisted out of the straps of the knapsack and began burrowing into it. "Oh Gosh!" she said. "The bag with those buns must be right at the bottom. They'll all be squashed."

"Better eat them," said Roger. "It's a good long time since we had dinner. And it was only sandwiches."

"Anyway, here's a tin of milk for Sinbad."

"Can't I let him out now?" said Bridget.

"All right if you're sure you can catch him again."

"He always lets me catch him," said Bridget. "He likes to be caught. Come on Sinbad. You're going to have some milk. Where's his tin. Do spike it, Roger."

Sinbad, who had been mewing impatiently, put his head out of the basket the moment it was opened. Then a paw showed, then another. After that there seemed to be no more hurry. He stepped slowly out, and stretched first his front legs, then

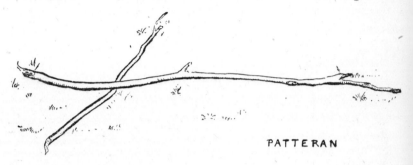

PATTERAN

his hind legs, then his furry back, as if he had never been in a hurry at all.

Roger drove the spike of his scout knife twice, at opposite sides, into the top of the little tin. He looked round. "What about a saucer?" he said.

"Shove a bit of chocolate in your mouth," said Titty. "Here you are. Go and look for a dock leaf for him, and let him lick the milk off that. Bother those buns. I'll have to unpack everything."

Roger went off with a well-stuffed mouth. Titty emptied the knapsack out on the ground. It was as she had feared. Susan must have been very bothered about the telephoning to forget that cream buns had gone in first when she dropped things like sugar, cornflakes, biscuits and chocolate on the top of them. The cream buns were in an awful state. Roger was right. It would be just as well to let him and Bridget eat what they could of them, and see if Sinbad would lick up as much of the cream as they had not been able to scrape off the inside of the paper bag. Gosh! If she'd known they were as badly squashed as this there would have been no need to open that tin of milk. Titty set aside the least damaged of the buns and let Bridget do her worst with the others. "You'll jolly well have to get the mess off your face before Susan turns up."

Bridget set earnestly to work.

"Oh look here," said Titty. "You must keep your hands off Sinbad while you're eating them. Just look at the mess in his fur."

"Sorry, Sinbad," said Bridget.

"Hullo!" Roger came into sight.

"Where's the dock leaf?" said Bridget.

"Come along," said Roger. "There's a whole lot just round the corner. And there's a creek. It's dry, but there are two boats in it, and there's an old fisherman with another boat upside down on the bank. He's putting tar on it. I asked him where the creek goes, and he says it goes into the channel by the town. We ought to put it on the map. Come along. You could have a look at it while Sinbad's hogging."

It was the mention of the map that did it. After all, Susan had said they needn't hurry, and they had come pretty fast from the town, and were quite close to the Red Sea. And if there was a creek here, it was much more important to put it on the map than just to get home early and put the kettle on the fire. And anyway, she had laid a patteran. The others would know where they were. Titty re-packed the knapsack, being careful to put the bag with the more fortunate of the buns on the top instead of at the bottom.

"Come on, Bridgie," said Roger. "You bring Sinbad. I'll take his milk."

"And you've got to carry those squashed buns somehow," said Titty.

"Inside or out?" said Roger.

"Anyhow you like," said Titty, "but leave enough for Bridgie."

"Daisy said I had to eat them," said Bridget.

"Open your mouth," said Roger, "and I'll push this one in. You'll want both hands for Sinbad."

"Mou ... fffffff ..." said Bridget.

"Don't choke her," said Titty. "That'll do. She can carry it like that." Bridget, gagged with a cream bun, and with Sinbad in her arms, twisted her head away from Roger who was afraid the bun was not far enough in, and started along the path.

"Don't go and bite it," said Roger, "or you'll lose more than half."

Titty, lugging the knapsack and Sinbad's empty basket, hurried after them. A pity she hadn't got John's compass. But of course John had never guessed she would find a new bit for the map on the way home. She stopped, dumped basket and knapsack, and pulled out of her pocket her rather crumpled copy of the map. She put a cross to mark the place where they had turned off the lane, and dotted in a bit of the footpath. Did it really lead to a creek? She picked the things up again and hurried on.

An old man in a blue fisherman's jersey was working at a boat. Roger and Bridget were already talking to him. Sinbad was on the ground licking milk from a dock leaf that made a very good saucer. As Titty came up to them she saw a narrow ditch at her feet. A duck-punt and a small boat with a mast and a bit of rag at the masthead were lying on the mud. But there was not a drop of water to be seen.

"Oh well," said Titty to herself, "Those boats didn't walk here."

The old fisherman swept his brush to and fro, spreading shining black tar on the bottom of his boat. The air was full of its pleasant smell. He dipped his brush in an old paint tin. Drops of tar fell on the ground.

"Don't put your feet in it, Sinbad," said Bridget, much as if she had been Susan talking to Roger. "Oh! He has. I was just too late to pick him up."

"Oh, Bridgie," said Titty. "He's smeared the front of your frock. And there's that tear as well."

"It would have been much worse if he'd rolled in it," said Bridget.

The old fisherman was talking to Roger, who had asked just the question that Titty was going to ask herself.

"Swim in it when the tide's up," he said.

"Where does it go to?" asked Titty.

"That join the main channel, that do," said the old man. He pointed. "If you walk along to that hedge end, you'll see the tide acoming in."

Titty considered a moment. "I'd better just go and make sure," she said. "I'll be back by the time you've finished giving Sinbad his milk."

"May I put some tar on?" asked Roger.

The old fisherman handed over his dripping brush, and began to fill his pipe. He winked at Titty. "Always glad to see someone doing a bit of work," he said. Titty smiled. Roger busy with the tar and Bridget stuffing cream buns and feeding Sinbad, were likely to stay where they were. She hurried off along the side of the ditch, to make sure of things before putting them down on her map. That hedge did not look a long way off, and it wouldn't take a minute to fill in the map if she could see the mouth of the creek from there.

Time slipped on. She could not walk fast along the slippery path above the ditch. She came to the hedge end. The ditch had widened. It really was a creek. Sinbad's Creek, it should be, because if Sinbad hadn't needed a dock leaf for a saucer it would never have been discovered. Lumpy tussocks stood up out of the mud, with belts of green weed showing how high the water would come. And there was water, creeping along the bottom of the creek, which stretched before her, widening and widening, till it came to the main channel where she could see boats lying at anchor. If only she had a compass to make sure of its direction. She looked for a bit of dry ground, sat down, and began to sketch it in on her map. It was not a very good map, she thought, as she looked at it, but it was a beginning. Even the best of explorers cannot make perfect maps at first glance. Later, perhaps, she would be able to come with John and correct it. Anyhow, there it was, Sinbad's Creek, and, looking back past the hedge end and forward to where it opened into deep water (deep, because otherwise those boats would not be lying afloat), she was sure she had got it pretty well right. And then she noticed two things. First, that those anchored boats in the distance were all pointing north. Second, that the water at her feet was fast spreading out over the mud. When she had sat down to make her map the water had hardly come so far. Now, there was quite a lot of it, and as she looked down at it, she could see little white flakes moving with it, working their way inland.

She jumped to her feet, put the map in her pocket, and hurried back.

Roger, Bridget and the old fisherman were admiring the tarred boat.

"We've finished it," said Roger.

"Find your way all right, Missie?" asked the fisherman.

"Yes, thank you," said Titty. "Come on, you two. Where's Sinbad? I've been a lot longer than I thought I would be."

"There's a short way back to the road over that field," said the fisherman.

"We're not going back to the road," said Titty. "We're going across to the island."

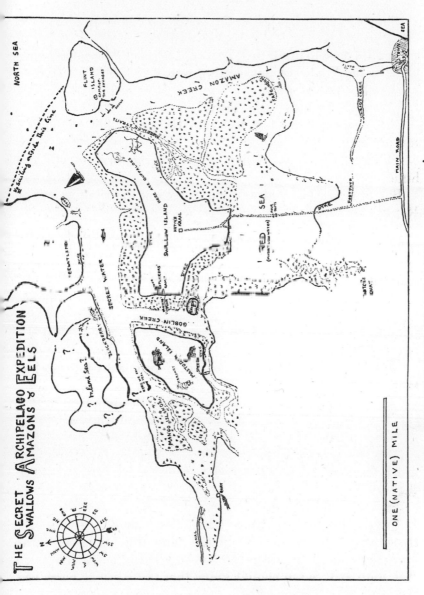

THE MAP: WITH THE ROAD TO THE TOWN AND SINBAD'S CREEK

The old man glanced at the water creeping up along the ditch.

"You'll have to jump to it, Missie," he said. " if you're going to cross the Wade without getting wet."

"Gosh!" said Roger.

"Where's Sinbad?" said Titty.

"He's somewhere close to," said Bridget. "He was here a minute ago."

"There he is," said Roger. "Skip along, Bridgie. I'll get him."

But Sinbad had no idea of hurry, except to keep just out of Roger's reach.

"Got him," said Roger at last, and bundled the mewing ship's kitten into his basket. Titty swung the knapsack on her shoulder, and started back along the narrow footpath.

"You've no time to lose," they heard the voice of the old fisherman. "That old tide come in quick, that do."

"Go it, Bridgie," cried Roger, as they caught up the ship's baby.

"He'll be seasick. I know he will if you shake him up like that."

"Can't be helped," said Titty. "Run, Bridgie, run."

They came panting out of the footpath into the lane.

"Good," said Roger. "They're not in sight yet."

"It isn't good a bit," said Titty. "We've stayed in there much too long. I say, Roger, did you kick my patteran out of the way?"

"Sorry," said Roger.

Titty's two sticks were lying just anyhow. She set them again in the middle of the lane, this time with the long one pointing down the lane towards the Red Sea, so that John and Susan should know that the advance party had gone on.

"Come on, Bridgie," she said. "Keep going. Stick to it. We may be only just in time. And if the others aren't quick they'll be too late."

"What for?" said Roger.

"Tide," said Titty. "We'll be Egyptians ourselves if we don't look out."

CHAPTER XXVI

RED SEA CROSSING: EGYPTIANS

"Stop," said Bridget. "Stop. I can't run any more."

"Only a few more yards," said Titty. "Keep going. We'll stop as soon as we're in sight of the Wade."

They came out of the lane and ran up to the top of the dyke. Before them stretched the desert of brown mud with the road running across it to the island. The road looked clear, but on either side of it, almost meeting across it, two wide tongues of water were spreading over the mud.

"The tide's come in a long way already," said Roger. "I bet the road's pretty wet where it dips in the middle. Shall I run on and make sure?"

"John knows about it," said Titty. "They're sure to be here before it's too late to cross."

Bridget sat down panting on the top of the dyke.

Titty stood beside her. Should she go on, or wait for the leaders of the expedition?

Roger went slowly down the dyke on the further side and a little way out on the road over the mud.

"What's Roger doing?" said Bridget.

"Looking for worms, probably," said Titty.

But at that moment, Roger, who was staring at something in the mud, suddenly turned. "Quick. Quick!" he shouted. "Titty! Bridget! Come on. They've crossed already."

"They can't have," said Titty, with a sudden tightening of the chest. "They can't have," she said again, as she ran down the slope. But in her heart she knew they could. How long had she been off the road, getting that creek to put on the map?

It had not seemed more than a few minutes. But minutes go fast when you are exploring. They, or at least Bridget and Roger, had never been very far from the place where the footpath turned out from the lane. They had heard nobody go by. But would there have been anything to hear? John and Susan, hurrying home, would not have been singing or even talking. They would have been just walking as fast as they could, expecting every moment to see the rest of the expedition somewhere in front of them. They must have passed the patteran without seeing it.

"Look," said Roger, pointing at the muddy road. "There are the tracks we made coming across ... all our boots going the same way. And there are theirs going back. ... Two pairs of boots. Two pairs. John's and Susan's. You can see the criss-cross pattern on the sole."

"Oh Gosh!" said Titty. "Bridget! Come on!"

Titty looked out ahead over the Red Sea of mud at those two arms of water creeping in, and the long low line of the island at the other side. The native kraal, red in the sunlight among its few green trees, looked very far away. There was no one on the island dyke. John and Susan must be already in the camp. Already they must know that Titty, Able Seaman, in command, had made a mess of things. Oh bother the ship's kitten. Oh bother Sinbad's Creek. If only they had never left the lane. If only there had been a dock leaf nearer at hand for Sinbad's milk. If only they had not come on the old fisherman. If only she had not tried to add that creek to the parts explored. If only. . . .

"They might have left us a patteran," said Roger. "Just to show they'd gone on."

"They thought we were ahead of them," said Titty. "They never saw ours."

They set out to cross once more that long road over the mud. Titty carried the knapsack, Roger the basket with the ship's kitten in it, and Bridget, the ship's baby, carried nothing at all and did not seem inclined to hurry.

Titty caught Roger's eye, looking at her doubtfully.

"We're in plenty of time," he said cheerfully, but she knew he meant it as a question.

"Lots," she said shortly, and Roger instantly slackened his pace.

"We've got to hurry just the same," she added quickly. "John and Susan must be in camp already and wondering where we are."

"They'll be jolly pleased when we show them we've got a new creek," said Roger.

"We oughtn't to have gone to look for it," said Titty. "It's my fault, but we ought to have kept to the road. Then they wouldn't have missed us."

"We wouldn't have found the creek if we had," said Roger.

"We had to stop somewhere," said Bridget. "I say, need we go so fast?"

"Remember the Eels are coming," said Titty. "And you mustn't be late, must you?"

"They'll wait for me," said Bridget. "They can sacrifice Daisy any time."

"You don't want them to have to wait?"

"No," said Bridget.

"Come on then," said Titty.

She glanced over her shoulder towards the mainland and then forward again to the low line of the island dyke at the other side of the Red Sea. The mainland already looked a long way behind them, but the island seemed hardly any nearer than it had seemed before they had started over the mud. It was going to be all right, so long as those two did not get frightened. But already there was water in those curling channels in the mud. And out in the middle of the Red Sea she could see that the water was close to the narrow brown line of the road. Away to the east where in the morning the mud had stretched almost to the opening of the Straits of Magellan there was water. Away to the west a wide river stretched to Goblin Creek. Gosh! If only they had not gone off along that footpath. If only they were more than half way across. She looked back again. Suppose they were too late and the waters met across the road, would they be able to get back to the mainland? If only she knew how fast the tide came in.

"Shall I go on ahead?" said Roger, "and signal if the water's beginning to meet?"

Titty looked at him. So the same ideas were in his mind too.

"We can easily go back if we have to," he said.

"We shan't have to," said Titty stoutly. "Go ahead if you like."

"Perhaps we'd better stick together," said Roger.

It was no good trying to go any faster. Bridget, a human sacrifice not wanting to be late for the ceremony, was doing her very best.

*

They were nearly half way across. The mainland behind them and the island before them looked equally far away. On either side of the cart track was water now instead of mud. The track was like a narrow bridge over the sea.

"The tide's a lot higher than it was when we came across," said Roger. "We'll be coming to the channel soon, where we had to splash through."

"It was only an inch or two deep," said Titty.

"Weren't there two channels?" said Roger. "We splashed through one and the other was nearly dry. Gosh! Look at it! . . ."

The road dipped before them, only a little, but even a little was enough to bring it below the level of the incoming tide. They had come to the first of the channels. For twenty or thirty yards the road was under water. It was not deep under water. Ripples over the ruts made the road still plain to see.

Titty looked back and forward and made up her mind.

"Keep along the middle where it's shallowest," she said cheerfully. "Don't splash more than you need."

"Come on, Bridget," said Roger. "We're more than half way."

He set out, with Bridget close behind him and Titty close behind Bridget. The water on the road was an inch deep round the soles of their boots. After the first few yards it rose to their ankles.

"Which channel was the deepest?" said Roger over his shoulder.

"Both about the same, I expect," said Titty. "This one's all right."

"Look out, Bridgie," said Roger. "Don't put your foot in the rut. You'll have it over the top of your boot."

Close ahead of them now were the four stout posts between which *Wizard* had sailed. There the road was still dry. It rose inch by inch out of the water, firm honest cart-track. In another few moments they would be on it. The water was already not so deep. It was well below the tops of their boots. It was lapping round their ankles. It hardly covered the road, though of course it was deeper in the ruts. Roger broke into a run, sending mud and water flying.

"Roger!" exclaimed Bridget. "You've splashed me all over."

"Never mind," said Titty. "Come on. Once we get across the next channel we'll be all right. . . ."

"I say," said Roger. "I believe the next one's the deep one. Look at it."

Beyond the place with the four posts the road dipped again and disappeared and here there were no ripples marking the ruts. The road simply went down into the water as if it ended there. Only, nearly fifty yards away, they could see where it

THE ROAD ACROSS THE RED SEA · AT HIGH AND LOW TIDE

came up once more and ran straight over the mud to the island.

"It really *is* a Wade," said Roger.

Titty looked back. They were more than half way across. If only they could wade through this bit they would be all right. "Poor old Pharaoh," said Titty to herself. Well, they would have to try it. And if it was too deep they'd just have to splash back and run for the mainland, before it was too late.

"Careful where you step," she said. "Keep on the hard part."

They went on.

"It's all right," said Roger. "It's no worse than the other bit."

He was wading on with the water just above his ankles. Bridget was close behind him, and Titty ready to give a hand to Bridget.

"Ouch!" said Roger suddenly. "Look out for that hole."

"You haven't got it into your boots?" said Titty. "Keep in the middle. Look far ahead where the road comes up again. It's no good trying to see the road at your feet with all the mud in the water."

Roger stopped, standing on one foot and prodding at the bottom with the other.

"Deeper," he said. "I'm going to take my boots off."

"Don't waste time," said Titty. "Do remember the tide's coming in."

Roger took a step forward and one leg went in over the knee.

"There," he said. "Now I've done it. Soft mud. I must be on the edge of the road."

"It's over my boots," said Bridget. She stood still and looked round at Titty.

"Never mind if it is," said Titty. "You've often got them wet before. Roger, you stay where you are. Let me feel for the way."

"I'm wet anyhow," said Roger. "And I know where the

road is now." He plunged forward and found the water well above his knees. The next moment the basket with Sinbad swung up in the air and Roger floundered, tried to keep his balance, lost it, and fell with a tremendous splash.

"Come back," cried Titty.

"Lost a boot," said Roger struggling to his feet. "It's all right. Sinbad's basket never even dipped."

Titty waded towards him and took the basket. Roger, wet from head to foot, tugged at a boot that was stuck in the mud and wholly under water. It came free with a jerk and Roger took another step and all but fell again.

"It's jolly soft," he said.

"You must be off the edge of the road," said Titty.

"Am I to come on?" asked Bridget.

"No," said Titty. "Stand still. Look here, it's hard where I am."

Roger floundered a step or two and stood beside her. "On the road now," he said. "But the water's deeper than it was."

"Of course it is," said Titty almost crossly. "Tide's coming in. Stand here a moment. Take Sinbad. I'm going to try again."

She looked far ahead at the line of withies marking the invisible road, and waded on. Good. The road was still hard beneath her feet. Just a few inches of mud but hard gravel underneath it. It must begin to get shallower quite soon. If she could only be sure herself, sure enough to tell the others to follow her and splash right through. She took another step. Water trickled cold down the inside of first one boot and then the other. And Bridget's legs were much shorter than her own. She stopped, and almost before she knew it the water was tickling her knees. She made up her mind. They could not get through. The only thing to do was to turn round, get through the splash they had already passed and race back along the road to the mainland and safety.

"Turn round, Bridget. And you, Roger. Don't hurry.

Get back. Get back to the dry place by the four posts. . . . All right, Roger. . . . I'll take Sinbad again."

"But what are we going to do?" said Bridget.

"Go back to the mainland," said Titty. "It'll be all right. We'll make a fire and get our things dry."

"But what about the feast?"

"John'll come for us as soon as he can bring the boat."

Titty glanced back towards the island. There was nobody in sight. One of the buffaloes lumbered up to the top of the dyke, stood there looking at her without interest and settled down to graze. Not a human being was about.

They waded carefully back to the bit of the road that was still dry between the shallow splash they had crossed and that other that was already too deep for them.

"Now then, run," said Titty, as soon as they were all three out of the water. "No time to lose. Tide's rising all the time, and that other place'll be deeper than it was."

"It jolly well is," said Roger a moment later. "It's over my knees already."

"You take Sinbad and the knapsack," said Titty. "And I'll carry Bridget. She handed over knapsack and basket, and stooped, soaking the edge of her skirt, while Bridget, beginning to be worried, climbed up out of the water on her back. She staggered on.

"You're a good weight," she said, cheerfully.

"That's why they said I'd be better than Daisy," said Bridget.

"It's too deep," said Roger suddenly, and Titty lost her footing, and fell, with Bridget on her back.

"Gosh!" said Roger.

"I'm wet right up to my head," said Bridget.

"No good," said Titty, struggling up. "We can't get through. We've got to get back to the posts. Keep hold of my hand, Bridgie. You can't get any wetter."

"But how'll we get ashore?" said Roger, when the three of them had struggled back to the bit of dry road.

"John and Susan'll come back as soon as they find we aren't in the camp. They'll see us and bring a boat. We've only got to wait. Empty the water out of your boots."

The bit of road with the four posts on it, in the middle of the Wade, was shorter than it had been. At each end of it was a widening channel of water. On each side of it the water stretched as far as they could see, on one side to the Magellan Straits and the passage to Cape Horn, on the other side to Goblin Creek and the island of the Mastodon. And the water was rising, rising fast. Crossing the Wade in the morning Titty in imagination had been under water, looking up at the keels of boats passing overhead. And now they were not Israelites, crossing dryshod, but Egyptians. They were trapped there in the middle of the sea. They could go neither forward nor back and must wait there, watching the narrow island of the road shrink under their feet.

What would John do if he were in command? Swim and fetch a boat? It would not be far to swim to the place where the road climbed once more out of the water. She was on the point of flinging off her clothes when she remembered that Roger and Bridget and Sinbad would be left there waiting in the middle of the sea. Then she thought of telling Roger to swim for it and bring help. But supposing there was a current. Supposing he were to be swept one way or other away from the road. Everywhere else was soft mud. And if he were to get stuck in it (and she had seen how easily that might happen) she would have to leave Bridget alone while she swam to help him. Bridget was all right now, but it would never do to leave her alone. . . .

"Do you think they'll see us soon?" said Bridget.

"Sure to," said Titty. "Give them time to get to the camp and to find we're not there." She spoke calmly, keeping the fear out of her voice as she looked along the island shore. Never had the island looked more utterly deserted. Even the buffalo had left the dyke.

"It's covered that pebble already," said Roger. "I'll put another one further back."

He scrabbled in the mud for pebbles, and laid a row of them, each one about a foot further than the last from the edge of the water. Before he had laid the last the first had disappeared.

"What are we going to do?" said Roger.

"Wait," said Titty. "We've only got to wait. And I'll serve out a ration of chocolate."

"Why not?" said Roger.

They went to the four posts, at the highest point of the road. That would be the last part to be covered. Roger hung Sinbad's basket from the top of one of the posts. Titty hung the knapsack from another, after burrowing into it for a slab of chocolate, which she broke into three equal pieces. Bridget and Roger nibbled chocolate. Titty took a bite of hers but found to her surprise she did not want it. Just for a moment she thought she was going to be sick. Why didn't somebody come up on the dyke and see them?

"It's like the Flood," said Roger. "It's a pity we haven't got an ark. I say, is it any good our yelling?"

"Too far," said Titty. "They'd never hear. But we might as well try. We'll all yell 'Ahoy' together."

Roger wasted a bit of chocolate by swallowing it.

"Now then," said Titty. "One . . . two . . . three . . ."

"AHOY," they shouted.

"Again," said Titty. "One . . . two . . . three, AHOY . . . OY . . . OY!"

In spite of all three voices, well timed and doing their best, "Ahoy" sounded very thin when shouted from the middle of that great space of water and mud.

"Ahoy," shouted Roger.

"Shut up," said Titty. "Keep a look out and yell when you see anybody. No good just shouting at nothing." A little more shouting into emptiness and she knew the others would begin to be as worried as she was herself.

Roger went along the little bit of dry road. He came back, looking grave.

"All my stones are under water," he said.

"Well, naturally," said Titty. She caught his eye, scowled at him and glanced over her shoulder at Bridget who was talking to Sinbad through his basket. If Roger knew things were pretty bad, it was no use pretending to him, but, whatever happened, they must keep Bridget cheerful.

Roger understood. There was no need to do any explaining.

"Gosh!" he said suddenly. "I wish I had my penny whistle. What about singing? Come on, Bridget. Let's have 'Hanging Johnny'. See if you've forgotten the words. . . ."

Titty wished he had chosen a livelier tune, but "Hanging Johnny" was better than nothing.

"And then I hanged my granny," sang Bridget.

"That's not the first verse," said Roger.

"Haul away, boys, haul away," sang Titty, her eyes on the distant dyke.

"I hanged her up so canny," sang Bridget.

"So Hang, boys, Hang," sang all three.

Hanging Johnny worked through his relations in the wrong order and did not explain that people said he hanged for money till the last verse. But Roger made no more complaints and the choruses went with a will, though both Roger and Titty were thinking of something else. Surely someone would appear somewhere, and the sooner the better, before Bridget realized that their tiny island of road would shrink to nothing and that they would be left in the middle of the Red Sea, the waters of which would stretch from shore to shore.

"You sing one now," said Bridget.

"What shall we do with a drunken sailor?" sang Titty. Was that John's head moving above the dyke? "What shall we do with a drunken sailor?" No, whatever it was it was gone. "What shall we do with a drunken sailor?" And no one on the mainland either? "Early in the MORNING." Well, Bridget was all right so far. Keep going. "Way, hay, up she rises. Way, hay, up she rises." Has Roger spotted someone? "Way, hay, up she rises." No. He's only looking at the shore. Gosh, I wonder if we ought to have swum for it right away. "EARLY in the MORNING." . . . Too late now.

"Go on, Titty," said Bridget. "Brasswork comes next. . . ."

"You sing it," said Titty. "We'll chorus."

"Set him polishing up the brasswork,
Set him polishing up the brasswork,
Set him polishing up the brasswork,
EARLY IN THE MORNING"

"What about a fire?" said Roger. "A good column of smoke so that nobody could help seeing."

"No firewood," said Titty. "You can't burn mud. . . . I'll tell you what though. We can unwrap the parcels and burn all the paper. . . ."

"Lucky he wrapped everything up," said Roger. "He never guessed it'd be so useful. 'What I always say is they ought to make the clerk of the weather. . . .' Good old grocer. . . ." Roger laughed again. "I bet he didn't know why I had to bolt."

"Let me light it," said Bridget.

"All right," said Titty.

"You must do it with one match," said Roger.

"If it doesn't blow out," said Bridget. "And it won't, unless you go and blow it. There's no wind really."

"There isn't much paper," said Titty, digging parcels out

of the knapsack. Look here, Bridgie. You and Roger eat the last of those cream buns. We can use their bag."

"The lump sugar's in a cardboard box," said Roger. "The sugar'll be all right without it till we get to the camp."

"The ginger biscuits are in a paper bag," said Bridget.

"Let's have it," said Titty. "And the cornflakes have got a good burnable box. And he's put paper round the tins of milk and cocoa."

"I say," whispered Roger to Titty. "Ought we to burn Sinbad's basket? There's nothing else in the way of sticks."

"Can't," said Titty. "We can't have Sinbad loose if we have to swim."

Roger looked at the widening water between them and the island shore.

"We'll manage, if we have to," said Titty quietly. "You and me with Bridget between us. Or I'll take Bridgie and you keep the basket as dry as you can."

"The ground's not very dry," said Bridget, who was busy arranging the fuel. The paper gets wet as soon as it touches it."

"All the more smoke," said Titty.

Roger pulled out his knife and attacked one of the four posts on the high bit of the Wade. He got a shaving or two. "Jolly damp," he said. "I suppose they would be, going under water every time the tide comes in. . . ." His face changed as he spoke. Titty knew that he too was thinking how deep the waters would flow over the spot where they were standing. She scowled at him furiously. "Good for you, Bridget. Here's your match. Get the paper well lit and then the cardboard. . . ."

"There's some seaweed round that other post," said Roger. "That ought to make some smoke."

"Done it with one match," said Bridget. "I knew I could. I wish Susan had seen me."

"So do I," said Titty, and glanced again at the distant dyke.

The paper flamed up, burning much too fast, but the cardboard box, torn to narrow bits, caught fire, and a column of smoke drifted up and away. Roger put the seaweed on the top. The fire nearly went out, but heartened again, with a smell of burning kelp. Roger frantically cut a few more shavings, but nobody can make a big fire with nothing to burn, and presently the paper had burnt out, and they were simply wasting matches lighting and relighting small bits of charred cardboard and trying to light wet shavings that needed drying before they would kindle. The fire was over. The smoke signal had been made. There was not a sign that anybody had seen it.

"What'll Susan say when she finds sugar and ginger-breads and cornflakes all mixed up in the knapsack?" said Bridget.

"Tell us to separate them," said Roger.

The water was lapping over into the ruts on each side of the bit of road that was still uncovered in the middle of the Red Sea. The road was getting shorter and shorter. All was covered except that bit between the two pairs of wooden posts.

"Are we going to get wet?" asked Bridget suddenly.

"You can't get wetter than you are," said Titty. "You've been in once when I fell down. Look here. Don't let the ship's kitten get frightened. You tell him they'll be coming for us in a minute."

"All right," said Bridget and went to the post on which Sinbad's basket was hanging, to give the kitten words of comfort.

Titty and Roger went to the water's edge.

"Hadn't we better swim now?" said Roger.

Titty looked towards the island. "No," she said. "Not till we can't help it. Remember what that mud's like by the shore. We've got to wait till we can land on hard ground."

"It'll be jolly deep here by then."

"I know," said Titty. "And it's all my fault. We ought to have gone right on and not stopped till we were on the island."

SIGNAL OF DISTRESS

"It was Sinbad's fault really," said Roger. "And mine a bit."

"No it wasn't," said Titty. "Why can't one of them look this way?" she added almost angrily. "Look here. We'd better take our clothes off for swimming, and make a bundle of them with Sinbad's basket on the top."

"Bridget knows how to float," said Roger. "And she'll keep still if you tell her to."

"Gosh!" said Titty. "It's the worst mess we've ever been in."

The water lapped about their feet, and they went back to the posts. The water crept over the road. The ruts were filled. The middle of the road was a thin line that disappeared. They were standing in water that stretched almost from the mainland to the island.

Roger suddenly began to struggle out of his wet shirt.

"Not yet, Roger. Not yet," said Titty.

"Signal of distress," said Roger, wringing out the water.

"There's nothing to hoist it on."

"Give me a leg up," said Roger.

"It's worth trying," said Titty.

"Whistle for a wind," said Roger. "It's too wet to wave."

Bridget obediently tried but failed. The ship's baby was beginning to lose faith in the able seamen.

"Go on, Bridgie," said Roger. "'Spanish Ladies' is an easy one. Lick your lips first."

Some noise did come from Bridget's lips, and sure enough the light wind that had just rippled the water strengthened a little, as Titty took one of Roger's feet in both hands and hoisted him up, while Roger scrambled up the post, and sat on the top of it, taking a grip of it with both legs. Over his head, one hand above the other, he held his shirt. A gust, that sent little waves lapping round the tops of Bridget's boots as she stood at the foot of the post, blew out the signal of distress and kept it flapping.

"Jolly good flag," said Roger. "It'd be better if it wasn't so beastly wet."

"Can you see anybody?" said Titty.

"The water's over my boots," said Bridget.

"Look here, Bridgie," said Titty. "You know how to float. Well, you're going to. You'll just have to lie on your back and keep still, and I'm going to swim you ashore. It's going to be as easy as easy."

"But I can't," said Bridget. "Not for as long as all that. Isn't anybody coming? You said they were coming. And what about Sinbad?"

"Roger'll take Sinbad. It'll be all right. And then we'll run and get dry, and everybody'll be awfully proud of you."

"Would Susan let me?" said Bridget.

"Of course she would. And so would John. It isn't as if you were too young."

Bridget gulped.

"There's no other way," said Titty. "I'll keep tight hold of you all the time."

"When are we going to start?" said Bridget.

"Now," said Titty.

"And Sinbad'll get wet too."

"Roger'll keep him as dry as he can."

"And what about the things in the knapsack. The sugar and the biscuits for the feast?"

"Can't be helped," said Titty. "And I don't see how we can save our seaboots. Oh yes we can. We'll tie them to one of the posts and come and get them when the tide goes down again. There's some string in the knapsack. You stay here, and I'll go and get it from the post. We won't take Sinbad's basket off his post till we're ready to start. Better get out of your clothes. . . ."

"Will we lose them too? . . ."

"AHOY!" There was a sudden yell from the human

flagstaff above their heads, and a frantic flapping of the signal of distress.

"What is it?" cried Titty, and at the same moment she saw.

"Saved," said Roger.

Far away, in the mouth of the channel leading to Goblin Creek a black speck of a boat was moving over the water.

Titty suddenly felt like laughing and crying at the same time.

"There you are, Bridgie," she said. "No swimming after all. He'll be here before the water's up to our middles."

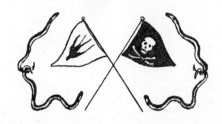

CHAPTER XXVII

RESCUE AND AFTER

"THE water's a long way above my knees," said Bridget.

Titty judged the distance to that far away boat. The water would be a good deal higher before it could reach them, and already felt swirly and strong.

"Come on, Bridgie," she said. "We'll perch you on that other post."

"Shall I let go of this one?"

"Hang on to me."

She waded across the road, stumbling at one place where she suddenly found deeper water in a rut. The water certainly was coming in very fast. But nothing mattered now. The boat was coming. Only now she let herself know how she had feared the moment when, if there had been no boat, she and Roger would have had to get somehow across that wide water, with Bridget, who did not know how to swim, and Sinbad who would for the second time in his short life have been in danger of drowning.

"Up you go."

She hoisted Bridget up to the top of the post, left her there, perched like Roger, and herself stood, waiting at the foot of it.

"What about you?" said Bridget.

"I'm all right," said Titty. "We all are."

"It was my shirt that did it," said Roger. "Hullo, it's not John. It's the Mastodon."

The water rose higher and higher, but Titty cared no longer. The boat, with the Mastodon rowing as if in a race, was coming fast towards them. Wet? They were all wet.

Roger had sprawled in mud and water. Titty had fallen down. Bridget had fallen with her. But wet clothes were nothing. Much worse things had seemed like happening. The Red Sea had closed over the road but, after all, they had not had to swim for it.

Bridget, perched on the top of her post, watched the boat and the quick flash of the Mastodon's oars. Titty too had no eyes for anything else. But Roger, now that his efforts as a flagstaff had been successful, was thoroughly enjoying himself, and was looking round to see if anyone else had noticed his signals and seen the Egyptians out in the middle of the Red Sea.

"Hullo," he shouted. "Titty! More boats!"

Three small boats were in sight coming from the other entrance to the Red Sea, from the channel between Cape Horn and the mainland. They had no sails or masts. The people in them were rowing, and rowing fast. Someone waved.

"Karabadangbaraka!" A breathless shout came from the Mastodon's boat, now quite near.

"Akarabgnadabarak!" Titty, Roger and Bridget turned round and shouted together.

In another minute the Mastodon, resting on his oars, floated up to them. He could hardly speak, he had been rowing so hard, and he looked much more worried than any of the Swallows.

"You're pretty lucky," he panted. "The tide comes in jolly fast. In another half hour you'd be swimming. What are you doing here? You might have drowned yourselves."

"Did you see the signal of distress?" said Roger.

"Lucky I did," said the Mastodon almost crossly. "I say, you know there's deep water over here at high tide."

"We didn't mean to be Egyptians," said Roger.

"All jolly well," said the Mastodon. "John and Susan must be mad to let you."

318

"They didn't know," said Titty. "It was my fault ... though I did put a patteran to show them." She took Sinbad's basket, and put it in the boat. "Come on, Bridget. Let yourself slip. I'll catch you." Standing nearly up to her waist in water, she helped Bridget down from the post and aboard.

"You get in now," said the Mastodon. "And then I'll go alongside Roger."

"Won't we be too many?" said Roger. "I'm all right. I can wait for one of the other boats. Hullo. What's happened to them?"

The people who had been doing the rowing in those far away boats had disappeared. Not a head, not a hand, showed above the gunwales. The boats were drifting like derelicts with the tide.

The Mastodon had been rowing with his back to them, and, when he came to the posts, had had eyes only for the explorers he was rescuing. He now saw the other boats for the first time.

"Gone adrift," he said.

"There were people in them rowing a minute ago," said Titty.

"There aren't now," said the Mastodon.

And then the outline of one of the boats changed. A lump, a head, showed above the gunwale. Someone was looking out.

The Mastodon laughed.

"It's all right," he said. "Come on down, Roger. Lots of room if we keep her steady."

"There's the knapsack on that other post," said Titty.

"We'll get it."

Heads and no more showed above the gunwales of the three drifting boats in the distance. The rescue of the Egyptians was being watched from afar, and the Mastodon had a broad grin on his face, as he pulled his laden boat across to the place where the road to the farm came up out of the water.

"What is it?" asked Roger.

"Are you laughing because we're so wet?" said Bridget.

"You might have been wetter," said the Mastodon, serious for a moment, and then, looking over his shoulder at those drifting boats he laughed again. Suddenly he stopped rowing, leant forward, gently prodded Bridget, and smacked his lips.

"Much plumper than Daisy," he said.

"We've been stuffing her with cream buns," said Roger.

"Good," said the Mastodon, and rowed on till the keel of the boat scrunched on hard gravel where the road came up again out of the water.

The rescued Egyptians stepped out.

"Thanks most awfully," said Titty.

"That's all right," said the Mastodon. "Better bolt to the camp as quick as you can. Your chiefs have been back ages."

"Aren't you coming?" said Roger.

"Not just yet," said the Mastodon, and rowed away towards the drifting boats.

*

"Come on," said Titty. "As fast as we can go. We'll have to change everything, and put our clothes to dry."

At a good jog trot, in soaked clothes, the water in their seaboots squelching at every step, they hurried in single file along the top of the dyke. Bridget, in front, set the pace, easing to a walk now and then, but never for long. Titty and perhaps Roger knew what a narrow escape they had had but for Bridget the adventure on the Wade was already no more than a wetting and a wetting already past. She was thinking of something else. To-night it was to be, to-night she would be taking Daisy's place, a human sacrifice, the very centre of the ceremony.

*

"Gosh! Look what they've done!" Roger was the first

to see the huge bonfire, ready for the lighting, that had been
built while they had been away.

They came into the camp, and stared about them. There
was Susan's fire, also ready for lighting, in Susan's neat fireplace, and there, below the dyke, was this colossal pile of
driftwood, and old bits of boats and sticks, and broken up
boxes and baskets, and bits of a broken barrel.

"It's a beauty," said Roger.

"What's this post for?" asked Bridget, looking at a stout
post driven firm into the ground.

Titty looked at it and then at Bridget. "Probably for you,"
she said.

"Oh," said Bridget rather doubtfully.

"More totems," said Roger.

"They must have brought theirs," said Titty. "That's
the Mastodon's. And look, they've hung a lot more shells on
ours. But where are John and Susan?"

The camp was empty but for themselves.

"They've been here," said Roger, looking into John's tent.
"Here's his map with the road to the town on it. They must
be somewhere about."

"Quick," said Titty. "Let's get our wet things off before
they come back. It won't be so bad if they find us all dry."
She squeezed out Roger's shirt which had served as a signal of
distress, wrung the last drops from it and spread it on a bush.

"Go on, Bridgie. Off with your things. Undies too. No.
Don't go all wet into Susan's tent. I won't be a minute
changing, and then I'll dig out a frock for you. You change
too, Roger."

"I'm going to get into bathing things," said Roger, "and
go down to the landing place and wash the mud off."

"Good idea," said Titty. "It's no good getting all muddy
into clean things. I'll do the same. But Bridget mustn't
bathe, and she isn't really very muddy, only wet. Here you

are, Bridgie. Here's a towel. You just rub down for all you're worth."

Titty's wet things and Roger's joined Bridget's spread to dry on the bushes. Six seaboots were stood upside down to drain. Titty and Roger, in bathing clothes, raced down to the landing place, splashed into the water, got the mud off, and splashed out again.

"I've got another lot on my feet," said Roger, as they staggered up through the mud of the saltings."

"So've I," said Titty. "Hurry up. We'll sit on the bank and dabble our legs in the pond."

"Look at Bridget," said Roger. "Going to a party. . . ."

Bridget, dry and in a clean white frock, was earnestly tying her hair ribbon. "Am I all right?" she said.

"Quite," said Titty. "Haven't you seen the others?"

"No," said Bridget. "And Sinbad's gone straight to sleep."

"Let's give a yell," said Roger.

"Ahoy!" they shouted.

There was no answer.

"Come on, Roger, let's get clean anyway," said Titty.

They paddled their feet in the pond, sitting on the bank, and were already drying themselves, when, at last, they saw John and Susan coming along the dyke to the north of the camp.

"Here they are," shouted Roger. "Hullo!"

Neither John nor Susan answered him. They came on in grim silence.

"Something's happened," said Roger as soon as he could see their faces.

John and Susan walked into the camp.

"Titty," said Susan. "Where have you been?"

"Look here," said John. "It's really rather too bad. We've been half round the island looking for you."

"We did leave a patteran," said Titty.

"Where?" said John, but did not wait for an answer. "We can't get the map finished, and it's your fault. Daddy's coming for us in the morning. Nine o'clock. I told him the map wasn't done and he said we'd have to leave it. He wants everything packed up and ready to put aboard at high tide, so as not to waste a single minute. He'd sent a message through the farmer. Didn't you see it stuck on the stick of the meal-dial?"

He held out a crumpled bit of paper, on which they read: "Your dad say he come for you at high water tomorrow. You was all away when I look for you."

"To-morrow!" gasped Titty.

"Oh Gosh!" said Roger.

"I'd got the rudder mended before three o'clock," said John, "and we got Daddy on the telephone first shot, and Susan and I raced home, and there'd have been just time for me to go and settle that North West Passage if only you'd waited in the camp instead of putting Susan in a stew and making us waste hours in looking for you. And now we can never do it. It's too late now, and the map's a failure without it."

"But we weren't in the camp," said Roger.

"Bridget!" said Susan, "Who told you to put on a clean frock?"

"The other one was wet," said Bridget, looking at the bushes, where clothes of all kinds were drying.

"Bridgie ... Oh, I say, Titty. You haven't let her fall in. ... And Roger too. And you. What on earth have you been doing?"

"We couldn't help it," said Roger. "It might have happened to anybody. It did happen to the Egyptians, only much worse."

"We got caught," said Titty. "You see...."

*

A long shrill whistle sounded from somewhere behind the dyke. Susan started, dipped into a pocket, and brought out her hand empty.

"My whistle," she exclaimed. "Nancy must have got it, or Peggy. But what were you doing to get wet all three of you?"

"Sinbad discovered a creek," said Roger. "It wasn't Titty's fault."

A curious drumming noise sounded from somewhere north of the camp. It was answered by another, like that of two sticks being rapidly beaten together, somewhere to the south.

The explorers looked about them.

The drumming noise came again from close behind the camp.

It came again as if from the landing place, and again from somewhere else.

"What's that?" said John.

And then from all directions came the noise, not deep enough for a drum, a thin quick rattle, as if half a dozen corncrakes were calling to each other. There was nothing to be seen, but the noises were coming nearer and nearer, from all sides.

The story of the Egyptians was not told until much later, for suddenly wild yells sounded close at hand, "Kara . . . Kara . . . Kara badang . . . Baraka . . . Baraka . . . Karabadang-baraka!"

Two seconds later the savages rushed the camp.

CHAPTER XXVIII

CORROBOREE

THE explorers, caught unprepared, had no time in which to make ready for defence. Nobody had expected anything quite like this. At one moment they had been standing rather miserable in the camp. Everything had gone wrong. Each one of them, except Bridget, was feeling somehow to blame and therefore ready to be cross with all the others.

And then, at that blast of Susan's whistle, blown by someone who had no right to have it, at that noise of drumming, now here, now there, now all about them, everything was changed. The savages were among them. Six of them, not four. And what savages! Feathers in their hair, bodies striped and splashed with mud for war-paint, faces patterned with mud, black bars on cheeks, rays of mud upwards from each eye, like the rays of the setting sun; Nancy had done her work well; even the Eels, who had helped her at it, had hardly known each other, when she had finished. And as for the explorers, when that howling mob rushed the camp from all sides, they stood there dithering.

But they had small time to dither. John, Captain John, the leader of the explorers, found himself hurled to the ground with two savages, striped like tigers, on the top of him. A noose was slipped over his kicking ankles and pulled tight. The rope was taken twice round the middle of him and knotted, and the two savages, leaving him trussed and helpless, rushed on to help a small and rather skinny savage who was struggling with Susan. Roger found himself lifted off his feet by a savage of enormous strength, who cried, "Eels for ever! Don't

wriggle like a lugworm. My warpaint's hardly dry." Roger
put his knees together, planted them in the stomach of the
savage and straightened out. The savage lost grip. Roger
fell, was up in a moment and away. The powerful savage dived
after him and caught him by the ankle. This time there was
no escape. The savage sat on the top of him, roped his ankles
and tied his wrists behind his back. The small and skinny
savage had been having a difficult time with Susan who stood
firmly on her feet fending off attack after attack, but three to
one was too much, and while the two savages who had made
short work of John held the struggling Susan, the small
and skinny one wound a rope about her, binding her elbows
to her sides and hobbling her legs. "Eels! Eels for ever!"
they shouted, and left her beside John and Roger, just as
two other savages, with black bodies and striped arms and
legs, brought along the captured Titty, wound round and
round with rope, one carrying her feet, the other her shoulders.

"Don't frighten Bridget!" whispered Susan urgently.

The savages laughed and ran back to join the others.

Bridget, standing in the middle of the camp, had watched
the swift defeat of the explorers. Just for one moment she had
been startled by those leaping painted creatures. Then she
had understood. She had seen John, Susan, Titty, Roger
brought to the ground and roped as prisoners.

"What about me?" she said. Susan need not have worried.

"Food . . . Food . . . Food. . . ."

The savages were closing in around her.

"Food . . . Food . . . Food. . . . Food for the Sacred Eel."

They were dancing in a circle, leaping and shouting. The
moment had come, and Bridget, in her clean white frock, stood
in the midst of a ring of jumping whirling figures. She stood
there, smiling, wondering what was going to happen next.
She began to recognize the savages. That large, long-
legged one must be Nancy. She knew the tear in the back of

PUTTING ON THE WAE-PAINT

Nancy's bathing dress. She knew the Mastodon by his stiff mop of sandy hair. Those two who had set upon John in the first attack must be Dum and Dee. She could not tell them apart any way, and certainly not when they were all over stripes of mud. And that skinny one, who danced more fierily than any of the rest, must be Daisy who would have been the human sacrifice if they had not found a better.

Bridget waited eagerly. What exactly were they going to do?

The fiery, skinny savage left the ring for a moment, dived into the long grass and was back again, dancing nearer and nearer with something in her hands. She swung it to and fro, she waved it before Bridget's eyes, darted backwards, shot forward again and suddenly flung the thing over Bridget's head. Bridget clawed at it and was relieved to find that it was only a necklace of seashells.

"Marked for the Eels," sang the skinny savage, her eyes sparkling through black rings of mud.

"Marked for the Eels," she sang and the others took up the chorus.

> "Marked for the Eels,
> A juicy dish
> To feed the wrig-
> liest of fish.'
>
> 'Marked for the Eels,
> So plump and fat
> They'll smack their lips
> To think of that."

There was a loud noise of smacking lips as the savages came nearer. Bridget, in spite of herself, drew back from them. First one finger then another prodded her plump arms. They were all round her. She moved again. Foot by foot she moved as a savage finger touched her now here now there. Suddenly she found that she was close to that big post that had been driven into the ground.

"Keep your arms down," said the skinny savage.

Another savage was busy at her feet.

They drew back. Bridget, standing against the post, was roped to it, with a rope round her middle and another round her ankles.

"Grab her and hold her," sang the Eels.

> "Grab her and hold her,
> Bind her tight.
> The noble Eels
> Feed well to-night."

The skinny savage darted away and came back with the lid of a tin. She was stirring something in it with a finger. She danced up to Bridget, one finger dripping red. Bridget felt something cold on her forehead, as the skinny savage drew a wriggling eel on it. The others danced before her, pointing at her.

*

The gloating of the Eels was violently interrupted.

Roger, from the moment he had been dumped beside the other captives, had been working to free himself. He had held his wrists as far apart as he could while that strong savage tied them. Now he was holding them close together and was working one against the other.

The rope was already a little slack. From where he lay he could see the savages closing round Bridget. He wanted to shout to her to hold out, but changed his mind in time. That would have served only to warn the savages.

He whispered to John, "I'll have this hand loose in a minute."

John, who had been better roped than anybody, tried to turn over and failed.

"What are they doing?" he whispered.

"They've got Bridgie," said Roger.

Susan struggled in her ropes.

"I'll go for them in another ten seconds," said Roger.

"Don't be a donk," said John. "What can you do against the lot? You must untie Susan and me first."

"And me," whispered Titty.

"All right," whispered Roger.

"What *are* they doing to her?" said Susan. "Singing . . ."

"They've put something round her neck," said Roger. "They're roping her to the post. They're going to sacrifice her right away. . . . I'm out . . . at least one hand is. . . . And the other. Oh gosh! He's tied my legs with a granny and it's stuck. . . ."

"Cut it."

"It's one of our ropes."

"Never mind that," said Susan. "They'll frighten her."

"Roger, in spite of the granny, got his hands free. Keeping as still as he could, for fear a savage should be looking, he freed his feet, worked himself inch by inch nearer to John, and in a moment had untied John's wrists. The savages had laid their captives side by side, and John, after he had got the stiffness out of his elbows, was busy with Susan's ropes before Roger had had time to free his feet.

"Now," said John.

"Oh look here," said Titty, "I've got one arm out."

"Keep still," said Susan, "I'll cut it. I don't care whose rope it is."

"Any of them looking?" whispered John.

"They've tied her to the post," said Roger.

"They're doing something to her face," said Titty.

"Come on," said John, leapt to his feet and charged at the savages.

"A rescue. .... A rescue," shouted Roger, bowling a savage off his feet, stumbling himself, and going head first into the arms of the strong savage who had tied him up.

"Swallows for ever," shouted Titty, and threw her arms round the skinny savage with the red paint. The lid with the paint flew out of her hands and plastered itself on Bridget's white frock.

A huge splash of red paint on her white frock, and the red mark of the eel on her forehead made Bridget look indeed as if she were being slaughtered at the stake.

"All right, Bridget," cried Susan. "It's all right. We'll cut you free. You're going to be rescued."

"Oh go AWAY," shrieked Bridget. "Go AWAY. They're just in the middle of it. I don't WANT to be rescued."

*

Just for one moment the explorers wavered. But their rally so far, had been successful. The very strong savage had had all the breath knocked out of him by Roger's head, which had hit him in the middle like a cannon ball. He was doubled up, gasping, unable to speak. The smaller savage was still on the ground. John was struggling with two savages, one of whom exclaimed, "Jibbooms and bobstays!" and hurriedly put it right, by shouting "Congers!" Susan, with two savages hanging on to her, was forcing her way towards the post to which the human sacrifice was tied.

The strong savage, recovering his breath, panted the word, "Karabadangbaraka!" The other savages echoed him.

"A rescue!" cried the explorers.

"Go AWAY," cried the human sacrifice.

"Karabadangbaraka!" shouted Nancy, and then, "You idiots, are you Eels or aren't you?"

"Akarabgnadabarak," said Titty, clinging firmly to the skinny savage who was doing her very best to get her arms free.

"Akarabgnadabarak," said John. "Go on, Susan, say it too."

"Akarabgnadabarak," said Susan.

"Akarabgnadabarak," said Roger. "I say, I'm awfully sorry I winded you."

The battle stopped. Explorers and savages, now all savages, stood breathless and panting, looking at each other.

*

"What about lighting the fire?" said Nancy. "The whole tribe's here. Eels and blood sisters . . . and brothers. Daisy lights it, of course. Go on, Mastodon, and bring the sacred stew. Roger'll give you a hand."

"It's close here," said the Mastodon. "I ferried it across before the attack. It ought to be still hot. And anyway it has to be finished in the bonfire . . . with the human bits. . . ."

"Gosh!" said Roger. "Does Bridget know?"

Daisy made a poor start at lighting the fire. Match after match went out and nothing caught. Susan watched, and then could bear it no longer. She gathered a lot of dry grass, scrumpled it up into a wad and gave it to Daisy. "Try lighting this," she said, "and then push it well into the middle. Make a hole first."

The wad of dried grass made a good fire-lighter. Daisy, a skinny, but finely striped savage, pushed it well into the bottom of the huge pile of sticks and logs. There was a sudden heartening blaze. A noise of crackling came from the pile, and little flames could be seen, leaping and climbing in the middle of the pile. There was a roar as dry sticks in the heart of the pile caught fire, and flames shot up into the rising column of smoke.

"Eels. Eels for ever! Good. Here they are!"

Roger and the Mastodon came up from the saltings with

THE EEL DANCE

a huge two handled cauldron. Daisy darted at them and lifted the lid. Inside the cauldron was a saucepan in water that was still steaming round it.

"It's been simmering for ages," said the Mastodon.

"Now for Bridget," said Daisy.

The cauldron, with its lid off, was put on the ground close to the human sacrifice.

Daisy, with a scout knife, danced up to Bridget.

"A bit from there," she said, and made to carve a slice from one of Bridget's plump arms. She danced away, lifted the lid of the stew, and dropped the invisible piece into the saucepan. With the lifting of the lid a smell of stewed eels rose into the air.

"Beauties!" said Daisy. "You've never had such a lot."

"They'll be better with some Bridget," said the Mastodon, licking his lips. He too went up to the post, carefully chose his bit, and carried it to the pot, sniffing greedily at it on his way.

Nancy was particular about hers. "No bone," she said. "Fat and juicy. A good bit for sizzling. Nice crackling to it, like pork." She picked her spot, and carved out her bit so earnestly that Bridget winced though the knife never touched her.

"Don't frighten her," said Titty.

"I'm *not* frightened," snapped Bridget.

Everybody in turn carried tasty bits from Bridget and dropped them in the stewpot. Then the cauldron was pushed, not without risk of singed eyebrows, into the edge of the bonfire, and the exulting savages, clapping their hands in time, and shouting the words of the tribe, danced round the blaze.

Bridget, tied to the stake, a gory victim, watched them for a time. The sacrifice had been made. The best bits of her were cooking in the pot with the Mastodon's eels, and she began to feel they had forgotten her.

"What happens to me now?" she said, when Titty danced near enough to her.

"Human sacrifices always get rescued at the last minute," said Titty. "Half a minute and I'll cut you free. You've got to dance the Eel dance and take part in the feast."

A moment later the human sacrifice was capering with the rest.

"That's right," said Daisy. "As eely as you can. Wriggle and leap."

"Go it, Eel-baby," said Nancy.

The water in the cauldron came on the boil again. Susan, shielding her eyes from the flames, lifted the lid with a towel.

"Nearly ready?" asked the Mastodon. "They ought to be."

Nancy hurled herself on the ground. "I'm done," she panted. "Can't dance another minute."

"They'll be satisfied," said Daisy, dropping beside her. "Not even congers could keep it up for ever."

Bridget, who had started last, found herself dancing alone.

"I say," said Susan. "We haven't got enough plates."

"Who wants them?" said Nancy. "Fingers for bits of eel and Bridget, and we'll share porridge bowls for the juice."

"We'll have enough if half of us use bowls and half plates. And some people must use forks."

"Teaspoons," said Peggy. "There are six big spoons and six little ones."

"Roger, what are you doing?" said Susan, seeing Roger diving into the stores tent.

"Getting the grog," shouted Roger. "Come on, John. I can't carry enough bottles in two hands. You take the cake, Titty. We'll come back for the ginger nuts and bananas."

*

Sitting in the glow of the great bonfire, the blood brothers and sisters of the Eels feasted and drank. Two to a mug, for

Mrs. Walker had not provided for eleven to a meal, they toasted the sacred eel.

"Deep in the Atlantic he swims," said Daisy.

"Feasting on corpses," said Titty.

"Oh I say," said Peggy.

"Don't be a mudworm," said Nancy. "All the best eels feast on corpses. They like drowned sailors best."

Peggy pushed her plate away.

Nancy glared at her. "Like us feasting on Bridget."

"But I'm a human sacrifice," said Bridget. "Not a corpse."

"Just as good," said Daisy, licking her lips. "We've never had the eels tasting better."

"It's the bits of Bridget that make the difference," said the Mastodon.

"The Mastodon's got some of our blood in him, and you've all got some of his," said Daisy. "And we're all Eels together, and these eels we're eating will make us eelier."

"And the Bridget we're eating'll make us plumper," said Roger. "Ha! I had a lovely taste of her just then. Very nutty. Go on, Peggy, have another try."

Bridget ate silently for some minutes, chewing carefully. "I can't really taste myself," she said at last. "But I haven't eaten eels before anyway, so I wouldn't know the difference."

"What are we going to do to-morrow?" said Daisy, and suddenly more than half the Children of the Eel turned back into being explorers.

"Oh Gosh!" said John. "You don't know what's happened. There isn't going to be a to-morrow. It's all over. The *Goblin*'s coming to take us off at high tide in the morning and we won't be able to get here again till next year. And I've never done the North West Passage. Thank goodness you did Peewitland to-day."

"But we didn't," said Nancy. "There simply wasn't time. There was such a lot to be got ready for the eel feast. The

bonfire took ages to build. And then we had to go to Flint
Island to get the war drums and things. And then it was time
to come and meet the Mastodon. We were going to go round
Peewit to-morrow. I say, I'm most awfully sorry."

"It can't be helped," said John. "I ought to have done
the North West Passage and I haven't. And all that part of
the map's silly if we don't know whether it's islands or not. I
ought to have made sure long ago."

"It's all my fault," said Titty. "Going and looking at
Sinbad's Creek."

"It wasn't," said Roger. "It was the Captain's fault and the
Mate's. You made a good patteran and they never saw it."

"John told me to go home, and if we'd gone he'd have had
time to go through the North West Passage, if there is one,
instead of looking for us."

"Oh well, you'd have missed being Egyptians," said Nancy.
"Barbecued Billygoats! I did wish it was me when we saw you
perched on posts in the middle of the sea."

Susan stared with horror.

"What?" said John.

"Didn't you know we'd seen?" said Nancy. "We were
sneaking round with the tide, so as to meet the Mastodon and
paint him and get ashore where you wouldn't be looking for
us, and surround the camp, and do a proper eely attack, and
then we saw them. We rowed like fun, but the Mastodon
got there first, and we were in full war-paint, so we just had to
lie down in our war canoes. . . .'

"Was it you in those boats?" said Roger. "We saw people
rowing, and then nothing but empty boats drifting along."

"But were you out in the middle of the water?" said Susan.

"Waving a signal of distress," said Roger. "If the Mastodon hadn't been jolly quick we'd have been swimming. Titty
and I had everything planned."

"Oh Titty," said Susan.

"Jibbooms and bobstays," exclaimed Nancy. "Be an Eel, Susan. Nobody got drowned. They didn't even get wet. At least not very. And it was good exploring, too. We know now what the Red Sea can do."

"We knew without that," said Susan.

"We were only just too late," said Roger. "The waters had joined in front of us, and we tried to go through and it was a bit deep, and I went off the road by mistake. . . . And then we tried to go back, and it was too deep. And we lit a fire. And I got up on a post and waved."

"What did you say about Sinbad's Creek?" said Nancy.

"I'll show you," said Titty, and she went to her tent to get the sketch map made that day.

"Get the main map too," said John.

"Cheer up, Titty," said Nancy, as they were coming back. "Nobody can really mind now it's safely over."

"It isn't that," said Titty. "But it was my fault, and now we've got to go back with the top of the map not done."

Dusk was falling, and some of the striped savages were piling more wood on the flames. Some of the wood was old planking from a broken up boat with copper nails in it, and the copper made green flames in the fire. By the flickering light, explorers and savages looked at the maps, and shared their mugs of steaming cocoa.

"That bit fits in there all right," said John. "And I say, where does that creek come out?"

The Mastodon looked at Titty's sketch. "It's all right," he said. "It comes out in the main channel, just here. . . . Can I mark it?" He felt for his pocket to get a pencil, forgetting that he was dressed in stripes of mud and a pair of bathing drawers. He took a bit of charred wood from the edge of the fire and marked the place.

"If only we hadn't got to leave the north all question marks," said John, looking away in the dusk beyond the mouth of

Goblin Creek, over the Secret Water. "If we'd done that bit it wouldn't be so bad. All the rest's pretty good."

"Couldn't we do it in the morning?" said Nancy.

John groaned. "We've got to have every single thing ready to go aboard at high tide," he said.

"It's a splendid map anyway," said Daisy.

"Couldn't we finish it for you?" said the Mastodon.

Titty listened.

"No good," said John. "Savages are all right as guides, and jolly useful, but we've got to do a thing like that ourselves. Explorers can't mark a passage unless they've been through to know it is one."

Titty prodded Roger secretly.

"Ow," said Roger.

"Sorry," said Titty, and prodded him again a moment later. This time Roger understood. Presently the two of them slipped away from the circle round the fire.

Titty talked earnestly for several minutes.

"I've got a bit of string that's long enough," said Roger when she had finished.

"Good," said Titty, "I'll get the other things."

They went back to the others, and worked their way in among savages and explorers and had another look at the map.

Dark was closing in when from far away sounded a long drawn hoot on a foghorn, followed by two others. Daisy and her brothers started up.

"Missionaries," said Daisy. "Watch."

A rocket soared into the dark sky behind the island, and burst into a shower of sparks.

"We've got to go," said Daisy. "We promised to bolt the moment they gave that signal. That was one of our rockets and we've brought one with us to show we've seen it."

She darted off and was back in a moment with a rocket on its long stick. She fitted it in the ground.

"Are you going to fire it off?" said Roger.

"Bridget is."

The human sacrifice fired the answering rocket. It hissed up into the darkness and scattered falling stars.

"Now we must bolt for it," said Daisy.

"But where are your boats?" said John.

The Mastodon was already running, surefooted even in the dark down to the landing place.

"He's got them," said Daisy. "We landed and then he towed them round and anchored them out of sight behind the little island."

"Our clothes are in one of them," said Peggy.

By the time the Eels and their blood relations had come down to the landing place, they could hear the sound of oars in the dark, and presently the Mastodon came pulling in, with the three small boats of the savages towing astern.

A minute or two later, four of the savages were rowing away, the Mastodon to his lair, the other three to the mouth of the creek.

"It's been just gorgeous," said Daisy. "And what we won't do next year. . . ."

Five explorers and two striped savages stood in the dark at the landing stage listening to the splash of oars.

"Karabadangbaraka!" the call came over the water.

"Akarabgnadabarak!" came the answer from the shore and from the Mastodon already near the mouth of his creek.

"Come on, Peggy. Wallow a bit and get the war-paint off," said Nancy. "I've got something to say to you," she whispered privately.

"Yes," said Susan. "You'll never get the mud out of your sleeping bags if you go into them like that. And look here, Bridget. You ought to be in bed already."

Nancy and Peggy, back from their wallow, dried themselves by the embers of the bonfire. "Lucky it's too dark," said Nancy, "to see the blackness of the towels. But we won't want them again. Buck up with your drying. You've got to sleep while you can."

"What are you doing in the stores tent, Titty?" said Susan. "Putting things back? That's right. But we're not going to do any washing up till morning."

"Good," said Titty.

Bridget had gone unwillingly to bed, but slept as soon as her head was on her pillow. After all, she had been an Israelite in the morning, an Egyptian in the afternoon and a human sacrifice in the evening, and that was about enough for one day.

"It just can't be helped about Peewitland and the North West Passage," said John. "Daddy'll understand. Hullo, Titty. Have you taken the maps into your tent?"

"I've got them all," said Titty. "Do you want them?"

"No," said John.

"Aren't you going to bed?" said Susan. "We've got to be up early. It'll take us all our time to get packed."

"I know," said John.

He stood for a minute or two watching the dying fire, looking into the darkness and thinking over the exploration of the week. The map was not finished. They had failed after all. Well, it couldn't be helped. The main thing now was to have everything packed and ready before the relief ship came in. He went to his tent, pulled his clothes off and settled down for the last night in camp.

*

In the tent of the Amazons, Nancy poked at Peggy. "Look here, Peg," she whispered, "if you squeak when I wake you, I'll never speak to you again."

*

There was a whisper in Roger's tent also.

"Titty." A hand reached out under the tent wall and felt about till it met another groping hand. "Have you got hold of it?"

"Yes."

"Don't go and pull too hard. I can't spare a toe."

"All right. I won't. And don't you pull too hard either."

"Is that you, Titty?" John had heard the whispering.

"Good night," said Titty.

"Good night," said John.

In the darkness of her tent Titty tied her end of Roger's bit of string tightly round her thumb. It was not too easy to tie it one-handed in the dark, and she knew before it was done why Roger had tied his end round a toe instead. But it was done at last. She gave a gentle tug. A tug, not quite so gentle, answered her. She lay down with the tied thumb outside the sleeping bag. With the other hand she reached out and felt a small pile of things beside her. Yes, she had forgotten nothing. She firmly sent herself to sleep.

CHAPTER XXIX

PACKING UP

J OHN stirred in his sleeping bag. There was sunlight on the walls of his tent. Time to get up? He pulled the bag closer round his chin. A spider at the end of an invisible thread was dangling in the doorway. It dropped a few inches. He watched it climbing again, spinning as it climbed. There was sunlight outside. Yet he woke with a queer feeling of gloom. It was like waking on the day after he had written *parvissimus* instead of *minimus* in an examination paper. Something had gone wrong. Suddenly he remembered what it was. The expedition had failed. They would be embarking that day and sailing home with the map unfinished, the North West Passage undiscovered and the North East Passage, that would make Peewitland an island, still no more than guessed at. Nancy had failed him . . . even as he thought of it he could not help smiling at the thought of what she had done instead and at the memory of the savages ringed, straked and spotted in their war-paint of mud. Titty had failed him . . . no, that was not quite fair . . . he ought to have seen her patteran. . . . Still, the result of Titty's private exploration had been that he had not had time to do what he had planned . . . and very nearly there had been a worse disaster. The skin on the back of his hands tickled with horror as he thought of those idiots letting themselves get caught by the rising tide. . . . If only they had done what they had been told to do, they would have been in the camp when he and Susan had got home and he would have been able to make a dart for the North West Passage to get that question settled before Nancy and her savages took charge. And now the map would have to be left unfinished till they came again, if ever they did come again. And it wasn't as if the unexplored bits were well away in the corners where they would be natural, almost right. There they were, bang in the middle, on the very shores of the Secret Water, spoiling everything. Islands, or mainland? . . . Who could tell? No one had had time to go and see.

Daddy would be disappointed . . . and then John remembered that Daddy, too, was under orders. He might be disappointed about the map but he would be still more disappointed if he were to come sailing in with the relief ship and find that he had been failed by John and that the explorers were not ready with tents packed, ready to go instantly aboard.

What time was it? He pushed his sleeping bag down to his knees, and kicking free from it, crawled out of his tent. Susan had taken Nancy's watch into her tent. John went to have a look at the meal-dial. The shadow had not reached the breakfast peg by several inches. He grabbed bucket, soap and towel, and had a hurried wash at the edge of the pond.

"Stuffy little beasts," he said to himself on seeing the door flaps of Roger's tent and of Titty's, hanging down instead of being tied back to let in air.

He dressed, rolled up his sleeping bag and night things, slackened the guy ropes of his tent, jerked out the tent pegs, laid the posts aside and rolled up tent and ground sheet.

Susan put her head out. "'Sh!" she said. "Bridget's still asleep."

"She'll jolly soon have to get up," said John. "*Goblin*'s coming and every single thing's got to be packed and ready. I'm just going to wake the others."

"Give them as long as you can," said Susan. "They'll only wake Bridgie. Let me get breakfast going first."

"What's the time?"

"Half past seven. Here's Nancy's watch. Hang it on the totem so it won't get forgotten."

"I'll be lighting the fire, while you're getting up. But buck up. I've left the bucket by the pond."

There was no trouble to-day in finding fuel. Charred sticks lying in the still warm ashes of the savages' bonfire were piled together over a handful of reeds in Susan's fireplace and burst instantly into a blaze.

Bridget put her head out. "Isn't it time to get up?" she said.

"Good," said John. "She's awake anyhow. Take your toothbrush and come along. There's only time to slosh two buckets over you. We've got to get everything packed. Go on, Susan. Blow your whistle. Gosh! I wish we had a ship's bell. Ahoy, everybody! Wake up, Captain Nancy! Kick your mate out! Roger! Titty! Heave out, you able seamen! Show a leg!"

He stooped by the door of Titty's tent, reached in, got a good hold of the foot of her sleeping bag and hauled mightily, thinking to drag it out with Titty in it. He nearly fell, for the bag came very easily. There was nothing in it. Clinging to it with all its claws was a startled kitten, which, after one anxious moment, recovered its dignity, stood up, blinking in the sunlight, and began to stretch itself.

"Hullo!" said John. "Titty's up already. Out you come, Roger!"

There was no answer, and looking in he saw that Roger's tent was also empty.

John looked into the tent of the Amazons. Lumps in the sleeping bags showed where the explorers lay.

"Nancy!" he shouted. "Get up. We've the whole camp to pack."

There was no answer.

"Let me cold-sponge her," said Bridget, hopping round, holding up her pyjamas with one hand and squeezing a sponge in the other.

"Go ahead," said John.

"But they aren't there," said Bridget a moment later.

"Of course they are," said John.

"They aren't," said Bridget. "Look. They've just stuffed things in their bags to look as if they were."

"Bother them," said John. "This isn't April Fool's Day. But it's a good thing everybody's up. They were jolly quiet about it."

"Where are they?" said Susan.

"They'll have gone down to have a last wallow," said John.

He emptied the bucket over Bridget twice and a third time for luck and then set to work at the stores tent, slacking the guy ropes and pulling up the pegs. He saw Susan looking at a lot of bowls, and saucers still dirty from last night's eel stew.

"Oh gosh! I'd forgotten. All yesterday's washing up to do. Don't worry about cornflakes. Give them boiled eggs they can hold in their fingers. We're only just going to have time."

"All right," said Susan. "Two eggs apiece. You can eat two? Bridget? Done your teeth? Call that face washed?"

"Yes," said Bridget, "and so it is."

"Mother won't say so. You come along here and bring the bucket."

"Ow," said Bridget. "You're tearing the skin off my forehead."

"What on earth did Daisy use last night?" said Susan. "You're going to have that eel on your forehead for the rest of your life."

"Oh leave it for now," said John. "We'll get it off when we get home. But do let's have everything waiting when the ship comes in. Look here. Can I be taking down your tent? Skip to it Bridgie and pack your knapsack."

"I say," said Susan, ferreting among the stores, "who on earth mixed sugar and biscuits and cornflakes all together?" Titty had forgotten to tell her how the Egyptians had found fuel for their fire in the middle of the Red Sea. "And, what's happened to the chocolate? I'm sure we had more than two slabs left, even after the feast. And I didn't think anybody ate bananas last night."

John looked round, puzzled. "What's become of my compass?" he said.

"Oh dear," said Susan. "This is going to be as bad as packing to go to Holly Howe. Everybody always loses something at the last minute. The compass'll turn up when we get the other things packed. Let's get breakfast over. Eggs are ready. . . ." She blew a long blast on her whistle.

She was answered only by a startled curlew and a sudden stir of gulls along the saltings.

"Blow again," said Bridget.

"Ahoy! Breakfast!" shouted John. "Look here, Susan. I'll go down and chivvy them up."

*

Five minutes later he was coming back from the landing place, feeling pretty cross with everybody in the expedition except Susan and Bridget, who, at least, were where they ought to be.

"Boats gone," he said gloomily, scraping the mud off his boots against a clump of grass.

"Both boats?" said Susan.

"Yes," said John. "I bet Nancy put them up to it. The whole lot must have gone off to say 'Good-bye' to the Mastodon."

"Well, their eggs are getting cold," said Susan.

"They won't care," said John. "The Mastodon'll make them stay to breakfast, and they'll take ages over it, and, oh gosh! do look at the time. And their tents still to do, and the *Goblin* 'll be in sight before they've begun to pack."

"I think they might have invited us," said Bridget.

"They jolly well knew we wouldn't go," said John. "They know we've got to have everything packed."

"Come and eat your breakfast, anyhow," said Susan.

Susan, John, Bridget and Sinbad breakfasted almost in silence. Bridget talked to Sinbad, but not much. John and Susan kept looking, now at the things to be packed, the tents still to be dismantled, the whole camp that had somehow to be turned into packages for quick and easy stowage, and now towards the landing place, expecting every moment to see the others hurrying home.

Three small white sails showed at the mouth of the creek.

"It's the Eels," said Bridget.

A few minutes later the three savages were splashing across the saltings.

"Karabadangbaraka," they shouted.

"Akarabgnadabarak!" said the explorers.

"Where's Nancy?" said Daisy. "Where's everybody? I say, White Chief, we're awfully sorry about yesterday. I mean about there being no time to go round Peewit. We'd have gone if we'd known it was the last day. But Nancy said she thought you were going to stay a lot longer...."

"It's all right," said John as cheerfully as he could. "We'll fill that bit in next year. The bit I didn't do matters just as much. More, really."

"What about that eel on my forehead?" said Bridget. "Susan tried to scrape it off and it won't come."

Daisy looked critically at last night's work. "It's not a bad eel," she said.

"But what did you do it with?" said Susan. "Soap doesn't seem to touch it at all."

"Red paint," said Daisy. "It'll come off with a spot of turpentine. And so'll the gore on her frock. It's only a small eel. I had an awful time last summer, but that was when we

348

tried tattooing, and Dum and Dee painted eels all over me. You should have heard the missionaries afterwards."

"But where are the others?" asked Dum and Dee together, rather as if they wanted to change the subject.

"Gone to say 'Good-bye' to the Mastodon," said John. "And they jolly well ought not to have gone. Daddy'll be here in another half hour."

"I'll go and tell them to come back," said Dum.

"Here's the Mastodon," said Dee.

"Karabadangbaraka!" said the Mastodon, stamping his muddy boots.

"Akarab-gand-abarak," said Daisy.

"Gnad . . . gnad . . ." said Bridget. "I was listening to see if you'd say it."

Daisy fiercely champed her teeth. "We didn't eat enough of you last night," she said. "Nothing but chops and steaks. I never thought about taking a nice bit of tongue. Wish I had."

"What are the others hanging about for?" said John.

"Haven't seen them," said the Mastodon.

"WHAT? Then where are they? They've gone off in both boats. Nancy really is a bit too thick, and Titty and Roger ought to have more sense. We've got the whole camp to pack and they know it. And Daddy said there wouldn't be a minute to lose, and he wanted us to have the stuff all ready in the boats."

"I say," said Dum. "You know your relief ship. What colour is her sail?"

"Dark red."

"I thought it was. There's a dark red Bermuda sail coming in from the sea now. We saw her in the distance."

There was a stampede along the dyke to the point from which, looking east, they could see the open sea. Far away out there, a triangle of red sail was moving in towards the outer buoys.

"I'm pretty sure it's the *Goblin*," said John.

He looked up and down the Secret Water. Not another sail was in sight. "Every single thing's gone wrong," he said bitterly. "We've failed with the map, and now Daddy's coming for us, and nothing's ready."

"Come on," said the Mastodon. "We'll help. All hands to stow the camp."

"Wriggle, you Eels," said Daisy. "We'll have the camp stowed in two flicks of a fin."

There was a general rush back to the camp. Four savages and three explorers hurled themselves upon tents, stores and bedding. Down came Roger's tent, Titty's, and the bigger tent of the Amazons. John and Susan, packing hard, hurried from group to group to explain just how the folding had to be done, when the tents were ready to be stuffed into their bags. Susan for once had no hand in washing up. Daisy and her brothers were not, perhaps, as thorough as Susan would have liked. But there the things were, washed, and one of the Eels was giving a final wipe to the last of the mugs with the camp dishcloth. "What about all these eggs?" said Daisy. "I don't know," said Susan. "Empty the water out of the saucepan, and put them back in it. It's their own fault if they aren't here for breakfast. Bridget, do go and see if you can see them."

The Mastodon shouldered the long heavy bundle of the Amazon's tent.

"No good taking things down to the landing place till they bring the boats back," said John. "They'll only get all over mud."

"We'll put them into our own boats," said the Mastodon.

"The relief ship comes for the explorers, and the savages ferry things off in their war canoes," said Daisy.

"It'll save a lot of time," said Susan. "But I do wish they'd turn up."

To and fro, to and fro, explorers and savages staggered to

the landing place, dumped tents and bags and boxes and water cans into the boats of the savages, and splashed hurriedly back over the marshy saltings.

Bridget came running to the camp. "I can't see them anywhere," she said. "And it *is* the *Goblin*. Where's the telescope?"

"Where is it?" said John. "Has anybody seen it? And I haven't found my compass."

Nobody had seen the compass. Nobody had seen the telescope.

"Titty usually has it," said Bridget.

John and Susan looked round the place where the camp had been, at the pale places where the tents had stood, at the fireplace, where Susan's breakfast fire was smouldering out, at the big blackened ash-covered patch on which had blazed the ceremonial bonfire of the Eels. Nothing was left but the painted totem with a necklace of shells and Nancy's watch hung round the eel at the top of it and the meal-dial, the shadow of which had already left the breakfast stick behind. Everything else was packed in the boats of the savages ready to be ferried off. But what was the good of that with the explorers' boats missing and four explorers missing with them?

John was just going to pull up the long stick the shadow of which showed how time moved from meal to meal.

"Oh don't do that," said Daisy. "Do leave it for a relic."

"What about the totem?" said John.

"It's yours," said the Mastodon. "Isn't it, Daisy?"

"Of course," said Daisy. "Take it with you, and then, when you come again, you put it up and all the Eels of all the world will come wriggling to help."

John looked at Nancy's watch.

"Close on nine," he said. "Where can those idiots be?"

"Tide's slack already," said the Mastodon.

They went along the dyke to look out again.

Yes. There was the *Goblin*, the relief ship, sailing into the Secret Water. Already she had left the open sea.

"Westerly wind," said John. "She'll have to tack. That may take a little longer."

"But where *are* they?" said Susan.

Bridget was the first to see them. "Look. Look," she pointed.

"What are they doing in there?" said the Mastodon.

Almost opposite the place where they were standing, far up the wide creek that ran inland from the northern shore of the Secret Water a brown sail and a white were sailing together.

"Wave to them. Signal to them," said Susan.

John semaphored. B...U...C...K......U...P ... "I'm against the skyline all right," he said, "but they probably aren't looking."

"They're coming this way," said the Mastodon.

"Both of them," said Daisy.

"Starboard tack both of them," said Dee.

"They've simply gone off to have a last race," said Susan furiously.

"They'll never get back before the *Goblin* arrives," said John.

The relief ship was coming steadily nearer, beating to and fro across the Secret Water, now towards the north shore, now towards the island from which she was being watched by the explorers and the savages. The two small boats, sailing south down the creek had the wind on their beam, had no need to tack, and were coming at a great pace.

"They'll do it," said Daisy.

"They never will," said John, but in his heart began to hope they would.

"Which of them's ahead?" said the Mastodon. "White sail, I think."

"Brown," said Daisy.

"Jolly hard to see when they're coming straight at us," said Dum.

"Brown sail's to windward," said Dee.

"Go it, Titty," said Bridget.

"Go it, Nancy," said Daisy and then . . . "Sorry . . . Titty's all right but Nancy's more of an Eel."

BLUE PETER AT THE CROSSTREES

"They're both jolly well all wrong," said John. "Going off racing on the last morning when they know they ought to be here. But, I say, I do believe they *are* going to do it."

"Go it. Go it everybody," shouted Bridget.

"What's Daddy doing?" said Susan.

Everybody looked from the two small boats racing towards them down the creek on the further side to the relief ship steadily beating her way up the Secret Water. Someone, Daddy, was by the mast.

z

"He's sending up a flag," said John.

A small bundle climbed to the cross trees and suddenly blew out and fluttered in the wind, a dark blue flag with a white square in the middle of it.

"Gosh!" said John.

"What does it mean?" said the Mastodon.

"Blue Peter," said John. "Everybody repair on board. About to sail. He's in a frightful hurry. He's hoisted it before he's even got his anchor down."

"They're going to do it," said Daisy. "They'll be out of the creek in a moment, and then we'll see who's ahead."

"If only they get here before the *Goblin*," said John.

"Pretty good race," said the Mastodon. "Look at that."

"Go it. Go it," shouted the Eels, as the two boats left the creek, bore slightly to starboard, and came racing side by side across the Secret Water. Almost it seemed that both boats were a little uncertain in their steering for a moment, as, coming out into the open, their helmsmen saw for the first time the red sail of the relief ship which up till then had been hidden from them by the land.

354

CHAPTER XXX

NORTH WEST PASSAGE

Titty put herself firmly to sleep, but, at the same time, did her best to turn herself into an alarm clock. Sleep she must, but oversleep she must not. Roger, she knew, would sleep until she woke him. Whatever happened she must not fail to wake herself as soon as it was light. She slept for two hours and woke suddenly in the dark. How long had she been asleep? An hour, half an hour, four hours? She did not know. Too early anyhow. She tried to sleep again, but could not. Everything depended on her waking at the right moment. She lay there, fingering the string tied round her thumb, and seeing in her mind's eye that blank space at the top left-hand corner of the map where John had drawn a question mark. What was it like through that gap? Perhaps it was only a creek leading nowhere. Well, the only way to find out was to go and see, and to-morrow morning early (or was it already to-day?) was the only chance to put things right and make up for the mistakes of yesterday. She began in her mind to dot in the lines of a channel. . . . The dots were like sheep. She counted them as she put them in, lost count and, as the map was only in her mind, had to begin again at the beginning. . . . Dot . . . dot . . . dot. . . . She woke again, and found the tent a little lighter. Almost she could see the shape of it. Well, this time it was not worth while to go to sleep. She would just lie there watching the light grow, and at the right moment pull the string for Roger. She heard gulls on the saltings . . . far away.

She woke next time in a panic. Daylight was in the tent. She could see everything, even the little pile of things she had

made ready the night before. She pulled the string, and heard
a startled grunt from the next tent. Then there was silence. It
would never do if Roger were to start up with a yell and wake
the camp. She pulled again gently. Nothing happened. She
pulled again, a long steady pull. There was a sudden answering
jerk that nearly tore her thumb off. Then another. She pulled
back, three short pulls. Then the string came loose. Roger had
freed his toe. She hauled it in, crawled to the mouth of her
tent, and put her head out into the cool morning air. Roger's
tousled mop was poking from his tent door.

"Are you really going?" he said.

Titty put her finger on her lips.

"Of course," she whispered. "Don't make a row." She
crawled out of her tent and shivered. Close to Roger, she
whispered in his ear. "Put on your woolly. Bring an oilskin
to sit on. It'll be warmer when the sun comes up. And don't
make a single sound. Pretend you're one of the Eels."

"Boots?" whispered Roger.

"Wet inside," hissed Titty. "Better without. Come on.
Look out for treading on a stick by the fire. . . . 'Sh."

For one awful moment she thought she heard a sound in
one of the other tents. Whatever it had been she did not hear
it again. Silent as the very best of Eels, they crept out of the
camp, down the dyke, and through the wet grass of the saltings.
There was no fog, but a thin morning mist was rising. Silently
they waded through the mud of the landing place. Silently
Roger hauled in the *Wizard*. Silently Titty lowered into it the
knapsack with the things she had thought necessary. All but
silently Roger coiled the rope and put the anchor in the bows.
The anchor just tapped the gunwale as he put it in, and, ankle
deep in mud, the explorers looked at each other, and then back
at the tops of the tents, just showing in the mist.

"Hop in," whispered Titty. "We'll clean the mud afterwards. Don't do any splashing now."

"Shall I row?"

"Not yet."

With Roger in the stern, Titty pushed *Wizard* afloat and
sat down, gingerly getting the oars out, one at a time. A rowlock squeaked as she took the first stroke. She unshipped her
oar, took out the rowlock, dipped it in the water and put it
back. She tried another stroke. The leather of an oar, working
in the rowlock, complained. She put the oar overboard, wetted
the leather, and tried again. That was all right. With quiet
strokes, dipping her oars without a splash, she rowed away,
keeping near the bank, so that, even if anyone had been looking
from the camp, there would have been nothing to see.

Slowly, for the tide was coming in, she rowed down the
creek and out into the Secret Water. She turned west and
stopped rowing. The banks slipped by. The tide, pouring up
the Secret Water, was with them now and carried them along.
The expedition was safely on its way.

"Roger," said Titty. "You'd better have breakfast."

"I think so, too," said Roger.

"Chocolate and bananas," said Titty, digging in her knapsack.

"It'll be warmer when the sun comes up," said Roger.

"It's warmer already," said Titty.

A low bank of cloud hid the horizon. Its upper edge was
tinged with rose. Already the sun was climbing behind it.
Ripples were crossing the water to meet them. A light wind
was blowing from the west. For a minute or two they drifted
with the tide. Titty got out the compass and put it at her feet.
She laid the telescope, ready for use, on the thwart beside her.
She unfolded a copy of the map, had a good look at it, and then
looked up the Secret Water. She took a good big mouthful of
chocolate and settled to her oars.

*

She stopped rowing only when they were close to the mouth of the gap that John had wanted to explore. There she shipped her oars and began desperate work with the compass.

"The point this side of Goblin Creek bears east by south," she said firmly. "Very near that anyhow. And the herons' trees on Mastodon Island are all in a row. Bearing south. We've got them marked all right. That fixes the gap. She put a cross to show where they then were, and lines with the compass bearings on them, one leading to the distant point, and one to the old heronry.

"Can't we sail now?" said Roger. "There's enough wind and we won't have to tack."

"We'd better," said Titty. "Then you can steer and I can have the map on the middle thwart. . . . We've done jolly well so far. It would have taken much longer if we'd tried to sail before."

She hoisted the brown sail. *Wizard* began to move through the water.

"Keep in the middle as well as you can, and let the sheet go if we touch. Whatever happens we mustn't sail hard on the mud and have to waste time getting off."

"Aye, aye, Sir."

"Don't let her go too fast. Keep the sail flapping."

"Aye, aye, Sir."

"Course is north-west," said Titty, looking at the compass and scribbling on her map.

"North-west it is," said Roger.

"You mustn't try to steer by compass though," said Titty. "Just try to keep in the middle, and I'll watch the compass and note down how she heads."

"Gosh," said Roger. "We're in for it now."

The banks on either side were closing in. They had left the Secret Water and were sailing with the tide up a narrow inlet. There was mud to right of them, mud to the left. Beyond the mud were low straight-topped dykes like the one on which their camp was pitched. Ahead of them, the dykes seemed to draw together and meet.

"Don't believe it goes anywhere," said Roger.

"It must," said Titty. "Look at the way the water's moving along the edge of the mud."

"It's coming to an end. . . . Hadn't we better drop the sail and go slower."

"We're all right so far. Gosh! What was that?"

There was a sudden soft bump. Titty dropped her pencil and hauled the centreboard more than half way up. Roger let the sheet fly. Titty stabbed over the side with an oar.

"Deep enough now," she said. "That must have been a shallow patch."

They slipped slowly on, but even Titty began to think that they were sailing up a blind alley.

The banks were now very near to them. In front of them a grass covered mound seemed to close the head of the creek.

"There's no way through," said Roger. "Hadn't we better turn before running aground?"

"If there isn't, there isn't," said Titty. "Anyway all that mattered was to find out. . . . Hullo. . . ." Her voice changed. "Look there. That lump doesn't join the dykes. . . ."

"Which way? . . . Quick," cried Roger. The channel, narrow as it was, divided into two.

"Right . . . Right," said Titty. 'Starboard, I mean."

"The other looks bigger," said Roger, but already that grassy lump was to the left of them, and, cut off from the wind, they were moving up a narrow ditch. Titty poked with an oar at the muddy bank. The ditch bent to the right, as if to end under the dyke, then bent to the left, and suddenly the wind came again, they had lost the shelter of the grassy lump, and saw water stretching before them, a channel winding its way over enormous mudflats.

A duck with red beak and wide chestnut waistcoat watched them from the mound.

"Shelduck," said Roger, "or drake," and then, "I say, that other channel was all right too. It's an island. Better make sure." Without another word he swung the little boat round, and, sailing slowly against the tide, drove back through a wider ditch than the one they had come through. The grassy mound was still on their left when they came back to the place where the creek had divided.

"Good," said Titty. "Shelduck Island. . . . That's one discovery anyway. Look out. She touched then. . . ."

But she touched only for a moment as she turned, and then, with wind and tide to help her, flew back up that western channel and out into the inland sea of shining mud and rippled water.

"What do we do now?" said Roger.

"She's heading north," said Titty. "Keep on. Keep in the middle."

"In the middle of what?" said Roger, and Titty had no answer for him. The water pouring in through those two ditches, one each side of Shelduck Island, was spreading over the mud. On their right was a built up dyke. Below the dyke was mud, then the channel in which they were sailing, and then, to the left a wider stretch of mud and beyond it, far away, another dyke, guarding no doubt the meadows of the mainland, for over there trees showed on the skyline.

Suddenly the dyke on their right ended. Mudflats stretched away as far as they could see. Their channel, now as broad as a very wide river, curved round over the mud.

"Heading east," said Titty. "We're behind the land. Look. Look. There's a creek, and there's another. But they don't go through, or we'd have seen them on the other side."

There was some quick work with compass and pencil.

"It's as big as the Red Sea," said Roger. "But where's the way out?"

"There must be another way besides those two ditches," said Titty.

She pulled out the inner tube of the telescope and searched the distant shores.

"Look here," she said. "There's nothing along this side, or John would have seen it that day when you were over here, and Bridget got herself captured."

"There isn't," said Roger. "I blackberried all along."

"It must be somewhere right ahead."

"But the water's coming to an end. There's nothing but mud."

"There's water beyond it."

"But the mud's in between. I told you so. We're stuck."

Titty hauled up the centreboard. *Wizard* drove on a few feet and stuck again. Titty hurriedly lowered the sail, and Roger got a crack on the head from the yard while trying to keep it from going in the water.

"What now?" said Roger, rubbing his head.

For a moment Titty did not answer. She prodded with an oar into the soft mud. The oar stuck. Shaking it backwards and forwards she pulled it free. She was just going to prod again. Then she remembered that even if they could go no further they were not trapped. The tide would rise and float them again and they could get back by the way they had come. No. There was no need for panic.

"What about more breakfast?" she said.

"I don't mind," said Roger.

"Two bananas left," said Titty.

The sun had risen clear of the clouds, there was blue sky overhead, and the explorers ate their last rations and looked about them.

"There's one thing," said Roger. "It's a jolly lot better to be stuck in good old *Wizard* than paddling about in the middle of the Red Sea. And if there isn't a passage there isn't."

Titty looked at the low shores east and south, and then back towards Shelduck Island. "We must be half way across," she said. "And there's more water ahead."

"Mud in between," said Roger.

Titty stepped up on the bow thwart, and stood there with a foot each side of the mast, holding the mast in one hand, and the telescope in the other. It was true there was mud in front of them. It was as if they had run aground in a sort of bay. The mud stretched right and left to the low green line of the land. But straight ahead, on the other side of the mud, there was water again, another bay cutting into the mud on the opposite side. Titty watched it carefully.

"I say, Roger," she said. "Could you go up the mast? The boat's sitting firm. She won't turn over. And I'll sit in the bottom."

"Of course I can," said Roger.

"Go up then, and have a look at the water the other side of the mud."

Roger was up the mast in a minute, and hung on there looking out.

"Just water," he said.

"Isn't it nearer than it was?"

Roger watched. "Of course it is," he said at last. "Tide's rising."

"Then there must be another way out," said Titty. "Or how does the tide get at it? Where does the water come from?"

There was no answer to that. From the masthead it was easy to see that there were two sheets of water creeping towards each other over the mudflats. One was the water that had brought them so far. The other was coming to meet it.

"How soon'll they meet?" said Roger. "Look here, I can't hang on for ever, I'm coming down."

"We're going to get through," said Titty.

Inch by inch the waters came nearer to each other. The *Wizard* stirred, floated, moved on and stopped again. Titty, busy with her map, sketched in as well as she could as much of the coastline as she could see. Roger watched.

"I've been at that creek," he said. "But it doesn't go through. John hoped it did but it doesn't."

"Did he mark it on his map?"

"Yes."

"Good," said Titty. "That'll help," and she carefully took a compass bearing of the deep cleft in the coastline. "South-east," she said, drew a line and pencilled the bearing beside it.

Inch by inch the water, not deep enough to float the *Wizard*, crept on to meet the water that was spreading on the further side of the mud. The wide mudbank that had divided them shrank and shrank. It became a narrow isthmus, joining two sheets of mud. It was an isthmus no longer. The waters met across it.

"Roger," said Titty. "That's the way we'll have to go. Towards the place that other water's coming from. About North-east."

"She's moving. . . . No. Stuck again. . . . She's moving. Let's get the sail up, to blow her across as soon as she can float."

They hoisted the sail, and because the rudder was lower than the keel, they unshipped it, and made ready to steer with an oar.

"Whatever happens we mustn't smash the rudder again," said Roger.

Every few minutes the boat stopped, moved on and stopped again. Suddenly she was off, moving steadily, faster and faster.

"North-east," said Titty. "North-east. Keep her steady with an oar. I'm putting the rudder back. We're off."

"Deeper water," said Roger. "And we don't need the centreboard with the wind aft."

"We'll do it," cried Titty. "We'll do it."

Faster and faster the little boat slipped along over the smooth water. The entrance by Shelduck Island was very far away. But there was no sign yet of any other opening. On port bow and on starboard the land was coming nearer. Even Titty began to fear that the two lines of the land were all one and that they were simply running into a bay. And time was going on. If they had to turn back, would they ever be able to get home to the camp before the *Goblin* came sailing in, when everything had to be packed and ready? "Oh gosh!" said Titty to herself. "Have I gone and made a mess of things again?" And then she remembered that though now the water was all one, there had been two separate sheets of it, and though one had come in past Shelduck Island, the other must have come from somewhere else.

"Weeds ahead," cried Roger. "Lots of them."

"I know," said Titty.

"Dykes," cried Roger. "I say, Titty. . . . We'll have to turn back."

"Keep her going as she is," said Titty.

"Aye, aye, Sir. . . . As she is."

The little boat ran on. Clumps of weed were sticking up out of the water to right, to left and straight ahead. The usual dyke, built up to protect the land from flooding was coming nearer. It looked as if there could be no way through.

"There's a gap," said Titty. "Those two dykes don't join."

"We'll be aground in another minute," said Roger.

"Marshes right across," said Titty.

"Shall I turn round?"

"Yes. . . . No. . . . Wait a minute. . . . Keep her as she is. . . . I can see water on the other side."

Nearer and nearer they came to the marshes, lumps of mud

edged with green slime, with narrow trickles of water, and tall weeds. There were little openings everywhere, but no proper channel. Not one of the tiny creeks seemed to go more than a few yards into the marsh.

Roger pointed. "That one's the biggest."

"Or that one," said Titty.

There was hardly time to choose. Hummocks of slimy mud were on either side of them. The narrow ditch, one of dozens, in which they found themselves, bent to the right, then left, then right again. They felt the *Wizard* graze the mud. She touched and touched again and stuck.

"Oh gosh!" said Roger, "and there isn't even room to turn her round."

"We've got to go on," said Titty. "There's open water the other side if we can only get her across."

They stepped out of the boat and, their feet slipping and sinking in the mud, tried to lift her on.

Roger staggered across one of the hummocks to look at another winding ditch. "I say, Titty," he called. "It's still pouring in. It must be ages before high water."

"Oh gosh!" said Titty. "I only hope it is. The camp's got to be packed by high water and if we're not back before they get up they'll be in an awful stew."

"Will Daddy wait for us?" said Roger.

"We've got to be back before he comes," said Titty. For one dreadful moment she saw the marooned explorers waiting on the shore, two able seamen missing, the relief ship sailing in, and John doing his best to explain. But how could he, when he did not know where they were? And they could go neither back nor forward, but were stuck here, within sight of open water.

And then, suddenly, she saw that all these tall rank weeds growing on the marshes had rings stained on their stalks.

"Roger," she said. "All this is going to be under water. We've only got to wait."

"But have we got time?" said Roger. "Look here. Hadn't I better get to dry land, and go and signal to them for help?"

"Oh no. No." said Titty. "You'd only get stuck in the mud. And anyway, what could they do? We've just got to wait till the water rises."

"All right," said Roger. He took the telescope. "I say, there are terns over there. Diving.... Having their breakfasts."

"You've had yours," said Titty. "You're not hungry again!"

"Not exactly," said Roger, and pulled the end of his belt a little further through its buckle.

"We've only got to wait," said Titty again. "Some of those hummocks are already under water. Look here. She's in an awful mess. Let's get some of the mud off her inside."

Inch by inch the water rose. The marshes turned into a lot of tiny islands. Weeds were standing in water. Titty, looking ahead, tried to fix in her mind where the water had showed first. There it would be deepest.

The little boat stirred, stirred again, and, with the sail still set, began to slip forward.

"I'll steer just till we're through," said Titty. "You keep a look out."

The boat moved on, Titty steering to avoid the places where the weeds were thickest. It was like steering through a flooded field and trying not to hit the clumps of thistles.

Suddenly Roger shouted. "A sail! A sail! I say Titty, they've spotted we've gone and John's come to look for us."

Titty groaned. That was the very worst thing that could have happened. If John had done that then the camp would not be packed in time, and the *Goblin* would come in to find nothing ready. Everything would have gone wrong, and once again good intentions would have come to a bad end.

"It's not John," said the look out. "It's the Amazons. He's sent them instead."

LIKE STEERING THROUGH A FLOODED FIELD

"Gosh! I wish I knew what the time was," said Titty.

The weeds were fewer in the water and lower. Twice the boat had touched but had not stopped.

"We're through," shouted Roger. "We've done it. I can see our island, and the native kraal."

"Come and steer," said Titty. She looked at the compass. "South. That's good enough. You steer and I'll get it down on the chart."

The other boat was beating to meet them. Peggy was steering, Nancy flourishing a paper.

"Ahoy!" she shouted. "We've done it. Circumnavigated Peewit. So that bit's all right. John'll get his map done after all."

Titty waved her own.

"We've discovered the North West Passage," she shouted. "What time is it?"

"Don't know. Susan's got my watch. I say, you haven't been right round?"

"Yes, we have," shouted Roger. "We had breakfast before sunrise."

"We didn't have any," said Peggy.

"We didn't want any," said Nancy firmly, and then. "Look here. We'll race you home."

Roger looked at Titty. She was the better steersman and he knew it.

"Go on, Roger," said Titty. "Do the best you can. I've got to finish the map."

And so, neck and neck, the two expeditions raced down the creek towards the Secret Water.

"Did you pack your tents?" called Nancy.

"No."

"Neither did we."

"I say, Nancy," said Titty, "there's no tide. It must be high water."

"Barbecued Billygoats, don't I know?" said Nancy. "But we can't go any faster. They won't mind when they know what we've done. And anyway the *Goblin*'s not in sight...."

But just then the two boats, side by side, shot out of the creek, and there was the *Goblin*, close at hand, beating up the Secret Water with the Blue Peter already fluttering from her cross trees.

"Gosh! Oh gosh!" said Titty.

"Giminy!" said Nancy.

"There they are. All of them," said Roger. "The Eels and the Mastodon and everybody.... And the tents are gone...."

"Stick to your steering," said Titty, and with fingers that would not keep steady, drew a line on her map that was meant to be straight but was not.

CHAPTER XXXI

FAREWELL TO THE EELS

THE two small boats swept into the creek together, *Firefly* half a boat's length ahead.

"We'd have won if you'd steered," said Roger.

"Couldn't," said Titty. "You did jolly well. And the map's done . . . well, done enough to be added to the rest . . . and we're not too late, and look, look, they've loaded all the camp into the Eels' boats." She crammed pencil and indiarubber in her pocket. "It's going to be all right after all." She looked back. The *Goblin* was already coming into the creek. Mother was steering, and Daddy was on the foredeck ready to drop the anchor. She looked ahead. All the four boats of the Eels were lying afloat, loaded to the gunwale, a savage at the oars in each boat. The tents had gone. John, Susan and Bridget were down at the landing place, the water lapping about their feet at the edge of the saltings. John was furiously beckoning. Bridget had Sinbad in her arms, and at the same time was trying to flap a handkerchief to welcome the relief ship. The saucepan must have been forgotten. Susan had it in her hand.

"Saved," said Nancy, who was by the mast of *Firefly*, all ready to lower sail. "Well done, the Eels!"

"Wait till he's anchored," they heard the Mastodon say, as the boats of the savages were moving out to meet the *Goblin*. "Give him room to round up."

"Titty," shouted John from the shore. "Get your sail down quick."

"Turn her into the wind just a second, Rogie," said Titty, "and then go straight for the landing. . . . NOW."

Down came the sail. Titty hauled up the centreboard and the *Wizard* slipped on and grounded at the landing place.

"Look here, Titty," said John. "It's really rather too bad. You could have waited to go racing till we got back to Pin Mill. You knew Daddy was coming at High Tide. . . ."

"Pipe down, skipper. Pipe down." *Firefly* had slid in alongside and Nancy had hopped out. "She didn't go out to race. Neither did we. They've done the North West Passage. We've done the North East. The map's finished after all. Show him, Titty." She flourished her map in John's face. "We've only got to put them in. Peewit's an island all right. So's Blackberry. And who's late anyhow? Nobody. Barbecued Billygoats! Don't you see?"

Titty said nothing. She simply handed John her map, with all the bearings marked, the coastline sketched in, and a row of dots marking the course of the *Wizard* through the gap and across the Northern Sea.

John stared at it and then, as a long rattling noise showed that the *Goblin's* anchor was down, he saw the boats of the savages, four of them, with all the gear of the camp aboard, shoot out from the shore. Everything was ready, just as Daddy said it should be. Not a minute was being lost. And, at the very last moment, failure had been turned into success. The whole map of the Secret Archipelago would be finished after all. There was nothing left to be done but to put the last bits in and to ink and colour it at home. He couldn't speak, but grabbed Titty's hand and shook it.

"What about us?" said Nancy. There was joyful handshaking all round.

"Did you have any breakfast?" asked Susan.

"Are those eggs?" said Roger, taking the lid off Susan's saucepan and looking to see what was inside.

"Hard and cold," said Susan.

"Who cares?" said Nancy. "Deal 'em out."

371

"Be quick," said Bridget. "We're waiting for your boats. Sinbad wants to go aboard."

*

The *Goblin*, rounding into the wind, had stopped moving.

SPLASH. . . . Grrrrrrrrr. . . . The anchor chain ran out. Commander Walker made fast, hauled on the topping lift, and had time to look about him.

"Well, Mary," he said. "They're a good lot. Tents struck and all ready. But how on earth have they managed to pick up such a lot of boats?"

Four boats, deeply laden, were rowing out towards the *Goblin*. Two others were at the landing place where people were busily rolling up their sails.

"But who are these?" said Mrs. Walker. "I've counted all ours. Bridget, Susan, John, Titty, Roger and the Blackett girls. All ashore. But these . . .?"

"Friends, I suppose," said Commander Walker. "That's why our rapscallions were sailing instead of packing. I was thinking I'd have to court martial them. But it looks to me as if they'd done exactly what I told them."

The four heavily laden boats came nearer.

"Hullo!" said Commander Walker. "And who may you be?"

Daisy stopped rowing, grinned as widely as she could, and pointed first at the *Goblin*, then at the bundles that almost filled her little boat, then at the explorers ashore and then at the *Goblin* again.

She spoke.

"Eelalog orusagoon."

"Beg your pardon," said Commander Walker. "Say that again."

"Eelalog," said Daisy, pointing to herself, "Orus," pointing to the explorers at the landing place . . . "Agoon . . ."

The other three had also stopped rowing, and were looking first at Daisy, and then at Mrs. Walker.

"Savages," said Mrs. Walker.

"Of course," said Commander Walker. "Might have known." He hung a couple of fenders over the side, and pointed to them.

"Savee?" he said. "Makee fast longside. Plenty quick."

Daisy pulled her boat nearer, and gave rapid orders in an unknown tongue.

"Catchee," called Commander Walker and threw her a rope. "Hey. You. Makee fast." He threw a rope to the quietly smiling Dum, and put over two more fenders on the other side. Presently two of the savage boats were tied alongside. "Now then," said the Commander. "Quick time topside all that. Plenty quick. Bimeby chow chow." He turned to Mrs. Walker. "Lucky you thought of bringing those bulls' eyes." And then, "You. Black fellow. Strong man. Makee fast astern. Come topside. Help stowee."

It was extraordinary how well the savages understood him.

In almost less than no time, *Goblin's* cockpit was crammed with rolls of bedding, tents in bags, and what not. Her decks were covered. Down below, Daisy and her brothers were stowing things, and talking together in a language which really sounded very like English, while Captain Walker and the Mastodon hove package after package down the companion way, and Mrs. Walker was dumping things down the fore hatch, and, at the same time watching the others at the landing place.

The boats of the explorers were coming off now, sails stowed, masts lowered, and hard-boiled eggs not wasted after all.

"Hullo, John," said Daddy. "Good man. I thought you were running it a bit fine when I saw your sails as we were coming in, but I was wrong. Everything going like clock-work and not a minute wasted. Let's have your painter."

John opened his mouth to speak and shut it again. After all, everything was all right. Nothing could have been smarter than the way in which the savages had brought tents and bedding and all the gear of the expedition alongside the *Goblin* the very moment her anchor had gone down.

"Hullo, Bridget," said her Mother. "I'll take the kitten. Now then. One pull and up you come. Hullo, Susan. All well? No accidents?"

"No need to ask," said Daddy. "Look at them. . . . Well, John, how did you get on with your map? I don't suppose you've had time to do much of it."

"Done it," said John.

"What? How much of it? I thought you said yesterday there was a lot to do."

"Only two bits," said John. "Titty and Roger did one. Nancy and Peggy did the other. We'll put them in on the way home."

He unwrapped the drawing-board with the map on it. Daddy looked at it.

"You've done the whole lot? . . . Well done, indeed. Why it's a blooming masterpiece. That's Titty's work, I know. That walrus . . . seal . . . I beg your pardon . . . beats the band. And I like your buffaloes. . . ."

"It isn't all inked, of course," said Titty. "I'll finish the inking to-night and put all our tracks in properly in different dots."

"It's pretty good as it is," said Daddy. "Just have a look, Mary. But what's all this up in the corner . . . "Secret Archipelago Expedition . . . Swallows Amazons and Eels. . . . Eels?"

"That's the tribe," said Titty.

"We couldn't have done it without them," said John.

THE MAP COMPLETE

"Every single one of them's helped. We had six boats when we were doing the upper waters and the Mango Islands. . . ."

"Useful kind of savages," said Daddy looking round at them. "What's become of that bag of bulls' eyes? Pass them round. Yes. That's the kind of savage to meet. Pity they don't know English. Hey, you. Chow, Chow. Suck 'em. Bulls' eyes. Plenty sweet . . . and a bit pepperminty too."

"How did you know they were savages?" asked Titty.

"Oh we knew all right," said Commander Walker. "They look it, don't they? There's a savage look in their eyes."

"You should have seen them yesterday," said Nancy, who had brought *Firefly* close to and was waiting till there was room to come alongside.

"Hullo the Pirates," said Commander Walker. "Your Mother's meeting you in London, to scrub and holystone you ready for school."

"We've had a lovely time," said Nancy and Peggy together.

"Hullo, Roger. Not down to starvation rations yet. Lucky we were able to pick you up before the grub ran out."

Just then the wind caught Bridget's hair.

"Bridget!" cried Mother. "What have you done to yourself? What's all that red on your forehead?"

"Blood," said Bridget. "Blood. I've been a human sacrifice. It's all right. Daisy says it'll come off easily with a drop of turpentine. And nobody's said 'Hullo, Sinbad'."

"Hullo, Sinbad," said Mother and Daddy together.

Presently the two boats of the explorers, *Wizard* and *Firefly*, lay astern, ready for the long tow to Pin Mill. Everybody was aboard. The *Goblin* swarmed with thirteen people and a kitten, Daddy and Mother and the whole blood brotherhood of the tribe of the Eel. They were standing on the foredeck, sitting on the cabin-top, going below to have a look in the crammed cabin, and coming up again. The bag of bulls'

eyes passed from hand to hand and a strong smell of pepper-
mint hung about the ship.

"What on earth's that?" asked Commander Walker as
Daisy, who had been carefully looking after it, passed the totem
to John.

"It's a totem," said John.

"It's the totem of the Eels," said Daisy and then, remembering she knew no English, she went on rapidly, "Eelalog . . .
orus . . . illa . . . illa . . . belango. . . ."

"Ah, yes," said Captain Walker. "Nothing could be
clearer than that."

"But are you going to take it with you?" asked Mother.
"Somebody must have taken a lot of trouble over it."

"The Mastodon made it," said Titty.

"Jolly good work," said Commander Walker. "Who's the
Mastodon?"

The Mastodon grinned rather sheepishly.

"You should just see his hoofmarks," said Roger.

"Won't he want to keep it?" said Mother.

The Mastodon shook his head.

"Orus belango," said Daisy.

"It's ours now," said Titty. "He gave it us. We're in the
tribe too."

"We're all full of Eel's blood," said Roger.

"Properly vaccinated," said Nancy.

"I bled more than anybody," said Bridget.

"It's all right, Mother," said Susan. "We used a lot of
iodine as well."

"Well, Mary," said Daddy to Mother. "We're going to
hear some travellers' tales when we get home. We ought to
carry that thing at the masthead. Give it Bridgie's hair-ribbon
for a pennant. And where are your flags? We'll fly them from
the cross-trees, as soon as we're off and I can take down the
Blue Peter."

"Have we really got to start right away?" said Titty.

"We have. . . . I ought to have come for you yesterday, but I couldn't get down from London in time."

"Oh, I say," said Nancy. "It's a good thing you didn't."

"Why?"

There was a general silence. The rudder being mended in the town. . . . Half the expedition looking for the other half. . . . The Egyptians surrounded by water in the middle of the Red Sea. . . . The savage attack. . . . Corroboree and human sacrifice. . . . The dreadful blank spaces that would have been left on the map. . . . Everybody could think of plenty of reasons why.

"Susan," said Mother. "I don't know their language, but you can translate. . . . Will you tell them we're sorry we have to go off in such a hurry, and that we must try to meet again next holidays."

"They've got a boat," said John. "Bigger than *Goblin*."

378

"Well, if ever they come round to Shotley we'll be very glad to see them."

"Thank you very much indeed," said Daisy surprisingly.

"I thought you didn't know English."

"Oh well," said Daisy, and laughed.

"All for the shore," called Commander Walker and went to the foredeck. There were hurried good-byes all round. John and Roger ran forward to help haul on the anchor chain.

The savages tumbled into their war-canoes, and cast off. Commander Walker broke into song:

"Farewell and adieu to you noble natives,
  Adieu and farewell to you bold savagees,
    For we're under orders
    For to steer for old England,
  And we must be sailing across the wide seas."

"Karabadangbaraka!" shouted the explorers.

"It's all right. They won't tell anybody," called Titty, seeing an anxious look on the face of the Mastodon as he glanced at Daisy.

"Akarabgnadabarak!" shouted three of the savages.

"Akarab*gand*abarak!" shouted the fourth.

"Anchor's atrip," called Captain Walker. "You take the tiller, John."

John ran aft to the tiller. Captain Walker was hoisting the staysail. The *Goblin* gathered way. At her masthead was the totem of the Eels, a monstrous eel in red and blue and green, with a long white ribbon fluttering from it in the wind. Nancy and Titty had taken the flags from their staffs, and, when the Blue Peter came down, up they went, the swallow flag to one cross-tree and the skull and crossbones to the other.

There was a cheer from the four boats of the savages and an answering cheer from the *Goblin*.

Then the savages' boats were hidden by the land. The

Goblin, with *Wizard* and *Firefly*, one behind the other, towing astern, bore away down Secret Water for the open sea. She passed the cross-roads buoy. *Lapwing*, the mission ship, lay at anchor. The explorers thought they saw the missionaries waving, but they were not sure. Then the mission ship was hidden by Flint Island, and the *Goblin* was heading for her home port. A fair wind and the ebbing tide hurried her out across the sparkling bay. The explorers, crowded aboard her, looked astern and saw the islands of the Secret Archipelago merge once more into a long unbroken line on the horizon.

SUDDEN

When he rode into Sandy Bend, there was a range war in the making. So he signed on with the Circle Dot outfit and started to poke around where others had been afraid to go. He called himself James Green, but wherever men talked low over a game of monte or a bottle of whiskey, he was referred to as Sudden!

Other SUDDEN Westerns

by Oliver Strange

SUDDEN—OUTLAWED
SUDDEN
THE MARSHAL OF LAWLESS
SUDDEN PLAYS A HAND
SUDDEN—GOLDSEEKER
SUDDEN RIDES AGAIN
SUDDEN TAKES THE TRAIL
THE RANGE ROBBERS
THE LAW O' THE LARIAT

by Frederick H. Christian

SUDDEN STRIKES BACK
SUDDEN—TROUBLESHOOTER
SUDDEN AT BAY
SUDDEN—APACHE FIGHTER
SUDDEN—DEAD OR ALIVE!

and published by Corgi Books

Oliver Strange

Sudden Makes War

CORGI BOOKS
A DIVISION OF TRANSWORLD PUBLISHERS LTD

SUDDEN MAKES WAR
A CORGI BOOK 0 552 08812 9

Originally published in Great Britain
by George Newnes Limited

PRINTING HISTORY
George Newnes edition published 1942
Fifth impression 1950
Corgi edition published 1961
Corgi edition reprinted 1962
Corgi edition reprinted 1963
Corgi edition reprinted 1963
Corgi edition reissued 1965
Corgi edition reprinted 1965
Corgi edition reprinted 1967
Corgi edition reprinted 1969
Corgi edition reprinted 1970
Corgi edition reissued 1971
Corgi edition reprinted 1972
Corgi edition reprinted 1974

This book is set in 9 pt. Times New Roman.

Corgi Books are published by Transworld Publishers Ltd,
Cavendish House, 57-59 Uxbridge Road,
Ealing, London, W.5.
Made and printed in Great Britain by
Hunt Barnard Printing Ltd, Aylesbury, Bucks.

TO
THE MEMORY OF
ROBERT P. DENNY
MY FRIEND

CHAPTER I

"I'm lookin' for a man."

The words—of sinister import in the West—arrested the attention of everyone within hearing, and had the desired effect of collecting a crowd of the curious. Yet the speaker had not the appearance of one engaged upon an errand of vengeance. A youthful cowboy—he was no more than twenty—in town for a spree, seemed to explain him. So thought at least one of the onlookers.

"Young Dan Dover o' the Circle Dot ranch over to Rainbow," he told an enquirer. "Now what in 'ell is he after? They ain't got no money to throw about."

" 'Pears like they have," was the reply.

For the object of their interest, standing on the raised platform before the Paradise Saloon, his Stetson pushed jauntily back to disclose curly hair of a particularly aggressive shade of red, had produced two gold pieces—double eagles—and a Mexican silver dollar. With these he began to perform the elementary conjuring trick of passing the coins from hand to hand, keeping one in the air. It was not much of a show, and in an Eastern town would have attracted little notice, but in this far-flung outpost of civilization, it held his audience and brought others.

"The man I'm in search of has gotta have nerve," the young man announced, his narrowed gaze sweeping over the spectators, "an' be able to use his hardware. The fella who can stand the test, pockets these two twenties an' gets the offer of a worth-while job. Don't all speak at once—I on'y got one pair o' ears."

"Good long 'uns, though," one of the crowd chuckled.

"An' that's terrible true, brother," the youth replied, with whimsical gravity. "I have to keep 'em pared down to get my hat on."

The onlookers laughed and continued to enjoy the entertainment, unaware that while the performer's eyes appeared to be occupied solely with his trick, they were, in fact, closely scanning the faces about him. Tradesmen, teamsters, half-breeds, drummers, and loafers—he could place them all, and shook his head slightly.

"I'm outa luck—there ain't an outfit in town," he muttered.

For Sandy Bend boasted a railway station, from which a single branch line travelled East, and was therefore a shipping point for cattle. Only among the reckless sons of the saddle could he hope to find what he sought. He let the coins drop into his right hand, closed, and opened it again. One was missing.

"Now where has that pesky Mex dollar got to?" he mused. With an exaggerated frown of perplexity he displayed the palms of both hands; they were empty. "Blame it, the twenties have gone too; must be floatin' around." His right fist clawed at the air, and when the fingers unclosed again, there were the three coins. "Dead easy," he commented. "The on'y difficult part is gettin' the gold to start with."

Applause greeted the feat, and some of the audience began to drift. The conjurer grinned knowingly.

"Don't go away, folks; this is a free show an' I ain't comin' round with a hat," he assured. "Shorely there must be one o' you who could use forty bucks."

He was talking at one man, whose presence the movement of others had uncovered. Tall, broad-shouldered, with a lithe, athletic frame, black hair, cold grey-blue eyes, and a lean, hard-jawed face, he was lounging against a hitching-post on the outskirts of the crowd, watching the scene with satirical amusement. No dandy cowboy this; the plain leathern chaps, woollen shirt, and high-crowned hat all bore signs of wear; even the silk kerchief knotted loosely round his neck was of sombre hue, and the two guns, hanging low on his thighs with the holsters tied down, were not fancy-butted. Red-head chinked the coins in his hand, eyes on the stranger.

"Who'll take a chance?" he asked.

The look made the words a direct challenge, and the man by the hitching-post seemed to accept it as such. He stepped forward, moving with an indolent ease which suggested the latent powers of a great cat.

"I'll try anythin'—once," he drawled. "What's yore proposition?"

The young man suppressed a smile of triumph. "It's right simple," he replied. Slipping his first finger and thumb round the silver coin, he held it at arm's length. "All you gotta do is let me shoot that out'n yore grasp at twelve paces."

The black-haired cowboy's face was expressionless. "Yu ain't lackin' in nerve yore own self," he said slowly.

The crowd agreed. The slightest deviation would result in a smashed hand for the holder of the target, and though there were many of them to whom forty dollars meant temporary affluence, not one was prepared to take such a risk. The maker of the offer knew what they were thinking, and confined himself to the man before him.

"The twenties is just a circumstance," he mentioned. "Point is, will you gamble?"

The grey-blue eyes studied those of the questioner with grave intentness, and then, "I tote two guns; cripplin' one paw won't stop me usin' the other."

"Which is where I gamble," the conjurer grinned.

"I'll go yu," was the quiet reply. "Yon's a good place."

He pointed to the blank wall of a stout log building across the street. Deftly catching the coin the other flipped in his direction, he moved through the crowd, which split into two lines. Dover followed, placed him in position, and then returned, counting off the paces.

"What's his game?" one of the bystanders queried. "He don't seem the showin'-off kind."

"You can search me, but he'd better make the shot," replied a neighbour. "That other fella's no kind to fool with. Look at him —just as unconcerned as a corpse."

It was true; resting comfortably against the building behind him, the man who was to be shot at appeared to be the least interested of those present. Only when he saw that the other had taken up his place and was waiting did he straighten up and extend his left arm. Framed in finger and thumb, the disc of silver twinkled in the sunlight; it presented a perilously small mark, but the audience sensed that something more than mere cowboy conceit was behind the exhibition.

"Gosh! there ain't no margin for a mistake, 'less he misses the hand complete," was one comment.

"He won't do that; these cowpunchers can all shoot."

Silence ensued as the marksman drew his six-shooter, flung the muzzle upwards, and chopped down on the target. For a long moment he held it poised, squinting through the sights, and then pulled the trigger. The report was followed by a cheer from the breathless watchers as they saw the coin driven from the holder's fingers, hit a log, and drop in the sand. Amidst a hum of approbation, the stranger thrust his left hand into the pocket of his chaps, picked up the silver piece and pitched it to Dover.

"Now it's yore turn," he said.

The grin of triumph on the young cowboy's face faded a little.

"What's the idea?" he asked.

"Yu mentioned a fella who can shoot," the other reminded. "I'm aimin' to ease yore mind thataway."

The grin had gone now, but a snigger from someone nearby brought it back. The boy was game.

"Fair enough," he admitted.

The crowd, eager for more excitement, lined up again as the two men took their places. The stranger, left hand still in his pocket, waited until he saw that Dover was ready, and then. . . . No one of the onlookers could have sworn to seeing the loosely-hanging right hand move, but the gun was out, hip-high, and the spirt of flame followed instantly. Again the coin was torn from its

9

frame and hurled against the timber. The speed of the draw, apparent lack of aim, and amazing accuracy had an almost paralysing effect on those who saw it.

"Gawda'mighty!" ejaculated one. "That's shootin', that is."

Dover himself was staggered, but he was also jubilant. He hurried to congratulate. "Never seen anythin' like it," he said. "Figured I could use a six-gun, but hell! I'm on'y a yearlin'. Say, my throat's fair crackin'; let's irrigate."

They adjourned to the saloon and selected a table in a quiet corner. Their drinks sampled, Dover fished out the Mexican dollar and examined it curiously; there was a dent in the middle, and another on the edge. He pointed to the former.

"Guess that's mine, seein' the care I took," he said.

The other smiled, reached out his "makings" and began to fashion a cigarette. There was a smear of blood on his left hand; the Circle Dot man's eyes widened.

"I'm guessin' again," he said. "I'm right sorry."

"Shucks, it's on'y a graze. Mebbe I moved a mite," was the careless reply. The tell-tale stain was wiped away. "Well, s'pose we get acquainted. I'm James Green, of No place, Nowhere, an' powerful fond o' new scenery."

"Pleased to meet you," the other replied. "I'm Dan Dover. My dad owns the Circle Dot range at Rainbow, 'bout fifty mile on from here. Mebbe you know it?"

Green shook his head. "This is my furthest west." His steady gaze rested on his companion. "What's yore trouble?"

"Did I mention any?" came the counter.

'No, but a fella doesn't come such a caper as this for fun. At first I thought it was a bluff, but when I called it an' yu went through, I knowed different."

"Well, yo're right, there's trouble to spare, an' more ahead unless I'm wide o' the trail. I want a man—a real one, to help me deal with it."

"My guns ain't for sale," the stranger said curtly.

"I don't want 'em, but the fella who comes to us has gotta be able to protect hisself; we've had a hand killed an' two more crippled pretty recent."

"How come?"

"Shot from cover—every time," Dover informed bitterly.

"Sounds bad. Got any suspicions?"

"Plenty, an' nothin' else. See, here's the layout: the Circle Dot ain't a big ranch—'bout a thousand head just now—times is poor, but it owns good grazin' an' water—a stream from the Cloudy Hills runs right through our land."

"Plenty water is shore an asset."

"Yo're shoutin', but it can be a liability. The Wagon-wheel, located east of us ain't so well fixed. They tried to buy us out—at their figure—but we wasn't interested, an' that started the feud."

"Feud, huh?"

"Yeah. I warn't but a little shaver in them days—mebbe it's ten year ago, an' Dad don't talk much. Gran'dad owned the ranch then. He was a hard case; straight as a string, but mighty set in his ideas—it's a family failin', I guess. He was the first to go; they found him laid out in a gully one mornin', with two slugs in his back. There was no evidence, an' not much doubt either—the Wagon-wheel had been pretty free with their threats. Tom Trenton, father o' the present owner, just grinned when my uncle Rufe —Dad's elder brother—taxed him with the crime. Rufe was a red-head—all the Dovers are—an' he pulled his gun, but bystanders grabbed his arms, an' Tom went away with a gibe. Oh, he'd 'a' shot it out willin' enough; there ain't no cowards in the Trenton family."

"Yore gran'dad was downed from behind," came the reminder.

"Yeah, that's one o' the things I can't understand; from all I've heard, finishin' a fella thataway wouldn't 'a' give Tom Trenton much satisfaction. Sounds odd, I guess, but . . ."

"He'd have wanted the other to know; I've met that sort."

"Well, however it may have been, he didn't have long to crow, for a coupla months later he was picked up half a mile from the Wagon-wheel with a bullet between the eyes; his gun was lyin' near, but it hadn't been fired. There was a lot o' talk, near everybody reckoned Rufe had done it, an' as the Trentons owned the sheriff—an' do now—he had to pull his freight. Allasame, that didn't end or mend matters; the quarrel dragged on, an' like a slow fire, flared up at intervals. Dad is carryin' round some slugs, but he don't weigh much anyways, an' Zeb Trenton has a limp he warn't born with. For some years now there's on'y been bad feelin' till a few months back when the trouble started again. That's why I'm here."

"Meanin' yu an' yore father can't handle it?" Green said.

"Just that," was the frank reply. "Dad ain't the man he was afore we lost mother—it seemed to take the heart out'n him—an' me, I s'pose I'm kind o' young. Our boys is a good bunch, but they need a leader, someone with more savvy than a kid they've watched grow up."

Green was silent for a while, considering the curious tale to which he had listened. He was not enamoured of the proposal, but liked the maker of it. The boy was straight, modest, and possessed the pluck to take his own medicine, as the shooting incident proved. His mind went back to a little ranch in Texas; he had been just such another youth. But the world had used him roughly since then, moulding him into a man, experienced, dangerous, and when occasion demanded, ruthless. It had also given him another name. For this was "Sudden," whose daring exploits and uncanny

11

skill with weapons had earned an unenviable reputation in the south-west.[1]

Presently he made his decision. "I'll see yore Ol' Man."

Dover's relief was obvious. "I'm right glad," he said, and then, awkwardly, "Anythin' holdin' you in this dump?"

The other smiled. "I can start straight away if yo're ready."

"I've got a call to make at a ranch 'bout five mile north. Mebbe you wouldn't mind goin' ahead. You see, I didn't like leavin'—Dad's venturesome—just refuses to realize how real the danger is."

"Then he won't be expectin' me?"

"No, but any traveller is welcome at the Circle Dot, an' once yo're there, I guess I can get him to see the light. I oughta told you this before, but——" He bogged down, and then added, "If he'd knowed why, he wouldn't 'a' let me come."

Green nodded; he had a mental picture of the rancher, proud, independent, a man who had fended for himself all his life, and little likely to admit that misfortune and growing years had lessened his ability still to do so. He knew the type, rugged, sturdy fellows, who would fight to their last gasp of breath against any aggression. The boy before him would follow the same pattern, if Fate so willed it. He grinned back at the smiling but anxious eyes.

"I'll take a chance," he said, and rose.

"Dessay I'll overtake you if I can persuade the owner o' that black in the corral to sell."

"He won't part."

"You seem mighty shore. Is he a friend o' yores?"

"That's somethin' I've never been able to decide," the gunman said with a sardonic twinkle. "Yu see, the black is mine."

Dover's expression was rueful. "Cuss the luck. Saw him this mornin' when I turned my bronc in; I never come so near to bein' a hoss-thief. Made up my mind to buy him if it busted me. He's a peach."

"He's a pal," was the grave reply, and the young man—to whom also a horse was more than a beast of burden—understood.

"Well, life's full o' disappointments, ain't it?" he rejoined cheerfully. "I guess I won't be overhaulin' you; Thimble is a good li'l cowpony, but in a race that black would make him look like he was standin' still. See you at the Circle Dot, an' o' course, we're strangers. If Dad thought I was puttin' one over on him, he'd dig his heels in an' a team o' mules wouldn't make him budge. But don't get a wrong impression; he's the finest fella I ever knowed, but he's got his own ideas."

Green laughed. "I'm a mite thataway my own self," he confessed. "A saplin' what sways with every wind ain't the tree to trust yore weight to."

[1] Related in *Sudden—Outlawed*. George Newnes Ltd.

CHAPTER II

"Shore is an up-an'-down country, an' any fella what likes his scenery mixed couldn't rightly complain."

It was late in the afternoon, and the black-haired man from Sandy Bend, in default of other companionship, was communing with his horse. The deeply-rutted trail he had been following, after a steady climb, brought him to a small plateau which afforded a view of what lay before. It was a daunting spectacle for the unaccustomed eye—a vast rampart of grey-spired, arid-topped mountains, their lower slopes shrouded by dense growths of yellow and nut-pine, stretched along the horizon beneath the slowly sinking sun. They did not seem remote, but the traveller knew they must be about forty miles distant. Between them and where he sat lay a jumble of lesser hills, interspersed by valleys, sandy stretches of sage, greasewood, and cactus, with innumerable tracts of timber.

"Reckon we can't be far from that Rainbow town," Sudden continued. "I guess we won't trouble it. If that young fella was correct, headin' south a bit should fetch us to the Circle Dot, havin' o' course, lost our way. Might happen to anyone, Nigger, 'specially a fool hoss, huh?" At the mention of the name, the black head swung round, the lips curled back from the white teeth. "That's right, grin while yu can, yu ol' pie-buster, for I've a notion we'll have little to be amused about as time ticks along."

He rode on for a mile or so and came to a spot where the wagon-road forked, one branch leading southwest. This was a smaller and less-used trail, formed—as the tracks showed—mainly by cattle and horses. Sudden swung into it.

"Shore oughta be a ranch at the end of it," he soliloquized. "Which one don't matter much to a stranger."

The trail proved easy to travel, winding snake-like to avoid obstacles such as steep inclines, gullies, and thick plantations of trees, all of which would render the passage of a herd difficult. Some miles were covered at an easy pace, and then the muffled report of a rifle shattered the almost absolute stillness. The horse pricked up its ears, and the rider spoke soothingly:

"Easy, boy, it can't be us they're after," he said. "Too far in front, an' we ain't got enemies around here—yet. Allasame, we'll be careful."

A pressure of a knee and the animal lengthened its stride. Sudden, no longer sitting slackly in the saddle, kept keen eyes on

13

the path they were following. There were plenty of quite innocent reasons for the shot, but he was reaching the region of a range war, and . . . A mile was traversed without further incident, and he was beginning to blame himself for over-caution when he turned into a sandy gully, the sides of which were hidden by brush. Here, nibbling at the tussocks of coarse grass along the edge of the trail was a saddled pony, and a few yards away, a man sprawled, face downwards.

To all appearance, he might have been thrown by his mount, but an ugly red stain between the shoulder-blades pointed to a more sinister explanation. Standing beside the body, Sudden saw it was that of a man on the wrong side of fifty, with thinning grey hair, and deeply-lined features. His eye caught the Circle Dot brand on the grazing horse; what Dan Dover feared had come to pass. The gunman's face grew grim.

"The cowardly skunk never gave him a chance," he muttered, and with a glance at the enclosing walls of vegetation, "Hell, he picked the right place too; small hope o' findin' any traces."

Nevertheless, he fixed in his mind the exact position of the corpse in case it might assist in locating the spot whence the shot was fired. Then he bent to examine the wound; the bullet had smashed into the spine, and death must have been instant.

"Stick 'em up, *pronto*!"

At the harsh command the stooping man straightened—slowly, to face four horsemen whose approach the soft, sandy floor of the ravine had deadened. Looking unconcernedly into the muzzles of four rifles, he raised his hands, but only far enough to hook the thumbs into the armholes of his vest.

"Howdy, gents," he greeted. "I'm glad to see yu."

"Mebbe," the one who had spoken before said dryly. "What's goin' on here?"

He was a short, weedy fellow of middle-age, whose naturally cunning expression was enhanced by a pronounced obliquity of vision. A straggling moustache drooped around and over a weak mouth and inadequate chin. Even the star, prominently pinned to his flannel shirt, could not endow him with dignity. Sheriff Foxwell, commonly called "Foxy" by friend and foe, was not a likeable person.

"Mile or so back on the trail I heard a shot, an' then I find—this," Sudden replied, pointing to the dead rancher.

"Why, it's Ol' Man Dover!" one of the party cried.

They closed in on the prostrate figure, thereby cutting off possible retreat by the man standing beside it. If he sensed the significance of this manœuvre—and he could scarcely fail to do so —his demeanour was unchanged. The sheriff climbed clumsily from his horse.

"Shore is," he said, "an' cashed all right. Plugged in the back, an' his own gun in the holster. Where's his rifle?"

"On his hoss," Sudden informed.

"Huh! Looks like a bush-wackin', but why?" Foxy questioned. He stooped and explored the dead man's pockets, producing a sizeable roll of currency. "That don't point to robbery, unless—the fella was interrupted." His squinting eyes rested on the stranger.

"Nobody in sight when I arrived."

"Mebbe this gent'll tell us somethin' about hisself," an older man suggested.

The sheriff looked sourly at him. "I'm handlin' this, Hicks," he reminded, "but as you've butted in we might as well know what this *hombre* is doin' around here."

"I'm on my way to the Circle Dot," Sudden said quietly, and anticipating the obvious question, "I was hopin' to land a job."

The officer's eyes were sharp with suspicion. "Happen to be acquainted with Dover?"

"Never heard of him till this mornin'," was the indifferent reply. "But I happen to be acquainted with cattle."

The sheriff shrugged his shoulders. " 'Pears an open an' shut case to me," he said. "You admit yore errand was to meet him, an' we find you standin' over his dead body, just about to search him, seemin'ly. Well, there's plenty trees, an' you got yore rope, Jed, I see."

The man addressed, a lanky, raw-boned individual, nodded, and patted the looped lariat on his saddle horn. Sudden looked at the puny maker of this swift decision with satirical disdain.

"If yo're tryin' to throw a scare into me I'm tellin' yu it's a waste o' time I'm no greenhorn," he remarked.

"Nary scare," was the cool retort. "We're just naturally goin' to hang you, that's all."

"Well, it's a relief to know yu ain't aimin' to roast me at a slow fire, but has it occurred to yu that as I entered the gully from this end, an' the shot—by the position o' the body—must 'a' come from the other, there's a flaw in yore evidence? Any one o' yu might 'a' done it, but I couldn't."

"Skittles! You'd make yore arrangements, o' course, shiftin' the corp to fit yore story."

"Knowin' yu were comin', no doubt."

"Naw, that's where you slipped up," Foxwell countered an ugly grin on his thin lips.

The threatened man realized that the fellow was in earnest, and would carry out this monstrous injustice. He appealed to the others.

"Yu standin' for this?"

Hicks answered. "It's the sheriff's business, but what about takin' him in, Foxy, an'——"

"Like you say, it's my business," the officer cut in angrily. "Here's a respected citizen foully done to death, an' we catch the culprit red-handed. Rainbow's had too many o' these killin's an' I'm goin' to stop 'em. Jed, git ready."

Before any of them could move, Sudden leapt backwards, thus bringing all the men in front of him. At the same instant, his hands swept his hips and both guns came out. So swift and unexpected had the action been that the riders had no time to level the rifles held across their knees. Now it was too late; the man they had deemed to be in their power, had them in his; and it was a different man, a tense, half-crouching figure instinct with menace.

"Get ready yoreself, Sheriff, to hop into hell," he said. "I can down the four o' yu in as many seconds." And to the horsemen, "Drop them guns an' reach for the sky, or by the livin' God . . ."

The weapons fell into the sand, and four pairs of hands were uplifted, but not in prayer. The sheriff's face had become a sickly yellow, and he was the first to obey the order, a fact which brought a cold smile from the giver of it.

"That's better," he commented. "Now yu be good li'l boys an' no harm will come to yu—mebbe."

"Yo're resistin' the Law," Foxwell spluttered fatuously.

"Me?" was the surprised retort. "Why, I ain't resistin' any. Start the game, Sheriff; it's yore deal."

The taunted officer was saved the necessity of replying by the arrival of a new factor. Into the ravine from the Sandy Bend direction loped a rider. He pulled up when he reached the group of men. Sudden swore under his breath; it was young Dover.

"You caught me up after all," he said. "But yo're too late."

The boy gave one glance at the body, sprang from his saddle, and knelt beside it. "Dad!" he cried, and then, as the full extent of his loss seeped in. "So they've done it, the murderin' curs; I should never 'a' left you." He looked up fiercely. "Whose work is this?"

The sheriff started to lower a hand but changed his mind and nodded towards the stranger. "That fella, I guess."

The reply come in a bitter sneer. "Yo're guessin' is like the rest o' yore doin's—pretty triflin'. So that's why yo're all lookin' paralyzed. You fools, this man wouldn't know Dad from Adam, an' moreover, he was expectin' to ride for the Circle Dot."

"That don't prove anythin'," the sheriff said sullenly. "Road-agents ain't in the habit o' askin' yore name an' address afore they salivate you. Anyway, the Ol' Man could have turned him down. He was robbin' the body when we arrove."

With shaking fingers, Dan felt in his father's pockets, and drew

16

out the roll of bills. "Seems to have made a pore job of it," he replied acidly. "Even a beginner couldn't 'a' missed this."

Hicks spoke: "Do you know this fella, Dan?"

"I met him this mornin' at the Bend, an' sent him along; we're short-handed."

The sheriff's mean eyes glittered. "Did you arrange for yore dad to come an' meet you?" he asked.

It was a moment before the shameful implication penetrated, and then the boy leapt to his feet, fury struggling with the grief in his face, and stepped towards his traducer.

"Pull yore gun, you coyote," he rapsed.

The officer had no intention of doing anything of the kind. "I've got my han's up, Dover," he reminded.

Sudden had watched the scene in silence, but now he spoke: "Yu can take 'em down, Sheriff—if—yu—wanta."

The drawl of the last three words made them a plain insult, but Foxwell had a thick skin, and an inordinate desire to preserve it; he did not avail himself of the permission, preferring to take refuge behind his badge.

"I was app'inted to keep the peace, not break it," he said, and looked round at his following. "You'd think a son whose father had been bumped off would be anxious to have the guilty party brought to justice, huh?"

"I am, an' I know what he was after, an' where to seek for him," Dover said savagely. "So do you, an' that's why you'd like to pin it on a stranger. Don't you worry; evenin' up for Dad is somethin' I can take care of. Now, get back to yore murderin' master an' tell him that you did all you could to blot his tracks—an' failed."

Sudden spoke again. "They're leavin' rifles an' six-guns here," he said quietly. "There's a heap too much cover, an' they may get notions."

Under the threat of his levelled weapons, they let fall their pistols, wheeled and rode down the ravine. The sheriff shouted a parting:

"Rainbow will have somethin' to say 'bout this."

"Shore, tell it how one man held up an' disarmed the four o' you," Dover retorted. "The town ain't had a laugh lately. I'll send yore guns to Sody's; they'll know then you ain't lyin'."

When they had vanished through the entrance to the ravine his anger evaporated, leaving only the dull ache of sorrow. In a voice hoarse with emotion, he asked:

"You ain't backin' out?"

"Not any. That imitation sheriff has got me real interested. Might as well be movin'."

The grisly task of roping the dead rancher on the back of his pony was accomplished in silence. Then Sudden put a question:

17

"Yu said yu knowed what the killer wanted. D'yu reckon he got it?"

"I dunno, but likely Dad wouldn't be carryin' it. Did you see any tracks?"

"On'y that."

He pointed to a kind of path, running at a right angle to where the dead man had lain, the sandy surface of which seemed to have been recently disturbed. Following it, they came to a bush at the side of the ravine. A white scar showed where a branch had been wrenched off, and in a moment or so they found it; the withering leaves were gritty.

"Wiped his trail out as he backed away," Sudden commented, and scanned the slope keenly. "He came down an' went up here—them toe an' heel marks is plain as print. I'll see if I can trace him. Yu fetch the hosses along an' meet me."

He climbed the bank and soon found indications that someone had preceded him. Trifles which would have escaped an untrained eye—bent or bruised stems of grass, a broken twig, the impress of a foot on bare ground, were all-sufficient to enable him to follow the path of the previous visitor along the rim of the ravine. For some two hundred yards he thrust his way through the fringe of bush and came to the place he was seeking. Shadowed by a scrub-oak, and screened from below by a rampart of shrubs, was a trampled patch of grass. Two flattened hollows about a foot apart caught his eye. He knelt down in them and looked along the ravine; the spot where he had found the body was plainly visible.

"Easy as fallin' out'n a tree," he muttered. A yellow gleam in the longer grass proved to be a cartridge shell. "A thirty-eight—they ain't so common."

Close by he picked up a dottle of partly-burned tobacco, tapped from the bowl of a pipe; the assassin had solaced himself with a smoke while waiting for his victim. There was nothing else, but in a nearby clump of spruce he found hoofmarks, a branch from which the bark had been nibbled, and several long grey hairs. He followed the tracks down to where they merged with many others in the main trail, and could no longer be picked out. Dover was waiting.

"Any luck?" he asked.

"Not enough to hang a dawg on," Sudden admitted, and told of his discoveries.

"Trenton uses a pipe," the boy said. "Let's be goin'."

They set out, and the sad burden on the third horse kept them silent. There was but a scant five miles to cover, most of it over open plain splotched by thorny thickets, patches of sage, and broken only by an occasional shallow arroyo. Soon they came upon bunches of cattle contentedly grazing on the short, sun-burned grass, and presently the ranch-house was in sight.

18

A squat building of one storey, solidly constructed of trimmed logs chinked with clay, it stood on the crest of a slope and afforded a wide view of the surrounding country. It had been erected for utility rather than elegance in the days when raiding redskins were not unknown, and save for three great cedars which provided a welcome shade, there was nothing bigger than a sage-bush for hundreds of yards all round. A little apart were the bunk-house, outbuildings, and corrals. At the foot of the slope a double line of willows and cottonwoods told the presence of a stream. As they pulled up outside, a grizzled, bow-legged little man came out, stared, and as he recognized the laden pony, ripped out an oath.

"Hell's flames, boy, what's happened?' he demanded.

Dover dismounted wearily. "They got Dad, Burke," he said gruffly. "Tell you about it presently. Help me take him in."

So the rancher came home for the last time. The sad spectacle was watched by a thin-featured, sunken-eyed youth of about seventeen who had crept to the door. He shrank aside to let the bearers pass, and then swung round, face buried in a bent arm, and shoulders shaking.

"It shore is tough luck," Sudden consoled. "Don't take it too hard."

"He was mighty good ter me," came the mumbling reply.

"We all gotta go—some time."

"Yep, but not that way—widout a chanct," the lad replied fiercely. "Gawd, if I was on'y a man, 'stead of a perishin' weed, I'd cut th' hearts out o' th'——" He finished with a torrent of vitriolic expletives.

"Yu ain't got yore growth yet, son," the puncher said.

"Growth?" the boy echoed bitterly. "What yer givin' me? I'm a lunger—one o' Gawd's mistakes what nobody wants, an' I'd 'a' croaked by now if it hadn't bin fer *him*."

A violent spasm of coughing racked his spare frame.

CHAPTER III

A few moments later, Burke reappeared. "Dan'll be along presently," he began. "He's told me about you, Mister, an' I wanta say right out that yo're mighty welcome, 'specially now. By the time we git shut o' the hosses, supper'll be ready; we got a good cook, if he is Irish."

As they returned from the corral, carrying saddles, rifles, and blankets, the little man spoke again:

"This is a knockdown blow for Dan, he fair worshipped his dad, which goes for the rest of us. It was fear o' this happenin' sent him to the Bend. 'I'm goin' to git a good man, Burke,' he told me this mornin', 'one who'll put the fear o' death into these cowardly dawgs.' He glanced sideways at the tall, lithe figure for each of whose long strides he had to take two. 'I'm thinkin' he was lucky.' "

"How many on the pay-roll?" Sudden asked.

"Eight of us in the bunkhouse," Burke replied. "I'm the daddy o' the outfit—bin here goin' on twenty year."

"I'm takin' it yo're foreman."

"We never had one—the Ol' Man ran his own ranch; you might call me sorta straw-boss."

"Yeah, but now——"

"See here, Mister——"

"Make it 'Jim'."

"I'm obliged. Well, Jim, it's thisaway: I'm a good cowman an' so is the boy; I'll fight to a fare-you-well an' he'll do the same, but that ain't enough in a war, which is what yo're hornin' in on. The Circle Dot needs a fella with experience; Dan ain't had none, an' I've had too much—old men git sorta fixed in their notions." A faint smile passed over the wrinkled, sunburned features. "Once I had dreams o' ownin' a ranch, but now I ain't got no ambition a-tall, but I'd like to go on bein' straw-boss."

Sudden nodded, realizing the tragedy behind the simple statement; the mounting years of hard, dangerous work for a bare living, the gradual extinction of hope, and the prospect of poverty when the heavy hand of Time prevented him from following the only occupation he knew.

The living-room of the Circle Dot ranch-house was spacious, with a great stone fire-place, in front of which lay a fine grizzly pelt. The furniture comprised a table, desk, and chairs, solid but suggestive of ease. Saddles, guns, and other ranch gear made it comfortably untidy for a man. Burke read the stranger's thought.

"Dave wouldn't have a woman in the place after he lost his wife," he explained. "I reckon Paddy—he's the cook—ain't got the instincts of a home-maker."

At that moment Dan came in, haggard, but grim-faced. "You'll feed with us to-night, Bill," he said. "We gotta talk things over."

The meal was brought in by the cook, a short and incredibly fat man, whose chubby countenance wore an expression of gloom utterly out of keeping with his deep-set twinkling eyes. While they were despatching it, Dan related the happenings of the day, and by the time the tale ended, Burke was regarding the newcomer with increased respect.

"How did Dad come to be on that trail?" Dan asked finally.

"Came to meet you," was the reply. "He had a message askin' him to, left by a stranger who claimed to have run into you; must 'a' bin soon after you started."

"I never sent it, an' didn't see a soul till I was half-way to the Bend; it was just a trap." Another thought brought his brows together. "Nobody outside o' here knowed I was goin—I on'y decided this mornin'."

"Either they're watchin' yu, or someone passed the word," Sudden remarked. "Shore o' yore hands?"

"They've all been with us some time 'cept one, who came a few months back. Dunno much about him—Dad warn't the suspectful sort, unfortunately."

Sudden smothered a smile; Dave Dover had passed on his trustfulness to his son apparently, as witness his own case.

"Flint is wise to his work, an' does it," Burke put in.

"If he's here for a purpose, he'd naturally wanta stay," Sudden pointed out. "Who's the boy?"

"Dad picked him up at the Bend 'bout twelve months ago. Just a hobo kid stealin' a ride on a freight car what come further west than he figured on. He was precious near starved, an' his lungs is all shot to pieces. Wouldn't give any name, but he talked a lot o' New York, so the boys christened him 'Yorky.' He's s'posed to help the cook, but spends most of his time smokin' cigarettes an' damnin' everythin' an' everybody.

"A queer li'l runt—'pears to have a spite agin hisself—but he's got guts. Soon after he arrived, he goes with one o' the men in the buckboard to Rainbow. Said the ranch was deadly dull, an' he wanted some excitement. He got it. The storekeeper's son, a big lummox of a lad an' the town bully, started on him. They fought, an' Yorky was fetched home with a bruise on every inch of his body. But not a chirp could we git out'n him.

"Dad was hoppin' mad. He rides into Rainbow next mornin', learns the truth, an' tackles the storekeeper. 'I want a word with your boy, Evans, he sez. 'You needn't to trouble, Dover, he had his lesson,' the storekeeper replies. 'Right now he's in bed, both eyes bunged up, two teeth missin', an' a neck what looks like he'd had a turn-up with a cougar.'

" 'Yorky was half-dead to begin with, an' yore boy twice his weight,' Dad points out.

" 'Mebbe, but the half what ain't dead is lively enough,' Evans retorts. 'He fought like a wild thing—fists, feet, teeth, an' nails, anythin' went, an' when I drags 'em apart, he stands there spittin' out blood an' curses. "No blasted hayseed can call me names an' git away with it," he sez, an' keels over.' "

Dan was silent for a moment, his eyes sombre. "That was Dad," he said. "Hard as granite at need, but with ever a soft spot for sufferin' in man or beast; I've knowed him mighty near kill a man for maltreatin' a hoss." He roused himself, striving to thrust aside the burden of grief which oppressed him. "Well, this ain't gettin' us no place. Burke, I'm minded to ask Green to be foreman."

"What you say, goes, Dan," the little man replied steadily.

Sudden shook his head. "That won't do nohow; I've a better plan," he said. "Burke here, knowin' the range an' the outfit, oughta be foreman; that's on'y right an' fair. I can be more use to yu if I ain't tied. Call me stray-man, say; that'll give me a chance to snoop around, learn the country; an' keep my eyes an' ears open."

Burke's despondent face brightened amazingly at this proposition, but Dover still seemed doubtful. "I'd like a lot for Bill to have the job—it's due him," he admitted. "But it don't seem much to offer you."

"Shucks!" was the smiling reply. "It ain't what a man's called but what he does that matters."

"If Jim slept here 'stead of in the bunkhouse he'd be less liable to have his comin's an' goin's noticed," Burke suggested.

"Which is one damn good notion," Dover said eagerly. "I'll be glad to have you, Jim; it's goin' to be lonesome . . ." He broke off and swept a hand across his eyes as though to disperse the mist of misery which enveloped him every time he thought of his loss. "Hell burn them," he burst out. "They shall pay, the curs." The moment of fury passed, and he looked up wearily. "Didn't mean to let go thataway. Burke, the boys will have the bad news by this; go an' tell 'em the good—'bout yoreself; I reckon they'll be as pleased as I am."

"I'm obliged, Dan," the foreman replied. "I'll do my best." He turned to Sudden. "I'm thankin' you too, Jim; mebbe I was lyin' about that ambition."

"Yu didn't deceive me, ol'-timer," the puncher grinned.

When they were alone, he looked at the boy into whose life he had so strangely stepped. "Yu got a good man there," he remarked. "Yu've done the square thing by him, an' yu won't regret it."

22

"No, Bill Burke's white, an' he was fond o' Dad," Dover replied. "Jim, the situation is more desperate than when I spoke to you at the Bend; it ain't too late to slide out—if you want."

"Forget it," Sudden said. "When I start anythin' I aim to go through. All I want now is a bed, an' it wouldn't do yu no real harm to try one. An' remember—there's allus light behind even the blackest cloud."

* * *

Breakfast was no more than over when Yorky came in to say that "a guy from town" was asking for Dan. The young man went out, and Sudden followed. The visitor proved to be Hicks.

"Mornin', gents," he said, pleasantly enough. "The sheriff's holdin' an enquiry into yestiddy's bad business, an' he'd like you both to be there. It'll be at Sody's, an' Foxy sez mebbe you could fetch along . . ." He broke off.

"You can tell him——" Dan began fiercely.

"That we'll be on hand," Sudden finished, and when the messenger had departed, added, "No sense in r'arin' up an' settin' folks against us."

"It'll be a mere farce," was the bitter comment.

"Shore, but we gotta play the game their way—for a spell," Sudden replied, and then, thoughtfully, "Some o' yore outfit might care to be present at the buryin'—Burke, say, an' three-four others."

"Yu think they'll try anythin'?"

"Oh, I guess not, but as a mark o' respect for the deceased, yu know."

So it came about that when the buckboard, driven by Burke, arrived in town, it was accompanied by five armed horsemen, a fact that caused a stir of excitement.

"Who's the black-haired *hombre*?" asked Seller, who, as carpenter and coffin-maker, had an interest in the proceedings.

"Must be the fella what found the body an' held up Foxy," Evans told him. Some of the sheriff's party had talked. "If he's throwin' in with the Circle Dot, gettin' rid o' Ol' Dave ain't goin' to help much."

"Ain't the Wagon-wheel dealin' with you now?" came the sarcastic query. "Or are you tired o' livin'?"

"They are, an' I ain't, but I don't like 'em none the more for that," the storekeeper retorted. "If this burg has to sit up an' beg every time Trenton gives the word, it's a mighty pore prospect."

"You said it. Dave Dover had a rough tongue, but he was a square shooter. Well, I got a box for him—it pays to keep one ready in this man's town—but I'd liefer some other fella was to fill it."

Rainbow was a small place, and utterly unlovely—a huddle of

23

primitive buildings flung haphazard along one side of a sandy but unfailing stream. It boasted a bank, stores, an hotel—so-called—eating-house, and a sprinkling of private habitations. It owed its existence mainly to the proximity of two ranches—the Circle Dot and the Wagon-wheel—and also to the fact that its location and supply of water made it a convenient halt for trail-herds from more distant ranges bound for the Bend.

Relaxation was lavishly catered for; a facetious citizen once remarked, "Take away her saloons, an' Rainbow very nearly ain't." The most important of these were the Parlour, and Sody's. It was into the latter that the corpse of the murdered man, covered with a blanket, was carried and laid at one side of the cleared space in front of the bar. The sheriff was seated at a table with half a dozen citizens ranged behind him; his eyes grew meaner when the Circle Dot contingent entered.

"Any need to fetch along them riders?" he snarled.

"They've as much right to be here as you have," Dan told him.

"Well, let's git on. Gotta be reg'lar, but I reckon we're just losin' time on thisyer enquiry."

"I didn't ask for it. Shore is a' waste o' time; even you can't make it anythin' but murder."

"That's for the jury to decide," Foxwell snapped. "I've selected 'em a'ready."

"So I see—all men who didn't think much o' Dad."

"It wouldn't 'a' bin easy to find six who did," the sheriff sneered.

"An' that's a damned lie," Dan flared. "So now what?"

Before any reply could be made, a man, who had been kneeling beside the body, stood up. Dressed in a skirted coat which had once been black, a dirty boiled shirt, coarse trousers tucked untidily into the tops of his boots, he presented a picture of gentility in the last stages of decay. And his gaunt, clever, but dissipated features, and long, untended hair, added to the illusion, though he was little more than thirty years of age. His red-rimmed eyes regarded the peace officer belligerently.

"Have you brought me from my bottle to listen to your wrangling?" he demanded, in a hoarse but cultured voice. "Of course, Foxwell, if—by a miracle—you are about to fight and provide me with a patient, I am not objecting."

The sheriff had no intention of fighting, despite the gibe; he found the interruption very timely.

"I'll take yore report first, Malachi," he said.

"Doctor Malachi, to you," came the correction. "What do you imagine I can tell you? The man is dead—been so for fifteen hours, or more; shot from behind, doubtless from hiding, as seems to be the chivalrous custom in these parts. Here's the bullet, from which you will learn little; contact with the spinal column

24

has distorted it." He tossed the bloodstained pellet on the table, wiped his long, thin fingers on a rag of a handkerchief, and added, "My fee is five dollars—cash."

Foxwell stared at him. "Hell, Doc, you ain't told us nothin' we didn't know," he protested. "Five bucks for diggin' out a slug?"

"That is my charge for extractions—teeth or bullets," Malachi returned serenly. "And remember, Sheriff, if you should chance to become ill, it would be most unfortunate if I were too occupied to attend you."

The officer glowered but gave in, not unmindful of the fact that most of those present were enjoying the incident. The doctor, despite his loose habits and acid tongue was, by reason of his profession and education, a privileged person; he was, in truth, the only qualified medical man within a radius of fifty miles or more. Malachi picked up the bill Foxwell produced, walked to the bar, and appeared to take no further interest in the proceedings. The sheriff examined the fatal fragment of lead.

"Like Doc said, it don't tell us a thing," he said, and Sudden could have sworn to the relief in his tone.

"My statement was that *you* wouldn't learn much," a voice from the bar interjected. "Weigh it, you idiot."

Foxwell had to comply. Scales and an assortment of cartridges were fetched; only in one instance did the weights tally.

"She's a thirty-eight," Hicks, who was making the tests announced. "That don't git us much further, unless——" His gaze went to Sudden. "What gun do you carry, Mister?"

"A forty-four," the cowboy replied.

"No good foolin' about over the slug, thirty-eights ain't so scarce," the sheriff said irritably. "We wanta hear how that fella found the body."

"I met young Dover in Sandy Bend an' mentioned I was needin' a job. He asked me to head for the Circle Dot, an' promised to follow later. On the way I heard a shot an', soon after, came upon the dead man. I was lookin' him over when the sheriff an' his posse turned up. Then——"

"Awright, I know the rest," Foxwell cut in hastily.

"A murdered man, and another on the spot, that should have been enough evidence for *you*, Foxy. Why didn't you hang him?"

The sarcastic question came from the bar, and the sheriff unthinkingly told a half-truth. "I changed my mind."

"I don't blame you," was the instant rejoinder. "If I had a mind like yours I'd do the same," A ripple of laughter followed, and the voice went on, "Don't you think the jury might like to know the reason for this astounding departure from your usual methods?"

"The jury knows all it needs to," the badgered man retorted.

25

"Including the decision it is to come to, I expect. Then why hold the enquiry? God! what a fool you are, Foxy."

Purple in the face, the sheriff turned on his tormentor. "When I want yore help I'll ask for it. Yo're——"

"Fee for a consultation is ten dollars, in advance—from you," the doctor finished.

"Obstructin' the course o' justice."

"Justice! Why, you couldn't spell the damn word, much less administer it," Malachi laughed, and presenting his back, poured another drink.

The sheriff breathed a sigh of relief; he stood no chance in a verbal contest with that man. In an effort to regain his self-respect, he glared round the room.

"You got anythin' to say, Dover?"

"Plenty," the young fellow replied, and told of the message his father had received. "It did not come from me—it was a trap, an' it's an easy guess who set it."

"Guessin' won't git us nowhere; the Law demands proof," Foxwell said unctuously.

"The Law here squats on it's rump an' does nothin'," Dan sneered. "This ain't the first time a man has been done to death by a yellow-livered sneak afraid to show hisself. Well, I ain't askin' yore help, Sheriff; the Circle Dot can handle it."

The officer scowled, and then, "What is it, Bundy?" as a lumpy cowboy in his early thirties, whose craggy face seemed to be endowed with a permanent sneer, stepped forward.

"All I wanta say is that yestiddy afternoon the en-tire Wagonwheel outfit was workin' ten mile from where the shootin' took place."

"Methinks the witness doth protest too much," came a comment from the bar.

The sheriff swore. But evidently the statement was what he had been waiting for. "We ain't gittin' no forader," he said testily, and turned to the men standing behind him. Then, "The jury finds that deceased died from a gun-shot wound, but there ain't no evidence to show who done it."

"Had any existed, there would have been no enquiry," Malachi added. "Foxy, when my commodious abode needs whitewashing, the job is yours."

"Who was it spoke for the Wagon-wheel?" Sudden asked.

"The foreman, as nasty a piece o' work as the Lord ever put breath into," Dan replied. "Sent a-purpose, an' the sheriff knew it."

"That sawbones ain't much respect for the Law."

"Devilin' Foxy is just pie to him, but it's a dangerous game. He's a queer cuss, but I like him."

CHAPTER IV

That afternoon another oblong heap of heavy stones was added to the little cemetery, a scant half-mile from the town. It was a pretty place, a tiny plateau of short grass, sprinkled with gay-coloured flowers, and ringed in with shrubs and trees through which the sun sent flickering shadows. Rainbow did not possess a parson, so there was no ceremony. The men present stood around, hats off, watching silently. When all was done, Dan, looking down upon the pitiful pile through misty eyes and gripping the brim of his Stetson with tense fingers, registered a vow:

"They shan't beat us, Dad," he muttered, and turned away.

As the empty buckboard, with its escort of stern-faced riders moved slowly towards the town, a stout, ruddy-cheeked horseman slowed up to allow the young cattleman to join him.

"I'm powerful sorry, boy," he began. "I've knowed the Ol' Man since you were knee-high to a sage-hen, an' knowed him well. He was hard-shelled, but inside he was the pure quill. He never let down a friend, or let up on a foe, an' for anybody in distress, he was a safe bet. Losin' yore mother shook him terrible, but if the preachers is right, mebbe they're together agin." He was silent for a moment. "What I wanted to say was, if there's anythin' I can do, any time, come to me."

"That's mighty nice o' you, Bowdyr," Dan replied. "I'll not forget. Guess I'll be needin' friends."

"Yore new hand looks a likely proposition. What do you know about him?"

"Not a thing; I took a chance."

"Fella has to—times," Bowdyr agreed. He studied the puncher —who was riding on the other side of the buckboard—for a while. "I'd 'a' done the same—with him."

When they reached Rainbow, Bowdyr drew rein at the Parlour Saloon, of which he was the proprietor, and voiced an invitation.

"I don't feel like drinkin', Ben," Dover said.

"A livener won't do us any harm, son," Bowdyr argued. "Frettin' ain't goin' to fetch the ol' boy back, an' I want a word with you."

The Parlour was very similar to Sody's but rather smaller. It had a long, highly-polished bar—the pride of its owner—facing the swing-doors. In front of it were tables and chairs. A roulette wheel, and other forms of gambling were to be found on the right side, while to the left was space for dancing, and a piano. Mirrors,

and brightly-coloured Navajo blankets served to relieve the bare-
ness of the wooden walls.

"Drinks are on the house this time, boys," the saloon-keeper
told the Circle Dot riders, all of whom he knew, save one. Dover
remedied this by introducing the new man.

"Ben, this is Jim Green; he's goin' to ride for us."

"Glad to meetcha," Bowdyr replied, and with a grin, "I own
this joint, though the Circle Dot fellas sometimes act as if they
did."

"If they make trouble, Ben——"

"Skittles, I was joshin'. They're a good crowd. I reckon a
cowboy with no devil in him is no more use than a busted bronc.
Ain't that so, Green?"

"It shorely is," Sudden agreed.

"We'll take our liquor over there," Bowdyr suggested, pointing
to a table in one corner. "No need to tell everybody our affairs."
When they were seated, he resumed. "Now, Dan, I'm goin' to ask
a straight question, an' I want the same kind o' answer. In Sody's
this mornin' you practically declared war on the Wagon-wheel.
Did you mean that?"

"Every damn word," the young man replied harshly. "They're
tryin' to smash the Circle Dot; they shoot down our riders, an'
now they've murdered Dad. Mebbe I'm next on the slate, but
until they get me, I'm fightin' back."

"Good enough," the saloon-keeper said. "What I can do, I
will."

"Thanks, Ben. They had their alibi all fixed, but it was a mistake to send a liar like Bundy."

"It's got me guessin'," Bowdyr remarked. "The Trentons was
allus high-handed an' disregardful of other folks' rights, but this
ambushin' ain't like 'em."

"That's so, but the fella who's been givin' the orders at the
Wagon-wheel for some time is that Easterner, Chesney Garstone.
I figure he's got Zeb hawg-tied."

"An Easterner, an' runnin' a cattle-range?" Sudden queried.

"Oh, Trenton does that; this jasper just runs Trenton," Dan
explained.

"Been around long?"

"Less'n twelve months, but that's too long. Hell, there he
comes. Don't often favour you, does he, Ben?"

"No, an' I ain't regardin' it thataway neither," the saloon-
keeper replied bluntly.

Chesney Garstone was a big man, physically, and in his own
estimation. About midway between thirty and forty, heavily-
built, his close-cropped fair hair, blue eyes, and somewhat square
head gave him a Teutonic appearance. He was meticulously
attired; trousers neatly folded into the tops of his highly-polished

28

riding-boots, a silk shirt, loosely-tied cravat, and soft black hat. Altogether a striking figure in any company. To their surprise, he stepped towards them.

"I came in to see you, Dover," he began. "I want to say how sorry I am—only heard the news two hours ago, when I rode in from the Bend."

Dan ignored the outstretched hand. "So you were there, huh?"

Garstone's eyebrows rose. "Certainly; I rode over yesterday morning and took the train to Washout, where I had business, and spent the night."

"Havin' given yore orders before you went."

"What the devil are you driving at?"

"Just this, Garstone. At the time my father was murdered, you claim to have been in Washout, Bundy says yore entire outfit was ten mile away, an' I s'pose Zeb has his tale all ready too."

"Are you suggestin——?"

"Not any—I'm statin' facts."

Garstone's eyes were furious, but he kept his temper. "Look here, Dover, you are talking wild," he said placatingly. "This must have been a terrible shock to you, and I'm willing to make allowances. My only object in coming here was to express regret, and see if we can come to terms. Listen: you have more water than you need, and we are short. Why not sell us the strip of land which would enable us to use the stream? I'll give you a fair price."

"How long have you owned the Wagon-wheel?"

"I don't, but I'm representing Trenton. What do you say?"

"One thing only: bring me the houn' who shot my father an' I'll talk with you."

Garstone made an impatient gesture. "You ask the impossible. Dave Dover had enemies, no doubt; he was the type to make them, stubborn, overbearing——" He paused as the young man's right hand moved threateningly towards his hip. "I'm not armed."

"No, an' I ain't got my back turned on you, have I?" Dan said meaningly. "Take notice, Garstone; if I hear o' you blackenin' Dad's name again, that excuse won't work; I'll horsewhip you."

Even this deadly insult failed to break the other's control, and he showed no sign of the fire raging within him. He appealed to Bowdyr.

"You are a witness that I tried to make peace," he said. "This hot-head boy insists on war, and by God! he shall have it—war to the knife."

"Meanin' a stab in the back, o' course," Dan retorted.

"Meaning the end of the Circle Dot," Garstone snapped.

As he went out of the saloon, the young rancher's voice followed him:

"Get yoreself a gun, Easterner; you'll be needin' one." He sat down again, drew a deep breath, and added, "That clears the air some."

Bowdyr shook his head. "He's a cunnin' devil; knowed you'd turn his offer down, but it puts the blame for any trouble on you, an' there's those in town will see it thataway."

"I ain't carin'," Dan replied. "What you think of him, Jim?"

"He's dangerous," Sudden said. "An' I wouldn't gamble too high on his not totin' a gun."

"I hope he does," was the sinister answer. "Time to be movin', Bill." This to the foreman, who promptly collected his men.

The ride home was very different to the usual hilarious return from town. Death was no stranger to any of them, but to-day farewell had been said to one they liked and respected, who, but yesterday, had been their leader. Stern-faced, the three cowboys paced behind the buckboard, speaking only rarely and then in lowered tones.

"Young Dan shorely made hisself clear to that dude," remarked Bob Lister, who was commonly addressed and referred to as "Blister."

"He did so, an' I'll bet he warn't wide o' the mark neither," Tiny—the heftiest of the outfit—replied. "What you think, Noisy?"

"Yeah," the third man said.

Tiny turned to the first speaker. "Allus the same. Ask that fella a simple question an' out comes a torrent o' talk like a river in flood-time. Honest, Noisy, if you don't hobble that tongue o' yores you'll git a bad name."

'He has that a'ready," Blister pointed out, and inconsequently, "There's goin' to be bustlin' times in this neck o' the woods. I'm likin' the look o' that new *hombre*—if he's on our side."

"Bill spoke well of him an' he's a good judge—he engaged me," Tiny said modestly.

"Yeah, I heard him apologizin' to the Ol' Man," Blister grinned, and Tiny—having no retort ready—the conversation languished.

The Circle Dot reached, horses unsaddled and turned into the corral, the rancher and Sudden were making for the house when a man emerged from a little shack near the wood-pile and came towards them. He was old, as his dead-white, untrimmed hair and beard bore witness, but in his prime he must have been both tall and powerful. Even yet, the broad but bowed shoulders suggested strength above the average. In one hand he was swinging a heavy axe, the blade of which shone like silver in the rays of the sinking sun. As he drew near, Sudden noted that his eyes were dull, expressionless.

" 'Lo, Hunch,' the young man greeted.

30

The man stared at him for a moment, and then, with apparent effort, stammered, "What's—come—o'—Dave?"

In a few sentences, and speaking very slowly, Dover told the tale. The other listened with seeming indifference, swung round without a word, and lurched away to the wood-pile. They saw the axe flash into the air and heard the thud of the blade as the keen edge bit deep into a baulk of timber; the blow was followed by others, each driven home with savage intensity; it almost seemed as though he were wreaking a vengeance on the tree-trunk.

"Another o' pore Dad's pensioners," Dan explained. "Drifted in 'bout two years back, sick an' starvin'. He lives in the hut, an' keeps us in fuel. O' course, he's kinda lackin'—lost his memory. For months we figured he was dumb, couldn't get a word from him; even now, it takes somethin' extra, but he 'pears to savvy what folks say."

"There don't seem to be much wrong with his muscles."

"He's as strong as a bullock—packs or hauls in loads you'd take a team for. He can't remember any name, but the boys a led him 'Hunch' on account of his stoop. Just worships that axe. I figure that he's been a lumberjack; every now and again, he'll be missin' for a spell, wanderin' in the woods."

"Ever have any trouble with him?"

"On'y once. We had a new hand—fella named 'Rattray,' an' the first half o' that described him. He was the kind what would tease a kid, an' he regarded a daft old man as the answer to a bully's prayer. It didn't come out just that way. Rattray got the axe an' started breakin' stones to blunt the edge. Hunch threw him clear across the bunkhouse, snappin' a leg, an arm, an' some ribs. Doc Malichi put him together again, an' when he was able to ride, Dad told him to. Rattray rode, but on'y as far as the Wagon wheel, so there's another who had reason to . . ."

Sudden switched the subject. "Odd number, that pill-merchant," he remarked. "What's he doin' here?"

"Committin' slow suicide," Dan replied. "It's a pity for he's a clever chap an' knows his job. Don't you pick holes in him; I've a notion he's a friend, an' we ain't overburdened with 'em."

"Well, there's one good thing about an enemy—yu know what to expect; friends ain't allus so dependable," was the puncher's cynical comment.

At the door of the ranch-house, Yorky was lounging. He scowled at the rancher.

"So now he's gone, yer t'rowin' me out," he said resentfully.

"Where did you get that idea?" Dan asked curiously.

"Flint said yer wouldn't be runnin' a home for hoboes no more."

"I don't consult Flint about my actions; you can stay as long as you want," Dan replied shortly, and went in.

31

Sudden hung back. "Why don't yu fork a hoss an' get out in the open, 'stead o' stayin' cooped up in the house, smokin' them everlastin' coffin-nails?" he asked quietly.

The boy's rebellious expression softened. "The Ol' Man useter talk that way, but it ain't no good," he muttered. "I told yer, I'm a weed an'—I can't ride, Mister."

"Weeds can grow big an' strong," Sudden smiled. "I'll teach yu to stay in a saddle. Think it over, an'—I'm Jim—to my friends."

He went, and Yorky slumped down on the long bench by the door. "Hell! I b'lieve he meant it, but what's th' good?" He reached out a screw of tobacco and papers, only to thrust them back again. "Awright—Jim—it's a bet."

So, on the following morning, when Sudden came to get his horse, he was accompanied by an unhappy-looking youth who stood and gazed doubtfully at the pony Burke had selected for him.

"Too old an' lazy to buck," the foreman said. "Been here damn near as long as I have. His name's 'Shut-eye.' Story is that one o' the boys—years ago—after a long an' tirin' day, dozed off in the saddle, figurin' his hoss would fetch him home. When he woke, hours later, they were in the same place an' the hoss was asleep too."

The average cow-horse, sensing that saddling is the prelude to hard work, resents the operation, but Shut-eye gave Tiny and Flint no trouble at all. But Sudden was not taking chances; even a mild fit of bucking might result in a fall which would send his pupil back to the ranch-house cured of any desire to ride. He meant to try the animal first.

"Shorely seems unenterprisin' but mebbe he's savin' hisself. If that's so, he's due for a surprise."

It was Sudden who got the surprise, for no sooner was he in the saddle than the pony, with a squeal of rage and pain, dropped its head and leapt into the air, coming down with feet bunched and legs like steel rods. So unprepared was the puncher for this display of temper that he lost his seat and only saved himself from being ignominiously "piled" by a swift grab at the saddle-horn, an act which brought a guffaw and satirical gibe from behind.

"Pullin' leather. Yorky'll have a good teacher."

Sudden did not look round—he was busy fighting the mad-dened beast beneath him—but he noted the voice. Back in the saddle, he gripped with his knees, dragged on the reins, and by sheer strength brought the pony's head up. Instantly the animal reared and would have fallen on him had not the rider flung him-self forward and driven home the spurs. A few more ineffectual efforts, which were deftly foiled, and Shut-eye appeared to realize it had met its master; trembling in every limb, the beast stood still.

Sudden got down, dropped the reins to the ground, and stroked the quivering nostrils. Then he loosened the cinches, raised the saddle, and swore as he saw the source of the trouble: a small section of cactus—the dreaded *choya*—had been so placed that any weight would drive the cruel, barbed, glistening spokes into the flesh. Well he knew the blinding agony they could cause, and it was not astonishing that the victim should forget its many years of training and relapse into savagery under the torment. With the point of his knife he wrenched the cactus free, and holding it on the palm of his hand, turned to the onlookers. Amid dead silence, he stepped to Flint, upon whose coarse features a half-sneer lingered.

"Why did yu put this under the saddle?" he asked sternly.

For a moment the man hesitated, and then, with an air of bravado, replied, "Just a joke; wanted to see if anythin' would wake the ol' skinful o' bones."

"An' it didn't matter if the boy took a tumble, which—sick as he is—would possibly kill him?"

"Oh, I figured you'd sample the hoss first," came the jaunty lie.

"Well, that makes it my affair. Any idea what the *choya* can do to man or beast?"

"No, allus avoid 'em m'self," Flint grinned.

Sudden dropped the torturing thing. "Yo're goin' to learn," he said, and with a lightning movement clutched the fellow by the throat, swung him off his feet, and sat him down on the cactus. With a howl of anguish Flint scrambled up and snatched out his gun, only to have it struck from his grasp and find himself sprawling on the ground from a flat-handed blow on the cheek. Frantically he tore at the cause of his suffering, and got more of the devilish spines in his fingers. A stinging, burning pain in every part of his body possessed him.

"Damn you all, git this cursed thing off," he shrieked.

The men looked at Sudden, who nodded. "Guess he knows what the *choya* can do now," he said, and turned away.

One by one, the terrible little thorns had to be ripped out by main force, and by the time the operation was completed, the patient appeared to be thoroughly cowed. Limping, he picked up his gun, made to thrust it into his belt, but instead, swung about and presented it full at the broad back of the man who had punished him.

"Freeze—all o' you," he rasped, and his face was a mask of murder.

"Pull, an' we hang you," Dan warned.

"This is atween him an' me," Flint retorted. "He gits his chance. You can face an' flash yore gun, Green." He would fire the instant the other was round, before he could draw.

That was what he meant to do: what he actually did was gape

with wide eyes at the muzzle of a six-shooter, levelled almost alongside his own, and pointed at his heart. The turn and draw had been one movement, executed at lightning speed. Behind the weapon, eyes of arctic coolness bored into his.

"Shoot, an' we'll go to hell together," said a mocking voice.

That was the position, and Flint knew it. If the thumb holding back the hammer—Sudden had no use for triggers—was released, even in the act of dying, he too was doomed. It was the acid test. One crook of his own finger, and . . . Those watching saw his hand sink slowly; the price of vengeance was too high.

"It can wait," he muttered thickly, and bent a malignant look upon his employer.

"I'm quittin'," he snarled.

"I fired you fifteen minutes ago," the rancher replied.

Flint's face took on a savage sneer. "Well, that suits me fine. Who wants to b'long to a pussy-cat outfit anyway?" He slouched towards his horse and was about to mount when Dan spoke again, brazen-voiced:

"That bronc bears my brand. When my father picked you out o' the dirt, you'd spent the last dime o' what yore saddle fetched."

The ruffian whirled on him. "You sendin' me off afoot?"

"You leave as you came," the young man retorted. "I don't even lend hosses to folk who misuse 'em."

"I'll make you sweat blood for this, Dover," was the fellow's parting threat, as he set out on the long tramp to town.

"I reckon I've lost you a hand, Dan," Sudden said.

"Take it you've done me a service," was the reply. "We can do without vermin around here."

CHAPTER V

Flint's departure was the signal for the outfit to get busy, and Yorky began to sidle towards the house. But Sudden was watching.

"Ain't yu ridin' with me?" he asked.

"Aw, Jim, I don't feel so good this mornin'," the boy said. "Can't we put off th' outin' fer a spell?"

The puncher saw the apprehensive glance at the pony, now standing head down, limp and dejected. He smiled as he replied:

"It's now or never, son. This is yore best chance. I doubt if even another dose o' cactus medicine would rouse a kick in that animile. Up with yu."

With obvious reluctance, Yorky climbed clumsily to the saddle; Sudden adjusted the heavy wooden stirrups so that the rider was almost standing in them, and gave him the reins. Shut-eye swung his head round, discovered that this new burden did not hurt, and again relapsed into apathy. The rest of the cowboys cheered and proffered advice.

"If you wanta git off quick, Yorky, don't slide over his tail or he'll h'ist yu into kingdom come," was Blister's contribution.

"Keep him awake," Tiny urged. "He snores awful."

"Talks in his sleep too," added another. "He's wuss'n Noisy for chatterin'."

The boy patted the neck of his now docile mount. "He can't answer," he grinned. "He dunno how ter bray."

Amid the laughter the retort evoked, Sudden stepped into his saddle and the incongruous couple set out, the boy bumping awkwardly up and down.

"Hold the reins short, an' shove yore feet well into the stirrups to take yore weight—yu don't need to ride like a sack o' meal," his tutor advised.

Moving at little more than a walk, they covered some three miles of plain, and reached a patch of pines. Sudden dismounted, trailed his reins, and told the boy to do the same.

"He won't stray then," he pointed out. "Reckon this'll be far enough to begin with, time yu get back. But first, yu gotta rest."

Lying on the soft, springy bed of pine-needles, Yorky gagged and choked as he drew in the odourful air. "Hell, this'll kill me," he gasped.

"No, cure yu," the puncher assured. "A dose o' this every day'll heal them lungs o' yores, but it's strong medicine, an' you have to get accustomed; it's the breath o' the pines."

"I ain't no sucker—trees don't breath."

"Every livin' thing breathes, trees an' plants too, an' when they're crowded, the weaker ones pass out for want of air," Sudden explained.

He rolled himself a cigarette and held out the "makings." Yorky's eyes gleamed, but he shook his head.

"I'm layin' off smokin' fer a bit," he said.

"Good notion," Sudden agreed. "Give the clean air a chance." He pondered for a moment. "Did Flint have anythin' against yu?"

"He was sore 'cause I cleaned him at poker. Say, you sports don't know nuttin' 'bout cyards. I was playin' th' game fer real money when I was a kid, an' I c'n make 'em talk."

"Was that all?"

The boy hesitated. "Yep," he replied.

The puncher knew it was a lie, but he was of those patient people who can wait. He pinched out his cigarette and got up.

"I have to be movin'," he said. "Stick around here for a while —no sense in gettin' saddle-sore."

With envious eyes Yorky watched the fine black lope away and vanish into the depths of a deep arroyo. "He's a reg'lar guy," he muttered. "Mebbe I'd oughter told him."

Sudden's mind too was upon his late companion, this pitiful product from the stews of a great city, pitchforked by circumstance into surroundings utterly at variance with all he had known, and where his handicap of ill-health told most heavily.

"Some folks is born to trouble, Nig," he mused. "Others, like you an' me, go huntin' it. An' we've shorely found some, spelt with a big T, if I'm any judge, an' I oughta be." A saturnine smile broke the line of his lips as he recalled the events of the last forty-eight hours, and he lifted his shoulders. "Fate deals the cards, an' a fella has to play 'em, win or lose."

Emerging from the arroyo, he crossed a stretch of plain and came to a double row of willows between which a clear stream moved unhurriedly. This must be the source of the dispute. It seemed a peaceful thing to war over, but the puncher was well aware of the value of water to a cattleman. Half a mile away on the other side, the land rose abruptly in a ragged ridge of rock running parallel with the creek. Groups of cows were grazing there; he was about to go over and investigate the brands when Dover rode up.

"Lost Yorky?" he asked.

"No, left him bedded down among the pines," Sudden smiled.

"You must be a magician. After that one trip to town, even Dad couldn't get him a hundred yards from the house."

"He's never had a break," Sudden said, and pointed to the ridge. "Yore boundary?"

"Yeah, this is the strip Garstone was speakin' of, but that wouldn't satisfy 'em. The Trentons is rotten right through, an' I'll never trust nor help one of 'em. As for that prinked-up Easterner ——" He spat disgustedly.

"Garstone will need watchin', he got all the points of a rattle-snake bar the good one—he'll strike without warnin'," was Sudden's opinion.

They rode along beside the creek, silent, the rancher studying this man of whom he knew nothing save that he could shoot like a master, used the saddle and long stirrup of the Californian "Buckaroo," but spoke with the slow drawl of the South. Western etiquette forbade a question, but there was no need.

"Tryin' to figure me, Dan?" Sudden asked, with a dry smile, and when the quick flush told he had hit the mark, added, "Shucks! yu have a right to know."

He spoke of a dying man, who, with his last breath, bequeathed a legacy of vengeance upon two scoundrels who had wronged him sorely, and of his own promise to pay the debt.

"That's why, like the creek there, I'm allus on the move," he said. "I ain't struck their trail yet, but I shall—one day." How that day did indeed come has been told elsewhere.[1]

Dover looked at the set face of the speaker; measured by time, he was not so many years older than himself, but in experience, twice his age. The similarity of their cases bred a feeling of brotherhood in his breast; he too had a score to settle. Impulsively he thrust out a hand, which was gripped in silence.

"Makin' for anywhere in particular, Jim?"

"Figurin' to have another look at the ravine—mebbe I missed somethin'."

"Then we part here," Dan said. "Yore line bears to the right."

Sudden had not gone far when a faint call of "Help!" reached him. It appeared to come from the vicinity of the creek and, swinging his horse round, he rode in that direction. A repetition of the cry served as a further guide, and in a few moments he was again beside the stream, at a point where after passing over a miniature Niagara, it widened out into a largish pool. The sight which greeted him was a singular one: a pale-faced girl, who appeared to be sitting in the water, and by her side a young man standing in it. The latter was Dover.

"Hey, Jim, don't come in," he warned. "Will yore rope reach this far?"

"Yeah, but it'll mean a rough passage for the lady."

"Can't be helped—it's our on'y chance. This damn quicksand has got us good."

Sudden leapt from his horse, walked to the water's edge, and swung his lariat. Carelessly as the rope seemed to be thrown, the

[1] Related in *The Range Robbers*. George Newnes Ltd.

37

loop dropped neatly over the girl's head. "Fix it under her arm-pits," he directed, and when this had been done, began to haul in swiftly. With a splash the girl struck the water, and in a brief space reached the bank, a limp, bedraggled specimen of humanity. The puncher helped her to stand up and removed the rope.

"Ain't no way to treat a lady, but I had to work fast," he apologized.

She fought for breath to answer, but failed to find it; this man who could throw an eight-hundred-pound steer had yanked her across the strip of shining water at incredible speed, and to her great discomfort. Sudden was not waiting for thanks.

"Hi, cowboy, need a hand?" he called out.

The leverage the empty saddle gave him had enabled Dan to free his feet from the clutching sand, and he was now astride the horse, only the head of which was visible.

"I can swim back," he replied.

By this time the girl had regained her breath. "Must I lose my pony?" she asked wistfully.

"A side-ways pull would break his legs," Sudden pointed out. A big cottonwood, one huge branch of which jutted out over the water, suggested something. "It's a chance," he said, and to Dover, who was preparing to plunge in, "Hold on a minute."

He sent his rope hurtling out again, and following his instruc-tions, Dover contrived to pass it under the pony's belly and tie it securely. Then he slipped into the stream and came ashore. In the meantime, Sudden had attached Dan's rope to his own.

"What's the idea?" the young man asked, as he emerged and shook himself like a wet dog. "That bronc is meat for the fishes."

"I'm one o' them obstinate folk an' need convincin'," was the reply.

Swinging himself into the cottonwood, he crawled along the great limb, passed the end of the joined lariats through a fork, and returned to the ground. The head of the pony was now almost submerged, and conscious of impending doom it uttered a shrill cry of fear.

"Awright, ol' fella, we're doin' our best," Sudden said, as he fastened the loose end of the ropes to the saddle-horn of his own mount. "This'll give us an almost straight lift, an' if the pore beggar's still got a kick in him, it may serve," he explained. "Steady, boy."

This to the black, which, with braced limbs, leant forward until the rope was at full stretch. The two men, intent on the operation, took no notice of the girl, but she too was watching anxiously. At a word from his master, Nigger advanced a pace, the muscles bunching beneath the satiny skin; the rope became taut as a bow-string, but apparently without effect. A second pace, another scream from the drowning animal, and Sudden chuckled.

"He's loosenin', 'less we've pulled his legs off," he said. "I can see the horn o' the saddle."

It was true; as the big horse slowly advanced, the smaller beast at the other end of the rope was raised clear of the quicksand to hang suspended, twisting in the air, and obviously beside itself with fright.

"Well, we got him, an' we ain't," Dan remarked quizzically. "What's the next move?"

"Drop him back in the water, an' yell," Sudden replied. "He won't stay to get mired again, an' he's carryin' no weight."

The rope was released and a piercing cowboy call rent the air; that, and the feel of the water sent the rescued beast scrambling frantically for solid ground, on reaching which it stood still, shivering and dejected. The lariat and saddle removed, however, it proceeded to roll contentedly in the grass, apparently little the worse.

"He ain't hurt none," Sudden said, adding with a grin, "an' what a tale he'll have to tell in the corral to-night."

"He's not the only one," a sweet but rather rueful voice remarked.

Engrossed in their task, the other rescuee had been forgotten, but now they turned to find her seated on a tuft of grass, trying to restore some sort of order to a wet mop of short, curly black hair. Little clouds of steam arose as the fierce rays of the sun licked up the moisture from her soaked attire. She was, as Dover confessed in an aside to his companion, "Sorta soothin' to the sight."

The description did her less than justice, for, despite her bedraggled state, even one of her own sex would have allowed her charm, at least. To the men, she was beautiful, and the fact that she could find a smile for them showed that she possessed the quality they most admired, courage. Sudden was the first to speak:

"How're yu feelin', ma'am?"

"Rather as though I ought to be pegged out on a line to dry," she replied. "The stream looked shallow enough to ride through, but half-way across I realized that my mount was in difficulties, and turned to go back, but it was too late. You see, I can't swim."

"You picked the wrong place," Dan told her. "The ford is a bit further down; there's a couple o' white stones to mark it."

"Being a stranger, I am afraid they wouldn't have meant anything to me." Her dark, long-lashed eyes regarded the tree-shadowed pool reproachfully. "Who would have dreamed that so charming a spot could be treacherous?"

"The Rainbow ain't to be trusted," Dan grinned. "She's as various as a——" He stopped abruptly.

"Woman," she finished, with a light laugh. "Please don't mind me—I am well aware of the failings of my own sex."

39

She stood up, her clinging garments revealing the youthful lines of her slim body. "I want to thank you both," she went on, her voice grave again. "But for your help, I might have . . ." She broke off, with a little shudder, and then, "My uncle will want to thank you too, and he'll be glad to see you at the Wagon-wheel—why, what is the matter?"

For Dan's face had suddenly become bleak. "Who are you?" he asked bluntly.

The girl's eyes flashed. "I am Beth Trenton," she replied. "And you?"

"My name's Dover, if that tells you anythin'."

"All I want to know," she returned coldly. "But I am still grateful for what you have done."

"Then don't be," the young man said vehemently. "Helpin' one o' yore family—even in ignorance—is somethin' I wanta forget."

"I have been here only a week, and have received nothing but courtesy from the men I have met; I am sorry to find an exception," was the cutting reply. She looked at Sudden. "If you will be good enough to bring my horse . . ."

When the puncher had roped and saddled the animal, she mounted with graceful ease, and without another word, rode in search of the ford. Dan's moody gaze followed her, noting how the proud, straight figure swayed easily to the movement of the beast beneath it; she could ride, and for a reason he did not attempt to analyse, the fact made him still more angry.

"Why in hell didn't I go some other place this mornin'," he fumed. "Zeb Trenton'll laugh hisself sick over this."

- "He oughta be mighty grateful."

"Ought means nothin' to him; he won't even pretend to be, the slimy ol' toad. Bet he's told her a pretty tale about the Dovers. If I'd knowed who she was— "

"Yu'd 'a' done just the same," Sudden smiled. "I'm allowin' it's rough it had to be yu, but rescuin' folks in distress seems to be a habit in yore family."

"She must be the niece I heard was comin' to live with him. I'd forgot about it. Damn the luck."

Sudden understood; the girl was very attractive, and had she been related to anyone else . . . His advice took a prosaic form:

"Better head for home an' get into some dry duds. I'll be on my way."

As he neared the scene of the murder, he left the beaten trail and approached obliquely, keeping under cover. It was unlikely that anyone could know of his intention to visit the place, but he was not one to take unnecessary risks. Peering through the branches of a tall bush, he could see where the body had lain. Someone was there, stooping over the spot, apparently examining

40

the ground intently. Presently the figure stood up, and Sudden recognized the bent shoulders, white hair, and big axe thrust through the belt.

"Hunch! What in the nation is that ol' tarrapin doin' here?"

Evidently he was engaged on the task Sudden himself had performed, that of reading the "sign" left by the assassin, for he climbed the bank of the arroyo at the same place and vanished. Sudden waited, but the other did not reappear, and the puncher returned to the Circle Dot in a reflective mood.

CHAPTER VI

An uneventful week passed. Sudden spent the time, as he put it, getting acquainted with the country. Somewhat to his surprise, Yorky was ready each morning to accompany him part of the way. The boy had made the most of his mount, which, carefully groomed, and with mane and tail combed, presented a much improved appearance. When the puncher remarked on this, Yorky flushed, and said:

"Th' boys figure he's played out but they's wrong; all he wanted was a bit of attention. We're pals, ain't we, Shut-eye?"

He stroked the pony's muzzle and Sudden smiled as he saw the piece of sugar pass from the boy's palm.

"A hoss is a good friend to have—'specially in the West," he said gravely. "Treat him right an' he'll not fail yu. I'm for Rainbow this mornin'. Comin' along?"

Yorky looked at his tattered raiment, and shook his head. "Nottin' doin'. Me fer another dose o' th' pine-breath; I'm gittin' so I don't cough me heart up—mos'ly."

"Good. Can I bring yu any smokin'?"

"Nix on that. T'ought I told yer I ain't usin' it."

"So yu did—I done forgot," the puncher lied. "So long, son."

"So long, Jim, an'—thanks," Yorky replied, and turned quickly away.

Sudden watched him trot off in the direction of the little pine forest. Still an awkward figure in the saddle, he was clearly improving. "The hell of it," he muttered softly, and started for the town.

He found the Parlour devoid of customers save for the unkempt person of Malachi, who, draped against the bar, was chatting with the proprietor. The latter welcomed the newcomer warmly.

" 'Lo, Green, you know the Doc, I reckon," he said.

"On'y by reputation," Sudden replied.

"Then you don't know him," Malachi said dryly.

"Well, I'm hopin' he'll drink with me allasame," the cowboy smiled.

"Sir, I'll drink with the Devil himself if the liquor is good—and there's no doubt of that here—but I warn you I am not in a position to return your hospitality."

"Aw, yore credit's good too, Doc," Bowdyr assured.

"Thanks, Ben, but I don't sponge on my friends," Malachi

returned, and to the puncher, "Folks in this locality are too healthy."

"I've been wantin' to speak to yu 'bout one who ain't," Sudden replied. "That kid at the Circle Dot."

The other nodded. "Old Dave got me to look him over, and that spawn of a city sink called me everything he could think of, and it was plenty. He finished by saying he didn't want to live in a God-forsaken place like this, and he'd be everlastingly some-thinged if he swallowed one drop of any blankety-blanked medicine I sent. My advice to Dave was to ship him back East and let him die in the gutter he had come from."

"He certainly can cuss," Sudden grinned. "Is there a chance for him?"

"Yes, if he spends all his time outdoors, and stops poisoning his system with nicotine—which he won't; he isn't the sort you can scare into doing a thing."

"But he might for a friend," the puncher suggested. "Well, Doc, I'm obliged for yore advice." He slid a ten-dollar bill along the bar, adding, "I think yu told the sheriff that was yore fee for consultation."

Malachi stared in amaze, and then a slow smile overspread his thin features; he pushed the bill back. "That was a special charge for Foxy," he said. "Besides, I've told you only what you knew already."

"Yu confirmed my own ideas, an' that's allus worth payin' for," Sudden insisted. "Yu can throw in a few doses o' physic if it will ease yore mind any; I'll see he takes 'em."

Malachi argued no further. "Next time you get shot up, I'll mend you free," he promised. "Ben, we shall need a bottle of your best to celebrate this unexpected appreciation of the medical profession in Rainbow."

Both the saloon-keeper and the puncher declined more than one small drink and the doctor tucked the bottle under an arm, bade them farewell, and hurried away. Bowdyr shook his head.

"It's a terrible pity," he remarked, "for, drunk or sober, he's a damned good physician."

Sudden's reply was cut short by the arrival of another customer, a tall, gangling man nearing sixty, who walked with a limp. He was harsh-featured, with a jutting, high-bridged, predatory nose, and close-cropped beard. Though dressed in range-rig, his garments were of better quality than those affected by the average rider. A heavy revolver hung from his right hip.

"Mornin', Trenton," Bowdyr greeted, in his tone more than a suspicion of coolness.

"Mornin'," the other said curtly. "Whisky—good whisky."

"If you can stand the stuff they peddle at Sody's, mine'll be a treat for you," Bowdyr said.

The rancher shrugged and looked at the cowboy. "Join me?"

Sudden pointed to his unfinished glass. "Obliged, but I'm fixed," he replied.

Trenton helped himself from the bottle before him, sampled the liquor, but made no comment. He turned again to the cowboy.

"I don't use this place, but I heard you'd ridden in, an' I wanted to see you."

"Yeah?"

"It appears I'm in yore debt for gettin' my niece out of a jam the other day," the rancher went on.

"Nothin' to that—I'd 'a' done as much for one o' yore steers," Sudden replied. "Besides, Dover——"

A scornful laugh interrupted him. "All that young fool did was to get himself in the same mess," Trenton jeered. "If it hadn't been for you, the pair of 'em might have drowned."

"Oh, Dan would 'a' found a way," Sudden defended. "I guess he was a mite impulsive."

"If he's expecting thanks from me he's liable to be disappointed; I don't owe him any. Yore case is different. What's Dover payin' you?"

The puncher chuckled. "Nothin'," and when the other's eyebrows went up, "Yu see, we ain't mentioned the matter as yet. I s'pose it'll be the usual forty per."

"I'll give you double that to ride for me."

"That's a generous offer to a stranger."

"I am under an obligation to you," Trenton explained. "Also, I can use a man who has ideas and acts promptly."

Sudden was silent for a space, and then, "I'm not in the market," he said. "Yu can forget about that obligation."

"But damn it all, I'm offerin' you more than I pay my foreman," Trenton cried.

"Which wouldn't make me too popular with him," was the smiling reply. "No, seh, money never meant much to me; I'm stayin' by the Circle Dot."

The rancher's face took on an ugly snarl. "That one-hoss ranch is might near the end of its rope. I'm beginnin' to think I misjudged you after all."

"It's happened before," Sudden said gravely. "I reckon I must be a difficult fella to figure out."

Trenton glared at him, realized that he was being gently chaffed and, with an oath, stalked out. The saloon-keeper looked at his remaining customer dubiously.

"It was a good offer," he commented. "Zeb ain't regarded as a free spender; he must want you bad."

"No, he's just tryin' to weaken Dan. At the end of a month, his foreman fires me, an' I'm finished round here," Sudden explained. "He must think I'm only just weaned."

"Nobody never does know exactly what Zeb Trenton thinks," Bowdyr replied. "It'll pay to remember that there's another way o' deprivin' Dan o' yore services."

The warned man laughed, but he paused at the door and took a quick look up and down the street before stepping out. Then he made his way to the store, to emerge presently with a bulky parcel which he strapped behind his saddle. He returned to purchase cartridges.

"Got many customers for thirty-eights?" he asked casually.

"Not any," the tradesman replied disgustedly. "Used to get 'em 'specially for a Circle Dot rider, Lafe Potter. He's bumped off, an' I ain't sold none since. Let you have 'em cheap."

"No use to me. Store-keeper I knowed once got landed the same way, an' I just wondered if he had company."

As he rode back to the ranch, he was thinking it over. The calibre of the weapon which had slain Dave Dover was not quite so common as the sheriff had attempted to imply; apparently nobody in Rainbow possessed one.

"O' course, a fella could buy his fodder elsewhere—the Bend, mebbe," he debated. "Wonder what became o' Potter's gun?"

That evening, after supper, he put a question.

"Yeah, Potter was wiped out some months back," Dan informed. "He was night-ridin' on what we call the creek line, an' was found in the mornin', after his bronc had sifted in without him. Same ol' story, shot, an' no evidence."

"What happened to his belongin's?"

"He owed money in the town, an' the sheriff claimed 'em," Dover said. "I never heard of any sale, but Evans was paid a matter o' ten dollars, an' I'll bet Foxy pouched the rest."

Which, having seen the officer, Sudden thought likely enough. The dead cowboy probably did not own even the name he was using, and there would be no one to make enquiries. Sudden saw that the trail had petered out for the present.

When he and Yorky set out in the morning, the boy was mildly facetious about the gunny sack tied to the puncher's cantle.

"That's a mighty gen'rous meal yo're packin', Jim. Goin' a long ways?"

"Bit further than usual. Can yu swim, son?"

"Yep, but I don't s'pose I c'd tackle the Pacific."

"Yu mean the Atlantic—we're headin' East, yu numskull."

"Shore I did. They's a chunk o' th' Atlantic in Noo York harbour. I useter go down ter see th' big liners come in. Oh, she's a swell city. I wish——"

"Yu were back there?"

Yorky shook his head. "Not now, it's different here these days, but I'd like fer yer to see Noo York."

"I have," Sudden grinned. "Wasted two whole weeks there

45

once, an' was thunderin' glad to get away. Them brick canyons they call streets——"

"Th' fines' ever."

"Mebbe, but they stifled me—I like fresh air. An' the crowds, everybody on the tear, like the end o' the world was due any minute."

The boy digested the criticism in silence. This capable man, who had handled Flint as though he were an infant, would not give an opinion lightly. Perhaps the one city he had known was not quite an earthly paradise after all.

"She shore is a busy li'l dump," he said, but less enthusiastically. "I'll bet yer met some smart folks."

"A few," Sudden smiled. "One of 'em tried to sell me a gold brick, but got peeved when I started to scratch it with my knife. Another said he'd returned recent from the 'per-aries' an' claimed to have met me somewheres, but after I allowed it was likely, as I'd been there, he lost interest."

Yorky wriggled delightedly. "He'd be a 'con' man; they's a slick gang."

"Shore," Sudden grinned. "Then three more invited me to play poker with 'em. Real nice fellas, they were—paid all my expenses, an' a bit to spare."

The boy's eyes went wide. "They let yer git away with it?"

"I had all my clothes on," the puncher replied, and Yorky had been long enough in the West to know what that meant.

They passed the customary stopping-place and about a couple of miles further came to a grassy hollow, shaded by pines. At the bottom of this, rimmed by sand, and shining in the sunlight like a huge silver dollar, was a tiny lake.

"There's yore Atlantic, an' if yu know of a better place for a swim, I'm listenin'," Sudden remarked as he dismounted.

In five minutes they had stripped, and the puncher, with a short run, shot into the water and vanished, to reappear ten yards from the bank, laughing and splashing. "C'mon, it's fine," he called. Yorky tried to emulate the feat, but only succeeded in falling flat on the surface and driving most of the breath out of his body. Then he struck off in the direction of his friend, beating the water with feverish rapidity which soon had him gasping.

"Take it easy," the puncher advised. "A slow stroke'll carry yu further, an' give yu a chance to breathe some."

Presently they came out, to lie stretched on the sand, where the increasing heat of the sun's rays soon dried them. Yorky was surveying his ragged shirt ruefully, prior to putting it on, when Sudden, reaching down the gunny sack, pitched it over.

"Ain't hardly worth while, is she? See what yu can find in this."

The boy groped in the bag, and produced a new, striped, flannel shirt, which he slipped into.

"Them pants o' yores is plenty ventilated but sca'cely decent," the cowboy went on. "Mebbe——"

Yorky was already searching; the pants appeared, followed by socks, and then something which made him gasp—a pair of the high-heeled boots affected by range-riders, and a broad-brimmed hat, the tall crown pinched in the approved fashion. Petrified, the boy stared at the garments, until Sudden's voice aroused him.

"Climb into 'em, yu chump. What d'yu reckon clothes is for?"

Dumbly, but with averted face, he obeyed; apart from Old Man Dover's, it was the only kindness he had received since coming West, and he was ashamedly conscious that his eyes were wet. The things fitted easily, but well, a tribute to the donor's gift of observation. When at length he spoke, his voice was shaky.

"Jim, I dunno——"

"Forget it, son. What's a few duds anyway? All yu gotta do now is get strong, eat more, an' fill out yore dimples. We'll make a cowboy of yu yet."

Yorky was silent; there was something he wanted to say, and it was difficult. With an effort he made the plunge:

"I'm feelin' mean. Jim, yo're swell ter me, an' I bin holdin' out on yer—'bout Flint. It warn't the cyard game; he wanted fer me to spy on the Ol' Man. I telled him where he c'd go."

"Good for yu," Sudden said. "Glad yu came clean about it. Flint was likely planted on us a-purpose. Yu see, the Wagon-wheel is out to bust the Circle Dot, so we gotta keep an eye liftin'. *Sabe?*"

"I get yer," the boy replied. "We'll beat 'em."

"Shore we will," Sudden smiled. "Now, I must be off; Dan don't pay me just to dry-nurse yu."

"An' them Noo York smart Alecks played him for a sucker," Yorky grinned, when he was alone, and went to survey his new finery in the mirror Nature had provided.

* * *

Beth Trenton sat on her pony regarding the scene of her recent discomfiture. She did not quite know why she had ridden there again except that, reviewing the incident in a calmer frame of mind, she had experienced qualms as to the way she had behaved. After all, the men had probably saved her life, and the fact that they were opposed to her uncle did not justify ingratitude. Looking at the placidly-moving surface of the stream, the danger beneath seemed incredible. Acting on a sudden impulse, she sent her mount down the shelving bank. At the very edge of the water, the animal shied away. She turned it again, and with a sharp blow of her quirt, tried to force it into the river, but with forefeet dug into the sand, the pony refused to budge. A satirical voice intervened:

"Well, of all the fool plays I ever happened on."

Angrily she jerked her mount round and saw one of the men of whom she had been thinking. Lolling in his saddle, hat pushed back, he was regarding her with unconcealed disapproval.

"It pleases you to be rude, sir," she said, with an attempt at dignity.

"It don't please me to see a hoss punished for showin' more sense than its rider," he replied brusquely. "What in blazes made you want a second dose o' that deathtrap?"

"I didn't, but I was curious to find out if the animal remembered," she said stiffly.

"An' if he'd lost his head an' rushed into the water, you'd 'a' been in the same pretty mess."

"From which you, as a gallant gentleman, would doubtless have extricated me."

"Yeah, at the end of a rope," Dan retorted. "You'd 'a' come out lookin' like a dish-rag, an' lost yore pony."

"Ah, yes, your clever friend not being with you." The gibe brought a flush, and her next remark deepened it. "What, may I ask, is your business on my uncle's land?"

The young man smothered his mounting wrath; after all, she was a stranger, and damnably pretty; and even as he loved spirit in a horse, he could appreciate it in this girl, lash him as she might.

"The land is mine," he told her quietly. "That rib o' rock is the Trenton boundary."

She did not doubt him, and the knowledge that he had scored in their verbal battle brought an added tinge of red to her cheeks, and took some of the harshness from her tone.

"Then I am trespassing?"

"You can come when you please, but that don't go for them other skunks at the Wagon-wheel."

Instantly he knew the slip had delivered him into her hands; the slow smile had begun, and it was too late to retract that one superfluous word.

"*Other* skunks," she said sweetly. "That means——"

"Yore uncle an' his outfit," Dan finished.

"Also—myself," she added, and waited for his apology.

She had mistaken her man; he was far too angry now, both with himself and her, to do anything of the kind. "Mebbe I ain't clever at stringin' words together, but I'm tellin' you this: on'y a skunk can live with a skunk," he retorted, and with an ironical sweep of his hat, spurred his horse, and was gone.

Beth Trenton stared after him in dumb amazement, and then— she laughed. "Maybe I did rowel him quite a lot," she murmured. "And I was a fool about the pony. All the same, you must pay for that, Dan Dover."

The Wagon-wheel ranch-house was a roomy, rambling one-storey building, standing at the top of a scrub-covered slope through which some sort of a road had been cut. It was flanked by the usual bunkhouse, barns, and corrals. A raised veranda extended along the front. On this, the ranch-owner was sitting when Beth, having handed her mount to a boy, approached the house.

"Where you been this mornin', girl?" he asked.

"Re-visiting the scene of my misadventure—I wanted another shiver," she smiled. "By the way, Uncle, did you thank those men?"

"I've seen Green, an' offered him a job here at twice what he's gettin'," Trenton replied. "He——"

"Refused," she said.

"How do you know that?" he asked sharply.

"Just a guess—he didn't seem the sort to be bribed."

"No question of that; he'd done me a service an' it was one way of payin' him; I didn't want the fella. As for that whelp, Dover ——"

"He risked his life," she reminded.

Trenton laughed sneeringly. "I wish he'd lost it," he said savagely. "He'll rot in his boots before he gets a word of gratitude from me."

The girl did not argue; she was beginning to discover unknown depths in this only relative who had befriended her since the passing of her father some years earlier, paid for her education, and was now giving her a home. Evidently the feud between the two ranches was more bitter than she had suspected. The knowledge both saddened and dismayed her.

CHAPTER VII

Trenton, Garstone, and the foreman were closeted in a small room used by the rancher as an office.

"So Green turned you down?" Garstone remarked. "It's a pity—we could do with him."

"An' we can do without him," Bundy growled. "There's other an' cheaper ways o' dealin' with his kind if he gits awkward."

"I'll have no bush-whackin', Bundy," Trenton said curtly. "There's been too much already, an' it's a game two can play."

"I warn't sayin' any different," the man lied. "But this fella man-handled Flint a bit back an' if he tries to level up that's no business of ourn."

Trenton took his pipe from his mouth and spoke through clenched teeth: "If he does, an' I know it, I'll hand him over to the sheriff right away."

"That'll shore scare him most to death," Bundy rejoined, with an impudent leer.

Garstone gave a gesture of impatience. "You said you had some news for us, Trenton," he reminded.

"I have information which may be of value—if we can use it," the rancher said. "It comes from Maitland, the new manager of the bank here. As you know, the cattle industry has had a rough time for some years, an' we're all working on borrowed money. The Circle Dot is in so deep that the bank holds a mortgage on the whole shebang, an' it runs out in less than two months' time."

Garstone looked sceptical. "They'll renew—these small-town concerns have to take risks."

"I doubt it; Maitland is scared—every rancher around owes him money, includin' myself." He smiled grimly. "Dave Dover gone, an' an inexperienced boy in the saddle makes all the difference. I guess he'd be glad to sell that mortgage."

Garstone sat up. "That's an idea, Zeb," he conceded. "What's the figure?"

"Forty thousand."

"Dave Dover must have been mad."

"No, the Circle Dot is worth more than that, an' he gambled on Lawson—the old manager—remainin'; they were good friends."

"Where's the coin coming from," Garstone wanted to know.

The rancher shrugged. "We've nearly a couple of months to raise it."

"And so has young Dover. Does he know?"

"I believe not, an' I suggested to Maitland, casually, that he might let the lad get over his father's death before pressin' him."

"Damn it, that was clever of you, Zeb," the Easterner complimented. "Gives us a start in the race, anyhow."

* * *

Yorky's new attire was as big a surprise to the outfit as it had been to him, and he had to endure a considerable amount of banter. But it was of the good-natured character—the kind they inflicted upon each other—for the boy's health aroused only pity in their robust natures. Also, Yorky's tongue had a razor edge, and, as Tiny once put it, "the li'l runt was shore raised on brimstone."

When Blister and Noisy rode in and beheld the resplendent figure leaning carelessly against the veranda rail, they gave a passable imitation of falling from their horses.

"D'you see what I see, Noisy?" Blister cried. "Dan has done sold the ranch from under us, an' there's the noo owner. I'm askin' for my time; I ain't ridin' for no dude."

Noisy nodded. They pulled up about ten yards away, removed their hats, and sat in silent admiration. A moment later, Tiny, Slocombe, and Lidgett arrived, and without a word, lined up beside them. Yorky, who was enjoying the sensation he was causing, spoke:

"Howdy, fellers."

"It can talk," Blister said in an awed tone. "An' somehow the voice seems familiar."

The voice continued to talk. It began by describing them as a bunch of locoed sheep-herders, and went on to become even more familiar, referring, with fluency of adjective, to the personal habits of each one in turn. All this with a grin on the sallow face.

"Why, it's Yorky!" Slow pretended to discover. "Sufferin' serpents, boy, where did you git them bee-yu-ti-ful clothes?"

"Bought 'em outa his savin's on smokin'," Tiny suggested.

"Couldn't be did in the time," Blister said. "Yorky don't earn more'n a dollar a week."

"He does, but he don't git more," the boy corrected.

"I b'lieve he's robbed a store," Lidgett laughed.

"Aw, go chase yerself," Yorky countered. "Me rich uncle in Noo York——"

A howl of merriment cut short the explanation; extravagant tales of this mythical relative had amused them on more than one occasion. Sudden had joined the group.

"Don't yu mind 'em—they're just jealous," he said. "Yu'll be the best-dressed Circle Dot fella at the dance."

"What dance?" several voices asked.

51

"I hear the town is holdin' one, at the schoolhouse, tickets a dollar a head—to approved applicants."

"That last oughta shut out them Wagon-wheel felons," was Tiny's comment. "When's she due to happen, this fandango?"

"Middlin' soon, but the date ain't fixed."

"It's two long weeks to pay-day, an' we couldn't raise a dollar in the outfit," Blister wailed.

"Shucks! Dan's got a slate, ain't he?" Sudden grinned.

That evening he told his news to Dover and the foreman, both of whom were inclined to be sceptical.

"Rainbow must be wakin' up," was the rancher's opinion. "How did you get the glad tidin's, Jim?"

"Met Malachi on his way up here. No, he warn't lit up, but I wouldn't say he was enjoyin' the ride. He's unusual, that *hombre*."

"Shore is, if he'd come ten mile to bring a bit o' local gossip," Dan said ironically.

"There was somethin' else; he said yu might find it worth while to make the acquaintance o' the new bank manager—soon."

"What the devil——"

"That's all he would say, but in yore place I'd take the advice. Malachi ain't a fool, 'cept to hisself."

Dan gave in. "I'll ride over in the mornin'."

"He also mentioned that the dance is bein' organized by Zeb Trenton, to introduce his niece," Sudden went on.

The young man's face flushed furiously. "Then the Circle Dot ain't attendin'," he grated.

"That'll disappoint the boys an' put us in wrong with everybody," the foreman dissented.

"He's right, Dan," Sudden supported. "Yu can't afford to stay away."

"Damnation, whose side are you on?" Dover asked irritably.

"Yores, an' I made it plain to Trenton yestiddy when he offered me double pay to ride for him," was the pointed reply.

"He—did—that? An' you sent him packin'? I'm sorry, Jim; I'm a sore-headed bear, these days."

"Don't need talkin' about. He put it that he owed me somethin'."

"Imagine a Trenton sufferin' from gratitude! All he wanted was to take a good man from me."

"The dance is also to serve as a welcome for another newcomer—the bank fella," the puncher added.

"That settles it—we just gotta be there," Burke said. "Yorky must 'a' had early news o' the party—he's all dressed up a'ready, an' got the boys guessin'."

"I saw him as I rode in, struttin' around like a young turkey gobbler," Dan smiled. "Yore doin', I s'pose, Jim?"

"Part o' the cure," Sudden replied.

* * *

In the private office of the bank Dover sat facing the manager, a smallish, undistinguished person, nearing fifty, with thinning hair, and pale, spectacled eyes.

"I wasn't meaning to trouble you yet, Mister Dover, in view of your bereavement," he said. "But I'm glad you came in; I wanted to see you."

"About anythin' in particular?"

"Er, yes. Are you acquainted with the state of your father's finances?"

"No. Dad was allus kind o' secretive, an' I ain't had time to look over his papers."

"Quite so. Well, Mister Dover, when I examined the books of this bank I was amazed and even alarmed by the amount owing to it by the local cattlemen."

"You tellin' me the Circle Dot is one of 'em?"

"Not only one, but the most deeply involved."

At this moment the door opened and a young, fair-haired girl stepped in. "Oh, Dad," she began, and stopped. "Sorry, I didn't know you had a visitor."

"My only child, Kate, Mister Dover," the banker explained. The young man stood up, shook hands, murmured, "Pleased to meetcha," and the girl withdrew, but not without a challenging glance of approval at the rancher.

"What's the position?" Dan asked.

"We hold a mortgage on your ranch for forty thousand dollars," came the reply.

Dan jerked upright, his eyes large. "The hell you say?" he gasped. "Forty thousand? That's a jag o' money."

"Much more than we can afford to lose. I understand the cattle business has been bad for some years."

"You won't lose a cent," Dover asserted. "There's better times right ahead."

"Mister Trenton, whose experience you must allow, doesn't share your views about that."

Dan's face darkened. "How came the Wagon-wheel into this?" He put a question.

"It is our rule never to disclose information about a client," Maitland said pompously.

"Then Trenton don't know about the Circle Dot?"

A second's hesitation, and then, "Not from us, Mister Dover," came the denial.

Watching the weak, irresolute features, Dan knew the words

53

were untrue. Long years of sitting on a stool, adding up figures, had given the man a position of some responsibility, but not the knowledge to use it. He would bully those beneath him, and be servile to his superiors, and of the latter he would regard Trenton as one.

"What do you want me to do?" he asked.

"The mortgage expires in a little less than two months, and as I am convinced our Head Office will not consider a renewal, it must be paid off."

"An' failin' that?"

The banker lifted his shoulders. "We have the power to sell."

To all the young man's arguments that a forced sale would not produce even the amount of the debt, let alone the value of the ranch, and that, by waiting, the banker would get the whole sum due, he shook a stubborn head. He had the interests of his employers to consider; his predecessor had been unwise; he was sorry, and so on.

Dover listened with a set jaw; he knew the mean, warped little soul was joying in the possession of authority for the first time. Mechanically he took the flabby hand extended when he rose.

"I shall hope to see you at the dance," Maitland said. "A very kindly thought on the part of Mister Trenton. It will give me an opportunity of meeting our customers in a more congenial atmosphere than that of an office. My wife and daughter will appreciate it."

Dan gave a non-committal answer, went out, and proceeded to the Parlour. Bowdyr was alone—yesterday's patrons were sleeping it off, and to-day's had not yet begun to come in.

"Where's Malachi?" the rancher enquired.

"At the opposition joint, I expect," Bowdyr grinned. "He's an odd mixture: allus pays cash here, but runs an account there—sez he'd hate to die in my debt, but it would cheer his last moments to remember that he owed Sody 'bout a million dollars. You want him?"

"I want a drink more—a big one."

The saloon-keeper looked at him keenly. "What's the trouble, boy?" he asked, pushing forward bottle and glass.

Dan swallowed a hearty gulp of the spirit, and then told the story. Ben's face grew graver as he listened.

"Hell!" he said, when all was told. "I knowed the Ol' Man was up agin it, but never suspicioned it was that bad. An' you think Trenton knows?"

"Shorely," Dan replied. "He'd milk that money-grubber dry. I've gotta raise that coin somehow, Ben, or he'll buy the Circle Dot for half its value."

"Well, Dan, any help I can give is yourn, but pore times in the cattle trade hits me too," Bowdyr said.

"I know that, Ben, an' thanks, but this is my job."

The entry of Malachi put an end to the conversation. He appeared to be sober, and helped himself to an unusually modest dose of his customary tipple.

"I'm obliged for yore message, Doc," the rancher said.

"You've seen Maitland? What's your opinion of him?"

"I think he's taken the place of a better man."

"Yes, it was an unlucky day for Rainbow when Lawson elected to go back East," the doctor agreed. "This fellow has always had a boss; he'll find one here."

"He's done that a'ready," Dan said bitterly. "Though mebbe he ain't aware of it yet."

Malachi nodded. "Trenton gets the town to give a dance in his niece's honour, an' tells Maitland it's for him." He laughed wryly. "Clever devil; wonder how much he owes the bank?"

"I dunno, but I'd like to," Dan said. "You goin' to this festive gatherin'?"

"I might. I'm told the girl is pretty. Have you seen her?"

"Yeah, she has looks," Dover admitted, and left soon after.

"He's missin' his dad," Bowdyr remarked.

Malachi nodded agreement. "Ought to take more liquor; drink is the sovereign cure for depression, old settler; lifts a man to Paradise——"

"An' drops him in hell next mornin'," the saloon-keeper finished. "You can't tell me, Doc; I sell it."

CHAPTER VIII

Dover spoke little during the evening meal, but afterwards, when he joined Sudden and Burke at the fireside—for the nights were chilly—he shared the burden which had been on his mind all day. The effect on the foreman was shattering.

"Goda'mighty, Dan, it can't be true," he cried. "Them bank sharks must be framin' you."

"I saw the deed," the rancher replied. "It's straight enough. We have to pay up, or let Trenton grab the Circle Dot."

"Is the Wagon-wheel in debt to the bank?" Sudden asked.

"Shore to be, but not up to the neck, as we are."

"Then they won't find it easy to put up the price."

"Not unless Garstone can get it back East."

"That'll take time, an' gives us a fightin' chance to beat 'em to it," the puncher responded. "Mebbe if yu reduced the amount . . ."

"I offered that, but he wouldn't listen. Trenton has painted a pretty gloomy future for cattle."

"Awright, we gotta make it so—for him," Sudden said grimly. "Meanwhile, we'd better keep this to ourselves; sometimes there ain't safety in numbers. Yu got anythin' in mind, Dan?"

"Yeah, but it's such a long shot that—well, it'll sound hopeless."

"Long shots come off-times."

The rancher pondered for a moment, and then, "Bill, you'll have heard o' Red Rufe's Cache?"

"Shore, but I never took much stock in it," Burke replied.

"It's true," Dan said, and went to an old desk in a corner of the room. They heard a click, and he returned with a creased half-sheet of paper. "Here's what it sez: 'Dear Dave,—I've made a lot o' money an' a good few enemies. In case one o' these last gets me, I'm lettin' you know that my pile is cached in the hills. When you reach the bowl on Ol' Cloudy's knees, watch out. West is north, an' north is noon, one half after will be too soon. I'm sendin' the rest o' the instructions by another hand. Yore brother, Rufe.' That was the last news we had of him, some three years ago."

"An' the second messenger never arrived?" Sudden asked.

"I dunno. A stranger was found two-three miles out on the Cloudy trail a little while later; he'd been shot an' robbed. The first chap got drunk in the town an' may've talked some. Any-

56

way, the story of the cache oozed out, an' there's been more than one try to find it, but Cloudy is big an' hard country."

"Yore father didn't attempt it?"

"I ain't shore; he was away for a week or more several times, but without the rest o' the directions, it's almost hopeless."

"An' it was this paper that——"

"Dad was killed for," Dan said gruffly. "Yeah, someone has the other. I figure Flint was sent here to steal it."

"That means Trenton has the other?"

"That's my belief, but I've no proof," the rancher admitted. "Yeah, I guess I could find this place the paper mentions, but without the further instructions . . ." He shrugged his shoulders helplessly.

"Well, it's a forlorn hope, like yu said, Dan," Sudden remarked. "We gotta keep eyes an' ears open. One good point to bite on is that whoever has the second message is wuss off than we are—he don't know where to begin."

"If on'y we could put our paws on that missin' paper," the foreman lamented.

"If—that's one hell of a word, ol'-timer," Sudden smiled. "Just the most provokin' one in the whole darn dictionary."

*　　　*　　　*

The evening of the dance arrived and found the Circle Dot bunkhouse in a state of feverish activity. Shirts had been washed, boots polished, and war-bags were being searched for a hoarded neckerchief or cherished tie, which was not always found in the possession of its rightful owner.

"Hi, who's rustled my red silk wipe?" Lidgett wanted to know, and then, detecting Noisy in the act of slipping the missing article out of sight, pounced upon it.

"Why, you gave it me," protested the silent one.

"It was on'y lent, you chatterin' son of a cock-eyed coyote," Lid retorted. "Think I got nothin' to do with my earnin's but keep you in clothes?"

"You don't earn a cent—what Dan gives you is part o' *our* pay," Noisy grinned. "We do the work."

Paddy, the cook, pestered by demands for hot irons to take the creases from seldom-worn coats, and the loan of his razor, which was known to possess an edge, energetically damned the dance and the fools who were going to it. He was remaining at the ranch.

"An', thank Hiven, it's a peaceful night I'll be enjoyin' for once in me loife."

"It's a mercy you ain't comin'—there'd be no space for any-body else," Slim unwisely told him.

"Shure an' there wud for you if the room was full, ye slice o' nothin'," the fat man retorted. "Yer partner'll think she's dancin' wi' a flag-pole."

Before Slim, who really did justify his name, could hit upon an adequate reply, Blister cut in. "They say the Trenton dame is awful pretty; wonder if she'll take a turn with any of us?"

"Zeb'll 'tend to that," Tiny said. "I'm told the banker's girl ain't exactly a grief to look at. I've most near forgot how to waltz; let's try her out, Blister."

It was an unfortunate rehearsal—for someone else. The two wash-basins were in great demand, and Slocombe, despairing of getting one, had brought in a bucket of water, and, stripped to the waist, was bending over it, sluicing his face, when the disciples of Terpsichore collided heavily with his rear. Head jammed in the bucket, the outraged victim rose to his feet, the soapy contents cascading down his person, and literally drowning the muffled maledictions which came from the interior of the utensil. Tiny, eager to make amends, tore the strange headgear from the wearer's head. The effort was well-meant, but Tiny was a tall man, his snatch was upward, and he forgot the dangling handle. With an agonized yell, Slocombe grabbed the offending pail, hurled it with a crash of glass through a window, and clutching his almost fractured jaw with both hands, capered around the room spitting out lather and profanity with every leap. The paralysed outfit fought its mirth—one laugh might have turned the comedy into a tragedy. Tiny broke the silence:

"Which I'm damn sorry, Slow," he said, and his voice contained no hint of the laughter bubbling within him. "We didn't go for to do it; we never saw you."

"Sorry?" Slocombe cried. "You lumberin', club-footed elephant—they oughta hang a bell on you to tell folks when yo're movin' around; yo're a danger to the c'munity, an' why in hell did you try to slice the face off 'n me with that sanguinary handle?"

"I acted for the best, Slow, honest I did," the big man replied, but his contrite expression was too much for the audience and a storm of merriment broke out.

Slow looked murder for a moment, and then—being a good sport—joined in. The appearance of Sudden stilled the tumult, and he had to be told the story.

"Yo're dead right, Slow," was his decision. "Tiny oughta have a corral all to hisself."

"You'll be late, Jim, won't you?" Blister asked, noting that the puncher had made no preparations.

"I ain't goin'," was the reply. "Someone has to stay an' keep house, if on'y to see that nobody steals our cook."

"Huh, they'd have to fetch a wagon to take him away," Slim chimed in.

"We'll cut the cards to see who stays home 'stead o' you," Tiny said, and the rest voiced approval.

"Mighty good o' yu, but it's all settled," Sudden replied. "An' I don't care for dancin', anyways."

Later, as Dan mounted to follow his men, he said, "Why not come along, Jim. Paddy can hold down the ranch."

"I'm playin' a hunch; mebbe there's nothin' in it."

When the hilarious whoops died away in the distance, he had an idea. Returning to the living-room, he opened the desk. Knowing where to look, it did not take him long to find the hidden drawer. Then, the paper in hand, he pondered. On a shelf, amid a dusty litter of odds and ends, was a spike file of paid bills. Sudden removed half, thrust on Rufe Dover's letter, and replaced them. Then he saddled his horse, leaving it picketed just outside the corral. These preparations made, he returned to his lonely vigil. Paddy was singing in the kitchen, and away over the plain the weird call of a prowling coyote came to him.

"The boys would say there ain't no difference, an' they'd be damn near right," he chuckled, as he lit a cigarette and settled down in his chair by the fire.

The hours crept by and the watcher was beginning to think he had foregone an evening's amusement vainly when a rifle-shot brought him to his feet; something was happening on the range. He stepped swiftly to the kitchen and awoke the drowsing cook.

"Get a gun an' keep yore eyes peeled," he said. "Somethin' odd goin' on."

He hurried to the hut by the wood-pile; its occupant was squatting by the fire.

"Hunch, I want yu to fork a hoss an' fetch Dan an' the boys; they're at the schoolhouse in Rainbow. Say there's trouble, an' hurry. Understand?"

The old man nodded, and the puncher wasted no more time. He reached his horse, coiled the picket-rope as he ran, mounted, and spurred into the open. He had not gone far when he saw a flash, followed by a crack—this time, of a revolver—and the bellow of a frightened steer. Rustlers! Sudden clamped his teeth on an oath and slowed down—he had no desire to run into a trap. Soon he could hear the beat of galloping hooves, and discern shadowy forms scurrying to and fro in the gloom. They were rounding up cattle in readiness to drive.

Sudden dragged out his Winchester, waited until he could see one of the vague figures, and squeezed the trigger. The crash of the gun was succeeded by a muttered curse which brought balm to the marksman; the bullet had not been entirely wasted. Three fingers of flame stabbed the darkness, but the Circle Dot man had moved immediately he had fired, and the lead hummed harmlessly past him. He replied, aiming at the flashes, three quick shots from

59

different positions, to convey the impression that he was not alone. Apparently he succeeded, for a hoarse voice said:

"Better be movin'—we've given 'em time enough. C'mon."

The puncher sent a couple of slugs to hasten their departure and then rode forward. A dark blot on the ground proved to be a dead horse from which the saddle had been removed. Nearby about a score of steers were milling. Sudden broke and scattered them; if the rustlers returned, they would have to start all over again. But he did not think they would; the remark, "given 'em time enough" was sticking in his mind, and realizing the impossibility of running down the raiders in the dark, he headed for the ranch-house.

Approaching quietly, he dismounted and slipped in by the back door. On the floor of the kitchen the cook was lying senseless. Sudden dashed into the living-room in search of whisky. The place might have been struck by a cyclone. Chairs and table overturned, the desk and secret drawer open, rug thrown aside, papers and other articles scattered broadcast. Sudden grinned as he saw that the shelf and its dusty burden had not been touched. There was no whisky, and a smashed bottle on the hearth supplied the reason. He was looking at this when a voice came from the doorway:

"Don't stir if you wanta go on breathin'."

There was no need to turn; a small mirror over the fireplace told him that a masked man, with a levelled gun, had followed him in from the darkened passage without. Sudden obeyed a further order, but did not raise his hands very high.

"Where's the letter from Rufe Dover?" the unknown barked.

"On the shelf behind me—there's a file," the puncher said.

In the glass he watched the fellow move, noted that as he reached for the shelf, his eyes instinctively followed his hand. This was the moment Sudden was waiting for. His own right dropped, whisked out a gun, reversed it, and fired over his shoulder, the whole action taking seconds only. He saw the intruder stagger under the impact of the bullet, drop his weapon, and lunge from the room. At the same moment a voice outside the window said:

"What's doin', Rat? Want any help?"

"No," Sudden gritted, and sent a slug crashing through the glass.

He heard the front door slam, and the same voice asked: "You got it?"

"Yeah, in the shoulder—that cursed gun-wizard showed up. C'mon, beat it."

A scuffle of hurrying hooves told the rest.

The puncher returned to the kitchen to find that the injured man had recovered his wits and was sitting up tenderly feeling a large bump on the back of his head.

"Glory be, an' phwat's happenin' this noight," he wanted to know.

"S'pose yu tell me," Sudden suggested.

"An' that won't take long," Paddy replied. "I'm settin' in me chair, an' hears someone come in by the front dure. I thinks it's yerself an' stan's up to welcome ye. An' thin, the roof falls on me."

*   *   *

The festivities at Rainbow were in full swing by the time the Circle Dot contingent arrived and had deposited hats, spurs, and guns. Desks had been removed from the floor, forms arranged against the walls, thus leaving space for the dancers. At one end of the room, a pianist and a fiddler—loaned from Sody's saloon—struggled for the lead in a polka, and bets were laid as to which would win. Trenton, his harsh countenance contorted in what he would have called a smile, had presented his niece to the more important of the townsfolk, and she was now dancing with Malachi. Her glance rested on Dover as the rancher and his men entered, but she at once looked away. The doctor danced well, and had taken the trouble to improve his appearance. But he was his usual flippant self.

"I will wager a waltz that I can guess your thoughts," he said: "Is it a bet?"

"Why, yes," she smiled.

"You are wondering what I am doing out here in the wilds." The girl flushed. "You win," she said. "Now tell me."

"I might answer with your own question," he parried.

"Mister Trenton is my sole remaining relative."

"Tough luck," he murmured, and noting the tiny crease between her level brows, "I mean, of course, being reduced to one. Now I had too many relations, and they all had ideas as to what I should do with my life, so I ran away."

"But why choose such a—sordid place?"

"Sordid? Well, I suppose to Eastern eyes it would seem so; a wit once said that Rainbow started with a saloon to supply the necessaries of life, and the store came later to provide the luxuries. But have you reflected that this same sordid settlement may one day become a great city, of which—as an early inhabitant—I may be regarded as a foundation stone?"

"Now you are laughing at me," she protested.

"No, I'm serious. 'Imperial Caesar, dead and turned to clay, may stop a hole to keep the rats away.' At present, I'm only stopping the holes these foolish people make in one another. Which reminds me, you must see our cemetery—it is really pretty."

"You would naturally be interested in it," she replied, paying him in his own coin of raillery.

"Very little," he smiled. "Most of those within it required no aid from my profession to enter the other world. Ah, the fiddle has beaten the piano by a whole bar. Hello, Dan, you've met Miss Trenton?"

The young rancher, by whose side they had stopped, looked into the girl's cool, unsmiling eyes, and said, "No."

"Well, you have now," Malachi replied. "Ask her prettily and perhaps she'll dance with you."

He left them, and Dan's gaze travelled over the slender, simply but perfectly-clad figure. "Will you?" he queried.

She made a pretence of consulting her card. "I have no vacancy," she said icily. "Besides, only a skunk can dance with a skunk."

Dan's mouth hardened; it had been an effort to ask, and the scornful reminder of his rudeness made him reckless. His eyes swept the room, noting that many Wagon-wheel riders were present.

"You shore fetched along plenty partners," he flung back, and turned away.

Garstone found her red and angry. "I don't like that young man," she told him.

"That's something else we have in common," he said. "I hate the sight of him."

He slid a possessive arm about her and steered into the throng. He was easily the best-dressed and most striking man in the company, and in spite of his bigness, light on his feet. Dan, watching with narrowed eyes, was conscious that they made a perfect pair. He was also painfully aware that everyone else seemed to be having a good time. As usual, on these occasions, males predominated, but this did not trouble the cowboys, for when ladies were lacking, they just grabbed another of their kind and jigged about, exchanging quaint expletives when a collision occurred. Blister and Slow—the late fracas now only a matter for mirth—were performing together, and a fragment of their conversation reached him. Blister was the gentleman.

"Never seen you lookin' so peart, pardner," he complimented in dulcet tones. "You bin washin', or somethin'?"

"Yeah, y'oughta try it," the "lady" instantly retorted.

"You'd dance well too, if you knowed what to do with yore feet," Blister went on.

"I'll shore know what to do with one if you trample on 'em any more," was the spirited response.

At any other time this, and the sight of Tiny, carefully convoying the school-mistress—an austere-faced lady of uncertain age—and holding her bony form as though it were a piece of delicate china, would have moved him to merriment, but now . . .

"Might be goin' to his own funeral," he muttered. "Hell, I'll get me a drink."

Again he met with disappointment; he ran into Maitland and

had to be introduced to the banker's wife—a colourless little woman with a tired face. Then he found himself dancing with the daughter.

"When we came here, I didn't think I was going to like it," she confided, "but I am. The cowboys are so picturesque, and I'm longing to see a ranch."

"You'd be disappointed," he told her. "Just a lot o' land, with some cows sprinkled around."

The expected invitation not having materialized, she changed the subject. "Isn't Miss Trenton charming—quite the prettiest girl here, but perhaps you don't care for brunettes?"

"If a fella likes a woman I reckon the colour of her hair don't matter," he fenced.

"See, she's dancing with that sick-looking boy; she must be real kind."

Miss Maitland was right, and wrong. Beth, anxious to humiliate the man who had again been rude to her, had hit upon a means; the honour he had solicited should be conferred upon the least important of his outfit. Yorky, feeling rather unsure of himself, despite his contempt for the "hayseeds," suddenly found the belle of the evening sitting by and looking kindly at him.

"You must be the boy Doctor Malachi was telling me about," she said. "Like myself, you come from the East."

"Yes'm, li'l ol' Noo York," he stammered, and added, "Allus sump'n doin' there."

"Far too much doing," she smiled. "Unending noise and hustle, never any rest. I didn't like it."

This was another blow to the boy's faith in "li'l ol' Noo York."

"Jim don't neither," he admitted.

"And who is Jim?"

"He's my pal," Yorky said proudly. "I useter loaf aroun' the house all th' time, but Jim sez, 'Quit smokin', go a-ridin' an' git th' breath o' th' pines.' So I done it, an' I'm better a'ready."

"The breath of the pines," she repeated. "Your friend must be something of a poet."

"Not on yer life," the boy defended. "Nuttin' slushy 'bout Jim. Gee! y'oughter see him stripped—I mean, he's——"

"A finely-made man," she helped him out. "You must tell me about him, and yourself, while we dance. You do dance, don't you?"

"I c'n shake a leg," he said; and conscious that he had omitted something, "but I dasn't ask——"

"Nonsense," she smiled. "I am going to enjoy it."

And enjoy it she did, for her partner had the gamin's instinct for rhythm in his toes. Thus she learned how Old Man Dover had brought the boy to the ranch, and how he had hated it until a black-haired hero had come to change his outlook entirely. She

63

was told about Flint, and what "fine guys" the boys were.

"And Mister Dan, is he a fine guy too?" she asked.

"Shore he is, white clean t'rough," Yorky said loyally.

Miss Trenton stole a glance at the rancher as he passed, and failed to experience the exultation she had expected. When the music ceased, she dismissed her partner with a gracious word of thanks. Garstone stepped to her side.

"Why on earth were you dancing with that tramp?" he asked.

There was a warning flash in the dark eyes. "I believe it is a lady's privilege to select her partner."

"Of course, but if you must take one of the opposite camp, surely it need not be the stable-boy."

"The stable-boy behaved like a gentleman," she said coldly. "No, I am tired, and wish to rest a little. Miss Maitland is looking appealingly in this direction; I am sure she will oblige."

"That's a good suggestion—we have to keep in with the fellow who holds the purse-strings," the big man laughed, but there was a frown on his face when he had turned away.

Meanwhile, Yorky's sharp eyes had noticed something, and he disappeared to investigate. He returned during the next interval, and got Dan's attention.

"Say, Boss," he whispered. "Five or six o' th' Wagon-wheel fellers, includin' Flint, has beaten it."

"Gone to Sody's to tank up," Dan suggested.

"They ain't—I've bin ter see. Their hosses is missin' too," the boy replied. "Man I asked said he hadn't seen Flint since soon after the second hop."

"That's certainly odd, Yorky; it ain't like cow-hands to run off from a dance—they don't get so many. Hello, Bill, wantin' me?"

"Hunch is outside—Jim sent him; sez there's trouble," the foreman said.

"Round up the boys, an' we'll be goin'."

In ten minutes they had left Rainbow behind and were riding for the Circle Dot. Silently, and with eyes alert, they pressed on through the still, dark night. When, at length, they reached the ranch, all seemed as usual. Then Sudden's voice challenged:

"Who's there?"

Dover replied, and a shaft of light appeared as the door opened; the puncher, gun in hand, stepped out.

"Sorry to have busted in on yore fun, boys," he said. "The excitement's all over, I guess, but when I sent Hunch I didn't know what was afoot." Dan asked a question. "Rustlers. I downed a hoss. They didn't get any steers."

"Durn the luck, it would 'a' bin a good finish to have a run in with cow-thieves," Tiny grumbled. "Jim had the best of it after all."

When Dover and the foreman followed Sudden into the living-

64

room they got a shock, and had to be told the rest of the story. Dan's face fell when he saw the empty secret drawer.

"So they got it," he said dejectedly.

Sudden grinned, reached down the file and stripped off the bills until he came to the letter. "Like hell they did," he replied. "I had a feelin' someone might know o' that hidey-hole an' come for it, so I put it in the least likely place for anythin' o' value. Now we'll make shore; three of us know the contents o' that bit o' paper, so we'll—burn it."

"Yo're right, Jim, an' I don't know how to thank you," Dan said. "It was a smart move."

"Shucks," the puncher replied, and dropped the document in the fire.

"Settles that," Burke remarked. "How did you get on to their plans, Jim?"

"I didn't, but I got to wonderin' why Trenton was keen on an affair which would leave the Circle Dot wide open. Some o' his fellas could show theirselves, ride here, an' get back before the dance finished; no one could prove they hadn't been in town all the time."

"Which is how it was planned," Dan said, and told of Yorky's discovery. "The raid on the cattle was a fake?"

"Yeah. When Trenton learned I wasn't comin'—he had a list, yu know—they had to get me away from the ranch-house. Why, they even fired a gun in case I didn't hear 'em. Havin' played safe with the paper, I went along; yu see, there was just a chance someone was after the cows."

"I guess you've got the straight of it," the foreman said. "Mebbe that dead hoss'll tell us somethin' in the mornin'."

But this hope proved futile; on the left hip of the animal a square patch of skin had been stripped off. The marauders had not overlooked any bets, as they believed.

CHAPTER IX

Yorky was the proudest member of the outfit. Not only had he eclipsed them all by partnering the peerless Miss Trenton, but promotion had come to him.

"That kid was the on'y one of us to notice that them Wagon-wheel outcasts had sneaked away from the show," Dan told his foreman. "He goes on the pay-roll at twenty a month, an' it's up to him to make it more."

To the surprise of the bunkhouse, the usually precocious youth accepted his good fortune modestly. "It's mighty good o' Dan," he said. "I ain't wort' a dime to him, but I'm aimin' ter be."

"That rich uncle——" Slow began.

"Aw, go an' fry snowballs," Yorky grinned.

"Honest, I'm glad, Yorky," Blister put in. "I was scared we'd lose you as well as Tiny."

"Lose me?" the boy queried. "An' where's Tiny goin'?"

"Well, I figured las' night you'd soon be ridin' for the Wagon-wheel," was the reply. "An' Tiny's fixed to marry the school-marm an' help lam the kids."

The big puncher addressed the company. "Blister ain't a natural liar; it's just that his tongue gits ahead o' his thoughts."

When Yorky appeared for the morning excursion, Sudden noticed, with inward satisfaction, a coiled lasso hanging from his saddle-horn.

"Ain't proposin' to hang yoreself, are yu, son?" he asked.

The boy was used to his friend's sardonic humour. "Naw," he replied. "Guessed yer might larn me to t'row it. C'n yer rope?"

"Well, I'm not as good as some, but I expect I can give yu some pointers," the puncher admitted.

When they reached the pool, and had enjoyed their swim, Yorky was instructed in the rudiments of roping, which he found to be a much more difficult art than he had imagined. Also, he was treated to an expert exhibition which caused his eyes to bulge, and filled him with an ambition to do the like. In the puncher's hands, the lariat seemed to become a live thing, obeying every twitch of the deft wrist.

"Gawd, I'd give a lot ter handle a rope like that," Yorky said admiringly.

"Yu'll have to—a lot o' time," Sudden told him. "Practice, son, just practice, an' a leetle savvy—that's all yu need."

As the teacher was preparing to leave, the pupil asked, "What will a gun cost me, Jim?"

"Probably yore life," was the grim reply. "Yu got enough to keep yu busy with ropin', hawg-tyin', an' learnin' to ride somethin' a bit more uncertain than Shut-eye yonder."

"I useter carry a gat."

"The devil yu did? An' what was yore other name—Bill Hickok?"

"Oh, I ain't no sharp-shooter, but I was in with a hard bunch," Yorky replied airily. "I knows which end of a gun th' trouble comes out of."

"It's the trouble that comes outa the other fella's yu gotta keep in mind," Sudden warned. "Yu leave shootin' be for a spell; get a grip o' them other things first."

And because of his faith in this man who had done so much for him, Yorky pushed into the background his most cherished ambition, and contentedly applied himself to the task of mastering his lariat. As Sudden had hoped, the fresh, bracing air, new interests, and the revival of hope, were working wonders, and "li'l ol' Noo York" was fast becoming a less glamorous memory.

*   *   *

It was some days later that Yorky went in search of adventure, and found it. He had not yet been raised to the dignity of being assigned a definite job, and time was more or less his own. He knew nothing of the country round, and determined to find out something about it. Particularly he wanted to see the Wagon-wheel ranch-house, perhaps cherishing a hope of getting a glimpse of the girl who had been kind to him at the dance—kindness, until he had come West, was a rare experience. So, when Sudden had left him, he set out. Casual questions in the bunkhouse had given him the route.

"Foller th' creek, ford her at th' white stone, an' bear right," he repeated. "Sounds dead easy, Shut-eye, but we gotta watch out —them Wagon-wheelers is mebbe feelin' sore."

Like the rest of the outfit, Yorky believed that a raid on the cattle had been attempted. Paddy had been sworn to silence, explaining the bump on his cranium by an invented fall over a chair in the dark, a solution which evoked ribald reflections on his sobriety.

He crossed the stream, and then headed north-east over an expanse of grass-land plentifully besprinkled with brush, which enabled him to keep under cover for the most part. The necessity for this was soon apparent, for he had gone less than a mile when a horseman swung into an aisle he was about to enter. Just in time he forced Shut-eye headlong into a thicket of thorn—to the discomfort of both of them—and waited while the rider went by.

"Flint!" the boy breathed. "That's onct I'm lucky."

When the man disappeared he resumed his journey, and presently, in the distance, saw what he knew must be the place he sought. The ground about it was too open to conceal a horseman so he hid his mount in a clump of brush, dropping the reins over its head as Sudden had told him, and advanced on foot, keeping to the right, stooping and running swiftly from one bush to another.

He had got within a hundred yards of the house when two men emerged and, to his dismay, walked directly towards the tree behind which he was hiding. He looked round, but there was no cover he could hope to reach without being seen. His eyes went upward; the tree was a cottonwood, thickly foliaged. With a bound he managed to grasp the lowest branch and, panting with the unusual exertion, climbed to the crotch above. Since he could only see below through one small opening, he judged he was safe so long as he stayed quiet.

"If I bark, I'm a goner," he murmured, and instantly a violent desire to do this very thing assailed him. Smothering it, he bent down to listen, for they had stopped beneath him. Garstone opened the conversation.

"Well, Bundy, why have you brought me out here?"

"Because it's quiet, an' to ask you one plain question: Are you at the Wagon-wheel to help Trenton, or to help yoreself?"

"What the hell do you mean? How dare you——"

"Easy, Mister Garstone," the foreman cut in. "Puttin' on frills ain't apt to pay in these parts where one man is as good as another, 'cept with a six-shooter. Now mebbe yo're fast with a gun—I don't know—but I'm tellin' you that I am—damned fast."

"Are you trying to pick a quarrel with me?" Garstone asked.

"No, I want you to talk to me as man to man, an' not as a boss to a dawg who works for him," Bundy returned sourly.

"I am here to help Trenton, and in doing so, I hope for some advantage to myself. Does that satisfy you?"

"It's a law-sharp's answer. I'll put it plainer: are you prepared to sit in at a game what'll help you, but not Trenton?"

Yorky, easing a cramped leg, made a slight rustling. Apparently the foreman must have glanced up, for the trembling boy heard Garstone say, "Birds," and add with a laugh, "Hope they don't forget their manners." After a moment's pause, he answered the question. "It would depend, of course, on what the game meant—to me."

"Half the Circle Dot, or around twenty-five thousand bucks, as we might decide," Bundy said coolly.

"You may deal me a hand," the big man replied. "If I like the cards, I'll play; if not, I'll keep my mouth shut."

"Good enough. Well, here's the layout; with forty thousand we could buy the Circle Dot an' run it ourselves, or sell it to Zeb for fifty thousand."

"Marvellous! Not suggested by our talk with Trenton, of course." His tone betrayed disgust and disappointment.

"All that jaw suggested to me was that we'd be fools to help another fella to a wad o' coin we could have ourselves," Bundy replied.

"And, of course, you know where to find the money?"

The foreman was losing his patience. "The mistake you make, Garstone, is to think everyone else a blasted fool," he said. "Shore I know; what'd be the sense in talkin' if I didn't?"

"That makes all the difference. Go ahead."

"The cash will be on the ten-fifteen from Washout to-morrow mornin', consigned to the bank at the Bend. It will be a small train, just the engine, one coach, an' a baggage-car, containing the coin."

"Coin? You mean bills, with the numbers known," Garstone commented. "Too dangerous."

"Part of it'll be paper, but by an oversight—the list o' numbers will be missin'—at the other end; that'll cost us a thousand. The rest will be in gold. There'll on'y be the engine-driver, his mate, one conductor, and the baggage-man to deal with. Three of us oughta be able to handle it."

"Three? Who's the other?"

"Flint. He gits a thousand too—that's arranged."

"So we lose two thousand?"

"What did you expect, money for nothin'?" Bundy asked, his voice pregnant with contempt.

"Oh, all right. What's your plan?"

"Ten mile short o' the Bend the line runs through a thick patch o' brush an' pine. One o' the trees dropped across the metals will stop the train. You cover the driver while Flint an' me take up the collection—we'll have to skin the passengers too an' make it look like a reg'lar hold-up. O' course, we cut the wires first."

"My size is rather outstanding," Garstone objected.

"We'll all be masked, an' dressed in range-rig, nobody'd reckernize you. I'll borrow Jupp's duds—he's about yore build—an' havin' strained a leg at the dance"—this with a wink—"he ain't usin' 'em."

"Well, it certainly sounds feasible," Garstone admitted.

"Feasible?" the foreman echoed ironically. "Why, it's cash for just stoopin' down."

"Not much of a stoop for you, perhaps, but it's a hell of a one for me, Chesney Garstone," was the reply. "However, the opportunity is there, and must be taken advantage of. By the way, what did Zeb expect to find at the Circle Dot?"

"I dunno—paper o' some sort, but they failed, so Flint couldn't tell me anythin'. Trenton's got some scheme for raisin' the wind, but he's pretty tight-mouthed 'bout it.''

"We'll help him," Garstone smiled. "The more money he has, the higher price he can pay for the Circle Dot. How did you get on to this, Bundy?"

"I ain't sayin'," the foreman replied. "You can take it the facts is correct; that's all as matters."

They moved away, and it was not until—peering between carefully-parted branches—he saw them vanish among the buildings, did the boy dare to move his stiffened limbs. Dropping to the ground, and bent double, he scurried from cover to cover, and, after what seemed to him an age, reached his pony.

"Us fer home, Shut-eye," he gasped, as he scrambled into the saddle. "An' we ain't losin' no time neither, git me?"

Following Sudden's instructions, he had taken note of landmarks likely to assist him in finding his way back, and presently came almost in sight of the ford over the Rainbow. Here he received a fright—a horse was splashing its way through the water. He was heading for the nearest shelter when a soft voice called, and he saw that the rider was Miss Trenton.

"Why, Yorky," she smiled, as she cantered up. "Were you running away from me?"

"I hadn't seen yer—on'y heard th' hoss," he explained. "It mighter bin—anyone."

"But surely none of our riders would harm you?" she said.

"I b'long to th' Circle Dot outfit—that'd be enough."

She shook her head, unconvinced. "Have you been to visit me?" she enquired.

Yorky's thin cheeks reddened. "Naw, I jus' wanted ter see yer home."

"And what do you think of it?"

"Betche'd be happier at the Circle Dot," was the unexpected answer.

It was now her turn to colour up, though afterwards she could not imagine any reason for so doing. There was a trace of reproof in her reply. "Thank you, but I am quite comfortable."

Yorky was not slow-witted; he saw that he had displeased her. "I warn't meanin' ter be rude," he apologized, and looked so downcast that she had to smile again.

"And I wasn't meaning to be cross," she said. "So we'll both forget it. Why did you leave the dance so early; weren't you having a good time?"

"The best ever, an' that goes for all of us." He was itching to get away; the trip had taken much longer than he had thought, and the sooner his news was told, the better. He did not realize the full import of what he had learned, but it was plain that a train was to be robbed and the plunder used to obtain the Circle

Dot, though how that was to be done without the present owner's consent was beyond his comprehension.

"Including Mister Dover?" she asked.

"I didn't hear no complaints."

"I think he might have let the men stay a little longer," she persisted.

"Dan's young, but he knows his job," Yorky said loyally—even this lovely girl must not find fault with his boss. He fidgeted in his saddle. "Guess I oughter be goin'; I bin out all day, an' th' boys'll be worryin'; I ain't wise ter th' country—yet."

"Running away from me again?" she teased. "Well, so long, Yorky, it is my turn to visit you now, and perhaps I will."

He snatched off his hat as she moved on, and it might have pleased her to know that it was probably the first time he had paid this tribute to a woman.

Splashing through the ford, he thumped his unspurred heels against Shut-eye's well-padded ribs in an effort to extract a little more speed from that lethargic but easy-going quadruped.

"Yer got four legs, pal—I've counted 'em—use every damn one," he urged. "If we'd met up with a Wagon-wheeler 'stead o' her . . ."

He reached the ranch without further interruption, and was un saddling at the corral when Tiny and Blister rode up.

" 'Lo, kid, Noo York glad to see you?" the former asked.

"I didn't git as fur, but Rainbow is warmin' up fer th' weddin'."

The big man swallowed the bait. "What weddin'?"

"Yourn an' th' school-marm's," Yorky cackled, and dodging Tiny's grab, made for the ranch-house. Blister's bellow of laughter followed him.

He entered by the back door, and the cook—noting the flushed, excited face—was moved to comment. "Phwat hev ye been up to, ye young divil, an' how much grub has passed yer lips the day?"

"Oh, hell, Paddy. Where's Jim?"

"In th' front room with Dan an'—Saints, he's gone."

The impetuosity which took him from the kitchen caused him to burst unceremoniously upon the three men. They stared at him in silence for a moment, and then the rancher said quietly:

"I didn't hear you knock, Yorky."

"I'm sorry, Boss, but I got noos, an' it won't keep."

"Take a seat an' tell us," Dan replied.

It came out with a rush. Ten minutes later they had heard the story of his adventure, minus the meeting with Miss Trenton, and were regarding the narrator with stunned astonishment. Sudden read the minds of his companions.

"Is this the truth, Yorky, or one o' those fine tales yu sometimes invent to amuse the boys?" he wanted to know.

71

"Cross me heart, it's true, Jim," came the instant reply.

"An' there is a ten-fifteen—I've travelled by it a good few times —a little train, made up like he said," Dan stated.

"Well, it shore beats the band," Burke said. "Garstone an' Bundy double-crossin' Trenton; that's a laugh I'll enjoy."

"I guess not, Bill," Dan said. "We've gotta stop it. With that cash they can make a deal with Maitland, an' we're ditched. They wouldn't buy till the hold-up was stale news, or Garstone would claim to have raised funds East. Oh, it's smart, an' I never suspected Bundy o' brains."

"There's more to him than folks aroun' here savvy," the foreman replied. "Have you noticed that he never wears a glove on his right hand?"

"Gunman, huh?" Sudden said. "An' advertises it. Shucks!"

Dover, remembering the shooting in Sandy Bend, understood the puncher's disdain, and smiled, but his face was soon sober again.

"Question is, what are we to do?" he asked. "If we tell the sheriff, he'll just laught at us, an' that's all; so would Trenton. We don't know who is sendin' the money so a warnin' ain't possible neither."

"Take some o' the boys an' catch 'em in the act," Burke suggested.

"One of 'em might get away with the booty, an' Foxy would turn 'em loose anyway. What's the joke, Jim?"

For Sudden's eyes were twinkling like those of a mischievous boy. "Just an idea," he said, and went on to tell them what it was; in a few moments they were laughing too.

"Gee! it'd be a great play to make," Dan chuckled. "But could we pull it off?"

"I'm sayin' we can," Sudden replied confidently. "Why not have a shot at it—just the three of us."

"Say, ain't I in on this, Jim?" Yorky ventured to ask. "I could hold th' hosses."

Sudden's shake of the head was definite. "No, yu've done yore share, an' we're all mighty obliged, but there'll be a lot o' hard an' fast ridin' to-morrow mornin'. Time'll come when yu can keep up with the best of us; just now, patience is yore strong suit. An' mind, not a word."

"I get yer, Jim," the boy replied. "I'm a clam."

CHAPTER X

Early next morning the three conspirators devoured a substantial breakfast, saddled their mounts and, in the grey light of the dawn, disappeared in the direction of Sandy Bend. They did not follow the regular trail, having no desire to be observed, or to visit the town itself. This meant a loss of time and speed, but was necessary, since to run into the Wagon-wheel men would be fatal to the success of their plan.

Leaving the Circle Dot range at the eastern limit, they plunged into an almost trackless waste of broken country, the natural difficulties of which made anything in the nature of a direct course impossible, but all three were expert in the art of breaking a trail, and having started in good time there was no need to force the pace.

The foreman led the way, and though they were often driven wide of their line, his sense of direction brought them back to it. Nature was awake, birds whistled and called, and in the undergrowth they could hear the stealthy movements of unseen denizens of the woods. Riding in single file, they spoke seldom; each of them was dwelling on the part he had to play; a slip might result in unpleasant consequences. The morning air felt chill on their faces, but the slowly-mounting sun would soon bring more heat than was comfortable.

At the end of several hours, the leader called a halt and got down. Pointing to a sharp ridge on their right, he said:

"Oughta be able to git a glimp o' the Bend from up there. I'll take a peep—better be shore than sorry."

He trudged away, and they presently saw him come into view on the peak of the height. He was soon back, a grin of satisfaction on his face. He waved a hand to the right.

"The Bend is over there, so we're pointin' slap on the target," he said, and with a glance at his watch, "Time a-plenty, too."

"An' it's a good place for the purpose, is it, Bill?" Dover queried.

"Couldn't 'a' found a better if I'd bin Jesse James hisself," Burke assured him.

Another five miles brought them to a small forest of pines, and threading their way through the slim, straight trunks they came to a strip of thick bush, on the other side of which ran a single line of railroad. They pulled up where the matted foliage of the trees afforded deep shadow.

"Here she is," the foreman said, unstrapping a small axe from behind his saddle.

"No need for that, Bill," Dan said. "That windfall will serve our purpose."

A rope was tied to the prostrate tree, and one of the horses dragged it to the side of the line. The three men then lifted and laid it across the rails.

"They'll have to get down to shift her," Sudden said. "Yu'll take charge o' them, Bill, while I deal with the passengers, an' Dan attends to the baggage-car. We'll spread along, keepin' in the bushes till the train stops. No shootin', 'less yu have to, an' then— miss."

The horses were concealed in a group behind the brush, and tied, in case the noise of the locomotive should startle them. Burke consulted his watch again.

"She's liable to be here any time now," he said. "Better pull down the blinds an' git to our stations."

With faces masked by bandanas in which eye-holes had been cut, and hat-brims drawn low down, they looked at one another and laughed.

"Shore does make a difference," Sudden admitted. "I wouldn't trust either o' yu with ten cents."

"Funny what a sense o' security that bit o' rag gives you," Dover reflected aloud. "I was feelin' a mite nervous about the job, but it's all gone."

"Me, I'll be glad when it's over," the foreman confessed. "Our intentions is good, but we're bustin' the law all to bits."

A puff of smoke down the line sent them under cover; the train was coming. Laboriously it approached, rumbling along the rails, belching white clouds, and then, with a screeching of brakes, slowed and stopped. The driver thrust his head out of the cab and stared at the obstruction.

"Hey, Luke, there's a blame' tree in the road," he called. "We'll hev to git down an' shift her."

Clumsily the two men clambered out and moved to the front of the engine. At the same moment, a masked figure stepped from the bushes and, in a gruff voice, said:

"Put 'em up, boys, an' you won't git hurt."

A levelled revolver, held in a steady hand, added weight to the command, and the railwaymen had no thought of disobeying. As their hands reached for the sky, the driver spoke:

"The pot's yourn, Mister. I'm too wicked to die—yet."

The train-robber grinned beneath his mask but made no reply. He had done his part, and was wondering how his friends were faring. Actually, they had picked their places to a nicety. The conductor, thrusting out his head to discover the reason for an unusual halt, nearly collided with the muzzle of a six-shooter.

"Shut yore trap an' do just what I tell yu, or . . ." The threatening gesture was unnecessary—the conductor's pay did not justify heroism. He fell back, and allowed the possessor of the weapon to board the train. The man handed him a small leather sack.

"Collect all the cash an' valuables in the coach, startin' with yore own," he was told. "I'm just behind yu, an' if there's any funny business, yu won't be here to laugh. *Sabe?*"

Evidently the conductor did, for he emptied his pockets with alacrity, and then entered the coach. There were only half-a-dozen passengers, and everyone of them protested, but the sight of the sinister figure stalking behind him silenced all argument. But, as Sudden afterwards related, "What they were goin' to do the railroad company would put it outa business."

When the ordeal was completed, and it did not take long, the bandit took the bag, stepped to the end of the coach, and addressed his victims:

"Listen, folks. When yu reach Sandy Bend, go to the bank an' yu'll get back yore property. This ain't a real stick-up—we're doin' it to win a wager, but—don't try no tricks, 'cause that'll make it serious." As he descended from the train, he motioned the conductor to follow. "I've told those people the truth, but I'm keepin' yu covered till my friend has finished."

A moment later Dan appeared, a corded, wooden box under one arm. He had experienced no difficulty—the baggage-man also was too sinful, or poorly-paid, to risk his life. Moreover, he had no knowledge as to the value of the purloined box, which, with some sacks of flour, comprised all his charge. So, white-faced, he watched the marauders vanish into the undergrowth. After all, the banker at Sandy Bend could afford to buy more gun-fodder, for the box—addressed to him was labelled, "Handle with care. Cartridges."

Sudden read the inscription and laughed grimly. "Golden bullets, but they won't be fired at the Circle Dot. Well, boys, we've done fine, but the job ain't finished; I've gotta get the plunder to the Bend an' beat the train. I reckon Nigger an' me can make it. Yu two point for home." They demurred a little at this, but he would not listen. "We settled it thataway, "he reminded. "I ain't knowed there an' yu are."

Rolled in his slicker, the box and leather bag were roped to his saddle, and just as the engine-driver and his mate pushed the obstruction clear of the line, he set out.

The train resumed its interrupted journey, the occupants excitedly discussing the incident, and speculating on the possibility of recovering what they had lost. The conductor was disposed to a sanguine view.

"No sense in tellin' us that if it ain't so," he said. "We couldn't

75

do nothin', an' it's just the sort o' mad caper them cowboys would indulge in on a dare. Anybody out much?"

"My wallet contains two hundred dollars I'll be glad to see again," a passenger replied.

Smaller amounts of currency, rings, and watches were claimed by the rest, and when the conductor stated that the baggage-car contained only sacks of meal and a box of cartridges, an atmosphere of optimism developed.

"If they're winning a worth-while sum—and they must be to risk a long term of imprisonment—they'll play safe and return the booty," the largest loser argued. "We'll know soon."

But their troubles were not yet over, for after travelling another five miles, the train slowed down and stopped with a jerk. The conductor stuck his head out—cautiously this time, and promptly drew it in again.

"Damn me if there ain't another tree on the line," he said. "What's the game? We got nothin' more for 'em."

The bewildered passengers heard a sharp order, accented by a rifle-shot, which brought the two men on the engine tumbling hastily to the ground, hands in the air. The tall, heavily-built cowboy who had given it slanted his smoking weapon on them, and said warningly:

"Stay put if you want to go on living."

Stealing a glance back along the line they could see that the previous procedure was again in operation; two other men, masked and with drawn pistols, had boarded the train. In vain the conductor—who at once realized that these were not the same visitors—tried to explain.

"Yo're too late, Mister, them other fellas has beat you to it; we're cleaned complete."

The bandit pushed the gun in his face. "What other fellas?" he barked. "Talk fast, or by the Devil's teeth . . ."

The trembling man talked fast, and called upon his passengers to support his story by an ocular demonstration—their empty pockets. The recital did not improve the intruder's temper.

"Can you describe 'em?" he asked.

The conductor's reply was hardly helpful. "They was cowboys seemin'ly, with their faces covered. Said they on'y did it to win a bet, an' we'd git our stuff back at the Bend."

The stranger laughed sneeringly. "An' on the strength of a lie like that you let 'em git away with it, you lousy cowards." He backed out of the coach, with a parting threat that anyone who stirred would be shot.

In the meantime the custodian of the baggage-car was telling the same story with less success. Bundy, who had allotted to himself the task of securing the real reason for the robbery, was not easily convinced. He, too, wanted a description of the unknown

76

hold-ups, and got no more than his confederate. Then he searched every inch of the van, even tapping the boards with the butt of his gun.

"What's in them?" he growled, pointing to the sacks.

"Meal, I s'pose," the man replied.

"Open an' tip it out," Bundy ordered, and when the fellow hesitated, jammed a six-shooter into his ribs.

This produced immediate action, the sacks were untied and up-ended, but no wooden box was forthcoming.

"Like I said, she ain't there," the train-man unwisely remarked.

"Can't I see? you —— yella dawg's pup. Go an' look some more, blast you," Bundy snarled.

With a savage swing he drove a fist behind the man's ear, flinging him, face downwards and well-nigh senseless, into the pile of flour, and went out. Flint was waiting for him, and a call brought Garstone. A few words revealed the position, and the big man's face—could they have seen it—might have caused trouble; it expressed only incredulity and rage.

"Are you asking me to believe that?" he cried involuntarily.

"Please yoreself," Bundy snapped. "Go search the train an' question those lunkheads, if you want."

"But it's impossible—only we three knew, unless . . ."

"Unless what?"

"That other fellow, who was to have a thousand, got a better offer and sold us."

"Well, he didn't, an' he's losin' his too," the foreman retorted. "He dasn't play tricks on me—I know too much about him. Somebody's got in ahead of us, either by accident, or because they heard somethin'. I'm for home; no good hangin' about here."

Three very disgruntled would-be train-robbers, each deeply suspicious of the others, climbed into their saddles and disappeared in the shadowy recesses of the pines. Once more the train went on its eventful way.

About the same time the rider of a black horse got down outside the bank in Sandy Bend, took from behind his saddle a box which seemed to be weighty and a small bag. Stepping inside, he asked to see the manager.

"What name shall I say?" the clerk enquired.

"Please yoreself, he won't know it anyway," the stranger smiled. "Just say it's real important."

After a short wait he was ushered into the private office. The manager, middle-aged, with an astute face and keen eyes, pointed to a chair.

"Have a seat, Mister ——. I failed to catch your name."

"That ain't surprisin'—I didn't give it," Sudden smiled. "My business is on'y to hand over somethin' I reckon belongs to yu."

He placed the box on the desk, and the banker's eyebrows rose. "It certainly does," he replied. "But you are not working for the railway?"

"I am, an' I ain't," the puncher said. "An', anyway, the train don't 'pear to 'a' come in yet. Yu came mighty close to losin' them —ca'tridges."

"I don't understand."

"Well, last night, me an' a couple o' friends chanced to learn of a plan to hold up the train this mornin'—the fellas was short o' feed for their guns, I expect." The story-teller's eyes were alight with mirth. "We hadn't much time, an' the on'y wagon-trail out we could hit on was to stage a stick-up ourselves—sorta forestall 'em, as it were—an' fetch the plunder to yu."

The manager stared. "That was a clever but very daring expedient," he said.

"Oh, I dunno, the odds are allus in favour o' the holdups," Sudden replied. "Yu see, they have the advantage o' springin' a surprise, an' the fellas on the train are covered afore they know it."

"You talk like an expert."

"I've studied the subject," the puncher grinned. "Fella can't tell what he may come to."

"Your knowledge seems to have served you well on this occasion. You had no trouble?"

"It was like money from the ol' folks at home," the puncher said easily. "There's one thing, we had to make it look right an' clean the passengers too. I told 'em to call here for their property —it's all in the small sack. Mebbe yu'll 'tend to that?"

"Most willingly," the manager replied, and laughed. "So the other gang must have held up a stripped train? The joke was certainly on them. Now, see here, my friend, you and your companions have rendered the bank and the railway a great service, and I wish——"

"It don't need speakin' of," Sudden interrupted. "We put this over for personal reasons, an' that's all there is to it."

The banker was studying him keenly. "I'm perfectly certain I've seen you before, and recently," he observed.

"No, seh, yu ain't seen me afore, nor even now," the visitor replied meaningly.

"Well, it shall be as you say, but if at any time I can help you, count on me."

"I'm thankin' yu," Sudden said, gripping the hand extended. At the door he turned. "Mebbe I oughta tell yu that the record o' the numbers o' them ca'tridges will be found—missin'.'"

He was gone before the astounded manager could say another word. An examination of the box revealed the expected gold and notes; in the bag were jewellery, bills, and small change. The banker scratched his head; in all his experience of the West, he had never heard of a prank like this.

The last drop in Bundy's cup of bitterness was added when he met his employer in the afternoon.

"I sent Rattray in to the Bend with the wagon to collect some flour I ordered from Washout," Trenton said. "It was to be on the ten-fifteen, and he should be back by this. Seen anythin' of it?"

The foreman said he had not, which, as he now knew, was a lie; not only had he seen it, scattered all over the dirty floor of a baggage-car, but he had sent a man squattering into the middle of it. The reminder of the chance they had missed seared like a hot iron, and when he was alone he told the world exactly what he thought of it in a flood of abuse which only ceased when a swift suspicion came and gave the Recording Angel an opportunity of re-charging his fountain pen.

Was it by accident that the Wagon-wheel flour was on that particular train? Had Trenton learned of their plan and made his own move to checkmate it? Bundy swore he would find out, and he finished with a blistering promise of vengeance.

CHAPTER XI

The news of the attacks on the train travelled fast, and soon reached Rainbow; the passengers had chattered freely of their unusual experience. Speculation as to the real reason for the quixotic behaviour of the first gang of bandits, and witticisms at the expense of the second, were on the lips of everyone. It therefore resulted that the Wagon-wheel foreman and his confederates had salt unwittingly rubbed into their wounds at frequent intervals. The identity of the actors in the comedy was still unsuspected, for the banker and his clerk both described the person who had returned the stolen property as just an ordinary cowboy. This did not satisfy Bundy, and two days after the event he made the journey to the Bend in the hope of discovering something.

During a round of the saloons, he heard himself ridiculed and had to agree that he was a blundering fool so often, as to make him wish he had not come, especially as he had learned nothing. But, at last, when on the point of giving up, and in a drinking hovel of the lowest type, he was rewarded. The talk was on the one topic, and for about the tenth time in various places he had said:

"Beats me how that fella could ride into a town like this, in broad daylight, an' git away unnoticed. Ain't all blind in the Bend, are you?"

"Not that early in the day," laughed a bystander.

"An' it warn't quite like that neither," chirped a dried-up old fellow. "I seen his hoss—leastways, I reckon it was his'n—the time fits—standin' outside the bank."

Bundy tried to appear indifferent. "Did ye now? What kind of a hoss was it?"

"Big rangy black, with a white blaze on the face; mustang breed, I'd say; a fine critter," the old man replied. "Worth a fortun' to a road-agent."

The foreman needed no more; there could be only one such horse in all the district. He came out of the dive afire with a fury which increased with every mile of the long ride home. So it was Green and two of the Circle Dot outfit who had cheated him—for so he regarded it. Had they kept the money it would have hurt less, but to be outplayed and made an object of derision by men he hated, cut him to the bone. Once, dismounting, he stood for a few seconds in a half-crouch, then snatched out his gun and sent the six shots in rapid succession at a thin sapling a dozen yards

80

distant. Stepping to the tree, he noted that every bullet had chipped the bark at the same height. Reloading the weapon, he got back into the saddle, his teeth bared in a Satanic grin of satisfaction.

"I'm as good as I ever was," he muttered. "Look to yoreself, Mister blasted Green."

Arrived at the ranch, he went in search of Garstone, but failed to find him. The Easterner had, in fact, ridden into Rainbow with Miss Trenton. On reaching the place, however, they had separated for the time and so she was alone when Dan almost bumped into her as he came out of the store. He raised his hat and would have gone on, but she stopped and smiled.

"Why do you always try to avoid me?" she asked.

Dan had little experience of the so-called fair sex, or he would have recognized the age-old device of putting an opponent in the wrong, so the accusation staggered him. But he was a fighter, and he had already decided that this slim, prepossessing girl could only be handled with the gloves off.

"I guess I must be hopin' you'd run after me," he smiled impudently.

The unlooked-for reply discomposed her, and all she could say was, "Not if you were the only man in the world."

The smile broadened into a grin. "You'd have to travel some then," he said. "Think o' the competition. Gee! I'd shore have to live in the tall timber."

Despite her irritation, the absurd picture he conjured up made her laugh. The parcel he was carrying provided a change of subject; the shape showed that it could only be a rifle.

"More preparations against your own kind?" she asked sarcastically.

"Precautions is a better word," he corrected. "An' don't you call the Wagon-wheel outfit my kind—they ain't. Anyways, this happens to be a present for a good boy. I fancy you know him."

"Yorky?"

"The same. He did me a service an' I want to even up."

"Wasn't there anything else you could choose? He's only a child." She herself was less than three years older.

"I reckon he never was that, but he's due to be some sort of a man, an' we'd like it to be a real one."

"And that will help?" she enquired, a little scornfully.

"Quite a lot. We're gettin' him interested in work on the range an' this is part of it. If you'd seen Yorky two months ago you wouldn't recognize him."

"Well, I hope he'll like his gift."

"Like it?" Dan laughed. "He'll take it to bed with him."

She laughed too, and then her face sobered. "I must go," she said. "Mister Garstone brought me in, and is waiting."

Hat in hand, he watched the two meet, and pass up the street together. The man's face was registering disapproval when the girl reached him, but all he said was:

"Had the cowboy anything of interest to tell you?"

She divined that he was jealous, and the thought thrilled though she had not yet troubled to analyse her own feeling regarding him. But she was young, and the admiration of a physically attractive man, who had at least a semblance of culture, could not be entirely unwelcome. Still, she had no intention of letting him suspect this, and it was in rather a distant tone that she replied:

"I was under the impression that Mister Dover owned a ranch."

"Thinks he does, but maybe he's mistaken," Garstone told her. "I wasn't asking out of curiosity, Miss Trenton. The Wagon-wheel and Circle Dot are practically at war, and that fellow might have let slip information of value to us."

"Our conversation was confined to the youngest member of his outfit—the boy they call Yorky."

"Member of his outfit—that's a good one," Garstone sneered. "I'd call him a bit of useless lumber."

"Hardly that, since Mister Dover has just purchased a present as a reward for good work."

"Dover must have wanted a pocket picked."

"You must not speak ill of my admirers," she said playfully. "Why, quite recently, he rode to the Wagon-wheel just to see where I lived. There's devotion."

"The devil he did?" Garstone said. "When was that?"

She thought for a moment. "Oh yes, I remember; it was the day before that amusing attempt to rob the train. How awfully sick the second party must have felt on finding they had been anticipated, but it was childish to vent their spite on poor uncle's flour."

Garstone had little to say during the rest of the ride home, and seeing Bundy as they approached the ranch-house, made his excuses to his companion, and rode towards him.

"Any news?" he asked.

"Plenty," the foreman frowned. "The fella who took the stuff back to the bank was atop of a black hoss with a white blaze."

"Green!" Garstone exploded. "I knew it."

"Then you might 'a' opened up an' saved me a journey," the other said sourly.

"I didn't learn of it until a little while ago," the big man replied, and repeated what the girl had told him. "We heard a movement in that tree we were talking under and put it down to birds. That young sneak must have seen us coming, and hopped up there to hide. He'd take the tale back to Green, and that damned cowboy out-planned and made monkeys of us. God! I'll bet the Circle Dot riders haven't stopped laughing yet."

"They'll have somethin' else to grin about afore I've done with 'em," the foreman growled. "As for Green . . ." He tapped the butt of his gun. "He's for hell."

"The trouble is, they know who were in it," Garstone said, rather uneasily. "If they split to Trenton . . ."

"Can't prove a thing—it's their word agin ourn," Bundy reassured. "As for puttin' Zeb wise, Dover wouldn't do that if he knowed the ol' fool was to be bumped off tomorrow. No, I ain't worryin' 'bout that; it's the pot we've bin done out of. Why'n blazes didn't I send a slug into that damned tree?"

"No use moaning over a lost opportunity; we must find another. Trenton has a scheme; perhaps that will be luckier—for us," the Easterner said meaningly. "How are you going to deal with Green?"

"Watch my smoke," the foreman said.

Garstone shrugged. "Watch your step; he doesn't look a simple proposition to me," was his reply. "He sports two guns."

"A bluff, meanin' nothin'," Bundy sneered. "Take it from me, the fella who can really shoot on'y needs one gun an' one shot; mos'ly there ain't time for more."

*   *   *

In the front room at the Circle Dot, Yorky was clutching the Winchester and scabbard Dan had brought home and presented to him. Usually loquacious enough, his gratitude and delight in this new possession nearly deprived him of speech.

"I dunno—how ter—thank yer, Boss," he stammered. "I didn't do nuttin'—it was jus' blind luck, an' I . . ." He bogged down completely.

"Cut the cackle, Yorky," Dan said kindly. "You did a-plenty, an' I'm rememberin' it. Jim'll show you how to handle the gun an' you got all outdoors to blaze away in. Now, I'm bettin' you wanta cut along an' show the boys."

"You win, Boss," Yorky grinned, and made for the door. There he paused to add, "I ain't forgettin' this—ever," and was gone.

"I'm thinkin' that li'l ol' Noo York has lost a citizen," Burke laughed.

"An' Rainbow gains one, thanks to Jim," Dover said.

"Rubbish," the puncher replied. "How long d'yu s'pose afore one o' them Wagon-wheel wastrels comes a-gunnin' for me?"

"But why?" they both asked.

"I rode my own hoss into the Bend; somebody must 'a' spotted it. I needed Nigger to make shore o' gettin' there before the train; I did it easy—the country bein' less difficult than I. figured."

"It was certainly a risk, but you would have it thataway," Dan said, so seriously that the puncher laughed.

"Shucks! Fella who never takes one, takes nothin'," he rejoined. "Mebbe I'm wrong."

And when a week passed without anything occurring to disturb the serenity of the Circle Dot, it began to appear so. Every morning Yorky would depart for what the outfit called his "cure," the cherished rifle slapping against his pony's ribs, and would be absent for hours, frightening the birds, and making life a misery for any wandering jack-rabbit or coyote so unfortunate as to come within range, to return, tired but happy, and with a capacity for food which drew from the cook the ironical suggestion that he had contracted "Wur-r-ms."

"Gwan, yer human gas-bag," Yorky retorted, when the accusation was made. "I'm a small eater."

"Shure it's so, but ye pack away enough for wan twice the size o' ye," Paddy told him.

When late afternoon came and brought no sign of the boy, the cook grew anxious, and went to the foreman. "Faith, he'll not be missin' a meal willin'," he said.

Burke looked grave; it was no country for a tenderfoot to get lost in, and there was a possibility of accident. He told the cook he would send the men out again as they came in. Sudden, with Blister and Tiny were the first to arrive, and they set off at once for the pool, which Yorky made the starting-point of his excursions. They found plenty of tracks, but it was impossible to tell which were the most recent.

"Spread out fan-wise, but keep within hail," Sudden said. "If he's hurt, whoever finds him may need help."

The ground was fairly open, with thickets of scrub here and there, most of them too dense and thorny for anything but a tough-hided animal to penetrate. Save for a brief glance, the searchers paid them no attention; neither Yorky nor his mount would fancy their exploration. The short, dried grass showed no marks, and Sudden rode straight on, trusting to luck. It came his way, for after they had left the pool several miles behind, a horseman loped from the far side of a larger patch of brush some hundreds of yards ahead, and at the sight of the newcomer spurred his pony in an evident attempt to escape.

Sudden shouted a command to halt, but no notice being taken, he spoke a word which galvanized the black into instant action; like a living thunderbolt, the animal shot forward, the ground sliding beneath the spurning hooves and the sound of them clearly reached the fugitive. A quick backward look, an oath, an something fell from his hand. Without slackening pace, Sudden swung down sideways, one leg crooked across the saddle, secured the object, and straightened up. A glance showed him that it was Yorky's rifle. He was now only a dozen yards away from his quarry; his hand went first to his gun, then to his rope. The coils

84

spun out, the loop settled over the shoulders of the runaway, and the black stopped as though shot. Seconds later, the snared man was plucked from his seat as by a giant hand, to be flung heavily on his back. Sudden dismounted, his face pitiless. The other two cowboys, who had heard his shout, now came up.

"Why did yu run, Bundy?" was the first question.

"Didn't wanta git shot in the back," was the impudent reply.

"Didn't like yore own medicine, huh?" Sudden went on, and did not fail to note the flicker in the man's eyes. "Yu came damn near gettin' a dose, would have, if I hadn't wanted some information."

"Go ahead. Mebbe I'll give it."

"Mebbe you'd better; I've got ways o' persuadin' folk—ask yore friend Flint, if yu ever see him again. Yu can stand up on yore hind-legs an' shuck the rope. I don't s'pose yu'll try anythin' but I hope—yu will." When the man was on his feet, he added sharply: "Where did yu get that gun yu dropped?"

"Found it."

"Right. I'm lookin' for the owner, an' yo're goin' to help. Lead his hoss, Tiny—the gent prefers to walk."

"Me, walk?" Bundy protested angrily. "You can't do that."

"Not likely, but yu can," Sudden grinned. "An' I hope, for yore sake, we don't have to go far."

The prisoner's fury deprived him of caution. "How'n hell should I know where the brat——" He stopped, aware that he had been betrayed into a folly. The grim faces of the three men apprised him that he was in grave peril. An inspiration came "Awright, I'll tell, though I promised not to," he said. "I met the hobo kid totin' that gun, which I figured he'd pinched. He sold it to me for twenty bucks—told me he was sick to death o' the West an' wanted to git to Noo York. Last I see of him he was makin' for the Bend."

Sudden stepped forward, snatched out the man's gun, and examined it; one chamber contained an empty shell.

"I shot at a rattler—an' missed," Bundy explained.

Bleak eyes bored into his. "Another lie from yu an' I'll be shootin' at one, an' I won't miss," Sudden rasped. "Climb yore hoss; if we don't find Yorky, alive an' well, yu hang."

"Say, Jim, why not string him up now, an' if the kid's all right, we can come back an' cut him down," Blister suggested.

Bundy's expression became more uneasy; he knew that the proposal was not so jocular as it sounded; there was no mirth in the speaker's voice.

"There was nothin' the matter with him when we parted," he said. "I'm tellin' you."

"What yu tell us ain't evidence," Sudden replied dryly. "Lead on to where yu last saw him, an' if yore memory fails yu, pray—hard."

Grey-faced, the prisoner got into his saddle, and Tiny dropped the loop of the lariat over his shoulders again. He was trapped, and the only hope of saving his skin lay in finding that accursed boy. For this saturnine, black-haired stranger, who had thwarted him for the second time, had not the appearance of one to make idle threats. So he obeyed the order, conscious that, at the least sign of treachery, the drawn guns behind him would speak. Fifteen minutes later he halted his horse.

"It was somewheres aroun' here," he said. "Wanted the way to the Bend, he did, an' I told him to point for that block o' pines, an' keep goin'."

They reached the trees, dark and forbidding in the fading rays of the sun.

"He wouldn't go through," Sudden decided. "Which way round did yu tell him?"

"To the left," Bundy returned sullenly.

"We'll try the right—he may not have believed yu neither."

They circled the little forest, and had gone less than half a mile when the search ended; at the sight of the boy lying beside the body of his pony, Sudden rapped out an oath, and the grip on his gun tightened; the Wagon-wheel foreman was very near to death at that moment. Had not Yorky lifted his head. . . .

"Jim," he cried. "I knowed yer'd come." His red, swollen eyes rested on Bundy, and then travelled to the new scabbard hanging on the puncher's saddle-horn. "Gimme my gat," he added hoarsely.

"Easy, son," Sudden replied. "What happened?"

The tale was soon told. He had strayed further than he intended, and had the bad luck to meet Bundy, who chased, roped, and threw him. When he stood up, he was knocked down again, despoiled of his rifle, and ordered to get out of the country for good, or he would be shot. "Then he killed pore ol' Shut-eye, the rotten, cowardly ——" The quavering, high-pitched voice trailed off in a venumous string of epithets to terminate in a spasm of coughing.

"Yu didn't go," Sudden said.

"I started, but when he rid off, I come back—ter my pal."

Bundy saw the faces of his captors grow more and more rigid as the damning recital proceeded. He must say something, or wish the world good-bye.

"All lies," he said. "I bought an' paid for his gun, an' he asked me to finish off the hoss—claimed to be scared the Bend folk might think he'd stole it."

"Blister, search the boy, an' his saddle pockets, an' see how much coin he has," the puncher ordered.

The cowboy did the job thoroughly, even making Yorky take

off his boots. "One dollar an' two bits," Blister announced, when the operation was completed.

Sudden looked at the convicted liar. "Get down," he said. A turn of the wrist sent the noose clear of the captive's head, and the puncher coiled the rope as he walked towards him, and threw it on the ground.

"I've met up with some pretty scaly reptiles, but yu top the list, Bundy," he began quietly. "Yu know this lad is in pore health, yet yu yank him out'n the saddle, beat him up, steal his gun, shoot his hoss, an' turn him loose to tramp to the Bend. Even if he knowed the way, with night comin' on, no food an' no blanket, it was a shore thing he'd never make it, an' yu meant he shouldn't. What yu aimed at was plain murder. Got anythin' against him, or was it just because he belongs to the Circle Dot?"

The foreman's face grew darker. "He's a dirty little snitch; it was him wised yu up 'bout the Bend affair, an' lost me twenty-five thousand bucks," he growled. "Ain't that enough?"

Sudden was surprised, but did not show it. Where had Bundy obtained this information? Only he, Dan, Burke, and Yorky knew the inner history of the hold-up; perhaps the boy himself had boasted. Anyway, that problem could wait; there was a more pressing one on hand. He replied to the ruffian's question.

"Dessay yu've killed for less," he said acidly, and paused, weighing the situation. "I oughta leave yu on a tree, but mebbe yu were a man once, an' yu shall have a chance to die like one." He threw Bundy's gun on the grass. "If yu get me, yu go free. Pick her up."

"An' be downed while I'm stoopin'," the other jeered.

"I won't draw till yo're all set," Sudden said contemptuously.

The promise—which he did not doubt—made the Wagon-wheel man think. To offer such a great advantage, his opponent must be infernally fast or a fool, and Bundy had good reason to know that he was not the latter. His confidence in his own prowess was shaken. Another thought came, a desperate expedient; if he could kill Green, he did not fear his companions—they would be taken by surprise and unable to act immediately.

He bent quickly, grasped the gun and, instead of rising, tilted the muzzle upwards and pulled the trigger. Even as he did so, Sudden—watching for some such act of treachery—drew and fired. Bundy's shot missed by a bare inch, and before he could repeat the attempt his weapon was driven from his grip by the puncher's bullet. He clawed for it with his other hand, but Sudden sprang in, kicked it away, and sheathing his own gun, cried:

"Stand up, yu yella dawg, an' take what's comin' to yu."

Bundy was ready enough; he knew that ninety-nine men out of a hundred would instantly have driven a bullet through him after the failure of his dastardly trick; he had been lucky to meet

87

the hundredth; but with the passing of the shadow of death, his hatred of the man who had spared him increased. Truly, with some natures, a favour from a foe is a bitter pill to swallow.

Bundy had one more remark to make. "Them friends o' yourn keepin' outa this?"

"They won't be my friends if they interfere," Sudden said.

"Good enough," the foreman replied. His confidence in himself was returning. He had a well-earned reputation as an exponent of the rough and tumble frontier method of settling quarrels. "I've bin waitin' to put my paws on you for an interferin' houn'."

"Yu couldn't find me, o' course," Sudden sneered.

"I bide my time. I got the kid, an' yo're here."

"Well, what are yu waitin' for, the dark, so that yu can run away again?"

The taunt got through the foreman's hide, tough as it was. "No," he bellowed. "Here I come," and rushed in with fists flying.

"An' there yu go," Sudden retorted, as he drove a lightning left to the face which sent the man reeling.

He staggered to his feet and fought back with blind fury, reckless of the hurt he received, driven by an insensate desire to get his enemy by the throat and slowly squeeze the life out of him. But he had little chance against one who used his head as well as hands; straight jolts to the jaw and body met his wild rushes, and battered down his feeble defence. Opposed to that scientific hammering, his savage lunges were of no avail.

Once only a swinging fist got past the Circle Dot man's guard, and floored him. But he was up instantly, and when Bundy, with a shout of exultation, dashed in, he was met with a tempest of blows which drove him back, foot by foot, until, with every bone in his body aching, and both eyes nearly closed, he dropped his arms. Only for a second, but like a flash, Sudden's right came over and sent him, spent and apparently helpless, to the ground. There he lay, breathing heavily, and making no effort to rise.

"I reckon he's through," Tiny remarked. All of them had watched the combat in silence. "There ain't a kick left in him."

Tiny was wrong; no sooner had he voiced the thought than Bundy's head lifted.

"Yo're a damn liar," he mumbled through puffed lips. "I'm goin' to show you."

Incredible as it seemed, after the punishment he had taken, he heaved himself upright, shook as a dog might after rolling, and stood, long arms swinging. Then he bent and plunged forward. Sudden waited, wondering; there could be no more fight in the fellow, and yet . . . The menacing figure was on him, fists raised, before he realized the fell design—he had but a second to act; the ruffian's right foot was sweeping up to deliver a savage kick in the stomach which might kill, or disable a man for life. Quick as thought, Sudden jumped aside, seized the ascending limb behind the ankle and forced it upwards. The foreman, thrown completely off his balance, struck the ground violently with the back of his head; this time, there was no movement. The victor cold, inscrutable, stood over him.

"Ain't bruk his neck, have you, Jim?" Tiny asked.

"No, that still remains for a rope," Sudden replied. "Put Yorky's saddle an' bridle on this brute's hoss."

Bundy heard the order, and had sufficient life left in him to understand what it meant. "You settin' me afoot—after this?" he snarled.

"Yo're gettin' a taste o' what yu cooked up for the boy, an' lucky at that—we oughta be plantin' yu."

The foreman knew it, and said no more. Not until they had melted into the growing dusk did he struggle, with many groans and curses, to his feet, and, carrying his riding-gear, set out on the nightmare journey to the Wagon-wheel. For to one who spent nearly the whole of his waking hours in the saddle, and whose body was one big bruise, the long march over rough ground could only be unspeakable torture.

Something of this was in the puncher's mind when Tiny reproached him for not settling the affair straight-away after Bundy's cowardly attempt had failed.

"I wanted him to suffer, an' I'll bet right now he's near wishin' I'd downed him," Sudden replied harshly. "After what he fixed up for Yorky . . ." He turned to the youth. "Mebbe yu oughta go away for a spell."

"I'm stayin'," Yorky said stoutly. "Me an' that foreman feller ain't finished yet."

The puncher smiled into the darkness, glad of this fresh proof that his protégé was game. "Well, keep clear o' the Wagon-wheel, though it bothers me how they got hep. Anybody see yu there?"

"I met Miss Trenton on th' way back," the boy admitted.

"She may've mentioned it, an' if my hoss was spotted in the Bend, that'd be enough," Sudden decided.

The whoop of welcome which went up when the rest of the outfit saw that the missing one was of the party, brought a warmth into the waif's heart; these were his friends. In that moment the big city lost him for ever.

CHAPTER XII

Trenton and Garstone stared in undisguised astonishment when, in response to a summons from the former, Bundy came to the ranch-house in the afternoon. He had reached the Wagon-wheel about sunrise, almost dead on his feet, and dropping on the pallet-bed—he had his own quarters—slept like a log from sheer exhaustion. Despite his attempt to do so, he could not remove all traces of the terrible treatment he had undergone; the blackened, swollen eyes, gashed lips, missing teeth, and battered face told an eloquent tale.

"What in hell's happened to you?" Zeb enquired. "Been trampled on by a herd?"

The foreman had his version ready. "I was ridin' back last evenin' when I run into Green an' two o' the Circle Dot fellas. They come on me unawares, roped an' threw me, an' got my gun. Then they set about me—I'd no chance agin three, an' one of 'em that big chap they call Tiny. When I was all in, they went off with my hoss. I had to hoof it home, an' I warn't in any good shape for that neither."

The rancher's face grew purple as he listened; he took the affair as a personal insult. "Three to one?" he cried. "It's a fine thing if my men have to ask the Circle Dot's permission to ride the range. I've a mind to call the boys an' have it out with Dover an' his bullies right away."

"What would that get you?" Garstone asked.

"Somethin' I've sworn to have—the Circle Dot," Trenton replied.

"No, only a forty thousand dollar mortgage which you couldn't meet," the other returned coolly. "I don't suppose Maitland would be any more generous to you."

Trenton's bluster collapsed like a punctured balloon. "Yo're right," he said moodily.

"I usually am," Garstone agreed serenely. Modesty was not one of his weaknesses.

"If yo're worryin' over payin' my score you needn't to," Bundy growled. "I'll 'tend to that my own self—int'rest an' all."

"Touching the acquisition of the Circle Dot, we don't seem to be getting any nearer," the Easterner remarked sarcastically. "Have you made any progress?"

"Very little. Maitland might renew on the security of the two ranches, though we owe him quite a lot already, but that would only mean gettin' deeper in. No, we'll have to fall back on the plan I had in mind—to find Red Rufe's Cache."

"A tale for a tenderfoot?" the foreman fleered. "If that's our on'y hope, we can wish the Circle Dot a fond fare-you-well as' no error."

The rancher's face stiffened. "The thrashin' seems to have destroyed yore manners as well as beauty, Bundy," he said coldly. "You can go."

Like a scolded dog the man came to heel instantly. "Sorry, Boss, I was disappointed," he pleaded. "If there'd bin anythin' in that yarn, the Cache would 'a' come to light by this; plenty has searched for it."

"True, but the Cloudy country is large and terribly difficult; unless one knew just where to look, findin' the proverbial needle in a haystack would be child's play in comparison."

"And you have this information?" Garstone asked eagerly.

"Not quite, or I should have made use of it before now," Trenton replied. "This is how the matter stands: Red Rufe was Dave Dover's elder brother. He left Rainbow, went further West, an' made a fortune and reputation as a gambler. Report has it that he sent a letter to Dave, statin' that he had hidden his wealth, an' givin' the approximate location—said to be in the Cloudy Hills. A second message was to follow with instructions for findin' the exact spot. This one miscarried, an', quite by chance, came into my hands."

"So that's why Flint and Rattray visited the Circle Dot?" Garstone said.

"Certainly. I hoped they would find the first letter. Flint was on the track of it when he made a fool of himself an' got fired."

"Then you are not sure it is concealed in the Cloudy Hills?"

"No, but the fellow who fetched the first letter said Rufe handed it to him there; that's all anyone knows except—Dover."

Garstone made a gesture of impatience. "That means our knowledge is useless," he said irritably.

"Yore wits don't seem to be workin' this afternoon, Ches," Trenton returned equably. "Listen: the Circle Dot needs money even more than we do; what do you suppose they will do?"

"Try to find the Cache, possibly."

"Certainly, I should say, an' in doin' so will give us the information we now lack," the rancher said triumphantly. "I'm havin' a watch kept on their movements, an' when they start, we'll follow. Once we know the locality, we have the advantage of being able to go straight to the hidin'-place while they are gropin' in the dark."

"That's a great scheme, Boss," Bundy complimented, his damaged features contorted in a painful grin. "If we can collect the pot, we'll have Dover an' his crowd yappin' for mercy—an' not gettin' it."

"It's undoubtedly a fine chance," Garstone admitted, and he was looking at the foreman when he spoke. "Any idea what the Cache consists of?"

"No one knows," Trenton replied. "Gold, in coin or dust, possibly paper too."

"What became of this Rufe person?"

"Vanished after the second message. Went back to his card-sharpin', I expect, an' got wiped out. He was a big fellow, very upright—his back was the only straight thing about him. He had red hair, like all the Dovers, an' a fiend of a temper, the sort of man to make more foes than friends."

"We oughta be ready to set out on the word," Bundy put in. "How many will you want?"

"We three, with Flint, Rattray, an' another should be sufficient. We'll need plenty of supplies, an' a small tent for my niece."

"Takin' her?" Bundy asked in surprise. "It ain't a job for a dame."

"Nonsense," the rancher said. "Just a little trip into the mountains; she'll enjoy it. We shall avoid trouble, an' probably not encounter the other party at all."

The foreman was not satisfied, but Garstone did not support him, and after the earlier rebuff he was taking no more risks; this thing was too good to miss.

Garstone had not objected because the presence of Miss Trenton fitted in with his plans, already partly formed, but which were now beginning to expand more widely than either of his companions suspected, even Bundy, who was having thoughts of his own.

* * *

That same evening, at the Circle Dot, a very similar conversation was taking place. Dan, who had been to Rainbow earlier in the day, broached the subject.

"I have a talk with Maitland an' there ain't any possibility o' the bank givin' us an extension," he began. "Told me his people wouldn't hear of it, an' that—as a business man—he agreed with 'em. So that's that."

"An' there's no other way o' raisin' the wind?" Burke asked.

"On'y one," the rancher replied. "We gotta find the Cache."

The foreman's face was anything but optimistic. "It's one hell of a chance," he muttered.

"Bill, if yu were in a poker game, with the cards runnin' badly, an' had just one stake left, what would yu do?" Sudden said.

"Bet it, o' course," was the prompt reply.

"Shore yu would," the other grinned. "Well, that's our position. So what?"

"I ain't baulkin', Jim," the foreman returned. "I've bin up agin the iron before. Whatever Dan sez, goes, with me."

"I know that, ol'-timer," Dover said. "An' because I do, I'm goin' to ask a favour; I want you to stay here an' look after the ranch; I'll feel easier in my mind with you in charge."

Burke made a brave effort to conceal his disappointment; he would have dearly loved to make one of the search party, but he recognized that his employer was right—it would be more than unwise for both of them to be absent; the Wagon-wheel might seize the opportunity to try something.

"Very well, Dan," he agreed. "Who you takin'?"

"No call for a crowd," Dan told him. "I figure that myself, Jim, Tiny, Blister, an' Hunch oughta be plenty."

"Hunch?" Bill said in surprise.

"Yeah, he knows the Cloudy district probably better than anybody around here, is a good woodsman, an' can cook an' make camp. We might take Yorky along to help—just as well for him to be outa the way till Bundy's bruises lose some o' their sting."

"When do you aim to start?"

"Soon as we can arrange things," Dan replied. "We'll want some stores, which I'll get in town to-morrow."

"An, no one must know a word about it, not even the rest o' the outfit," Sudden supplemented. "Also, we'll slide out in the middle o' the night."

The other two looked at him in astonishment. "What's on yore mind, Jim?" Dan questioned.

"Just this: the possessor o' the second part o' the directions don't know where to begin searchin', but he's on'y gotta trail us to find out."

"Holy Moses, he's right, Bill," the rancher cried. "We're a couple o' sheep-heads. Trenton may have this place picketed, an' be waitin' for us to move."

"We'll try to keep him waitin'," Burke grinned. "How long d'you expect to be away?"

"Can't say," Dan told him. "If we have any luck—but there's no sense in guessin'."

"Yorky'll be tickled to death over this trip," Sudden remarked. "How'd he get on with his new mount this mornin'?" They had not had their usual jaunt.

"Well, he got on, an' off in quicker time," the foreman twinkled. "Shore, it's a good little hoss, no vice in him, just a mite fresh. The boy warn't hurt, 'cept in his feelin's mebbe, an' he comes up smilin'. 'That's first t'row to you, partner,' he sez. 'Let's roll 'em agin.' He climbs on, an' gits piled, which makes him

93

scratch his head some. But he's game. 'Third time lucky,' he grins, an' by cripes, it was; we seen daylight between him an' the saddle pretty offen, but he hung on, an' it was the hoss got tired first. When the fun was over, Slow asked which o' the names Yorky' called the animile he was goin' to choose. 'I'm namin' him "Dancer"—he's so damn lively on his toes,' the kid sez."

Sudden laughed. "Yorky's all right; he's goin' to bring good luck to the Circle Dot, mark my words. Yu do well to take him with us, Dan."

* * *

In the morning Dover journeyed again to Rainbow, and to the youngster's extreme satisfaction, took Yorky with him. Arrived there, they separated, the rancher to deal with various business matters, and Yorky to do as he pleased. His first visit was to the post office, where he mailed a letter, with many furtive glances around to make sure he was not observed. Then he went to finish his "shoppin'." This actually meant displaying himself in all his glory to young Evans, who was now assisting his father in the store. Yorky hung about outside the place until he saw that the boy was alone, and then, hat pulled over his eyes, and regretful that he had not brought his rifle, he swaggered in.

"Got any feed for a Winchester forty-four?" he enquired, making his voice as gruff as he could.

"Yessir," the youth behind the counter replied, diving into a drawer.

Yorky choked down a chuckle; he was not recognized. Casually he examined the packet of cartridges, tossed down a bill, and received his change. The young salesman noticed that the customer did not appear to be wearing a pistol, and, anxious to do business, ventured to ask solicitously:

"C'd I int'rest you in a second-hand six-shooter, sir?"

Yorky squirmed with delight—this was better than his dreams. "Dunno as I care fer other folks' leavin's," he replied carelessly, "I'll take a peep at her."

The gun was reached from a shelf and the customer revolved the cylinder, cocked and pressed the trigger, tried the grip, and hefted the weapon as he has seen cowboys do when examining a new one.

"What yer askin'?"

"Twenty dollars—the price is on the ticket."

Yorky was aware of the fact. "I'd say fifteen's a-plenty," he said disparagingly.

"I'll see if Dad will take that," the salesman replied, and disappeared into the rear of the shop.

Yorky looked disconcerted; he had been showing off, and much as he would have liked to possess the weapon, had no intention of buying it. He was seeking a means of backing out without loss of dignity when Dover came in, and brought an inspiration.

"Say, Boss, c'n you let me have an advance?" he asked anxiously. "I've offered fifteen bucks fer that gun an' I'm shy th' coin."

Dan picked up the six-shooter. "She's good an' cheap at the figure," he said. "Here's the necessary."

"Thanks a lot, Boss," Yorky replied with great relief. "I didn't want ter eat dirt afore this kid. He don't know me: ain't it a scream?"

The "kid" returned and, after a very respectful greeting to the owner of the Circle Dot, addressed his other customer:

"I can accept yore offer, sir. Will you be needin' any cart-tidges?"

"Them I got will do—she's a forty-four, same as my rifle," Yorky said, and paid over the price. "Yer needn't to wrap her up, an' *yer can't int'rest me no more, neither.*"

He thrust the gun under his belt, pushed his hat back, and stood rocking on his heels. Goggle-eyed, the beefy boy on the other side of the counter gawped at him, remembered and suffered. The ragged, sick little tramp he had fought and beaten—as he maintained—had now beaten him, by becoming what he would have given his ears to be—a cowboy. He could strut into the store, and he—Evans—would have to serve and be polite to him; only a lad could plumb the bitterness of this. His job, of which he had been so proud, became as dust and ashes in his mouth. And then, unable to bear those triumphant eyes any longer, he bolted.

"I guess that levels up some with him," Yorky said. "I'll be outside."

"The durn li'l monkey," Dover muttered. "Fancy him thinkin' up a game like that."

The store-keeper came in, and his orders given, the rancher rejoined the boy. A little way along the street they met Foxwell, who stopped, his beady eyes alight with malice.

"'Lo, Dover, gittin' ready to quit the Circle Dot," was his greeting.

Dan suppressed a start. "Any reason why I should?" he asked.

"Well, everybody knows yore ol' man was up to his neck in debt, an' it's said now that the bank won't give you no more rope," came the insolent answer.

"Lies," Dan replied airily. "Big, fat lies which no respectable representative o' the Law should be passin' on. Lemme see, Sheriff, how long have you managed to hold office?"

The officer's not too acute intellect missed the innuendo. "Goin' on four year," he said, even rather pridefully.

"Yeah, I remember; it was you who found the murdered man on the Cloudy trail—the man who had neither money nor papers on him, not even a letter addressed to someone else, huh?"

The sheriff's gaze shifted uneasily. "That's so; the fella what drowned him took everythin'."

"I don't doubt it." Again the implication passed unobserved. "A month or two later you were elected by a small margin, one provided—so some folks said—by the Wagon-wheel outfit because you had done Trenton a considerable service."

"What are you drivin' at?" Foxwell cried, his face crimson.

"Lies, Sheriff, big, fat lies like I was tellin' you about," Dan retorted, and then, "God Almighty!"

They were standing a few yards from the Parlour Saloon. On the opposite sidewalk, Miss Trenton had apparently made up her mind to brave the terrors of the rutted and hoof-torn strip which was Rainbow's only thoroughfare; just past this point, the street took one of its uncertain turns. She was half-way across when, with a stertorous bellow, six wild steers, enveloped in a cloud of dust, charged down upon her. The girl saw the cruel branching horns, fierce eyes, and lolling tongues, and made a despairing effort to hurry. But this only led to disaster; her feet slipped in the powdery sand and she fell to her knees right in the path of the infuriated animals, behind whom now appeared a perspiring horseman, shouting and gesticulating.

Leaving the pop-eyed sheriff, Dover sprinted along the sidewalk, dragged out his revolver, and fired at the leader, a little in front of the herd. The brute hesitated, stumbled and went down, only a yard from where the girl lay. The fall of the foremost halted the others, but Dan knew it would be only momentary. Jumping into the road, he floundered to the spot, and raised the now senseless form. A man on foot has no terrors for range cattle, and the sight of him put them in motion again. By a superhuman effort, he regained the sidewalk with his burden; a grazed arm and a ripped shirt-sleeve from a slashing, needle-pointed horn was the only damage.

"Close work, boy," Bowdyr said. He had come out to see what the noise was about. "Bring her into my place.". .

"Ain't hurt, is she?" the sheriff enquired anxiously.

"I guess not," Dan replied. "If you wanta do Zeb another service, go an' ask that butcher's lout what he means by bringin' cows through the town an' drivin' 'em into a frenzy with his fool yellin'; must be mad or drunk." He caught the saloon-keeper's enigmatic expression, and added, "Might 'a' killed the pair of us." The sheriff went; he did not enjoy the company of Mister Dover in this mood.

When Miss Trenton returned to the world again, she was sitting in a strange room, with a rugged but kindly-faced man bending over her, glass in hand.

"Drink this, ma'am," he said. "It's good stuff, an' will put new life into you."

96

She obeyed, and the strong spirit—though it made her cough—sent the blood racing through her veins. She looked curiously at her surroundings.

"What place is this?" she asked.

"The Parlour Saloon an' I'm Ben Bowdyr, the proprietor," he explained. "Dan's gone for Doc Malachi, an' to git hisself another shirt."

"Is Mister Dover hurt?"

"Shore, no, just a spoilt garment," Ben assured her. "Ah, here's the Doc."

Malachi hurried in, the concern on his face giving way to relief when he saw the patient. "You are not harmed, Miss Trenton?"

"I foolishly fainted," she replied. "Mister Bowdyr kindly gave me some—medicine, and I am quite well again."

"Medicine?" Malachi echoed. He picked up the glass she had used, sniffed, glanced at the saloon-keeper, who had retired to h's bar, and smiled whimsically. "Then Ben has done all that is necessary and robbed me of a case. And from the way Dover carried on, I really thought it was a serious one."

"It would have been but for his courage and prompt action," she said soberly. "He also escaped injury I am told."

"Yes, these cattlemen are tough animals—very discouraging to a doctor," he mourned. "Fortunately they are quarrelsome. But you have made a conquest, Miss Trenton." He saw the colour creep into her cheeks. "That brandy—I should say, medicine—was laid down by Ben's grandfather, 'way back in Virginia, in the days when people of position had cellars, and he wouldn't take fifty dollars a bottle for it."

Her gaze went to the saloon-keeper. "He was most kind," she murmured.

"The first thing I learned out here was not to judge by appearances. Ben is a fine fellow, and one day, when settlements like Rainbow become cities, such men will be sent to Congress, and have a word to say, not only in the affairs of our country, but of the world."

"Still your dream," she smiled. "Why, isn't that Yorky?"

Malachi stared as the boy came to them. "By all that's wonderful, it is."

"I'm hopin' yer ain't hurt much, ma'am," Yorky said. "I seen it all an' shore t'ought yer was a goner."

"Thanks to Mister Dover, I am not a—goner," she smiled. "And how are you, Yorky?"

"Fine, an' I'm on th' pay-roll," he blurted out. "S'cuse me, I got a message for Ben."

"An amazing improvement," she said. "There's a case to make you proud of your profession."

"Not my work," he told her. "I prescribed a cessation of nicotine poisoning and fresh air——"

"The breath of the pines," she murmured.

"Precisely, but I didn't put it so prettily."

"No, I remember it was his friend, Jim."

"Really? After all, why shouldn't a puncher be poetical—he's at grips with Nature all day long. Anyway, Green saved that lad's life, by supplying the missing ingredient in my treatment." Her look was a question. "Yorky had lost his self-respect, and lacking that, my dear lady, a human being is—finished; he cannot fight disease." Then, in a flash, his gravity was merged in a laugh, as he added, "I should be a preacher."

She was about to reply when Dover came in, and before the door swung to again, she saw Miss Maitland pass.

"I must be going," Malachi said rather hurriedly, and as he departed spoke in an undertone to the rancher, "Not leaving town yet, are you?"

"I'll be here for a while," Dan replied, and stepped to where the girl was seated. "Doc tells me you ain't injured. I'm glad. Is there anythin' else I can do?"

His manner was stiff and distant, and she suddenly comprehended that the red-haired youth who so impulsively rushed to rescue her from the quicksand had—short as the time was—become a man. Grief and responsibility had brought about the transformation.

"I think you have done enough, and more," she replied. "It is hard to find words to express my thanks."

"Then don't try," he said bluntly. "I don't want 'em, an' if it will ease yore mind, I would 'a' done just the same for any tramp in the town."

"Very well, but you cannot prevent me feeling grateful," she said. "You risked your life."

"Which is no more than I've done many times for one o' my father's steers," he told her. "I'm not meanin' to be rude, Miss Trenton, but to be forced to help one o' yore family is plain hell to me."

"I understand," she said coldly. "But you must remember that to be forced to accept your help is also plain hell to my family."

With a slight inclination of her proud little head, and a smile of thanks to the saloon-keeper, she walked out. The rancher's gloomy gaze followed her. What had possessed him to speak that way? He recalled how his heart had seemed to stop beating when he saw her in the path of the cattle. Perhaps it was the reaction at finding her unharmed when he had feared . . . Or maybe it was the encounter with the sheriff, which still rankled? Well, what did it matter—she was a Trenton anyway. He went to the

98

bar, and Bowdyr's first remark might have been an answer to his last thought.

"She's a fine gal—even if she is kin to Zeb," he said.

"Looks ain't much to go on," the young man observed cynically. "The meanest hoss I ever owned was a picture."

The saloon-keeper, being a wise man, kept his smile and his thoughts to himself. Malachi, returning presently, found them drinking together, and to the surprise of both, declined their invitation.

"How's the arm?" he enquired.

"Fine, it was just a touch."

"Yes, touch and go; if you'd been two seconds later the horn would have pierced your heart," the doctor said. "I didn't tell Miss Trenton that."

"I'm obliged—she's over-grateful a'ready. You ain't here to ask after my health, are you, Phil?"

"No, my errand concerns my own. When are you going away?"

"So you've heard that damn silly rumour too?"

"I pay no attention to idle chatter, and get it into your head that I'm on your side," Malachi said seriously. "Listen: I happen to know—never mind how—that you have to raise a large sum of money in a short time."

Dan swore. "So my financial position is common property?" he said bitterly.

"Whose isn't, in this place?" was the rejoinder. "Where are you going for it? With the cattle business as it is, your chance with the Eastern capitalist is nil; north and south are only ranches in the same predicament as yourself; in the west, there is Rufe's Cache—if you can find it."

"What do you know about that?" Dan demanded.

"The story is common property also," the doctor reminded. "Your father himself gave me the facts, and asserted that if necessity arose, he could go to the spot. Probably that is why he did not worry about his debt to the bank."

Dan was silent; it was disturbing to think his affairs and plans were known. Then he said, "Who told you I was leavin' Rainbow?"

"No one. Aware of the difficulty you are in, I tried to reason out a line of action, that's all. The Cache would appear to be your best bet."

"What's yore interest?"

"The purely selfish one of wanting to go with you."

Bowdyr had been called away, so Dover got the full shock of the surprise, and it certainly was one. That this man, whom he liked, but had always regarded as an effeminate, should desire to undergo the danger and discomfort of a journey into the mountains seemed quite incredible.

"It'll be damned hard goin', we'll have to break trail a lot, live rough an' sleep in the open, an' it's cold too, nights," he warned. "Also, there's a risk o' fightin' if——"

"Trenton gets the idea. Yes, he needs cash as much, and perhaps more, than you do. Well, I can ride and shoot, I'm fitter than I look, and I'll obey orders. Also, if anyone gets hurt . . ."

The rancher voiced his last and chief objection. "You'll be a devil of a long way from a saloon," he said pointedly.

"Which is exactly why I want to come," Malachi smiled. "It is an experiment, Dan, and I'm asking you to help me."

They shook hands on the bargain.

CHAPTER XIII

Beth Trenton returned to the Wagon-wheel sound in body but perturbed in mind. Naturally generous by nature, the attitude her rescuer had adopted distressed and saddened her. Coming from the East, she could not comprehend the stark animosity which could keep two families at war for years. And rude, primitive as he seemed, there was much that was likeable in Dan Dover. If only she could bring about a peace.

Her uncle was alone in the living-room. As she related her adventure, she saw concern, relief, and then both were swept away in a gust of anger at the mention of her preserver's name.

"That fella again?" he stormed. "What cursed ill-luck arranges for him to be handy every time you get into trouble?"

"I am afraid I cannot regard it as ill-luck," she replied. "He saved me, and might have died himself."

"Bah! Only one thing kills that breed—a bullet," was the brutal rejoinder. "I'm not ungrateful, girl; any other man could ask what he liked of me, but Dover . . ."

"He does not want even thanks," she said. "He threw my own back in my face."

"The insolent young hound," Trenton growled. "He needs a lesson, an' by Christopher, I'll see that he gets one."

"Uncle, what was the beginning of the trouble?" she asked.

"Oh, it's a long story; I'll spin it for you one day, but you can take this to go on with—a Dover murdered my father," the rancher said, and stood up. "Yo're a Trenton, Beth, an' our enemies must be yores too; we don't forget or forgive."

He had meant to tell her of the coming trip into the hills, but judged this was not the time; better to let the memory of this latest obligation to Dover fade a little. Women were kittle cattle, and he wanted her wholly on his side. He struck another blow.

"Have you noticed Bundy's face?"

"Why, yes, he seems to have met with an accident."

"Yeah, the accident of runnin' into three o' the Circle Dot riders out on the range," Trenton said. "They threw an' savaged him, stole his horse, an' he had to foot it home, over ten miles, in the dark."

"Three to one?" she cried. "The cowards! Was Mister Dover there?"

"No, but his new man, Green, was, so you can be certain his boss approved; probably it was a put-up job, an' they were waitin' for the chance."

"But why?"

"Simply because he's foreman here; it's a blow at me."

She could not doubt, although she found it hard to credit that Green, of whom the doctor had spoken highly, could take part in such a sordid enterprise. But she was learning that the Westerner was a creature of fine impulses, strong in his likes and dislikes.

"Isn't there any law?" she ventured.

"No, only a sheriff," was the satirical answer. "Now, don't you worry yourself about these things, my dear. Bundy can take care of himself, an' so can the Wagon-wheel."

* o o

Dover also journeyed home in a worried state of mind. He had called on Maitland before leaving town, and the interview had been anything but helpful. It was, the rancher moodily reflected, a fitting climax to a thoroughly imperfect day. So Yorky, to whom it had proved exactly the opposite, found him a morose and pre-occupied companion. Jocular references to his encounter with young Evans met with no encouragement. In the bunkhouse, it was much the same; the boys listened to his story, but it failed to arouse the amusement he had looked for.

"Got back on him for the lickin' he gave you, huh?" Blister commented.

"Never did lick me," Yorky retorted heatedly. "He took as much as I did."

"Then you had nothin' to square up for," the cowboy replied.

Even Yorky's quick wits could find no answer to this, and he subsided into silence. It began to dawn upon him that he had not been so clever after all. This suspicion was strengthened when he showed his new acquisition to Sudden, with an account of how he had got it.

"She's good value," the puncher said. "Told the boys?"

"Yep, they didn't seem to think it funny," Yorky admitted, and repeated Blister's remarks.

"They were right—it ain't a bit funny," Sudden said gravely. "Yu fought Evans, an' come out even. Well, nothin' to that, but now yu've put yoreself in his debt by shamin' him, probably made him hate his job. That's bad."

"Never thought of it that way, Jim," the boy said contritely. "What c'n I do?"

"Next time yo're in town, go to Evans an' eat dirt," the puncher said. "That's a meal we all gotta be ready to take, an' if it gets yu a friend, it's worth while."

The boy promised. He had learned another lesson.

Not until the evening meal was ended did Dan unburden his mind to Sudden and the foreman. They had already heard of the cattle incident—Yorky having given a graphic and highly-ornamented version of it to the company in the bunkhouse.

"So you had to git a Trenton outa trouble agin, Dan," Burke remarked. "That girl didn't oughta be allowed out alone."

"It wasn't her fault," the young man found himself saying, and then, "We got somethin' more important than that to discuss. Maitland is beginning to put the screw on—he won't even let me have cash for runnin' expenses. There's tradesmen in town to be settled with, an' pay-day comin' along."

"The boys won't mind waitin'," Burke put in gruffly.

"I know, Bill, an' that's why I don't want 'em to," Dan said. "I've an offer for a hundred three-year-olds; the buyer will take over an' pay at the Bend. It's a poor price, an' will mean hangin' up our start for two-three days, but——"

"Needs must, when the banker goes on the prod," Sudden misquoted.

"You said it," Dan replied with a smile, the first they had seen from him all the evening. "Well, that eases my mind. I wouldn't like to go leavin' debts to folks who can't afford to lose, an' Bill here without a shot in the locker. An' talkin' of goin', Doc Malachi wants to come along; I said he might."

The foreman looked dubious. "Does he understand what he's lettin' hisself in for?"

"I made that plain," Dan replied, and repeated the conversation, finishing with, "He might be useful."

"Shore, but how come he knows we're in a jam?" Burke asked.

"He wouldn't say, but I can guess. He's been seein' a lot o' Maitland's girl since the dance, an' she helps in the bank. Her father trusts her—he told me as much."

"That explains the 'experiment' too," Sudden smiled. "I hope he wins out on it. What about hittin' the hay—we got a coupla busy days to shove behind us?"

With the coming of daylight, they were at work, rounding up cutting out, and road-branding the steers to be disposed of. Small as the herd was, these operations took time and entailed much riding, for the cattle were spread over a wide range. About half a mile from the ranch-house, a big bunch of steers was collected by four of the outfit, and from these Dover and Sudden roped the selected beasts, dragged them to the nearby fire, where Lidgett hog-tied them and Slow applied the iron.

The bellowing of the branded brutes, blinding sun, swirling clouds of dust, acrid smell of burnt hair, and the varied objurgations of the toilers, who sweated and swore with equal fervour, presented a scene of confusion from which it seemed impossible for order to emerge. By the arrival of dusk, however, the herd was ready to take the trail, and the discarded cattle dispersed again. the boys raced for the river, to rid themselves of the real estate they had acquired during the day. When they arrived at the bunk-house, Paddy affected astonishment.

"Shure, Dan should 'a' told me he was takin' on new han's," he said.

"Gwan, you ol' grub-spoiler," Slow retorted. "Hump yoreself. I'm hungry enough to eat you—raw—if I had a ton o' salt."

"An' it's on'y a mouthful I'd be for ye," the Irishman grinned, and Slow, whose mouth was built on generous lines, retired from the combat.

* o o

At daybreak the herd was on the move, Dover in charge, with Blister, Tiny, Noisy, and Sudden as his crew.

"They're in prime condition an' the trail ain't difficult," the rancher said. "If we drive 'em middlin' hard we oughta make the Bend before dark to-morrow. Me an' Tiny'll be in front, Noisy an' Blister on the flanks, an' Jim'll keep the 'drag' goin'."

Very soon the riders had the steers lined out, and travelling at a steady pace. Cattle on the trail can, in normal circumstances, cover from fifteen to twenty miles a day, according to the nature of the country. Dan was hoping to do better than this on a short drive, but he was too good a cowman to "tucker out" the animals by pressing them too early.

The hours slid by, and the drive proceeded uneventfully. Now and then an adventurous beast dropped out of line and made a break for freedom, to be chased, brought back, and called uncomplimentary things by a sweating rider. Sudden, in the rear, was kept busy hazing the few stragglers always to be found in any trail-herd.

The approach of night found them on a plateau some miles in extent and nearly half-way to their destination. As the feed was good, and a stream adjacent, Dan decided to halt there. The tired cattle were watered, bunched together, and the rancher, with Noisy, took the first spell of night-herding. The other three squatted round a fire, and having fed, smoked and talked. In the distance, where a black blob showed indistinctly in the half-light, they could hear the watchers crooning to their charges.

"Dan's a fine fella, but as an opery singer he'd shore be a total loss," Blister laughed. "Cows can't have no ear for music, or you couldn't soothe 'em down with a voice that'd scare a kid into convulsions."

"They sleep to git away from it," Tiny explained. "That's why I'm a pore night-herder—the critters stay awake to listen to me."

"That won't win you nothin'—you take yore turn," Blister chuckled. "Fancy tryin' that one; you got about as much savvy as a mule."

Before the outraged cowboy could reply to this aspersion, Sudden cut in: "An' there, though he ain't intendin' it, he's payin' yu a compliment, Tiny. Lemme tell yu somethin' I actually witnessed. An' ol' darkie was drivin' a buckboard behind a big, hammer-headed mule with ears like wings. All at once, the beast stalled on him, just stiffened his legs and stood stock-still like he'd taken root. Well, the nigger tried persuasion first; he got down an' talked.

" 'Now looky, Abram, dis ain't no way to act. Ain't I allus treated yoh well? W'at foh yoh wanter play dis trick on Uncle Eph?'

"He said a lot more, but it didn't do any good; Abram just curled his lips back over his teeth an' laughed at him. So the darkie goes to pullin' him, then to pushin' the buckboard on his heels, but he might as well have tried to shift a house. Then Uncle Eph got his dander up. He climbs into his wagon, unearths a stout ash-plant, an' lays into that mule like all possessed. Yu ever seen a fella beatin' a carpet what ain't been cleaned for years? Well, that was how it was. I reckon yu could 'a' heard the racket half a mile off, an' the dust came out'n that critter's hide in clouds—it was like a sand-storm. But Abram never stirred an inch, an' when at last the nigger dropped back on his seat too tired to lam any more, that mule lets out a sort o' sound—jeerin' like—which made his master madder'n ever.

" 'Light a fire under him,' one o' the onlookers advised.

"This put new life into Uncle Eph. He scouted round in the buckboard, produced wood an' paper, built his fire an' put a match to it. 'I burn de damn belly off'n yoh, Abram,' he said viciously, an' when the flames shot up an' the mule stirs hisself, he lets out a yell of triumph. But he was a bit previous; that durned animal moved just fur enough forward to bring the buckboard right over the fire, an' took root again; if Uncle Eph hadn't got mighty active he'd 'a' had nothin' but a fiery chariot to ride in. An' then Abram turns his head an' closes one eye in the most deliberate wink I ever saw. No, sir, don't tell me mules ain't got savvy."

They laughed at the story, and Tiny said, "I remember once——"

But what it was they were not to hear, for from over the plateau came the crash of guns and bellowing of scared steers, followed by the thunder of many hammering hooves.

"Hell's joy, the herd is gone," Blister cried.

Springing to their saddles, they scampered towards the hubbub, dragging out their rifles as they went. Sudden caught sight of a whitish object flapping in the gloom, and took a snap shot. The object vanished, but he did not stay to investigate—the important thing was to stop the stampeding cattle. By hard and, in the dark,

105

hazardous riding, they got ahead of some of the frightened brutes, turned, and drove them back to camp.

"Stay here an' ride hard on this lot, Blister," Sudden said "We'll go hunt for more."

On their way they met a horseman shepherding about a dozen steers; he proved to be Dover.

"We'd just got 'em settlin' down nicely when the hullabaloo began," he said. "Somebody loosed off a gun, an' another of 'em flapped a sheet or blanket an' shouted. You got some, you say? Good work. Lucky they was tired—ain't liable to run far. Yeah, Noisy's all right; he's takin' in a small gather."

Throughout the hours of darkness the search went on, and when dawn arrived, a count showed that they were only ten short.

"Better'n I hoped," Dan said. "We may pick up one or two more on the way."

As they returned to snatch a meal at the fire, a dark, huddled form, lying where the grass was longer, attracted their attention. A dead man, and beside him, a lightish slicker. Sudden remembered his chance shot. He turned the body over; the features were familiar. He visioned again the saloon at Hell City, into which this same Mexican had limped, footsore and weary, come to report failure and risk death at the hands of Satan, the master brigand. He had saved the fellow's life then, and now blind Fate had ordained that he should take it.[1]

"Couple o' twenty dollar bills with the Rainbow bank's stamp on 'em," Tiny announced. He had been searching the corpse.

"Better take those, Dan; we might be able to trace 'em," Sudden advised. "An' we'll bury this *hombre* if yu got no objection; I once saw him act mighty like a man—for a Greaser."

The drive was resumed, and as Dover had predicted, they came across several of the runaways, and so could deem themselves well out of what might easily have been a disaster. They saw nothing of their unknown assailants, and as the latter part of the journey was over a regular cattle-track, they reached their destination in good time.

The business of handing over the herd did not take long, and after a satisfying meal they drifted into the Paradise Saloon.

"Remember this joint, Jim?" Dan asked.

Sudden grinned; it was there he and the rancher had adjourned after the shooting test; somehow it seemed a good time ago Grouped at the bar, they discussed the question of the return trip, whether to start at once, or wait for daybreak. All of them were tired, but as Tiny finally expressed it:

"A bed listens fine to me, Dan, but you on'y gotta say the word an' I'm ready."

[1] Related in *Sudden Rides Again*. George Newnes Ltd.

"What do you think, Jim?"

Sudden did not reply for a moment; his gaze was on a short, shabby, bearded fellow sitting a few feet away. Then he asked, "Yu acquainted with the landlord o' this shebang, Dan?" And when the young man nodded, "Find out if he knows the whiskery gent just behind yu."

The rancher ordered another round of drinks and, after a whispered colloquy with the proprietor, turned to his friends. "Never set eyes on him afore, but that don't mean much—strangers ain't no novelty in the Bend."

"Mebbe not," Sudden replied, and raising his voice a little, "We'd better be on our way."

The last to leave, he saw—by the aid of a mirror—that the bearded man was also making for the door. Leading his party along the street, he swung round a corner and halted. Almost immediately the object of his suspicion appeared, and seeing the group of cowboys, hesitated and then slunk past.

"He was interested in our conversation, an' now he follows us. What d'yu make o' that, Dan?"

"I'm no good at riddles, Jim. You tell me."

"Those coyotes back on the trail missed the beef, but if they knowed when to expect us, they might try for the dollars."

"Likely enough, an' that *hombre* would have plenty time to get here ahead o' us," Dover admitted. "What's our best plan?"

"With that fella trailin' us we got no hope o' trickin' 'em. I vote we catch some sleep an' start in the mornin'," was Sudden's suggestion. "If they waylay us, we'll stand a better chance in the daylight."

The others agreed that this was the wisest course, and being already short of one night's rest, they gave the attractions of the town the go-by, and turned in early.

There was no sign of the bearded man when they set off soon after daybreak, but none of them doubted his being in the vicinity. Sudden only grinned when Tiny mentioned it. One precaution was taken: Dover called Sudden aside and slipped a packet into his hand; it was the money received for the cattle.

"You got the fastest hoss in the bunch," he said. "If things get tight, make a dash for it."

"Unless they're watchin' the trail, we'll have no trouble."

"They may be, or it's possible that jasper has gone on a'ready to tell 'em we're comin'."

"He ain't," Sudden chuckled. "Over-keen, Mister Whiskers. He took the room next to mine, an' when I found my key would open his door, I slipped in, hawg-tied an' gagged him, an' told the landlord my neighbour wanted to sleep late."

Dover laughed. "Gosh, Jim, you don't miss any bets," he complimented. "I'm damn glad you didn't go over to Trenton."

"Well, that settles Whiskers, but we still gotta remember that the others may be the patient kind."

The three cowboys had to be told, and they looked at Sudden with added respect. Blister's tribute amused them all.

"Jim," he said gravely. "One o' these days you an me *won't* have a game o' poker."

"Blister," was the solemn reply. "When it comes to cards, yu wouldn't believe how dumb I am."

"Yo're dead right, I wouldn't," Blister agreed.

Having no herd to hamper them, a good pace could be maintained. Sudden led the party, and Dan brought up the rear, each man riding a little behind the next so that all of them could not be covered at once. The first score of miles were negotiated without incident, and then they drew near to where the stampede had happened. The sun was climbing the sky, and in the growing heat they did not hasten; it was necessary to spare the horses in case speed should be urgently needed.

East of the plateau, as Sudden remembered, the trail traversed a shallow gully, both walls of which were hedged by thick brush. Immediately on entering this, he slackened pace still more, eyes alert. Half-way through the sun glinted on something in the depths of a bush; it was the barrel of a rifle, and directly opposite was another.

"Shove 'em up," barked a voice. "We got you set—both sides."

Sudden's reins were already twisted round the saddle-horn—his knees told the horse what to do. When, in apparent obedience to the order, his hands rose, a gun was in each, spouting flame and lead. Left and right, the shots crashed, the rifle-barrels disappeared—one exploding harmlessly—and there was a sound of breaking twigs and violent movement in the veil of vegetation. At the same instant, the black sprang onward, a few mighty bounds carrying it clear of the gully. The rest of the party followed, bending low and raking the brush with their revolvers. Scattered, ill-aimed replies came from the ambushers. When he had ridden about a mile, Sudden waited for his companions.

"Anybody hurt?" he wanted to know. "What's the matter with yu, Noisy?"

"Ain't nothin'," the silent one replied. "Just a graze."

"We'll tie it up," the puncher said. "I figure them fellas have had a full meal."

The "graze" proved to be a nasty flesh-wound in the forearm, and when this had been attended to they went on their way. Blister and Tiny, riding together, discussed the occurrence.

"I never see his han's move, but both guns was out an' workin'. I'll bet he got both them smarties," the big cowboy remarked.

"Smart nothin'—a pair o' bunglers," said a quiet voice behind. "Lemme give yu a tip, Tiny; next time yu go bush-

108

whackin', don't show yore gun; the slant o' the barrel tells the other fella where to aim."

"Speakin' from experience, Jim?" Tiny came back.

"Shore," Sudden grinned. "I was a road-agent afore I came down in the world an' had to take to punchin'."

In due course they reached the Circle Dot, and once more the bunkhouse had a story to hear. Blister told it, finishing in characteristic fashion:

"An' after the ruckus, the on'y trouble we had was listenin' to Noisy yowlin' like a sick cat over that triflin' scratch he got."

"Turn anythin' Blister sez the other way round an' yo're liable to git the truth," the wounded man replied, a statement which evoked a general chorus of "Yo're tellin' us."

CHAPTER XIV

Miss Maitland and Malachi had walked as far as the cemetery. It was, as he had told Miss Trenton, a pretty place, though the oblong mounds of stones—several with staggering, home-made wooden crosses—did not add to its beauty. The customary bitter expression was absent from the man's clever face.

"They all seem to be nameless," the girl commented.

"Rainbow has no monumental mason yet," he told her, and pointed to the most recent heap. "That is the resting-place of Dave Dover, who was kind to every living thing—except an enemy." A touch of his old sarcastic humour returned. "Yet, if any other citizen had brought you here, the grave he would have shown with pride would have been that of a scoundrel who killed seven people—and he wasn't a doctor. The town hanged him, most justly; he was a fool—he should have taken a degree before indulging his appetite for blood."

She did not smile. "I don't like to hear you joke about your profession," she said. "Great soldiers, who use their lives to take life, are honoured, but a doctor, who devotes himself to saving life receives—what?

"All that every human being wins in the end—that," he said flippantly, and pointed to the nearest grave.

"You are not yourself to-day," she reproved.

"That's the trouble—I am," he replied cynically. "Forgive me, Miss Maitland; I sometimes talk, and act, like an idiot. What I really wanted to tell you was that I am going away."

The colour came into her cheeks and receded; she had suddenly realized what this man's absence would mean. It had begun in pity on her part for one who, still young and talented, was leading an aimless, sordid existence. A bed in a shabby hotel, meals at an eating-house, and many hours of every day in saloons; the tragedy of it shocked her. And now . . . She tried to speak casually:

"Are you going for good?"

"For my own good, I hope," he smiled. "Would it matter?"

"I have not so many friends," she told him, and there was a note in her voice which brought a gleam into his eyes.

"I expect to be away only some two or three weeks," he said. "Where, when, and why, I am not at liberty to tell even you. The town—if it troubles to ask—will be informed that I have gone East, and supply its own reason—a debauch."

"But—you have been——"

"Abstemious lately? Precisely, and therefore the wiseacres will argue that a breaking-out was inevitable." He saw the fear in her glance. "No, it isn't that; if it were, I would stay here and be damned to them."

She smiled again; this was the old Malachi, reckless, contemptuous, but likeable. They spoke only of trivialities on the way to Rainbow, but when parting, Malachi said, "You will be glad when I return, Kate?"

"Yes—Philip," she replied.

"That is all I need to know," he murmured. "I shall come back—sane."

* o o

The same evening, the doctor visited the Parlour Saloon, as usual, but drank nothing. He left early, and some time later rapped at the door of the Circle Dot ranch-house. Dover opened it, and conducted the visitor to the front room, where the rest of the party to go into the hills were assembled. Burke was also present, having taken his final instructions from the owner. After greetings had been exchanged, the doctor said:

"I enquired about those two twenties, Dan; they were paid by the bank to Trenton a week ago, but they could have changed hands more than once, so it doesn't prove much."

"Mebbe it don't, but it shore looks like he'd got news of our drive an' hired some scallawags to bust it," the rancher replied. "That's my view, an' I'm holdin' it till I know different."

"He wouldn't risk usin' his own men," Burke contributed.

"I'm obliged, Doc. Got all you need in the way o' gear?" Dan went on, and receiving an affirmative nod, reached a bottle from a cupboard. "We'll have just one li'l drink to success—it's the last liquor we'll see till we reach town again."

"Leave me out, Dan," Malachi said quietly.

"Me too; I don't use it," Yorky echoed.

They all laughed at this, save Hunch, sitting in one corner, a big revolver thrust through his belt, and the great axe between his knees. He took the spirit handed to him, tipped it down his throat with a single gesture, and replaced the glass on the table. The action was that of an automaton, no expression showed in the blank face. The doctor was studying him curiously. Dover looked at the tall old grandfather clock.

"Gone midnight, Bill," he said. "Might as well be on the move."

One by one they stole out, secured their mounts, and with Hunch astride a huge rawboned bay as guide, and Blister, leading a pack-horse loaded with supplies, bringing up the rear, they were swiftly merged in the murk. Silence reigned, but for the far-off

111

cry of a questing coyote, and the plaintive hoot of an owl in trees they could not see. There was no moon, but the velvet sky was pricked with a myriad pin-points of light which only seemed to make the obscurity more profound. They moved slowly but surely, the leader appearing to know his way despite the darkness. So far, all had gone well.

But no one of them had seen the lurking man in the shadow of the corral, who, having watched their departure, ran to his hidden horse, and stooping low over its neck, followed them. The first news they had of him came as a finger of flame and the crack of a rifle. Blister reeled and would have fallen but for the quick clutch of the rider next him, Tiny. Sliding to the ground, the big cowboy lifted the hurt man down and laid him on the turf. Sudden raced in the direction from which the shot appeared to have come; nothing was to be seen, but he could hear the diminishing beat of hooves.

"On'y one of 'em," he muttered, and returned to his friends.

Malachi, by the light of an improvised torch, was making an exclamation. "Bullet struck the thigh and went through," he said. "Nice clean wound, but it will keep you on your back for some weeks, my lad. Give me some water." A canteen provided this, and he washed and deftly bandaged the injury. "He'll have to go back to the ranch."

"Shore, one of us will take him," Dover agreed.

"Aw, Boss, there ain't no need," Blister protested. "Doc's fixed my pin fine, an' I can make it; I ain't no kid. It's just too bad, missin' the trip, damn the luck."

"I'll go tuck him in his li'l cot, an' catch you up," Tiny offered.

"You won't know the way, an' if that snipin' houn' has gone to wise up the Wagon-wheel, we can't afford to wait," the rancher said perplexedly.

"I don't want no nussin', specially from a ham-handed freak," Blister declared. "Lift me into the saddle an' Paddy will be loadin' steak an' fried into me in less'n an hour."

Tiny obeyed, adding solicitously, "Rest all yore weight on the sound leg."

"Awright, Solomon. Which rein do I pull if I wanta go left?"

"Neither of 'em; you just naturally jump off, pick the hoss up an point him that way. Gwan—an' take care o' yoreself," Tiny chuckled.

They watched him start, sitting straight up, but they could not see the lean brown hands clutching the saddle-horn, nor the clamped teeth as the throbbing pain of a damaged limb increased with every movement of his mount. Dan was anxious.

"Think he'll be all right, Phil?" he asked. "I'd sooner lose the damn ranch than anythin' should happen to Blister."

112

"He'll get there," Malachi said confidently. "He's got grit, that boy." And added, under his breath, "He makes me ashamed."

*　　*　　*

Zeb Trenton was awakened early by the announcement that a visitor was waiting to see him on urgent business. Going down to his office, he found Garstone, Bundy, and the bearded man from the Bend, whom he greeted with a frown.

"Well, Lake, you've been long enough comin' to report," he said aggressively.

"I'd nothing' but bad news to bring," was the sullen answer.

"So you failed?"

"You can call it that. We stampeded the herd awright, but the beasts were too tired to run far or scatter enough. The punchers rounded 'em up again, an' they got one of us—Benito."

Trenton shrugged impatiently—the passing from life of a Greaser was of little moment to him. "Well?" he snapped.

"Havin' lost the cattle, we decided to try for the money on the back trip," Lake proceeded. "I went on to the Bend, figurin' to shadow Dover an' give the boys word. It didn't work out thata-way." He paused for a second or two, and then, in a voice which dripped venom, he told of the trick Sudden had played on him, and the subsequent abortive ambush. "Two of our chaps was crippled, an' by the bastard who tied me up, a prisoner in a damned hotel bedroom for half a day—tall black-haired cow-punch, with a coupla guns. I'm a prompt payer, an' I meant to git that hombre, so I goes to the Circle Dot an' lays for a chance."

"Don't tell me you downed him," Bundy said. "He's my meat.'

"He's still yores—if I don't see him first," Lake replied. "I didn't have an openin'—too many others around, but just after midnight I got on to somethin' I figured might interest you Dover an' six more, with a pack animal, sneaked away from the ranch-house an' headed for the Cloudy country. I follered, an' sent 'em a slug for luck; nailed one, for shore, but I'll bet it warn't the perisher I was after."

The effect of his news was electrical. Trenton's face grew purple, as he rose to his feet and stamped with rage. "Blast them, they've diddled us an' got a start," he cried. "You any good at trailin', Lake?"

"I can read sign better'n most," was the modest answer.

"We'll take you with us; you'll be well paid, an' have an opportunity of wipin' out your score against Green. Is everythin' ready, Bundy? Right, we set out as soon as we've eaten."

In less than two hours they were on their way. Avoiding Rainbow, they cut across the wagon-road leading to the Circle Dot, forded the river, and rode in the direction of Dover's western boundary. Presently they came to the spot where Lake had ceased his spying. It was daylight now, and the marks of a group of horses were easy to find. Lake pointed exultantly to some burnt-out matches, and a smear of blood on the grass.

"Told you I got one," he cried. His eyes swept the ground. "On'y winged him, seemin'ly—they sent him back. Well, that's one less to deal with."

Trenton asked a question. "We'll catch 'em whenever you say," was the confident reply.

"We don't want to," the rancher warned. "An' it is important they they shouldn't know we're followin' them."

"I get you; tailin' 'em will be just too easy," the fellow sneered. "These cow-thumpers don't know nothin' 'bout hidin' tracks."

There he was wrong, for one of the despised "cow-thumpers" —to which class he himself once belonged and disgraced—had the redskin's skill in detecting or concealing a trail. Sudden's childhood had been spent with an old Piute horse-dealer, who, in his sober hours, taught him the craft of his race. The puncher had never forgotten that early upbringing which, on more than one occasion, had stood him in good stead.

A mile or so later, the leader halted, and when Trenton wanted the reason, had to admit that the tracks had ceased on the edge of a small stream. Obviously the quarry had taken to the water.

"No call for that if they don't know we're follerin'," Lake grumbled.

"O' course they know," Bundy said. "You told 'em yoreself when you fired that fool shot." He did not approve of the man's inclusion in the party.

"How the devil was I to guess what was afoot?" Lake threw back.

A search of the banks of the stream in both directions resulted in the trail being again picked up, but not until considerable time had been consumed. A recurrence of these delays at frequent intervals soon showed that they were not accidental, and drew another caustic comment from the foreman.

"I'd say there's a cow-thumper ahead who's smarter at blindin' tracks than you are at findin' 'em," he jeered. "Is there anythin' yo're good at?"

The little man glared at him through reptilian, half-lidded eyes. "Yeah, killin' vermin," he said quietly.

Garstone had early attached himself to Miss Trenton, and if he admired the trim figure in its neat riding-suit, the skirt reaching only to the tops of her high boots with their dainty silver-spurred heels, and the soft grey hat above the ebony curls, she too could not but admit that he looked well on horseback. As usual, he was carefully dressed: his cord breeches, top boots, loose coat, and soft silk shirt and tie, lent him distinction among the roughly-garbed others of her escort. She was full of curiosity about the expedition, for her uncle had told her little.

114

"Why do we have to wait about like this?" she asked, while the trail was being found again. "I understood it was to be just a pleasure trip."

"Business and pleasure, especially the latter, for me," Garstone smiled. "The fact is, Miss Trenton—and I tell you this in confidence—we are on a treasure hunt."

"Really?" she cried. "But how exciting. "What form does the treasure take?"

"We don't know—gold, money, or jewels, maybe all three. It is reputed to have been hidden somewhere in these hills by an outlaw named Red Rufe."

"What became of him?"

Garstone shrugged. "Who knows? Probably returned to his old haunts for more plunder and got wiped out."

"And Uncle Zeb knows where the treasure is?"

He smiled into her sparkling eyes. "No, it isn't so easy as that; he has certain indications, but it may take time." His tone grew warmer. "I hope it does."

She reddened a little under his ardent gaze. "But why is it necessary to search for tracks; they cannot be Red Rufe's."

"No, others have got wind of our enterprise and stolen a march upon us; we want to know where they are bound for. You see, success means everything to your uncle. Cattlemen have had a lean time for several years, and he is heavily in debt."

"Poor Uncle Zeb," she said. "I always thought him wealthy."

"Most people think so—he has his pride," Garstone returned. "I have a great regard for him, and after the fine fight he has put up against overwhelming odds, it will be too terrible if he should lose the Wagon-wheel."

"Is it as bad as that?"

"Yes," he replied gravely. "And your uncle has ideas for the development of Rainbow; it will break him up if he is not able to carry them out. He doesn't talk of these things, but I am in his confidence."

"Who are the others you spoke of?"

"Who but the Circle Dot? Dover would sell his soul to see your uncle ruined," came the bitter reply.

She did not doubt it; Dan had shown his animosity plainly enough. "We must find that treasure," she said.

"We certainly will," he assured her. "I'm prepared to do anything rather than let Zeb go under."

"I'm sure we all feel like that," she agreed.

This being the admission he was waiting for, he dropped the subject, satisfied that he had done a good day's work for his employer, and a better one for himself. Which was as it should be, according to the ethics of Chesney Garstone.

CHAPTER XV

Sudden was the culprit. He it was who devised those vexatious and time-eating problems which were exercising the wits of the bearded man, and fraying the tempers of his companions. The Circle Dot puncher had little expectations of throwing the pursuers entirely off the trail, but the greater the distance between the parties, the more chance there was of doing so. So, whenever they encountered a rivulet, they splashed along it, either up or down, before crossing; patches of hard ground, which would record no hoof-prints, were traversed diagonally at the widest points, and once the tracks led straight to the edge of a morass and ended, with no turn to right or left.

This apparent miracle was accomplished by patience and the alternate use of blankets, of which each man carried a couple; the first was spread—from the saddle—at right angles from the trail, and the horse led on to it, then the second, and before the animal moved from that, the first again. By this means, Sudden, who took the lead, covered a considerable space without leaving a mark, and the others followed his actions exactly. When they had all reached him, he returned on foot, with a pair of blankets, and brought the pack-horse. The operation took time, but would cost those who followed much more.

"That was a smart ruse, Jim," Malachi complimented, as they went on their way. "Do you think it will baffle them?"

"It's an old Injun caper," the puncher replied. "If Trenton has a real tracker with him, he'll guess it, but they've still to find our trail again."

Soon afterwards they reached the verdure-clad foothills and, plunging into the welcome shade, began a gradual rise. Hunch, jogging steadily along at Sudden's elbow, spoke never a word, but his usually lack-lustre eyes were a little brighter as they neared his beloved forests. Through an occasional break in the trees they caught a glimpse of the distant snow-capped peak of Old Cloudy, thrusting up into the azure sky.

As Dover had warned the doctor, they were breaking their own trail, winding in and out through thick brush, along stony ravines, climbing up-flung ridges of rock, yet making for a definite point. Once or twice, Sudden spoke to the old man, but getting only a gesture for answer, made no further attempt; his Indian training had taught him the value of silence.

Mile after mile they paced on, treading at times a tortuous

116

path through tall timber, in a twilight due to the matted, leafy roof overhead. Frequently they had to turn aside to avoid a prone monarch of the forest, snapped off and thrown down to rot by a greater monarch—King Storm. Only in places where the trees thinned out did a shaft of sunlight came to tell them it was still day. There was little life in these dim solitudes.

The nearness of night found them on a grassy ledge hemmed in by vegetation, save at the back where a plinth of gaunt, grey stone rose straight up for a hundred feet. Here Sudden called a halt.

"Best camp here, Dan," he said. "There's feed for the hosses an' the smoke of a fire won't show against that bluff."

The beasts were picketed, lest a prowling bear or mountain lion should stampede them. Hunch and Yorky soon had the fire blazing, and the music—to hungry men—of sizzling bacon mingled with the odour of boiling coffee.

"Likin' it, son?" Sudden asked, as Yorky passed him with an armful of dead wood for fuel.

"I'll say I am," was the enthusiastic answer. "Why, Jim, this beats a dance all ter blazes."

During the meal, Sudden asked how they were getting on.

"I reckon we're about half-way, but it's on'y a guess," Dan told him. "What d'you think Hunch?" He got the invariable nod for reply, and in a lower tone continued, "I believe he came up here with Dad, though he wouldn't know for what purpose; that's one o' the reasons why I fetched him along. How you feelin', Phil?"

"Tired, but never better," Malachi smiled. "A few weeks of this and I'll give up rolling pills to ride for you."

"You could do a lot wuss," Tiny told him. "Plenty o' fresh air, exercise, an' four squares a day, when yo're to home—which ain't offen. What more does a fella want?"

"A stated number o' dollars per month an' time off to throw 'em away, I find," the rancher grinned. "An' let me tell you, when Tiny does miss a meal, he makes up for it at the next. Pleased to have you, Phil, so long as you don't give the boys anythin' to improve their appetites."

Soon afterwards, one by one, they rolled up in their blankets; it had been a long and strenuous day, and their surroundings held out no hope for a less arduous one on the morrow. Only Sudden remained awake, squatting cross-legged by the fire, his Winchester by his side. Though every sense was alert for any sound he could not explain, his mind was on the curious enterprise to which he found himself committed. He fell to considering the men of the other faction. That Trenton was following he had no doubt; the rancher was an astute and unscrupulous man, aggressive and intolerant of opposition. Bundy he dismissed with a ges-

117

ture of disdain, a common enough rogue, who would commit any crime for sufficient gain. Garstone he had not yet fathomed; one thing seemed certain—he was not the type to serve as jackal to one of the rancher's calibre. What was the fellow doing so far from the East? He could hit upon no satisfactory answer, and presently, when Tiny—rubbing his eyes—came to relieve him, he sought sleep.

* * *

At a camp some fifteen miles away, much the same procedure had taken place, save that there were two fires—one for the rancher, his niece, and Garstone, the other for the men. Bundy had protested against this arrangement, but had been curtly ordered to do as he was told. The fires were sufficiently far apart to prevent conversation being overheard, and near one of them stood the small tent in which the girl was to sleep. Despite the fact of their slow progress, Trenton was in high spirits.

"Well, Beth, how does roughing it in the open appeal to you?" he asked.

"Very much indeed—it's so thrilling," she replied. "Do you really think we shall succeed?"

Neither of the men answered until Rattray—who was acting as cook, and serving them—had retired to his own fire, and then Garstone said:

"I told Miss Trenton of our main object in coming here; she is very interested."

"Indeed I am," she agreed eagerly. "But very sorry it should be—necessary."

"That's all right, my dear," Trenton said heartily. "Every man who gets anywhere has to face up to a stiff fight now and then. We'll make the grade."

"To be sure," Garstone supplemented. "That red-headed rascal, Rufe, is going to put us all on the top of the world."

"Had he red hair?" she queried.

"I really don't know," the big man prevaricated. "I presumed it to be the origin of his nickname."

"He might have got that as a killer," Trenton suggested, in a voice which had suddenly lost its geniality. A burst of laughter from the region of the other fire seemed to remind him of something. "Bundy expected to feed with us—he's been gettin' uppity lately. I had to remind him that I'm boss."

"Quite right," Garstone concurred. That the foreman and his employer should not be on the best of terms might well further the nebulous schemes beginning to take shape in his brain. "He appears to have got over his grouch."

"Just as well. People who work for me have to obey, without question."

118

The Easterner did not subscribe to this sentiment quite so entirely, and said nothing; it sounded too much like a hint to himself. And he felt convinced that the foreman had not forgotten.

In this he was right, for even as the rancher spoke, Bundy was inwardly brooding over what he regarded as an insult, and vowing it should be paid for. Nevertheless, having been driven to "herd with the hands," as he phrased it, he might as well be comfortable, and so devoted himself first of all to smoothing the ruffled plumage of the newcomer.

"Well, Lake, I'm allus ready to own up when I'm wrong, an' I was 'bout you," he commenced. "Yor shore can read sign; that dodge they tried at the bog would 'a' razzle-dazzled an Injun."

"It gave us a lot o' trouble," the tracker said modestly.

"Warn't yore fault; you tumbled to the trick; it was pickin' up the trail agin that cost the time."

The bearded man was not proof against this fulsome flattery. The foreman, he thought, was after all not such a bad chap. So prone are we humans to approve those who approve us.

"Thanks, friend," he said. "But there's one puzzle 'bout this trip I can't find the answer to, an' mebbe you—as foreman—can tell me."

"Give it a name," Bundy replied, pleased in his turn by the use of his title.

"What are we after?"

"Well, I dunno as there's any need to keep it quiet now," the foreman said, but lowered his voice. "Treasure, that's what. Mebbe you've heard o' Red Rufe's Cache?"

Lake laughed derisively. "Heard? I've looked for it—like a-many other idjuts. Still, I don't mind wastin' some more time if I'm well paid."

"You didn't know where to go, seemin'ly." This from Rattray, a spare-built but wiry cowboy, whose features suggested that the first syllable of his name could not possibly be accidental.

"Yo're damn right, I didn't, or would I be here?" the other retorted. "But is Trenton any wiser? If he is, why are we moseyin' along on the heels o' them fellas in front?"

He got no answer to his questions. Flint and Rattray could not give him one, and Bundy was far too cunning to empty his bag— yet. The appearance of knowing a little more than they would give him a hold over them. So all he said was:

"There's a good reason for that, an' you can gamble on it; Zeb ain't a fool—in some ways."

"I take it we all git shares," the new man said, his eyes agleam with greed.

"Seein' as we're four to two—not countin' the gal—we'll be dumb if we don't," the foreman replied meaningly.

Flint and Rattray nodded their agreement with this view. Lake said, "Pardner, I like you more'n more."

Bundy was satisfied; if the rancher did not treat him fairly, he had a card up his sleeve. Also there was Garstone, who had shown himself quite willing to double-cross his employer in the affair of the train robbery; he provided another card, making three in all, counting Trenton.

"An' if you play 'em properly, Bundy, ol' scout, yo're on velvet," was the conclusion he came to.

CHAPTER XVI

Throughout the greater part of the next day, the Circle Dot men pressed steadily on. Though they deemed themselves to be well ahead of possible pursuit, they neglected no opportunity of blinding their trail, and were successful—had they but known it—in straining the vituperative powers of the bearded man to the utmost.

The scenery on all sides was wild and awe-inspiring. Dense masses of pine which defied the sun, thickets of thorny scrub, clumps of bright-flowering bushes, and, from time to time enormous chunks of rock weighing thousands of tons, "fragments" which had broken away from the mother mass towering in the distance. The slope was slight but definite, and sometimes they advanced across wide, almost level benches of grass and cactus. They skirted deep, wedge-shaped gorges where the side of the mountain appeared to have split open, treading narrow ledges where a slip would have spelt destruction.

Game seemed to be plentiful, quail, squirrels, rabbits, and once they came upon a small herd of deer feeding in a patch of lush grass. For a few seconds the dainty beasts stared in amaze at the unwonted intrusion of their domain, and then, in a flash, were gone. Yorky, fingers itching for his rifle, looked longingly after them.

"Lots o' time for that," Sudden consoled. "Business first, an' there ain't no sense in advertisin' our whereabouts."

The boy sighed. "I wouldn't know where to aim, anyways."

"Just behind the left shoulder—the heart's there," the puncher told him.

As the climb continued, the trees became smaller and less numerous, a sign that a higher altitude was being reached. Then, when the westering sun was rimming the mountain tops with gold they came to a spot entirely at variance with all they had seen.

It was a shallow basin, perhaps a hundred feet deep at the centre, and less than half a mile in diameter. The sides sloped gently up to the encircling lips of ragged rock. The surface was a grey, powdery sand, and the only vegetation, scattered greasewood and cactus. On all four points of the compass, V shaped breaks provided openings to the basin. Hunch got down, stepped to Dover's side, and gestured with one hand.

"Is this where you came with Dad?" the young man asked, and getting a nod of assent, went on, "Well, boys, this appears to be the scene of operations."

Right ahead, seeming to loom over them, although many miles distant, was Old Cloudy. Sudden, studying the mountain, saw that the round knobbed top, and wide sloping flanks might well suggest the head, shoulders, and dropping arms of a sitting man and that viewed from where he stood the basin might—with no great stretch of imagination—be described as a bowl on the knees of this Gargantuan figure behind which the sky was now turning to a blood-red.

"What d'you think of it, Jim?" Dover asked.

"Seems to fit. What's the next move?"

"We gotta settle which way to go—this is no place to camp." He tilted his hat back and scratched his head reflectively. "West is north," he repeated. "Well, that gap in front of us is west."

"We gotta reckon it as north," Sudden said. "An, north is noon, that is, twelve o'clock. We were told on reaching here, to watch out. Now that might be a warnin', but I figure it's a pointer." His gaze swept round the almost perfect circle of the basin. "S'pose we're lookin' at a mammoth watch-face, with that western break as twelve. Then the one we came in by must be the half after the hour which would be too soon. That means our way is by the opening on the left, which would be three-quarters past."

"Holy cats! I believe you've hit on it, Jim," the rancher cried. "Can we stop 'em followin' us, in case they get so far?"

"I'll 'tend to that. Yu take the boys an' ride in single file till yo're clear o' the basin."

Starting from where the trampled sand plainly showed that a group of horses had paused there, he galloped straight for the gap to the right. Reaching it, he found it to be a little pass with a stony surface which would show no tracks. Returning to the basin, he backed his mount along the line by which he had approached. Repeating this operation twice resulted in a trail apparently made by six riders, the hoof-marks all pointing in the same direction. He then followed his companions, dragging a rolled blanket attached to his rope, and thus obliterated the traces of them all.

Passing out of the basin, he found himself in another narrow gorge, the floor of which consisted of rock detritus, with frequent patches of cactus and coarse grass. The wall on the right was much higher than that on the left, and along the foot of both were bushes; above these, they were bare and inhospitable. Half a mile from the basin, under an overhanging shelf of cliff, camp was being established. There was sufficient feed for the animals, and a few yards away, a rock pool, fed by a trickle from the height above.

During the meal, the puncher explained what he had done. "It may keep 'em outa here for a spell, but I guess they'll try all the outlets in turn, an' we don't have to waste time."

"How about playin, their game—lettin' 'em find the stuff, an' takin' it away from 'em?" Tiny suggested.

"That would mean a fight, an' I'd ruther avoid that, if possible," Dover replied. "But the money is mine, an' I intend to have it, one way or another."

"We've no actual evidence that anyone is dogging us," the doctor pointed out.

"Shore, but I know Trenton," Dan said grimly. "Dad's death, the searchin' o' the Circle Dot, an' the attempt to scotch our drive to the Bend happened for a purpose. Zeb is comin', an' he'll have some o' the Wagon-wheel scum along."

Therefore they kept watch, and in the early morning, Sudden —relieving the doctor—caught him in the act of re-corking a bottle, which he had been holding near his lips.

"Cure for headache, Doc?" he asked superciliously.

Malachi looked rather shame-faced, and with an effort at bravado, replied, "More often the cause of one, Jim." And then, "God! what weak creatures we are—some of us."

He opened his hand, disclosing a small medicine phial, quite full, as the puncher guessed, of whisky. "You know why I came here," he went on bitterly. "Well, it seemed to me that I was running away from temptation, so I brought temptation with me. I fancied myself strong enough to have the odour of it in my nostrils and resist. I was wrong—it makes me mad for the taste."

"Is that all yu fetched?"

"Yes, and had you not come, it would have gone, and at dawn I should have been sneaking off for Rainbow—to get more."

"No, to lose yoreself an' die in despair," Sudden told him. "Yu never could make it; yu gotta stay."

"You don't realize what it means," Malachi cried. "Have you ever had to combat a craving which, like a devouring flame, possessed your body and mind so utterly that all else in life became of no importance?"

Sudden laughed harshly. "Listen," he said. "Once I was left, tied hand an' foot, in the middle of a desert, by a Mexican guerilla chief, the most inhuman devil I ever met. After usin' nearly all my strength to free myself, I set out to walk endless miles of sand in search o' water. My tongue was swollen—I couldn't close my mouth, I was near blind with the glare, my body was dried an' scorched till it felt like a red-hot coal, an' if ever a man suffered like a tormented soul in hell, I did. My limbs were lead, an' every movement—agony. What I had to beat, Malachi, warn't thirst, but the desire to lie down, an' die.[1] That's yore case, man; yu have to fight, not the want o' liquor, but the urge to give in. Now, drop that bottle an' put yore foot on it."

"I can't, Jim; don't ask me," the doctor pleaded.

[1] Related in *The Marshall of Lawless*. George Newnes Ltd.

"Then drink an' be damned," the puncher said roughly, and turned away.

The brutal contemptuous tone had its effect; he had moved but a yard when there was the tinkle of glass on stone, and the grind of a heel. The doctor had won a victory.

In the early morning, the search of the gorge was begun, any feature which might suggest a hiding-place being carefully examined. The only discovery of any value was a cave, and as it was dry, and large enough to conceal the horses if necessary, they moved the camp there. It proved to be more spacious than they had imagined, with a high vaulted roof from which hung hundreds of stalactites, flashing like spearheads in the leaping flames of the logs. Seated round the fire after a tiring and fruitless day, the adventurers looked about them with some misgiving; in the darkness, the cavern appeared to have no limits.

"If this is Red Rufe's bank he's shore given us a job to tie into," Tiny informed the company, and thereby expressed the thoughts of all.

"We'll give the outside another look-over before we tackle this," Dan replied.

"Looks a likely spot, till yu get inside, an' then it don't," was Sudden's contribution.

Malachi took no part in the conversation and ate almost nothing. He seemed to be ill and depressed, evidently suffering from the lack of his customary stimulant. There had been no sign of other visitors in the vicinity.

"Either they ain't come or you've fooled 'em, Jim," the big cowboy decided.

"Yu can bet on both them reasons an' still lose," Sudden told him. In the afternoon, Malachi, alone, sick and oppressed by the intense heat, and not conscious of where he was going, wandered out into the basin, and suddenly saw the world go black. When he recovered his senses there was a familiar taste in his mouth, and a voice he knew was speaking:

"That's better, Doc. Burn my soul, but I thought you was cold meat. Take another sup o' corpse-reviver."

A flask was held to his lips and tilted. He took a big gulp, and the fiery spirit steadied his shattered nerves and cleared his vision. He was in the basin, sitting with his back against a small boulder, and Bundy was kneeling beside him.

"Stupid of me—must have fainted—touch of the sun," he muttered.

"Shore, might happen to anyone," the foreman agreed. "But what in hell are you doin' up here? Thought I was dreamin when I clapped eyes on you."

The liquor, working on an empty stomach, was muddling the medico's mind, but he had a hazy idea that he must not tell

124

the truth. "Just taking a little vacation, Bundy," he replied. A happy thought occurred to him. "I've always wanted to shoot a big-horn." He pushed away the proffered flask.

"Oh, come, Doc, it ain't like you to refuse good liquor, an' this is good—some o' Ben's best ol' bourbon—not a headache in it. You know the stuff."

Malachi did—too well. He heard the swish of it against the glass, the pungent smell assailed him as the foreman removed the cork, and his whole being thirsted for it. His hand, trembling, came out.

"Just—one small sip."

"Drink hearty," Bundy replied generously, and whether the doctor heard or not, he obeyed.

This further dose completed the job, the drunkard's eyes glazed a little, and his voice thickened as he said, "Thanksh, Bundy, but what bringsh you to Ol' Cloudy?"

"Same as yoreself—takin' a holiday," Bundy grinned. "Trenton wanted his niece to see the country, an' I had to come along."

Malachi blinked at him owlishly. "Mis' Tren'on here? Thash wrong; no place f'r lady. Have to shpeak to Zeb when I shee him." He hoisted himself to his feet. "Mus' go now. Goo'bye."

Staggering and stumbling through the sand, he reached the gorge, and, in the shade of a bush, lay down and slept. At the evening meal, when they were wondering what had become of him, he walked in, his face deathly white, hands shaking.

"Dan, I've done an unpardonable thing—betrayed you," he began, in a harsh, unnatural voice, and not sparing himself, told his story.

They listened in silence, and then Dan said, "So they are here. How many?"

"I have no idea; I was too drunk to try and find out anything," Malachi replied miserably. "All Bundy said was that Miss Trenton is with them."

Dover stared. "Did you say *Miss* Trenton?" he asked. "Zeb must be loco to drag a girl into this. If he fancies her presence will help him, he'd better think again."

"Worth while gettin' acquainted with this place—we may have visitors in the mornin'," Sudden said, and as he passed Malachi, added, "Don't yu fret, Doc, we all make mistakes, an' they were bound to find us sooner or later."

The doctor looked at him dumbly; these men were beyond his comprehension. He had failed them—terribly, perhaps destroyed their hope of success, and instead of reproach, there was only a calm acceptance of the situation, and a readiness to face it. He shook his head.

"I'm just a cheap Judas, who has sold his friends for fifty cents' worth of whisky," he said moodily. "And I'm a poor fighter, Jim."

"Shucks! the man who never lost a battle ain't been born yet," the puncher consoled.

With the help of blazing pine-knots, they carried out an inspection of the cavern, to the apparent concern of thousands of bats in the dark dome above, but no indication that any human being had ever before set foot there rewarded them. Sudden was curious about the back of the cave, where the walls and roof closed in leaving only what seemed to be the mouth of a tunnel leading into the bowels of the earth. The floor was fairly level, as were the walls, but it was clearly Nature's handiwork. Probably, he conjectured, many thousands of years ago, it had formed a channel for a great volume of water.

Anxious to know whether it provided another exit, he went on and had proceeded something less than two hundred yards when an intuition of danger caused him to pull up sharply and hold his light lower. His nerves were in perfect condition, but what he saw sent a shiver up his spine. A stride from where he stood yawned a gap in the floor, about twelve feet across, and extending from wall to wall. He knelt on the brink, moving the torch to and fro, but could only see that the sides of the abyss were perpendicular, and hear, from far below, the rumbling roar of a racing torrent.

"An' I nearly walked into it; fools for luck," he soliloquized, as he turned to retrace his steps. "I must warn the boys that this ain't no way to run."

CHAPTER XVII

Bundy, having watched his drunken victim out of sight, hurried with all speed to his own camp, and called his employer aside. His cunning eyes were alight with triumph.

"Boss, I got news—big news," he cried. "I've found out where them Circle Dot dawgs is holed up. They never come this way a-tall, they just tricked——"

"Never mind that," the rancher said impatiently. "Where are they?"

"The other side o' that hollow, right opposite to here."

"Have you seen any of them?"

"Yeah. Come across Doc Malachi."

Trenton regarded him with disgust. "You've been drinkin', or dreamin'," he sneered.

"Damnation, I'm tellin' you the truth," Bundy raged.

"Don't strain yore system," the other said acidly. He was in a bad temper; they had lost the trail, and this fool had raised hopes only to dash them again. "Get on with the fairy tale."

The foreman swallowed his wrath, and explained. Trenton listened to the end, still only half-convinced.

"Malachi," he muttered, "Why should he be with them?"

"Claimed he was takin' a holiday—to get a sheep," Bundy jeered. "Wanted me to believe he was alone." He laughed.

Trenton did not join in the mirth; the presence of the doctor seemed to worry him. As he turned away, he said, "Well, if what you say proves to be correct, it will add, maybe, a hundred dollars to yore share, my man."

He did not see the grimace of hate this patronizing speech produced, nor hear the hissed words: "Throw yore chicken-feed to them as needs it, you stingy ol' buzzard; I'm helpin' myself, an' be damned to you."

When Garstone, who had been riding with Beth, returned, the rancher told him of the foreman's discovery.

"Good," the Easterner said. "We'll pay them a visit in the morning. You got that paper all safe?"

"Do you think I'm dumb enough to bring it here?" Trenton enquired satirically. "No, sir, it might get into wrong hands. I played safe, an' destroyed it, after learning the contents."

Chesney Garstone concealed his chagrin only by an effort. "My God, you took a risk," he said. "If you should—die . . ."

"The secret would be lost. I appreciate yore anxiety, but would that matter to me?"

The big man forced a smile. "I suppose not, but——"

"I have a niece. True, but I'm a selfish man, an' I don't care two flips of a cow's tail what happens in this world after I've left it," was the callous reply.

There was a great deal of low-toned conversation that evening round the men's fire. The foreman could not keep his achievement to himself, though he took care to make clear that it was due mainly to his sagacity, and not—as in fact—to blind chance.

"So now, thanks to me, all we gotta do is walk in an' collar the plunder," he concluded.

"Have to locate the Cache first, ain't we?" Lake wanted to know.

"No trouble a-tall," Bundy assured him. "The Ol' Man has a paper givin' exact directions, which is somethin' them other guys ain't got, or they'd 'a' bin off by now."

"Sounds good," Rattray remarked casually.

"Shore does," Bundy said ironically. "Why, in three-four days we'll be back in Rainbow, git our two hundred bucks apiece mebbe, an' live 'appy ever after."

"Two hundred—hell," Lake ejaculated. "Is that Trenton's notion o' things?"

"He half promised me an extra hundred for what I done to-day," was the sneering reply. "Figure out yore chances."

No one answered, but the black looks of his hearers betrayed their feelings plainly enough. The foreman said no more; he had sown the seed, and was willing to await the harvest.

In the morning, Garstone approached the rancher. "What about Miss Trenton? Taking her along?"

"Nothin' else for it," was the reply. "Can't leave her in this wild spot, unless you'd keep her company."

The suggestion was not at all to Garstone's liking. "I would enjoy it, of course, but I want to be in on this thing," he said. "And I doubt if it would be wise to weaken our force; we don't know how strong Dover is."

"Oh, he won't fight," the rancher returned contemptuously. "But perhaps yo're right. You can look after Beth."

A little later Trenton led the way across the basin, his men in pairs behind, the girl and Garstone in the rear. Excitement shone in her eyes, and there was a tinge of colour in the slightly-tanned cheeks. A wave of passion swept over the man by her side. He bent towards her.

"My dearest ambition has come to pass this morning," he whispered.

"We haven't found the treasure yet," she replied, wilfully ignoring his meaning.

"I have found mine already, and have been deputed by your uncle to take care of it—for to-day. I would like the task to last longer—a lifetime. Do you understand, Beth?"

128

The words, spoken in a low, ardent tone, quickened her pulses and brought a hot flush to her face. For days she had expected the avowal, had almost decided to accept, but now that the moment had come, she hesitated.

"Yes, I understand," she said gently. "But we have known each other such a little while. You must give me time."

"Well, that's fair, my dear," he replied. "Perhaps when this trip is over, you will know me better."

She thanked him with a look which bred a desire to take her in his arms then and there, but he fought down the impulse; with this girl—even had they been alone—it would be an act of folly.

"What has become of the Circle Dot people?" she asked. Evidently, Trenton had told her only that they were to unearth the hidden wealth.

"We are on our way to visit them," he said. "They are camped on or near the spot we wish to search."

"Do you think Mister Dover will be—difficult?"

"No, since your uncle knows where to look, and he doesn't, a wise man would admit that he has lost."

"I'm afraid he's not very wise."

"A hot-headed young fool describes him better," Garstone said. "If he asks for trouble, he'll get it."

By this time the gorge was reached. Beth Trenton was conscious of a cold tremor as she looked at the barren, sterile walls, broken only by stunted growths clinging precariously where fissures in the cliff provided a semblance of soil; she had a premonition of impending tragedy. Despite the bright sun, and the twittering of birds in the bushes which lined their path, the place seemed to convey a threat. A sharp command rang out.

"That'll be far enough, Trenton."

The Wagon-wheel owner dragged on his reins. "Who the devil are you to give me orders?" he called. "Afraid to face me?"

Dover stepped from behind a shrub some twenty paces away. "No, but I'd think twice o' turnin' my back on you," was his cutting reply. "What's yore errand here?"

"None of yore business."

"I'm makin' it mine."

"How long have you owned the hills," Trenton retorted. "I go where I please."

"An' it pleased you to follow my trail, foot by foot," Dan sneered. "Quit lyin'; you've come to steal somethin' that belongs to me, but I got here first."

Anger and surprise betrayed the rancher into forgetting his customary caution. "You've found it?" he cried.

Dan's laugh was not mirthful. "The cat's out," he said. "Found what? The charmin' view you came all this way to show yore niece, an' fetched along five armed men to help you locate it?"

The taunting tone and the fear that he might be too late after all, roused the rancher to fury. "You damned whelp," he stormed. "If it weren't for my niece——"

.."Skittles!" Dan interposed. "She'll be in no danger 'less you all try to hide behind her. Set yore dawgs on when you've a mind."

Without looking round, Trenton gave an order. "Scatter and take cover; we'll cut this cockerel's comb right now."

Even as they moved to obey, he snatched out his revolver and fired at Dover. He was too late; the young man had guessed right and vanished just in time. A volley from the Wagon-wheelers followed but was ineffective since they had not even a protruding rifle-barrel to aim at. Trenton, with a curse of disgust at having missed, jumped his horse for the bushes. At the first shot, Garstone had seized the rein of Beth's mount and dragged it to the side of the gorge.

"Get off and sit down," he ordered, and set the example. "We should be safe here if the idiots don't aim low." He noticed her expression of surprise. "I'm from the East, and I don't hold with these primitive ways of settling differences," he went on. "Maiming or killing an opponent only proves proficiency with a weapon, so the greater ruffian is always right."

She did not reply; it was all very plausible, but even with her own Eastern upbringing, the sight of this big fellow sitting beside her in probable security while his friends fought, seemed wrong.

"What did Dover mean by saying the treasure belongs to him?" she asked.

"Obviously a lie," he replied carelessly.

The crash of the firing increased as the defenders of the gorge got busy, and several bullets zipped through the branches above their heads, sending down a shower of twigs and leaves.

"Damn them, they're shooting wild," Garstone muttered. "Lie close."

He took her hand, but she drew it away. "I'm not afraid," she told him.

"I am—for you," he replied warmly, but got no response.

The spiteful crack of the rifles continued for a space, and then came a long-drawn groan. Garstone, peering from their retreat, saw Trenton, his gun falling from nerveless fingers, stagger from the bushes and fall headlong in the open.

"Damnation! the swine have got Zeb," he cried.

Beth scrambled to her feet. "I must go to him," she said, and disregarding his remonstrance, ran to where her uncle was lying.

Bundy was already kneeling beside him, apparently searching for the injury. Garstone followed the girl, calling out for the firing

130

to cease, and energetically waving a white handkerchief. He need not have troubled; even the appearance of Dover and Malachi produced no shot. The latter's examination was brief.

"He's not dead," he announced. "But the wound is serious."

"Can we take him away with us?" Garstone enquired.

.."Yes, if you want him to die," the doctor replied tersely, and looked at Dover. "His only hope is to remain here, and in my care."

"Anythin' you say, Doc," Dan agreed. "We'll do all we can."

"I shall stay to nurse my uncle," Beth said quietly, her steady eyes challenging a refusal.

Dover lifted his shoulders. "I ain't objectin', but we're not fixed to entertain yore sex."

The Easterner drew Beth apart. "My mind is made up, so please don't attempt to dissuade me," she told him.

"I should not dream of doing so," he said. "You are acting bravely and rightly, but there is something I must tell you. These scoundrels have tried to kill your uncle because he alone knows exactly where the treasure is hidden; they have failed to find it. You will admit that they should not benefit by this dastardly deed."

"I will do anything to prevent that," she replied, her face cold and set.

"Good. Zeb has set his heart on securing this money and so saving the Wagon-wheel. We must try to carry out his wishes. Listen: he may become feverish and talk, or recover consciousness long enough to confide in you, Keep everyone away from him, except the doctor, of course, and if you learn anything, let me know at once."

"How can I do that?"

"You know the place where we sheltered? I will come there every evening soon after dark in the hope of seeing you. Is it agreed?"

"Yes," she replied. "I care little about the money, but I want to see this gang of murderers defeated."

By this time the wounded man had been bandaged and laid on a blanket. "Two of you take him to our camp," Dan directed, and when Bundy and Flint at once stepped forward, added brusquely, "Not you."

The scowling pair fell back; Tiny and Hunch raised the burden and carried it carefully away. The doctor and the girl went with them. Dan turned to Garstone.

"You an' yore pack o' curs can scratch gravel, an' if you got any regard for yore skins, you'll keep clear o' here," he warned.

"You're taking a high hand, Dover," the other replied. "Miss Trenton is my promised wife, and I shall certainly come to see her."

131

"At yore own risk; if I catch you near my camp, I'll shoot you, an' that goes for yore thievin' bunch too. Now, roll yore tails; the play's over."

Garstone's face became ugly. "That's where you're wrong," he snarled. "This is just the first act—there's a second to come."

His four followers were behind him, waiting for a word. But Dover's men were back now; Sudden, thumbs hooked in his belt, watching sardonically, Hunch, indifferently swinging his great axe in one hand so that the sun flashed on the gleaming blade; Dan and the big cowboy, alert and ready, and Yorky, his new gun gripped in both fists, eyes alive for the least movement. Garstone did not give the word—the odds were not sufficiently in his favour. So he sneered and went in search of his horse. The others tailed in after him, but presently Bundy spurred alongside.

"We could 'a' cleaned 'em up," he said regretfully. "But where's the use? Zeb didn't have it on him."

"Didn't have what?"

"The paper, o' course, tellin' where the dollars is cached. Why'n hell d'you s'pose I downed him?"

For an instant Garstone gazed at him, petrified, unable to credit his ears, and then, "You—shot—Trenton?"

"Shore, I'd never git a better chance," came the callous reply. "He was just in front o' me, an' with all that firin' . . ."

He paused, aghast at the fury in the other's face. "You clumsy bungler," the big man rasped. "Why don't you leave the planning to those whose heads are not solid bone throughout? Did you imagine that Trenton would carry a secret like that on his person for rogues like you to steal?"

"Where else?" Bundy asked sullenly.

"In his brain, you dolt, after destroying the paper," Garstone told him harshly. "So you've probably slain the only man who can tell us where the treasure is, damn you."

The foreman was too appalled by the magnitude of his mistake to resent the abuse showered upon him; it seemed to be the end of their hopes, and if the other men got to know . . . "Mebbe Zeb'll come round enough to talk," he faltered.

"Yes, to them," Garstone snapped.

"There's the gal," Hopefully.

"You're a little late with that idea," came the sneer. "What do you think I was speaking to her about? She's our one chance, and until I get news from her, we can make no move. Understand?"

Bundy nodded. He did not like the tongue-lashing, but he liked still less the prospect of losing his share in the contents of the Cache, so he endured the first in the hope of getting the second. Which did not mean he forgave. A cowboy once described the foreman as having been "raised on vinegar," and the only comment from the company was, "an' the meanest vinegar, at that."

132

CHAPTER XVIII

The Circle Dot men watched the discomfited band leave the gorge, and then returned to the cave. Dover walked to a small recess near the entrance, where a second fire had been lighted, and the wounded cattleman made comfortable on a pile of blankets. Miss Trenton was seated on a chunk of stone at his side, and the doctor was standing near.

"How is he?" Dan asked.

"Pretty bad," Malachi replied. "Bullet through the chest, but he's physically fit an' has a chance—a slim one. I've done all that is possible."

Dover nodded, and the doctor went, leaving the young man staring moodily at the helpless form of his enemy. He was recalling the stark, outstretched figure of his father. What part had Trenton played in that tragedy? Was this retribution, or . . . His reverie was broken by a cold, scornful voice:

"Admiring your work?"

"This is no work of mine," he returned quietly.

"Why quibble? You or your men—it is the same thing," she said passionately.

"Trenton fired the first shot, direct at me, without warnin'," he reminded.

"You had insulted him," was all she could find to say.

Dan's laugh was bitter. "So, a Trenton may lie, steal, or murder, but he must not be insulted. Oh, yo're one o' the breed, all right."

"I'm glad of it."

"An' so am I, otherwise——"

He did not finish, but her woman's intuition told her what was in his mind—that he might have cared for her. She bit her lip, conscious of an intense desire to hurt this man who showed his scorn so plainly.

"You would have been too late," she said. "I am already——"

"Promised to Garstone," he ended. "He bragged about it just now, this brave fella who cowered with you behind a bush while his friends fought."

He had seen that. The hot blood in her cheeks was partly due to the taunt, but also to the fact that the Easterner had taken her consent for granted, "He was asked to look after me and did so."

"An' his own skin at the same time. Well, let's drop an unpleasant subject. I want to know whether you'd ruther feed with us, or over there?"

"I am not used to the company of ruffians," she said loftily.

"You oughta be, by this time," he retorted. "One thing more: you are not to go more'n twenty yards from this camp without my permission."

"And if I do?"

She saw his jaw harden. "I'll put you across my knee an' spank you good an' plenty," he said.

Before she could reply to this amazing threat, he had joined the others at the fire. Tiny was chaffing with Yorky.

"How'd it feel to be loosin' off yore gun at a human bein'?" he wanted to know.

"I warn't—I was aimin' at Bundy," the boy grinned.

The chuckle this produced reached the girl's ears, and she shivered; she found herself unable to fathom these men, who slew or attempted to, and in the same hour, could be amused by trivialities. She looked at her charge; only the faintest rise and fall of his breast showed that he still lived. He, too, was of the same type, hard, relentless, violent, in keeping with the savage character of the country. She gazed round the gloomy cavern, rendered even more eerie by the dancing flames of the fires, and it all seemed like an evil dream. The low, clear voice of Dover came to her during a lull in the chatter.

"What you say don't surprise me none, Doc," he said. "All the more reason why we gotta pull him through."

Beth had not heard Malachi's remark, but it was evident they were speaking of her uncle. It set her wondering. Why should Dover be anxious to save the life he or his had tried to take? Then she remembered what Garstone had told her.

"They shan't know," she murmured, through shut teeth. "I'll beat them, the brutes."

But she could not dismiss Dover from her thoughts. The red-haired boy who had so gallantly twice come to her aid, had become a stern, harsh-tongued man, lacking even the common courtesy accorded to her sex. Anger welled up as she recalled his threat.

"And he would do it," she reflected. "He—hates me—just because I am a Trenton."

A more sophisticated woman would have solved the secret, divined that Dover's attitude was due to anything but hatred, and that in the blundering fashion of an inexperienced youth, he was trying to build up an impassable barrier between them, lest worse befall. Her mind failed to envisage the completeness of a malignity which could hand down a war from one generation to another.

Later, when she was striving, unsuccessfully, to arrange the blankets upon which she was to sleep, she heard the rancher say,

"Tiny, go an' help Miss Trenton," and to Malachi, "Hell! a woman who can't make a bed."

The big cowboy came over, gave one glance at the tumbled coverings, shook the sand out of them, and started from the beginning. In five minutes an attractive couch was awaiting her. He threw more logs on the fire.

"Lie with yore feet to the flames an' you won't git cold." He gazed curiously at the sick man. "Any better?"

"There is no change," she replied.

"Well, he shorely asked for it," Tiny said. "Shootin' at Dan thataway was a dirty trick."

" 'Like master, like man,' " she quoted to herself, thanked him, and lay down. It proved to be very comfortable, and her last waking thought was that she must get one of the cowboys to teach her the knack. After all, a woman really ought to know how to make a bed.

Sudden, Malachi, and the rancher spoke together when supper was over.

"Phil has some news for us, Jim," Dan began. "He claims that Zeb was shot by one of his own outfit."

"Likely enough," the puncher said.

"More than that—certain," Malachi pronounced. "The bullet entered the back, travelled upwards, and through the chest; it must have been fired by someone behind and near."

"Bundy was the first to reach him," Sudden reminded. "Also, he was too long lookin' for a wound in plain sight."

"After the instructions for findin' the Cache, huh?" the rancher asked.

"There were no papers on Trenton," Malachi remarked. "I made sure of that when dressing his hurt. Unprofessional, I fear, but . . ."

"Then Bundy may hold the key."

"I guess not," Sudden said. "Trenton's no fool; that document would be a dangerous thing to carry about; he would learn and destroy it, as we did."

"Yo're probably right, Jim," Dan agreed, and to the doctor, "Miss Trenton thinks one of us shot her uncle; don't put her wise. No need to tell the boys either—yet."

In the morning Malachi came to inspect his patient. Dover was with him. Having satisfied himself that the dressings were in place, the doctor said, "Well, he is no worse. Anything to report, nurse?"

"Once in the night he groaned, and I think, tried to move."

"Shows there's a kick still in him. He's a tough old sinner is Zeb, and he'll fight."

"Did you sleep well?" Dover asked the girl, and when she nodded, went on, "I've told Hunch to get some birch." The flash in her eyes advised him that she had misunderstood. "Birch twigs make the best bed one could wish for," he explained dryly.

"I see," she said slowly. "They have, I believe, other uses."

Dan hit back. "I told him to fetch in plenty." As he stalked off, his reflection was, "Damn the girl. Why can't I keep away from her?" The eternal call of youth to youth was the answer, had he but known it, but he blamed his weakness. "Like a fool moth, flutterin' round a flame an' on'y gettin' singed," was his angry conclusion.

Yorky, who had been on guard, arrived with a vent for his annoyance. "Say, Boss, that Garstone guy is a piece down th' alley. I told him to stay there till yer came."

"Is he alone?"

"Couldn't see no others."

"Ask Jim an' Tiny to be on hand," Dover said, and went out.

The visitor had dismounted and was leaning against the tree to which he had tied his horse, smoking a cigarette, and with a small grip-sack at his feet. No greetings were exchanged.

"I've brought some things Miss Trenton may want," he began. "I wish to give them to her."

"I'll take 'em," Dan said, picking up the bag. "What's inside o' this?"

Garstone looked indignant. "I wouldn't presume——"

"Then I will," Dan said coolly, and opened the grip. On the top lay a loaded revolver. "That's somethin' she won't need—don't s'pose she ever pulled a trigger in her life. Wonder where she got it."

"Provided by her uncle, I imagine."

Dan laughed, unpleasantly. "Yeah. Zeb would know the company she had to ride with." He slipped the weapon into his own belt. "I'd give it to you, but I don't want to walk backwards to my camp."

The obvious implication brought a venomous expression to the big man's face. "Scared, eh?" he sneered.

"Scared nothin'," the rancher said harshly. "I'm on'y rememberin' that Trenton was shot from behind."

Garstone's start of surprise was quite well done. "Impossible!" he cried.

"Doc Malachi knows his job."

"And is on your side."

"True, he ain't a skunk neither."

"You keep adding to the score, Dover. Don't forget that there'll be a day of reckoning."

"My memory's fine," was the nonchalant answer. "Wait here; I'll send the girl to you."

Indifferently he turned his broad back and strode away. Garstone watched him with a brooding frown, fully aware that

136

Sudden and Tiny, rifles across their left arms, were in sight. That they knew the manner of Trenton's hurt was disturbing. Had they informed his niece? But when she presently came to meet him, he did not ask. His first enquiry concerned the patient. She told him the little there was, adding that she believed the doctor was doing everything possible. Garstone saw his opportunity.

"Yes, having done their best to take his life, they are now desperately eager to save it," he said bitterly. "And we know why."

"It would seem so," she admitted.

Her reply was a great relief to him; evidently she had not been told. At the same time, he sensed a change in her; she did not appear to be so pleased to see him as he would have liked.

"Are these fellows treating you decently?"

"Yes, but I am virtually a prisoner."

"It won't be for long," he consoled. "Once we get the location from your uncle, you will be released, and I will deal with these dogs as they deserve."

She found herself wondering what form this promised retribution would take, and how it would conform to his views as to the use of violence in quarrels. Before she could come to any decision, he spoke again:

"We must be vigilant, my dear—everything depends on your being present when Zeb regains consciousness. I don't trust that tippling doctor; he is working for them."

"I think he is honest," she said. "There are worse things than love of liquor—greed of gold, for example; the first may kill one man, the second, many."

"I thought you were anxious to discover the treasure," he protested.

"For my uncle's sake, but if it is to cost lives . . ."

Garstone was a gambler; he played a desperate card, to win or lose all. "If you've changed your mind, we'll give up the affair and sneak back to Rainbow with our tails tucked in," he said. "The Circle Dot will be delighted."

The fire in the dark eyes told him he had won. "No," she replied, through clenched teeth. "I will do my part; they shall not profit by an attempted murder."

"That's the Trenton spirit—I knew you wouldn't back down," he cried exultantly. "And soon, when the old man is on his feet again, and the ranch in the clear, we'll——"

"I must get back," she interrupted hurriedly. "Even now, uncle may be needing me."

He let her go without demur—it would be a calamity if the enemy learned the secret first—but his expression, when she had turned, was anything but that of an adoring lover.

*   *   *

137

A week passed, spent by the Circle Dot in a continuance of the search. The gorge had been gone over with a fine-tooth comb, and every foot of the floor of the cavern probed, but beneath the layer of sand only rock was encountered. The task appeared to be hopeless, yet they persevered.

The condition of Trenton had improved, the wound was beginning to heal, and his pulse was stronger. Between long spells of sleep, he would lie like a log, gazing vacantly into the vaulted roof. He knew no one, and uttered no sound. Beth, watching constantly by the bedside, earned the admiration of all, save Dan, for her devotion.

"Got the right stuff in her, that gal," Tiny remarked. "If she hadn't enough to do a'ready, I'd fall sick my own self."

"We'd have ter send fer th' school-marm then," Yorky grinned, and then went in pursuit of his hat, which had been sent spinning across the cave.

Malachi was optimistic. "He's better in body, but doesn't seem to get his wits back," he reported to Dover.

"If he don't, it looks like a stalemate for all of us," the young man said despondently. "That damned banker will sell us out."

"Well, the Wagon-wheel can't buy anyway. What has become of Garstone and company?"

"They're around. He sneaks up the gorge every night, an' the girl goes to talk with him. They think they're puttin' one over on me."

"Aren't you a trifle hard on her, Dan?" Malachi suggested. "She's having a middling rocky time and standing up to it well."

The rancher laughed ironically. "Do you know why she offered to nuss that o' crook? Not because he's a relative, but to get a line either from him or us, on where to look for the dollars. So far, she's had nothin' but failure to report to her—boss."

"If that's so, Garstone has lied too, and is using her," the doctor asserted. "The girl is not mercenary."

Late that evening, with only the stars to light her path, Beth slid noiselessly out of the cave and crept through the bushes to meet Garstone. He was there, and greeted her with outstretched arms, but she recoiled.

"I must hurry," she whispered. "I believe Dover suspects we are meeting. Thank Heaven, this may be the last time I need come here."

In the excitement her words caused, he forgot the rebuff. "You have news—at last?"

"Yes, my uncle spoke, to-day, when we were alone," she replied. "Only two sentences, but they may supply the clue."

"Quick, tell me, girl; at any moment we might be disturbed." In his anxiety, the mask of culture he affected slid aside, and she saw the gleam of covetousness in his eyes, heard it in his husky

138

voice. At that moment she knew that she was nothing to him but the bearer of tidings which might make him rich.

"His speech was faint, and very slow, like that of one trying to remember," she said. " 'The—cave—of—the—bats.' There are hundreds of them over our heads. Then, after a long pause, he went on, 'The—finger—of—the—ages—points—the—spot.' "

"And that was all?" His disappointment was patent.

"He has not said anything more."

"The devil, it only sets us another problem. The cave is probably the right one, though there may be others with bats in them, but what does finger of the ages mean? Has the place any unusual feature?"

Beth strove to visualize her prison. She was weary of the daily and nightly vigil, sick of the whole sordid business. "It contains many stalactites, hanging from the roof like great fingers——"

"By the Lord, you've got it, girl," he burst in. "Fingers of the ages—the products of millions of years. It will be under one of them, but which? Surely the longest or largest; we'll find it."

"Don't be too sanguine," she warned. "Dover and his men have scanned every foot—the floor is rock."

He laughed confidently. "Never fear; with the tip you've given us, it'll be easy. Now, cut along back, in case of accidents. By the way, what sort of guard do they keep?"

"They take turn, in pairs, through the night. What do you intend to do?"

"No plans yet, but be prepared for quick action," he said briskly. "We'll have you free, *pronto*, as these barbarians put it."

With scant ceremony, he left her, and as she returned to the cave her thoughts were not of the pleasantest. Without being yet in love with the man, his bigness, good looks, and evident knowledge of the world had made that an undoubted possibility. He had put the money first, and herself second in the night's enterprise, and she knew that was how they ranked in his mind. The fact disturbed her. Creeping along under the cliff, she reached the entrance to the camp, and stole through. Her patient was asleep, and four recumbent forms round the fire showed that all save the sentries had turned in. With a sigh of relief, she followed their example, and, despite her anxiety, slept soundly.

CHAPTER XIX

Garstone drove his horse hard in his haste to deliver the good news to his companions. They had been difficult to control for the past week, though he had made it clear that, in consequence of Bundy's blunder, patience was their only policy. Lake had been the principal objector.

"Drive 'em out'n their camp an' we got as good a chance as they have," he argued. "While we're messin' about here, they may find the stuff an' light out."

"My information is that they're no nearer success than when they started," Garstone had retorted, and as the other three supported this view, he won his way. And now he could enjoy his triumph.

He must tell them, for he needed their assistance, but when it came to a division of the spoils, he saw breakers ahead. His brow became furrowed as he dwelt on the problem. Their idea was equal shares—as much had been said—and the very thought of it filled him with rage. He found himself regretting his cavalier treatment of the foreman, but the fellow was an ignorant boor, anyway, and could no doubt be talked over.

They were sitting round the fire, smoking and chatting, when he arrived. Their changed attitude towards him was clearly shown by Lake's greeting:

"Yo're back early, Garstone. Warn't yore Lulu too kind this evenin'?"

The Easterner drew himself up. "Use a civil tongue when you speak of that lady," he said. "And for myself, remember that, in the absence of Trenton, I'm your chief."

"Oh, yeah," the other sneered.

"If you don't like that, you can clear out—now," Garstone added.

"Who's makin' me?" The fellow's hand was stealing towards his gun.

With amazing speed for one of his bulk, Garstone leapt, pinned the threatening wrist, and wrenching away the weapon, flung it down. Then his great fingers closed on Lake's throat, lifted and shook him with such ferocity as to well-nigh dislocate his neck.

"You insolent hound," he gritted between his teeth. "I've a mind to tear you in two with my hands."

He shook him again as though about to carry out his threat, and then hurled him to the ground, to lie there panting and beaten. Garstone turned to the others, who had watched the scene in silence.

"Curse the foul-mouthed fool," he growled. "He might have been useful to-night in the clean-up, but we must do without him."

"The clean-up?" Bundy cried.

"Certainly—that's what I said," Garstone replied coolly. "Miss Trenton, as a great sacrifice of her personal comfort, has found out what we wanted to know, and this—reptile—insults her."

The "reptile" was climbing to his feet; he had heard, as the speaker intended, and was not going to be left out if he could avoid it. Vengeance would wait.

"Aw, Boss, I warn't meanin' nothin'," he whined. "Just a bit o' joshin', that's all. Us fellas is a mite loose speakin' of women, but I reckon we all respec's Miss Trenton."

Garstone hesitated—purposely. His gust of passion had been partly premeditated, an attempt to regain the authority which had been slipping from him since the rancher's injury, and he had no desire to lessen the number of his force, few enough already for the task in view. Also, a dismissed man might turn traitor, warn, or even join, the enemy.

"That type of humour does not appeal to me," he said coldly. "I am willing to overlook it, this time, but you fellows must understand that what I say, goes, or I am finished with the business."

Being completely in his hands, for the present, there could be only one answer to this, and Bundy voiced it:

"I guess we're all agreed on that." The others nodded assent, Lake leading the way. "That's all right, Boss. I s'pose with what Miss Trenton has told you, we can go straight to the Cache?"

Garstone suppressed a smile at this clumsy attempt to pump. "Hardly so simple, Bundy," he replied. "My information will enable me to find the treasure only when we have driven Dover and his men away."

"Why can't we make tracks with the dollars an' leave them Circle Dot pilgrims to go on lookin' for what ain't there?" Rattray wanted to know.

"Because, my clever friend, the said pilgrims are camped right on top of the dollars," was the crushing reply.

Shortly after midnight, they set out, crossed the basin, and entered the gorge. Fortune favoured them, for the night was dark, and they were able to approach unseen. Fifty yards from the cavern, they dismounted and continued the advance on foot. Moving slowly and silently against the black background of the bushes, they presently paused at the sound of a voice—the doctor's.

"Did you hear anything, Hunch?" it enquired.

141

No reply came; they did not know that the old man had answered with his customary movement of the head, useless in the darkness. So they waited, and then went a few more paces. The shadowy forms of the sentries could now be dimly discerned.

Flint and Rattray crept up behind them, the soft sand muffling their tread, a rifle-butt rose and thudded on the head of Hunch, spreading him senseless on the ground. At the same instant, vicious iron fingers encircled Malachi's throat from behind, preventing the escape of any sound, he was flung down, tied, and effectively gagged by men who, accustomed to handling cattle and horses, found his spare frame an easy task. That they went to this trouble in his case was due to Garstone.

"Mustn't damage the doctor," he had said grimly. "We may need his services."

Leaving their victims on the ground—having first bound the old man in case he recovered—the attackers moved towards the cavern. The glow of the fires, while emphasizing the darkness, enabled them to see the blanketed sleepers, four at one, and two at the other. The latter interested them not at all. With cat-like tread, and invisible until they got within the circle of light, they spread out and then closed in on the larger fire. A low whistle from their leader, and they charged.

Outnumbered and taken by surprise, the Circle Dot men had little chance. Sudden, awakened by a stumble followed by a stifled oath, only thought it was his turn to take guard, and got to his feet. Then, across the flames, he saw Yorky, kicking and struggling in the grip of a formless shadow, and heard him yell:

"Look out, Jim; they's on to us."

He turned just in time to escape a swinging blow from a gun-stock. His hands dropped to his belt, but ere he could pull a weapon, his arms were pinioned in a band of steel and he was dragged violently backwards. He saw Yorky felled to the earth by a savage fist, and a fitful flare showed him that it was Garstone who dealt the blow; the sight of this big fellow beating up a boy disgusted and infuriated him.

With a swift wrench, he got one arm free, and twisting, drove a fist where he imagined the face of his assailant must be. His guess was a good one, he felt his knuckles connect with flesh and bone. The man fell away, but before Sudden could make any use of this advantage, another hurled himself upon him, clutching and grabbing for a hold. Every muscle braced to keep his feet, he struck fiercely right and left in an endeavour to break away and use his six-shooters, but the two men gave him not a second's respite.

Guns began to crack spitefully, but in the flickering light and violent action, aim could only be erratic. In one flash, Sudden saw Tiny drop, and his opponent run to the aid of the two with whom Dan was fighting furiously. Biting on an oath, he redoubled his efforts, shooting out short-arm jabs with such speed and venom that one of the clawing forms fell back, and panted:

"We got you to rights, Green. Give in, or I'll blow you apart." The words were followed by the click of a cocked revolver.

It was Flint's voice, and the puncher was about to tell him where he could go when a woman's shrill shriek of despair rang out, and he saw Beth Trenton—apparently panic-stricken—running in the direction of the tunnel. The memory of the abyss awaiting her chilled his blood.

The interruption had startled his adversaries into a moment's slackness. Stooping, he snatched a blazing pine-knot from the fire and thrust it into their faces. Scorched and half-blinded by this unexpected weapon, they recoiled, and dashing between them, he followed the girl, calling her by name. Only the hollow echo of his own cry came back to him.

He raced on, realizing that her life depended upon his overtaking her in time. Fit as he was, his breathing power, already taxed by the fight against two, began to weaken under the strain he was now putting upon it. Moreover, his high-heeled cowboy boots were built for riding, not running, and the uneven nature of the ground provided another obstacle to speed.

But Sudden was not the man to boggle at difficulties, he had met and overcome too many; so he stumbled on as best he could, and in silence, for he needed all his breath. Presently, a scuffling step warned him that she could not be far away. He dared not call out, lest he frightened her; the death-trap must be near. A moment later, holding his torch high, he saw her, only a few yards ahead, staggering blindly on, apparently oblivious to all save a desire to escape. With a last desperate effort he reached and dragged her back on the very brink of the chasm.

"It's all right, Miss Trenton," he said. "Yu were headin' for danger."

She looked at him with dazed eyes, made a feeble effort to release herself, then saw the gaping void before them and shuddered violently.

· "I lost my nerve," she murmured. "The shooting and fighting, I couldn't bear it. I wanted to get away—anywhere."

"Shore, I understand," he replied.

Behind them in the tunnel, a shout, followed by two shots which whistled by them in unpleasant proximity, reminded Sudden that he was a hunted man. He had no intention of allowing himself to be taken, and if he left the girl, she might be hit in the random shooting. He took a quick glance at the bar to their retreat; it appeared to be about twelve feet wide, and the far side was slightly lower. The pursuers, who had no light, were still a little distance off and advancing slowly. It was a hazardous chance, but still—a chance. He pitched his torch carefully, saw it fall safely on the other lip and remain alight. Then he turned to his companion.

"Feelin' better?" he asked.

"Yes, I am all right again," she replied. "What are you going to do?"

"We gotta get over that—ditch," he said.

"Impossible," she cried.

"Or stay an' be shot."

As if to drive home his grim alternative, the tunnel reverberated with two more reports, and the bullets chipped fragments from the rock walls; they were shooting at the light. Sudden acted promptly. Seizing the girl's arm, he stepped back ten careful paces, then stooped and lifted her.

"Keep still, an' don't be scared," he said.

Filling his lungs, he started to run, gaining momentum with each stride and counting them. At the tenth, with a mighty effort, he launched himself and his burden into the air. Sickening seconds, more like long minutes, ensued, during which they seemed to be hanging over the unseen, terrible trough of blackness beneath. Sudden felt that the girl's weight was dragging him down, and the fear that he had failed to jump far enough flashed through his mind. They were falling—falling, and then his feet jarred on solid earth, he stumbled, and went headlong. Beth, forced from his grasp by the impact, was lying, faint and dizzy, just in front of him.

"Don't move," he whispered.

He need not have troubled; she had no desire or strength to do so. Prone in the darkness they waited; the torch had flickered out. Steps sounded, and a voice:

"C'mon Flint. We must be most on to him now."

"Don't like this damn place—too much like a perishin' grave," was the grumbling reply. "I'm for goin' back; can't see his light even."

"Must 'a' died on him, 'bout here too. Thought you wanted this *hombre*?"

"Shore do, I'd like to flay him alive."

"Same here, an' I ain't losin' a—Christ!"

The imprecation was succeeded by a blood-curdling shriek of terror, and then a second, dulled, like a weird echo, appearing to come from the depths below.

"What's happened, Rat?" Flint cried anxiously. "Where are you?"

A match spluttered in flame. Evidently the surviving ruffian was investigating. Then came a horror-stricken "Gawd-a'-mighty!" and the pad of hurried footsteps dying away in the direction of the cave.

144

Sudden pawed about, managed to find and light his precious pine-knot, and then assisted the girl to stand up. She was unhurt, but trembling as one in an ague.

"He has died—a terrible death," she whispered. "Why did I come to this awful country?"

Sudden's reply had a touch of sternness. "Don't blame the country because there are evil men in it, they are everywhere, in the big cities as well as the small settlements. What has happened is just that one o' them has gone to the hell waitin' for him, an' the world is the better for his goin'. Now, we ain't quit o' trouble yet—we gotta find a way out."

His cold-blooded view of the tragedy steadied, if it did not convince her. They resumed their journey, the puncher slightly in advance, and keeping a wary eye for further pitfalls. Beth was silent for some time, and then asked:

"What do you suppose has happened in the cave?"

"Most probably yore friends are on top by this," he replied dryly. "Tiny and Yorky were out of it when I left, an' Dan was battlin' against three—big odds for any man."

"Why did you run away and leave him?" she demanded, and there was something of anger in her tone.

The darkness hid his grin. "I was scared," he said.

The answer, coming from one who had recently dared that desperate leap, was too absurd. "I don't understand."

"Scared you would suffer Rattray's fate," he told her.

The blood raced into her pale face, and she was thankful he could not see it. "Forgive me," she murmured. "You knew of that awful place then? I should have guessed there was a good reason for your leaving Mister Dover. You saved me, and I haven't even thanked you."

"I'd like yu to forget it, ma'am," he said, supremely uncomfortable. "Ain't that a blink o' daylight ahead?"

She failed to see anything, and small wonder, for it was still night outside, as the puncher well knew, but it served his purpose. Presently he noticed she was limping, and asked the reason.

"It is nothing—just a bruise, when we fell," she explained. "Why didn't you leave me on the other side? Those men would not have harmed me."

"They were shootin', in the dark, an' might have hit yu," he pointed out. "Mebbe I took a risk, but there warn't much time to chew things over."

After another silence. "You could have warned Rattray."

"Did yu hear what they wanted to do to me?" he asked caustically, and when she could not answer, added, "They would have thanked me with bullets."

They plodded on, resting on the ground at intervals. Progress was tedious, for the friendly pine-knot had burned out, and they had to grope their way through the blackness. At length, however, Sudden was conscious of a freshness in the heavy atmosphere, and away in the distance there really was a spot of faint light. Beth saw it also, and it revived her flagging energy.

"An opening," she breathed. "Heavens, I feel as though I had been buried alive."

They reached it, and stepped out into the chill air of the dawn. They were on the side of a steep hill; the country below was shrouded in mist, and from out of it came the roar of a river.

CHAPTER XX

In the cavern, the battle was over. Tiny, smiting lustily, had held his own against Garstone and Lake until a wild shot from Bundy, intended for his own antagonist, struck the big cowboy above the knee and brought him down. Having first secured his six-gun, the released pair went to help the foreman, who was wishing he had taken on an easier task than the owner of the Circle Dot. Awakening to find himself already in Bundy's clutch, Dan had fought furiously. Hammered relentlessly, the attacker had to let go, and both pulled their guns. Dodging about in the uncertain light of a fire, however, does not make for good shooting, and beyond a graze or two, both were unhit.

"Best give in, Dover, we're three to one," Garstone urged, as he and Lake arrived.

"You can go plumb to hell," the young man panted.

They came upon him from all sides. He fired once, doing no damage, and then the weapon was struck from his hand. He had a glorious moment when he felt his fist smash into Garstone's lips, and that was the end; someone jerked his feet from under him, and though he continued a hopeless struggle, they soon had him bound and helpless. The Easterner, blood drooling from his gashed mouth, bent down, eyeing him with malevolent satisfaction.

"Well, Dover," he jeered. "You've made a pretty mess of things. But for you, we'd never have found this place. Thanks."

"Which takes in the pretty mess I've made o' yore face, I s'pose," Dan countered.

"No, I'll be showing my gratitude for that later," Garstone frowned. "After we've collected the dollars."

Dan managed a laugh. "Oh, I can wait; I ain't one o' them impatient fellas."

"What's a few hours anyway?"

"If you think Zeb'll talk that soon, yo're wrong; you did too thorough a job."

It was the other man's turn to laugh. "That's where you're wrong—he has talked," he said triumphantly. "I had the news I was waiting for last evening."

This time he scored. Dan understood; it was the girl who had brought this disaster upon them. In fairness, however, he could not blame her; she was on the other side, and he should have remembered. He had missed a bet.

"What's come o' the two men who were outside? Did you kill them?"

"Certainly not. We had to tie them up, and I fancy your aged lunatic got a rap on the head. You have yourselves to thank for any rough treatment."

"We can take it," Dan retorted. "I noticed you picked on the kid for yore share. Where's Green?"

The taunt penetrated the big man's skin. "I neither know nor care. When Miss Trenton lost her wits and ran screaming for that opening at the back of the cave, he appeared to lose his courage, and followed her. Two of my men went in pursuit, and have not returned."

Even as the words left his mouth, Flint staggered into the firelight. His labouring lungs told that he had been hurrying.

"Well, did you get them?" Garstone asked.

"Get *them*?" the man repeated.

"Yes. Green and Miss Trenton."

"My Gawd! Was she there too? Funny, I had a notion Green was chasin' somebody; that explains it."

"Explains what, you idiot? Tell a straight tale," Garstone said impatiently.

"Me an' Rat was scrappin' with Green when, all unexpected, he grabs a chunk o' the fire, shoves it in our faces, an' runs hell for leather into that hole over there, with us on his tail. It's a kind o' underground passage, black as the inside of a nigger, but we could see his light dancin' ahead so we kept on. It was chancy work, runnin' in the dark, an' he was goin' fast. We couldn't gain any, so we spilled lead, but that didn't stop him. Then he seemed to slow down, an' his torch dropped an' went out."

Flint paused to draw a deep breath, and resumed, "Rat was a bit in front, an' called me to hurry. Afore I can git to him, there's an awful screech, follered by another, kind o' smothered, like it came from deep down. I yelled to Rat but got no answer, so I crept forward on han's an' knees, feelin' the floor in front till—there ain't no floor. I struck a match, an' I was kneelin' on the edge of a big crack, wide—an' deep? well, I'd 'a' figured it dropped clear to hell if I hadn't heard runnin' water below."

His ghastly effort to be facetious drew no smile from his audience.

"What do you suppose happened?" Garstone asked sharply.

"I guess Green an' the gal got catched in the trap, an pore ol' Rat blundered in after 'em."

Garstone's face shoed no emotion. "We'll look at this place," he said.

"Turn me loose," Dan pleaded. "I give you my word I won't try anythin'—I just wanta help."

"No doubt—help yourself," was the sneering reply. "Flint,

148

you and Lake keep an eye on the prisoners, see that they don't 'try anything.' You come with me, Bundy."

Armed with lights, the pair traversed the tunnel and reached the chasm. The foreman lowered his torch and pointed to some small footprints.

"She got as far as this, anyway," he remarked.

"Obviously," Garstone agreed curtly.

He stepped to the brink of the rift and stood peering down into the abysmal depths, listening to the murmur of the subterranean river hundreds of feet below. Callous as he was, the vision of Beth, young, beautiful, instinct with life, hurtling to a dreadful death in the darkness chilled him. But the feeling soon passed; there were many other women in the world, and ere long, his crafty brain was considering how he might turn even this tragedy to his advantage.

"It would seem that Flint was right," he said. "A fine athlete could get over, if he knew the danger was there, but with the girl . . ." He shook his head to complete the sentence. "Bad news for Zeb; she was his only relative."

"If he cashes, who gits the Wagon-wheel?" Bundy enquired.

"I have an interest in it," Garstone told him. "I shall arrange with the bank to take over the ranch."

"Trenton ain't gone yet," was the sour reminder.

"True, but I do not think he will recover."

"Well, if he don't, an' you git the Wagon-wheel for the mortgage on it, you'll owe me somethin'," the foreman said brazenly.

"Yes, I shall owe you a lot, Bundy, and I always pay my debts," Garstone replied. "Singular spot this; I should say that anyone so unfortunate as to fall in there, would never be seen again, alive or dead. Well, we can do nothing; let's get back."

The foreman was more than willing; his companion's tone made him uncomfortable. One who accepted the tragic loss of his lady-love so cold-bloodedly would have little hesitation in sending a man he feared to keep her company. Garstone, physically, was more than his match if it came to a tussle. So, until they were well away from that gaping black gulf, Bundy carried his torch in the left hand, keeping his right close to his gun.

The cave was as they had left it, save that the early light of day was stealing in. Flint and Lake were busy at the fire, preparing breakfast. The captives sat or lay in a group apart. Garstone went to inspect them, something in the manner of a conqueror. The sentries had been brought in.

"Sorry to find you in such bad company, Malachi," he said.

"I couldn't prevent you and your friends coming," the doctor retorted. "Did you discover anything about Miss Trenton?"

"I am afraid there is no hope," Garstone said. "I imagine that, fleeing down the tunnel in a distraught state of mind, the

149

approach of Green—also running away, these gunmen are all cowards at heart—would seem like pursuit and hasten her destruction. He also appears to have perished, for which I am sorry; a rope would have been a more fitting end."

"You quite shore they weren't killed by yore toughs, an' that Flint's yarn isn't just a cover-up?" Dan asked, adding with a reckless disregard of the fact that the man was one of his gaolers, "Lyin' is the thing Flint does best."

The big man turned away without answering, and went to where Trenton was lying. Dan got a poisonous glare from the receiver of his compliment, but that did not worry him. The bottom had dropped out of his world, and though he tried to persuade himself this was due to the loss of his friend and ranch, he knew it was not so; a dark-eyed slip of a girl, with an oval, slightly tanned face, and firm lips which could smile so sweetly, meant more than all. He had striven to erect a barrier between them, and, so far as he was concerned, had failed. And now, Death had done a better job. He could see that slender young body, battered and broken, the plaything of some rough torrent in the dark depths of the earth. He closed his eyes in an effort to shut out the picture, and groaned.

"Hurt, Dan?" Malachi whispered.

"Yeah, but it's somethin' you can't cure, Phil."

The doctor understood. "Don't give up hope yet," he consoled. "I've a lot of faith in Green."

"That's th' talk, Doc," Yorky chipped in. He was next the rancher. "Jim'll show up—he'd git outa hell if th' lid was on. Me? I'm awright; th' big stiff knocked me cold, that's all. One day he'll come up agin a feller his own size an' run like a scaldedcat."

Garstone, who had returned in time to hear this unsolicited testimonial, kicked the author of it savagely in the ribs. "Keep your dirty tongue still, you city vermin," he flared, and to Malachi, "I am releasing you to nurse Trenton. Come over now, I don't like the look of him." He cut the doctor's bonds, and added, "If you take any other advantage of your freedom, you'll be shot."

Malachi's eyes were blazing. "Garstone, if ever I have the pleasure of performing an operation upon you, I shall forget my profession and do the world a service," he said.

"Meaning you'd murder me, eh?"

"Yes, but I should call it an 'execution.' "

Garstone's laugh was ugly. "No wonder Zeb is not getting better," he fleered.

The wounded man was motionless, eyes closed. The doctor turned down the blankets, examined the wrappings, and felt the pulse.

"He's no worse," was his decision.

"But he hasn't got his sense back," Garstone expostulated. "He opened his eyes just now and didn't know me."

"Which might indicate that he had," Malachi said caustically. "I am doing all I can to remedy your foolish blunder—if it was one."

"What the devil do you mean by that?" Garstone demanded. "By God, I'll——"

"You know what I mean, and your threats don't frighten or interest me. The Almighty gave you a fine big body, and by a mischance put into it the soul of a louse."

Turning on his heel, he walked back to his companions, leaving the Easterner white with fury, and yet a little afraid of this quiet-spoken, acid-tongued man who defied him so openly. The fellow knew too much, and must be dealt with. The approach of Bundy gave him an idea.

"Just been talking to Malachi," he remarked carelessly. "He seems to think his patient will pull through."

"Good," the foreman replied, trying to speak as though he meant it. "I hope he's right."

"You have every reason to, for if Trenton doesn't recover it becomes murder, and as the doctor knows who fired the shot, his evidence would be awkward."

Both fear and suspicion were in the look Bundy darted at the speaker. "How in hell——?" he began.

"I didn't tell him, my friends," Garstone interposed. "These scientific gentry have their methods, and the nature of a wound may tell them much. Did you have anything to say to me?"

"The boys wanta know when we start searchin' out the gold."

Garstone did not reply at once; recent developments had altered the situation. Now that he found himself practically sole possessor of the secret, he was not eager to unearth the booty. His cunning brain had been busy with the idea of securing the whole of it for himself, but he could see no way—no safe way. He had told his followers that he could find it, and if he did not . . . . So he replied jovially:

"No time like the present, there's plenty of light now. Get the men and the tools."

Walking to the centre of the cave, he gazed up at the dark, domed roof from which hung scores of stalactites, like gigantic icicles their points sheathed in steel by the incoming daylight. They were of varying size, and one—almost in the middle—exceeded the others in girth and length.

"The finger of the ages, indeed," he mused. "Strange; nature toils for millions of years to make this marvel, and a gambler uses it to mark his hoard—I hope." And as the men came up, "We'll try here."

Flint, stepping forward with his pick, glanced up. "Hope the

151

shock won't shake that damn spike down on me," he grinned.

"You needn't worry, it would take an earthquake, and a big one at that, to shift it," Garstone assured him.

The man swung the tool, brought it down, and dropped it; the resounding clang of metal upon rock was followed by an oath from the striker, whose arms were jarred to numbness. Lake took up the pick and tapped all over the spot indicated; in no place did it penetrate more than an inch or so, and he threw it aside in disgust.

"That ain't no use—giant powder's what we need," he said.

"Shore you got the right location?" Bundy asked.

"Certain," Garstone replied, with a confidence he was far from feeling, and not unmindful of the doubtful looks directed at him. "Clear the muck away and let's have a view of this rock."

This was done, exposing an uneven stone floor which promised little. Garstone was puzzled. Was there a further clue which Trenton had not mentioned? He did not know, but the demeanour of his companions was beginning to disturb him. Flint flung down the spade he had been using and commenced to roll a smoke.

"Wonder how long it took the fella to dig a hole here?" he speculated.

"Mebbe he found one ready," Lake suggested. "Then he'd just have to plant the *dinero* an' ask the rock to kindly grow over it."

Bundy laughed sneeringly, but the sarcasm brought a glint into Garstone's eyes. "Even the bray of an ass may be useful," he snapped, and, snatching off his hat began slapping the cleared space vigorously, sending the dust flying in clouds. The others watched his antics in amazement, fully convinced that he had suddenly gone mad. On his knees, he studied the ground closely, and then rose.

"I was right," he said exultingly, and pointed to a crack which the displaced dust had revealed. "There's a loose piece, and I'm betting it's the lid of the treasure-chest."

This magically renewed their activity. Bundy seized the pick, drove the point into the crack, and threw his weight on it. A small, roughly rectangular section of the floor moved. Flint went to the foreman's assistance, and they managed to lever up one side. Garstone bent, got his fingers under the raised portion, and with a mighty heave overturned what proved to be a flattish slab of stone. Beneath was a shallow hole, and in it a stout rawhide satchel. At the sight Flint let out a whoop and made a grab, but the big man pushed him back.

"Hands off," he said. "The first thing is to find out what the contents are, and it is for me to do that."

He lifted the satchel, and undid the two straps by which it was secured.

"It's heavy, but not so large as I expected," he said, but went no further with the opening; his gaze was on the place from which he had taken it. "You were right, Lake, that's a natural hollow. All he had to do was find a lid to more or less fit; the dust would do the rest. A perfect hiding-place—it might have remained undiscovered for a thousand years."

"Seein' it ain't, s'posin' we git on with the business," Bundy suggested impatiently.

Garstone had to comply. Squatting round, their avid gaze following his every movement, the others waited. He might have been a conjurer, about to perform an intricate trick, and perhaps the fear that he would was at the back of their minds; honour among thieves is only proverbially prevalent. Their attention entirely occupied, they failed to see Malachi creep round the wall of the cavern, glance at his principal charge, and slip out.

Garstone's hand came from the bag holding a short roll of paper which, unwrapped, revealed a row of golden coins. He counted them, and the musical chink as they dropped from one hand to the other, set the eyes of his audience aflame.

"Fifty yellow boys—double eagles—a good start," he announced. He rolled them up again, and reached out a second, so obviously a replica of the first in size and weight that he did not trouble to open it. One by one, similar packages appeared until a score were stacked beside him on the ground. The men were breathing hard, so absorbed by the fascination of a visible fortune as to render them an easy prey had the prisoners been free. The lure of the gold held them; they could not wrench their eyes from it.

"Twenty thousand bucks," Bundy said thickly. "That bag ain't empty yet."

"I'm aware of the fact," Garstone replied, "But the dollars should more than satisfy our claim, and the rest belongs to Trenton."

"To hell with Trenton," the foreman growled. "We found, an' we keep it."

"That goes," Lake added. "Out with it—Boss."

The last word was a palpable jeer, and Garstone knew it. He looked at Flint, but saw no support in that quarter. There was nothing for it but to continue. A thick wad of paper currency came next, bills of large denomination mostly, all of which had to be duly counted; they amounted to forty thousand dollars. Then, two at a time, Garstone handed out small buckskin bags, heavy, and tightly tied. He opened one, and gloated over the yellow dust within. Gold! His lips curled into a sneer as he reflected that men had sweated under a blistering sun to fill those bags, only to throw them away on the turn of a card. The men passed them round, hefting them, and grinning widely; they were in high good humour.

153

"Can't tell what they're worth without scales, but I'd guess all o' ten thousand," Bundy remarked. "We can take three apiece."

Garstone began to replace the treasure in the satchel. "It will be handier to carry in this," he said. "We can divide later, after cleaning up here."

Rather to his surprise, they made no protest, and the fact caused him some inquietude. Had they a secret understanding to obtain his share? Well, that was a game at which more than one could play. He looked round. "Any suggestions for dealing with our friends yonder?"

"Send 'em to look for Rattray," Bundy proposed.

Garstone, who saw at once that such an infamous act would leave him at the mercy of his companions, promptly objected. "I am opposed to violent measures unless they are necessary, and safe," he said. "This would be dangerous—very dangerous. No, when we go, they will remain—alive. Of course, they will free themselves, but with no weapons or horses, and three sick people to tend, it will be a long time before they return to Rainbow, and then it will be too late—our story will have been told, and we shall be in possession."

"You don't suggest we should burden ourselves with a dying man?"

"Shore not, but we gotta do some explainin'."

"Quite simple," was the reply. "We came in search of the Cache, and found it. The Circle Dot—of whose presence in the mountains we were, of course, ignorant—attacked and tried to rob us. They killed Trenton, his niece, and Rattray. We beat them off."

"Straight as a string," Flint grinned.

"How come they wiped out the gal?" Bundy wanted to know.

"She tried to escape in the fight, Green pursued her, and they ran into trouble."

"Which fits the facts," Lake put in. "Yo're a pretty neat liar, Garstone; I gotta hand it to you."

The Easterner forgot to thank him for the compliment, but did not fail to note that the fellow had regained his air of insolent familiarity; it was another danger-signal.

"What's come o' that damn doctor?" Bundy asked.

Garstone strode over to the prisoners. "Where's Malachi?"

"Haven't a notion, an' if I had, I shouldn't tell you," Dan replied.

"Sore, eh?" the big man gibed. "So would I be, after sitting on the top of seventy thousand dollars for over a week, and losing it." His contemptuous gaze went to the trussed-up form of Yorky. "Makes you hunger for your open road again, doesn't it, hobo?"

The boy did not reply—he had no desire to be booted—but as

154

the bully turned away, he muttered, "Aw, go an' swaller yoreself an' be sick, ye . . ." He trailed off into a brief biography of Garstone, whose origin, appearance, habits, and future were luridly described.

"If cussin' would help, you'd be a while team an' a spare hoss," was Dover's dry comment, when the tirade ended.

"It eases a fella some," Yorky excused. "Do you figure th' Doc has skipped, Boss?"

"He's no quitter," Dan told him.

"What they goin' to do with us?"

"Can't say. Scared, son?"

"I dunno," Yorky admitted. "Couple o' months back I wouldn't 'a' cared, but now . . ." He was silent for a moment. "A man must take his medicine, Jim allus said."

The disappearance of the doctor caused some consternation, to Bundy in particular. Flint and Lake were despatched to find him, and Garstone seized the opportunity for a quiet word with the foreman.

"Splitting the dollars four ways doesn't help our plans," he commenced meaningly. "We won't have enough between us to get the Circle Dot, much less the Wagon-wheel."

Bundy realized that he was needed. "They ain't done much," he said. "Oughta be well satisfied with five thousand apiece."

"That or—nothing," Garstone said deliberately. "You agree?"

"Shore I do," was the reply. "Nothin'—for choice."

The men under discussion came in at that moment. "Can't find a trace of him," Flint reported. "We combed the gorge thorough. All their hosses is gone too—they had 'em picketed further along; looks like someone stampeded 'em."

"That cursed sawbones," Bundy exploded. "Wish I'd put his light out earlier."

"Well, they won't see the horses again, and it's a long walk to Rainbow," the Easterner said. "But it makes one difference: with that fellow at large, we can't leave Trenton here."

CHAPTER XXI

Beth sat down; daylight was a very welcome experience after the long lack of it, and she was terribly tired. Soon, however, sex asserted itself, and the task of neatening her appearance occupied her. Sudden too, inured as he was to physical exertion, found a rest acceptable; sitting cross-legged, he rolled a cigarette, wondering the while where the twistings of the tunnel had brought them. On their right towered the great head of Old Cloudy, and far away to the left the sky glowed faintly red, telling of the coming sunrise. Below, a sea of purple mist eddied and swirled.

The girl was studying this grave-faced, saturnine man who, having saved her life, had not hesitated to risk it again in the presence of another threat. The memory of that fearful leap sickened yet thrilled. What were they to do now? She put the question.

"Wait till it clears lower down," he said. "I reckon we've both had enough o' walkin' blindfold."

"I am anxious to get back to my uncle," she pointed out. "I shall never forgive myself for running away."

"Natural enough—yu been raised different," he excused. "The cave can't be far off; we'll find it."

"You think they will remain there?"

"I reckon," he told her, a wisp of a smile on his lips. "They won't find that Cache, 'less Trenton has talked, which ain't likely."

"He did talk—to me, though I don't think he knew I was there," she confessed. "I told Mister Garstone."

"The devil!" His bleak expression alarmed her.

"My uncle needed that money urgently," she explained.

"So did Dover, an' he had a right to it, which Trenton did not," Sudden said sternly. "Red Rufe was Old Man Dover's brother."

The statement shook her, but she was loyal to her kin.

"Then I am sure Uncle Zeb was ignorant of it."

"For years it has been common knowledge in the town."

"My uncle would not do anything dishonourable," she replied stubbornly.

"If that goes for his men, mebbe it's no good tellin' yu somethin' else," he returned. "Trenton was shot from behind."

Her eyes flamed. "I don't believe it; you're just trying to prejudice me, and whatever I may owe you——"

"Which is nothin' a-tall," he broke in. "Ask Doc Malachi." And as if to end the matter, "There's somethin' worth lookin' at."

156

Away on the eastern horizon, the grey had given way to a rosy glow, deepening towards its source, the flame-red disc of the sun, moving majestically up from behind the rim of the world. A growing golden light spread its radiance over the earth, softening the harsh outlines of crag and cliff.

"It's wonderful," the girl breathed.

"Shore is," the puncher replied. "Pity we humans can't grade up to the beauty o' the universe we live in."

"Some of it is ugly," she protested.

"On'y where man has interfered," he said cynically. "All nature has beauty of some kind."

"When I came to Rainbow we crossed a hideous desert, nothing but sand, cactus, and desolation."

"See that same desert by moonlight an' it'll beat the finest picture yu ever saw—if yu ain't thirsty," he added whimsically. "That scurry 'pears to be on the move; we'll start."

Side by side, they set off down the slope. The coarse grass, dotted with patches of greasewood, stunted mesquite, and cactus, made progress difficult and speed impossible. Before they had travelled far, a harsh warning rattle sounded, and from a bush just in front of Beth, a repulsive flat head shot up and swayed back to strike. Almost before she could cry out, a flash and roar came from her companion's hip and the reptile subsided, its head smashed by a bullet. Sudden drew out the empty shell, reloaded, and holstered the weapon. The girl stared at him in amazement.

"You were—so quick," she murmured, speaking her thought.

He grinned at her, and, in that instant, seemed almost boyish. "No time to waste when Mister Rattler goes on the prod—he's a fast worker."

"I have—to thank you—again," she said.

"Shucks," he replied impatiently. "I sorta got yu into the mess, an' it's up to me to look after you."

This brought Dover into her mind. She would never understand these Western men; they resented any expression of gratitude, and could even be rude about it.

He had picked up the still quivering body. "A biggish one. Would you like his rattles?"

"Heavens, no, I hate snakes," she shuddered. "They are of no use, surely."

"The buttons? In Virginia the niggers make bracelets of 'em; they're claimed to keep off evil."

"I should have brought one when I came to Arizona," she said bitterly.

When they continued the journey, he went in front, "to deal with varmints," but they encountered no more, and presently reached a level ledge of short grass. By this time the first slanting rays of the sun were splitting the mist into filmy, opalescent veils which rose and melted away, revealing that they were on one side of a deep canyon, the walls of which dropped sheer to a tumbling, riotous river hundreds of feet below. It seemed likely to Sudden that the stream they had jumped in the tunnel might empty itself into this one, so the broken body of Rattray could be returning to Rainbow.

"Where now?" the girl asked.

"We'll follow the canyon, east, an' get around this hump," he decided. "Then a twist to the north should fetch us somewhere near the cavern."

They tramped on, pausing only to drink at a rivulet which crossed their path. But the hump was succeeded by more high ground, steep and brush-clad, an insuperable barrier which pinned them to the canyon-side. They spoke little, but once or twice, to take her mind from the fatigue he knew she must be enduring, the puncher remarked on the marvel of the painted walls of the gorge, purple, green, brown, and red, brilliant beneath the burning rays of the sun, and the grotesque pinnacled and turreted masses of grey rock which served as a background.

"Yes, it's all very lovely," she sighed, and tried to smile. "But it only proves that even beauty can breed monotony. I'd give it all for something to eat."

"We'll have breakfast right soon," Sudden told her. "Wait here; I'll be within call."

He plunged into the undergrowth. After a while she heard the crack of his revolver, and he reappeared carrying a young rabbit. She watched interestedly as he lit a fire, deftly skinned the animal, and toasted it on pointed twigs. Again she was impressed with his competency. The meat proved delicious, and the ice-cold water of a nearby rill, completed the meal.

"You have done that before," she complimented, as they set out again.

"Shore," he agreed. "There's been times when I've had to live on the country for days. We could have tried that rattler."

She shivered. "But no one eats snakes."

"Yu ain't never known *real* hunger," he smiled. "I've been told rattlers is pretty good grub. In Texas the wild hawgs hunt 'em, an' I'll bet they don't do that for fun. White men eat frawgs an' snails, an' pay high for the privilege."

The long looked-for break in the barrier appeared at last in the form of a gully. They turned into it eagerly, but, though taking them in the right direction, it was not—as Sudden soon divined—the one leading to the cave. For one thing, it was narrower, and much cumbered with boulders and rank growth of thorn and cactus, difficult, and at times, painful, to penetrate. Also, they had lost sight of Old Cloudy, a fact Sudden did not like.

158

"Take a rest," he said, pointing to a flat stone. "I'll scout around an' see if I can pick up a landmark."

He thrust through the scrub, and by the movement of the foliage she saw that he was climbing the wall of the gully; he seemed to be made of steel. She herself, though the food had given her new strength, was exhausted, and glad enough to sit down. She fell to musing on the few moments of panic which had brought such misfortune upon her, and others. One man had died horribly, and perhaps her uncle, lacking her care, had . . . She would not think of that. Her thoughts came back to her companion in this astounding adventure. She hoped he would not be long, for while she still regarded him as one of the enemy, he created a curious sense of confidence, and the prospect of facing the wilderness alone was terrifying. Her reverie was shattered by the clink of iron against stone, and an amazed expletive.

"My God! it's Beth!"

The familiar voice brought her to her feet. Garstone was staring as though unable to believe his own eyes. Springing from his saddle, he ran to her.

"My dear girl, how in the world do you come to be here?" he cried. "Bundy, Miss Trenton has returned to life."

The foreman, followed by Lake, rode up. "Mighty glad to see you, Miss Beth," he said, but there was no warmth in tone or look. "We figured we'd lost you for good an' all."

"We certainly did," Garstone agreed. "How did you escape?"

She gave a brief account, and concluded, "We are trying to find the cave."

"Where is this fellow?"

"He went to look for a way."

"Get under cover, you two; we'll nail him when he comes back," Garstone ordered.

Too late, the girl remembered that Green belonged to the Circle Dot. "He saved me from death, and must not be touched," she protested.

"He forced you to go with him in order to drive a bargain with us," Garstone invented. "Also, he is your uncle's foe, and therefore should be yours."

"Does my life mean so little to you?" she demanded.

"No, but I am not going to let emotion blind you to the truth. That man is a killer; in all probability it was he who wounded Zeb."

"The truth," she cried. "Is it that Uncle was shot by one of his own men, and that Red Rufe was the brother of old Mister Dover?"

"Both are lies," Garstone said evenly. "I see that Green has made good use of his opportunity. You have sealed his fate."

She saw it was hopeless. "Where is Uncle Zeb?"

"Not far away; Flint is taking care of him."

Bundy and Lake had already concealed themselves, and their leader was on the point of doing the same when Sudden stepped from the bushes. A glance, and his guns were out, one of them covering the Easterner.

"Tell yore men to come out, with their paws high," he ordered. "You have one second to choose between that an' hell, Garstone."

The eyes of the speaker were chips of blue ice, and the threatened man did not hesitate. He called out, and the hidden pair emerged, biceps cuddling their ears.

"Where's Flint?" Sudden asked the girl.

"I've not seen him," she replied. "I'm told he is attending my uncle."

"An' yu believe it?"

It was Garstone who answered. "Of course she does. Isn't it natural that Trenton should be with his own people?"

"Who left him with his enemies when it suited their purpose," was the sarcastic rejoinder. "Well, Miss Trenton, yu remainin' with yore own people?"

"Certainly. I wish to be with my uncle."

Sudden nodded, and backed into the middle of the gully, his guns menacing the three men. "I s'pose yu've stolen the dollars, Garstone, but don't get too brash, mebbe there's another trick to be tabled yet."

"The big fellow's wooden face had changed. "I think, perhaps, you are right," he replied. "We want him alive, Flint."

At the same instant, the girl—eyes wide with dismay—uttered a warning, "Behind you."

Sudden spun round in a flash, and fired. Flint, who had crept upon him unperceived, had his gun out and was in the act of pressing the trigger; the bullet ploughed up the ground a few yards in front of him, and with a howl he dropped the revolver and grabbed a smashed elbow.

The puncher swung his weapon back on Garstone, but that astute person had moved to Miss Trenton's side, and he dared not risk a shot. So, with a scornful laugh, he turned and charged at the wounded man, who, having no stomach for the encounter, jumped away. It was an unlucky move; a gun roared and Flint went down, a bullet in his brain. Sudden sprinted along the gully he was not pursued.

"Why the devil did you shoot Flint?" Garstone asked angrily, as they gathered round the fallen man.

"He run into it—I was tryin' for Green," Bundy explained.

"Damn raw work—he was a coupla yards off," Lake jeered. "I thought you could shoot."

"I can, an' I'm ready to prove it." Threateningly.

The bearded man was not to be bullied. "Right now, if you want," he growled.

Garstone interposed. "Cease squabbling; we're few enough as it is."

"Yeah, three to divide instead o' four," Bundy leered.

"Four in place of five—Miss Trenton takes her uncle's share," the big man corrected, and the look which passed did not escape him. "Speaking of Zeb, we can't now leave him in the old camp; you two must fetch him."

"Like hell we will," Bundy retorted. "An' you wait here, I s'pose?"

"No, that would ruin our plans—we should arrive in Rainbow too late," was the cool reply. "Also, with that cursed cowpuncher at liberty, we may lose all we've gained. Of course, if Trenton should be dead, you can catch us up."

The inhuman suggestion was not lost upon the pair of rogues. They did not fancy leaving this fellow with the booty, but holding a poor opinion of his courage, they felt confident that they could force him to keep faith. They agreed, and Garstone rejoined the girl, who was impatiently awaiting him. As he expected, her first question was respecting her uncle.

"The journey was tiring him—a rest was imperative," he explained. "Flint stayed too, and the poor fellow was doubtless here to report when that scoundrel Green slew him."

"Green fired once only, and crippled Flint's arm," she said. "The fatal shot came from Bundy."

"Is that so?" he cried, in affected surprise. "Bundy, of course, would be aiming at Green; Flint was unlucky. I didn't see it; I was so concerned about you——"

"I noticed it," she said coldly. "You were saying?"

"I am sending the two men back to bring your uncle."

"Don't we accompany them?"

"No, we have to go on." He saw mutiny in her eyes and chin. "It is of vital importance to Trenton, and his wish, that we should get to Rainbow with all speed. You won't mind spending a day or so in the forest with me, Beth, will you?"

"I very much mind further separation from Uncle Zeb," she fenced.

"It cannot be helped," he replied, a touch of hardness in his tone. "I have a duty to him, and intend to fulfil it."

Which highly virtuous sentiment produced less effect than he had hoped. However, she said no more. Truth to tell, physical weariness, anxiety about the old man who had been good to her, incipient doubts, and a sense of disappointment in one she had almost decided to link her life with, had, for the time, broken the girl's spirit. Certainly, Garstone's welcome had been less warm than she expected, in fact, at that first moment of meeting, he might have been sorry to see her. She told herself that this was absurd, that the shock of encountering a person one had mourned as dead would be numbing, but the feeling remained.

Having disposed of the dead man, Bundy and Lake prepared for their journey. The girl watched them impatiently as they stowed food in the saddle-bags. Fortunately for her peace of mind, she could not hear their conversation.

"Think we can trust him?" Lake asked.

"No, but I guess we can handle him if he double-crosses us," the foreman replied. "An' mebbe we'll catch 'em."

"Totin' a sick man?" Incredulously.

"I didn't say that."

Lake digested this. "Even then they'll have a good start."

"Oh, yeah," Bundy grimaced. "Garstone an' the gal are both from the East. How long afore they lose theirselves?"

"An' our money."

"We can trail 'em, an' there's going to be on'y two sharin'—you an' me, *sabe*?" Bundy rasped. "Then the Circle Dot an' the Wagon-wheel can go to hell. I'm for California. With seventy thousand bucks—between us—we don't wanta fool with cattle."

Lake regarded him through narrowed lids; he had noted the interjected words, and they gave material for thought. But all he said was, "Sounds good to me."

When they had gone, Bundy having pointed out, tongue in cheek, the route Garstone should take, the latter returned to his companion. He was in a much more cheerful mood.

"Well, that's that," he said, "I'll get a fire started, and I hope you can cook—we'll have to fend for ourselves. This isn't the way I hoped we'd begin housekeeping together, but we'll get along."

She did not respond to his elephantine playfulness, and his clumsy attempts to help prepare a meal only reminded her, oddly enough, not of the efficient cavalier she had parted from, but of his friend, Dan Dover. Would he be pleased she had not perished, even though she was a Trenton? She stifled the thought resolutely, and busied herself brewing coffee.

CHAPTER XXII

The bound men in the cave watched the preparations for departure and wondered what was to happen to them. They saw the wounded rancher carried out, and Dan's protest that he was not fit to be moved was ignored. When their weapons and stock of provisions were also taken it began to look grave. A remembrance of Sudden's description of the gulf in the tunnel was not comforting. When all was in readiness, Garstone strolled over, and stood, contemplating Dover with malignant contentment.

"You have lost everything, or nearly," he said. "Treasure, ranch, and paid gunman; only your life remains. Well, I give you that; violence is not to my liking."

The suave, insolent voice made the young man indifferent to consequences. "Yo're tellin' me," he flung back. "Even when you rob a train, you pick the safe job—the men on the engine ain't never armed."

It was a guess, but a good one, and the gibe went home. But Garstone was a winner, and could afford to laugh; he did not.

"Keep clear of Rainbow, if you're wise," he warned. "And if you meet Malachi, tell him my promise will be kept."

"He won't believe me," Dan replied.

Garstone shrugged away the insult and looked at Yorky. "And you, get back to your sewer, you rat."

"Rats has teeth an' can bite," the boy spat out, and waited for the expected kick.

It did not come and, despite his hardihood, Yorky breathed more easily when the bully had vanished through the exit from the cave. He was silent for a time, wresting with some problem and then asked, "Does the mails from theseyer hick towns ever git lost?"

"I reckon, now an' then," Dan replied. "Why?"

"Ain't heard from me uncle in Noo York——"

"Don't you pull that stuff on me, son," the rancher cut in. "Hello, who's that?"

A slight figure had slid cautiously into the cave; it was Malachi. "So the buzzards have flown," he greeted. "And how are my patients?"

"Yo're one shy—they took Trenton," Dan told him.

"Damnation! it will probably finish him," Malachi exploded, and busied himself with their bonds.

"They've also collared our food, weapons, an' I s'pose, hosses."

"No, I set them adrift—thought it was a bright idea at the time, but afterwards I wasn't so stuck on it," the doctor said ruefully. "I forgot they'd be lost for us, too."

"You did yore best, Phil, an' there's a chance some will drift back. Grub is goin' to be the worry—we'll have to trap. By the way, Garstone said for me to tell you he would keep his promise. What was it?"

"Oh, nothing of consequence," Malachi smiled. "I was to be shot if I made any use of my liberty. Just a bluff."

He went away to attend to the hurt men, and the rancher's eyes followed him with a new expression. "A bluff. Huh? But you had the nerve to call it, Phil," he said softly.

After a while the doctor came back. "They're both going on well, but I can't understand Hunch," he reported. "That crack on his skull isn't serious, but it seems to have destroyed his memory."

"What, again?"

"Odd, isn't it? But he failed to recognize me, and appears to have no recollection of the Circle Dot, or how he came to be here."

"Mebbe the big axe would start his rememberin' machinery," Dan suggested.

"I tried that, but he just stared as though he'd never seen it before. Physically, he's perfectly sound."

"Well, Tiny'll keep us tied here for a spell," the rancher said. "Hi, Yorky, rustle some fodder for the fire; I'm goin' to see if I can knock over a cottontail or two."

"We'll be awright when Jim comes along—he's got his guns."

"He'd shorely be a cure for sore eyes," Dan replied moodily. He could not share the boy's confidence.

"Stranger things have happened," Malachi said. "The blackest moment is the turning-point, you know."

* * *

Meanwhile, the man of whom they were speaking was not many miles distant. The gully in which the Wagon-wheel party had surprised him was, he had discovered, considerably east of the one he was making for, but with Old Cloudy in sight again, he had a mark to steer by. He did not fear pursuit; they had the treasure. He wondered where was Trenton. Behind, perhaps, in the charge of Flint. But how were they transporting him? His mind went to his late fellow-traveller. A nice girl, he admitted, but somewhat lacking in savvy.

"Young women is apt to take a fella at face-value," he mused, and then came the cynical addition, "Wouldn't take 'em a-tall if they didn't, I s'pose."

Sudden was no misogynist, but so far the fair sex had not figured largely in his life. He was to meet his fate, but the time was not yet.

164

He trudged on, crossing ridges, threading arroyos, circling thickets of impassable brush, steadily advancing towards the mountain. The sun was still high in the heavens when, in a strip of sandy soil, he noticed hoof-prints. They pointed eastwards, and a careful scrutiny revealed five different sets. The prints of his own horse, Nigger—which he could recognize at a glance—were not among them.

"Four riders, one of 'em Garstone," he deduced, "an' a pack-hoss. Or mebbe they've distributed the baggage an' tied Trenton on the fifth."

That the tracks were not those of his friends he was quite sure. Exactly what had happened to Malachi and Hunch he did not know, but he had seen Tiny shot down, and it was most improbable that he would be able to sit a saddle so soon.

He set himself to follow the trail, and at the end of an hour's hard work reached what he knew must be the deserted Wagon-wheel camp. Standing in a small grove of trees, and sheltered by a cliff, was a canvas tent; only the presence of a woman could account for such a thing in that place. The ashes of the two fires were cold. Hanging from a branch was most of the carcase of a newly slain deer. He stepped to the opening of the tent and peeped in. A man, swathed in blankets, was lying on the floor. The puncher did not need two guesses—it was Zeb Trenton.

"The murderin' swine," he muttered. "They leave him here, helpless, an' to cinch it, hang a bait outside that would fetch any mountain cat gettin' scent of it." He bent over the rancher. "Trenton, it's Jim Green."

The eyes remained closed and there was no movement. Sudden seized one of the ice-cold hands; a faint flutter of the pulse informed him that the flame of life still flickered. A quantity of stores, flour, bacon, coffee, caught his eye, and the packages seemed familiar. With them, guns and six-shooters, thrown in an untidy pile on the ground. He picked up one of the rifles; it was Yorky's prized Winchester, and he understood; this was the loot from the cavern. What had become of his friends?

Only in one way could he find the answer, and, granite-faced, he set out, carrying his own rifle—which he had found among the rest, and the boy's. Exhausted and hungry as he was, his magnificent muscles did not fail him. Moving with the effortless swinging stride of an Indian on the trail, he crossed the basin, and entered the gorge. Apprehension grimmed his mouth as he approached the cave.

"Hello, the house," he hailed.

"It's Jim," he heard Yorky yell. "Didn't I tell yer he'd make it?"

The boy was the first to reach him, closely followed by Dan and Malachi. Judged by the standards of the East, their welcome was little more than casual, but Sudden was a Westerner himself, and he understood.

"Jim, I'm powerful glad to see you," was what the rancher said, but the clasp of his hand told a great deal more. And so with the others, but they all wanted to know what had befallen him.

"Well, we got away——" Sudden began.

"We?" Dan cried. "Then Beth—Miss Trenton—is alive?"

"Shorely," the narrator smiled. "Tryin' to find a way back here, we ran into Garstone——"

It was the doctor who cut him short this time. "See here, Jim, we like you a lot, but you'll be as unpopular as a drunk at a temperance meeting if you don't tell a complete story."

"Shucks, I'm doin' just that," the puncher protested. "I caught the girl in time—there was a bit of a crack in the floor o' the tunnel. Flint an' Rattray started shootin' an' I had to get her outa there."

"How did you cross that bit of a crack?" Malachi demanded. "I was looking at it a while ago; it nearly froze my blood."

"Jumped it, o' course; think we growed wings on the spot?" Sudden replied, and divining the coming question, added, "Well, she warn't so heavy."

"My sainted aunt," Malachi breathed. "How many lives have you, Jim?"

"I started level with a cat, but mebbe I've used up a few," the puncher grinned.

"All right," the doctor smiled. "Get on with your—bragging."

"Like I said, we got clear an' bumped into the other crowd. Garstone told Miss Trenton that he had her uncle safe an' she decided to stay with 'em. He tried to persuade me, but I warn't willin'. Then Flint objected to my goin' an' I had to argue with him; his arm was hurt."

"Bruised, no doubt," Malachi commented ironically.

"Mebbe," the puncher agreed. "He jumped aside when I charged, an' Bundy shot him in the head."

"Why'n hell—" Dover began.

"He'd claim to be aimin' at me, though I was six feet from Flint; it was either mighty good, or mighty bad, shootin'. Now I'm comin' to the important part; I wanted to tell you right off, but Doc would have his dime novel." He grinned at Malachi. "I'm headin' for here, as near as I can guess, when I stumble on tracks. I back-trail an' they lead me to the Wagon-wheel camp. There, inside a tent, is Zeb Trenton."

"Alive?" This from the doctor.

"On'y just, I'd say."

"They left him alone. Why, it's plain murder."

"Yu said it—'specially the way things was fixed," Sudden agreed, and told of the deer-meat.

166

Dover's face grew dark. "We can trump that trick, anyway, by fetchin' him here," he said. "You were goin' to suggest that, Jim?"

"Yeah, the more so as they seem to 'a' got our stores an' weapons there. I didn't see no hosses."

"They never got 'em," Dan said, and explained.

"Well, yu can't have everythin' in this world o' sin an' sorrow; we'll have to hoof it." He looked at the big cowboy, who, squatting near, was energetically cursing his crippled limb. "If I leave yu my rifle, Tiny, can yu deal with any visitors?"

"Betcha life, an' I hope it's that dawg's-dinner of a Wagon-wheel foreman."

"Don't let yore prejudice blind yu to the merits o' Garstone an' Lake," was Sudden's sardonic advice. "What is it, Yorky?"

"Is my gun among them at th' camp, Jim?"

The puncher shook his head, but the boy's crestfallen expression was too much for him, and he pointed to the weapon, lying with his own, where he had laid them when he came in. "Guessed yu'd be losin' sleep over it," he smiled.

Yorky secured the gun, examined it anxiously, and then appealed to the others. "Ain't he th' ring-tailed wonder o' th' world?"

"Yu wanta hang a weight on that tongue—it moves too easy," Sudden said, and closed him up like a clam.

On their way across the basin, the rancher—by what he regarded as artful questions—dragged a few more details from his companion.

"So she ain't believin' Zeb was got by one o' his own gang?"

"Well, she didn't exactly call me a liar, but it amounted to that," the puncher admitted.

"A Trenton never listens to reason," Dan said, but the accent of bitterness was less marked. "It musta been a tough experience for one with her raisin'."

"She's got plenty pluck—an' didn't complain, not once, but she don't like rattlers."

"You shore do surprise me," Dan grinned.

They dropped into a silence. Behind them they could hear Yorky chattering excitedly, and the doctor's amused and sometimes caustic replies.

"That boy's havin' the best time of his life," the rancher remarked presently. "I'm havin' my worst. I'm right sorry I dragged you into this, Jim."

"Forget it. Did yu promise me a picnic?"

"No, but I'm finished; this was my ace in the hole. The Circle Dot——"

"Ain't changed han's yet. I don't know what Garstone's game is, but he's clearly reckonin' Trenton out of it. If we can take him back alive, it'll put a kink in his plans that'll need straightenin'."

"By the Lord, yo're right," Dan cried, and with a grim smile, "I never dreamed a day'd come when I'd wanta keep Zeb outa hell, but it shore has. Hope we ain't too late."

To Sudden the camp appeared just as he had left it, except that he could not remember having closed the flap of the tent. He went across, raised it, and looked inside, only to start back in astonishment. The rancher was still there, rolled in his blankets, but a few feet away, lying with arms flung wide and sightless eyes staring, was the bearded man, Lake. A revolver lay near Trenton's right hand, which was slung across his body.

"They came back then," Dover said.

This explanation did not satisfy Sudden. The doctor, after one glance at the dead man, turned his attention to the rancher.

"He's alive, and certainly no worse; in fact, his pulse is stronger," he pronounced. "He must have the constitution of a horse."

Sudden's eyes were busy. "Lake wasn't shot here; see the marks of his spurs as he was dragged in and put in position to make it appear Trenton killed him? Raw work, but whoever did it reckoned on some wild beast comin' to muss things up. I'd say Bundy an' this *hombre* came back—mebbe the girl insisted—an' she's waitin' with Garstone."

With a scowling brow Dover allowed this to be a possible solution of the mystery. "If that bloody-minded foreman is around, the sooner we get Zeb to our camp the better," he said. "Do we have to bury this carrion?"

The puncher lifted his shoulders. "I'm allowin' it's rough on the buzzards, but there's a spade handy."

So Lake got his grave. Stout saplings, with cross pieces, and a blanket provided a litter for the sick man. Sudden and Dover acted as bearers, the other two following with weapons and provisions, including a haunch of the deer-meat. They left the tent standing, an object to spur the imagination of some future visitors.

They reached the cave without incident, and having announced their arrival loudly—Tiny had an impulsive and suspicious nature —marched in. The crippled one welcomed them with an eagerness not entirely free from personal regard.

"Food!" he yelped. "You Yorky, git busy with a skillet an' some o' that hunk o' meat; my belly's that flat you could slide me under a door."

"Doc sez yo're feverish an' gotta go light on grub," the boy chaffed. "Mus' take care, ol'-timer; breakin' th' sad noos to ye widder——"

"I ain't married none."

"Good as—the school-marm would feel like one," Yorky grinned, and, nimbly avoiding the rock heaved at him, went to his culinary duties.

Trenton having been made as comfortable as circumstances permitted, the party sat down to a meal they all needed. Tiny, after pushing about half a pound of broiled venison into his mouth, spluttered a compliment:

"You cook pretty good, Yorky. If you live to be a hundred, an' practice reg'lar, you'll come mighty close to Paddy at slingin' hash." He choked and had to be thumped on the back.

"Serves you right for talking with your mouth full," Malachi told him.

"Not full, Doc, or there'd be none fer us," Yorky chipped in.

The conversation took a more serious turn when Dan raised the question of what they were to do. "With hurt men an' no hosses, we 'pear to be hawg-tied," he said.

"How long would it take one of us to reach the Circle Dot?" the doctor asked.

"Best part of a week, if he knowed the country," Dan stated. "It's fierce travellin' afoot."

They discussed the project for a while, but the rancher did not favour it. "Where's the use?" he argued. "I guess we've lost the Circle Dot anyways. Best stay here an' give our invalids a chance.'

Soon afterwards they turned in, leaving Yorky—who was to take the first watch—sitting at the entrance to the cave, his rifle across his knees. With the potential presence of an assassin in the neighbourhood, no risk could be run.

In the morning, when the doctor visited his principal charge, he received a pleasant surprise: Trenton was conscious, and could speak.

"You, Malachi?" he greeted. "Where am I?"

"In our camp. But you mustn't talk."

"I must—I've a lot—to say," the sick man replied, with a touch of his old fire. "What happened—after Bundy—shot me?"

"You knew that?" Malachi cried.

"I saw his hand—grippin' the pistol—behind me. That was my —last memory. I——" His voice trailed off weakly.

"Let it wait, Trenton," the doctor urged. "You'll get well, but are pretty bad still, and must rest."

"I can't—unless I know. It won't harm me—to listen."

Stonily silent, the wounded man heard a brief recital of what had taken place. Only when Malachi concluded somewhat bitterly, "So your friend Garstone is safely on the way back to Rainbow with your niece and the plunder," did his expression change; fire flamed from the cavernous eyes in the emaciated face as he said hoarsely:

"My—friend—Garstone. Doc, you must patch me up—strong enough to get to Rainbow—an' settle with that double-crossin'

169

hound an' his murderin' tool, Bundy. I'll obey any orders, meet any bill——"

"Never mind that," the doctor smiled. "You're better, and I hope I haven't set you back telling you this."

"I'll rest easier," the rancher assured. "It wasn't all news. I was awake when Green found me; didn't know what he was after, so I shammed dead. Later on, Bundy an' Lake arrived, an' I played the same trick on them; Bundy had his gun out." He paused for a moment. "I lay limp an' still; he shook my shoulder, lifted my hand—which was cold—an' let it fall.

" 'He's cashed,' I heard him say.

"They went outside an' Lake suggested plantin' me, but Bundy wouldn't agree. They quarrelled, there was a shot, an' Bundy dragged Lake's body into the tent an' dumped it on the floor.

" 'One from three leaves two,' he said. 'Now it's between me an' you, Mister Garstone—the gal don't count. As for you, Trenton, I'm sorry yo're dead. For years you've hazed me, an' I wanted to squeeze the breath out of your rotten carcase with my hands. May you roast in the hottest corner of hell.' With that, he drove a boot into my ribs, an' I didn't know anythin' more till this mornin'."

Trenton sank back with a sigh of relief; the story had called for an heroic effort. Malachi was concerned.

"I ought to be kicked myself," he said contritely.

"Don't think it," the old man said. "You've given me somethin' to live for, an' by Heaven I'm goin' to live." A ghost of a grin trembled on the thin lips. "Appetizin' smell from somewhere."

"Yorky is stewing some of that deer. Are you hungry?"

"I could eat it raw."

The doctor's negative was emphatic. "You may have some of the broth," he conceded.

"All right, broth goes," the patient said resignedly.

As Malachi continued his "round"—as he termed it, he met Dover. "How's Trenton?" the young man asked.

"Conscious and hungry," Malachi smiled. "He knows the facts, and is wise to Garstone and company."

Dan's eyes rested dismally on the hole where the treasure had been. "Help me put that stone back, Phil; it makes me damned mad every time I see it," he said.

CHAPTER XXIII

Garstone had hoped that the despatch of the two men would satisfy the girl, but in this he was disappointed. His suggestion of an immediate start produced only the plea that she was tired—which could not be gainsaid—and needed a rest.

"But you will be riding," he protested.

"Is that so easy in these hills?" she parried. "Apart from that, I wish to wait until my uncle joins us."

Garstone concealed his anger; he alone knew how futile her desire was. "It means a loss of precious time for no useful purpose—Zeb could not possibly travel at the speed we must go."

"I should see him, and be sure he is getting better," she persisted.

"It will probably retard his recovery to find us here," he retorted. "If I know Zeb, he will be absolutely furious."

This was a powerful argument; she was well aware that the old man had all the Trenton temper. "What is the reason for the urgent haste to reach Rainbow?" she queried.

This was the question he had been waiting for. "Do you remember my telling you how important the finding of the treasure was to your uncle?"

"Yes, you said it meant keeping or losing the ranch."

"That's the position. The Wagon-wheel and Circle Dot are both deeply in debt to the bank. The mortgages expire in a few days, and if the money is not paid, the bank will sell the properties."

"But surely Mister Maitland——"

"A branch manager—an insignificant cog in a machine," Garstone said contemptuously. "Had Zeb or I been there, something might have been arranged, but in our absence . . ." He finished with an expressive shrug.

"I see," she said. "Of course, you found the money?"

"Good Lord, fancy forgetting to mention it," he laughed. "Yes, we found it, thanks to you, and there it is, strapped to my saddle. About seventy thousand dollars, enough to clear the Wagon-wheel and realize Trenton's dearest ambition, the purchase of the Circle Dot."

"Mister Dover may not wish to sell."

"Possibly, but the bank will," he replied. "We have that young pup where the hair is short."

She was silent, disturbed by a sentiment she did not trace to its source. In spite of his rudeness, she could feel no animosity towards the red-haired young rancher, and no satisfaction in the prospect of his humiliation and ruin. She did not want to dwell on it.

"Uncle Zeb should be very grateful to you," was all she could find to say.

This gave him an opportunity to strike another blow, lest she should still be obstinate. "Oh, I'm no philanthropist," he smiled. "I'm working for myself too. You see, when I came to your uncle, I put all I possessed into the Wagon-wheel, taking a third share. I am not anxious to be a pauper—especially now—but that's what I'll be if we reach Rainbow too late."

She stood up. "We will get away at once," she told him. "I did not understand how much depended on us."

"Of course not," he rejoined. "These matters of finance are not for pretty heads to worry over, but you're a true Trenton—you have to know, and then you see it through, sink or swim. That's the quality I most admired in Zeb."

They set off. Garstone dispensed with the pack animal, deciding that they could carry sufficient supplies without it.

"Shouldn't take us more than a couple of days," he said. "Bundy gave me the direction."

Quick-witted as he believed himself, it had not occurred to him that the foreman might designedly have pointed out a much longer route than was necessary, and he certainly did not realize that finding a path through the tangled mass of up-ended country which lay ahead of them was no task for a "tenderfoot."

*   *   *

Two days after the rancher had been brought to the cave, Sudden and Yorky were returning along the gorge from a hunting expedition, the spoil being the most toothsome portions of a young buck.

"Say, Jim, this is th' life, ain't it?" the boy said jubilantly. He had shot the deer, under his companion's guidance, and it was his first. "I don't care how long them cripples takes gittin' well."

"Yo're a selfish li'l devil," the puncher replied, with a severity which was only on the surface; he had planned that the lad should love this outdoor life, as he did himself. "So you want Dan to lose his ranch, an' them crooks to win out, huh?"

"Cripes! I didn't think," came the hasty denial.

His companion was not listening—to him. From somewhere near had sounded the call of a horse. Sudden uttered a long, low whistle, and waited. A crash in the undergrowth, and out stepped his own mount—Nigger. An instant it stood, looking at him, and then, with a little whinny, trotted to his side and rubbed its muzzle on his sleeve. The puncher pulled one of the soft ears.

172

"Where yu been, yu black rascal?" he asked. The animal's head dropped, as though it sensed reproof in the tone, but lifted again when a shrill neigh came from behind; two other horses were standing in the open. "C'mon," the puncher ordered. "Yore va-cation is over; we'll collect them playmates o' yourn afore long."

With never another glance round, Nigger followed its master like a docile dog.

This acquisition greatly improved the position of the party. That afternoon, Sudden rode away carrying three ropes on his saddle-horn. He made no attempt to guide his mount, riding with a slack rein, and, as he expected, Nigger went in search of its companions. In a grassy glade about a mile from the camp they came upon four. Sudden ran down and roped three of them, tying each as it was secured, and after a busy couple of hours, returned with his unwilling captives.

"I got yourn, Dan, Yorky's, an' the big roan that lets Tiny stay on him," he reported, with a grin. "I'll try again to-morrow, an' yu might have a look round their camp; they must 'a' let some go."

So the morning found the rancher combing the neighbourhood on the other side of the basin. He unearthed, and caught two ponies, one he believed to be Trenton's, and the other—still saddled—he surmised to have belonged to Lake. On his way back he stopped at the camp, got down, and entered the tent. Everything had been taken away, no, not quite everything, for a gleam of yellow caught his attention. He picked up the object, an oval locket of gold. From within, a face smiled at him, familiar, yet not the same, and older; a relative, no doubt.

He slipped it into a pocket—he would send it to her. He frowned at the thought that he might have to address her by another name. Well, she would still be a Trenton. And Zeb? He could have left him there to die, but the Dovers fought fairly, even against a treacherous foe. He did not want, or expect, thanks.

"It'll hurt the ol' devil more the way it is," he reflected.

Arriving at the cave, he found that Sudden had been equally successful, so their remuda was complete. The question of when they could start for home was the subject at supper. Everything depended on Malachi's report.

"You're all right, Hunch, aren't you?" the doctor asked.

The old man looked up, nodded, and went on feeding. But for his bandaged head he appeared much the same, save that he did not know them, and the big axe, once so carefully tended, was now stained and rusty.

"Possibly Tiny could sit a horse," Malachi said doubtfully.

The cowboy's protest was instant and emphatic. "Say, Doc, I

could ride afore I could walk. With one leg an' two arms, I'd stay on top of a blizzard."

"That leaves Zeb," Dover said.

"He's picked up wonderfully, and is in a fever to go," the doctor admitted. "I fancy it may do him just as much harm to wait. With short stages and long rests, we might manage it."

"Ain't there a nearer way, Dan?" Sudden questioned.

"Yeah, we took a twisty trail comin' to fog any who might follow. That place you struck on gettin' outa the tunnel must 'a' been Rainbow Canyon. The stream runnin' through it forks a piece along, an' the right arm is our river. If we keep by that, I reckon we'll cut down the distance quite a bit, which would make up for slow-movin'."

It was decided that, if the rancher were no worse, the journey should begin in the morning.

CHAPTER XXIV

Dame Fortune was frowning upon the foreman of the Wagon-wheel. On the morning after he had left the lifeless body of Lake lying in the tent, and set out hot-foot in pursuit of Garstone, a calamity which threatened to thwart his schemes befell him. Slithering down the sandy side of a ravine, his horse trod on a loose rock, lurched and went over, Bundy jumped clear, landing on hands and knees. He rose with an evil look, grabbed the rein and savagely jerked at it. The beast struggled to regain its feet, but could not, one leg had snapped. With an oath the man pulled out his gun and sent a bullet crashing into its brain.

"Damn an' blast the mouldy luck," he growled, as, carrying his saddle and rifle, he resumed his way. "Satan hisself must be workin' for Garstone, but I'll beat him yet."

Further reverses were to come. His own cunning—after the manner of a boomerang—returned to hit him; the round-about route he had foisted on the Easterner now meant weary miles afoot for himself. And since the cattleman's fondness for humping a saddle is about equal to that of the Devil for holy water, a few hours saw the article hurled into the brush with a curse.

He had little difficulty in following the trail, for Garstone had not the skill to conceal it. This ignorance, however, frequently drove the foreman to frenzy, for the big man had blundered through places hard for a horseman, and doubly so to a pedestrian. Often also, Bundy found himself tramping long miles which he knew were taking him no nearer to Rainbow.

"Hell burn him," he muttered. "I told the fool to head for the sun, but if he's goin' to do it allatime, he'll finish where he started."

Four days passed, and in the early afternoon another blow fell —he lost the trail. It had led him to the verge of a large pine forest. There were no hoof-prints, right or left, and he could only conclude that they had kept on through the gloomy aisles of the trees; but the deep mat of pine-needles would retain no tracks. He spent hours circling the forest in the hope of finding where they had emerged, but without success. Sitting down to rest, he arrived at a decision.

"I'll get me to Wagon-wheel an' deal with Mister Garstone there. Anyways, thirty-five thousand is a sizeable stake, an' mebbe . . ." A sinister scowl ended the sentence, and then, "The

175

Rainbow River comes out'n these hills. I gotta find it I'm fair sick o' traipsin' this Gawd-damned wilderness."

He picked up his rifle and blanket-roll containing his scanty supply of food, and set out, heading south-east. An hour later he was standing on a high bench screened by bushes, whence the ground dropped abruptly, flattening as it reached a great crack in the surface which he guessed to be Rainbow Canyon. He was about to descend and verify this when a horseman came in view. Bundy swore, and ducked under cover; it was Dover. Peering through the sheltering foliage, he watched Tiny, Hunch, and Yorky follow, with a pack animal. Then, after a brief interval, Malachi, with a companion at whom the foreman gazed with bulging eyes.

"Trenton," he whispered, as though afraid they might hear though they were nearly a thousand yards away. The man he had left for dead, riding to Rainbow, with his—Bundy's—enemies. Trenton would know all, the murder of Lake, and his own duplicity. The completeness of the catastrophe stunned him. But stay, the rancher might have been unconscious during that last visit to the tent. But if not, they would hang him in Rainbow; Trenton would see to that. It was too big a risk to run.

"I'll have to close yore trap, Zeb," he growled. "Anythin' you've told them others don't signify, an' Garstone can't *prove* nothin'. But this ain't the place; I gotta have a good getaway."

Rifle in hand, he slunk along after the unsuspecting travellers below, his callous brain at work. With the rancher silenced, he must again seek Garstone.

"Couple o' slugs'll give me the dollars an' a pair o' hosses to carry me out'n the Territory," he told himself. "My luck must 'a' turned or I'd 'a' walked right into Rainbow to git mine."

Considerably cheered by this reflection, he began to watch for a suitable spot. He had no difficulty in keeping up, for the quarry was moving slowly. Presently he noticed that the bench was dipping and bringing him nearer to his target. Gripping his rifle in feverish eagerness, malignant eyes on the man he meant to slay, he suddenly saw the opportunity slipping away. The horsemen had reached a point where the walls of the canyon closed to within forty yards of one another and abruptly widened again. This narrow gap was spanned by a natural bridge of rock, bare, and offering no cover. If they decided to cross this, trailing them would be well-nigh impossible, the land on the far side of the river being open, and almost treeless, offering few chances of concealment. As he had feared, they turned.

The sight spurred him to action; it must be now or never. The passage across the gulf was narrow, the surface rough; they would ride it in single file. This would give him time to get close—there must be no mistake. He scrambled down from the bench, fighting his way through the scrub until he reached the edge. There he knelt, panting, weapon levelled; he was only two hundred yards distant.

"I'll hold off till they're all over," he decided. "If any o' the rest git curious, I can send 'em after Zeb, one at a lick."

He watched them negotiate the bridge, singly, as he expected, and his lips drew back in an ugly snarl of satisfaction when he saw that Trenton was the last. Sighting full at the broad, bowed shoulders, he steadied himself and pulled the trigger. Through the smoke of the discharge he saw the rancher fall forward on the neck of his horse, which, startled by the report, leapt onwards.

"Got him," he gritted.

Even as he spoke, two quick reports rang out, a bullet shattered twigs just above his head, and a second smashed into the breech of his rifle and ruined the mechanism. With an oath he threw aside the useless weapon and turned his eyes to the right, whence the shots had come. A black horse was thundering down upon him, and the rider, standing in his stirrups, was assiduously pumping lead from his Winchester. Sudden, staying behind with the idea of obtaining fresh meat, had come on the scene just as the assassin fired.

The foreman shivered; he hated, but also feared the hard-featured puncher who had thrashed him so severely. In the moment of triumph, he had met disaster. He must do something. Escape through the brush was hopeless against a mounted man, he would be ridden down, trampled under those iron hooves. The drumming beat grew louder, bullets were humming past his ears; in a moment or two . . . A desperate device suggested itself. The widening of the canyon below the bridge brought the rim of it within a hundred yards. If he could reach that, the cowboy's horse became useless; they would be on equal terms.

Keeping under cover as long as possible, he then abruptly swerved into the open and raced for the canyon, zigzagging to avoid being picked off. He reached the edge safely, saw, some fifteen feet below, a narrow ledge running along the rock face. A break in the rim enabled him to clamber down and breathe again; he could not be seen from above.

So quickly had the whole affair happened that when he looked across the canyon the rancher's companions were only then lifting him from his saddle. But a bullet which chipped the cliff below showed that he had been observed. It would also tell the pursuer where he was. Bundy pulled his gun.

"If Green follers me here, I'll nail him," he grated. "An' with his hoss an' rifle . . ."

During the brief suspense, doubt crept in. His foe was fast—terribly fast. Bundy remembered that other time, when a lightning draw had foiled a foul trick which few men would have survived, and death had stared at him out of grey-blue eyes. What was it like to die? The violent jarr of the bullet, seconds—perhaps moments—of merciless pain, and then—nothingness. The look of blank amaze on Lake's face returned to him. Would he too——? He strangled the thought. His mind raced. Seventy thousand bucks; there must be a way.

A fiendish look told that he had found one. Changing his gun to his left hand, he picked up a chunk of rock with his right, leaned limply against the cliff so that the missile was hidden, and waited. The scrape of slipping boot-heels on a hard surface warned him that the puncher was descending. A moment and he appeared, six-shooter levelled. The foreman's face was a pasty yellow; he made no attempt to raise his weapon, seeming to be exhausted.

"Don't shoot, Green," he cried hoarsely. "I give in."

"Chuck yore gun towards me, an' put yore paws up," Sudden said sternly.

Bundy obeyed, lifting the left arm only. "Can't manage the other," he whined. "Damn bronc fell, bustin' a leg an' my collar-bone. I had to finish him."

The story was plausible enough; the man was apparently minus mount and rifle. All the same, the cowboy was not convinced. Unhurriedly he moved forward and half-stopped to lift the surrendered weapon. Like a flash, Bundy's "injured" arm flew up and down. Too late, Sudden detected the action and straightened; the great stone struck him on the chest instead of the head. Reeling back under the force of the blow, he lost his foothold on a slippery incline and vanished into the abyss.

Bundy, beads of cold sweat on his forehead, heard a shout of rage from the distant spectators, but no bullets came. Wondering at this, he secured his revolver, and creeping to the edge of the ledge, peered over. What he saw nearly sent him after his victim. Twenty feet below Sudden was clinging to a dwarfed mesquite growing from a tiny cleft in the rock. For a moment the astounding sight paralysed him; then, with a blasphemous imprecation, he prepared to deal the finishing stroke. Sudden saw the threatening muzzle, and nerved himself for an effort of despair.

"Might as well go one way as another," he muttered.

He still had his left-hand gun, and hanging by his right arm only, he swept it out and drove a slug into the evil, gloating face above just as Bundy fired. Sudden felt the wind of the bullet, and then saw the ruffian's body dive past him into the depths. But he was not out of the woods yet. His friends were coming to help him, but an upward glance told that they could not be in time— the root upon which his life depended was loosening. He looked down; there was another bush a little lower, in a direct line; if he could grab that as he fell . . . Far below, he could see the red-

178

brown river raging along the bottom of the canyon, hurling itself at the jagged, tooth-like boulders which strove to bar its progress.

Grim of face, he let go, felt the air whistle in his ears, then branches struck him, and he clutched; the bush withstood the shock of his weight. Arms aching until it seemed they must leave their sockets, he dangled there, and waited for aid. It seemed long in coming. Actually, as they told him later, Dan, Hunch, and Yorky were on the ledge less than ten minutes after the daring drop. His first news of them was the loop of a lariat which slid past his face. Slipping his weary arms through, he was hauled up, bruised, but little the worse.

"Shore, I'm all right," he replied to Yorky's shaky enquiry. "Injuns think a lot o' the mesquite; I'm agreein' with 'em. Did he hit Trenton?"

"No, Zeb 'pears to have collapsed just as Bundy fired—the journey's takin' it out of him, an' there ain't much to take." Dan replied. "Thought we'd lost you, Jim. How come?"

"He fooled me—good an' proper," Sudden confessed, and told about it.

When they rejoined the others, Trenton had recovered, and was chaffing at the delay. He scowled at Sudden. "So you wiped out Bundy? I wanted him myself, an' I don't thank you," he said.

"Did I ask yu to?" the puncher retorted, and rode on.

"By God!" Tiny swore. "Next time Jim sees someone takin' a pot at you he'll let 'em git on with it, I reckon."

Trenton asked curtly what he was talking about. The cowboy told him, and put it plainly. Followed another question.

"Wasn't it Green an' two-three more o' you who beat Bundy up for no reason?"

"Jim thrashed him—alone—for ill-treatin' Yorky. Bundy knocked the boy down, stole his rifle, shot his pony, an' set him afoot out on the range, a sick kid, with night comin' on. No reason, huh?"

"Is that true?"

The cowboy's good-humoured face became bleak. "If you wanta call me a liar, Trenton, wait till yo're well."

The rancher dismissed the threat with a grimace of disdain. "How long have you known Green?"

"Not near so long as I have you, but I like him a damned sight more," was the candid reply.

And that concluded the conversation.

Two more days of travel brought them within a mile of Rainbow, and there, in a wooded hollow well away from the trail out of the town, Dover called a halt.

"Before we decide anythin' I'll slip in an' get word with Bowdyr," he said. "It'll be dark when I reach the Parlour, an' I'll take care not to be seen."

When he returned, he was excited, and a little jubilant. "We're in time," he announced. "Maitland is offerin' the ranches for sale to-morrow mornin', at eleven o'clock; all the cattlemen in the district have been notified. He's in a hurry, curse him; that's the day my mortgage expires."

"Mine too," Trenton growled.

"Well, mebbe he'll get a surprise," Dover went on. "We'll camp here to-night. The sale is to take place in the Parlour, an' we can sneak in through the back—I've fixed it with Ben. Our game is to lie low until Garstone has showed his hand—if he's there. He won't be expectin' any of us, an' he's figurin' Trenton cashed. We can hear everythin' from the room behind, an' sift in at the right moment. All agreed?"

The assent was general. Trenton, a tired and sick man, sustained solely by his thirst for vengeance, asked one question:

"Anythin' been seen of Garstone an' Beth?"

"No, but they may've gone straight to yore ranch."

Dover's surmise was correct. Garstone and the girl had actually arrived in the vicinity of Rainbow several hours ahead of the Circle Dot, and Beth had insisted they should avoid the town. Garstone had no objection to offer. His comment, if uncomplimentary to his companion, was true—neither of them was fit to be seen. The homeward trek had been an ordeal for both, and to the girl a nightmare. Many times they had lost all sense of direction, and in the end had blundered blindly on the wagon-road to the settlement. Taking so much longer than they expected, food ran out, and though the man could shoot, he was so poor a woodsman that he frequently frightened the game and returned empty-handed.

The stress of the journey had shown Garstone to small advantage. Obsessed by his eagerness to get on, he showed less and less consideration for his companion, and any delay infuriated him. At such times he was almost brutal in his insistence, and she began to divine that his customary suavity was but a mask. The plea that he must save the ranch did not satisfy her. Any expression of anxiety concerning her uncle only irritated him.

"You didn't expect them to catch us up, surely," he said. "They would have to travel slowly, and you must remember that Zeb is not young, and sorely hurt; anything may have happened."

He had intended to prepare her for the news he hoped Bundy would bring, that the rancher had succumbed to his injury, but he only succeeded in frightening her.

"You mean he is—dead?" she asked fearfully.

"Of course not, but he may have had a relapse, which would delay them," he replied quickly. "On the other hand, Bundy would know a shorter way than we found, and they may be waiting at the ranch."

This did not prove to be the case; at the Wagon-wheel nothing had been heard of the owner or the foreman. When the travellers had washed, dressed, and eaten, Garstone was in a more pleasant frame of mind.

"Well, my dear, we're only just in time," he said. "I have a notice from Maitland that the Wagon-wheel and Circle Dot ranches will be sold to-morrow morning."

"But isn't that rather high-handed?" Beth asked.

"It certainly is, and I cannot understand Zeb giving them the power to do it. Either he is a poor business man, or he was in desperate need of the loan. However, we'll give that money-grubber a jolt."

"We? Surely there is no necessity for me to attend?"

"On the contrary, it is most essential. In your uncle's absence, you represent the family, and—I don't think he'd mind your knowing this—you are his heir."

"What have we to do?"

"Clear the Wagon-wheel and buy the Circle Dot," he replied triumphantly. "The two will make a fine property—for us, Beth. We shall also fling that red-haired boor into the mire."

The venom in his voice revolted her. "I have no wish to see Mister Dover ruined," she said coldly.

His surprise was genuine. "Why this sudden solicitude for the enemy of your family?"

"On one occasion, at least, he saved my life," she reminded.

Garstone shrugged. "I doubt if the cattle would have hurt you," he said. "Perhaps we'll make Dover foreman at the Circle Dot."

"Which would humiliate him still more."

Her vehemence brought a thoughtful expression to his face. "No, that wouldn't do—he must leave Rainbow. A disturbing element, but I can deal with him."

She looked at him with stormy eyes. "Which means that you will get someone else to do it, I suppose," she said cuttingly. "I am tired of this hatred and violence. I will have no part in it."

Her mind in a tumult, she sought solitude in her own room, to sit, staring blindly at the peaceful scene without. Something had happened to her; it was as though she had awakened from an evil dream. She had not yet said "Yes" to Chesney Garstone, and knew now that she never would.

The man himself was not perturbed by her outbreak. "Over-wrought," he decided. "She'll learn." The game was in his hands now. He had the money, and Trenton was dead—he felt sure of that, though the non-appearance of Lake and Bundy was perplexing. One bold stroke would put him in possession of both ranches. He went to Trenton's office to prepare it.

CHAPTER XXV

When the Circle Dot men awoke in the morning it was to find one of their number, Hunch, missing; no one had seen him go, and his horse was still there.

"Reckon he warn't interested," Dan opined. "Hiked off to the ranch, or back into the woods—he was allus happier there. His testimony wouldn't count anyway. You got any ideas, Doc?"

"No, he beats me," was the reply.

Breakfast was eaten, razors produced, and they made themselves as presentable as possible. "No 'casion to look like a lot o' bums if we are busted," Dover remarked, and Malachi, for one, agreed with him. Then they sat down to wait the word from Bowdyr.

By the hour advertised that portion of the Parlour usually devoted to dancing contained almost the whole male population of Rainbow, and a few of the women. There were also strangers, cattlemen from the outlying ranges, and a sprinkling of others whose garb told that they were alien to the West. Lounging against the wall at the back glum-faced, were Burke and the rest of the Circle Dot outfit.

On the little platform the piano had been pushed aside, and a table, with several chairs, substituted. At this sat the banker, his daughter beside him. Prompt to the moment he rose and briefly explained the purpose of the meeting, concluding with the remark, "Some of you may regard this action as inconsiderate on the part of the bank, but I must remind you that business is business, and a financial institution cannot be conducted on philanthropic lines."

He waited for the perfunctory applause of this oratorical gem to die down, and was about to continue when there was a stir at the door; Garstone and Miss Trenton entered. The big man had timed their arrival to the instant. He had the leathern satchel under one arm. Maitland stepped from his platform to meet them.

"I am delighted to see you both," he greeted. "I could get no news of you at the ranch. I trust Mister Trenton is well."

Garstone drew him apart, and a whispered conversation ensued. At the end of it the banker was all subservience. "Of course, as a man of affairs, you will understand how I was situated," he excused. "My head office——"

Garstone cut him short with a gesture, and conducted his companion to the platform, where seats were provided. The banker again addressed the audience.

"The arrival of Mister Garstone with funds to liquidate the bank's debt disposes of the Wagon-wheel," he announced. "Is there anyone here to represent the Circle Dot?"

"Yeah, me," Burke called out. "An' I say it's a damned shame to sell Dan Dover's property behind his back."

The applause which followed this outspoken statement brought a flush to Maitland's pale face. "Have you the money to pay off the mortgage?" he asked.

"You know thunderin' well I ain't," the foreman replied. "Dan went to git it, an' may be here any ol' time."

Beth Trenton rose. "Mister Maitland, the Wagon-wheel will advance the necessary sum to the Circle Dot," she said.

Garstone's expression became one of fury. Gripping the girl's arm, he forced her to sit down, whispering savagely, "Don't be a fool, Beth." Turning to the banker, he went on, "The Wagon-wheel will do nothing of the kind, Miss Trenton is allowing her heart to overrule her head; we expect that from her sex, but it is not business. What is the amount owing to you?"

"Forty thousand dollars."

"I will buy the Circle Dot for that figure if there is no better offer."

None came, and Maitland smiled his satisfaction; that the bank should not lose was his sole concern. He had risen to terminate the meeting when the Easterner again whispered.

"Mister Garstone has something to say to you," he stated.

Standing there, big-framed, carefully-dressed, a genial look on his fleshy face, the man made an imposing figure. He dispensed with any preamble.

"I am going to tell you why Zeb Trenton is not here to do this job himself, and it's quite a story. Most of you have heard of Red Rufe's Cache. Well, some weeks ago, Trenton, his niece, myself, and some of our men went in search of it." Several in the audience sniggered. "Yes, I know others have tried and failed, but we succeeded, and there it is"—he pointed to the satchel—"somewhere about seventy thousand dollars."

There were no sniggers this time, but envious eyes rested on the container of so much wealth. It had been for anyone to find.

"Unfortunately, a gang of ruffians from the Circle Dot——"

"You better lay off that kind o' talk," Burke warned, and was supported by a growl from his men.

"Were also after it," Garstone went on. "They attacked us, but we fought them off. Two of our men, Rattray and Flint, were killed, and Mister Trenton so severely wounded that I had to leave him in the charge of Bundy and another, since it was urgent I should be here to-day. So Miss Trenton and I came on, and

183

though it was a terribly arduous journey, I could not wish for a more plucky fellow-traveller."

Beth received the compliment with stony indifference, but the speaker was too full of his own success to notice. As owner of two ranches, Rainbow must learn to recognize his importance. These hucksters and the like had to be told that he was no mere servant, and Beth brought to heel.

"It may interest you to know that I own one-third of the Wagon-wheel; should Trenton not recover, it becomes two-thirds, the rest going to his niece. The will, which I have here, substantiates this. It is in accordance with his desire, often expressed to me, that we should wed, and the lady, I am happy to say, has consented."

If the spectators expected blushes and confusion they were woefully disappointed. Red of cheek she certainly was as she sprang to her feet, and her eyes were flaming.

"That, like some of your other statements, is a lie," she said, in a clear, ringing tone. "Nothing in this world would induce me to marry you. As regards the two men who died, Rattray perished by accident, and Flint was shot by Bundy, as you well know. My uncle——"

"Is here to speak for himself," a weak but stern voice interrupted.

Through the door leading to the living part of the establishment, near the platform, Trenton, supported by Dover and the doctor, followed by Tiny and Yorky, entered, Garstone's features underwent a swift transformation from rage to joy, and he was the first to reach the rancher's side.

"My dear Zeb, so those two fellows have got you here at last. I never was so pleased to see anyone," he cried, and in a whisper, as he dragged forward a chair, "All is fixed; we have the Circle Dot. I can explain everything."

Trenton did not reply. Sinking into the seat, he looked round the room, and then darted a finger at Garstone.

"That man is a liar and a cheat," he said. Heads craned forward, and no one now thought of leaving. "His story of what happened in the mountains is as false as his own black heart. We attacked the Circle Dot, an' I was shot by Bundy, my own foreman. When the money was found, this skunk cleared out an' left me, dyin' an' helpless, alone in the wilds, to be the prey of any savage beast. Later, he sent Bundy an' Lake back to finish me. They thought I was dead a'ready, an' I heard them talkin'. They quarrelled about buryin' me, an' Bundy shot Lake, threw him down beside me, an' put a pistol by my hand to make it look I'd done it. The Circle Dot found an' fetched me home. On the way, Bundy saw us, an' tried again to get me, but Green got him."

He paused, breathing heavily, Garstone, who had listened to

184

this terrible indictment with well-simulated incredulity but a very pallid face, addressed the doctor:

"He's mad, raving; illness has turned his brain."

"No," Malachi said sharply. "He is saner than you are."

Trenton spoke again. "One thing more. That rascal has no share in my ranch, an' the so-called will of which he is boastin' is another lie."

Garstone whirled on him. "Lost your memory too, eh?" he sneered. "That document was dictated to me by you a few days before we started for the hills, and the signature was witnessed by two of your men, Flint and Rattray."

"Who are conveniently dead," the rancher retorted.

"I shall hold you to it, and claim one-third the value of the ranch, and the same proportion of this," Garstone replied, striking the bag beside him on the table.

"That is mine," Dover put in quietly. "We were camped on the spot where it lay when the Wagon-wheel took us by surprise. Moreover, it was put there by my father's brother, an' there-fore——"

"It belongs to me," another voice broke in.

All eyes went to this new actor in the drama, a man who had been sitting unnoticed at the side of the room, chin on chest, hat slouched over his brow, and apparently taking little count of the proceedings. Now he rose, leant forward, and pushed his hat back.

"Do you know me, Zeb Trenton?" he asked vibrantly.

The rancher might have been looking at an apparition. Others, too, stared in speechless amazement, for despite the absence of the unkempt white beard and long hair, they recognized the gaunt, stooping frame of Hunch, the silent woodsman of the Circle Dot. But this fierce-eyed old man was very different to the one they had known as a semi-witless vagrant.

It was a full minute before the answer came. "Rufus Dover, by God!"

"Yes, Rufus Dover, the man you drove out o' Rainbow."

"You killed my father."

"True, but not as he killed mine—by shootin' him from ambush," was the stern reply. "I met Tom Trenton the night he died; boastin' of his deed, he dared me to draw; I beat him to it— he was dead before he could pull trigger. There was no witness. You called it murder, raised the town against me, an' I had to fade. In California I was knowed as Red Rufe, made my pile, an' runnin' with a rough gang, cached it, an' sent two messages to my brother. Then a tree fell on me, an' when I recovered my mind was a blank. Years later, I drifted in to the Circle Dot, blind instinct, I reckon, for I didn't even recognize Dave. But he knew an' took care o' me. He showed me the first message I'd sent, but it recalled nothin'; the second did not reach him." He bent his piercing gaze on the sheriff, who was sitting near Maitland. "An' you know why, Foxwell."

The officer seemed to shrink into his clothes; he read danger in those accusing eyes. "He was dead when I found him," he quavered. "I on'y——"

"Stole the letter an' sold it to Trenton for that badge you disgrace," the old man finished. "Who murdered my brother Dave?"

The sheriff shivered. "I—I dunno," he said hoarsely.

Sudden stepped forward. "Trenton, where did yu get that thirty-eight we found on yore saddle?"

The rancher's reply came promptly. "Bundy gave it me, just before we left for the hills; my forty-four was out of order."

The puncher looked at Foxwell. "An' Bundy had it from yu; don't trouble to lie. Scratched on the stock are the letters, L.P., the initials of Lafe Potter, the Circle Dot rider whose belongings yu sold, mebbe. Dave Dover was drilled by a thirty-eight, an' the empty shell was left in plain sight, with a dottle o' baccy beside it. Yu smoke a pipe, don't yu, Trenton? An' then he plants the gun on yu—the on'y one o' that calibre in the district, so far as I could learn. That was why yu wasn't keen on weighin' the bullet at the enquiry; yu knew the guilty man."

"I didn't," the sheriff protested. "I never thought o' Bundy. I figured it was——" He stopped, his frightened eyes on the owner of the Wagon-wheel.

Trenton stiffened in his chair, and his fingers closed convulsively. "You suspected me, you whelp?" he rasped. "By Heaven, if I had my strength——"

The cowering wretch was not to escape. In two strides, Dan had him by the throat, his badge was torn off, and after being shaken until his teeth clashed in his jaws, he was flung on the floor.

"Get out before I tear you apart," the young man panted. "If yo're in town one hour from now, you hang."

Foxwell did not doubt it. Scrambling to his feet, he stumbled towards the door, amid the jeers and curses of the onlookers, many of whom struck at him as he passed.

"That lets you out, Trenton," Red Rufe said. "I've one thing to thank yore people for: when they clubbed me up on Ol' Cloudy, they brought back my memory, though I didn't let on—for reasons. Sorry I had to make a fool o' you, Doc."

"You didn't—I've always been one," Malachi smiled. "But I'm wiser now." His gaze was on Kate Maitland.

Rufe addressed the banker. "I'll trouble you to hand over my money."

Maitland, conscious that he was wading in deep waters, did not

186

know what to do. He appealed to Trenton, and got a snapped, "Give it to him, of course."

It took both arms and an effort on the banker's part, but Red Rufe held it easily with one hand. "Now I'll tell you somethin' else, Mister," he said. "The Circle Dot is also mine—Dave was on'y my manager, an' he had no power to raise cash on it. Yore mortgage ain't worth a cent." Maitland's face grew white. "But, though I don't like yore methods, the Dovers pay debts—of any sort. You'll get yores, on one condition." He bent over and whispered.

"Certainly, Mister Dover, anything you say," the banker promised eagerly, colour returning a little to his cheeks.

Garstone, slumped in his chair, brow furrowed in a heavy frown, was silent. He had failed; just when all seemed secure, his edifice of fraud and treachery had toppled about his ears. But something might still be saved from the wreck. He drew himself up and looked at Trenton.

"I want my third share of the Wagon-wheel."

The rancher's clamped lips writhed in a bitter smile. "Better apply to Maitland," he replied. "Mebbe he'll accept yore lyin' paper. The Wagon-wheel is no longer mine."

The enormous strain to which he had subjected it was telling upon his enfeebled body. Beth, now sitting beside him, put a protecting arm about the bent shoulders.

"Don't fret, Uncle Zeb, everything will come right," she whispered.

Maitland, who appeared to have recovered his poise, spoke plainly: "I shall certainly require definite proof that the will is genuine."

One of the two strangers who had been chatting with Yorky pushed forward. He was a keen-eyed, poker-faced fellow, dressed in the fashion of the big cities.

"If it's a question of handwriting, gents, perhaps I can help," he said. "I'm a bit of an expert."

Garstone believed he had found a friend. "I shall be indebted," he replied, with a marked emphasis on the last word.

On receiving the document, the unknown turned to Maitland. "You got a known specimen of the signature on this?" he enquired.

The banker fumbled among his papers. "Here is a draft which Mister Trenton signed in my presence."

The expert compared the two signatures, discussing them with his companion, who had joined him. "I guess that settles it," he said, handing back the draft, and put the will in his pocket.

"Here, I want that," Garstone cried.

"So do the New York police, and they want you with it," the

man returned dryly. "So bad, too, that they've sent me to fetch you."

The blood drained from Garstone's face, but he made an attempt to fight the fear which possessed him. "You are making a mistake," he said. "I am Chesney Garstone——"

"Yep, that's a swell monicker," the man replied, and beckoned to Yorky. "Now, son, this is the guy you wrote us about, ain't it? Tell him who he is—he 'pears to have forgotten."

"Look at that kid's face," one of the crowd whispered to his neighbour. "Nothin' you could offer him would buy this moment."

He was right; Yorky would not have sold it for the contents of Red Rufe's Cache. Pointing to Garstone, he cried shrilly, "That's the Penman—Big Fritz, forger an' bank-buster. He done the Burley Bank job an' killed the night-watchman. I've seed him scores o' times in O'Toole's joint on th' Waterfront."

To the breathless spectators of the scene the man seemed to become older before their eyes; instead of a confident, bumptious bully they saw a haggard craven. Even his voice had changed.

"He lies, I don't know the Waterfront. I never heard of Mike O'Toole——"

The stranger's laugh stopped him. "Maybe, but who told you it was *Mike*?" he asked. "Well, we all make slips, and we had you fixed anyway."

"You can't arrest me here for an offence committed in another State," Garstone said desperately.

"That's my part," the second man said. He flicked aside his coat, showing the badge of a deputy-sheriff. "You'll be taken to Tucson, and sent on to New York."

Garstone shuddered. There was no escape; these cold-featured men would take him away to—death. He cursed the luck which had sent him to Rainbow; cursed that other fugitive from the underworld who had brought about his undoing. He visioned again the cave in the mountains, and heard a voice, "Rats has teeth, an' can bite." The rat had bitten, even then, and the wound would be fatal. The thought that this puny brat had bested him bred a madness in his brain. If he must die, it should not be alone; that grinning little beast . . . Livid with fury, he snatched a pistol from beneath his open coat and levelled it at Yorky's breast.

"You first—vermin," he hissed.

The words were his last mistake. Ere he could press the trigger, a gun cracked, and he staggered, pitched sideways, and rolled off the platform, the weapon dropping from his twitching fingers. Sudden shoved his smoking six-shooter back into his belt.

"I had to do it," he said to the officers. "Yo're journey has been wasted."

"Oh, I guess not," the New Yorker replied callously. "Dead

or alive was my instructions; he'll be less trouble in a box." And, as the puncher turned away, added, to his companion, "Did you see it? Hell! I'm glad they didn't ask me to collect *him*."

In the midst of the excitement, as the jostling crowd surged forward to get a sight of the corpse, someone touched his elbow— a very pale and trembling Yorky.

"Say, Mister, d'yer think Clancy'll git promotion fer this?" he questioned.

"Sure, he won't be a common flat-foot no more," the man replied. "There's a reward too; you both ought to come in on that."

"I don't want none of it—tell 'em Clancy can have my share," Yorky said quickly. "He's got a wife an' little 'uns. He was kind ter me. I'd like fer him to know I'm well an' doin' fine."

"I'll tell him my own self, son," the detective promised, and when the boy had gone, "Clancy said he was a lunger, but hell, he don't look it. Pity more of our slum lads can't git out here and have a chance of becomin' real men."

CHAPTER XXVI

Two weeks later, Dan, following the course of the Rainbow on his way to the Wagon-wheel, came upon two saddled ponies contentedly cropping the rich grass of the river bank. Rounding a clump of willow, he discovered the owners, Malachi and Kate Maitland, sitting very close together, and so completely oblivious to the rest of the world that they failed to notice his approach.

"Space on this range bein' limited, folks naturally has to crowd one another," he mused aloud.

The girl started, flushed, and tried to draw away, but her companion clasped her waist more firmly, looked up, and grinned.

"Dan, I've the greatest news for you," he said. "We are to be married."

The rancher laughed. "You call that news? Why, Rainbow has knowed it ever since we got back from Ol' Cloudy. I've on'y one thing to say, Phil—yo're a lucky fella."

"And that is no news to me," the doctor returned gravely. "Riding far, Dan?"

"I have business at the Wagon-wheel."

Malachi's eyes twinkled. "He has business at the Wagon-wheel," he told the girl beside him. "And maybe that range is lar̄e̅ and folks don't have to crowd one another."

They both smiled broadly, and it was Dover's turn to get red. "Aw, go to—Paradise," he said, and rode away.

To his mingled relief and disappointment, Zeb's old housekeeper answered his knock, conducted him to the sick rancher's room, and left them together. Trenton, sitting up in bed, welcomed his visitor grimly.

"Well, come to give me notice to quit?"

"No, just wanted to see if you're feelin' strong enough to tear this up," Dan replied, and threw a paper on the counterpane; it was the mortgage on the Wagon-wheel.

"What's the idea? Didn't you buy the ranch?"

"The Circle Dot took over the debt, an' you can pay in yore own time—I figure the cattle business is on the upgrade," Dover replied. "I've told our outfit that yore cows can graze to the river. That's all I gotta say." He turned to go.

"Wait a minute," Trenton said. "A week back I was called a stiff-necked, stubborn ol' fool; o'course, she didn't put it in those words——"

"She?" Dan wanted to know.

"Shore, my niece, Beth." The harsh, bony features had softened, and there was a shadow of a smile on the bloodless lips. "She's got pluck—nobody ever dared bawl me out, sick or well. It made me think, an' this clinches it. On top of savin' her life an' mine, you hand back my property. It shames me, boy. I've allus sworn I'd never thank a Dover, but I'm doin' it."

The young man gripped the proffered thin hand willingly enough, and the Trenton-Dover war was at an end.

"I owe a hell of a lot to you an' yore men—'specially Green," the invalid said presently. "If you agree, I'd like to offer him his own terms to come here."

"I wish you could persuade him, for we've failed," Dan replied sadly. "Claims he has a promise to keep, which means pullin' out soon. You'll never budge him, he's as obstinate as a—Dover," he finished, with a grin.

The old man smiled too. "I've treated him middlin' shabby," he said. "I reckon I'll have to eat crow."

"Jim ain't that sort," Dan assured him. "He's the best friend I ever had, an' he won't let me do a thing—just says 'Shucks' an' changes the subject. I'm damned sorry he's goin'."

"Ask him to come an' see me," the rancher said.

Dover promised, and was about to leave when he remembered something—the locket. He laid it on the bed.

"Guess this belongs to yore niece; I found it in the tent," he explained, and came away.

As he stepped into the open, he met the girl herself. She had no smile of welcome for him, and her greeting told why.

"When do we move out?"

"I've been seein' yore uncle about that," he replied.

"You might have waited until he is stronger," she said heatedly. "I must go to him at once."

She left him standing there, and did not see the whimsical look which followed her. Dan hoisted himself into the saddle and set off, but he had gone less than fifty yards when he heard her call.

"Mister Dover."

He grinned wickedly, but took no notice, until the cry was repeated, breathlessly. He stopped and dismounted; the girl was hurrying towards him; her face was flushed, eyes moist.

"You are the meanest man I ever met," she began. "You save my life, restore my uncle's property after he has used you badly, and even bring back something the loss of which grieved me deeply—my mother's portrait, and you refuse to accept a word of thanks. Why have you always disliked me? I couldn't help being the daughter of a Trenton."

The curious mixture of indignation and gratitude made her so provokingly pretty that he had hard work to refrain from putting

191

his arms about her and telling the truth—that he didn't care if she was the daughter of the Devil himself.

"I was afraid," He saw she did not comprehend, and went on. "Afraid I'd get too fond o' you, so I tried to build a barrier between us."

"And it had to be barbed wire?" she said.

"Yeah, but I found out that barbed wire won't keep thoughts from strayin', an' is liable to hurt those who handle it."

The soft dark eyes faced his bravely for an instant and then dropped. "I learned that too—Dan," she murmured.

It was quite a time before she had an opportunity to speak again, and, as she strove to rearrange her hair, it was a truly feminine remark:

"I expect I look a sight; I don't know what you must think of me."

"I think yo're the most beautiful girl in Arizona," he told her.

"Only in Arizona, Dan?" she teased.

"Arizona is my world," he replied.

"Mine too," she whispered, and brought about another interlude.

* * *

Sudden and Yorky were paying a final visit to the Pool of the Pines, for—as Dan had predicted—Trenton's inducements and pleas had proved vain as his own. They had enjoyed their swim, and Nigger was waiting. The boy's expression was woebegone.

"I'll be missin' yer, Jim. Wish I c'd come too," he said, for about the twentieth time.

"So do I, but it's too chancy," the puncher replied. "Best yu should stay here, learn yore job an' get them bellows o' yourn sound again. Then, mebbe, when I'm free, yu an' me'll go take a look at the country somewheres."

Yorky's eyes shone at the prospect. "Gee! Jim, that'd be swell," he breathed.

"So long, son," Sudden said, as he swung into the saddle. "Keep outa trouble, but if that ain't possible, see it through."

The boy watched the black horse and its rider until they were blotted out by a mist which was not of Nature's making; there was an unaccustomed lump in his throat.

"Just th' greatest guy—ever," he told the silence.

THE END